STEPHEN GALLAGHER

Comparative ANATOMY:
the best of STEPHEN GALLAGHER

Comparative
ANATOMY:
the best of STEPHEN
GALLAGHER

Subterranean Press 2022

Table of
CONTENTS

What's
UNDERNEATH

An Introduction to
Comparative Anatomy: The Best of Stephen Gallagher
By Stephen Volk

T'S NO GREAT secret to say Mr Gallagher and I have been travelling on parallel tracks.

We were both born in 1954. Myself in July, whereas he was an October child, and that already had an appropriately Ray Bradbury ring to it. My first proper job was in advertising; he cut his teeth in the Granada TV presentation dept, creating the bits between the programmes rather than the programmes themselves. (That was to come later.) Still, Granada was renowned as a hotbed of mavericks, and I think that rubbed off, unless it was in his genes. Fast forward to the 1980s. I got my first screen credit writing a Ken Russell movie, *Gothic*, while he worked on *Doctor Who*. Both of us splashing in puddles of the phantasmagoric. Having fun, I suspect, in ways neither of us had felt even vaguely possible ten years earlier. In the early 90s I got *Ghostwatch* on the box while he authored the mini-series *Chimera*—both genre flagpoles fondly remembered by fans some thirty years later. By coincidence, in the mid-nineties we both worked (separately) on spooky anthologies: yours truly on BBCTV's *Ghosts*, Mr G on ITV's *Chillers*. And by the time 2006 swung round, I'd created my ITV paranormal series *Afterlife*, and he'd created *Eleventh Hour* starring Patrick Stewart. Two shows that, I reckon, have strong echoes back to dramas we'd loved and been influenced by in our formative years, from *Doomwatch* to *Department S*, from Nigel Kneale's *Quatermass* to Brian Clemens' *Thriller*.

We were cut, you see, from pretty much the same cloth.

And so we plied our trade, we doppelgangers—the two Steves—selling and telling the stories we needed to. Always with a genre bent, sometimes with a horror or sci-fi bent, and all too often what the television companies didn't want. Writers interested in the bizarre, the weird, the scary, and the downright imaginative as opposed to cobbled northern backstreets were as rare in British TV as hen's teeth.

So much so that, soon after we finally met, Steve joked that whenever he went in to see a TV executive for a meeting, he always had the feeling I'd already warmed the seat for him.

I might have replied, "…or vice versa."

What I didn't convey enough, I suspect, on that first meeting, was that I was in awe of him.

Alongside the likes of Richard Matheson and Robert Bloch, who alternated between work for the page and the screen with equal skill and dedication, Steve was one of my heroes. And, get this—he was *British*. So every time I saw his name on the spine of a novel or on the telly it proved it was *possible*. That I wasn't a misguided nincompoop or misfit. Or if I *was* a misfit, I was in the very best of company.

My first experience of Stephen Gallagher's voice—and what a voice—was his novel *Valley of Lights*. To say it was gripping would be a gross understatement. It was miss-your-station gripping. One-more-chapter-before-you-switch-off-the-light gripping. A narrative with all the immersive drive of a great movie or TV show: and I mean that not as a putdown (as he would understand all too well), but as high praise.

Then—as with every story in this volume—I knew from the first sentence I was in the hands of a master. And there is no better feeling in the world.

Steve's writing is immaculate and enviable. I say that because I *do* envy it. Hugely. Each and every one of his books carries the weight of his confident economy of style, a surefootedness without ever a curlicue of cleverness to draw attention to the author. He is able to "get himself out of the damned way" and use precise and uncluttered language at the service of pure storytelling. Because that is what he loves. And it shows.

The great TV dramatist Jimmy McGovern once said in an interview that people often say to him: "That story wrote itself". It didn't, laughed McGovern. *It never does.* It requires immense hard work to get to the point where the story seems "effortless". And that is Steve Gallagher's talent to a tee. He is able to craft stories that seem to be plucked out of the air, whole and unadorned.

But what I also love about Steve as a writer and a person is that he is never embarrassed to talk about his influences, be it Dante or *The Dandy*; *Nineteen Eighty-Four* or *Supercar*; that spooky episode of *Cheyenne* with the grizzly bear ravaged by a forest fire or BBC2's infamous *Late Night Horror* episodes, half-hour classics in vivid colour—the tapes now wiped, lost forever, except in our scarred and sacred memory.

I've often said I believe that the life of a creative artist starts at about the age of twelve or thirteen. They experience, or see, or read, something that captivates them and they spend the rest of their lives trying to catch an approximation of the same kind of excitement. As we were born, misbegotten creatures, of the same era, I'd suggest that in Steve's case that would be a compendium of Patrick McGoohan going mad in *The Prisoner*, the chalk circle in *The Devil Rides Out*, Steed and Emma in "The House That Jack Built", the giant cyclops in *Lost in Space*, and absolutely anything that involved Ray Harryhausen. When it came to the written word, Captain Nemo, Sherlock Holmes, James Bond, and Rider Haggard were far more important than our school textbooks. And the Pan Books of Horror Stories paved the way for short stories of our own.

What could be more astounding, to our adolescent eyes, than having your name on the cover of a book? Or next to the words "created by" in the title sequence of a TV drama series? Not much, by our reckoning. For working class lads the idea was absurd, of course. But someone had to do it...right?

Which brings us to the present volume.

Best of.

Indeed. Relish that thought for a moment, please…

Because each short story that follows is a gem of the art form. Every one of them will make you shudder or chuckle—sometimes both. They might bring a tear to the eye, an unbidden question to the brain, or leave you with more than you bargained for. Whether they are tips of the hat to *Tales from the Crypt* or Robert Aickman, the wry tension of Roald Dahl or the musty dread of M.R. James, all are quintessentially Stephen Gallagher.

A man I would rate as, without doubt, the best British genre writer in my lifetime. Something he would no doubt reject with the full force of modesty I'd expect of him. Nevertheless, it's true.

Which is why I consider this book to be gold dust.

Best of.

Precisely.

In one of my favourite stories in the collection, "The Backtrack", the main character, a writer, says "I like the feeling of making something. Same as anyone who creates a pot or a painting. Everything beyond that is a bonus." I'm sure that is Steve's attitude at his core. But a few lines later he says: "The real story's always in what's underneath."

And that's what makes these pieces sing.

I confess I have favourites, as you will have yours. "Shepherd's Business" is one of the most perfect, and absolutely chilling, stories I have ever read. (In fact, I selected it for my top twelve of all time when a website asked me to.) I loved "Magpie" and "The Boy Who Talked to the Animals" as two massively different peeks into childhood, which Gallagher pulls off with consummate ease. "O, Virginia" had a cheeky and memorable charm, "One Dove" reminded me how much I adore the Sebastian Becker novels, while "Doctor Hood", "The Governess" and "Twisted Hazel" were so in my wheelhouse my heart literally quickened. But the masterpiece herein, for me, is "In Gethsemane"—a rare tale I immediately wanted to read again, and one I will treasure.

One final note, and a personal one.

At a career low point of my own, I don't remember when, I once asked Steve: "Do you ever think of giving up?" His reply, reassuring and inevitable, was: "I can't do anything else."

I took great inspiration from that, and remember it often.

Too frequently we seek the validation of others before we write, and we are almost always wrong to do so. The only true validation we need comes from ourselves.

Dickens, Dumas, Verne, Poe, Conan Doyle, Machen…all knew that we write because we have to. We know nothing else. And I for one would put Steve Gallagher on a par with those titans of literature whose work will always be with us. Will always shine. And shine its light in our very darkest places.

Stephen Volk
Bradford-on-Avon
June 2021

Twisted
HAZEL

FROM THE WINDOW I can see them coming and going. They're not the same people as before. Most of them are men, though I've counted two young women. They're working in the marked space in front of the house, the safe space, the space inside the ropes. Where the big lawn used to be, and where they won't get blown up. First they laid out poles on the ground, and then put them together into a low framework. Then they dragged a big canvas all the way over; it took ten of them to do that. Now they're all at the corners, winding at handles and calling out to each other. And as they wind the big marquee is slowly rising up, like a circus tent.

So much happening. Nothing ever happens here. It's no wonder I can't take my eyes off them.

I'd love to get closer, but I can't. I can't leave the house unless it's to go into the garden at the back, which has a wall around it. I can't go past the walls. Don't ask me why. If I ever knew, I don't remember.

So I watch.

Everything started the day the soldier and the woman came. They arrived in a Land Rover. He was in uniform, she very elegant, with perfect hair, and carrying a leather folder. I looked at her and saw everything I dream of being. Strong and gorgeous and she just didn't care. She stepped down onto the weeds and gravel as if the driveway was a red carpet. While the soldier was sorting out his big bunch of keys she was looking all around, taking everything in. I ran down the stairs to be there as they came in through the door.

She took a few steps into the gloom as he closed the door behind them, and when the floorboards creaked she turned and said, "Is it safe to walk around?"

"On tiptoe, yes," he said. And I think he was making a joke that didn't quite work because then he said, "No, we're fine."

It's a big hallway, with columns and a big wide stairway. The only light is from a glazed dome in the roof, high above the upper landing. There was a click and I saw that in her free hand she had a flashlight, not much bigger than a pencil, and she was directing its beam onto a carved and lacquered cupboard with Chinese figures all over it.

She clicked off the light and said, "Your Colonel wasn't wrong. The house is a real time capsule. Who's had access?"

"Since they sealed it up?" he said. "I couldn't tell you. I do know that only three of us can lay hands on the keys."

"An empty manor and you've had no break-ins. That's rare."

"I'd say it's largely down to being surrounded by a minefield."

They moved on through into the first of the rooms. The one I call the Horse Room, because of the picture over the fireplace. The furniture in here had all been moved over to one wall, and some of it was covered over.

She lifted a corner of the sheet and said, "Is there a plan of the floors?"

"'Fraid not," the soldier said.

"I'll have to make one."

The soldier had crossed the room and was standing in front of the fireplace, shining his own light up on the horse picture. The picture was mildewed along the top and sagging in its frame. The fireplace had more carving, all fruit and violins.

He said, "I don't know what the Colonel told you about the contents, but I wouldn't get my hopes up."

"I never do," she said, and let the dust sheet fall. The soldier was now tugging at a corner of hanging wallpaper alongside the fireplace, peeling it away from the wall like a piece of skin.

He said, "See what I mean? This is what happens when the damp gets in."

She glanced back. "But there's always room for surprises," she said. "Glass and fine china don't spoil. Metal and marble clean up. And a good enough picture can be worth the restoration."

He returned his beam to my horse picture. "What about this one?"

"Maybe not. Look, give me a chance to get my bearings. I'll call out if I need anything."

He got the message. "Yes, ma'am," he said.

"What do I call you? Captain? Adjutant?"

"Harry."

"Olivia."

"I'll be unlocking the cellars," Harry said, and went away.

I followed Olivia around. She fascinated me. She was so focused, so organised. She used the leather folder as a rest for her notepad and worked up a map of the ground floor as she went from room to room, inspecting all the things and making notes. She didn't see me. No one sees me.

Then I ran ahead of her upstairs. It had been so long since I'd been around anyone new. Some men had come once and boarded up the windows. For a while the army had used some of the bigger rooms to store boxes and equipment, but much of what they'd brought in had been cleared out again. Mostly the days were long and empty and to be honest I seem to prefer them that way. I might spend my time yearning for company, but whenever there are strangers around I get all excited and then after a while I can't wait for them to go.

Olivia would be different, I thought. I'd taken to her. She was making a second diagram of the upstairs rooms beginning with the one with the stuffed animals and the doll's house. I wished that I could tell her how this was my favourite but it would be pointless, she wouldn't hear me. She picked up the bear and sniffed it, made a face. She seemed more interested in the framed alphabet pictures around the room. She lifted one away from the wall to look at the back and then wrote something down.

The four-poster in the biggest of the bedrooms took her interest as well. She pulled on the heavy cover until she'd dragged it onto the floor and completely clear of the bed, and then she took hold of the frame and braced herself against it, trying to make it wobble. It didn't even creak, and she seemed impressed. She didn't replace the cover but she made a note.

Captain Harry was waiting at the foot of the stairs when we were done. He was still dusting cellar dirt off his hands when we reached him and he said, "There's a big wine collection. Wish I'd known."

"Most likely undrinkable," Olivia said. "Which may not deter a collector."

"I know plenty of chaps it wouldn't deter," Harry said.

Olivia's work here was all done, it seemed. She now began to gather her notes into the folder and said, "You say the building's safe?"

"The sappers looked it over and gave it the all-clear."

"Sappers?"

"Royal Engineers. They reckon the timbers are too rotten for saving but nothing's about to fall down. Did you see everything you wanted?"

"Enough to get my colleagues in and make a proper inventory. Can we get those windows unboarded? Maybe a generator and some lights?"

"You think it's worth the trouble?"

She zipped the folder. "I think it's worth doing the diligence."

"How long can I say will that take?"

"A couple of days at least. We'll go through all the rooms, tag and photograph everything that isn't nailed down, and make a spot valuation of each item for the catalogue. I'm thinking we should have the actual sale on-site."

"How would that work?"

"A country house clearance makes quite an event. We put a marquee on the lawn and open up the house for the viewing. Bidders get to see the lots in their original situation."

Harry seemed doubtful. "That could be tricky."

"It's an unusual venue. I can see it getting a lot of attention."

"A public auction on a firing range?"

"Your Colonel's the one who suggested it," she said.

"Then I'm wholly in favour," Harry said without hesitation.

Olivia indicated that she was ready to leave, and they made a move toward the door. She said, "How do I arrange access?"

"Through me," Harry said. "I'll sort you out with whatever you need."

I watched them leave. Captain Harry locked the big door from the out-side. They seemed nice.

SOMETHING MUST HAVE been set in motion, because some days later an army truck came down the long road from the trees on the hill. Along with the driver came a dozen squaddies and a sergeant. They unboarded the win-dows and then set about spraying weeds and roping off a safe area in front of the house. On other visits I'd heard them talk about all the 'live ordnance' that might still be lying in the fields hereabouts; people wandering outside designated areas might step on something that could explode, which is why the marked road is the only way in or out.

Olivia came back while the yard work was going on, and she didn't come alone. She arrived with her team in two escorted buses. Captain Harry opened up the house and then went off to talk to the sergeant. Olivia gath-ered everybody in the hallway and stood on the third stair to give out her instructions. Everyone, Olivia included, was wearing a security pass today. I was able to read their names, which is how I learned the rest of hers.

Olivia Lloyd. I like it. I wish it was my own.

She said to them, "I've been told the building's sound, but go carefully. The west wing and the ballroom seem to have suffered the least."

The ballroom was obvious but I never even knew we had a west wing. An older woman named Geraldine Logan asked, "Is the kitchen range to go?"

"Everything's to go," Olivia told her, and then they all dispersed off to their assigned parts of the house.

I wandered from room to room for a while, watching different people work. At this stage the presence of company was still a novelty. They made careful notes and took lots of photographs and left paper tags on everything. I could tell they'd done this many times before. They were in the attic, they were down in the cellar with portable lights. Out in the walled garden, two of them were pulling down ivy and cutting back bushes to reveal urns and statues long untouched by daylight. One tried to open a door in the wall to see what was beyond, but a gnarly corkscrew shrub had grown wild and spread across and there was no shifting it.

I went back in to look for my new friend, and found her talking to one of the men.

"Christopher," she said to him. "You look excited."

Going by his security pass his full name was Christopher Holland, and if he was excited, the signs of it were too subtle for my eye. He said, "There's one picture in the study I'd like moved today."

"The Stubbs copy?"

He chose his words carefully. "Let's call it that for now."

Shortly after that, two of them put on cotton gloves and carried my horse picture out to their bus. There was nothing I could do.

Geraldine Logan told Olivia, "There's some local interest to be found in the books, but they're all in a bad way."

"Pick out anything saleable and box up the rest in job lots," Olivia said, and so it went on.

They worked until the light faded, then came back the next day and the day after that and worked some more. Just as I was beginning to get used to them, they stopped coming.

Left alone again I wandered from room to room, looking at the notes and the labels they'd left on everything. Most of the notes meant nothing to me. I'd seen the people cleaning off some of the objects with soft brushes but otherwise they'd left everything dusty. *In context*, they called it.

I no longer had to go up to the attic to look out of a window. The view up there was limited but sometimes the sky beyond the trees would light up with explosions to the sound of distant gunfire. There was no firing tonight. Just clouds and stillness and stars.

It was quiet for a while and then all the activity started again. The tent people turned up this morning. The marquee is raised now, and they're setting out chairs under the canvas. There must be a hundred of those. They've got a generator, lights, loudspeakers. And now more strangers, different strangers, bussed in on coaches down the safe road, swarming over the house, catalogues in hand, poking into everything. There's a member of Olivia's team in every room to answer questions and forbid any handling. I'm already liking this part less.

I find Olivia with Captain Harry. He's always around somewhere, keeping an eye on everything, staying out of it.

He says, "Well, my boss is happy. What about yours?"

"He's Swiss," Olivia says. "So I never quite know."

I MIGHT AS well admit it, I'm miserable. It's auction day and there are men in brown coats and those same white cotton gloves moving to and fro, carrying everything out of the house and across to the marquee, one piece at a time. I hadn't understood their plan. I think I'd imagined they were here to bring the house back to life. I can hear the loudspeakers over there, but not well enough to make out what's being said. Every now and again there's a small ripple of applause from the tent.

They're dismantling my world and there's nothing I can do.

I try to stay close to Olivia but she's constantly on the move, only in the house for minutes at a time. I look for her upstairs and find two of the men carrying my doll's house out of my favourite room.

My doll's house!

I ask them to stop and they don't hear. I try to get in the way but that doesn't work. I'm just driven on before them, down the stairs, paper label on the dollhouse flapping while they navigate with care. I can't obstruct them, I can't get their attention. They've a special trolley waiting to take it across to the sale. They're setting it down on the trolley and again I beg them to stop.

Once it leaves the house, I can't follow. What can I do? I have to do something.

I get right into the face of the older man and I scream as hard as I can. There's no response. He doesn't hear, he doesn't see.

But behind me there's a crash of porcelain hitting the floor.

I turn.

It's Geraldine Logan and she's looking straight at me, pale as the white figurine she just dropped.

I move toward her. She sees me. Her eyes show it. Her gaze stays on me as I move. She takes a step back and then turns and runs before I can make my appeal. Within seconds she's out of the door and I can't go after her.

I stand there in the doorway, hoping she'll look back and relent. She does, she looks back from the driveway; but it's in fear, and I can tell that she no longer sees me.

Whatever the moment was, it's over.

My doll's house passes me by.

From behind me inside the house I hear Olivia call out, "Who did this?"

You did, Olivia, you did. You and your people. Why are you doing this to me? I have so little and you're taking my life apart.

For the rest of the afternoon I just sit on the stairs while the house empties around me. Things I don't treasure, some things I even hate, but that's not the point. It's my world.

Geraldine doesn't come back. From what I overhear she's left the site, and hasn't said why. Everyone thinks she's embarrassed by the breakage. She's the books and manuscripts person, I hear them saying. She shouldn't even have been handling china.

When they stop for the day, the house empties out and eventually there's only Olivia and Captain Harry left. She goes around all the rooms with her big list, checking things off. He waits to lock up. I've heard her say that she's worried about security now that the public have had a chance to look the house over. There are gangs that target country houses. They use auction catalogues and Country Life magazine as shopping guides.

She says to him, "I asked for someone to keep watch overnight."

"That would be me," he says.

"Oh," she says. "Sorry about that."

"I've had worse billets."

We're in my Horse Room, the one I've heard them call the study. Though the work's over for the day, neither of them seems in any particular hurry to leave.

Captain Harry says, "Can I make a confession?"

"Do I look like a priest?"

"Before your people took the inventory, I picked out a bottle and hid it."

"From the wine cellar?"

He nods.

Olivia is shocked. "You didn't."

"Army property," he says. "At least at the time."

"But still…"

"It was fair game," he says. "Your lot had a chance to find it."

"Where?"

He goes over to the big wooden desk where there's a bronze of a Greek lady dancing or tripping along or something. The statue's about two feet high. Olivia winces as she sees him take hold of it and tip it at an angle. She tries to say something but it's already too late, he's got it tilted. The inside of the bronze is hollow. He reaches in and slides a wine bottle out of it.

"I don't believe this," Olivia says.

Captain Harry blows some of the dust off the bottle and holds it up to the light. Then he sniffs around the cork, but you can see that he doesn't really know what he's doing.

"I know you deal in this kind of thing all the time," he begins, "but haven't you ever wondered…"

"I should stop you right there."

He reads her tone. "But you won't."

She takes the bottle from him and inspects it. My Olivia, she does know what she's doing. Even though she's brought disruption into my home, she's everything I want to be.

"Chateau Montrose, 1939," she says. "A high to mid shoulder fill."

"Is that good?"

"Wine loses volume through the cork as it ages. The less that it's lost, the better its chances."

He digs around in his pocket and brings out a pocket knife; opens it up and it's a corkscrew.

"Join me?" he says.

"You're kidding."

"Think of it as army surplus."

"The rest of the case went for six thousand pounds."

"But this one didn't."

She shakes her head in disbelief. I don't even know how many bottles make a case but I can see that, to her mind, what he's proposing is something outrageous and unimaginable.

Then she says, "Oh, fuck it. Yes."

She goes looking for some glasses. He clears off an old chesterfield and sets a low table in front of it. Then he hunts around and I think he's looking for a silver tray that he may have noticed in here one time, but that's gone.

Olivia comes back with two long-stemmed crystal glasses that I can't recall seeing before. They sit, and he strips the end of the bottle to get to the cork.

"I feel like a criminal," Olivia says.

"Exciting, isn't it?"

All three of us are transfixed as the first glass is poured. I don't know what I was expecting but to me it just looks like wine.

Harry takes a good mouthful and sits there holding it for a while, considering. I'm watching, Olivia's watching even more closely, and I don't think either of us can tell what he's thinking.

Eventually he swallows and gives his verdict.

"I've had worse," he says.

Now it's Olivia's turn. She swirls the wine, breathes in from the glass, then takes a sip. She gives it a few moments, then shrugs.

"'Salright," she concedes.

They both relax back. Captain Harry says, "So what's after this?"

"We'll move all the lots to our warehouse in Northolt," she says. "Buyers arrange collection from there."

"Hmm."

"That's not the 'after this' you had in mind."

He made an open-hands gesture, a plea of innocence. "Most people reckon my mind is a blank."

"Will you patrol the place like a watchman or do you plan on sleeping tonight?"

"You'll laugh."

"Try me."

Glass in hand, he stands. Picks up the unfinished bottle and indicates for her to follow. They go upstairs with me right behind them.

He's laid out a sleeping roll and made a camp on the four-poster bed.

"That's it?" she says.

"All I need," he says.

She laughs and pushes him and then the mood goes all strange and they start wrestling, except that it's actually hugging and kissing while they pull at each other's clothes.

I don't understand but it stirs something in me. Not so much like something I've forgotten, more like something that I've been trying to forget. Now they're on the bed and squirming around and she's making noises like he's hurting her, calling out and scratching at his back, and I want them to stop.

I don't know why, but I'm afraid. I can't take my eyes away but I really, really need them to stop. I can't be sure but I think I'm starting to sob.

Then suddenly she's looking straight at me and I know she can see me, just like the woman who dropped the jug.

She scrambles back up the bed, right up against the headboard. She hits it with a bang. He doesn't know what's wrong. He thinks it's something he's done. I take a step back. She's looking all around the room and now I can tell that she can't see me any more.

"What is it?" he says. "What did I do?"

"Nothing," she says.

"*What?*" he presses.

"I said, nothing."

He keeps asking but she won't tell him. She's pulling her clothes back on and she keeps looking around the room as if she fears seeing whatever spooked her again, but now she's looking in all the wrong places.

The mood is broken. When Olivia's dressed, she leaves in her own car. Captain Harry spends the rest of the night walking around the house, drinking the rest of the old wine, flicking at the paper tags on everything.

I walk with him, for the company. He seems sad.

TODAY IS THE second day of their sale. The final day, if I've heard it right. More people have turned up and they say that's because they've been holding back some of the more popular things. That doesn't include my horse picture, by the way. That's going to be sold in New York when they've finished fixing it up. I'll never see it again.

The desk and the sofa and the bronze lady, all gone. There are men taking measurements in the kitchen to get the old stoves out. They'll be sizing up the fireplaces next, and who knows what else. They were even looking at the stairs, but decided that the wood's no good.

Again, when Olivia's in the house, I stay close. She's looking out of a window at the back, into the walled garden. The statues are gone but there's a man out there on his own.

Straight-faced Christopher sees her by the window, and he stops to look out as well.

She says, "I'm keeping an eye on that one. He's registered as a buyer but he's made no move to the bidding tent."

"That's the head gardener's lad," Christopher says. "He won't be bidding. He told me he only signed up for the sale so he could see the house again."

"He's a bit old for a lad."

"Then imagine the state of the head gardener."

Olivia finds his name on her list. Then she goes out into the garden to speak to him. He's looking at the gnarly bush, the one that's grown over and blocked the gate. He's pretty gnarly himself.

"Mister Gilbert?" she says.

I can see that he's wearing a hearing aid, but he seems to hear her all right. Without actually looking at her he gestures toward the shrub and says, "There's nothing left of the garden. This is all I can recognise and it's the one thing they'd never let us touch. It's tragic," he says, "what's happened to the estate."

"You lived here?"

"My dad had one of the cottages." Another gesture, to somewhere vaguely beyond the walls. "Over there. Before the army took it on. That's gone."

"So you'd be just a boy."

"I was."

She glances back at the house and then picks her next words with care.

She says, "Was there ever talk of a ghost?"

Well, now he looks at her. His eyes are very pale, like they've been boiled. He doesn't give a direct answer but says, "Have you seen her?"

"Have *you?*"

He returns his attention to the old tree, growing out of control along the wall.

"No one knows who she was," he says. "Just that her bones were under the twisted hazel. I bet if you dug there you'd find nothing. But you can imagine how we all stayed clear."

Then he smiles to himself, as if at some old folly.

"Twisted Hazel," he says. "That's what we called her."

Olivia stays for a while after he's gone. I try to work out what she's thinking. She's just standing there, stroking her upper lip with a forefinger, looking at the shrub without really seeing it. The same way that, apart from that one moment in the bedroom, she always looks through me.

She starts shaking her head. I realise that she's quite upset.

"I'm so sorry," she says quietly, and goes inside.

I look up, and see Harry watching from the window.

IT'S ALL OVER. The marquee team begin taking down their canvas even as the last of the visitors are leaving. There was a smaller tent selling lunches and that's gone already. With its rooms mostly stripped bare, the house seems twice as big as it did before. I can't settle anywhere. I stand in one room or another and screw my eyes shut and summon it all back, reassembling in my mind one piece at a time, but when I open my eyes nothing's changed.

I stand at the window where Captain Harry stood, looking down into the garden as he did. When I see the twisted hazel I think of the old man and his silly stories. I've been here all this time and I've never seen any ghost.

Captain Harry's walking through the house. I follow him. He's looking for Olivia and he finds her in the morning room, counting rubbish sacks. There was a lot of debris and litter left scattered and not all of it's been gathered up.

I think he's been waiting to get her alone. He's nervous and doesn't know how to begin.

He says, "Are we...?"

And she immediately catches his meaning and says, "Yeah, we're fine. I'm sorry. I never meant for that night to get weird. Can we just forget it?"

"As you wish." I can't tell if he's relieved or disappointed. I think it's some of both.

She says, "We're all but done, here. What happens when everything's gone?"

"You mean, tonight?"

"I mean in general. What's the army's plan for the house?"

I can see that he's happier with the change of subject. He says, "There was talk of using it for urban warfare training. You know, dressing the place like an embassy and putting in a squad to practice room-to-room clearance and such. But then they'd have to fix it up for health and safety, which is kind of absurd."

"So it'll be left empty again?"

"Not for long. Artillery can always find a use for a new target."

"You're going to bomb it."

"Not me, personally. But yes. Come back in a year and chances are there'll be nothing to see."

She looks around. "It seems a shame."

"It is. But what can you do?"

"Lend me your knife," she says, but she won't tell him why.

That isn't quite the end of it. There's a gap of a few days and then men come in and start smashing through walls in the kitchen to get the oven ranges out. That takes them most of a week. The fireplaces go, and one entire three-part window at the top of the staircase. They lift the whole thing out of the wall, leaving the house wide open to the wind and the rain.

I don't keep track of them. I've no interest in who they are, or what they do. Mostly, I hide.

At nights I go and stand where the window was and look out toward the trees on the hill. With the window gone, it's almost like being outside. They've started their night firing again and it lights up the sky like fireworks. It takes my mind off things for a while.

Before she left for the last time, Olivia went down to the garden. She looked around to be sure no one was watching and then used Captain Harry's knife to take a cutting from the twisted hazel.

The night fireworks seem to be getting closer every evening, but I think that's just my imagination.

I don't know where I'll go.

I know there's a place for me somewhere.

If Olivia ever comes back, perhaps I can go with her.

There's always hope.

The Back of
HIS HAND

BILLY HAD DONE a lot of walking and pacing that morning, mainly to keep himself warm. He'd marked out a stretch of the pavement across the road from the tattoo parlour, and by now he knew it like…well, like the back of his hand. As long as he kept to this same piece of ground, he'd know the minute that anybody came along and went inside. He'd tried the door several times already.

But it was still early.

There was a greasy-spoon café almost opposite the parlour. It opened at eight, and Billy was on the doorstep when the proprietor came down and drew back the bolts. The proprietor was a stocky man, dark-haired and not so tall, and he seemed to be in sole charge with no help. He made no comment as Billy shouldered past him, leading with his well-stuffed kitbag. The café interior didn't look much, but it was clean. The warmth of the place folded itself around him like a blanket. He let himself relax a little, almost as if he'd been wound up tight by the cold.

He picked out a table that was close to the café's paraffin heater but which also was near to the window. The window was already beginning to mist up on the inside. He could still see the tattoo parlour from here.

When the man came over to take his order, Billy kept his gloves on and his hands under the table. The man seemed not to notice. Billy ordered the full breakfast with nothing spared.

Though Billy had his problems, lack of money wasn't one of them.

The man went around into the back, where he had a radio playing, and Billy could hear kitchenware being moved around on a range. It was a reassuring, almost homely combination of sounds. He yawned, and stretched his back. He'd been hitching all through the night, and had landed here in this seaside town at some utterly godforsaken hour of darkness. He'd zigzagged the country, leaving a trail that he was pretty sure would be hard to follow, and he'd kept his gloves on all of the time apart from when he'd needed to pee, and that he'd done only in locked cubicles on motorway service areas. Two gloves weren't necessary, but one glove would have looked odd. It might have attracted attention to him.

And attention was the last thing that Billy needed right now.

He'd never been here before. But the name of the place had stuck in his mind from just a couple of years ago when about a thousand bikers had descended on the place and settled in for a long Bank Holiday weekend. The bikers had been able to protest to the TV cameras about how misunderstood they were, the police had picked up plenty of overtime and had the chance to wear all their spiffy new Darth Vader riot gear, and the local traders had made a mint out of everybody; in fact, just about everyone had gone home happy although not one of them would ever have wanted to admit as much.

The town looked different now. The dawn sea battered at an empty promenade, and the wind howled through the deserted spaces of the new shopping centre. Most of the guest houses had hung out their *No Vacancy* signs and roped off the two-car parking spaces that had once been their front gardens. He might find a place here tonight where he could go to ground for a while, but it might be better to move on. It depended on whether he could face another night in transit. He'd never thought of himself as a soft case, but the last few hours had been the most miserable of his life. He'd waited out the time before daylight in the town's bus station, sitting with his bag and drinking weak piss-flavoured tea from a machine and trying to look like a legitimate traveller between destinations. A soldier on his way home, maybe; he reckoned that he could look the part and he carried a genuine forces kitbag as well, bought from Mac's Army Surplus Store. He'd watched a total of three buses come and go, all almost empty. In the phone booth he'd found a Yellow Pages with most of its yellow pages ripped away (there was no paper in the squalid toilet, and it didn't take a genius to put two and two together) but there had been enough of the directory left to tell him what he wanted to know.

He looked out through the fogging window again. No action across on the far side of the road. According to the listing, the tattoo parlour was the only place of its kind in town. The whole biker scene had led him to expect more but, what the hell, one was all that he'd need as long as it was the right kind of a place.

It looked like the right kind of place.

There was no shop window. The entire facade apart from the entrance had been boarded up and painted white, and this had become a background for a riot of hand-drawn lettering by someone who clearly had an eye for colour and design, but who equally clearly wasn't a trained signwriter. The style fell somewhere between 'sixties psychedelia and freehand baroque; across the top it read *steve, "professional" tattoo artist,* and the rest of it crowded out the frontage completely. From here, it was almost as if the building itself had been extensively tattooed, as an example of the owner's craft. It was the inverted commas around "professional" that had impressed Billy the most. That showed an education.

Breakfast came.

Billy realised almost too late that he'd pulled his gloves off without thinking, and his hands were on the table. He quickly drew them back and slid them underneath as the proprietor set a huge plate before him. "It's hot," he said, and the stuff on the plate was still sizzling.

Billy waited until he'd walked away, and then he rearranged the sauce bottle and the cruet set and propped up the plastic menu wallet so that it would screen his hands from the counter.

He kept an eye on the parlour as he ate. It was his first genuine meal in more than twenty-four hours, not counting grabbed snacks and chocolate bars along the way. A couple of transport drivers came into the café shortly after he'd started, but they didn't sit close. On the pavement opposite a few people walked by the parlour, but no one went in.

He'd finished. He ordered something else. It was starting to feel as if this was an open-ended situation that could last indefinitely. His attention began to wander, so that after a while he only belatedly realised that he was actually watching someone over at the door who had stopped and seemed to be about to enter.

He sat up, and paid attention.

It was a man. A youngish man, tall and skinny, with an unkempt thatch of hair and some kind of a beard. He wore thrift shop clothing and carried a plastic Sainsburys bag. Billy didn't get the chance to see much more because then the man was inside, the darkness of whatever lay beyond swallowing him up as the door swung shut to keep out the rest of the world.

He finished, and went over to the counter to pay. He held the canvas handles of the kitbag with his gloved hand and paid with the other, so that nothing looked suspicious.

Then he crossed the street to the tattoo parlour.

There had been a padlock on the door, now there was none. The hasp and staple, both new-looking, hung open; the hasp had been crookedly fitted and secured, not with screws, but with nails. One of them had been bent over and hammered flat—either the work of an amateur, or the world's least "professional" carpenter. As before, there was nothing in the frosted glass of the door to say whether the place was open for business, or what its hours were, or anything. Billy pushed, and it opened. He went inside.

There were no lights on downstairs, but a door stood open to the daylight of a grimy kitchen beyond the main room in which he stood. Billy could hear somebody moving up above.

"Hey," he called out. "Anyone around?" and he heard the movement stop. A moment later there was the sound of a hurried tread on an uncarpeted stairway, coming down. As Billy waited, he looked about him in the gloom. The walls showed the signs of bad plaster under too many layers of cheap redecoration, none of them recent. There were signs in the same flamboyant, spidery lettering as the frontage outside (*Strictly over 18s only—proof of age may be required*, and, somewhat less tactfully, *Not having a tattoo? Then Fuck Off*) and then poster after poster showing about a hundred different designs. He saw cats, dragons, jaguars, skulls, women, swords, daggers, scrolls…

"What is it?"

The man stood in the kitchen doorway. Seen from closer-to, he had the look of an aged juvenile. His eyes were of a blue so pale that he would probably always seem to stare no matter what he might actually be thinking, and his hair had a coarse, faded texture like curtains left hanging for too long in the sunlight. He seemed a sensitive type.

Unlike Billy.

"Look," Billy said, "before anything else, I'm talking five hundred quid and no questions asked. If that interests you, then we'll take it from there. If it doesn't, then I'm walking out now and I don't want to be followed. Is that understood?"

And the man said, "Five hundred quid? For real?"

"I can show it to you if you don't want to believe me."

"I'm interested," the man said.

And Billy, looking at him, thought Yeah, I reckon you are…because he knew a Junkie when he saw one, and this starved-looking specimen had to be one of the classic examples. So then he looked around and said, "Well then, how about some light?" And the Junkie, suddenly spurred into nervous action as if being jerked out of a trance, turned around and seemed confused for a moment as if he was so overcome by the idea that he'd forgotten where the switches were.

The overhead tubes flashed once or twice, and then one of them came on. The other just glowed orange at both ends, as if in resentment of its brighter neighbour.

The room didn't look any better. Quite the opposite. There were old grey vinyl tiles on the floor, the self-stick kind that often don't. A few of these had lifted and shifted, exposing the grimy wood flooring underneath. There were four straightbacked chairs over against the wall, and in the middle of the room a single padded chair with a headrest that was somewhere between the kind that you'd find in a hairdresser's and the kind that you'd find in a dentist's. The dentistry image was continued in the form of the hanging tattooist's needle on the end of its balanced and jointed support arm, with a system of long rubber drivebelts and gearwheels running all the way back to the motor at its base. On the table alongside the chair were a rack of needles, some dyes, and a bottle of Savlon antiseptic.

Billy said, "Show me your hands."

The man frowned, puzzled.

Billy said, "If I'm going to pay you that kind of money, I want to see steady hands first."

"I've got steadier hands that you," the Junkie said, offended, and held them out; they weren't exactly rock steady, but they weren't unusually shaky either.

Billy said, "You shoot up already this morning?"

And the Junkie said, "That's none of your damned business. Now show me the money."

Billy put the kitbag on the padded chair, and unzipped it a little of the way. It was enough to show some of the bundles of used notes, most of them still in cashiers' paper bands, that were inside. The man stared.

Billy said, "You haven't even asked me what I want you to do, yet."

And the man shrugged.

"For five hundred, who gives a shit?"

This was going to work out.

So Billy zipped up the kitbag again and then removed his glove and rolled back his sleeve and he held out his clenched fist, knuckles upward to show the dragon tattoo.

"I want this taken off," he said.

The man looked at it. Billy guessed that he had to be casting a professional eye over the design. It had cost Billy a lot of money, some ten years before; his friends at the time had told him that the man they were taking him to was the best in Europe. He'd been a big fat slob who hadn't looked like the best anything of anywhere, but Billy had been interested enough in the designs he'd been shown. They made the ones on the walls around here look like finger paintings.

The Junkie looked up at him. "Taken off?" he said.

"Completely off," Billy said. "You can do that? I mean, you can do it here and I don't have to go into a hospital or anything?"

"I can do anything you want," the man said. "But am I allowed to ask why?"

"No, you aren't," Billy said. "Lock the door, and let's get down to it."

The man looked again, and shook his head in disbelief. And then he made a little shrugging gesture as if to say *Well, it's your tattoo and it's your five hundred, so what does it matter to me?*

And he went to bolt the door from the inside.

Billy looked at the chair. It had a padded arm support at right angles to the seat, and the armrest had worn right away to the dirty-grey foam at its end. He felt his heart sink. Much as he knew he needed this, he hadn't been looking forward to it. Billy hated physical discomfort, not least his own. That ten years before he'd almost fainted when, after much more than an hour with his eyes screwed shut and his teeth gritted and his insides scrunched up tighter than a wash leather, he'd finally looked at the new pattern on the back of his inflamed hand and seen the tiny beads of blood that had been welling up from every needle strike. This was why he'd only had the one hand tattooed, instead of the matching pair that he'd intended. Much as he'd wanted the dragon design in the first place, he'd never been able to bring himself to go through the experience again.

And now he was sorry that he'd ever had it done at all…now that it was *that* close to landing him in jail.

"Shall I sit here?" Billy said as the Junkie turned from the door.

"Wherever you like," the Junkie said.

"Will it take long?"

"I shouldn't think so."

Billy took off his coat and climbed into the chair, and laid his arm on the rest. It was at right angles to his body, and raised as if to fend off a blow. As he was doing this the Junkie was scratching at his beard, looking down at the tattoo needles and other implements on the table.

"Is this going to hurt?" Billy said.

"Oh, definitely," the Junkie said, nodding absently.

"What about blood?"

"Lots of it," the Junkie said. "You don't make an omelette without breaking eggs."

"Oh, shit," said Billy, and turned his face away.

The Junkie said, "If it was me sitting there, I'd take something for it. Painkiller. You know what I mean?"

Billy turned his head back again and looked at him suspiciously. "You mean smack," he said.

"Not necessarily. There's other things you've never heard of. You wouldn't feel a thing and, even if you did, you wouldn't much care."

"These other things. Do they have to go in through a needle?"

"For something like this, yeah."

"Oh, shit," said Billy, "I hate needles."

"It's okay," said the Junkie. "I think I've got a clean one."

"Oh, shit," said Billy.

So the junkie asked for another fifty and Billy offered another ten, and they finally settled on the fifty because Billy had no idea how much the stuff was really worth and, besides, a hard light seemed to come into the Junkie's eyes suggesting that he'd conducted this kind of negotiation a thousand times before.

Also, Billy was getting scared.

"Wait here," the Junkie said finally, and disappeared upstairs.

Billy slumped back in the chair with a feeling of miserable resignation. He wished that he didn't have to do this. He liked his dragon tattoo, and would be sorry to see it go; he'd had it for so long that it was like a part of him, and he was hardly even conscious of it for most of the time. That, in a way, had been his downfall. When he'd been standing there at the Building Society counter with the replica Luger and the open shopping bag and the ski mask (courtesy of Mac's, once again), the last thing on his mind had been the chance of his tattoo being picked up by the cameras. He'd been wearing his gloves, but the glove had ridden down the back of his hand and uncovered almost all of the design.

And then two nights ago there he'd been, sitting at home with a few cans of Draught Guinness in front of the TV while his mother pottered around upstairs, when up had come one of those *Crimewatch* shows where they asked for help with real-life cases and all the TV people who wished they were working in movies got the chance to ham it up doing crime reconstructions. He'd been watching it all with a sense of professional interest when, in a segment that they called *Rogues' Gallery*, he'd found himself looking at his own last job from an unexpected angle. He hadn't recognised himself straight away, but then he'd felt an inner leap of joy at the realisation that here he was, making the big time at last.

But then the joy had turned to ice as they'd taken a part of the picture and blown it right up and there was his one-of-a-kind tattoo, filling the screen from side to side and clear enough to be recognisable.

He'd packed his kitbag and been out of the house without any explanation that same night, almost within the hour. They were saying that the police had linked him with a string of other jobs. There was even a reward. Some of the people that Billy knew, they'd have sold their own parents for medical experiments if there was a drink in it for them. And the worst of it was that the people that Billy knew, also knew Billy.

Millions of people watched that show. Those who made it crowed about their successes every week, and Billy sure as hell didn't want to become one of those. Even if his own friends didn't turn him in for the reward money, he'd inadvertently given the police a gift that they couldn't ignore. Small-time though he was they'd stay after him, like a man scratching around in his own behind until he dug out the peanut.

Somewhere upstairs, coming down to him through the ceiling, there was the sound of a floorboard being lifted.

Less than a minute later the Junkie was coming back down the stairs, and when he appeared in the doorway he was holding the same supermarket carrier bag that he'd had in his hand when Billy had first spotted him. In his other hand, he held an ordinary kitchen plate. On the plate lay a hypodermic syringe, an unlit candle, and a soot-marked spoon.

"Oh, shit," said Billy, and looked away again.

"I told you, it's clean," the Junkie insisted, setting everything down on the worktop. "It's a brand-new needle. I take the old ones down to the clinic, and they do me a trade."

"Wait a minute," Billy said, and even in his own ears it sounded like the beginnings of a whine. "I'm not so sure this is a good idea. I don't want to get hurt but I don't want to get hooked on anything, either."

"Nah," said the Junkie, undoing Billy's cuff button and starting to push back his sleeve. "That whole thing's just a myth."

"Really?"

"Really," said the Junkie. "I've been using this stuff every day for the past four and a half years. If there was anything to it believe me, I'd know."

"I'm just going to look over here," said Billy.

The Junkie seemed amused. "You really that scared of needles?" he said.

And Billy said, "I'm not scared of anything, I'm just going to look over here."

A couple of minutes later, he said, "Was that it?"

"That was it."

"You're pretty good at this."

"Thank you. Just relax and let it start to work on you. I've got to find a few things in the kitchen."

Billy lay back and closed his eyes. Maybe he could feel something already, he wasn't sure. He thought you were supposed to get a rush all at once like you were coming your brains out, but it wasn't happening that way. He wondered what would be next.

He knew even less about the art of tattoo removal than he did about the art of tattooing. Some people said it simply couldn't be done with any success, others that you had to go to a really expensive clinic and maybe even have skin grafts and everything. But then he'd heard that what they did was to use needles to hammer bleach down into the skin, deeper even than the inks that they were being used to eradicate, and he'd thought Well, it doesn't sound pleasant but it doesn't sound too complicated, either.

And then he thought, the kitchen?

And he thought Oh my God, he's going to use ordinary household bleach, and he started to sit up with the intention of getting out of the chair and heading for the door without a single look back; he could maybe just wear a bandage and tell people that he'd been burned and his hand was taking a long time to heal, and then he could settle in a new town and meet new people and he wouldn't have to go through anything like this at all...

And then a great sense of warmth and well-being hit him all at once, and it was better than coming his brains out because, to be honest, he'd always had this little problem of self-control that he never liked to talk about and always had to apologise for, and he sank back into the padded seat and, hey, wasn't it just the best and most comfortable chair in the history of mass-produced furniture?

"Getting any effect yet?" the Junkie said as he laid a few things out on the table alongside, and Billy said, "I dunno. Maybe."

He let his head fall back. It felt as if it was sinking into the padding about a foot deep or more. He smiled stupidly.

"Last chance to change your mind," the Junkie said.

And Billy said, "Do it."

The Junkie asked him to flex his fingers and he did, and then he had to ask the Junkie if anything was happening because he couldn't feel any feedback at all. The Junkie told him that was fine, and so Billy turned his face to the sweat-scented vinyl in the knowledge that when he sat up again, it would be over. He could move on, start again; and if anyone came looking, he could hold up his hands and say *Who, me?* with total confidence.

Move on. That was about what it entailed, because with or without the tattoo there was no going home. Thought about in the abstract, back when he hadn't actually been obliged to make the break, the notion had even held certain attractions; there was a lot of shit in his life that he'd always reckoned he could happily leave behind, a lot of arguments and all kinds of resentments, but somehow he couldn't see it that way any more. He kept thinking about his video collection. Every Saturday afternoon he liked to hang around street markets and car boot sales, looking for old stuff that the video libraries were selling off. He had all the *Halloweens* except for the first one, every one of the *Friday the 13th* movies, and almost a complete set of the *Police Academies* except for the one that was too new to have made it through the system yet. All lost. His mother would probably give them away or even just throw them out, the way she had with his comics all those years ago. Some of those comics would have been worth real money today. If he'd still had them, he'd never have needed to turn to crime at all.

Obviously, his troubles were all her fault.

He winced. Something hurt.

"Sorry," the Junkie said. "This isn't quite as sharp as I would have liked."

He'd been drifting. That wouldn't do. The last thing he needed would be to fall asleep and then wake up with the job half-done and the Junkie gone and his bagful of money gone with him. Even worse…what if the Junkie followed *Crimewatch?* Stranger things had happened. He'd know that the reward was more than the five hundred that Billy had offered, and Billy could wake up surrounded by police.

But if the Junkie had ever owned a TV, Billy reckoned that he'd probably sold or hocked it long ago. Not much danger there. But as far as the security of his kitbag was concerned, he'd already shown the Junkie what was inside.

Better to stay awake.

Concentrating his attention as best he could, Billy searched around for a conversational opener and then said, "How long have you been doing this?"

"About ten minutes now," the Junkie said. "It's not quite as easy as I thought. I'm trying to do it neat and there's all kinds of stuff in the way."

"I meant, how long have you been doing tattoos?"

"I don't do tattoos," the Junkie said.

This struck Billy as not a bad joke at all. He said, "So what's the big sign over the door and all the needles and stuff?"

"Oh, they're Steve's. He's the tattooist. But he doesn't open the shop on Wednesdays."

Billy frowned in his stupor. "So, who are you?"

"I'm Kevin. I just rent the upstairs from Steve. The roof leaks and it's a dump, but he lets me have it cheap as long as I pay him cash. I think it's a tax dodge. But I owe him more than a hundred in rent and he was going to throw me out; this means I can pay him off and have some left over."

Billy let his mind work on this one for a while, to no great effect.

And then he said, "But if you're not a tattooist, how come you know how to do a tattoo removal?"

There was a long silence.

And then the Junkie, his voice sounding as if it was coming from a long way away, said, "You wanted someone who could take off the *tattoo?*"

Billy sat up. He could only manage about halfway.

He looked.

The Junkie was sitting there on one of the hard chairs from by the wall, looking politely puzzled. He was spattered with red from the chin down, as if he'd been mixing up something nasty in a blender and had forgotten to put the lid on. In one hand there was a big, none-too-sharp looking kitchen knife; in the other, a towel that he'd been using to dab his working area clean. On the padded support before him, Billy's wrist had been tied down with a length of bandage that appeared also to be serving as a tourniquet.

But the most curious thing about the entire scene was the clear piece of daylight that was showing between Billy's hand and arm.

The Junkie said, "Don't judge it by what you see right now. It'll look much better when it's finished."

Billy gawped at the sight. Couldn't take it in. Still he felt no pain, no sensation at all from the shoulder down. The Junkie was watching his face, trying to guess his mood.

He was lost for words. Except, perhaps, for the phrase *Hanging by a thread*, which dropped into his mind unbidden and wouldn't go away.

He didn't dare move.

Not an inch.

He looked at the Junkie.

And the Junkie said hopefully, "Do I still get the five hundred?"

Little
ANGELS

I T WAS YEARS since I'd last been up there. They'd replaced the old train with one of those silver bullet things. It was automatic, and had no driver. They cleared the platforms and closed airtight doors in the station before we pulled out. The fit of the modern train through the opening of the tunnel was so close that anyone standing around, they said, would be sucked into its wake by the sudden drop in pressure.

Of course, this being the Alps, they said it in French.

We climbed up the inside of the mountain in darkness. I watched hewn rock passing through the squares of light that fell from the train. The interior of the carriage was bright and chic but the tunnel outside was more than a hundred years old, a product of sweat and dynamite. It was another world out there. Cruder, and more primitive.

And then there were the people, of course. People always mess up a neat picture.

I'd counted a few walkers and skiers, but mostly I'd seen tourists. They were going to look at the observatory on top of the mountain, and the man-made Ice Palace carved out of the nearby glacier. They were of all nationalities, and almost all of them had cameras. No one was dressed for the weather at the top. Most were in light jackets and windcheaters, and there was one stone-faced Japanese woman in a kimono and sandals. Her outfit looked more like stage costume than a person's regular clothes.

I knew what would happen. They'd get there and instantly register astonishment at the cold. Words like 'ice', 'glacier' and 'altitude' clearly hadn't been much of a warning. They'd spend a minimum of time looking around and then be on the next train back down into the valley. Some of the bolder ones would venture beyond the observatory, but most would wait out the time in the triple-glazed and heated tea-room.

From behind me I heard, "You're horrible, Grandma. We hate you."

"Yes," said another. "You're sad."

Inwardly, I sighed.

These were the first English voices that I'd heard on this trip, and I'd been hearing them throughout the morning. They belonged to two young boys travelling with their grandmother. They weren't from my hotel, but they'd come into town on the same bus and their table had been close to mine in the coffee shop at the foot of the mountain. By now I could cheerfully have strangled them.

They were about nine or ten years old—whatever their ages, there wasn't much between them. One was short and round and had red cheeks that looked as if they'd been touched up with a wire brush. His mouth looked weak and wet. The other was mousy, and thinner.

They'd been taunting her relentlessly. Or at least, they'd been trying to.

"You smell," I heard one of them saying.

"Your house smells," said the other.

"Does it really?" the woman with them said, unperturbed.

She wasn't rising to the bait and she wasn't letting them get any satisfaction out of her, either. I looked back and caught her eye. She was a perfectly ordinary-looking old lady. A little bit plump, a rinse of blonde highlighting her mostly white hair. She saw me but she didn't acknowledge me.

"Your house smells of wee," one of the boys said.

"Language," she said with perceptible sharpness.

I wasn't about to interfere. It was none of my business. But clearly the boys were out to push the limits for all they were worth. They probably had it in their minds that Grandma was an easy touch and that regardless of what they said to her, they were safe from all consequence.

We came out of the tunnel and up into daylight. The tinted glass of the train's windows took out the worst of the glare. We were above the snowline and the high peaks were all around us. The mountains looked like great sides of butcher's beef, muscled and veined with white fat. Everyone crowded up to the windows, and the first of the pocket cameras started to flash.

Well, I've seen more ridiculous things. I've seen someone take a flash photograph of a cinema screen before now.

We all disembarked at the topmost station. The walkers and the skiers were out of there in an instant and I was left amongst the tourists, almost all of them voicing their shock as the cold mountain air hit them through their thin clothes.

And through the crowd I heard:

"You're too slow, Grandma."

"You walk like a cripple."

This time, it was she who caught my eye. This was almost certainly because now that I was on my feet I was walking with two sticks, and at the kind of speed that's most prudent when you've a newly-healed artificial knee and you're walking on compacted ice.

"I do apologise," she said.

"Don't apologise," I told her. "I think you're a saint."

"I have five children and thirteen grandchildren," she said, which I took to mean that whatever they might throw at her, she'd probably dealt with worse. She moved to follow her charges, who'd run on and hadn't waited.

I wondered what the setup was, and where their parents were. Probably thinking what a treat it was for the old girl, spending a day of her trip alone with her grandchildren. The parents were probably back at their hotel, drinking the minibar dry and screwing the afternoon away, or trying to remember how to after years of no peace and little privacy.

Not everyone had dispersed when I reached the outdoors. The Japanese woman was having a terrible time on the deep snow in her wooden sandals; except for thin white nylon socks, she was all but barefoot. No one in her party had stayed to help her out, and I was struggling enough on my own. Even at my speed, I soon left her behind.

I had to see it all for one last time. They'd told me that the new knee was just the start of my problems, not the end of them. I'd walked and climbed for several summers here, back when I'd been in training. That was when I'd had the agility of a cat and the endurance of a dog. It irked me now to be stuck in the wake of these others as they picked their way along, fussing like chickens in a yard. But what else could I do? I wouldn't be climbing again.

I suppose my body was now paying the price for all of that hard effort and abuse. You push an engine to its limits and never let up, and what are you going to be left with at the end of its run? Scrap.

No point complaining about it. They were great days while they lasted.

I just wished they could have lasted a little while longer.

The track zigzagged out across the glacier to the observatory. The way was marked by ropes that ran between metal poles thrust into the snow. There was enough movement in the ice to make a permanent way an impossibility. Over time, the poles would move out of alignment and the way would have to be reset. I stopped often, not always because I needed to.

We were a mile high. The air was impossibly clear and, apart from where it had been churned and trampled underfoot, the snow was impossibly clean. It was as if everything in my field of vision had been etched with a diamond. A vast snowfield sloped down and away from me, and I could see where it bent and swirled down the pass like a river of cold lava.

The highest of the peaks surrounded and sheltered this spot. Much of the time, there was no wind. There were avalanche warnings along the track, and I could remember how avalanche had always been a danger in this area; the snow just sat there, warming in the day and freezing in the night, forming layer upon unstable layer until something happened to set the layers sliding.

I seemed to be alone now. The Japanese woman had given up and gone back to the railhead. Everyone else had reached the observatory and headed indoors, straight for the gift shop or the tearoom.

By the time I reached the buildings, my lungs hurt and my head was spinning. I was pacing myself because I knew that if I overexerted and got altitude sickness, I'd feel lousy for days.

The mountain under the observatory had been hollowed out, and here could be found the Ice Palace. It was no palace, more a warren of tunnels and carved shapes that had been made slick and smooth by use. It stayed frozen all year round, and they put new sculptures in every tourist season. There was usually an ice swan and a Little Mermaid, and one year there had been a Michael Jackson hacked out by ice pick.

I stopped to get my breath. It hung in the air before me, a slow-dispersing cloud.

And I heard, echoing from deep inside the labyrinth, a call of *"Fat cow! Fat cow!"*

I saw their shapes flickering within the ice. I couldn't see details, just the moving blocks of colour. They were running through the Ice Palace tunnels. Two offensive little pains in the rear, their energy undiminished by the altitude.

I thought I saw another shape moving after them. Bigger, darker, slower. They flickered ahead of it like two flames, darting and taunting.

"Prune tits! Pissy-knickers!"

Fainter now.

I WAS BEAT. I sat in the tearoom with the tourists, sipping hot chocolate and feeling my energy slowly being restored. All right, I'd done it. I'd wanted to see it all for one last time, and I had. But it wasn't the same. It never could be.

I don't know how long I sat there. At least three distinct sets of people came and went around me. Eventually the waitress gave me a warning, and I checked my watch. It was later than I'd realised. I knew I'd better set out in good time if I wanted to make the last train off the mountain.

When I got there I dropped into a front window seat, and then over the next ten or fifteen minutes the carriage filled up behind me. These were the stragglers, the last visitors of the day, the ones who'd hung on to the end even though the light was dying and the cold air was turning bitter. There was a blue cast to the snow outside, while right up on high the peaks were touched with reddish-gold from the sunset in the valley beyond. I knew what it could be like up here; in minutes the last gleam would fade and a darkness would slide in across the glacier.

A warning bell sounded, and all the doors closed. Our train eased out of the deserted station and began the descending journey. This was a subdued crowd, but I heard someone say, "Avalanche," and felt the ripple of interest that ran through them as everyone craned to see. Some got out of their seats and moved across the train to my side for a better look.

It was a minor avalanche, although I suppose you'd call no avalanche minor if you happened to be underneath it. Snow was pouring like a water-fall from a higher slope to a lower, two or three miles away on the far side of the glacier. I'd seen falls like it on my climbs. From here inside the carriage, I missed the distant-thunder sound they always made.

But then my attention was caught by something else.

There were two figures on the lower slopes. There was just enough light to make them out. They were a long way from the marked paths and they were dancing around on the snow like savages, their arms raised in the air and making two-fingered gestures in the direction of the train. They reeled like a couple of drunks, giddy with their own defiance, way out there on the wide white stage of the glacier.

They were like tiny matchstick people, small charcoal strokes on chalky paper, and then they were gone.

No one else seemed to have noticed them and, in the fading light, even I wanted to look again to be sure. But it was too late. The train had taken a bend and the tunnel was ahead. I looked around for someone to speak to but, of course, the train was automated and there would be no one until we reached the valley.

Maybe there was a phone for emergencies. Would it work inside the mountain? I turned in my seat to see if I could spot something like one.

Instead, what I saw was the boys' grandmother. She was sitting about three rows back from me.

I looked for the boys, but she was sitting alone. She saw me looking at her, and I started to say something.

Somehow, it didn't come out. It died when I saw the expression on her face.

"I have five children and thirteen grandchildren," she said.

She said, "They can't *all* be little angels."

RESTRAINT

"**D**ID YOU GET a look at the driver who forced you off the road?" The woman in uniform had pulled up a chair to put herself right alongside Holly's hospital trolley, so that she could speak close and keep her voice low.

Holly made the slightest movement of her head, not even a shake, and was instantly sorry.

The policewoman spoke again.

"Your son thinks it was your husband's car. Could that be right? We've called your house and there's nobody there."

Holly meant to speak, but it came out in a whisper.

"Where are the children?"

"Out in the waiting room. They've been checked over and neither of them's hurt. Your neighbours said you left after some kind of an argument."

"I'd like some water."

"I'll have to ask if that's all right."

Holly closed her eyes, and a moment later heard the sound of metal rings sliding as the policewoman stepped out of the cubicle. Only a curtain separated her from the Saturday night crowd out in Casualty, and a pretty lively crowd they sounded. She lay with a thin blanket covering her. They'd brought her back here after the X-rays. It was a relief to hear that the children were unhurt, even though it was what she'd half expected. That short trip down the embankment would have shaken them up, but it was only their stupid mother who'd neglected to put on her own seat belt after making sure of theirs.

That car. It had come out of nowhere. But if there was one thing that Holly knew for certain, it was that Frank couldn't have been at the wheel.

Why? Because she and Lizzie had struggled to lift him into the boot of their own car, not forty-five minutes before. And assuming he hadn't leaked too much and no one had lifted the lid for a look inside, he had to be lying there still.

He certainly wouldn't be going anywhere on his own.

The young policewoman was back.

"I'm sorry," she said. "I had to stop an argument. I forgot to ask about your water."

"Where's the car?" Holly croaked.

"Still in the ditch," the policewoman said. "The accident unit can get it towed away for you, but you'll have to sort out the rest with your insurers."

This was seductive. The linen smelled clean, and felt fresh. Holly was all but exhausted. She'd been lifted, laid down, tended to. It would be so easy to drift. The racket right outside was almost like a lullaby.

But her husband's dead body was in the boot of her car, and the police were all over it even as she lay there.

"Can I get that drink now?" she said.

As soon as the policewoman was gone, Holly tried to rise up on her elbows. The effort it called for surprised her at first, but she made it on the second attempt.

She was in her underwear, her outer clothing piled on a chair that stood against the wall. She started to climb off the trolley and it hurt, but it wasn't too bad; nothing grated and nothing refused to take her weight. Her head ached and she felt a great overall weariness, but there was no one part of her that screamed of special damage.

The floor was cold under her bare feet. She stood for a moment with her hand resting on the trolley, and then she straightened.

At least she could stand.

She tweaked open the side-curtain and put her face through the gap. In the next cubicle sat a young man on a chair, holding a spectacularly bloodstained dressing to the side of his head. He was in formal dress, with a carnation in his buttonhole and his tie all awry. He looked like the type who owned one suit and wore it for all his weddings, funerals, and court appearances.

"I wouldn't call you a shitsucker," Holly said.

He blinked at her, uncomprehending.

"The man you came in with just did," she said.

He was up on his feet in an instant, and as he flung back the outer curtain she got a glimpse of the scene beyond it. The rest of the wedding party was out there, arguing with the staff and with each other. The bride in her gown could be seen in their midst. They rose in a wave as the bloodied guest was spotted hurtling toward them, and then the curtain fell back as if on the world's most energetic Punch and Judy show.

That ought to keep her policewoman occupied for a while.

Holly could feel the adrenalin pumping now, flushing her of all weariness and pain, leaving her wired and edgy and ready to roll. She dressed as quickly as she could, and then instead of emerging into the open she started to make her way through one dividing curtain after another toward the end of the row. In the next occupied cubicle, an elderly West Indian man lay huddled under a red blanket. In the last sat a scared-looking woman with a small boy. They looked up apprehensively as she appeared out of nowhere.

"Sorry to disturb you," Holly said. "Where's the children's waiting room?"

IT WAS AROUND a corner and separated from the main area by a short passageway and a couple of vending machines. Under a mural of misshapen Disney characters stood a basket of wrecked toys, some coverless picture books, and some undersized chairs across which a sleeping form lay. She woke up Lizzie, and dragged Jack protesting out of the corner playhouse in which he'd made a den. He quietened suddenly when he looked at her face.

She took them both by the hand and they followed a yellow line on the hospital floor toward the exit.

As they approached the automatic doors, Holly saw herself in the glass. But then the doors slid apart, and they sailed out into the night to look for a taxi.

In the presence of the driver they asked her no questions, and they gave her no trouble. Lizzie was twelve. She was dark, she was pretty, good at her lessons and no good at games. Jack was only six, a beefy little fair-haired Tonka truck of a boy.

The roads were quiet and the taxi got them to the place on the ring road in twenty minutes. It was a good half-mile on from where she'd expected it to be. The police were gone but the car was still there.

"Do you want me to wait?" the cab driver said, but Holly said no and paid him off.

She waited until the cab was out of sight before she descended to her vehicle.

The children hung back on the grass verge, by the deep earth-gouges that marked the spot where their car had left the carriageway. Spray-painted lines on the grass and on the tarmac showed where the accident unit had taken measurements. Down in the ditch, they'd left a big *Police Aware* sticker on the back window of her Toyota.

The Toyota was old and it wasn't in the best of shape, but it was a runner. Usually. Right now it was stuck nose-first in the bushes along with all the windblown litter at the bottom of the embankment.

The keys had been taken, but Holly groped around in the wheel arch where she kept a secret spare. As she crouched there, she glanced up at the children. They were watching her, two shapes etched against the yellow sodium mist that hung over the road.

Her fingertips found the little magnetic box right up at the top of the arch, deep in the crusted road dirt.

"Got them," she said. "Come on."

Lizzie was nervously eyeing the Toyota as she and Jack came scrambling down.

"What are we going to do?" she said. "It's stuck here. We can't go anywhere."

"We don't know that for certain yet," Holly said, tearing off the police notice and then moving around to open the doors. She didn't know what the procedure was, but they couldn't have looked inside the boot. However quick the glance, Frank would have been hard to miss.

Jack climbed into the back, without an argument for once, and Lizzie got into the passenger seat.

Once she was behind the wheel, Holly checked herself in the rearview mirror. At least when she'd hit her head on the roof, her face had been spared. Her vision had been blurred in the ambulance, hence the need for an X-ray, but that had mostly cleared up now.

Still, she looked a sight. She ran her fingers through to straighten her hair and then she rubbed at her reddened eyes, but of course that only made them worse.

"Here goes," she said, and tried the engine.

It started on the second try. It was sluggish and it didn't sound at all right, but it caught just the same.

There was no point in trying to reverse up the banking, but she tried it anyway. The wheels spun and the car went nowhere. So instead she put it into first gear and tried going forward, squeezing on through the bushes.

For a moment it looked as if this wasn't going to work either, but with a jarring bump they lurched forward into the leaves. Switches bent and cracked as the Toyota forced its way through. She glanced in the mirror and saw Jack watching, fascinated, as foliage scraped and slid along the window only inches from his face. God alone knew what it was doing to her paintwork.

They came out onto what looked like a narrow limestone track, which was actually a soakaway at the bottom of the ditch. Staying in low gear, she began to follow its irregular line. After about a hundred yards she was able to transfer across to a dirt road, which led in turn to a lane. The lane took them under the ring road and then around and back onto it.

Once they were on hard tarmac again, Holly permitted herself to breathe. But not too much. There was the rest of the night still to be managed.

And then—perhaps even more of a challenge—the rest of their lives thereafter.

∽

SHE HADN'T SEEN it happen. She hadn't even been in the house. She'd come home to find Frank lying awkwardly at the bottom of the stairs and Lizzie sitting with her head in her hands at the top of them. It might have passed for an accident, but for the letter-opener stuck in Frank's neck.

He wasn't supposed to be in the house. The restraining order was meant to take care of that. He wasn't even supposed to come within a hundred yards of his daughter, regardless of where she might be.

So, technically speaking, by being in the boot of the car he was in breach of the order right now.

Holly's first thought had been to pick up the phone and call the police. Her second had been that perhaps she could first wipe off the handle and put her own prints onto it and take all the blame. Then a sudden rage had risen within her. She'd looked down on his twisted body and felt no horror, no awe. No anguish or dismay. Just cheated. Frank had contrived to poison their existence while he was around; was there to be no end to it even with him gone?

She'd made the decision right then. They would not enter that process. If they moved quickly enough, they could put him right out of their lives and make a clean beginning. It would be a credible move; Frank could make an enemy in the time it took him to buy a newspaper, and any suspicion would be dispersed among the many. She'd looked at Lizzie and told her exactly what she had in mind.

We can't, Lizzie had said.

So Holly had sat her down and for ten solid minutes had laid out the choices for her, making sure that she understood how much depended on the next few hours. What was done was done, she'd said to her, and there's no changing it now. Don't feel you're to blame. It isn't a matter of right or wrong. Your father made all the choices that caused this to happen.

It had worked. Kind of.

They couldn't use Frank's car. Being in the motor trade he'd use whatever vehicle was going spare on the lot, and of late he'd been favouring a red coupé that was hardly practical for the job in hand. So Holly had backed her Toyota into the garage on the side of the house, lined the boot with a plastic decorating sheet, and together they'd dragged Frank through the connecting door and manhandled his body into it. Handling him was less of a problem than Holly had expected. In the unpleasantness stakes, Frank dead was hard-pressed to match up to Frank in life.

Once he was safely stowed and covered in a couple of old towels, they'd driven out to collect Jack from school and then set off for the coast. Fish and chips on the pier, Jack. It's a surprise treat. We just have to make a call somewhere, first. Somewhere quiet. You'll stay in the car.

And then the accident, and the plan forced off-course.

But back on it, now.

FROM THE RING road, they got onto the motorway. The traffic was heavier here, and it slowed when the carriageway narrowed to a single lane. For a long time there was no visible reason for it, and then suddenly they came upon a surfacing crew laying down new tarmac under bright work lights; a colossal rolling tar factory that belched and stank like a dragon as it excreted a lane-wide ribbon of hot road, men with shovels and brushes working furiously in its wake, supervisors in hard hats chatting by their vehicles.

"Look, Jack," Lizzie said. "Big trucks."

"Big, big trucks!" Jack said with awe, and turned in his seat to watch through the back window as they left the staged drama behind.

"You like the big trucks, don't you, Jack?" Holly said as the lanes cleared and the Toyota picked up speed again, but Jack didn't answer.

Holly couldn't put a finger on it, but the Toyota didn't feel quite right after the accident. She could only hope that it wouldn't let them down, and that the outside of the car wasn't messed up too much. A police stop was something that she didn't dare risk.

The next time she checked on Jack, he was asleep. His mouth was open and his head was rocking with the rhythm of the car. He slept the way he did everything…wholeheartedly, and with a hundred per cent commitment.

For a moment, Holly experienced a sensation in her heart that was like a power surge. This was her family. Everything that mattered to her was here, in this car.

And then she remembered that Frank was in the car with them, too. Good old Frank. Consistent as ever. Bringing a little touch of dread into every family outing.

They left the motorway, took a back road, and drove through a couple of darkened villages. There was a place that she had in mind. Out to the north and west was a great bay whose inland fields and marshes were almost unknown beyond the region. At low tide, saltings and sand flats extended the land almost to the horizon. Much of what was now solid ground had once been part of the sea. In places the sea was claiming it back, pushing the coastline inland so that fields and even some roads were being lost forever. Hide something here well enough, and…

Well, she'd have to hope. It was the best she could come up with.

Somewhere along here there was a causeway road that had once led to a farm, long-abandoned. People had trekked out to it for a picnic spot when there was something to see, but then the shell had become unsafe and it had all been pulled down. Now there was just rubble and the lines of a couple of walls, and that only visible at a low spring tide.

They crawled along, following the causeway with the Toyota's dipped beams. It didn't so much end as deteriorate steadily for the last couple of hundred yards. The concrete sections of the road had become tilted and skewed as the ground beneath them had given up any pretence of permanence. The sections had drifted, and in places they'd separated completely.

She had to stop the car and get out to locate the cesspit. When she turned back, Lizzie was out of the car and standing beside it.

She was looking around and she said, "Have I been here before?"

"Once," Holly said. "Before Jack was born. I brought you out here to show it to you, because it was a place my mother and father used to bring me. But it had all changed."

Lizzie tried to speak, but then she just nodded. And then her control went altogether, and her body was suddenly convulsed with an air-sucking sob that was shocking both in its violence, and in its unexpectedness.

Holly moved to her quickly and put her arms around her, holding her tightly until the worst of it passed. There in the darkness, out on the causeway, with the moon rising and this thing of such enormity to be dealt with. It would be no easy night, and no easy ride from here. Holly was only just beginning to appreciate how hard her daughter's journey would be.

"I can't do this," Lizzie whispered.

"Yes we can," Holly told her.

They got him out of the car into the pool and he floated, just under the surface, a hand drifting up into the pale shaft of dirtwater light from the Toyota's beams. The first stone sank him and then they added others, as many as they could lift. A sudden gout of bubbles gave them a fright. Holly was convinced that it caused her heart to stop beating for a moment.

They stood watching for a while to be sure of their work, and Holly sneaked a glance at Lizzie. Her face was in shadow and impossible to read.

"We should say a prayer," Lizzie said.

"Say one in the car," Holly said. "We need to get back and clean up the stairs."

Back on the motorway she watched for police cars, but she saw none. She *did* become aware of some lights that seemed to pace her for a while, but when she slowed a little the vehicle drew closer, and she was able to see that it lacked the telltale profile of roof bar and blue lights.

They had unmarked ones, of course. There was always that risk.

After a while, the headlamps in her mirror began to irritate her. She slowed even more to let the car pass, but it didn't. So then she picked up speed and tried to leave it behind; two minutes later and as many miles on, it was still there.

It surely meant nothing, but now it was making her nervous. Lizzie seemed to pick up on this. She saw Holly's frequent glances in the mirror and turned herself around in her seat, straining at her belt to look out of the back window.

"It's the same car," she said.

"What do you mean?"

"The one that pushed us off the road."

"It can't be," Holly said.

Lizzie clearly wasn't certain enough to argue the point.

"Well, it's similar," she said.

Holly increased her speed even further, up and over the limit, and the wheel began to vibrate in her hands as if the Toyota was beginning to shake itself apart. It couldn't be the same car. She couldn't imagine who'd want to follow her, or why.

It seemed to be working. They were leaving the other car behind, but then she saw something out of the corner of her eye. She looked down. The oil light was on, the brightest thing on the dash, and the one thing she knew about a car's oil light was that on a screaming engine it signalled imminent disaster.

She slowed, but it didn't go out. Other warning lights started to flicker on around it. So Holly quickly put the car out of gear and indicated to move off the motorway and onto the hard shoulder.

They coasted to a halt. The engine was already silent by the time they reached a stop. It had died somewhere during the deceleration, she couldn't be sure when. As they sat there, the cooling engine block ticked and clanked like coins dropping into a bucket.

In the back, Jack was stirring.

"Fish and chips on the pier," he said suddenly.

"I'm sorry, Jack," Holly said. "It's got too late. Another time."

The other car was pulling in behind them, hazard lights flashing. Right then a big bus passed them at speed in the inside lane, and its slipstream rocked the Toyota on its wheels.

"Who is it, then?" Lizzie said, peering back as the other car came to a halt about fifty or sixty yards back.

"I don't know," Holly said. "Nobody."

Jack said, "Is it Daddy?"

Holly looked at Lizzie, and Lizzie looked at her. There was a risk that Jack might have picked up on something then, but all his attention was on the road behind them. The following driver was getting out. Just as the car was an anonymous shape behind the glare of its own headlights, the driver's figure was a slip of shadow against the liquid stream of passing traffic.

"No, Jack," Holly said, an inexplicable anxiety rising up within her. "It can't be your daddy." She glanced down at the dash. All of the warning lights were on now, but that meant nothing. Everything always came on when the engine stalled.

"It *is*," Jack said.

Holly could tell him it wasn't. But she couldn't tell him why.

She heard Lizzie draw in a deep and shuddering breath, and let it out again. She found her daughter's hand in the dark and squeezed it once.

Traffic flew by, and the driver kept on coming. He was silhouetted against the flashing hazard lights of his own vehicle, pulsing like an amber heart.

Maybe he was your regular Good Samaritan, coming to offer them a hand.

Or maybe he was one of any number of things, as yet unrecognised and uncatalogued.

"He's been in the rain," said Jack.

Forget the oil pressure. Forget the ruinous cost of a thrown piston or a seized-up engine. Suddenly it was far more important to get herself and the children away from this spot.

But all the Toyota's power seemed to have gone. The engine turned over like an exhausted fighter trying to rise after a long count. She tried turning off the lights, and as their beams died the sound of the starter immediately improved.

It barked, it caught. All the warning lights on the dash went out, including the oil. She crashed the gears, checked her mirror once, and pulled out. Right now her only concern was to get moving again.

Jack was turned around in his seat, straining to see.

"Who is it, if it isn't Daddy?" he said.

"It's nobody," Holly said. "Face forward."

"He's running after us."

"Jack," she said sharply, "how many times have I got to tell you?"

She was expecting him to give her an argument. But something in her tone seemed to make him decide, and he complied without another word.

Nothing that she was supposed to hear, anyway.

"It *was* Daddy," she heard him mutter.

SHE KNEW IT wasn't, but the thought was planted now and it spooked her. The sooner this was over with, the better. She wondered how they'd recall this night. Would it be etched in their minds so they'd relive it, moment by moment, or would it move to the distance of a remembered nightmare?

Jack must never know the truth. For him, the story would have to be that his daddy had gone away. He'd keep on looking forward to his father's return, but in time he'd grow and the hope would fade and become part of the background noise of his life.

For Lizzie it was going to be a lot trickier. But at least she was safe from her father now. Whatever problems she might have in dealing with the deed and its memory, that was the thing to keep in mind.

Over a wooded hill, down into a valley, heading for home. Out there in the darkness were the lights of all those small towns that didn't rate exits of their own, but were linked by the road that the motorway had replaced.

That following car was back in her mirror. Or perhaps it was some different car, it was impossible to say. All she could see was those anonymous lights. This time they were staying well back.

Here came the roadworks again. Same stretch, opposite direction. Again, one lane was coned off and the carriageway lights were out. A few moments after they'd crossed into this darker territory, the driver behind her switched on his beams. They were the pop-up kind. She saw them swivel into view like laser eyes.

Just like on Frank's coupé.

Jack said, "Can we have the radio?"

"Not right now," Holly said.

"It was working before."

"I'm trying to concentrate."

He was closing the distance between them. Holly knew she couldn't go any faster.

She looked down and saw that her ignition lights were flickering and that, once again, her oil warning light was full on.

They passed what remained of a demolished bridge, with new concrete piers ready to take its wider replacement. Beyond the bridge site, just off the road, stood a mass of caravans and portable buildings. It was a construction village, a shantytown of churned up mud and giant machines. A temporary sliproad had been bulldozed into the embankment to give access to works traffic.

Holly waited until it was almost too late. Then she swerved across the lanes and into the sliproad.

Something thumped against the car, and in the mirror she saw one of the cones go tumbling in her wake. The car behind her was swerving to avoid it. It made him overshoot the turnoff, so he couldn't follow her. Now he'd be stuck. The traffic wouldn't allow him to stop and back up again. He'd be heading in the same direction for miles and miles.

Good Samaritan? Good riddance.

All the lights in this temporary settlement were on, yet nothing moved. Jack was craning, eagerly looking around the various site office buildings as they entered the main area. But Holly got in first.

"Yes, Jack," she said. "They have big trucks here."

IT WAS ALMOST as bright as day, and completely deserted. The yard was floodlit and every portakabin office had its lights on. Holly could see through all the uncurtained windows that every one of the offices was empty.

She slowed, and stopped, and looked around.

A few vans, a couple of big diggers. Some concrete bridge sections waiting to be trucked out and assembled elsewhere. The site had the look of a frontier fort, obviously not intended to be here for ever; but it was hard to believe that the scars it would leave on the land could ever easily heal.

They would, of course. The big machines would simply put it all back when they'd finished. It wouldn't quite be nature, but everybody would be going by too fast to notice.

She got out. There was the sound of a generator, banging away somewhere in the background.

"Hello?" she called out, and then glanced back at the car.

Jack and Lizzie were watching her through the side-windows. Pale children, out on the road past their bedtimes. They looked hollow-eyed and tired. Jack with his little round face, Lizzie like a stick-version of the teenager she'd soon be.

Holly gave them a brief smile, and then moved out to look for someone. She didn't want to get too far from the car. She didn't want to let them out of her sight.

She called again, and this time someone came out from behind one of the buildings.

He stood there, and she had to walk over to him. He looked like a toothless old shepherd in a flat cloth cap, knuckly hands hanging down by his sides. He could have been any age, from a well-preserved seventy down to a badly done-by fifty. Too old to be one of the road gang, he looked as if he'd been on road gangs all his life.

She said, "Is anyone in charge around here?"

"Never, love," the man said. "They all do what they sodding well like."

"Well…what do *you* do?"

"I'm just the brewman."

Holly looked around her at some of the heavy plant that stood under the lights, looking as if it had all been airdropped in to remodel the face of Mars.

She said, "I've been having trouble with my car. Is there anyone who could have a look at it for me? I've got some money."

"Andy's the mechanic," he said.

"Is he here?"

"He's never here."

"Is it worth me waiting for him? Can I do that?"

"You can do whatever you want," and then added, as if it was his all-purpose charm to ward off evil, "I'm just the brewman." And then he trudged off.

She went back to the car.

"I'm fed up of this," Jack said.

"I can't help it, Jack," Holly said. "Try to understand."

"No," he said, barking it out like a little dog with all the passion and venom he could manage.

Rather than argue or get angry, Holly got out of the car again to watch for Andy the Mechanic.

The site wasn't quite as deserted as it looked, but it took a while to become attuned to it and to pick up the signals; the sound of a door opening and closing somewhere, a glimpse of a figure passing from one building to another.

She paced a little. She looked toward the motorway. For something to do, she raised the Toyota's bonnet and took a look at the engine in the vague hope that her car problems might have some blindingly obvious solution. But it looked like engines always did to her, grimy and complex and meaningless. There was a smell as if something had been burning, and when she held her hand out over the block she could feel the heat rising from it. She poked at a couple of the leads, to no effect other than to get her hands dirtier than they already were.

A voice called out, "Are you looking for someone?"

A man was walking across the open ground toward her. He was short, dark, powerfully built. He had at least six upper teeth missing on one side, but from the way that he grinned the loss didn't seem to trouble him.

"Would you be Andy?" she said.

"I might."

"Then I'm looking for you."

She quickly explained her problem in case he started to get the wrong idea, and he moved her out of the way so that he could take a look. It didn't take him long.

"Look at your fanbelt," he said. "If your drawers were that slack, they'd be down around your ankles. When that starts to slip, your battery runs down and you run out of power."

"Is it hard to fix?"

"If I said yes, you'd be more impressed," he said, and it was then that he noticed the two children inside the car. They were staring out at him.

"Yours?" he said.

"Yes," Holly said. "We've been to the seaside."

He looked at her, and then he looked at the car.

And then he said, "You take the kids and wait in the brew hut while I have a go at this. Tell Diesel to make you a cup of tea."

"Is Diesel the brewman's name?"

"It's what his tea tastes like, as well."

The brew hut was the oldest-looking and most battered of the site buildings. It was up on blocks, and reached by three stairs. The floor sagged as they stepped inside. There were about a dozen folding card tables with chairs around them, and a sense of permanent grime everywhere; it was as if engine oil had been ground into the floor, rubbed into the walls, coated onto the windows.

The brewman was sitting by a plug-in radiator, reading a copy of *The Sun*. It wasn't a cold night, but the radiator was turned up high and the air inside the hut was stifling. He looked up as they entered.

Holly said, "Andy told us to wait in here. Is that all right with you?"

"Whatever you like," the brewman said. "I'm Matty."

"He said you were called Diesel."

Matty's face fell, and he looked out of the window.

"The bastard," he said, and he got up and stamped off.

Given his mood and the likely state of his crockery, Holly decided not to press him about the tea. She ushered the children onto grimy plastic seats that stood against the wall. On the wall itself was tacked a selection of yellowing newspaper cuttings, all of them showing the debris of spectacular motorway crashes.

Jack said, "It stinks in here."

"Shh," Holly said.

"It *does*."

She couldn't tell him it didn't, because it did. And she couldn't agree that it did in case Matty was listening. So she only said, "It won't be for long."

They waited. There was a clock on the wall, but it was wrong. Jack swung his feet, Lizzie stared at the floor. Outside, a massive engine began to rev up somewhere close behind the building, making their chairs vibrate.

Jack said, "I'm bored."

"Play I-spy," Holly suggested.

"I'm not playing with him," Lizzie said. "He can't spell."

Holly said, with an unexpected tightness in her tone, "Then why don't we all just sit here quietly?"

There was silence for a while and then Lizzie muttered, rebelliously, "It's true. He can't."

And Jack agreed with her. "I've got a giant brain," he said, "but I can't spell."

Holly covered her eyes. She wasn't sure whether she was laughing or crying and the two children, equally uncertain, were watching her closely for clues.

This night would pass. It would somehow all be fine.

Keep thinking that, she told herself, and it might even come true.

"Mum…" Lizzie said.

Holly looked at her and saw the unease and the apprehension in her eyes. She might be sharp, but she was still only twelve years old.

"When this part's over," she said, "what then?"

She was choosing her words carefully because of Jack, but Holly knew what Lizzie was trying to say.

"We'll carry on as normal," she said.

"Can we do that?"

"We'll have to," Holly said.

There was a tap on the window. Andy was standing there outside, raising himself up on tiptoe so that he could look in, and he beckoned to her.

She went out, and they walked over to the car together. He told her he'd left the keys inside it.

"Best I can do," he said. "I've tightened your fanbelt and cleaned off your plugs. They were blacker than Matty's fingernails."

"Thanks, Andy."

"You've got a lot of oil down there. I don't know where it's coming from. You might need a new gasket."

He showed her what he'd done and got her to feel the difference in the fanbelt, which she pretended to appreciate. She offered him twenty quid and he took it with no embarrassment. Then she went back for the children.

The brew hut door was open. Lizzie was alone inside.

Holly said, "Where's Jack?"

Lizzie had slumped down into her coat as if it was a nest, hands in her pockets and legs outstretched, looking at the toes of her shoes as she clacked them together. She said, "He followed you outside."

"I didn't see him."

"He wanted to look at the big trucks."

Holly went out. Jack hadn't gone over toward the car, or she'd have seen him. She stood in front of the brew hut and called out his name.

Nothing.

Lizzie was in the doorway behind her now.

"It's not my fault," she said defensively.

Holly went around by the side of the brew hut and found herself in an area lit by the most powerful of the overhead floodlights. Under the lights stood a few parked cars and a variety of dormant machines. She could hear the massive engine whose note had been shaking the brew hut's foundations, and could tell that it was somewhere close.

She looked back and saw that Lizzie had followed her some of the way.

"You look around the buildings," Holly said. "I'll look here."

She didn't wait to see how Lizzie responded, but started to make her way through the machine yard. It was like a giant's bazaar of heavy engineering, the night sun casting deep, dark shadows under the gear. These were machines for ripping up the land, and they had spikes and claws and teeth on a saurian scale. Encrusted with clay and battered by hard use, they stood like bombed-out tanks.

She hauled herself up and looked in the cab of a well-rusted bulldozer on tracks. Jack wasn't in it, but by hanging on she could look out over the yard. Down the next row, a wagon was being inched up onto a flatbed trailer by some driver she couldn't see. The tyres on the wagon were enormous, and the ramps were bending under its weight.

She looked all around and called Jack's name, but she had little chance of being heard. The big engine roared and the great tonnage slowly rolled. In her mind's eye she saw Jack crushed or falling or struggling to get free of some unexpected snare. She saw gears turning, teeth meshing, pulling him in.

She called his name again, louder, and then hopped down to continue the search. She stumbled a little when she landed. The ground here was nothing more than churned-up dirt into which stones had been dumped to give it some firmness. It was no playground.

"Jack!" she called, moving forward.

As she came around by the bulldozer onto a firmer stretch of concrete road, she saw him. She could see all the way to the perimeter fence, where he was climbing.

Climbing? What was he *doing*?

And then she understood, and started to run.

IT WAS A storm fence, about eight feet high. Jack was already over the top of it, and climbing down the other side. The fence rocked back and forth under his weight as the concrete posts shifted in their holes, but he clung to it like a bug; its close weave offered ideal purchase for his small feet and fingers.

Holly stumbled on the rough ground, but caught herself and went on. On the other side of the perimeter fence was an unlit country lane.

Out on the country lane stood the red coupé with the pop-up headlights.

"Hey," she shouted. "Hey, Jack, no!"

He was descending with his face set in a look of utter concentration. Behind him, the car was making a low purring sound with its engine off but its electric fan sucking in the cool night air. The driver hadn't stepped out, and she could barely see anything of him. She could only guess that he was watching her.

Holly reached the fence, looking through it and up at him. "Jack," she said. "Come down, Jack, please. You can't go over there. That's not your daddy. Believe me. There's no way it could be."

But Jack didn't look at her, and didn't even show any sign of having heard. He was moving like a monkey. He reached down with his foot, found another space in the diamond pattern, and hooked his scuffed trainer into it before lowering the rest of his weight.

She could touch his fingers as they hooked through, right in front of her eyes; her breath through the wire could fall onto his face. "Jack," she said, "no!"

But he wouldn't look at her, and although he was only inches away she couldn't reach him. She was powerless.

"Jack," she said, "Look at me, please. Don't do this. Don't go to him."

She made a move as if to try and catch his hands through the wire, but it was pointless. She couldn't hold him if she caught him. All she could do was risk hurting him.

"Lizzie's looking for you as well," she pleaded. "Oh, *Jack…*"

He jumped, and hit the dirt on the far side with a thump. Holly made a leap at the wire and felt the entire fence lean before her, but she didn't have his agility and couldn't begin to climb the way that he had.

He was running for the car, now, and the car's passenger door was opening to receive him.

Holly was screaming, although she didn't immediately realise it. The car door slammed and its laser eyes opened. The engine started, and its nose swung around as it began to turn in the narrow lane.

Her hands were up at the sides of her head. She'd heard of people tearing at their hair, but she'd always thought it was just an expression. She looked around wildly.

Then she started to run along the inside of the fence, ahead of the turning car.

The country lane ran close on the other side. If there was a gap anywhere, she'd get through it. The car wouldn't pass her. No way was she going to let that happen.

Here was a gate. It was a back way into the site, little-used. A big double gate, wide enough for a lorry but chained and padlocked in the middle. There was enough play in the chain to make a gap of a foot or so.

It was a squeeze, but not an impossible one. She came out on the other side and all that she could see were the twin lights, the laser eyes of the beast that she had to impede.

She put on a burst and dived into its way, sliding to a halt in the middle of the lane and raising both of her hands. When it hit her, she felt nothing other than her own sudden acceleration; no impact, no pain, just the instantaneous switch from rest into motion as her legs were knocked from under her and she was spun down the side of the car.

Afterwards she'd never know whether she really saw it or only imagined the memory, but Holly went down hard in the wake of the moving car with a mental picture of her son's blank face only inches away on the other side of the glass.

She lay there.

She couldn't move. She could hear that the car had stopped and she wanted to lift her head to look, but nothing happened. Oh God, she was thinking, I'm paralysed. But then when she made an enormous effort, her hand came up and braced itself against the ground. As she was doing it, she heard a car door opening.

She wasn't paralysed, but she'd no strength. When she tried to push down with her hand to raise herself, her arm trembled and nothing happened.

Someone was walking up behind her.

Before she could muster the energy to turn and look, strong fingers gripped the back of her head and thrust her face down into the mud. In an instant, she was blinded and choking.

She found her strength now, all right, but it did her no good as a sudden knee in her back pinned her further to the ground. She struggled and flapped like a fish, but her face stayed under. The blood roared in her ears and lights exploded before her eyes.

Then in an instant, the pressure was off.

That first deep breath nearly drowned her on the spot, as she sucked in all the mud that had filled up her mouth. She retched and coughed, blowing it out of her nostrils and heaving up what she'd both swallowed and inhaled.

She felt a lighter touch on her shoulder and lashed out, only to hear a cry from Lizzie. She was there when Holly's vision cleared, keeping back and holding her arm where she'd been struck.

"I'm sorry, mum," she said.

Holly stared dumbly for a moment before an understanding started to form. Lizzie was backing toward the waiting car.

"No, Lizzie!" she said. She tried to rise, but one of her legs wouldn't support her.

"I know how you want me to feel about it, but I can't. I wish I could. I'm sorry. It's never going to be right after tonight, whatever we do. Ever."

Holly made another massive effort and this time made it up and onto her feet, putting all of her weight onto the uninjured leg.

"Wait," she managed.

Lizzie had reached the car.

"I'm the one that he wants," she said. "But he'll take Jack if I don't go with him."

The passenger door popped open about an inch.

"I'm sorry," she said again, and she reached out and opened it all the way.

Holly wasn't close enough to see how it worked, but Jack popped out of the vehicle as if propelled on a spring. He landed on both feet, and Lizzie quickly slipped around behind him and into the car.

The door closed like the door on a well-fitting safe, and the car's engine started to rev. It was all as swift and as decisive as that.

Holly started toward them, half-hopping, half-limping, but the car was already moving off and starting to pick up speed.

"Frank!" she shouted. "You bastard! Give her back!" and at the sound of her voice, Jack seemed to wake as if from a daze.

He looked about, as if suddenly remembering something, and spotted those red tail lights receding off into the darkness.

He gave a strangled cry.

"Dad!" he called out, and started to run down the lane after the car, slapping down his feet so hard that the ground almost shook.

Holly hadn't yet reached him, and her cries couldn't stop him. Neither of them had any chance of catching the car. But both of them tried.

She caught up with him a full ten minutes later, still standing on the dark spot where his breath and his hopes had finally given out.

"He forgot me!" he wailed. Holly dropped to her knees and pulled him to her.

For once, he let her hold him.

The
BOX

I T WAS A woman who picked up the phone and I said, "Can I speak to Mister Lavery, please?"

"May I ask what it concerns?" she said.

I gave her my name and said, "I'm calling from Wainfleet Maritime College. I'm his instructor on the helicopter safety course."

"I thought that was all done with last week."

"He didn't complete it."

"Oh." I'd surprised her. "Excuse me for one moment. Can you hold on?"

I heard her lay down the phone and move away. Then, after a few moments, there came the indistinct sounds of a far-off conversation. There was her voice and there was a man's, the two of them faint enough to be in another room. I couldn't make out anything of what was being said.

After a while, I could hear someone returning.

I was expecting to hear Lavery's voice, but it was the woman again.

She said, "I'm terribly sorry, I can't get him to speak to you." There was a note of exasperation in her tone.

"Can you give me any indication why?"

"He was quite emphatic about it," she said. The implication was that no, he'd not only given her no reason, but he also hadn't appreciated being asked. Then she lowered her voice and added, "I wasn't aware that he hadn't finished the course. He told me in so many words that he was done with it."

Which could be taken more than one way. I said, "He does know that without a safety certificate he can't take up the job?"

"He's never said anything about that." She was still keeping her voice down, making it so that Lavery—her husband, I imagined, although the woman hadn't actually identified herself—wouldn't overhear. She went on, "He's been in a bit of a funny mood all week. Did something happen?"

"That's what I was hoping he might tell me. Just ask him once more for me, will you?"

She did, and this time I heard Lavery shouting.

When she came back to the phone she said, "This is very embarrassing."

"Thank you for trying," I said. "I won't trouble you any further, Mrs Lavery."

"It's Miss Lavery," she said. "James is my brother."

In 1950 the first scheduled helicopter service started up in the UK, carrying passengers between Liverpool and Cardiff. Within a few short years helicopter travel had become an expensive, noisy and exciting part of our lives. No vision of a future city was complete without its heliport. Children would run and dance and wave if they heard one passing over.

. The aviation industry had geared up for this new era in freight and passenger transportation, and the need for various kinds of training had brought new life to many a small airfield and flight school. Wainfleet was a maritime college, but it offered new aircrew one facility that the flight schools could not.

At Wainfleet we had the dunker, also known as The Box.

We'd been running the sea rescue and safety course for almost three years, and I'd been on the staff for most of that time. Our completion record was good. I mean, you expect a few people to drop out of any training programme, especially the dreamers, but our intake were experienced men with some living under their belts. Most were ex-navy or air force, and any romantic notions had been knocked out of them in a much harder theatre than ours. Our scenarios were as nothing, compared to the situations through which some of them had lived.

And yet, I was thinking as I looked at the various records spread across the desk in my little office, our dropouts were gradually increasing in their numbers. Could the fault lie with us? There was nothing in any of their personal histories to indicate a common cause.

I went down the corridor to Peter Taylor's office. Peter Taylor was my boss. He was sitting at his desk signing course certificates.

I said, "Don't bother signing Lavery's."

He looked up at me with eyebrows raised, and I shrugged.

"I'm no closer to explaining it," I said.

"Couldn't just be plain old funk, could it?"

"Most of these men are war heroes," I said. "Funk doesn't come into it."

He went back to his signing, but he carried on talking.

"Easy enough to be a hero when you're a boy without a serious thought in your head," he said. "Ten years of peacetime and a few responsibilities, and perhaps you get a little bit wiser."

Then he finished the last one and capped the fountain pen and looked at me. I didn't quite know what to say. Peter Taylor had a background in the merchant marine but he'd sat out the war right here, in a reserved occupation.

"I'd better be getting on," I said.

I left the teaching block and went over to the building that housed our sea tank. It was a short walk and the sun was shining, but the wind from the ocean always cut through the gap between the structures. The wind smelled and tasted of sand and salt, and of something unpleasant that the new factories up the coast had started to dump into the estuary.

Back in its early days, Wainfleet had been a sanatorium for TB cases. Staffed by nuns, as I understood it; there were some old photographs in the mess hall. Then it had become a convalescent home for mine workers and then, finally, the maritime college it now was. We had two hundred boarding cadets for whom we had dormitories, a parade ground, and a rugby field that had a pronounced downward slope toward the cliffs. But I wasn't part of the cadet teaching staff. I was concerned only with the commercial training arm.

Our team of four safety divers was clearing up after the day's session. The tank had once been an ordinary swimming pool, added during the convalescent-home era but then deepened and re-equipped for our purposes. The seawater was filtered, and in the winter it was heated by a boiler.

Although if you'd been splashing around in there in December, you'd never have guessed it.

Their head diver was George "Buster" Brown. A compact and powerful-looking man, he'd lost most of his hair and had all but shaved off the rest, American GI-style. With his barrel chest and his bullet head, he looked like a human missile in his dive suit. In fact, he'd actually trained on those two-man torpedoes toward the end of the war.

I said to him, "Cast your mind back to last week. Remember a trainee name of Lavery?"

"What did he look like?"

I described him, and added, "Something went wrong and he didn't complete."

"I think I know the one," Buster said. "Had a panic during the exercise and we had to extract him. He was almost throwing a fit down there. Caught Jacky Jackson a right boff on the nose."

"What was he like after you got him out?"

"Embarrassed, I think. Wouldn't explain his problem. Stamped off and we didn't see him again."

Buster couldn't think of any reason why Lavery might have reacted as he did. As far as he and his team were concerned, the exercise had gone normally in every way.

I left him to finish stowing the training gear, and went over to inspect the Box.

The Box was a stripped-down facsimile of a helicopter cabin, made of riveted aluminium panels and suspended by cable from a lifeboat davit. The davit swung the Box out and over the water before lowering it. The cabin seated four. Once immersed, an ingenious chain-belt system rotated the entire cabin until it was upside down. It was as realistic a ditching as we could make it, while retaining complete control of the situation. The safety course consisted of a morning in the classroom, followed by the afternoon spent practising escape drill from underwater.

The Box was in its rest position at the side of the pool. It hung with its floor about six inches clear of the tiles. I climbed aboard, and grabbed at something to keep my balance as the cabin swung around under my weight.

There had been no attempt to dress up the interior to look like the real thing; upside-down and six feet under, only the internal geography needed to be accurate. The bucket seats and harnesses were genuine, but that was as far as it went. The rest was just the bare metal, braced with aluminium struts and with open holes cut for the windows. In appearance it was like a tin Wendy House, suspended from a crane.

I'm not sure what I thought I was looking for. I put my hand on one of the seats and tugged, but the bolts were firm. I lifted part of the harness and let the webbing slide through my fingers. It was wet and heavy. Steadying myself, I used both hands to close the buckle and then tested the snap-release one-handed.

"I check those myself," Buster Brown said through the window. "Every session."

"No criticism intended, Buster," I said.

"I should hope not," he said, and then he was gone.

It happened again the very next session, only three days later.

I'd taken the files home and I'd studied all the past cases, but I'd reached no firm conclusions. If we were doing something wrong, I couldn't see what it was.

These were not inexperienced men. Most were in their thirties and, as I'd pointed out to Peter Taylor, had seen service under wartime conditions. Some had been ground crew, but many had been flyers who'd made the switch to peacetime commercial aviation. Occasionally we'd get students whose notes came marked with a particular code, and whose records had blank spaces where personal details should have been; these individuals, it was acknowledged but never said, were sent to us as part of a wider MI5 training.

In short, no sissies. Some of them were as tough as you could ask, but it wasn't meant to be a tough course. It wasn't a trial, it wasn't a test. The war was long over.

As I've said, we began every training day in the classroom. Inevitably, some of it involved telling them things they already knew. But you can't skip safety, even though some of them would have loved to; no grown man ever looks comfortable in a classroom situation.

First I talked them through the forms they had to complete. Then I collected the forms in.

And then, when they were all settled again, I started the talk.

I said, "We're not here to punish anybody. We're here to take you through a scenario so that hopefully, if you ever do need to ditch, you'll have a much greater chance of survival. Most fatalities don't take place when the helicopter comes down. They happen afterwards, in the water."

I asked if anyone in the room had been sent to us for rebreather training, and a couple of hands were raised. This gave me a chance to note their faces.

"Right," I said. "I'm going to go over a few points and then after the break we'll head for the pool."

I ran through the routine about the various designs of flight suits and harnesses and life vests. Then the last-moment checks; glasses if you wore them, false teeth if you had them, loose objects in the cabin. Hold onto some part of the structure for orientation. Brace for impact.

One or two had questions. Two men couldn't swim. That was nothing unusual.

After tea break in the college canteen, we all went over together. Buster Brown and his men were already in the water, setting up a dinghy for the lifeboat drill that would follow the ditch. The students each found themselves a suit from the rail before disappearing into the changing room, and I went over to ready the Box.

When they came out, they lined up along the poolside. One of the divers steadied the Box and I stayed by the controls and called out, "Numbers one to four, step forward."

The Box jiggled around on its cable as the first four men climbed aboard and strapped themselves into the bucket seats. Buster Brown checked everyone's harness from the doorway, and then signalled to me before climbing in with them and securing the door from the inside. I sounded the warning klaxon and then eased back the lever to raise the Box into the air.

In the confines of the sea tank building, the noise of the crane's motor could be deafening. Once I'd raised the payload about twelve feet in the air, I swung the crane around on its turntable to place the Box directly over the pool. It swung there, turning on its cable, and I could see the men inside through the raw holes that represented aircraft windows.

Two divers with masks and air bottles were already under the water, standing by to collect the escapees and guide them up to the surface. Buster would stay inside. This was routine for him. He'd hold his breath for the minute or so that each exercise took, and then he'd ride the Box back to the poolside to pick up the next four.

Right now he was giving everyone a quick recap of what I'd told them in the classroom. Then it was, Brace, brace, brace for impact! and I released the Box to drop into the water.

It was a controlled drop, not a sudden plummet, although to a first-timer it was always an adrenalin moment. The Box hit the water and then started to settle, and I could hear Buster giving out a few final reminders in the rapidly-filling cabin.

Then it went under, and everything took on a kind of slow-motion tranquillity as the action transferred to below the surface. Shapes flitted from the submerged Box in all directions, like wraiths fleeing a haunted castle. They were out in seconds. As each broke the surface, a number was shouted. When all four were out, I raised the Box.

It was as fast and as straightforward as that.

The exercise was repeated until every student had been through a straightforward dunk. Then the line reformed and we did it all again, this time with the added refinement of a cabin rotation as the Box went under. It made for a more realistic simulation, as a real helicopter was liable to invert with the weight of its engine. To take some of the anxiety out of it, I'd tell the students that I considered escape from the inverted cabin to be easier—you came out through the window opening facing the surface, which made it a lot easier to strike out for.

Again, we had no problems. The safety divers were aware of the non-swimmers and gave them some extra assistance. The Box functioned with no problems. No one panicked, no one got stuck. Within the hour, everyone was done.

At that point, we divided the party. The two men on rebreather training stayed with Buster Brown, and everyone else went to the other end of the pool for lifeboat practice. I ran the Box through its paces empty yet again, as Buster stood at the poolside with them and ran through his piece on the use of the rebreather unit.

The rebreather does pretty much what its name suggests. Consisting of an airbag incorporated into the flotation jacket with a mouthpiece and a valve, it allows you to conserve and re-use your own air. There's more unused oxygen in an expelled breath than you'd think. It's never going to replace the aqualung, but the device can extend your underwater survival time by a vital minute or two.

Both men looked as if they might be old hands at this. Their names were Charnley and Briggs. Even in the borrowed flight suit, Charnley had that sleek, officer-material look. He had an Errol Flynn moustache and hair so heavily brilliantined that two dunks in the tank had barely disturbed it. Briggs, on the other hand, looked the non-commissioned man to his finger-tips. His accent was broad and his hair looked as if his wife had cut it for him, probably not when in the best of moods.

Buster left them practising with the mouthpieces and came over to pick up his mask and air bottle. I was guiding the empty Box, water cascading from every seam, back to the poolside.

"Just a thought, Buster," I said, raising my voice to be heard as I lowered the cabin to the side. "Wasn't Lavery on the rebreather when he had his little episode?"

"Now that you mention it, yes he was."

"How many were in the Box with him?"

"Two others. Neither of them had any problem."

I didn't take it any further than that. None of our other non-finishers had been on the rebreather when they chose to opt out, so this was hardly a pattern in the making.

The rebreather exercise was always conducted in three stages. Firstly, the Box was lowered to sit in the water so that the level inside the cabin was around chest-height. The student would practise by leaning forward into the water, knowing that in the event of difficulty he need do no more than sit back. This confidence-building exercise would then be followed by a total immersion, spending a full minute under the water and breathing on the apparatus. Assuming all went well, the exercise would end with a complete dunk, rotate and escape.

All went well. Until that final stage.

The others had all completed the lifeboat drill and left the pool by then. The Box hit the water and rolled over with the spectacular grinding noise that the chain belt always made. It sounded like a drawbridge coming down, and worked on a similar principle.

Then the boomy silence of the pool as the water lapped and the Box stayed under.

The minute passed, and then came the escape. One fleeting figure could be seen under the water. But only one. He broke surface and his number was called. It was Briggs. I looked toward the Box and saw Buster going in through one of the window openings. My hand was on the lever, but I waited; some injury might result if I hauled the Box out in the middle of an extraction. But then Buster came up and made an urgent signal and so I brought the cabin up out of the water, rotating it back upright as it came. Tank water came out of the window openings in gushers.

Buster came out of the pool and we reached the Box together. Charnley was still in his harness, the rebreather mouthpiece still pushing his cheeks out. He was making weak-looking gestures with his hands. I reached in to relieve him of the mouthpiece, but he swatted me aside and then spat it out.

Fending his hands away, Buster got in with him and released his harness. By then, Charnley was starting to recognise his surroundings and to act a little more rationally. He didn't calm down, though. He shoved both of us aside and clambered out.

He stood at the poolside, spitting water and tearing himself out of the flotation jacket.

"What was the problem?" I asked him.

"You want to get that bloody thing looked at," Charnley gasped.

Buster, who had a surprisingly puritan streak, said in a warning tone, "Language," and I shot him a not-now look.

"Looked at for what?" I said, but Charnley just hurled all his gear onto the deck as if it had been wrestling him and he'd finally just beaten it.

"Don't talk to me," he said, "I feel foul." And he stalked off to the changing room.

The two of us got the Box secure, and while we were doing it I asked Buster what happened. Buster could only shrug.

"I tapped his arm to tell him it was time to come out, but he didn't move," Buster said. "Just stayed there. I thought he might have passed out, but when I went in he started to thrash around and push me away."

So, what was Charnley's problem? I went to find him in the changing room. Briggs had dressed in a hurry in order to be sure of getting out in time for his bus. As he passed me in the doorway he said, "Your man's been wasting a good shepherd's pie in there."

Shepherd's pie or whatever, I could smell vomit hanging in the air around the cubicles at the back of the changing room. Charnley was out. He was standing in front of the mirror, pale as watered milk, knotting his tie. An RAF tie, I noted.

"Captain Charnley?" I said.

"What about it?"

"I just wondered if you were ready to talk about what happened."

"Nothing happened," he said.

I waited.

After a good thirty seconds or more he said, "I'm telling you nothing happened. Must have got a bad egg for breakfast. Serves me right for trusting your canteen."

I said, "I'll put you back on the list for tomorrow. You can skip the classroom session."

"Don't bother," he said, reaching for his blazer.

"Captain Charnley…"

He turned to me then, and fixed me with a look so stern and so urgent that it was almost threatening.

"I didn't see anything in there," he said. "Nothing. Do you understand me? I don't want you telling anyone I did."

Even though I hadn't suggested any such thing.

There was a bus stop outside the gates, but Captain Charnley had his own transport. It was a low, noisy, open-topped sports car with a Racing Green paint job, all dash and Castrol fumes. Off he went, scaring the birds out of the trees, swinging out onto the road and roaring away.

I went back to my office and reviewed his form. According to his record, he'd flown Hurricanes with 249 Squadron in Yorkshire. After the war he'd entered the glass business, but he'd planned a return to flying with BEA.

Hadn't seen anything? What exactly did that mean? What was there to see anyway?

I have to admit that in a fanciful moment, when we'd first started to suspect that there might be some kind of a problem on the course, I'd investigated the Box's history. But it had none. Far from being the salvaged cabin of a wrecked machine, haunted by the ghosts of those who'd died in it, the Box had been purpose-built as an exercise by apprentices at the local aircraft factory.

It was no older than its three-and-a-half years, and there was nothing more to it than met the eye. The bucket seats were from scrap, but they'd been salvaged from training aircraft that had been decommissioned without ever having seen combat or disaster.

When I went back to the sea tank, Buster Brown was out of his diving gear and dressed in a jacket and tie, collecting the men's clocking-off cards prior to locking up the building. The other divers had cleared away the last of their equipment and gone.

I said, "Can I ask a favour?"

He said, "As long as it doesn't involve borrowing my motor bike, my missus or my money, ask away."

I think he knew what I was going to say. "Stay on a few minutes and operate the dunker for me? I want to sit in and see if I can work out what all the fuss is about."

"I can tell you what the fuss is about," he said. "Some can take it and some can't."

"That doesn't add up, Buster," I said. "These have all been men of proven courage."

Suddenly it was as if we were back in the Forces and he was the experienced NCO politely setting the greenhorn officer straight.

"With respect, sir," he said, "you're missing the point. Being tested doesn't diminish a man's regard for danger. I think you'll find it's rather the opposite."

We proceeded with the trial. I found a suit that fitted me and changed into it. I put on a flotation jacket and rebreather gear. No safety divers, just me and Buster. Like the tattooed boys who ride the backs of dodgems at the fairground, you feel entitled to get a little cavalier with the rules you're supposed to enforce.

I strapped myself in, and signalled my readiness to Buster. Then I tensed involuntarily as the cable started moving with a jerk. As the Box rose into the air and swung out over the pool, I looked all around the interior for anything untoward. I saw nothing.

Buster followed the normal routine, lowering me straight into the water. The box landed with a slap, and immediately began to rock from side to side as it filled up and sank. It was cold and noisy when the seawater flooded into the cabin, but once you got over that first moment's shock it was bearable. I've swum in colder seas on Welsh holidays.

Just as it reached my chin, I took a deep breath and ducked under the surface. Fully submerged, I looked and felt all around me as far as I could reach, checking for anything unusual. There was nothing. I wasn't using the rebreather at this point. I touched the belt release, lifting the lever plate, and it opened easily. There was the usual slight awkwardness as I wriggled free of the harness, but it wasn't anything to worry about. I took a few more moments to explore the cabin, again finding nothing, and then I went out through a window opening without touching the sides.

I popped up no more than a couple of seconds later. When Buster saw that I was out in open water, he lifted the dunker. As I swam to the side it passed over me, streaming like a raincloud onto the heaving surface of the pool.

By the time I'd climbed up the ladder, the Box was back in its start position and ready for reboarding. I said to Buster, "So which seat was Charnley in? Wasn't it the left rear?"

"Aft seat on the port side," he said.

So that was the one I took, this second time. Might as well try to recreate the experience as closely as possible, I thought. Not that any of this seemed to be telling me anything useful. I strapped myself in and gave Buster the wave, and we were off again.

I had to run through the whole routine, just so that I could say to Peter Taylor that the check had been complete. It was second nature. In all walks of life, the survivors are the people who never assume. This time I inflated the rebreather bag while the cabin was in midair, and had the mouthpiece in by the time I hit the water. Again it came flooding in as the cabin settled, but this time there was a difference. Almost instantly the chain belt jerked into action and the cabin began to turn.

It feels strange to invert and submerge at the same time. You're falling, you're floating...of course people get disoriented, especially if they've never done it before. This time I determined to give myself the full minute under. Without a diver on hand to tap me when the time was up, I'd have to estimate it. But that was no big problem.

The cabin completed its turn, and stopped. All sound ended as well, apart from boomy echoes from the building above, pushing their way through several tons of water. I hung there in the harness, not breathing yet. I felt all but weightless in the straps. The seawater was beginning to make my eyes sting.

I'd forgotten how dark the cabin went when it was upside down. The tank was gloomy at this depth anyway. I'd heard that the American military went a stage further than we did, and conducted a final exercise with everyone wearing blacked-out goggles to simulate a night-time ditching. That seemed a little extreme to me; as I'd indicated to the men in the classroom, the Box was never intended as a test of endurance. It was more a foretaste of something we hoped they'd never have to deal with.

I found myself wondering if Buster had meant anything by that remark. The one about men who'd been tested. As if he was suggesting that I wouldn't know.

I'd been too young to fight at the very beginning of the war, but I joined up when I could and in the summer of 1940 I was selected for Bomber Command. In training I'd shown aptitude as a navigator. I flew twelve missions over heavily-defended Channel ports, bombing the German invasion barges being readied along the so-called "Blackpool Front".

Then Headquarters took me out and made me an instructor. My crew was peeved. It wasn't just a matter of losing their navigator; most crews were superstitious, and mine felt that their luck was being messed with. But you could understand Bomber Command's thinking. Our planes were ill-equipped for night navigation, and there was a knack to dead reckoning in a blackout. I seemed to have it, and I suppose they thought I'd be of more value passing it on to others.

My replacement was a boy of no more than my own age, also straight out of training. His name was Terriss. He, the plane, and its entire crew were lost on the next mission. I fretted out the rest of the war in one classroom or another.

And was still doing that, I supposed.

How long now? Thirty seconds, perhaps. I breathed out, and then drew warm air back in from the bag.

It tasted of rubber and canvas. A stale taste. The rebreather air was oddly unsatisfying, but its recirculation relieved the aching pressure that had been building up in my lungs.

I looked across at one of the empty seats, and the shadows in the harness looked back.

That's how it was. I'm not saying I saw an actual shape there. But the shadows fell as if playing over one. I turned my head to look at the other empty seat on that side of the cabin, and the figure in it raised its head to return my gaze.

The blood was pounding in my ears. I was forgetting the drill with the rebreather. Light glinted on the figure's flying goggles. On the edge of my vision, which was beginning to close in as the oxygen ran down, I was aware of someone in the third and last seat in the cabin right alongside me.

That was enough. I didn't stop to think. I admit it, I just panicked. All procedure was gone from my head. I just wanted to get out of there and back up to the surface. I was not in control of the situation. I wondered if I was hallucinating, much as you can know when you're in a nightmare and not have it help.

Now I was gripping the sides of the bucket seat and trying to heave myself out of it but, of course, the harness held me in. My reaction was a stupid one. It was to try harder, over and over, slamming against resistance until the webbing cut into my shoulders and thighs. I was like a small child, angrily trying to pound a wooden peg through the wrong shape of hole.

Panic was burning up my oxygen. Lack of oxygen was making my panic worse. Somewhere in all of this I managed the one clear thought that I was never going to get out of the Box if I didn't unbuckle my harness first.

It was at this point that the non-existent figure in the seat opposite leaned forward. In a smooth, slow move, it reached out and placed its hand over my harness release. The goggled face looked into my own. Between the flat glass lenses and the mask, no part of its flesh could be seen. For a moment I believed that it had reached over to help me out. But it kept its hand there, covering the buckle. Far from helping me, it seemed intent on preventing my escape.

I felt its touch. It wore no gloves. I'd thought that my own hand might pass through it as through a shadow, but it was as solid as yours or mine. When I tried to push it aside, it moved beneath my own as if all the bones in it had been broken. They shifted and grated like gravel inside a gelid bag.

When I tried to grab it and wrench it away, I felt its fingers dig in. I was trying with both hands now, but there was no breaking that grip. I somehow lost the rebreather mouthpiece as I blew out, and saw my precious breath go boiling away in a gout of bubbles. I wondered if Buster would see them break the surface but of course they wouldn't, they'd just collect and slide around inside the floorpan of the Box until it was righted again.

I had a fight not to suck water back into my emptied lungs. Some dead hand was on my elbow. It had to be one of the others. It felt like a solicitous touch, but it was meant to hamper me. Something else took a firm grip on my ankle. Darkness was overwhelming me now. I was being drawn downward into an unknown place.

And then, without sign or warning, it was over. The Box was revolving up into the light, and all the water was emptying out through every space and opening. As the level fell, I could see all around me. I could see the other seats, and they were as empty as when the session had begun.

I was still deaf and disoriented for a few seconds, and it lasted until I tilted my head and shook the water out of my ears. I had to blow some of it out of my nose as well, and it left me with a sensation like an ice-cream headache.

My harness opened easily, but once I'd undone it I didn't try to rise. I wasn't sure I'd have the strength. I gripped the seat arms and hung on as the Box was lowered.

I was still holding on when Buster Brown looked in though one of the window holes and said, "What happened?"

"Nothing," I said.

He was not impressed. "Oh, yes?"

"Had a bit of a problem releasing the buckle. Something seemed to get in the way."

"Like what?"

"I don't know."

He looked at the unsecured harness and said, "Well, it seems to be working well enough now."

I'd thought I could brazen it through, but my patience went all at once. "Just leave it, will you?" I exploded, and shoved him aside as I climbed out.

I never did tell Buster what I'd seen. That lost me his friendship, such as it was. I went on sick leave for three weeks, and during that time I applied for a transfer to another department. My application was successful, and they moved me onto the firefighting course. If they hadn't, I would have resigned altogether. There was no force or duty on earth that could compel me into the tank or anywhere near the Box again.

The reason, which I gave to no one, was simple enough. I knew that if I ever went back, they would be waiting. Terriss, and all the others in my crew.

Though the choice had not been mine, I had taken away their luck. Now they kept a place for me amongst them, there below the sea.

Wherever the sea might be found. Far from being haunted, the Box was a kind of tabula rasa. It had no history, and it held no ghosts. Each man brought his own.

My days are not so different now. As before they begin in the classroom, with forms and briefings and breathing apparatus drill. Then we go out into the grounds, first to where a soot-stained, mocked-up tube of metal stands in for a burning aircraft, and then on to a maze of connected rooms which we pump full of smoke before sending our students in to grope and stumble their way to the far exit.

They call these rooms the Rat Trap, and they are a fair approximation of the hazard they portray. Some of the men emerge looking frightened and subdued. When pressed, they speak of presences in the smoke, of unseen hands that catch at their sleeves and seem to entreat them to remain.

I listen to their stories. I tell them that this is common.

And then I sign their certificates and let them go.

Comparative
ANATOMY

THERE WAS A pall of late-evening mist out over the harbour, and no one to be seen in the ferry-service waiting room. The ticket office alongside it was closed down and dark; somebody had left a jacket on a chairback in there but, unless I was misreading all the signs, he was unlikely to be returning for it tonight.

I could see a handwritten notice propped up by an old brass paperweight on the other side of the ticket window. I couldn't even begin to translate what it said, although the indication seemed to be that the office had closed down at five. But the waiting room had been left unlocked, and the lights were still on, and inside I'd found timetables in three languages that showed a once-hourly service running on almost until midnight. I walked back to the car and, as I drew level with the open window on the passenger's side, I stopped for a moment.

"I think it's going to work out," I said. "If I've got it right, there should be a boat along in about twenty minutes."

Deborah was looking up at me; not apprehensive, not even tense.

"Can you be sure the information's up to date?" she said. "I don't see much happening around here."

"I don't know. Just keep your fingers crossed."

"Well," she said, "if it doesn't happen, it'll be no great disaster. We passed a few decent-looking inns on the road coming down."

I kind of smiled. But I don't think I said anything.

You'd have to see Deborah to know what I mean. Right then I'd say that I was still in the last part of that happy, stupid phase of a relationship where you can hardly feel the ground that you're walking on. Until she'd come along I'd almost forgotten the sensation; I'd been assuming that I'd grown out of it, I suppose, but then all in the space of a couple of weeks I'd discovered that one never really does. It simply lies there within you, dulled by habit until some major personal upheaval opens its way to the surface; and then all you need is the kind of luck that makes you want to check on your soul in case you've unwittingly put it in hock to Satan, and you're away.

Deborah was—*is*—quite something to see. A great-looking, intelligent blonde, and neither a juvenile nor a bimbo; nature had been getting more than a little help when it came to the hair colouring, but she made it no big secret and the effect wasn't cheap. Well, I never thought so, anyway, although I know that there was all kinds of stuff being said behind our backs once our secret had started to leak out. I really didn't care, and you'd have to have been in my shoes to understand why. We were a long way from home and all of home's problems and, as far as I was concerned, in a state damned close to paradise. I'd managed to get a last-minute rental on a summer house on the northernmost point of the biggest island in the group, and we'd gone there together. The summer was over and the autumn had set in, and it was a time of deserted beaches, shuttered cafés, long empty roads…

And—I have to say it—a set of charges on my credit cards like you wouldn't believe.

I went around and got into the car. The loading area had been marked out into lanes, but mine was the only vehicle in it. I'd owned it for less than a year, and it was fast and sleek and red—your basic male midlife crisis car, but I still thought that it was a great thing to have. It had pop-up headlamps and everything. Dark grey cloud seemed to be pressing down over the masts of fishing boats in the harbour, but that was mostly because it was getting late. I'd seen some empty fish boxes on the quays, but nobody working.

Deborah was looking through the dozen or so cassettes in the rack that was a part of the dashboard.

"I can't find a single one that we haven't played to death already," she said.

"Give the radio another try," I suggested. "See what it comes up with."

"Right."

She worked the auto-search button as I cranked my seat back a couple of notches and tried to relax. It would be all right. It was all going to work out. We'd make it across this short hop and then onto the last big scheduled boat of the evening that would take us back to the island and our rented cabin. Which was just as well, because I was so close to broke by now that a night in a hotel would have sunk me completely.

"I really thought we'd had it with that big lorry," she said, for no apparent reason and without taking her eyes off the rapidly-changing frequency numbers in the radio's LCD.

"We had a few yards to spare," I said.

"He was going too fast."

I didn't comment. But she was saying it to make me feel better, that much I could tell. If anyone had been going too fast it had been me, and I think we both knew it.

And as for how it had all come about...

Well, it had started that morning when we'd set out in the car for a two-hour boat trip to a part of the mainland from which we could drive to the capital. This wasn't a big country, but it was broken up and had so much coastline that there was no straightforward way of covering any distance. We'd ventured little further than the house and the beach in the past ten days, unless you count the odd trip into the nearest town for supplies, and I think that both of us were feeling ready for a change.

It was almost a mistake. Almost. The capital was downbeat and crowded and a total waste of time, and it threatened to disrupt the mood of the entire trip. But then we'd altered our plans and driven north to what the guidebook seemed to feature as the only other attraction in the area, which turned out to be a fairytale castle in a perfect state of preservation and with its atmosphere undimmed by the handful of late-season tourists who, like us, had fallen across the place almost by accident. It had everything—courtyards, chambers, dungeons—and it as good as saved the day for us. Afterwards we'd dined in a small restaurant in the shadow of the castle's walls, tables aglow from the shaded lamps that stood on each; and as I looked at Deborah across the table I was beginning to think that life couldn't get any better than this, that everything had magically come together and that my child's bright vision of the future, which had been so painfully dismantled on the route to maturity, had been returned to me complete...

And then I happened to look at my watch, and I began to panic.

Time had been slipping by us like a well-trained, silent army. We now had less than two hours to make it back to catch the last island ferry of the day. Two hours; there was no way that we could cover the distance and still make it. Even if the car was fast, the roads weren't; but I had to do it somehow, and I had to do it without knuckling down and admitting that the only reason for my haste was financial. The cost of the meal I could manage, just; Deborah tried for the bill but, fool that I was and so eager to keep up the illusion of the effortless high life, I got to it first.

But then it was Deborah who, back at the car, had spotted an alternate route on the map that had a chance of getting us to the quayside with only minutes to spare. It was a short dotted line linking two horns of land, a small local ferry service that, if it was still running, would cut a big piece out of the journey.

"Great," I'd said, "Let's go for it," and I only hoped that it wouldn't be an expensive crossing. According to the figure on the map, it would take about twenty-five minutes. How costly could that be? I pointed the car's nose in the right direction and put my foot down, and as we came out of the car park I checked the traffic on the wrong side and sailed out almost under the wheels of a big sixteen-wheeler truck. Haste, pure haste, and it almost got us killed. I don't know how we made it through, and I can hardly believe how our luck held; Deborah sat and said nothing for a long time, and her remark of a couple of minutes before had been her first reference to the incident.

She found a signal on the radio, and leaned back. I don't know what it was, perhaps one of the stations in Eastern Europe. She sighed. Out over the water, a couple of gulls hung and turned against the evening sky.

"I don't want this to end," she said simply.

"Me neither," I said.

But both of us knew that it would and, no matter how we eventually sorted out the problems that we'd left behind us, that no time would ever be quite like this again. Magic always stops at midnight. Understanding this, neither of us said anything more; because I think we both knew that talking about it too much would carry the risk of killing it stone dead before its time.

The boat was coming in.

It slowed and came to at the harbour's tiny quay, dropping its metal ramp with a crash. A couple of battered old cars, shapes that I recognised with European marques that I didn't, came rolling off and scooted away through the docks as if glad to hit land again, their drivers indistinct shadows at the wheels. I started my own engine and backed around to face the ramp. A solitary figure, muffled against the evening's chill, waited with a book of tickets and a well-worn leather money pouch. Mine was still the only car in the line, and I wondered if they'd stick to the timetable or wait around for latecomers before setting off.

Being kind of in a hurry, I hoped they'd just go.

I drew level with the ticket-taker. When I asked him how much, he held up the fingers of his cut-off gloves by way of reply. Well-wrapped was hardly the way to describe him; there was a scarf around his head that was held in place by his peaked seaman's cap and, apart from his fingers, only the tip of his nose was on show. All that I could think was that it must be pretty damned cold, out there beyond the harbour.

He waved us aboard with a big flashlight and as I was driving us forward onto the car deck, Deborah said, "Was there somebody inside of all that?"

"Yeah," I said. "Popeye the sailorman with an embarrassing case of herpes."

Nobody waited to direct us any further, so I stopped in the middle of the deck and we got out. There was room for a couple of dozen cars, at the most. The deck itself was of wood, oil-stained and worn, and it ran through the middle of the ship like an open-ended tunnel. Drive on at one end, drive off at the other. There were doors to either side of us, a couple of them open but most of them bearing *No Entry* symbols; only one of them carried an image of a stick figure ascending a stairway in the direction of an upward-pointing arrow and that one, I guessed, would take us to the passenger deck.

Deborah shivered slightly as I locked the car. I didn't know what kind of facilities to expect on a boat like this, but I wasn't expecting much. It looked really old, a real warhorse of a vessel that had probably been chugging back and forth across this same part of the seaways since God was in short trousers. If the noise coming up through one of the open doorways was anything to go by, the engines were of a pure vintage rustbucket type; the sound was like that of a couple of dozen three-year-olds having a good time with frying pans and hammers.

"Looks like we're going to have it all to ourselves," I said to Deborah and she shrugged as if to say, *Fine.* As we were crossing to the stairway, I glanced back at the car. Sitting there in the middle of the open deck, it looked as if it had been set up for an ad agency's photo session for one of the glossy Sunday colour supplements. The sky beyond the deck was now the colour of new lead, with all the yellow shore lights beginning to show up in the dusk. Everything else was turning to shades of blue and grey as the air grew noticeably sharper.

Life could be worse than this, I thought, and I followed Deborah inside.

The stairway was narrow and steep, and it led us to the passenger deck. What we found up there reminded me of the kind of no-space, ingenious, squeeze-it-in kind of carpentry that you used to find in wooden caravans and steam-age railway sleeping cars…all deep brown varnish and brass-headed screws, a real museum-piece of a vessel. There were three lounges at slightly different levels, none of them a regular shape and all linked by tiny passageways where two people could pass face-to-face, but only just. I hit my head on something as we moved to look into the first of the lounges, a squarish, low-ceilinged room set out with chairs and half a dozen card tables. On the nearest of these had been left three packs of playing cards, each held together by a rubber band and all looking as if they'd been handled by someone who was taking a break while draining oil sumps. The second room was hardly more than a cupboard, and had a couple of benches and no legroom. It ended in a narrow doorway with another of the *No Entry* symbols. The third ran almost the length of one side of the boat and was, apart from the underside of a stairway that cut down on the headroom at one end, the least claustrophobic.

There was a table under each porthole, and at the far end were two coin-operated drinks machines and a plastic crate for the empty bottles.

Basic? The word seemed to flatter it.

"This'll do us," Deborah said, and started to shed her coat. It was pretty warm once you were inside, probably from the surplus steam heat being piped around. "For half an hour, anyway."

I couldn't help smiling as I looked about us. The ferry that had brought us out from the island, and which would soon be waiting to take us back, had been huge and modern and like a floating hotel. This was more like a cafeteria at a dog track, but Deborah hardly seemed to mind.

I said, "How about a drink?" and she looked toward the machines. One was a big chilled-bottle dispenser—I wondered how they'd managed to manoeuvre it up the stairs—and the other was for hot coffee and soup.

"Dare we risk it?" she said; but the machines were more modern than the boat, and they were all lit up and humming, so I reckoned that it was probably worth a try. Having said which, we couldn't make up enough change between us; and so, leaving Deborah to wait in the lounge, I went back down to the car to see if there was anything in the meter money that I'd been keeping in one of the door pockets.

I saw no crew along the way. And then when I got to the car deck, I was surprised to see that we'd already cast off and were moving away from the shore; I'd heard no change in the engine's note, and even now I'd no sense of movement. I stood for a moment, looking out over the raised metal ramp that now formed a part of the ship's rail, and watched as the shore lights receded.

I think that I wanted to feel elated. I wanted to feel satisfied, at peace, content…all of those things that cluster around happiness and yet vanish the moment you try to give it the name.

But when I listened to the echoes inside, all that I could detect was a far-off note of regret; and I'm not sure that it was entirely because I was taking in a sunset.

I went back up to the passenger deck. She was by one of the portholes, looking out, and I went over and stood close behind her.

"How are you doing?" I said.

"Fine." She'd relaxed back against me a little, but she was still looking out. The land was receding from sight, and we were passing an orange marker buoy. We seemed to be heading into deeper and deeper shadow as we steamed out toward the open sea.

She said, "I've been watching for the crew."

"See anyone?"

"No."

"Me neither. They probably like to stay out of the way."

"In that case, they're experts. I've been keeping an eye on the bridge, and I've seen nobody moving around."

"I can't see the bridge from here."

She led me through to the smallest of the three passenger areas, the compartment with no legroom and a no-access door. The door itself had a porthole window, and I squeezed in alongside her to look through it.

We were looking forward. Just outside was a short exposed gangway, with a pitted safety rail on the seaward side and part of a davit from which, I assumed, would be slung one end of a lifeboat just beyond my line of sight. Jutting out ahead of us was a corner of the ship's bridge. I could see inside, but I couldn't see much.

"They've got lights," I said.

"Those have been on since we boarded."

"Still nothing for us to worry about."

We went back into the section with the dispensing machines, and I banged my head again on the way through. We used up my change and took the drinks over to one of the tables, which vibrated slightly with the beat of the engines as they drove us onward. I was wondering if we shouldn't have been able to see land, or at least the lights of land, ahead of us already; but the whole area was pretty remote, and so perhaps there was nothing to see. My impressions of the countryside so far had consisted of rolling fields, some of them of burned-off straw, and the occasional hi-tech windmill like a marker set down on the high ground by some alien civilisation—very few buildings at all, and these mostly modern and standing in isolation. I'd look at places like that as we drove by, and I'd try to imagine the lives of the people inside. But I never could, not convincingly, because I didn't even know how to begin; and yet I'm sure that as far as they were concerned, they probably reckoned that they were looking out at the world from its centre.

"What are you thinking about?" Deborah said.

"You," I told her automatically, even though it wasn't true.

"You mean about how I'm plain and half a stone overweight?"

"I can't see any of that."

"Then you have my permission to keep on thinking." She reached across the table and took my hand. Something inside me still leapt at her touch.

She said, "We're on our own, there's nobody waiting. So why's it so important to you that we get back tonight?"

"No reason," I said. "I just like where we're staying." And then I turned my wrist slightly so that I could see my watch again. "Less than ten minutes to go. We should be landing pretty soon. What do you say we go back to the car and get ready to roll?"

She shrugged, and I could see that I hadn't exactly convinced her. But what more could I have said? That our time together had been bleeding me dry, and that now it was starting to hurt? Perhaps I should have told her exactly that, I don't know. I only know that the best that I could manage was this lame-sounding excuse.

The car deck looked strange and unreal, the yellow deck lighting in contrast to the black square of night at its end. There was an edge to the sea breeze that was being drawn through, and it was tainted with the smells of oil and something else that I couldn't quite identify. The bulkhead lights were undiffused, and all of the deck's fittings—the pipes, the joints, the rivets, the cabling—were thrown into sharp detail like the bones and sinews on a dried-out butcher's carcase. Against this, the lines of the car were less harsh, more welcoming. The car was home on wheels, here in the belly of the whale.

As I was turning the key to pop all the locks, I looked forward into the night. I saw no moon, no stars, no suggestion even of the line between sea and sky.

"I still can't see any land," I said.

Deborah paused as she was opening the passenger door, and she looked for a while. I saw her eyes narrow slighly, as if the lack of expected detail bothered her.

But she said, "There's probably mist over the water. We have to be closer than it looks."

And she got into the car.

Mist over the water. That sounded reasonable to me. The sailing time was nearly over, there couldn't have been more than a few hundred yards left to cover to the far shore. The pilot wouldn't need much in the way of visual information if he had radar. And these kinds of ships always had to have radar these days, didn't they? There was probably some kind of regulation on it.

I heard the rumble of the automatic aerial as it telescoped up out of the bodywork somewhere behind me. Deborah was trying the radio. Where there had previously been at least a faint signal, now there was nothing. She tried all the preselects, and then she hit the search button again.

"It'll work better when we're out in the open," I said.

Deborah said nothing.

With only a couple of minutes left to go, I started the engine. It was a more reassuring sound than that of the dead radio; the automatic search was stopping at certain frequencies, but no signal was coming out. She tried it on the FM band, the AM, the longwave. There was a hint of something at one point on the longwave, a man's voice speaking emphatically in some strange language. It sounded as if it was coming from about a million miles away, and it faded quickly and didn't come up again.

After a while, she switched off and sat back. The aerial telescoped itself back into the bodywork again. She didn't look entirely happy.

"I think we're going to miss the connection," she said.

"We can just about make it."

"So you can nearly get us killed again? No thanks."

And in that moment I looked across at her and I thought, You know, you're right; maybe you *are* about half a stone overweight.

I switched off the engine and got out of the car. The through-breeze was clearing the exhaust fumes, but slowly. She had a point. We'd been out on the water now for nearly fifteen minutes longer than we should have. I went forward to the rail, and looked for some indication of what lay ahead.

Away from the glare of the deck lighting, my eyes began to adjust. It wasn't quite as dark out there as it had seemed; now I could make out a the last streaks of day in the form of a few fading grey bands across the sky, not much in the way of illumination but enough to counteract the impression of a featureless void.

Whichever way I looked, I could see the moving surface of the sea.

Nothing else.

So then I turned and walked the length of the deck to the other end, thinking that perhaps there was some fancy manoeuvering going on which would involve some kind of a reverse approach, but I think I knew the likely outcome of that particular line of speculation even before I'd reached the stern rail.

As I walked back to the car, I tried to tell myself that my anxiety came entirely from the need to meet a schedule while having no control over the means. But it was too late anyway, wasn't it? I'd already been working on the basis of my best estimate, with no margin. Now that I hadn't even the slightest chance of making it, I ought to be able to relax at least a little.

I got inside. Deborah had been trying the radio again. She looked up at me, and made a weak smile.

"Look, I'm sorry," she said.

"No," I said, "you were right. I was pushing it too hard. I got careless for a minute. I won't make the same mistake again."

"I think I can guess what was worrying you."

"Nothing was worrying me."

"We're still going to have to find a hotel for tonight, but it's going to be on me. That was always my intention. And before you start to object, can I point out that you've hardly let me pay for anything yet?"

"You think I was worried about money?" I said, sounding suitably astonished.

"Come the end of the trip, we'll settle accounts. Fifty-fifty, all down the line."

"Forget it," I said.

"We came into this together, and it's got to be fair."

"I don't even want to talk about it," I said.

"Hey," she said, "wait a minute. What does that make me?"

I didn't exactly know how to answer. The whole money thing was so sensitive, and I'd been brooding over it for a while now. I suppose I'd become like a wounded dog that bares its teeth at anyone trying to help.

"It's…it's not an issue," I said. "All right?"

"Fine," she said. "You go broke, but at least you can keep your pride."

She grabbed up a tape, and banged it into the cassette slot without even looking to see what it was. She probably didn't care, as long as it was noise and it filled up what otherwise would have been a stony silence. We both of us sat there, looking out of the car in different directions.

And when the tape finally ran out we both looked at it in the same moment, and I expect that we probably shared the same thought.

Because it meant that an entire half-hour had passed, and there was still no sign of us making a landing.

"Something's wrong," she said. And she didn't sound angry any more, she sounded sick and scared.

"There must have been a misprint on the map."

She turned to me. "What did the timetable say?"

But I dodged the question, because the timetables back in the harbour waiting room had indicated exactly the same thing; a twenty-five minute journey, made at hourly intervals throughout the day. No other boats were shown, no other sailings listed.

"I'll see if I can find out what's going on," I said.

I got out and went down to the rail and looked again. The sky was completely dark now and I saw no shore lights, no stars, nothing—just the ferryboat's own navigation lights and their limited spread across the near surface of the water. The sea around the vessel was cold and dense and unwelcoming. Where the lights were caught and reflected, they plated the waves in yellow and silver.

I looked back at the car. Deborah had climbed out and was standing alongside it, watching me, waiting for me to do something. So then I tried walking to the nearest of the ship's doors and knocking on it. It was like the door on a meat safe, solid metal and with a big lever handle. I hurt my knuckles on the paintwork but I don't think I made any sound that could be heard on the other side, especially not over the steady beat of the engines. When I tried the handle, it wouldn't move. The next door opened for me, but only to reveal the inside of an unlit deck locker full of mops and rags and other cleaning stuff.

I don't know what was making me more nervous, our increasingly belated arrival or the thought of being caught like a prowler in some area that I shouldn't have entered. The door to the engine room was still open and I stuck my head into the vertical shaft and looked down. The noise enveloped me and drowned out everything else, a raucous hammering like the heartbeat of a beast; I couldn't see a thing apart from the first few rungs of an iron ladder that was bolted to the side directly beneath me, and the indication seemed to be that whatever lay below, it lay in total darkness. I didn't get it. As far as my limited knowledge went, ship's engines didn't run unattended; not on a vessel of this size, anyway, and not for the length of time that we'd already been at sea. Perhaps there was a second door down below somewhere, and there were working lights and people beyond it.

But I really didn't feel like climbing down into the darkness to find out.

When I pulled myself out and turned back to face the deck, Deborah was waiting for me. She'd brought the road map over from the car, and for the moment it seemed that the spark of our near-argument had been forgotten.

"Look at this," she said. "I've been comparing some of the distances. There's only one direction we could have been going in, and that's due north. Any other way, and we'd have reached some kind of land before now."

"Unless we've been circling."

"The wind direction's pretty much the same as it was when we set out. I don't think so."

There seemed to be only one course left for us to take; to the bridge, and I led the way up the narrow stairs. The only explanation that I could think of was that perhaps the man at the helm had suffered an attack of some kind and that he was lying there now, unconscious—dead, even—while the boat continued to drift away from its regular course. *But surely he wouldn't be out there alone,* I was thinking as we entered the smallest of the three passenger lounges and I reached to open the forbidden door at its end; others had to be there with him, and someone ought to have been able to step in and take over. I'd heard of big modern ships that ran almost entirely on automatics, but even they were supposed to have a minimum bridge crew to keep an eye on everything. And this wasn't a modern ship, not by anybody's standards.

The crosswind hit me as I stepped out, and I reached for the safety rail. We'd been sheltered down on the car deck; this wind was bitter and cold, and it tasted of salt. It was just a couple of strides across the open to the bridge, and we didn't wait around. We went in through another one of those big watertight bulkhead doors, and even before we'd got it closed behind us we'd been able to gather that my heart-attack theory had been wrong.

Nobody lay slumped over the wheel.

Nobody was up here at all.

There were all the signs of life. Just no life itself. Most of the illumination came from the green nightlighting of the instruments, apart from a single downward-pointing spotlight over the chart table. The chart was recognisable from our road map by its land shapes, but all the concentration of detail was reversed from land to sea. Grease pencil lines showed our supposed course from quay to quay; they'd scuffed almost to nothing, as if they'd been drawn a long time before and went more or less unchecked by the crew on what had to be a more than familiar route. Close to this was the radar screen, which I wouldn't have known how to read; there was this sweeping line and a couple of repeating blips just like in every submarine movie you've ever seen. At each crew position there was a swivel chair bolted to the floor. I checked, but none was even warm.

"Someone had to have taken us out of the harbour," I said. I was moving by the helm to look at the ship's compass, one of those gimbal-mounted affairs designed to stay more or less stable in a rough and stormy sea. "We didn't just drift out."

As far as I could tell, the compass was reading due west. But if we'd actually been heading due west, then it was as Deborah had said; we'd have reached land long before now, and probably not too far away from our original destination. I gave it a push. It swung easily on its bearings—it hadn't jammed at all, that was for sure. And when it settled down again, its reading was unchanged.

"Try the radio," Deborah said.

I tried the radio. Try was about all that I could do, because nothing about it made any sense to me at all. There were little dymo-printed labels over some of the switches, but they were all in the local language and I couldn't understand what they were saying. I found the switch that turned up the volume on the loudspeaker, but all that I could get out of it was static.

"There's got to be someone around," Deborah said with rising desperation in her voice. "Where's the man who took the money?"

I turned on her.

"How the fuck would I know?" I roared. "Have I got X-ray eyes?"

Her mouth dropped open. I've never seen such blank, uncomprehending shock.

And I quickly said, "I'm sorry, I didn't mean that. But I don't know anything more than you do. So don't ride me as if I'm your father or something, all right? I mean it, I'm sorry."

But I wasn't. Not entirely. If anything, I felt slightly better. I don't blow off like that often, but I've sometimes wondered if people wouldn't treat me better if I did.

There was another exit at the back of the bridge, one that led down into the part of the ship that couldn't be reached directly from the passenger areas. Crew quarters, at a guess. Just before I led the way down, I took another glance at the radar; the picture had changed slightly from what it had been, the distance between the centre and the most significant blip having narrowed. And then I tried a half-turn of the ship's helm. The wheel moved with almost no resistance; and then when I took my hand away, it slowly began to move back. It took about thirty seconds altogether and, when we finally left the bridge, it had reset itself with the same silent efficiency as the ship's compass.

Down below we found a small common-room for the crew, a galley with every surface so covered in burned grease that it looked as if it had been painted with tar, and beyond that three double-bunked cabins that all smelled stale and sour, like unchanged sickroom linen. I was thinking about the radar, and wondering about the significance of the blip. The problem was that I didn't know how to interpret the screen; the most obvious explanation was that it was a much larger vessel catching up on us from behind, but it could just as easily have been some stationary object lying somewhere ahead just off our course. If it was another ship, then perhaps we could signal it; and I was just beginning to wonder how when Deborah called me along to another of the cabins.

"I recognise these," she said.

Hanging on a hook behind the door were an overcoat, a scarf, and a battered leather pouch. I raised the pouch and shook it, but it made no sound.

"The ticket money's gone," I said. "But he still could be somewhere on board."

"Or maybe there was nobody inside the coat after all," Deborah said. I suppose she meant it as a joke, but somehow after a moment it didn't seem to strike either of us as being too funny.

In one pocket of the coat I found a pair of gloves, in the other the flashlight with which the ticket-seller had beckoned us on board. It was an old flashlight, its handle taped to give a better grip. I tried switching it on and off, and the batteries seemed well up to strength.

Perhaps when we'd looked everywhere else, then I might even be able to raise the nerve to climb down to check the engine room with it.

But now I was moving with a little more confidence. Finding the ticket-seller's coat had given an extra little kick to my determination. It confirmed that someone had been around here after all, and it rooted the entire, increasingly strange experience in a kind of reality. The rest of the crew-only area took only a few minutes to investigate, and turned up nothing. There were upright lockers, but no corpses toppled out when I opened the doors. There was a washroom with shower cubicle, but no body lay curled up behind the curtain. No severed head glowered up from the toilet pan, no hanged man swung on a creaking chain from the overhead pipes as we descended a different stairway that would take us back down to the car deck. We came out on the opposite side to the passenger stairs, and I swung the heavy door shut behind us. The slam echoed across the deck.

I said, "There's only the engine room left to check out. You want to wait in the car for me, or what?"

She wanted to wait in the car. I can remember how, when I was a child, climbing into a wardrobe and pulling all the heavy coats around me in the corner had produced a tremendous sense of security; I could see the increasing uncertainty in her eyes and I guessed that being in the car might give her the same kind of primitive reassurance now. I was nervous and confused, I'll admit it, but she was actually scared; it almost made me want to shake her, but I didn't. Instead I gave her the keys, and I took the flashlight across to the engine room access shaft.

The door to the shaft appeared to be kept permanently open; someone had fixed its handle back against the bulkhead by winding several turns of stiff wire between it and some bracket. I switched on the flashlight and aimed it down the shaft. It ended about twenty-five feet below me, in a grey metal gridiron floor. Beneath the floor I could see a reflected glint of water. Bilgewater, probably, backed-up from some blockage.

Oh, great, I thought resignedly, and I swung myself in and started to climb down the ladder.

I wasn't exactly good at this. The flashlight beam was swinging about all over the place and my feet kept missing the rungs. Every now and again I'd stop and check below me, just in case something was coming up. Not that I was irrationally nervous, you understand. But you know how it is.

At the bottom I was expecting a door of some kind, not an open doorway with a warehouse-sized sense of dark space beyond it. I shone the light through and it hit grey-painted metal, all pipes and angles and dials exactly like you'd expect from a ship's engine room. The noise was terrific. I moved inside, shining the light around so that the machinery threw big, hulking shadows across the ceiling. There was no mistaking that this was a working area; no panelling, no attempt to conceal the wiring, not much in the layout to accommodate the human form. This was the machines' home territory, and anyone who entered it had to enter on their terms.

And I, it seemed, was the only one to have done so. At least on this trip.

A mistake has been made, was all that I could think. A major mistake. The equivalent, perhaps, of leaving your car on a hill with its dodgy handbrake applied and then finding it gone when you returned. I swung the light; the shadows zoomed. And then I swung the light back, because I'd caught something in the beam that hadn't registered until after I'd passed it by. Targeting in, I felt my way across. The entire floor was of the same kind of grating as the bottom of the shaft outside but instead of waste water underneath, there were conduits and dusty runs of cable.

What I'd seen was a coffee mug, perched on the flat upper surface of something like a flywheel cover. It wasn't much, but it was a sign of life and worth a closer look. The mug was full, and the surface of the coffee was quivering in a series of rings from the vibration of the housing on which it stood. I checked all around for spanners, rags, any sign of someone who might have been working close to the spot, and then I looked at the mug again and reached out to touch it.

The coffee was still hot. Too hot to drink, if anything.

So then, very tentatively, I touched the flywheel housing on which it stood. I was expecting to find the metal of the housing to be at the same fierce temperature, which would have explained it.

But the metal surface was barely warm.

It was exactly the kind of sign that I'd been looking for.

And suddenly, I didn't want to be here any more.

An empty ship, adrift, was one thing. But this hinted at something else, almost as if the vessel was being run by ghosts who popped out of existence the moment that one of us looked their way, and then faded back and quietly went about their jobs when our backs were turned. I shone the flashlight all around from where I stood and I was pretty sure that nobody was hiding, although I couldn't be absolutely certain; but who would work away in the dark like a troll, and then hide from the light so completely?

If there was an answer to that one, I no longer wanted to know it. All I wanted was to get back up to the car deck, preferably as quickly as possible and with nothing hanging onto my leg in an attempt to drag me back down. The manner in which I climbed up wasn't any more efficient than my earlier descent.

But I did manage it in about half the time.

I could hear the music the moment I stepped out. It came across the deck like the distant sound of a loud party and for a moment, I wondered how she was standing it. She'd switched on the car's interior light and I could see her there, looking straight ahead like some pale sketch in a badly-illuminated display case. I didn't know what I was going to do next. Search the place, find somebody, find out exactly what was going on; that had been the total of my strategy, and all that I'd found was a series of meaningless details that had built up to an unsettling and inexplicable effect.

I went to the stern rail. I was thinking about that blip on the radar screen, and wondering again at its significance. I could only guess at the horizon now, an indistinguishable line where one profound darkness met another. I could see nothing.

So I went back to the car and got in.

The music was so loud that it hurt; she'd got it cranked up even louder than the noise of the engine room, and I could hear the door speakers beginning to bend and tear under the pressure of being driven so hard. She didn't look at me as I turned it down to a level where I could make myself heard.

"Look," I said. "We're going to be all right."

"Are we?"

The way she said it, she was obviously throwing it down as a challenge. I said, "We're in no danger. The ship isn't sinking or anything. And unless I'm wrong, there's something going to be passing close by to us sometime soon. I've got the flashlight, I can give them a signal."

Now she turned her head to look at me. I looked into her eyes and saw a total stranger.

She said, "You don't understand anything, do you?"

"What's to understand?"

"It's wrong. It's all wrong. And it's just getting worse and worse."

"Now you're being stupid."

"Don't you call me stupid," she said, her cheeks bright with irrational fury. "You're not bright enough to call anybody stupid."

And then when she cranked the music back up to its earlier level, I reckoned that this was effectively the end of that particular conversation.

I left her to it. I couldn't talk to her, I didn't even want to sit with her and have that kind of mood in the air. Maybe it was unfair but I was thinking that everything good about the last few days was being blown away. I'd really believed that everything was going to be different this time. And it wasn't.

I think it was the biggest disappointment I'd ever known.

Going up through the passenger deck again—the thought of returning via the crew's quarters gave me a lingering, haunted feeling that I was no longer ready to confront—I went out onto the open walkway and so back onto the bridge. Nothing here had changed. I planned to try every setting on the radio, to study the charts and compare them to anything that I could find on the radar screen, to see if I could knock out whatever automatic pilot we were running on and turn us right around...the one thing that I wasn't going to do was sit in the car and listen to the fucking Beach Boys.

I looked at the radar screen. That second blip was still showing, only now it was much closer. It was so close to the centre of the image that in a minute or so it would have passed by.

I dived out onto the walkway again, and held onto the rail as I looked out. A few more seconds, and I'd have been able to see it from inside the bridge anyway. It was coming up from behind and closing fast; huge in comparison to our own humble little ferry, and moving in silence. For one panicky moment I thought that it was on a collision course, but then I realised that it was simply going to pass with little room to spare, a matter of a hundred metres or less. Its bow was cutting through the waves like a guillotine through so much paper.

Some kind of an inshore freighter, I suppose you'd call it; too big for the kind of run that we were supposed to have been doing, but hardly world cargo class either. Its plates were streaked with slime and rust, no paint left visible at all; chains and lines were trailing from its sides as if it had simply broken free from the shore and struck out on its own. Where there were portholes, they were the same opaque, muddy colour as the rest of the ship.

From the deckrail down, it resembled a salvage job. From the deck up, it blazed like the day.

The best way that I can try to describe it is to say, think of a football field at night; all of the overhead floodlights on but with no players, no crowd, none of the usual signs of life at all. Just this well-lighted container deck without a single freight container on it, nothing at all other than the squared-off hulk of a big sixteen-wheeler truck that had been roped down in the middle of the open space as if in anticipation of rough seas. Behind the cargo deck rose the main superstructure, and every one of its windows was as blank as camouflage paint. The closer this semi-derelict came, the more I was in its shadow and the less I could see.

I can't say that I recognised the truck. And I can't say that I didn't, either.

As the ship came level, shaving it about as close as it was possible to get without the risk of taking a piece of us along, I looked up and saw that there was a man standing at the rail. He was holding on with both hands and he was looking down. All the light was behind him, so he was nothing more than a silhouette. He didn't wave, he didn't move, I couldn't see anything of his face or his expression. He stood there with his hands on the rail, and he looked down as if in judgement. He might have turned his head to keep his eyes on me as the two of us passed, I don't know. The whole thing was going to be over in less than a minute.

The flashlight was still back inside, on the map table by the radar. I didn't run to get it.

The cargo vessel ploughed on past, still in silence until the regular chopping of its engines came by with the stern. Its wake was a river of foam that rocked the deck under my feet as the swell hit us. I tried to see if there was any name across the back, but all that I could make out was the place where a name had once been.

Wherever it was going, both of our ships appeared to have the same destination. Maybe it was just my imagination, but I was beginning to think that I could make out a faint glow of some kind on the horizon ahead.

I watched it for a while longer. And then when it was almost out of sight, I went inside and watched it on the radar.

And then I went back down to the car deck.

The same tape was still playing. She must have had it going around and around on the auto-reverse. Both doors were locked, and she didn't look up at me when I tried to open one. I knocked on the glass and called to her, but she stared straight ahead and didn't respond in any way at all.

So then I went to the car deck's forward rail.

I hadn't been imagining it. I was looking at the horizon ahead to where a greenish light was beginning to show in a thin band like the lights of a drowned city. I knew that I ought to have been feeling that this was something promising and I wished that I could, but all that I felt was a growing sense of dread.

NOW I'M WAITING for an education that I know I'd prefer not to receive. Below me the engines beat their steady beat, and around me the cold sea rushes by. Deborah can't be planning to stay in the car forever. The horizon's drawing nearer, and the light just beyond it is becoming more intense.

What's coming? God only knows. But if hell's the place where you get what you want most only to find that it all turns sour on you, then I suppose that it's as good a name as any.

That big truck. I was so sure we'd made it.

What a killer.

Blame the
FRENCH

THE PUB WAS called The Antigallican, but everyone knew it as The Ship because of the picture on the sign.

In its day it was a relatively respectable, end-of-the-street, no-frills working-class tavern with a men-only snug and brassware in the lounge. Shift workers would call in on their way home and at weekends put on a collar and tie and bring their womenfolk. In the long summers, we children would sit out on the pavement with crisps and lemonade while our parents were inside. The landlord had a dog named Charlie.

The building still stands, but the sign's long gone and it's been boarded up for ages. I'm here to tell you about the night that closed it down.

It was decades after my dad had taken me there for my first pint and I was making a few bob as the weekend potman, clearing up glasses and stacking them for washing. Times had changed, the work had gone, and the area had the worst of the town's declining fortunes. Apart from the Gardening Club that met once a fortnight with free sandwiches, the main clientele consisted of solitary old men drinking themselves to death, and young thieves.

Eileen and her husband had run the place as a couple. After he left her, she kept the license and ran it alone. Things stayed much the same for a few weeks but then she moved in a lover who, at twenty-two or three, was half her age. His name was Kieran and he knew a good thing when he saw one. He and his mates made the place their own. I don't know if boys like him are born with the looks of a thug, or what process shapes them if they aren't. He was long-limbed and skinny, with a bony-hard skull and small, squinty eyes. A dangerous weasel of a boy, and I don't mean just screwed-up squinty. He'd one eye so badly turned inward that it might have been comical, if the look of it wasn't so terrifying. No one ever commented on it. Of his mates, I think only two of them had jobs.

Early one Friday evening I was setting up chairs and mats when the first customer of the night came in. I looked twice because I'd never seen him before and we got very few strangers. At first glance you'd have thought he was homeless: the Big Issue-selling kind of homeless, not the ones who beg. His hair was long like a 'sixties hippy, his beard similarly untrimmed, and the coat he wore was one of those long German Army parkas that can be had cheap on the market.

I called up the stairs to Eileen and he stood with his hands on the bar, looking around, waiting until she came clattering down to serve him.

"What can I get you, love?" she said, unlocking the cash drawer under the optics, showing no reaction to his appearance.

"Pint of best," he said, and his voice was low and a little raspy. "Please."

He counted out the money in small change. His hands were filthy, the nails bitten right down. Eileen pulled the pint, let it settle while she banked the coins, then topped it off. One thing about her, she looked after her beer. He took a sip from his glass and then cast another glance around the lounge.

By now Eileen had relocked the till and gone back upstairs, and it was just him and me. I tried to guess his age. I couldn't. He was probably quite young.

"Something's changed," he said, and he nodded in the direction of the dartboard on the wall. "There used to be a picture. Right there."

"Are you from around here?" I said.

"I just remember the picture," he said.

"You mean the old sailing ship," I said. "The Antigallican. Same one you see on the sign. They moved it into the snug to make space for the darts. Everyone wonders about the name. It means—"

"I know what it means," he said, and he took his glass over to the door of the snug and pushed it open.

"Suit yourself," I said as it swung shut behind him. At that moment there was a burst of loud music through the ceiling from upstairs. Eileen shouted something and it was cut off as abruptly as it had begun. Kieran at home, was my guess.

I went about my business. So he didn't care for my stories. Antigallican means "enemy of the French". Why anyone would want to make a pub name out of that, I've no idea.

When I'd done, I looked over the counter and into the snug, which had a small counter of its own on the other side of the bar. I couldn't see the stranger. Behind me, some of the regulars had begun to arrive. They came in alone and they'd mostly sit in silence. I called up to Eileen and then went through into the back room to see what was what.

He was sitting across from the picture, contemplating it as he drank. It was nothing special. Not an original. Not even a very good print.

I said, "You might want to sit somewhere else."

He looked at me. "Why?"

"Frank likes to sit there. Frank's a regular." I didn't add that Frank was also a day patient who talked to himself in a bitter, incoherent tirade.

He didn't seem impressed. "There are plenty of seats," he said.

"That's what I mean," I said. "You can sit anywhere."

"So can Frank," he said.

He didn't move. I leaned in and said, in a low voice so Eileen wouldn't hear, "You don't want to risk trouble. Frank's touchy. And this isn't one of the good pubs."

"It used to be," he said, and returned his attention to the picture.

Well, I'd done what I could. I went back into the lounge and left him there, sipping his warm beer and watching a listing ship on a flash-frozen sea, going nowhere.

Kieran's friends turned up a short time after that. Four of them, the main gang; drooly Doug and stupid Steve, and the one who worked in the park for the council, and the one who'd been sacked from Kwik-Fit. They must have called him up as they were walking toward the door because Doug still had his phone in his hand and Kieran appeared just as they entered.

"Where've you all fukkin bin?" he said.

"Fukkin town," said the failed Kwik Fit fitter.

They always behaved themselves around Eileen, paying for their drinks and knowing better than to annoy her, though when she was out of sight they'd lean over the bar and top up their own glasses from the pumps. The first time I caught them, Kieran said, "I told them it's all right." After that, they'd catch my eye and grin at me while they were doing it. Did I ever say anything? No I did not. I was only the potman. And whatever soft spot Eileen had for her thick-as-pigshit squinting stud boy, I wasn't going to risk trespassing on it.

That evening they gooned around and every now and again one of them went outside with his phone where the signal was better, and the place filled up as much as it ever did on a Friday night. At one point Kieran disappeared upstairs and came down with a Macbook hidden under a towel. Origin unknown, but it wasn't hard to guess: some student's bedroom, or a momentarily unattended bag in the middle of town. He showed it around, but no one wanted to buy. He took it into the snug and came out a few moments later; making the kind of face you make behind someone's back to ridicule them. The stranger was still alone in there.

A hen party came in and brightened the place for a while, half a dozen of the local chip-fed beauties meeting up for a taxi on their way to the clubs. The boys tried to flirt, but the girls were too sharp, and their powder was reserved for better prey.

Then Frank showed up.

I don't know what Frank's exact problem was, or what had led him to this point in his life. Eileen had barred him a couple of times, but he kept coming back. He was a cursing machine, low and under his breath and entirely self-directed. She'd eventually realised that the drink calmed him and that the best thing to do was to let him settle in his corner and self-medicate. After twenty minutes or so he'd go quiet and for the rest of the evening he'd be docile.

"Hey, Frank," Kieran shouted across the pub. "You know there's some fukker in your seat? Says he'll fight you for it."

Eileen was in the back changing a barrel, but she came running at the shouting and the sound of breaking glass.

Everyone piled into the snug behind her. By everyone, I mean me followed by Kieran's gang, who came along more as eager spectators than useful supporters. There was beer on the floor and broken glass underfoot.

Frank was sitting quietly. He was trembling and the stranger's hand was on his shoulder. It was hard to say whether it was a grip of reassurance or whether the stranger was holding him down.

The stranger was looking at me. "You didn't tell me he was troubled," he said.

Kieran said, "You. You're barred. Get out."

"I say who's barred," Eileen said sharply, and Kieran shut up.

The stranger looked down at Frank and said, "He wasn't always like this." Then he released the older man's shoulder. Frank stayed put. He didn't look up. He was in his usual seat, now.

The stranger looked at Kieran and said, "Are you the one who tried to make him fight me?"

"So?" Kieran said.

Eileen said, "Did you?" And he flushed and said, "No."

She didn't bother to call him on the lie. She said, "Clean this up while I get the man another drink."

"Me?"

"You heard."

He just stood there, and Eileen lost patience with him.

"Oh, for fuck's sake, Kieran," she said. "Start earning your keep."

"I don't work here."

"You don't work, full stop. It's time you did something useful."

The stranger said, "Sounds like one of us has to go."

Kieran snorted and started to glance around to share the moment with his mates, looking for solidarity at the same time.

"I'm not going anywhere," he said.

His mates all seemed to agree that going anywhere was an unlikely option under the circumstances.

"Are you a sportsman, Kieran?" the stranger said.

"What do you mean?"

"You've been all mouth so far. Stirring up trouble and throwing your weight around. But can you back it up?"

"I can fukkin take you," Kieran said.

"Only if you want to see this woman lose her license," the stranger said. "If you want me out of here, let's make a bet for it."

Kieran didn't know what to make of this.

The stranger looked at Eileen. "He's not your son, is he?"

"No," she said. I couldn't quite tell if she was amused or offended.

"Is there anything he's good at? If he wins, I'll clean up the mess and leave. If I win, he's the one who has to go. What happened to the pool table?"

"The brewery took it out when it broke," she said. "There's just the dartboard now."

"I can manage darts," the stranger said. "A bit rusty but, you know. How about it, Kieran?"

"Darts?" Kieran said.

"Arrows. Don't you play?"

One of the others spoke. "Go on, Kieran," he said. "You can chuck arrows."

"Well, now I'm worried," the stranger said, although he didn't sound it. "You understand the bet. If I lose, I clean up here, walk out that door, and never come back. If I win, you do the same."

"I'm not cleaning up."

"You're missing the point. You don't just clean up, you clear out. For good."

"But I live here," Kieran protested, and looked to Eileen for support. I enjoyed the expression on his face when he found none. She was looking at him with a spectator's interest.

At that point, someone started making clucking noises. Like a chicken. We all looked around. They were coming from Frank. He didn't look up. But I'd never seen him smile before.

That did it. We all went through into the lounge and a couple of Kieran's friends cleared the tables away from under the board. The house darts were produced from behind the bar. It was a brass set with Union Jack flights, in a green plastic box with a cracked lid.

The board was like some rotted cork float that had spent years in the sea. The wood had been picked away and only the wire held it together, so heavily had it been used. But it would serve. Kieran had his confidence back now, and while I hoped to see him thrashed, I didn't expect him to honour any outcome that went against him.

However, something had changed in Eileen. The novelty of Kieran's company must have been wearing thin. He and his friends stole so much from the bar that their custom can't have been an asset. She was a middle-aged woman, unexpectedly single. Everyone had a good idea of why she'd taken Kieran in. His looks and personality had little to do with it.

Sometimes there's a moment in your day when the worst junk food is just what you need. But that doesn't mean you'll feel good about it afterwards.

"You go first," Kieran said, and held out the arrows.

"How do you want to do this?" the stranger said as he took them from him. "Three darts, highest score?"

"Whatever."

I saw a look pass between a couple of the yobs. Kieran had all the unproductive status skills of the urban youth. He knew pool, pinball and platform games on his mobile phone. He might never read a book, but the nudges, holds and bonus functions on a slot machine were no mystery to him. At the dartboard he'd screw up his wonky eye like Popeye and he had a weird, little-finger-out throwing motion that looked odd and effete, but he tended to hit what he was aiming for.

The stranger squared up to the throwing line.

"Highest score with three arrows wins it, then," he said. He raised a rock steady hand and sighted down the dart. I didn't like how close Doug the drooler was standing behind him.

And I was right, because as the stranger threw, Doug body-bumped him and spoiled his aim. The arrow ricocheted off the edge of the board. The stranger turned and Doug just smirked, secure in the numbers behind him.

Eileen said, "Take that one again."

And the stranger said, "My own fault. My hand slipped." But he stared Doug in the eye until Doug moved back, trying to pretend that moving was his own idea.

The stranger squared up to aim again. He had only two darts now and I didn't see how he could hope for a winning score with such a disadvantage. Why had he refused the chance to void his mis-throw? It was Eileen's pub. She could set the rules and no one was going to argue with her. I could see her eyes tracking the stranger, wondering what he was about. The boys, unable to imagine much beyond the obvious, pictured nothing but his impending humiliation.

Frank had joined us to watch. That was a first. And he was silent, which was another.

The stranger said, "I once asked my dad what Antigallican meant. He said that a soldier who came home from the Napoleonic Wars saved up his pay to open an alehouse. It was his dream. He called this place The Antigallican to commemorate his service. But you know the irony? He'd brought home a French wife and after he died she wouldn't change the name."

The second arrow hit with a thunk and went in deep. It was a clean throw, straight and forceful. Top half of the board, just right of centre.

"Life can be strange," he said.

Score one. One point. And I'll swear it was exactly what he'd been aiming for.

The boys all hooted and Kieran said, "That's it. Pack up. Fuck off."

"I still have one throw," the stranger said. "And then it's your turn. A lesson for you, Kieran. It's not actually over until you've counted the score."

He looked at Eileen. Eileen's expression didn't change. Then he raised his last dart and started to aim.

The entire pub was silent.

As if to draw out the moment, he said, "This morning I went to see the house I grew up in. All those memories. And what did I find?"

We all waited to hear what he'd found.

"Cockroaches," he said.

He turned as he threw. The arrow flew straight, but it wasn't toward the board. I saw it cross the room and slam into its target.

Which was Kieran's good eye. Yep. Right in, to the hilt. I heard him gasp and his hands flew up. They stopped inches short of touching the dart, which was now firmly planted in his face and wasn't about to fall.

"Your throw," the stranger said.

Kieran started making a sound. It grew louder. His hands were flapping around close to his face, wanting to pull out the arrow but not daring to touch. His other, inward-turned eye must have had the perfect view.

The sound he made was hardly human.

Everything kicked off then. The people at the back of the pub made for the doors. Kieran's friends made for the stranger, and the stranger jumped over the bar. There was a hard wooden baseball bat kept underneath, hung in a special bracket made by a previous landlord, and the stranger knew exactly where to reach. He came up swinging and took Doug down with his first, drove one of the others back with his next, and I think the one after that broke somebody's arm. I grabbed Eileen and pulled her over to the wall, which was about all that I could do.

The police didn't take long to arrive. It was an area they knew too well and there was always a car within speeding distance. By then Kieran was sobbing, holding a bar towel to his face as he waited for an ambulance, and Eileen was giving first aid to the one with a broken arm. One of the others was throwing up in the Gents and the fourth one had disappeared. There was a growing crowd on the pavement outside. I don't know where Frank went.

The stranger had returned to the snug. I looked in and saw that he'd kicked the broken glass aside and was sitting, once more contemplating the ship on the wall. The Antigallican. He'd drawn himself a fresh pint.

I said, "Navy?"

He shook his head.

"Special Forces?" I watch a lot of those films.

No.

"What, then?"

Out in the next room, paramedics were trying to move Kieran and he was getting hysterical.

"Just a local man looking for a quiet drink," the stranger said.

Cheeky
BOY

(Heroes and Villains)

YOU CAN BARELY hear the bell from my office at the top of the museum. He must have pressed it four or five times before I went down and unlocked the door.

He was about twenty-five. Certainly not much older. He stood there in his parka with a parcel under his arm and a sad-eyed Hippie Jesus look, and I said, "The museum's closed on Wednesdays."

But he said, "I'm here about the ad?" in the manner of someone venturing onto untested ground.

"Which ad would that be?"

"The one in *The Stage*."

So I moved back to let him in. "I called first," he said as he stepped past me. "I thought I was expected."

"You probably spoke to Miss Pope," I said, closing the door behind us. "She isn't here today. It doesn't matter. I'm the one you need to see."

We went up the stairs, past the stuffed birds and the civil war armour and the grandfather clock. Ours is a small town museum. Though we make the best of what we have, we don't have much of real importance. Our art collection is mostly minor Victorians and a few of the Cornwall Sunday painters from the 1920s. Our best Roman artefacts were taken by the British Museum, leaving us with a few clay lamps and one sandal.

My room is right up in the eaves, with a circular window overlooking the park. The door has an etched glass panel that's frosted and marked Private. Beyond it you'll find exactly the kind of overcrowded space you'd expect of a curator's office. Things waiting to be dealt with, and things already dealt with but awaiting some inspiration for where they might go. I've been there ten years. I believe Miss Pope has been around for longer than the sandal.

I asked the young man his name and he said, "It's Wallace. Alex Wallace."

"Can I offer you a drink or anything. Alex?"

"Some water would be great."

"Take a seat. I won't be a second."

When I came back with the glass, he'd opened up his parcel. It was a Morrisons' bag wrapped around an inch-thick album.

"I brought my cuttings, in case you wanted to see them," he said, offering it to me.

"Of course," I said, taking the album and laying it to one side on my desk, but before I could go on he said, "I won't be able to leave it with you. Those are my only copies."

So then, feeling self-conscious under his gaze as he sipped at his water, I sat down and opened the book. It was a photo album rather than a scrap-book. The pages were of thick card with the cuttings behind a clear plastic layer. A few were from newspapers but most were printed-out screen grabs from websites. Festival fringe reviews, mostly, all positive and some of them five-starred. In one photograph he looked about twelve years old, standing in front of a display of vintage puppets. The album was only one-third filled.

I was trying to give it my attention, just reading a line here and there, and after a few moments I was aware that he wasn't watching me at all. He was looking at the third chair in the office, the one where I'd placed one of our storage crates. The crate was wider than the chair, and sat across it like a child's coffin.

I closed the book.

"That's all fine," I said. "When you spoke to Miss Pope, did she explain what we're looking for?"

"Not really," he said.

"You've heard of Max Hudson?"

A nod of his head told me that he had.

"Next year we're holding a festival to celebrate five hundred years of the town's Royal Charter. The Council got hold of some Lottery funding and came up with a theme of Heroes and Villains. For villains they're having a Highwayman Day with coaches in the market square and a sponsored zombie shuffle for charity. A Witches' Ball in the Winter Gardens and that's about it." I didn't add that for real villainy there had been a couple of quite nasty murders in the 'fifties, but no one was allowed to mention them.

"On the good-guys side, it's slim pickings. The British Legion's organising a parade to honour local servicemen and women, which doesn't leave the rest of us much to play with. We've got an Olympic Bronze medallist from the 1984 relay team and a merchant sailor whose family claims he served under Nelson but wasn't at Trafalgar. We needed a proper local hero so we put out the word through the media. We were basically fishing for suggestions.

"Then the Telegraph printed a letter about Max Hudson. Seems he was more than just an entertainer. He was the hero of the St Joseph's Sanatorium fire in 1952 when he was killed trying to save some of the children. The letter came from a pensioner named Alice Bridges. Her younger sister was one of those who died with him."

I stood up. Alex rose with me and we went over to the chair.

"This was his dummy," I said, folding back a layer of tissue paper to uncover a shabby mannequin that fitted none too comfortably into the storage box. Two knotted linen strips held it secure.

"Square Bash Willie," my visitor said, reaching out to push back the tissue that was threatening to fold itself in again. The mannequin was dressed in army khaki. He added, "A vent would call it a figure, sometimes a doll. Never a dummy."

"I stand corrected," I said. "The doll was found in the building after the fire. Alice could remember attending a ceremony with all the other families where Max Hudson's parents presented Square Bash Willie to the Council. It was supposed to go on permanent display but I couldn't find any record of that. I finally came across the doll itself, packed away and stored in the basement. I'm not sure it was ever shown at all. It had been miscatalogued in the 'sixties and no one had seen it since then. You'll probably know more about it than I do."

"I don't know anything about the fire," he said, studying the figure without touching it, "But Max Hudson's a name in the business. He won a talent contest and worked in concert parties as a teenaged magician. During the Second World War he joined the army and ended up in ENSA. The unit he was assigned to already had a magician so that's when he switched to a vent act."

ENSA was the Entertainments National Service Association, a wartime division of the military set up to provide live entertainment to the armed forces. It was a refuge for enlisted show folk who couldn't fight to save their own lives or anyone else's. I'd seen no record of Hudson the young magician, but Hudson the ventriloquist had developed an act based on army humour.

"Square Bash Willie," Alex said again, looking down on the figure with obvious affection and respect. With his big eyes and wispy beard Alex might look like some species of young urban male, the kind that's educated but aimless. Yet here, on his own turf, I sensed some authority.

I'd struggle to imagine him as a performer, though, despite what his scrapbook might say. On stage or in a crowd, you just wouldn't notice him.

I said, "We could just display the doll downstairs, but it's an opportunity to get local groups and children more involved."

"What have you got in mind?"

"We're looking for someone who can take Square Bash Willie into schools and interact with the kids. There'll be other events as well. It'll be a big part of the festival and if it drives some traffic to the museum afterwards, we'll all be happy."

"You want a vent to put a voice into Max's figure."

"That was the point of the ad."

"That's quite a challenge," he said. "Can I ask, what's the fee?"

"We can't offer a fee," I said. "But you'll get publicity out of it. We're hoping to have someone film it and put it on YouTube. It's a civic event. A lot of people will be giving up their time."

I took his silence for agreement.

"And it'll look good on your CV," I added.

He looked at the doll again, and said, "Can I...?" And then, with care, he tugged at the first of the linen strips to undo the bow that secured it.

With the second strip untied, he carefully lifted the figure. I said, "The museum catalogue had it listed as a Cheeky Boy Figure. That's why no one knew what it was."

"The description's accurate," he said. "The Cheeky Boy is a traditional knee figure style. Look at the face."

The face was the kind that you'd associate with most of the old-school ventriloquist acts—wide-eyed, apple-cheeked, alert, and equally capable of mischief or horror. At home on the body of a schoolboy or a Toff or, as in this case, an unreliable-looking army private. The papier maché was cracked with a few flakes, but the head was intact. As to the works, I didn't know. I'd taken a careful look inside the body but the complex mass of rods, ropes, levers and rings had deterred me from investigating any further.

Alex said, "You need to be careful who you let handle this. A lot of modern vents use a soft figure which is basically a glove puppet. A hard figure's a completely different proposition. This one has a control stick loaded with three different actions." He worked his hand into the back of the figure and spent a few moments in exploration. "Four actions," he amended. "We've got lower lip, upper lip, side moving self centering eyes and a blinker. The upper lip's leather. That can dry out so I'm not going to risk it. Were you planning any restoration?"

"Just conservation. Can you say what it needs?"

"Don't let anyone touch it. I'll give you the names of some people."

He ran through the actions and the head came to life, swivelling and clattering with more noise than I might have expected. I have to say that this kind of handling went against all my instincts as a curator. But the people who pay my salary had ordered a civilian hero.

Alex said, "It's an Insull head. Len Insull was the top man for figures in England. This one's based on one of his stock designs." As he spoke he shifted position, settling the figure on his free arm so that their faces were almost on a level. Its own arms hung boneless, swinging with the weight of the figure's solid hands. "He supplied Lewis Davenport's magic store, back when it was on Great Russell Street. I think it's a Number One. On this model the blink would be an extra."

The eyes closed and the head rolled from side to side, and already it was eerie, like a bizarre little man working out the kinks after so long in a cramped position.

I said, "What kind of voice do you think?"

"Don't arsk him, he wouldn't have a farkin clue."

Seriously, I jumped. Alex looked as surprised as I. The head swivelled to make it seem as if the figure looked back and forth between the two of us.

"What?" it said.

"We weren't expecting you to speak yet," Alex said.

The figure seemed to look him in the eye. "Well," it said, "he has a good excuse. But what's yours?"

"That's very good," I said, and they both ignored me.

"Who's he talking to?"

"He's talking to you."

"Then why's he looking at you?"

"Because I'm the boss."

"What am I?"

"You're nothing."

"So you're the boss over nothing."

"That's a very old joke."

"I've been in a fucking box since nineteen fifty-two."

I said, "We'll have to keep it clean for the kids."

Square Bash Willie turned his face toward me and, with half-lowered lids, affected the accent of a stage cockney aping an aristocrat.

"Would these be the children wot I will be obliged to entertain with tales of other children being burnt to death and kippered and such like?" he said. "Why, I can 'ear their merry larfter already."

I'd been wrong about Alex. I could see it now. His diffidence was actually the key to his performance. It meant you paid him almost no attention while the dummy—sorry, the figure—was speaking. To my untrained eye his technique was good. He had the slightly mournful expression that many a ventriloquist has to adopt, but that was how his face looked all the time. The occasional slight movement of his throat was the only giveaway.

"I can't gnoove ne lip."

Square Bash Willie had inclined his head toward Alex who now had him speaking in a low voice, as if I wasn't to hear.

Alex said, "You mustn't move your lip. The leather's cracking."

"That's not a crack, it's a cold sore."

"It's a crack."

"It's a cold sore."

"How can *you* get a cold sore?"

"I picked it up on a weekend pass," Willie said, at full volume with the plosives clear and perfect. "While proposing to a petite young lady."

"Where?"

"I kissed her under the aqueduct."

"There's no aqueduct around here. I think you're attempting a *double entendre*."

"Like fucking ballet dancer? With these legs?"

"You know what I mean."

"All right, it was a passenger bridge. But you try saying that with only one lip."

"Look," I said, "This is fine. Everything's fine. Except for the effing and blinding. That will have to go."

Willie swung around to me. "You sound like Mother Teresa's life coach."

I'm not proud to admit it. But I gave up and talked to the dummy. It was so much easier.

I said, "Have all the fun you like and make them laugh, but here's what we need to put over. Today's kids don't know anything about Max. After the war he kept the character and the uniform and made the act over into a National Service routine. He appeared on the BBC a few times, but none of the footage survives. It was the variety circuit and summer seasons back then."

As I was speaking, Square Bash Willie kept his gaze on me but I was aware that his top lip kept trying to creep up, baring his teeth in a kind of sneer. Alex would notice and nudge him, and his lips would clamp shut. Then, after a few moments, the same thing again.

I stopped.

"I'm fucking with you," Square Bash Willie said.

"I know you are," I said. I was beginning to wonder if Alex was such a great choice after all. There was no doubting that he had the necessary skill, but I was getting the feeling that his skill might be hard to contain. On the other hand, his had been the only response to our ad.

I pressed on.

"Max's parents ran a working men's club in the town. Whenever he was touring in the area, he'd come for a visit and stay with them. There was always publicity. He'd be asked to open some event, judge a beauty contest… One time he and Willie showed up at the football ground for a match and posed with the team. It always gave out the same message, that he never forgot where he came from. They value that around here."

Willie seemed attentive. It was rather unnerving. His eyes had inset irises of coloured glass, so they had depth without life. And every now and again, he'd blink.

I looked pointedly at Alex. "It was a clean act," I said, and Alex shrugged and glanced at Willie, as if to say, *Don't tell me, tell him.* "Respectable enough for the nuns at the TB Sanatorium to ask for a visit as a treat for the children. He went, of course. He toured the wards and gave an hour-long show. About twenty minutes after the show, there was a fire in the basement. It started in the laundry room and got into the stairwell, and after that no one could reach the exit.

"Max went back in and tried to lead the children to safety. When he couldn't find a way out of the building he got them into a storeroom with a heavy door and closed it to keep out the fire. It held back the flames but not the smoke, so in the end it was for nothing and he died along with them. They found Square Bash Willie with the bodies.

"There was some controversy. No one wanted to blame the nuns but the fact is, doors that should have opened were kept locked. They didn't clear the building when they could have. But we're not going to get into that. It's not an occasion for opening old wounds."

Willie said, "Speaking of nuns, do you know the difference between a nun in a choir and a slapper in the bath?"

Alex said, "Not now, Willie."

"One sings with a soul full of hope, while the other..."

"I said not now," Alex interrupted. "Is all your material like that?"

"I'll be honest with you. Some of it's not as good. How much is he paying us?"

"Who?"

Willie turned and leaned toward me and fluttered his eyelashes. There was a clattering as the paired lids went up and down. If there's any more disturbing sight than a cracked-up grinning moon-faced papier maché Cheeky Boy giving its most seductive leer, I don't ever want to see it.

Alex said, "We've already covered that. There's no money."

The doll's head snapped around to look at him.

"No money," Alex repeated.

"No money?"

"No."

"Excuse the anachronism," Willie said, speaking slowly. "But—*W...T...F?*"

"It's to honour a fellow professional."

Willie put his face up close to Alex's, their foreheads almost touching. "The point of a professional," Willie said slowly, with Alex flinching at every plosive sound, "is that a professional gets paid. *Compadre.*" Alex's reaction made it look as if real spit was hitting him.

"We'll get a lot of publicity out of it," he said.

I was expecting some comeback with a joke, but Willie said nothing.

"And we might get something on YouTube."

Still nothing. Willie was staring and Alex seemed increasingly uncomfortable.

"It'll look good on my CV," he added.

Willie's head turned slowly. Now he was looking at me. Then back to Alex.

"Remember when you were twelve?" he said. "Eh, boy? Remember? It was never Disneyland with you. The one place you wanted to go was Vent Haven. Your parents saved up for three years to take you. That's love for you. Love for their strange little boy. To see all the figures from the acts who'd passed on."

Alex looked down. I remembered the picture in the cuttings book, the boy in front of row upon row of vintage dolls, each with a card bearing details too small to make out.

Willie said, "What's the unwritten rule in Vent Haven?"

Alex tried to look away, and he seemed to mutter something. But Willie wasn't letting him off the hook.

"I can't hear you."

"You never put a voice in a dead vent's figure," Alex said, clearly this time, and with some embarrassment.

I said, "But you're doing that now."

"That's because he's broke," Willie said. "He thought it was a paid job. And he's too polite to tell you to stick it."

"But you're not."

"That's the beauty of me," Willie said. "And while we're being honest, do you want to know what really happened in the fire?"

How do you answer that?

"Go on," he said. "You know you do."

I made a vague and helpless gesture.

He went on, "Picture the scene. There's Max. The show's over. Everyone's off to bed. He's given his time but he's been promised expenses. Without his expenses he can't get home. When you're a name in the business, everyone thinks you're rich. And that's what you want them to think! They don't call it show business for nothing. I'm packed away in the dressing room and he's arguing with the nuns while they bilk him out of his bus fare. Nuns, eh? Always quick to plead poverty."

Clack. He winked, and then continued.

"Then come the flames. A man on the street sees them first and bangs on the doors. The doors are locked. All the doors are always locked. Those young girls have to be protected. Or controlled. Little man-hungry minxes that they are. The fire brigade's on its way and the fire's down in the basement, so Mother Superior makes them stay in the building. Why? Because if they go outside, men will see them in their night clothes.

"Now the fire's in the stairwell and the stairwell's roaring like a chimney. The girls downstairs can't get out, and the girls upstairs can't get down. Then a voice is heard. Far away. From the store cupboard they'd given us for a dressing room."

"You?" I said.

Willie took a little bow. Then he switched his voice to something tiny and far away. A doll with its own ventriloquist skills.

"Don't leave me, Max. Come and get me." And back to normal—"Max couldn't ignore it. He could never ignore me. He ran through the flames and up those stairs, and the girls on the landing saw him and followed. He was the man with the funny little friend who sat on his knee and made them laugh. He'd look after them, wouldn't he? He must know the way out. When the fire came up the stairs they all crammed into the storeroom and by then it was too late. And all of them died."

"Except you."

"Except me. How about that?"

"Wait a minute," I said. "What am I saying? There was no one calling. None of that happened. Did it?"

"Are you going to argue with a witness?"

"You're not a witness." I looked at Alex. "You're not a witness."

Alex took a moment to react. As if he'd been caught up in the conversation and wasn't expecting to be included.

Willie said, "You can tell it your way. I'll tell mine." He rolled his head around to look at his handler.

"Bad news, sunshine," he said. "I don't think we're getting the gig. But you did a good job. Are you all right?"

"Yes, Willie," Alex said. "I'll be fine."

"Are you sure?"

"Yeah."

"I think we're done."

"I think we are."

"You can put me back now."

The life went out of Square Bash Willie when Alex disengaged his hand from the controls.

As Alex was laying the figure back in its storage crate I said, "You can't give the people a story like that. It's nothing but tragedy. We're trying to find something to celebrate."

"Then perhaps," Alex said, "it's better if you don't ask the dead to speak."

After arranging the figure, he tied up the linen strips to secure it and put the tissue paper over. Then with a brief and polite smile he picked up his book of cuttings and moved to the door.

I followed him down the stairs.

"You knew there were no other replies," I said. "Did you all get together and have a meeting? Are you the one they sent?"

He opened the main door and looked back at me. And I was thinking that if the dead ever could speak, then by today's example all of history would probably be fucked.

I said, "Money or no money. You never had any intention of taking the job, did you?"

He said nothing.

"Did you?" I said, and he still said nothing.

Then he went out, and closed the door behind him.

The
PRICE

A S FAR AS Lisa was concerned, weekends were for catching up. This weekend had been something of an exception, mostly because of Richard DeSimone; he was the record company executive who'd done most of the dealing with them since Nick had signed the new contract, and he'd driven up late on the Friday night to spend the next two days being flattered and feted and generally treated as if his opinions were worth anything more than the handful of mouse droppings that Bob Ingram would have given for them under any other circumstances. Ingram's act was a model of restraint, and a constant entertainment to Lisa. He stayed close to DeSimone, nodding at his wisdom and showing all the right reactions to his insights, of which he seemed to have a bottomless store. DeSimone had jet-black hair and the seamless good looks of a public schoolboy; these were spoiled by his eyes, which were small and squalid and snakelike. He had to be older but he seemed to be about twenty-four.

It was generally acknowledged that Nick couldn't hit the side of a slow-moving bus with a shotgun, and so it was no surprise to anybody when he didn't appear at the Saturday shoot. Nothing was in season yet, but there was a skeet range up on the moors that was reached by a wet and bumpy drive in one of the estate's Land Rovers. DeSimone contrived to sit next to Lisa, and to press against her for most of the journey. Lisa had worked as the organization's press secretary from the very beginning, and she'd believed that she was familiar with every species of media creep; but now she could only stare out of the Rover's window and try not to shudder.

DeSimone—whose country-squire jacket and green wellingtons looked suspiciously new—had been secretary of his college rifle club, and he'd made sure they knew it. Unfortunately his targeting also turned out to be in the slow-moving bus league, and Ingram and Lisa had a difficult time making certain that he stayed ahead. He talked about the bad light, the unfavorable wind, and how much better this kind of thing tended to be up in Scotland. It was his theory on the genetic basis of a woman's inadequacy with any kind of firearm, meant as a reassurance in the light of Lisa's miserable score, that finally caused her to catch Bob Ingram's eye. Ingram's response was a slight, resigned shrug, as if he'd already seen the likely results of the weekend and knew that there was little they could do to change anything.

DeSimone's next attempt was a double-miss. Lisa quickly raised her own gun, and blasted both of his clays out of the air before they'd even begun to fall.

They sat on opposite sides of the cab for the return journey.

On Saturday evening they gave him the works—a long dinner, a log fire, single malt whisky and the best grass available to supplement the small complimentary pharmacy that had been laid out in the guest bed room before his arrival. By then the strain was starting to show on Bob Ingram, and a couple of times when DeSimone's back was turned Ingram had run through a rapid-fire range of derisory gestures so sudden and intense that Lisa had to stage a coughing fit or be caught laughing.

On Sunday, they finally got down to business.

Lisa stayed in the ground-floor room that had been set aside as her office, catching up on some letters. Bob Ingram's office was a larger suite next door, and that was where he and Nick and Richard De Simone spent the entire afternoon without even calling for coffee. There was a tense kind of atmosphere over the whole house; Tony Patranella, Nick's longtime driver and more-or-less bodyguard, came wandering through on the pretext of wanting to ask Lisa something, and then forgot what it was. He kept glancing at the connecting door through to Ingram's suite, and the small talk would falter and his apprehension would show. Like everyone else in the organization—the "shareholders," as Ingram called the core group—his future depended on Nick Fulton. And Nick Fulton's own future was the subject under discussion.

When Tony was finally out of the way, Lisa checked her watch. She hadn't counted on him hanging around for so long, and now she hadn't much time. From the desk drawer beside her she took the small bundled up package that she'd prepared in the hours before DeSimone's arrival and then, leaving the electric typewriter running as an indication that she'd only stepped out for a moment, she left her office and headed for the stairs.

The house dated back to Georgian times, the lease to a more recent era when it had been the form for every big rock star to own a manor in the country. The kids loved to see it, all those Sunday-supplement features with the latest mad, bad upstart lounging around in leather trousers against a baronial backdrop. It seemed the ultimate put-down of everything that had gone before, to fill such a place with hangers-on and to treat it carelessly. Bob Ingram had let the situation run until they'd got the publicity that he wanted, and then he'd ruthlessly cleared out the human debris and brought the decent furniture back out of storage. The image now was more sedate; Nick's fans had grown up, and most would have homes of their own.

Ingram was sharp, all right.

The main guest bedroom was down at the end of the upper hallway. The hallway itself seemed as broad as the deck of a liner, broad enough to have full-sized tables set with flowers down its centre with still a car's width of space on either side. There was nobody around; the housekeeper didn't come in on Sundays, and everybody else was lurking downstairs hoping to hear something of the closeted discussions. The guest room wouldn't be made over until the morning, which suited Lisa's plans exactly.

The curtains were half-drawn, and DeSimone's suitcase lay packed but open on the bed. He was a messy packer, she noted as she went around the bed to the dressing-table, and even though he'd only spent two nights in here the air was distinctly unfresh. She resisted the urge to open a window; she didn't want to leave any signs that she'd been around.

She removed the rubber band that had been holding together the package that she'd taken from her drawer, and she spread the contents out on the dressing-table. One thin plastic trash bag, holding everything together. A roll of smaller polythene bags with wire twist-ties. Tweezers. Scissors. An eyedropper in a brown glass bottle. One clean bedsheet, folded. A pair of pink rubber gloves.

She put the gloves on before she did anything else, and then she lifted the open suitcase from the bed and set it on the floor without disturbing anything. She threw back the duvet cover, and carefully removed and folded the lower sheet; this went into the trash bag, which she then knotted to keep it sealed before she remade the bed—not too well—with the new sheet and replaced everything as it had been before.

The next stage was the part that she'd been looking forward to the least. Collecting her kit together, she went through into the bathroom.

DeSimone had been as messy in here as he'd been outside. The floor was awash with cold, soapy water from the shower, and he'd thrown down most of the clean towels to soak this up so that he could walk around. On the tiled floor of the shower stall a ring of shampoo suds had dried hard, and a few tiny hairs like dark question marks lay beached around the drain. Using the tweezers and fighting her revulsion, Lisa gathered these together and dropped them, tweezers and all, into one of the smaller bags.

Now came the worst.

She lifted the toilet lid. As she'd expected—hoped was too strong a word for it—the toilet hadn't been flushed. Essence of DeSimone was held there, tanked and rank, and she was going to have to reach down into the bowl and gather some in with the eyedropper. Her hands were sweating inside the rubber as she did it, feeling unclean and tainted by the closeness even though there was no actual contact. Nurses do this all the time, she told herself.

They're welcome to it, was her next, unbidden thought.

As soon as she'd finished she slammed the lid down and stood up and took her first breath in more than a minute. The bottle went into another bag, twisted and wire-tied, and then she resisted the urge to gather her stuff together and run for as long as it took to lift the cistern lid and reconnect the rod that linked the flush to the handle. She'd unhooked it herself, only hours before as the others had been finishing breakfast.

She made one stop on the way back, to stow everything in the bottom of the wardrobe in her own room. She'd burn the gloves at the first opportunity; but for the moment, she was going to go back to her typewriter as if nothing had happened. On the way down the stairs, she checked her watch; she'd been gone for little more than six minutes.

Around four-thirty, Lisa took off her audio headset just in time to hear a car being started outside. She went to the big window and checked and saw that, yes, DeSimone was leaving. It was almost worth a celebration. She'd known illnesses that had been more welcome.

She gave it a couple of minutes, and then went to the connecting door.

Bob Ingram was sitting in the big padded swivel chair, the one he didn't like to use. He'd pushed it away from the desk, and tilted it so that he could sit back and look at the ceiling. One of the shotguns, the one with the expensive engraved scrollwork that they'd bought in for DeSimone, lay across his knees.

Lisa said, "Things aren't that bad, are they?"

Ingram looked down at the gun as if he'd forgotten that he was holding it. "They're not so great, Lisa, old girl," he said, and he tipped himself forward and laid the gun carefully on the desk.

"I thought you were going to present him with that at the end of the stay."

"Well-greased and up his back passage with both barrels ready to fire, maybe. But I'm not wasting seven hundred quid of Nick's money for no results, and that's what we'd get."

Lisa looked around. Ingram seemed to be alone. She said, "Where is Nick?"

"He lost interest and wandered off toward the end. I can't honestly say that I blame him."

"No good news, then," Lisa said, as if she really had to ask, and she hitched herself up to sit on the corner of Ingram's desk. There was plenty of room.

Ingram sighed, the sound of anger that had been suppressed for so long that it had become stale. "They've screwed up the last two years, and they're not prepared to lose face in front of each other by admitting it.

Nick Fulton's sales are trying to crawl under a duck, so Nick Fulton has to carry the can. Regardless of the fact that they sneaked out two albums in the slowest part of the year, and then picked out a singles track with a reference to oral sex in the lyric so blatant that it was guaranteed no radio station in the country would give it airplay. They probably let the cleaning ladies pick the album covers while we didn't even get a look in on the marketing side, and now they've got the utter brass to say that Nick can't hold his sales any more. No," he concluded, getting to his feet, "the news is not good."

And then he went out to break it to the others, leaving Lisa alone.

And thinking.

Late that evening, she drove out to the station to meet a train. Nothing much ran on the line any more and Sunday was its slowest day, and so she found herself waiting alone in the old Victorian ladies-room with an old-fashioned iron stove fighting the chill from the corner. The place was a dusty relic of days gone by, and when the line closed down it would probably stand empty and ghosted for a few years until somebody bought it and turned the offices into bedrooms and set tubs of bright flowers out along the platform. They'd probably keep bees, and maybe a goat to crop the grass down where the rails had been. Nothing like it would ever be built again; it was a piece of the past, and the bubble was closing.

The train was late, and came in at eleven.

Only one passenger got off, a middle-aged man in jeans and an American Air Force flying jacket. He had a straggly, curly beard, and his long hair had been tied back with an elastic band to hang in a ponytail. His only luggage was a canvas tote bag. He came down the platform to Lisa, recognizing her instantly even though it had been a couple of years since they'd last met. They made an awkward handshake. He hadn't changed and neither, Lisa supposed, had she. They then went out to her car; he slung his bag into the back, and then they both climbed in for the return to the manor.

"So," she said, half an hour later, "how's Jim?"

They were in the kitchen now, sharing a late supper. Jim Louri was his name, and he was tearing through the game pie as if he hadn't eaten in a week. "Jim's fine, family's fine," he said as she slid a can of beer across the table to him. "Sharon brought her first boyfriend home last weekend. Words cannot describe how that made me feel."

"And business?"

"Lousy. Nobody's touring. I don't suppose there's anything going with your boy?"

"Touchy subject right now. Times have been brighter."

Louri had been a bass guitarist in a third-division heavy metal band until early arthritis had found its way into his hands; now he mostly made his living as a gofer and fixer for other acts on tour. The disease in his knuckles had at least saved his dignity, because the band had been going nowhere. Louri was the only one of them who'd stayed in the business, the rest going back to regular jobs.

"Okay," he said at last, pushing himself back from the table, "that's the small talk out of the way. Now tell me who you want to hurt."

Lisa was taken aback by this directness; uncertain of her ground and working with an understanding that had been founded mainly on rumour, she'd been wondering how she was going to introduce the subject that had been uppermost in her mind when she'd telephoned Jim Louri on the Thursday evening. "Simple as that?" she said, and Louri nodded.

"Simple as that. We do it now, you pay me tonight, and I leave in the morning. No guarantees on results and no second tries, either. You want to mess around some more, you do it on your own. That costs you nothing. I'm just a consultant here."

Lisa hesitated for a moment, and then she took the plunge.

"His name's DeSimone," she said.

"Would I know him?"

"I don't think so. He's a little fish who thinks he's a shark. He knows nothing, which is just enough to make him a problem for us."

"A problem how?"

"He's the record exec in charge of Nick's case. That means that when he screws up—which he's doing—Nick's career goes down the toilet and the rest of us follow."

Louri nodded again, thinking it over. "So what you really need is a charm for success."

"Nick doesn't need any charms for success. He's a solid-gold talent. What he needs is the debris taken out of his way."

Louri watched her for a moment. She didn't doubt that her determination was there for anyone to see. Then he said, "Okay. Did you get everything like I told you?"

"I got it," she said.

She left him for a while as she went upstairs; she'd a vague explanation in mind that she was going to use if any of the others should see Louri and wonder why he'd come to visit, but everything was quiet and it seemed unlikely that she'd need it. All the same, she was hoping that she'd be able to get him away in the morning without anybody else even knowing that he'd been around. Louri had a certain reputation, after all, or Lisa would never have known to contact him.

She collected everything that she needed from her wardrobe and left her room, closing the door quietly behind her. She could hear faint music coming from Nick's own suite at the far end of the landing. Tony Patranella and a couple of the others would probably be playing cards for Monopoly money in one of the other rooms, but everybody else seemed to have gone to bed, probably to lie awake worrying about whatever was going to happen. They had good reason, because when Bob Ingram became despondent it was a sure sign that things were going really badly. He was, in his unpretentious East End market-trader's way, a strategic genius in business matters, and if he said that the outlook was bleak then it was something that you had to believe. Bleak was what he seemed to be saying now, and so as far as Lisa was concerned this opened the way for desperate measures.

Down in the kitchen, Jim Louri had unpacked his tote bag and set everything out; Lisa saw a big cheap edition hardbacked book, some handwritten notes, scissors, tape, and a stick of stationery paste. She also saw that he'd cleared the kitchen table and dragged it across the stone floor so that it now stood under the old ceiling-suspended drying rack over on the far side of the room. He'd spread out a sheet of new brown wrapping paper shiny-side-up on the tabletop, and now he was unwinding the waxed line from its cleat so that he could lower the rack to within reach. Lisa set her own collection down alongside his.

"What did you get?" he said, coming over, and so she showed him the bagged hairs from the shower stall and the tiny bottle of diluted urine.

"Just don't ask how I got it," she said.

"You've got his sheet?"

"In the laundry bag."

"And what about a doll for the Volt?"

Now, faintly embarrassed, she brought out the last of her items; not anything that she'd taken from DeSimone's room, but something that she'd bought from the charity shop in the village on Friday morning. "I didn't make anything," she said, "but I got this. I was never much at art. Will it do?"

He took it from her, with a look that said that he'd seen some weird interpretations of a Volt before but never one quite like this. It was an Action Man combat soldier, the kind with the movable Eagle Eyes; its limbs had all twisted at odd angles in the bottom of the bag, like those of a body hit by a severe shockwave that had left the skin intact whilst breaking every bone inside. He hadn't been too well cared for, because his dogtags had gone and one of his plastic boots was missing. Louri held the doll in his own somewhat distorted hand and said, "Well, it's novel. But I don't see why not." And then he held it out for her to take back. "Look, you work on this while I see to the sheet. You want to cut a hole in the chest big enough to take an egg, and then we'll need an egg to go in it. One that was bought without any haggling over the price. Is that any problem?"

"Nobody haggles these days, not in a supermarket. I'll get one from the fridge."

Cutting the chest open with a Stanley knife was tough going, and faintly unpleasant; the doll's Eagle Eyes seemed to be watching her with reproach, and she reached to turn its head aside. Louri, meanwhile, carefully unfolded the sheet on the wrapping paper and pegged its corners to the rack so that he could hoist it up to hang straight. When he'd done this he took a broad kitchen knife and began to tap gently at the flat centre of the sheet. Nothing spectacular happened, but after a couple of minutes there was a discernible buildup of white flecks on the paper beneath.

Skin scales.

Lisa finished her work on the Volt as Louri was gathering the scales and the hair together on a piece of cling-wrap. The hole that she'd made was just about big enough now that she'd cut away some of the interior moulding as well, but it was ragged around the edges. Louri told her that this didn't matter as he tucked the twist of cling-wrap down into the body cavity, and then he turned to the egg.

Lisa must have been looking doubtful, because he said, "Something wrong?"

"I suppose not," she said. "It's just that… I didn't really think of stuff like cling-wrap and factory-farm eggs having much of a place in something like this."

"Got to adapt, use what you can," Louri told her. He was starting to make a careful cut into the shell at the broad end of the egg. "Have you ever actually tried to get hold of milk that three bats have drowned in?"

"We get stuff that tastes like it, sometimes."

"Well, you see the problem. If you want to pay really big money I can put you onto someone who'll turn up all dressed in black and he'll talk like he's in an echo chamber all the time and he'll tell you that he uses nothing that isn't one hundred percent authentic. You need a piece of a virgin's liver, he's got it. Babies' blood, no problem. His day job's a technician in a hospital pathology lab, see? He'll put on a good show, but in the end he won't give you any better guarantees than I will."

"I thought you didn't give guarantees."

"That's right. Pass me the sticky tape, will you?"

After opening the egg, he'd drawn out the white but let the yolk stay in, and then he'd filled up the space inside the shell with urine from the eye-dropper. Now he put a piece of clean paper over the hole, and sealed this in place with a piece of tape. The complete egg was then fitted into the prepared chest of the Volt, and the whole thing taped around several times. It looked swollen and deformed, faintly obscene.

"Now, what you do," Louri said, "is bury this somewhere that it won't be disturbed. As the egg rots, your man gets jaundice. You want to put an end to it, you dig it up and you burn the egg. Otherwise it just gets worse until he dies." He shrugged, but his eyes were serious. "If that's what you want, it's what you want. Here."

And he handed her the Volt. It was just a toy and an egg and a few scraps of nothing, but the real weight was in the responsibility that came with it. And the responsibility was all hers now. She looked at Jim Louri; but Louri was already repacking his tote bag.

She gave him DeSimone's room, although she didn't tell him that, and she left him with the envelope of money that represented all of her easily accessible savings. She carried the Volt carefully, well away from herself as if it was a hot source, and in her own room she laid it in a drawer so that she could close it away and not have to look at it. The bulge of the egg under the tape was like some gross tumour. She was nervous, and she was more than a little awed at the process she'd started.

And what if there was nothing in it? There probably wasn't. She knew that her faith was only the faith of desperation, the powerful will to believe in anything at all that offered hope in a hopeless situation. She also knew that she was too old to be starting in a typing pool for peanuts-by-the-hour. The desk in the corner, the coffee break, the quick dash out to get some shopping in the lunch hour. Leaving collections. The Christmas party.

She shivered, closed the drawer on the Volt's sightless Eagle Eyes, and started to undress. She tried not to think of the egg yolk in the middle of the tumour, already under attack and beginning to curdle.

"Do you ever check up on your results?" she asked Louri the next morning as they drove out again toward the railway station. She'd taken him breakfast in his room, and smuggled him out via the back stairs; nobody, as far as she could tell, had seen them go. As far as history was concerned, Jim Louri's visit hadn't even taken place.

"I never check," he said. "For all I know, it's just a big waste of time. And if it isn't, I don't want to know."

"If it all works out. I'll send you a bonus."

"No bonuses. It's all in your hands now. But I'll give you one last piece of advice."

She glanced across the car at him. "What?"

He wasn't smiling. "Don't let it go too far. Because you may get what you want, but there's always a price and I'm not talking about money. Whoever makes these things happen, he's got a weird sense of humour."

Louri's words were still in her mind as she drew in by the small country station. The stopping-train wasn't due for another hour, but by unspoken agreement she wasn't going to wait with him.

"Bye, Jim," she said as he got out of the car under the station's wooden awning. The building behind him looked like an old gingerbread house in fading red and cream. "Best of luck."

"And you," he said as he shouldered his tote bag, and then he slammed the car door and walked away. He didn't look back; services had all been rendered, responsibility had all been transferred.

And his warning was still in Lisa's mind as she turned the car around and headed for home.

The first thing that she noticed on her return was that Nick's Porsche was missing from the gravelled turnaround in front of the house. Bob Ingram collared her as she came in through the main door and said, "Lisa? You free?"

"Far as I know," she told him. He seemed to be in a hurry, but there was also something else; it was almost a sense of oiled gears turning fast as a smooth machine ran, the unmistakable buzz that Bob Ingram gave off when he was setting something up. And Bob Ingram was always setting something up, although last night Lisa had received the impression that their options and their opportunities to act had been reduced almost to zero.

He said, "Staff meeting in the main lounge in half an hour. Not the whole staff, just the shareholders."

"But Nick isn't here, is he?" Lisa said, thinking about the missing Porsche.

"That's the whole point," Ingram told her. "I'll explain everything then."

Lisa went up to her room to take off her jacket. Could it be that Ingram had a plan for getting them out of this? She only had the undercurrent to go on, but she certainly hoped that she'd read it right—because apart from assuring their futures, successful action from Ingram now would make her own tawdry little scheme unnecessary. It was looking pretty stupid in daylight, anyway; but stupid or not, there was still something about the nature of it that scared her. She could assert her disbelief as much as she liked, but she couldn't get rid of that small, cold pebble of fear.

The explanation was simple. She'd believed that she was ruthless enough, but now she'd found that she wasn't. As long as the Volt existed, regardless of any of its dubious magical properties, it was a testament to a personality that she didn't want to own. Perhaps that was the true value of the magic, as balm to those who were sick with the desire for vengeance or fulfilment and who were simply sent to sit in a corner where they could nurse their obsessions as the world turned without them.

If this was what the Volt truly said about her, then she didn't want any part of it.

But what could Bob Ingram be planning?

It might simply be that he was going to break the bad news to the shareholders in a formal way. Their stake in Nick Fulton was, after all, legal as well as professional; it all dated back to a time five years before when Nick had missed three concert dates because of his involvement with "That Chinese Kid," to quote Ingram's phrase. Ingram had personally tracked the two of them down and yanked Nick out of the seedy hotel room where they'd been hiding, and the subsequent out-of-court settlement with the tour promoter had wiped out the organization's cash reserves for a three-month period. The shareholder group had been created then, all of them agreeing to work on without pay for a four percent stake in the big guy's future. None of them had drawn a salary check since, but they'd all done pretty well out of it.

The Volt stared up at her from the open drawer, a bland mask of a face that even looked a bit like DeSimone if you ignored the macho little cheek scar that the manufacturers had added. She was going to get rid of it.

Eventually.

She went down to the main lounge before the half-hour was up, but the meeting had already started without her. The four others were sitting around as Bob Ingram stood before the log fire. Tony Patranella was saying, "So what's the exact score?" as Lisa let herself in and joined them.

"We've got two more years of contract to run," Bob Ingram said, and he started to tick off on his fingers. "They'll schedule two albums, but with no new production; both are going to be patched together from the tracks we haven't released. They'll float a couple of singles, but there's no question of any promotional budgets, no videos, nothing. They'll just cream off the easy revenue from the hard-core fans, and that's it."

"And after the contract?"

"Zero, zilch. No suggestion of renewal, and it's going to be difficult to get anyone else to look at us seriously after that. Meanwhile I'm supposed to be assured that they know what they're doing after listening to that little snot" (DeSimone, without a doubt) "lecture me on the music business for two hours. I was making a living out of the music business while he was sitting in his own cack watching Camberwick Green."

It certainly seemed that, after taking a hand in Nick's decline, those involved had come to an unspoken agreement that their own careers now depended on his continued failure. Anything else, any new ideas, could only reflect badly on their own earlier efforts. Success following a change of direction would be an unpleasant kind of exposure.

Lisa said, "How did Nick take it?"

"Not a crack," Ingram said with dry precision. "I hate to think what it's really doing to him. If they'd presented us with a series of straight, expedient business decisions, then that wouldn't have been so bad. But they've made business decisions and tried to pretend they're artistic judgments, and that stinks."

"You never wanted it in the first place, did you?" Lisa said. She could remember Ingram at the time of the negotiations; he'd tried to argue Nick out of the deal, but it hadn't worked. Nick had kept on looking at the magical figure of one million plus, unable to believe that a kid from nowhere could come to command such a price. And, of course, he didn't; there were clauses and subclauses and separate arrangements dependent on market performance, each of which took a chunk of the cash away and put it back in the company's hands to be earned all over again. Nick had seen none of this. He'd been unable to take his eyes off that long line of zeros.

Ingram said, "I advised against him signing. Then he signed, and I shut up."

"And that," Lisa said, beginning to perceive that there was rather more going on in Ingram's mind than the despondency he was allowing to show, "was the day you started planning for when everything turned out like it has."

"I took a couple of precautions," Ingram said with airy modesty.

"Like what?" Patranella said, scenting good news but uncertain of how that could be.

"Like the clause in our contract with the old company that prevents them from releasing any compilation albums without our say-so. Also the fact that there's nothing in the present contract to prevent Nick from making personal appearances with his own early material. We can do a back-door deal with Eagle and stage our own relaunch in around eighteen months. Eagle aren't too thrilled with us for walking out on them, but at least they know what Nick's worth."

There was a silence of realization, all around the lounge. Compilation albums tended to follow when any artist made a major switch of record label. Tbe old company, finding themselves sitting in the dust behind the bandwagon, would hurriedly bring out a "greatest hits" collection as their last chance to cash in. Eagle Records hadn't been able to do this, and even Lisa hadn't been able to understand why; but now she could see the purpose behind Bob Ingram's strategy.

She said, "Well, it'll give Nick something to hang onto," but Ingram looked at her with a warning in his eyes.

"Nick doesn't know what I've got in mind," he said, and he glanced around at all of them. "I don't want him finding out yet, either."

"Are you serious?" Anne Digby said.

"Deadly serious. The one bright spot in all of this is that when Nick's insecure the songs get better, and we're going to need that."

"So in the meantime," Patranella said, "we sit tight and wait it out."

"Yeah," Ingram said. "Nobody's going to starve, but we'll have to get lean. We can't count on royalties, and we can't count on a so-called falling star commanding much of a contract advance until he's proven himself all over again. Which he will."

Lisa didn't even think to question Bob Ingram's judgment; he'd steered Nick for too long, and certainly knew him better than anyone else around.

She said, "You've got a lot of faith in him, haven't you?"

"I love the guy. I'd kill for him. And if it ever actually came to that, I'd probably start with Creepo DeSimone. Until that opportunity comes around, we'll just have to be satisfied with settling in here and shaving all the extras off our operation. This is where you all come in."

The next hour was spent in a detailed run-through of Ingram's ideas for making savings, with contributions and suggestions from everybody. Lisa made notes under the heading of "getting lean," with the intention of drafting a show-and-destroy set of minutes on the meeting to make sure that proposals didn't get lost in the onward rumble of enthusiasm. She'd done this kind of thing a thousand times before and reckoned that she could handle it in her sleep, which was as well because her full attention wasn't on it now. She was thinking of the Volt and what it represented to her, and she was thinking of how she was soon to be released.

The meeting broke up in time for lunch, with Lisa saying that she'd follow the others through as soon as she'd locked the notes away in her desk drawer. What she actually did was to wait in her office until she'd heard their voices pass on through the hall, and then she slipped out and ran up the wide stairs. A minute later she was descending again with the Volt wrapped in an old silk scarf that had been in the same drawer. Burn it to stop the process, Louri had advised her; might as well follow form in this, she told herself, and she took the Volt through into the now empty lounge with its log fire. The hearth was old, ash-stained, and the rug before it was pocked with burns. She took the scarf from the Volt, and looked at it for one last time; just a kid's plastic toy, taped like a mummy and bulging with an obscene pregnancy, its face impassive and its limbs still twisted. She straightened them out, for no particular reason, and then she bent and quickly placed it on the topmost log.

It lay there, neat and rigid, Eagle Eyes staring up into the darkness of the chimney, but it didn't burn. The tape around its middle began to char and to give out thin tendrils of smoke as the adhesive melted, but Lisa realized that she'd made a mistake in placing it too high. It needed to be down in the white-hot centre of the fire. She could leave it and go to lunch and it would burn eventually as it lay, but somebody else might see it and—worst of all— might even rescue it. And besides, she wanted to see its end, and to be certain that she'd closed the business that she'd started.

Stupid idea, anyway. She should have had more faith in Bob Ingram, and held onto her savings. She reached for the iron poker that stood leaning against the corner of the surround, and used it to try to push the Volt deeper into the flames.

The doll had gone soft, which she hadn't been expecting; it slid from the log almost like a living thing, and when it hit the embers underneath it began to twist and stretch like a body in agony. She knew that it was just the plastic distorting in the heat, but still the sight made her feel faintly sick. There was a high-pitched whistling of escaping gases that might almost have been a scream; and as she watched, the Volt's taped middle split as the egg inside exploded and threw out rotten green ropes that were like guts.

She'd seen enough. She took the poker again, and thrust it at the Volt to bury it deeper in the fire where it couldn't be seen. But the doll folded itself around the poker and seemed to cling to it, distorted and disembowelled and melting but still eager to escape. She tried to scrape it off but didn't succeed the first time; the Volt was blackened now, charred like a body from a car wreck, only its eyes still showing white.

She heard them pop, one at a time, and then the Volt finally seemed to release its grip.

Lisa covered it over with ashes, and put a new log on top. Then she held the poker with its tip in another part of the fire to cleanse it, before replacing it by the surround and going through to join the others.

That faint wheeze of escaping gas could still be heard as she walked out of the lounge. But it would soon end, and then it would be over; a piece of the past, the bubble closed.

Bob Ingram was called out at ten o'clock that night, and within a few minutes of his leaving the news was all through the house. It was one in the morning before he got back, but nobody had gone to bed; they all stood in the big entrance hall like chessmen on the black-and-white tiles, and Ingram walked right through without looking at or speaking to anybody. He stalked into the lounge and slammed the door behind him, and that seemed to be that.

They could hardly go crowding in after, but neither could they leave it this way. Somebody was going to have to follow Ingram to find out what had been happening; and most of the others were now looking at Lisa, which meant that she was elected.

She closed the lounge door softly behind her. Ingram was over by the fireplace with a tumbler almost filled with scotch, and he was standing with his elbow on the high mantle and his head resting against his arm. He looked weary, totally spent. It was a few moments before he lifted his red-rimmed eyes to look at Lisa; she saw a kind of welcome there, and so she drew closer.

"They didn't need me," he said. "Apparently there wasn't even enough of him left to recognize."

"Oh, Bob," she said sadly, and she took his hand. He gripped hers for a moment, and then let go.

"It was DeSimone," he said. "He was responsible for this."

"What do you mean?"

"He was there. He was in the car with Nick. The only bright spot in this whole lousy mess is that he got torched, too. I hope it hurt. I really hope it did."

Lisa was beginning to say that she didn't understand, but then she realized that Ingram was telling her anyway. "It was the Chinese kid all over again," he said. "Remember? Nick's little humiliation trip that we went to so much trouble to cover up? When he drove into town on his own it was because he was meeting DeSimone. That oily little piece of germ warfare was getting his kicks out of slapping Nick around in private while he messed up the rest of his life in public. And Nick, poor bastard, couldn't get enough of it."

"What exactly happened?"

"They were both in the Porsche, on the motorway. Nick was driving. They came to one of those crossover sections where there were roadworks, and apparently Nick didn't even see the signs. He went straight through the plastic cones and hit a tarmac spreader at sixty. There was no one in the truck. The car blew up, and the tar got so hot it started to burn."

The door to the hallway opened a crack then, and Tony Patranella peeked in; but Lisa quickly waved him away and so he withdrew and closed the door, again without making a sound. Bob Ingram didn't even seem to have noticed; he moved across to the sofa and lowered himself onto it like a man at the end of a thousand-mile walk.

"You know what really gets to me?" he said. "I was the one who invited that shrimp here for the weekend. The two of them were probably in the same bed under this roof and I didn't know a thing about it."

In the same bed, Lisa was thinking; on the same sheets.

She was also thinking of the Volt as it twisted and screamed in the fire, its two eyes exploding like popcorn, one for each life that it carried. But Louri had told her that burning would end it, hadn't he?

And it had, hadn't it?

"Listen," Ingram said, getting up suddenly and leaving his drink untouched on the floor beside the sofa, "I've got calls to make. Tell the others, will you?" And he walked over toward the other door out of the lounge, the old service entrance that would allow him to get around to the phone in his office with less chance of having to face anybody along the way.

As he opened the door, Lisa said, "You want me to tell them everything?"

He considered for a moment. "Don't make Nick look bad," he said. "We owe him that much. Especially since he's going to make us all rich."

"What do you mean?"

"The guy's a dead rock star," Ingram said, letting the weight of the words hit her for the first time. "You know what his back catalogue's suddenly going to be worth? This is the gravy train, and DeSimone isn't even around to stop it any more." His voice was flip, but his face was bleak and his voice was coming dangerously close to the edge of cracking. "Solid gold again, Lisa," he said. "Solid gold."

And then he turned and went through, softly closing the door behind him. Lisa was left in an empty room with the fire burning low.

Whoever makes these things happen, he's got a weird sense of humour.

But nobody was laughing.

Not down here, anyway.

EELS

HE SAID, "GIVE me a minute and I'll shut the dog in."

The dog was a little Jack Russell terrier and its owner was Johnny Clifford, whom I saw most days of my working life but barely knew. He was middle aged, shaved infrequently, dressed like a tramp, and was never seen without the same shapeless hat. He owned the big house at the mouth of the quarry where all the lockup garages were.

Back then I rented one of the few lockups that wasn't burned out or falling down. I used it to store tools and scrap and sometimes as a workshop, if I was on a job that needed one. I'm a plumber.

I could never quite work out how Johnny Clifford made his living. It was always one scheme or another. For a few weeks after any big storm, he'd be a roofer fixing broken slates. In the record summer of '03 he'd been seen selling ice cream. Turning his hand to anything, chasing the money wherever it was.

I reckon he just scraped by. His house was big but he spent nothing on it, or on the battered old Transit that he drove. The only new-looking feature of the place was those two plastic shelters that had appeared around the back of the property. They'd arrived on a truck and gone up in a day, tent-like structures of thick polythene stretched over hoops. They looked like a little space colony in his back yard. The polythene was cloudy, and you couldn't see through it.

He said he had a job for me. So right now, on what felt like the coldest day of the year, I was about to get a peek at whatever new scheme he had going back there in Moonbase Alpha.

Once the Jack Russell was out of the way, I followed Johnny around the back of the house. His dog had never given me any problems apart from the times when I had to chase it out of the garage for trying to pee somewhere. But it would bark ferociously whenever anyone approached the house, and I was happy to see it secured. Dogs change when they're on their own turf.

We went into the first of the plastic shelters.

"Watch your head," Johnny said as he ducked in the entranceway.

It was warmer in here than outside, but not by much. The two domes were linked by a tunnel and I could see into both. Because of the plastic the light was soft and pure, like you'd imagine the light in heaven to be.

My first thought was that he was making wine. There were six big vats like those above-the-ground swimming pools that you get in suburban gardens. You fill them from a hose, and water pressure keeps the sides up. He'd insulated and put covers on them, and they were linked with pipes and filtration units.

He'd done all the assembly himself, but I could see why he needed me because his plumbing skills had their limits. On the ground before one of the vats lay an immersion heater coil, in pieces. I'd no idea what he'd been trying to achieve with it and, by the evidence, neither had he.

He said, "Can you do anything with this? I've been trying to rig up something that'll keep the water at a steady twenty-five degrees."

"What's it for?" I said.

"Never mind what it's for."

At this, I bristled a bit.

"It'll make a difference," I said. "Are we talking average or ambient?"

He looked at me as if I was trying to put one over on him. I actually was bullshitting, but he couldn't be sure of it. After a few moments he walked over to one of the other vats and drew the canvas back.

I went and stood beside him, and looked into the water.

"Fish?" I said.

"Eels."

Now that he said it, I could see that they didn't move like fish. They rippled. They were all down at the bottom of the tank and were sliding around one another in one seething, living knot. Their sizes varied.

I said, "What are you doing? Breeding them?"

"You can't breed eels," he said. "You buy in the young and then raise them 'til they reach a commercial weight. It's supposed to take about eighteen months, but these aren't thriving. Doesn't matter what I feed them on. It's this winter that's doing it. I've insulated the tanks, but they lose too much heat. The cold stops the elvers from growing."

"Who do you sell them to?"

"Smokehouses. Top class restaurants. They're a delicacy."

He got a net and fished one of them out for me to see. It looked like the devil and fought like one, too.

"They don't *look* very delicate," I said.

"They're tough little buggers, I can tell you that. If I'd known what it took to kill them, I'd have thought twice about taking them on."

He lowered the net into the water and tipped it so that the creature could swim out and rejoin the others. It quickly settled amongst them, a dark sliver of pure muscle flexing its way through the complex maze of its kin.

Johnny told me that he'd picked up all the gear from a would-be eel farmer who'd gone bust. Personally I'd have taken that as a warning sign, but I said nothing. He explained how he bought the live elvers straight from the fishing boats. How eels lived in freshwater but they spawned out at sea, and the young were caught as they swam inland.

"Everything's got to be just right," he said. "The people you're selling to...they won't take less than perfect."

He wasn't looking at me as he said it. He was looking down at his eels. His face was set and grim. I got the feeling that 'less than perfect' was something that had been dogging him for all of his life.

He left me to it and I got on with the job

JOHNNY CLIFFORD HAD been married once, and for a long time, but his wife had left him about three years before. She'd stuck by him for long enough to earn people's sympathy for the leaving, rather than their disdain. She was a pleasant, practical woman, and Clifford was the village grump who always looked as if he'd choke or cross the street rather than bid you good morning. Most people reckoned her a saint, and weren't scandalised even when it was revealed that her new partner was female. If anyone could drive a woman to that kind of thing, the feeling seemed to run, then Johnny Clifford was the man.

When she first left the village some joked that, irritated by her patience and good humour, he'd probably done her in and buried her on the moor behind the quarry. But she turned up every few weeks to collect her maintenance money. I'd seen her myself, a couple of times. She arrived in a silver car, driven by a woman who waited in it. She stayed for about an hour and I reckon she was probably making sure that Johnny had at least one decent meal in his month.

I don't believe he actually owned his house. If he did, then he could have sold it and moved into a smaller place and his money worries would have disappeared. I think he inherited the tail-end of a lease when his parents died, and there weren't enough years left on it to have any market value. So there he was, stuck with it—not so much a home, more a gigantic brick albatross. Not worth selling, nor worth investing in. If a window broke, he simply closed up the room and stopped using it.

He tried to bargain down my hourly rate, but I told him to take it or leave it. I think he knew what I'd say, but he tried it anyway. With that settled, he left me to work on my own.

In the course of the morning I rebuilt the heater unit and replaced the thermostatic control, and then I installed it and gave it a test. This tank, as he'd explained it, was the fingerling tank, for the most critical growing stage in the eels' life cycle. Eels thrive in warm water, which is why you get so many eel farms alongside power stations. They grow quickly in the waste heat from the cooling towers.

Johnny Clifford reappeared when the job was all but done. Most punters make a point of looking in every now and again to see how it's going, maybe offer you a brew, but not Johnny.

He stood there for a while as I put away my tools. I saw him check his watch and then he said, "I suppose you'll want paying."

"I'll drop off a bill when I've worked it out," I said.

"Listen," he said. "I showed you what I've got going, here, but I'd prefer it if you don't broadcast what you've seen. All right?"

"Okay," I said. "Why's that?

"I don't want everyone to know my business."

"Well, good luck keeping it quiet around here," I said. Here, where everybody seemed to find out everyone else's secrets before too long.

"I've got my reasons," Johnny Clifford said.

WITH AN HOUR or two of daylight left I had a couple of things to finish off for customers in the village, small tidy-up jobs. Fitting a vent cowl. Bleeding the air out of a system that I'd installed the week before. By the time I'd done, the light was gone and my working day was over. I picked up a pint of milk from the local Spar store and drove home to my cottage, which stood on the lane heading out toward the town.

The lane was on the other side of the moor from the quarry. From my upstairs window I could just about see Johnny Clifford's chimneys beyond the moor's distant edge. Whereas Johnny's house was huge and a burden to run, mine was tiny, and just turning around in it could be a challenge. Especially with the new bath standing upright in the hallway, waiting to be fitted. I was sprucing the place up, planning to put it on the market in the spring. I'd always promised myself that if I wasn't married by fifty-five, I'd retire early and move up to Scotland while I could still enjoy the walking. I'd scouted an area and had my eye on the shell of a house that I could renovate, but I had to sell this one to raise the capital.

You always need a plan. Something to aim for. In pursuing mine I spent little and I saved everything. Every job took me a little closer to it.

I typed up Johnny Clifford's bill and put it in a brown envelope, ready to drop through his letterbox the next morning.

Over the next couple of weeks, two things happened. The cold weather grew even colder, and I didn't see any sign of my money, if that counts as a thing. Late one afternoon, after taking the battery out of my van to give it an overnight charge, I set out across the moor to seek out Johnny and give him a shake for it.

There hadn't been any snow, but all the grasses had frozen. The sky was grey and the air was clear and it was as if the entire moor had been fossilized with a single breath. I followed the old mill path as far as the quarry's edge; the quarry had been the source of stone for the original houses in the village, and was like a bite out of the side of the moor. From where I stood I could look down onto the roofs of the lockup garages and the back of Johnny Clifford's place.

The lights were on in his eel farm. I could see the vague dark shape of him through the polythene, about his no-longer-secret business. I'd no idea how the news had got out. But even in the post-office pension queue they were talking about Johnny Clifford's mad venture in the quarry.

I followed the safety fence down. It was broken in lots of places and I was able to step over it into Johnny Clifford's yard. When I reached the bubble I stopped, and then I banged on the plastic with the flat of my hand. It made a muffled, thundery sound, like a drum. I waited a moment and then opened the door to look inside.

I didn't spot Johnny straight away. He was in the adjoining bubble and I saw him through the linking tunnel, up on a set of steps and stirring something in one of the vats. He was leaning into it like a gondolier, the pole supporting a part of his weight. He looked my way and I assumed he'd seen me, so I started toward him.

The next thing I was aware of was a frenzy of yapping and a sudden, sharp pain in my right thigh as Johnny Clifford's Jack Russell took a running leap at me and nipped my leg. Johnny Clifford looked up in shock and I realised that he hadn't seen me after all. He jumped down off the steps and came toward me, shooing the dog back as he did.

"What do you mean," he said, "just walking in like that on somebody else's property?"

"He's torn my trousers," I said.

He had, too. The dog's teeth had ripped a triangular flap that now hung loose. I rubbed around inside it, easing the sting of the bite and looking for signs of blood.

"It's just a scratch," Johnny said.

"You can get rabies from a scratch."

"Don't be so soft," Johnny said. "Come into the house."

HE SAT ME down in the kitchen and gave me a glass of cheap brandy. It was early for me but, what the hey, I was possibly the first man in the village to get a drink out of Johnny Clifford. The dog got shut into the next room and stood right up close on the other side of the glass door, glowering at me through the frosting.

"Has it broken the skin?" Johnny asked.

"No," I had to admit. "It still hurts, though."

"I expect you'll live," Johnny said, and went over to the mantelpiece. On it stood an old clock with its hands at a quarter to two. He reached in behind it and brought out what I recognised as my own envelope, with a slender wad of folded banknotes poking out of the top.

He'd have counted it already but he counted it again, lips pursed, breathing loudly through his nose.

I kept rubbing the bite. "A word of apology would be nice," I said. The skin hadn't broken but the place was staring to throb, and I could bet that it would bruise.

Johnny looked up from the money, and he didn't seem repentant.

"You swore to me that you wouldn't tell anyone what I'd showed you," he said.

"And I haven't."

"No?"

"No," I said. "And if you're astonished that word still managed to get around the village in spite of that, then you must be a bit simple."

"Certain people could make a lot of trouble for me," Johnny said.

I was starting to get angry now. "And you'll be wanting someone to blame for it if they do," I said. "Well, leave me out of it. Just pay up what you owe me and the next time you think of calling on me for something, don't."

I made a point of re-counting the money for myself once he'd handed it over. Then something happened that I hadn't been expecting at all.

"All right," Johnny said. "I got it wrong. I'm sorry."

And there was more to come.

The cheap brandy went away and a good whisky came out. "See if this helps," he said.

I'd never seen him unwind like this before. He even took the hat off.

I asked him what he was so worried about and his answer could be summed up in two words: animal welfare. He feared being raided by the animal welfare people.

I couldn't understand why. From what I'd seen, he took unusually good care of his stock. I wondered if he was operating without some licence that he needed to have, but it wasn't that.

"You keep this to yourself," he said. "Okay?"

He took me into one of the back rooms. It was empty apart from a row of domestic freezers along one wall, all rescued from scrap and no two alike. They were rusting but functional. He opened one of the freezer doors and inside it I saw newspaper-wrapped packages stacked three or four deep on every shelf. They were end-on, like bottles in a wine cellar. Each package was the size of an adult eel.

I didn't get it.

I said, "So?"

Johnny said, "They're alive when I put them in there."

Now I got it.

"Why?" I said.

"The traditional slaughter method is to pack them in dry salt and then eviscerate them. The salt deslimes them and then it's the disembowelling that kills them. Can you imagine that?"

"It sounds barbaric."

"Exactly. I tried it once." He shook his head. "Never again."

I looked at the stiff little corpses in their newspaper shrouds. They made the inside of the cabinet look like one of those Parisian catacombs filled up to the roof with skulls and bones. If it had been a freezer full of meat,

I wouldn't have thought anything of it. But meat's already dead when you put it in.

I said, "Is this not just as bad?"

"I hope not," Johnny said. "But who can say? I keep 'em in cold water for a week. Cleans out their intestines and slows them right down. Then I wrap them up and put them in the freezer and it's like they go to sleep."

"Up at the trout farm they use a stunning tank."

"Up at the trout farm they can afford one. She's bleeding me dry. The only thing the judge wouldn't let her do was pack me in salt first."

We went back to the kitchen. Johnny's dog joined us and showed me no hostility now, apart from a growl when I reached for my glass and he thought I was going to pet him.

Johnny elaborated.

"She reckons that taking money from me is the way to guarantee her independence," he said. "I told her, try earning your own, that's how you guarantee your independence. It didn't go down well."

There was more like that, all about his ex and her new relationship, and I have to admit that after a while I started tuning out.

"You know what gets me most?" he said. "Her turning up every month in a fucking Mercedes to collect it."

I shouldn't have walked back across the moor in the dark, but I did. Blame the whisky. There was just about enough spilled light from the village and the lane to keep me on track, but I could easily have stuck my foot in a rabbit hole or missed my way and taken a tumble into the old mill pond. I stopped at one point and looked back; the lights were still on in Johnny's eel farm, making the domes glow like winter beacons. Then I walked on and they were lost from sight.

IT WASN'T THE start of anything. I mean, no blossoming friendship. The next time I saw Johnny the hat was back on and he was his old morose, eye-contact-avoiding self. But I felt differently toward him. Behind the façade was a man who sought to spare his charges pain and to give them a gentler death than the rules required, even if it meant breaking them. Sometimes the gruffest people are the most sensitive. It's the way they protect themselves.

Although often, of course, you're cutting them slack they don't deserve and they're just bastards.

I was busy that winter. Whenever there's a cold snap, lots of ageing boilers fail and need to be repaired or replaced. I was doing a job for an old dear in the sheltered housing and it needed a valve they don't make any more, and rather than have to replace an entire section of her system I remembered that I had something compatible in my lockup.

When I went to get the part, I saw that there was a silver Mercedes parked outside Johnny Clifford's house with someone inside it.

I'd a rough idea where the valve was, but I had to rummage for it. I'd saved it from an old job for an occasion like this. I save everything. If I don't use it again, I'll eventually weigh it all in and get the scrap value. It won't be much but it'll be something.

I became aware of someone watching me from the open garage doorway. It was the woman from the car.

She was in her forties and what my mother would have called 'well turned out'. Tailored clothes, powdered skin, hair in a neat professional set. Kind of like a younger version of the Queen, if the Queen had worked in admin for the local council.

She didn't introduce herself. She just indicated the polythene outbuildings behind her and said, "Are those greenhouses?"

"Sort of," I said.

"What's he growing?"

"Tomatoes," I said, and the lie came out easily and without any forethought. I'd nothing against Johnny Clifford's wife, but this woman had annoyed me in an instant and without effort.

"Hardly the weather for it," she said.

"That's why you need a greenhouse."

She looked at me again, with one eyebrow raised. "Do I take it you're a friend of his?"

"Not particularly," I said.

"You don't surprise me. He doesn't exactly strike me as a kind man."

"Actually," I said, "I'm not sure that's true."

She took it no further than that, but shrugged and went back to her car to continue the wait. When I'd finally located the valve and emerged from my garage about fifteen minutes later, the car was gone.

I WAS WATCHING *Gladiator* for the umpteenth time on DVD when someone rang my doorbell. I don't get evening visitors. If anyone calls by, they're either lost or they want something.

I opened my front door to find a uniformed policeman standing there. My cottage fronts onto the lane itself, so his car was right behind him with his partner inside it. Things have changed and coppers don't look like they used to. The old Boys in Blue now dress like action figures with every available accessory hanging from their flak jackets.

This one said, "Which one of these is Quarry Bank House?"

"None of them. You're coming out of the wrong end of the village."

"But isn't that the quarry right there?"

"Different quarry. There's three."

He looked around with a sense of repressed frustration, as if he'd half known that they'd gone wrong somewhere but had been hoping not to get it confirmed.

He said, "Anywhere along here we can turn around?"

"Not until you get to the Saab garage," I said. I didn't have a driveway. There was the lay-by where I parked my van, but I wasn't about to move it.

I went to my window and watched the car move off, along with the two police vans that were following right behind. The Saab garage was about half a mile down the lane, and the management had become so pissed-off with people using their forecourt for a turning circle that they'd installed bollards that locked into the ground at night. Something I'd failed to mention.

I picked up the phone and called Johnny Clifford.

"Coppers and vans asking for your place," I told him. "Don't know why. Now you know." Then I hung up.

I watched another twenty minutes of the film but my mind wasn't on it. After the first five minutes, I heard the police convoy going back in the opposite direction. When I went up to my bedroom window and looked across the moor, I was half-expecting to see the police helicopter with its searchlight shining down on Johnny Clifford's house.

Was this the raid that he'd feared? It seemed awfully heavy-handed if it was. When he'd referred to the animal welfare people, I'd imagined a daylight visit from a couple of officials with clipboards and maybe a threat of prosecution to follow. This bunch were going in like the SAS.

It was a cold, wild night, and I'd little inclination to go out. I gave it a while longer, but I couldn't settle. So in the end I caved in and went over to see what was happening.

By then I'd missed most of it. The vans were in the quarry and the car was in front of the house, and there was a lot of flashlight work going on around the back. I could hear Johnny Clifford's dog barking inside. Most of the coppers were just standing around, and one was making a phone call.

I caught the attention of one who was standing alone by the car. He was young, with a thin fringe of a moustache, and he looked too little and fat to be in the police force.

I said, "What's going on?"

True to his training, he didn't give me a straight answer but said, "Would you know anything about this?"

"About what?"

"You see many strangers coming and going?"

"Only you lot."

The one from my doorstep had spotted me, and now came over. He had the air of a much harder customer.

Slapping his gloves together and with his breath feathering in the cold air, he said, "Do you ever have dealings with John Clifford? Do you know how he makes his living?"

"This is supposed to be a drugs raid," I said. "Isn't it? I know how it looks, but those aren't greenhouses. You'll have seen it for yourself, there's no plants growing in there. If anyone's told you different, they've been winding you up."

"Have you seen John Clifford tonight?"

"No." Which was true.

"Or spoken to him?"

I shook my head.

"If he isn't here," I said, "then I've no idea where he is."

I WAS HALF expecting to find him waiting for me when I got home, and I wasn't sure what I'd do with him if I did. But he wasn't there.

It wasn't hard to see who'd made a call to the police. The woman from the Mercedes, I supposed. The 'why' of it was a little bit harder to imagine. Maybe she was just anti-drugs. Or maybe she'd seen a chance to destroy Johnny Clifford's source of income and thereby her lover's small measure of independence. Some people are like that. They can only feel at ease with another person if they've absorbed them.

Whatever the reason, it wouldn't work. There was no net result beyond an hour of needless panic.

His dog was still barking when I went by the next morning, though.

The lower half of the kitchen window was a smeary mess of saliva and paw marks. The kitchen door was unlocked when I tried it. Remembering my previous experience with the dog I stood well back as I pushed the door open, but the terrier was desperate and paid me no attention at all. It shot out, started hunkering down while still on the move, and crapped its way to a tottering halt. That should have been funny, but it wasn't.

I went inside and called Johnny Clifford's name. I made a cautious ascent upstairs but he wasn't in his bed. When I came back down, I was uncertain of what to do.

He'd fled at my call, that much was clear. But with the door unlocked and the dog shut in, it was equally clear that he'd intended to return. Why hadn't he?

When I went into the room where all the old freezers were, I found three of them with their doors wide open and all of them shut down. Two of those with open doors had been emptied. The third had been partly cleared. The freezer motors must have laboured on into the night until they'd tripped a fuse and cut the power to all the sockets in the circuit.

The packages must have been thawing for some hours, because they settled and shifted as I walked out of the room. I heard them move.

I started to get an inkling of what might have happened.

I checked the eel farm, but he wasn't in there. The police hadn't disturbed anything. The first confirmation that I was on the right track came when I found Johnny Clifford's hat on the far side of the safety fence. I suppose I shouldn't have picked it up, but I did. With the hat in my hand, I ascended to join the mill path.

All trace of the mill itself had been erased from the village before I was born, but the name remained in the Mill Field below the moor and the mill path that ran across it. This was the way trodden by weavers a century before. As a boy I'd played by the mill pond, and over the years I'd seen it polluted and spoiled when a local farmer used it as a dump for rubble and sheep carcases. It was half the size it had once been, and the banks were treacherous because they were nothing but dirt, loose bricks and bones.

That was where I found Johnny Clifford.

The water was a grey, cloudy slush. He'd broken through the ice and it had re-formed over him. He was like something suspended in a paperweight; I could see him lying below the surface, face-down with his arms above his head as if frozen in the act of a butterfly crawl. All around him in the slush hung sheets of half-unfurled newspaper, like snapshots of waking birds.

My guess was that he'd been using the pond as a place to ditch the evidence from his freezers. The soft bank had given way on his second or third trip, pitching him headfirst into the water. I picked my way down to the edge with care.

There was nothing I could do for him. I wondered if he'd suffered, or if he'd even known anything at all after the initial shock of the cold. I wondered if it really was just like 'going to sleep'.

Then I saw something move under the ice.

Nothing was clear. It was like looking through the opalescent plastic of the farm. The further from the surface an object was, the less detailed it became. But something rose, passed over his body, and sank from view again. It moved slowly. Slowly enough for me to see the shape and length of it and be certain that it was an eel.

Another coiled around his head and then faded off into the murk, just as another rose and slipped between his ankles. Sleek ribbons, moving in slow motion. I watched in fascination as they orbited Johnny Clifford's corpse, sliding around him like a lover's caress.

DIFFERENT POLICE CAME. They put canvas screens around the pond and divers hacked through the ice to get him out. They found no eels in there, or so they said. I wonder if they even looked. Perhaps they should have dug down into the mud.

Anyway, I don't care. I know what I saw.

I've described it to people, and they always make a face and shudder. But I don't think that's right. I don't think it was anything sinister at all. I think it was beautiful, in its way.

And I sometimes wonder what Johnny Clifford would have made of it, if he'd been able to foresee his own end. I doubt that it was like anything he might have envisaged. And I doubt that it was like anything he would have chosen.

But that's probably true for most of us, however our lives may turn out. We can dream our dreams, write the scenarios in our heads. Scenes of valour, scenes of peace, scenes of farewell in the arms of those we love. We die like heroes, like knights, like champions. Our lives count for something, and in death we're always missed. Not for us the ignominious slip, the lonely conclusion.

We can always dream.

But when it finally comes, the chances are that we'll have to settle for something that's less than perfect.

To Dance by the Light
OF THE MOON

A T ELEVEN O'CLOCK on New Year's Eve, Mercedes Medina read the news.

She was the only newsroom staffer on the station at this hour, and so the bulletin was no more than an update from the IRN teletype: she was off the air at three minutes past, the red light in the news studio dying as the all-night DJ pulled the sound fader out. Mercedes could see him through the double-thickness window along with his tech operator, Derek, who'd got his chair tipped right back against the wall by the door. As she stood, Derek rocked forward and signaled to show that he wanted to speak to her; so she mimed holding a coffee cup, and then she went out.

There was an empty-office silence out in the corridor, and the musty new smell of carpets recently relaid. Mercedes had been with the radio station since its second year of operation, when money had been tight and everything had been run on a shoestring, and she wasn't sure that she liked the new image that the place was now taking on. It had all started to happen when they'd swung into profit; everybody started getting more image-conscious with the next round of franchise competition only two years away, because in a field where most people were newcomers there was an edge to be gained in becoming the Establishment as quickly as possible.

Everything considered, Mercedes didn't like the new situation much. But she doubted that she'd be saying so.

She stepped into a small room beside the promotions office. It had one low vinyl settee, a drinks machine, a food machine, and one bag-lined waste bin. Mercedes dialled the code number for a black coffee, and decided to stick at that because the drinks were free while the crisps and snacks weren't. The second machine also had a habit, seemingly inherited from its predecessor that had been around the corner before the big overhaul, of keeping money and delivering nothing—a tendency that had earned it the nickname of the Diet Machine.

"Had someone on the line for you before," Derek said from behind her as a cup dropped and something that would (she hoped) be coffee started to run. "I told her to call you back." Mercedes turned. Derek was unbelievably tall, around six four, and unbelievably thin. His sweatshirt sleeves had been rolled back to show arms that looked as if they'd just been cut out of plaster casts.

She said, "When was this?"

"Just as you were getting ready to go on-air. She said she'd call you on the newsroom line right after the bulletin."

"You didn't give her the number, did you?"

Derek held up his hands in a kind of defence. "Not me," he said. "She already had it, but don't ask me how. You going to talk to her?"

Mercedes half shrugged. "What was it about?"

"Could be a hot tip. Deep Throat stuff, you know."

"Yeah, I bet," Mercedes said disbelievingly, and she bent to raise the machine's Perspex gate and take out her coffee. It seemed to be more or less what she'd wanted, not counting the slight odor of chicken soup. "What's happening at your end?"

"Don's usual bunch of rough schoolgirls are due to arrive anytime now. He's put on something long and slow so that he can run down and let them in." Something long and slow, in this case, meant an album track that would play to an empty studio during the time that it took for the OJ to race down to the ground-level fire door where his friends/associates/hangers-on would be waiting. Don's taste seemed to be for noisy, knowing, underage girls. Derek shook his head and said, "I don't know where he finds them."

"I don't know how he gets away with it."

"Only because the ones with the big tits get passed along to the boss. You think if I had a perm and got some tinted glasses, I'd have the same kind of luck?"

"No," Mercedes told him as she shouldered the door open to leave. "Those are just accessories. It's the basics you're missing."

"Like what?"

"A total lack of discrimination, and an ego bigger than a telephone box. See you later."

Derek held the door as she slid through it, her cup in one hand and the yellow flimsies of the eleven o'clock bulletin in the other; and then, as she started off down the empty corridor toward the newsroom, he called, "Hey, Mercedes!"

She turned to look back; he was still in the doorway, a huge stick insect less than a year out of college, mousy-haired and with something that, in better light, might have been the beginnings of a beard. He said, "In case you're busy. Happy New Year."

"I'll be seeing you at midnight," she told him, and walked on.

The newsroom corridor was low-lit and silent, and windowless like the rest of the complex. In the background was the murmur of the late-night show being relayed through corridor speakers turned as low as they would go. The station was in a tiny corner of a huge plaza of shops, offices, a multi-level car park, and a high-rise hotel; at this time, when all of the office staff had gone home and there were barely more than a handful of people in the entire building, it was possible to detect a once-a-minute vibration that rumbled through the floors and the walls as if the whole plaza structure were in tune with the deep heartbeat of the city.

The phone had started to ring even before she was through the door; half hoping that it might cut out before she had to answer it, she went over to the big table that ran down the middle of the room and put the bulletin sheets on the spike for the office junior to sort out and file in the morning. Over by the window, the IRN teletype was already hammering out updates for the midnight news; the full-length glass behind it looked out into the main concourse o(the darkened plaza, a goldfish-bowl effect that all the staffers hated because of the crowds of kids who gathered in the afternoons to gape and to tap on the glass as if they were trying to wake the lizards in the reptile house. Now Mercedes saw only herself, a half-real reflection in a room that was a mess of half-read old newspapers, dead press kits, and stacks of directories: a ghost-girl that stared back at her, the skin of a dusty olive and hair of the blackest jet.

And the phone was still ringing.

She hitched herself onto the side of the desk and moved aside somebody's discarded pullover to reach the receiver. "Hello?" she said cautiously, expecting to find herself landed with some long and involved message for one of the other staffers. They weren't supposed to give out this unlisted number for personal use, but they all did it.

"They said to call back," a woman's voice said. It was a terrible line. "Can you talk to me now?"

"How did you get hold of this number?" Mercedes said. Not a message for someone else, after all; her interest began to warm a little.

"That doesn't matter. What I need to know is, can I trust you?"

"That depends. What are you going to tell me?"

"You're recording this," the woman said suspiciously.

"We don't record calls. We're just a small station and this is just an ordinary phone. Is it something you've done?"

"No. But I know someone who has."

"Tell me about it," Mercedes said. "Perhaps I can help." Or perhaps you're just going to waste my time as you try to make trouble for somebody you've decided deserves it; and then you won't give me your name, and then I'll forget all about it. She lowered herself into one of the well-worn typist's chairs and reached for a note block. Just in case.

"It's about that girl," the woman's voice said. "The student who was killed. You did a story on her last week, and tonight you said that the police aren't getting anywhere. Well, I know the person who did it."

Mercedes was bolt-upright now, looking desperately around for the portable UHER recorder that was supposed to be kept on permanent standby in the office. Either it was buried under the rubbish somewhere, or else someone had taken it home. "Do the police know about this?" she said, swearing to herself that she'd find whoever was responsible first thing in the morning and dig out selected internal organs with a rusty fork.

"I can't trust the police," the woman said. "The question is, can I trust you?"

"Yes, you can," Mercedes said firmly. "I've never let down a source yet." Or even had a source worth letting down, she thought as she hitched the chair in close to the table and started to jot down verbatim everything that had been said so far. "What's his name?"

"I can't tell you that. He's someone close and it would come back to me, you see what I mean? He needs to be caught, I think he even wants it. But he mustn't ever know that I had anything to do with it."

"Is he your boyfriend? Your husband?"

"I'm going to hang up," the voice threatened, and Mercedes scrambled to give reassurance.

"Wait wait wait," she said. "All right. I'm not going to push you. But with something like this, you get calls from all kinds of people and they aren't always 100 percent genuine. Now, I'm not suggesting that this means you… but you see my problem? You've got to give me something I can show around. I'm talking about credibility."

A breath. Then: "She was wearing powder-blue underclothes. A matching set. He took a piece away with him."

"Okay," Mercedes said, soothingly, as if a big hurdle had just been overcome here. The truth of it was that she had no idea whether the information was accurate or not; the body had been discovered only half a mile away across the city center and she'd been the first of the press to reach the scene, but the actual information that she'd received from the investigating officers had been the same as that in the official release. The important thing was that her caller didn't know this; and if the detail was as genuine as it sounded, it already gave her an edge on the competition.

Big time, here I come, she thought, and prepared to apply the squeeze. "So you're not giving me your name," she said, "you're not giving me his name, you won't even say what your relationship to him as. Why exactly are we talking here?"

"I told you, he needs to get caught. I know he left things, and the police didn't even see them."

It really was a lousy line; and the woman seemed to be trying to disguise her voice as well, which didn't help. Mercedes said, "What do you mean, things? You mean clues?"

"He even wrote on the wall, right there where it happened, and they didn't even see it. They probably thought it was kids. You could make them listen, though."

"And what exactly did he write?" An even darker possibility occurred to Mercedes. "Were you with him?"

"I've got to go."

"No, I didn't mean…"

"He's coming. He'll hear me."

"Well, let's work out some way that we can talk again…" she began, but she was wasting her time; the line had already gone dead.

Mercedes hung up; gently, reverently, as if the receiver were of thin glass and filled with gold dust. And then, alone in the newsroom with just the quiet clatter of the teletype as background, she took a moment to think.

She knew as well as anybody the dangers of believing in hoax calls in a case like this. That would be how she'd have to treat it, until she knew better; but it was the detail about the powder-blue underwear that already had her halfway convinced. She couldn't confirm it, but it hadn't sounded like an off-the-cuff invention. Now, to keep it 100 percent legal and by the book, she ought to call the police and tell them what she had.

Which meant that they'd move in and take over. And what would she get out of it? She was the one who'd been singled out for the call, hadn't she?

By the clock on the wall, she had forty-five minutes before her next on-air appearance. She started to move.

First she dug out the contract list and phoned out for a taxi to meet her out in front of the plaza right away. She knew that they'd all be busy so late on the eve of the New Year, but she also knew that contract work took precedence over casual bookings and that they'd probably bounce back some party pickup for a half hour or so in order to fit her in. Then she went around all the desks, opening their drawers and looking for any kind of torch or flashlight; she found one belonging to Bob King—it was in with the rest of his stuff, anyway, amongst the pens and the stale cough drops and his dirty-book collection—and she took it out and checked it. It wasn't much, just a cheap plastic thing running off a couple of pen cells, but the batteries were good and it would be better than nothing. Then she took her heavy winter coat from its hook behind the door and put it on.

She was in the middle of winding her long scarf around her neck when the phone rang again.

She almost strangled herself in her haste to answer it this time, snagging her scarf on the door handle and jerking herself up short; she snatched up the receiver and said a breathless, "Hello?"—but all that she could hear was the electronic echo of her own voice on a dead line.

After waiting a while and hearing nothing, she hung up. Don's regular soiree—cheap wine as well as cheap women—would probably be well under way by now, and since Mercedes didn't want to interrupt or even to get too close, she decided to call Derek via the talkback system from the adjacent news studio. She stood in the narrow booth and leaned across the microphone to the talkback switch; "Derek?" she said, and through the soundproofed glass she saw his attention snap around to her. He'd been sitting with his chair tilted back against the studio wall again, well apart from Don and his friends and with his face a careful mask of nothing. The main desk was out of the line of sight from where she was standing, but she could see a reflection in the window of the music studio opposite; Don was sitting with one of the girls on his knee, showing her how to run the desk and how to trigger the sequence of loaded cartridges for the commercial break. Mercedes wouldn't have cared to guess exactly how young the girl was, but she made Don look very old.

Mercedes told Derek, "I'm going out for half an hour to check on a late story. I'll be back in time for the midnight bulletin. I'll ring you from the box outside to let me in, OK?"

Derek signalled OK through the glass, but otherwise he didn't move. Nobody else paid any attention. She felt sorry for him; he could get up and wander around the empty station every now and again, but his job required him to base himself in the main studio to act as technical troubleshooter on the show and to handle the incoming calls when the OJ decided to open up the lines for requests or a competition. There was nothing much more for him to be doing at the moment other than to sit as witness to the spectacle of a middle-aged man trying to camp it up like some juvenile stud. Mercedes left them to it. She had forty minutes left, or half an hour in realistic terms, because she'd still have to time and prepare the next bulletin when she got back. She hurried down the whisper-quiet corridor; past the managing director's office and the sales suite, and let herself out through the door that was the boundary between the private working areas of the station and the public access, pub-lic-arena zone of the foyer. People could come in here from the plaza to drop off requests, pick up station merchandise, or get signed photographs of the presenters; they came through an outer glass door that could be unlocked only by remote control from behind the receptionist's counter, so that the worst of the weirdies could be kept at bay. The counter was unmanned now, the small switchboard lit up and locked through to an answering machine. Once out of the foyer, she'd be effectively sealed out of the station until Derek emerged in response to her call to let her in.

Stepping out through the door into the chill of the big enclosed mall, Mercedes was thinking ahead. The first and most obvious scenario that had come into her mind—apart from that of the whole thing being a motiveless hoax—had been one in which the sicko who'd killed the student persuaded an accomplice to phone and set up his next victim for him. But what did they think she'd do, walk the half mile alone in the middle of the night? As she moved out past the boarded gaps of the plaza's unsold shop units, she made a firm decision that she wasn't even going to step out of the locked cab if she could help it.

There was almost no light out here, but she was sure of her way; at the far end of the mall stood a half-hearted attempt at an indoor garden, and beyond that a bank of escalators that would take her down to ground level. The escalators wouldn't be running at this time, but there was rarely more than one of them in service anyway. At the bottom, an outward-opening fire door would let her out into the plaza's service road where her taxi would be waiting. Derek would have to make the same trek, remembering to wedge open the foyer door with a chair on his way out, in order to readmit her. It was an informal system and something of a pain, but what else could they do? The high number of unlet units in the plaza meant that the management couldn't afford round-the-clock security. They were lucky if they got a nightly visit from a man and a dog.

The contract minicab was waiting outside, its engine running and its headlights steaming faintly in the cold. Mercedes recognized the driver as someone who'd picked her up several times to run her home after night shifts; the big sedan was his own, its seats shiny and worn and the side pockets stuffed with colouring books and other children's debris. She settled gratefully into the back, the warmth of the heater already seeping into her as they rolled out of the alley and into the main street before the plaza.

"Where to?" he said. "Home so early?" But she said no, and gave him the first direction that would take them through an area of old warehouses and old pubs and nightclubs that changed names and nominal owners every few months. Gradually the pubs would get rougher and rougher, and more of the warehouses would be standing empty, and then, finally, true dereliction would take over.

What a place to die, she thought. The last sight your eyes ever see.

"You have a good Christmas?" the driver said over his shoulder, which brought her attention back to the present.

"Working for most of it," she said. "Was OK, though."

"Yeah, me too. To be honest, I don't mind it. Glad to be out for a bit. Couldn't move in our house without getting a frisbee in your ear."

The driver lapsed into silence again, and Mercedes sat back. The urban landscape outside was already beginning to deteriorate; the suppressed excitement of all those New Year's parties boiling away behind steamy lit windows was starting to thin out and disappear, giving way to the blind shells of Victorian buildings marked for demolition and, with increasing frequency, open tracts of wasteland where demolition had already begun.

They called it an Enterprise Zone; there was a big hoarding, or billboard, somewhere around here to say so, a desperate sign of a too-late attempt at renewal. The businesses that were supposed to be forced to relocate in the city-center developments had somehow dropped out of sight along the way, scared off by the high rents and the overheads. And now this…a nineteen-year-old girl, student at the Poly, fan of Bronski Beat and Spandau Ballet, smashed over the head with a length of railing and her already-dead body dragged into an empty side street to be stripped, stabbed, and slashed twenty-three times, and then partly re-dressed and covered over with her own coat. Or maybe this wasn't the kind of enterprise that they'd had in mind.

Mercedes now leaned forward again; the first turnoff was coming up soon, and a number of the sodium lights along the road were either out or else giving the dull cherry glow of a failed element. "Here it is," she said; and she could sense the driver's sudden confusion as they made the turn and the saloon's headlight beams swept across a cobbled street that was strewn with rubbish.

"Isn't this where they found that kid?" he said, slowing and watching for anything that might rip at the tires. The carcass of a thirty-year-old washing machine lay on its side in the road, rusty works spilled all around it.

"This is the place," Mercedes confirmed. She'd seen it only in daylight before, and hadn't thought that it could look any worse than it did then; but it was possible, she had to concede, it was definitely possible.

"You're not getting out here, are you?"

"Not if I can help it. Can you just cruise down slowly with your lights full on?"

It was a slow, careful, bumpy ride over bricks and glass and rotten timber. The houses on either side were rootless shells, sometimes with entire walls pulled out so that the upper stories hung in midair. Mercedes was watching the shadow play of light over brickwork, watching for the evidence that she'd been led along here to see; she wasn't entirely sure of where she ought to be until they passed a couple of plastic traffic cones and some flapping shreds of barrier tape that had marked the sealed-off zone of a careful police search. Suddenly she could see it, that grey morning reconstructing itself in her mind.

"Just stop here," she said, "for two seconds. And whatever you do, don't go away."

"Roger-dodger," the driver agreed as the saloon came to a halt, and Mercedes got out.

She shivered in the night chill after the warmth of the car. But there was more to it than that; evil still lay over this place like a radiant imprint slow to fade. She could sense it, read it, feel its touch. The tiny pencil beam stabbed out into the darkness. There was the spot where the dead girl had been lying, a second tarpaulin cover over her to keep off the rain but unable to stop the blood from washing out underneath; and here was the place where Mercedes had been standing, shakily recounting her impression into the UHER's microphone until the officer from the Community Affairs Division had firmly guided her away as the screens had been brought in. It had all gone out, virtually uncut, the officer's words included.

She ran the light over the walls, looking for writing. There was a spray-canned GAZ in four-foot letters, but it was old and already starting to flake away. Nothing else. Picking her way carefully over the rough ground, she went over for a closer check.

Halfway there, she glanced back at the taxi for reassurance. The interior light was on, her beacon of safety and retreat, but it seemed much farther away than the few steps she'd taken. Shape up, she told herself, and moved on.

Her first impression had been right; there was nothing written on any of the walls, anywhere, that looked either recent or meaningful. She was about to tum and head back to the cab when the figure in the corner raised its head and stared at her.

It was sitting, shapeless and slumped like a tramp, and it moved with a stiff, crackling sound like a dead bird's wing. The head came up and two dim, spit-coloured eyes blinked as if coming awake; they lingered on her for a moment as if recognizing and remembering, and then the head slowly lowered and the eyes were gone. Mercedes turned the light toward it so fast that she almost dropped the torch.

What she saw was two black plastic trash bags, stuffed and loosely knotted and piled one on top of the other. The topmost bag had come undone, perhaps pulled open by some scavenging dog. As she watched, the breeze lifted a fold of the plastic like a sail.

She took a deep breath, and tried to will her hammering heart back to something like normal rhythm. But her heart didn't want to know, and Mercedes had to concede that it was probably right. She turned her back on the scene and made straight for her transport.

By the time they were rolling out of the far end of the derelict street and turning back toward the main road, most of her panic had turned to anger. She was cold, she'd been scared, she'd probably messed up her boots. The driver said, "Find what you were looking for?"

"Different kind of evidence," Mercedes said.

"Oh, yeah? Evidence of what?"

"The fact that there are people out there with a pretty sick idea of what makes a joke. Fast as you can, will you? I've got another bulletin at midnight."

"Yeah, midnight," the driver said with a trace of despondence as the street-lights came back into view. "Another year gone, and nothing to show for it."

There was more life around here; some of the houses had been taken over by squatters before the vandals moved in, and even a couple of shops had managed to stay open. Beyond them were the outer-ring tower blocks, distant grid-patterns of coloured stars against the night sky. The buses stopped running to them at eleven; that was why the girl had been walking home, because somebody who'd promised her a lift back from a party had disappeared and she didn't have the money for a taxi.

"You were there, weren't you?" the driver said, breaking into her thoughts. It was like he'd just come up with something that he hadn't expected to remember.

"Not when they found her," Mercedes said.

"But you did all those interviews straight after."

"Yes. They went out on the network."

"So did you see the body, or what?"

Mercedes looked out of the side window at the passing traffic. "They'd covered it up by the time I got there," she said.

The cab driver was shaking his head. She saw his eyes as he glanced in his mirror, but he wasn't looking at her. "What makes somebody do something like that?" he said. "To a kid, as well?"

"I can't tell you."

"I mean, you see some of them…whenever there's a trial, the papers dig out their wedding photographs or whatever. And they're just ordinary blokes—you'd pass 'em in the street and you wouldn't even know. So where does it come from? Is it supposed to be in everybody, or what? Because I'm bloody sure it isn't in me."

"Well," Mercedes said, "people used to talk about evil. No one really does that any more."

"Yeah, I know. Couldn't come up with anything better to replace it, though, could they? Everyone's a bloody social worker now."

She checked her watch. Fifteen minutes to the hour. This was going to be one hell of a tight squeeze, and all over a hoax. The plaza was coming into sight now, the dark mass of the shopping mall topped by the linked tower of the hotel; they floodlit the hotel at night, giving its concrete a warm glow that it didn't have in the day. A couple of minutes, and she'd be there.

In the meantime, she was still thinking about evil. She'd been thinking about it a lot in the past few days. She hadn't exactly led a sheltered life, but that morning's visit to the murder scene had been her first exposure to the after-presence of something awesome and real. That evening, when she should have been out celebrating her first major-league report, she'd sat at home in her studio apartment and begun to shake so much that she finally had to go and throw up in the basin. She felt tainted, she felt scared. She'd seen it in the faces of the detectives, that they were in the presence of an old, old enemy, and she now had the sense that she was an unwilling member of their circle.

The nearest thing that she'd ever known to it had been about seven years before, when she was still living at home. The house next door had been broken into and vandalized, everything thrown around and furniture smashed. Nothing had happened to their own place, but a shadow had passed over and changed all that it touched. What she sensed now was something even worse: the passage of a malign intelligence, something whose agents had names and lives and family backgrounds, but which simply drew them on as a temporary human skin to carry out its work.

She'd sensed it, all right. And what now made it worse was that she felt that it had sensed her.

She had the taxi drop her by the phone booth at the front of the plaza. There was nobody in it, which was a piece of luck.

"All seems a bit dead," the taxi driver said doubtfully. "Is this OK for you?"

"I'll ring from here and somebody will come down to let me in," Mercedes assured him. "I'll be fine. You go on." He nodded, and reached under the dash for his radio mike to report in. Contract rides never tipped, Mercedes knew, and her excursion had probably cut into his side earnings for the night. "Happy New Year," he said, and as she slammed the rear door she said, "Same to you."

She was already in the booth as he was driving away. She dialled the studio's unlisted number. It was engaged. So was the newsroom number, which would have flashed a telltale in the news studio that Derek would have been able to see. In desperation she tried the request line, and hung up when she heard the beginning of the usual recorded message.

What were they doing up there? Didn't they know that she had to be on the air in—she checked her watch—just under ten minutes? To miss the broadcast would be the absolute pits of unprofessionalism, whatever the reason…and the reason she had wasn't even a good one. She tried the studio number again, once, for luck, but her luck was out.

Mercedes stepped from the booth and started toward the service road at the side of the plaza, half walking and half running. The pavement was a mess of grit and sand from a solitary and short-lived snowfall a couple of weeks before. Her only option was to try the door that she'd left by, to hope perhaps that Derek was already down there and waiting for her.

The service road itself was hardly more than a concrete alley, lit by a single bulb at its end and crowded with the hulking shadows of wheeled trash hoppers. She ran flat out, skidding and almost falling when she hit some sodden cardboard that had lain in the road for so long that it had greyed down to its colour. She was half expecting, half hoping for Derek to step out of the shadows and wave her in; but he didn't and she arrived at the doorway panting and angry and completely at a loss for what to do next.

There was no official procedure for something like this. Nobody was supposed to enter or leave the plaza until the morning security shift clocked in at 5:00 am. for any emergencies, the station crew was supposed to call a key holder. Why couldn't she simply have passed the hoax message along to the police, as she undoubtedly was going to be told that she should have? Off-the-record approval might have been given if her information had turned out to be worthwhile, but she didn't even have that to look forward to. Less than five minutes to go. Even if she went back to the phone and tried again, she still wouldn't make it. An hour ago she'd been a competent professional on top of her job; now she was feeling like a child again, sick and awed as she realized too late that simple events were running quickly out of her control.

Shivering and unhappy, she leaned on the door.

It gave silently inward.

She clattered up the dark escalator, slowed by the unfamiliar pitch of its motionless steps. God, the timing of this was going to be tight! She couldn't even hope to grab a spare minute by cheating with the clock as she'd done at least once before on the graveyard shift, probably setting a few people tapping their watches in puzzlement. This would be the one night of the year when everybody was counting down to midnight. Once inside the station, she'd have no time to do anything more than grab the eleven o'clock bulletin from the spike and repeat it. There was the warm light of the foyer, a small pocket of welcome over in the far corner of a vast space of darkness. Her footsteps echoed flatly on the ridged plastic floor; the distance seemed to stretch even as she covered it, almost as if she were flying nowhere in a bad dream. She didn't dare to check the time again, but it must be down to under a couple of minutes. Don was probably getting ready to read out the teletype himself. Don was a lousy newsreader, even worse than he was a DJ.

Mercedes almost slammed into the glass door. It didn't give.

She tried again in disbelief, but it was definitely locked. She pressed the buzzer a couple of times to get Derek's attention, and then she backed off, hopping nervously from one foot to another like a duck on a hot plate, ready to go and animated by her frustration. As she waited, she moved along to take a look in through the newsroom window. She'd have bet anything that

Don had been encouraging his schoolgirls to call up all their friends on the company phones. Looking through glass that was smeary with the prints of the noses and hands of daytime spectators—they called the newsroom the only zoo around where the animals were all on the outside—Mercedes saw nobody. The newsroom was as she'd left it.

So where was Derek? She moved back to the foyer and, as she tried the buzzer again, saw the sweep hand of the reception clock covering the last half minute to the hour. She started to pump the button, wondering if it was working at all; it should be sounding right down in the studio corridor, and surely Derek would be listening for it. She put her ear to the glass, holding the button down as hard as she could; but she didn't hear any faint and far-off bell, just the muted sounds of the late-night music show on the reception speakers that couldn't be turned off. The track faded, and the drumroll jingle that always heralded the start of the news began.

The news at midnight, she heard the heavily processed recording say, With Mercedes Medina.

She winced. This was terrible. Not only was Don about to screw up the news, but he'd now made it obvious to everybody that the regular newsreader wasn't even supposed to be missing. Thanks a million, she thought.

And then she heard her own voice.

The sound was blurred by the thick glass, but there was no mistaking it. She was too stunned to be relieved. She was past the headlines and into the first item before she realized that what she was hearing was a tape playback of the eleven o'clock broadcast.

It was unlikely that anyone would notice. News content tended not to vary much around this time of night, anyway, and sometimes it could be a difficult job putting a new-sounding slant on items that were going around for the fourth or fifth time. What she couldn't understand was, where did the recording come from? Station output wasn't regularly taped—at least, not in any form that could be retransmitted. She hadn't been aware of anything being done about this one.

Derek must have done it; he was the only technical operator on the station, and it was well within his province. Don probably wouldn't even know how to patch the signal into one of the studio decks. No, Derek it had to be.

But at eleven, Derek hadn't known that she'd be going out. Even Mercedes herself hadn't known it yet.

So what was the game?

Suddenly, Mercedes didn't like it. She didn't like it at all. She moved back along to the newsroom window and took another look, and this time she was almost prepared to swear that the chair and the phone and the mess on the desk were exactly as she'd left them. Never mind that she couldn't remember the exact details, she knew. Nobody had been in that office or used that phone, but still she'd been unable to ring in. There was only one possible reason for this that she could think of, an old journalist's ploy for tying up a phone line so that you could get to someone before the opposition could reach them; you dialled through, waited for the other party to reply, and then made some excuse about a wrong number so that they'd hang up. What you didn't do was hang up at your own end, effectively blocking the line for all other calls.

Oversensitive? Perhaps. But the newsroom phone had rung a second time before she'd gone out, and nobody had been there. With that and the studio phone out of use, the station had been effectively isolated from all input.

Reasons: none that she could think of. A joke, perhaps. A really strange one.

Maybe she could ask Derek for the explanation now; because here was his shadow in the light from the foyer, and there was the sound of him opening the spring catch from the inside. The heavy glass door swung inward, and Derek's gangling silhouette moved into the frame.

In the time that it had taken for him to unlock the door and emerge, Mercedes had backed around behind the nearest concrete pillar. She was barely aware that she'd done it until she felt the coldness of the untreated surface against her hands. Derek stood, bony-awkward and almost comically skinny, and he peered out into the darkness.

"Mercedes?" he said softly; so softly that it was almost impossible to hear. And then he moved out, letting the door swing shut behind him. From her place in the shadows behind the pillar, she saw that this man of sticks and bones, this sudden stranger, was carrying a large insulated screwdriver from the electronics workshop. Its narrow shaft was almost a foot long. He let it swing by his side, a natural extension of his arm.

He obviously hadn't seen her, because after calling her name he was now walking straight out across the middle of the plaza, toward the escalators. Foyer music was seeping out as the glass door closed slowly on its spring; it was the sound of a Scottish accordion band, something traditional for the season, and it was growing fainter and fainter as the gap narrowed and Mercedes wondered if she could make a run for it and catch it before the lock would re-engage.

Several times she almost went, and each time she told herself to wait another second so that Derek couldn't dash back and reach her before she could get the door closed against him; until finally, the faint click of the door told her that the chance had slipped away with all her hesitation. She heard the distant echo of Derek as he started his descent of the escalator; he seemed almost jaunty, as if he were out on a job that was no more than routine.

But his eyes. His eyes had been like dead scales.

If the plan had been to give her a scare, then he'd done a first-class job. But she couldn't persuade herself that this was the explanation, partly because it was too much part of a sequence that linked back all the way to the bitter rainy morning in the derelict street. She'd been sensed, she'd been seen; and now she was to be gathered in. Derek—strange, gangling Derek—was the arm of the reaper.

What was he doing, down below? Perhaps he didn't know that she was already inside the plaza, and had gone down to wait for her. Or else—and this seemed more likely—he'd given her time to get in and now he was securing the door in some way so that she wouldn't be able to leave again.

There was only one way for her to go. Upward, to the rooftop car park. The prestige hotel's main entrance was on that level, reached from the street by a spiraling ramp. If you didn't come in a car, preferably one with a high showroom tag, then the hotel didn't want to know you.

At least she'd be safe up there. She'd find people, probably a big New Year's party in one of the conference suites. She'd stay there until dawn, and to hell with explanations.

Moving as silently as she could, Mercedes set out to cross the plaza. She felt as conspicuous as a fly on a white rubber sheet. The entrance to the stairway was an anonymous pair of red ply doors situated between the frontages of a bridal-wear store and a toy shop that had recently gone belly-up. The big shopfront sign with its bunnies and frolicking ladybirds was still in place, but the window beneath it was empty and drab. With a slight sense of relief and a prayer that the doors shouldn't creak, Mercedes let herself through into the stairwell. It was narrow and undecorated, and it smelled of drains. She took out the small flashlight and shone it ahead to find her way; three floors up to the roof, she reckoned, and then another fire door with a push bar just like the one to the service road. The flashlight, hardly stronger than a decent candle, threw out long, angular shadows and moving bars across the walls as she ascended. Somebody had used the middle landing as a toilet, more than once.

At the top, she had to put all of her weight against the bar. She didn't weigh much, and the bar didn't seem to want to move. It was waist-high, and it was supposed to hinge downward under pressure to withdraw the long bolts at the top and bottom of the door; That was the theory, anyway, but the practice didn't seem to be working out. What was supposed to happen if they ever had a fire? Wasn't somebody supposed to check these things?

She tried to imagine smoke and flames, a panicking crowd. They'd come up those stairs at quite a lick, and they wouldn't be about to stop for anything; so Mercedes took a few paces back and then ran at the door, hitting the bar as hard as she could.

The door flew open, and hit the wall to the side of it with a crash that echoed all the way back down the stairwell.

But it wouldn't matter if Derek heard it, because by the time he could get up the stairs, she'd be across the roof and into the hotel. For the second time she emerged into the cold of the night, but this time it was like a release rather than a chore; the sight of stars and the low cloud that glowed faintly as if the city burned beneath it had never been more welcome to her. She was at a corner of the roof, the stairwell head being a brick tower close to where the station kept its radio car. She could see this in the shadows only a few yards away, grimy windscreen reflecting the neon tracery of a department-store sign on the next block. Straight ahead, less than a hundred yards across the asphalt, was the painted-on driveway and the entrance to the hotel.

It was wide and glossy and glassy and bright. Automatic doors led through to the lobby, where expensively carpeted steps climbed past display cases to a mezzanine level with reception desk, low sofas, and coffee tables amongst the potted plants. Hotel staff in dark suits or crisp whites could be seen moving around inside.

And between the hotel and Mercedes stood a roll-across metal gate.

She ran to it, grasped it, shook it; the barrier hardly moved at all. It was eight feet high and topped with spikes. A monkey might have made it over or a snake might have made it through, but Mercedes had no chance at all.

People were coming out of the hotel, and she called to them; "Hey," she shouted. "Over here, help!" But as the automatic doors hissed open, the group of seven or eight came spilling out with a party roar that drowned her completely, and within seconds they were at their cars and switching on their music systems in a kind of stereo war so loud and so discordant that she couldn't even hear herself. The cars started out in a jerky convoy, windows open and blasting as they drove off in a swirl of abandoned streamers and festive debris. As the last set of tail lights disappeared into the downward spiral, they left behind a windblown silence in which Mercedes was calling hoarsely to the night air. Five floors below, some body was sounding off as the traffic before him made a slow start at the lights.

Mercedes let go of the barrier. She'd been holding on so hard that it was now difficult to get her fingers to disengage. What was she going to do now? Go. back below, and risk meeting Derek on the stairs?

Or was Derek up here with her already?

She moved to the nearest shadow; and just in time. She saw the stairhead door swing outward in silence. Derek stepped forward in the doorway and waited, listening. Mercedes held her breath. He turned his head slowly from side to side like a blind thing, as if trying to locate her with some deep radar sense that went beyond sound or vision; and then, moving with a stealth that looked faintly absurd in one so tall and so angular, he melted off to check around the back of the stairhead.

He'd left the fire door wide open. It wouldn't take him long to check around behind, and then he'd be back and he'd see her as she ran. She'd hesitated once already and missed an opportunity at safety; now she was on her way even before she was certain that her decision was a wise one.

He appeared so fast that he must have expected this, been listening for her; but even so, he mustn't have been prepared for her to jump so soon, because she was just able to get in and slam the door before he could dive through after her. She wrenched up on the bar as hard as she could; Derek's weight on the other side of the door actually helped her, because he unwittingly pushed it home that last vital fraction of an inch that allowed the long bolts to engage with a bang.

Mercedes was in darkness now, and again she fumbled out the flashlight in order to check that the bar was secure. As she ran the light over, a soft tapping that was almost a scratching began.

"Mercedes?"

The door began to rattle; just faintly, as if under no more than fingertip pressure.

"Mercedes?"

Three round, crashing blows against the door that echoed like explosions in the stairwell and made her step back in fright; but the door held solid, and then came that soft whisper again.

"It's me, Mercedes." And then, slyly: "You know who I mean, don't you?"

She began to descend, the flashlight showing the way ahead once more. The batteries were starting to fade now, the light yellowing and getting dimmer, but she couldn't bring herself to switch it off even for a moment. She wondered what on earth she was going to do when she reached the plaza level again.

She'd be shut in, but Derek would be shut out. So far, so good. But she was guessing that he'd maybe pulled the wires on the buzzer, which meant that she wouldn't be able to get Don's attention inside the station; which left the option of perhaps trying to break into one of the shops in order to get to a phone and call the police. She'd never broken into anything before, and wasn't even sure how she'd go about it.

And suppose she got to a phone. What then? What exactly was she going to tell them? Because what had actually happened? She'd made an unofficial trip out, and she'd missed a broadcast. Derek had covered for her, and then emerged to come looking. He'd followed her to the roof, where she'd locked him out. There wasn't one element in the sequence where all the unreasonableness didn't seem to be on her side. All that she could offer was her fears, and her reading of the undercurrents of the situation. It was like a perfect melody with wrong harmonies that only she could hear.

It didn't help. She knew, deep down where it counted; there had been a mutual recognition between her and the presence at that derelict site, and now that same presence was wearing Derek like a glove. Perhaps it had even caused him to make that phone call to the newsroom that had sent her out in the first place; the station's commercial production studio had harmonizers and equalizers that could turn a man's voice into a reasonable facsimile of a woman's, if the added on-line interference was bad enough to cover the deceit.

It wasn't Derek, not in the true sense; this was the sandman, and he was bringing her a dream. But it wasn't the kind of dream that anybody would want to lie half-awake for, in drowsy anticipation.

Down on the plaza again, she went across to the indoor garden near the top of the escalators. It was a half-hearted affair, with most of the borders just empty dirt because all of the plants had starved away from daylight. There were small trees in barrels, a few rustic benches for shoppers, and a wishing well for local charities that had a stiff wire mesh just under the surface of the water to stop kids from reaching down and helping themselves to the pennies. Mercedes chose a fair-sized stone from one of the border walls and tried its weight. It was loose-laid, and so no problem to move, and she found that she could just about carry it.

Staggering along like the world's most heavily pregnant woman, Mercedes headed for the radio station foyer. Halfway there she stopped a moment to rest, and that was when she heard it; the sound of a lift somewhere else in the plaza, a sound that would be lost during normal shopping hours but that was now like a warning signal in the cavernous silence. It said that Derek was back inside. It said that he was coming for her.

Her first attempt to smash the big foyer window had no effect; she couldn't believe it, but the stone simply bounced back in her hands and set the whole pane shivering. The second time, she threw it hard and let go; this attempt put a sudden and terrifying split into the glass that travelled outward from the point of impact like forked lightning. For one moment she stood in deep awe of what she'd done, and then she set about breaking enough of a hole out of the reinforced window for her to step through.

There was no time to feel guilty, or even to begin to enjoy it. The glass fell out in big plate-sized pieces onto the foyer's carpet, and she felt something catch and tear at her coat as she bent to crawl through the opening that she'd made. Inside, as she straightened, she was taken by the bizarre feeling that she'd squeezed out of one world and into another; here it was warm, and the lights were late-evening soft, and the foyer speakers were relaying *Here Comes Summer* at a low murmur. Odd choice, she thought as she pushed into the inner corridor, a degree of professionalism reasserting itself as she entered home territory; but then, as she moved down past the offices toward the studio and what she'd been certain would be a degree of safety, she heard the record ending and the DJ coming on-air to link into the next track.

The DJ wasn't Don.

In fact, he wasn't anybody who worked at the station at all; his name was Dave Cook, and he'd left six months before on the promise of a contract in television. The contract had never materialized, and now he was working at some really tiny new station over on the Welsh border. Mercedes started to run toward the studio, already half knowing what she was going to find; the sound of the long-departed Dave Cook was a strong indication, and the absence of the red transmission light over the studio door seemed to confirm it.

She burst in. There they were, a neat triptych behind the sound console: Dan and his two young ladies, one on either knee with his arms flung around them, their faces black as old iron and their necks wired together with microphone lead. Their eyes were all bulging and their tongues were all sticking out; Yah Boo, they seemed to be saying, Sucks to the World.

The door behind Mercedes closed on its damper with a quiet thump, tapping her on the back and pushing her to go forward into the studio. She took one halting step, and looked around her in bewilderment. Her place of safety was suddenly old, bad news. Over by the big surprise behind the console was the sight that she'd been on the way to expecting: four full twelve-inch metal spools of tape in a stack, with a fifth playing on the deck. These would be the standby tapes, the emergency fallback material kept in a locked cupboard for occasions of serious equipment failure or evacuation of the station. It was supposed to be somebody's job to keep them up to date, but that somebody obviously hadn't.

It almost didn't shake her to walk around to the other side of the desk; Don and the two girls didn't even look real and their expressions were nearly comic, as if death were a bad joke that had simply jerked them away in the middle of its punchline. One outflung, long-nailed hand brushed at her coat as she carefully squeezed by them, and she delicately drew herself aside to avoid further contact.

Mercedes had been shown the basics of driving a desk on her first day in the station, but the details had gone whistling down the same hole as so much of the useless information that they'd been throwing at her around that time. She saw a long bank of colour-coded faders, another of equalizer dials, a row of needle indicators that bounced and bopped along with the outgoing musk; there were pieces of masking tape making crude labels with messages like *off-air p/bk* and *tx* and *Do not use!*, this last with a small skull and crossbones added, and the whole array was topped with a mess of running order sheets and unsorted commercial cartridges.

The absurd thought that occurred to her, as she tried to make sense of the layout, was that at least she'd now have no problem in convincing anybody that she'd been in real danger. All that she needed to do now was to find a way to get a Mayday message out, and fast. Derek might have tied up the phone lines somehow, but he'd had to leave the station's output running. She could make her plea for help live and on-air, and somebody would come.

Somebody would.

Wouldn't they?

None of the sliding controls on the desk seemed to be making any damn difference to anything; the transmission lights stayed dead, and the Beach

Boys played on as the tape reels turned. She looked frantically from one side to the other, knowing that she had minutes or less to get her message out and then to find somewhere to hide. Every fader was up, but the mike still wasn't open—which could only mean that Derek must have pulled the necessary patch leads around the side of the desk. With no technical knowledge, Mercedes didn't have a hope of putting herself on-air.

He'd killed the studio. He'd tied up all the outgoing phone lines. What did that leave?

It left the incoming request line, the one that would be hooked up to an answering machine. The signal fed directly into the desk, but Mercedes had seen the TOs using a white phone to speak to callers off-air during tracks. She had to reach across Don to take it from its hook; it was an awkward manoeuver because she didn't want to touch him, and managing this wasn't easy because she didn't want to look at him, either.

Lifting the phone had automatically switched the line to the handset. She broke in on what sounded like a couple of giggling kids phoning in for a dare.

"Listen," she said, "this is an emergency. I want you to put your phone down and then call the police. Tell them…"

"Hello?" one of the kids said.

"Yes, hello. My name is Mercedes Medina. I'm a newsreader here. Please call the police and say…"

But whoever it was on the other end of the line, she wasn't listening; Mercedes heard the scuffling of a hand being placed over the mouthpiece, and an awed voice saying, "It's her that does the news!"

"I know," she said, "please! I need your help for something very important…"

"Hello?" the kid said, returning.

"Please listen to me! Don't talk and don't go away! People are dead here!"

But the voice that answered her then was not that of a child; it was one that she recognized instantly and with a cold, crawling sense of helpless fear. It was the heavily processed facsimile of a female voice that she'd first heard only an hour before.

"Happy New Year, Mercedes," it said. "I've got a present for you. Want to come and see what it is?"

Heard now and without the disguising overlays of fake interference, it wasn't so convincing; it didn't even sound human any more. "Derek," she said, "it's you, isn't it?" But the voice went on as if she hadn't spoken.

"All right, then," it said with faked resignation. "I can see I'll just have to bring it to you myself." She dropped the phone. She'd taken too long, allowed herself to be trapped; she looked around for a way out, a weapon anything. With sudden inspiration, she moved to the tape deck and ripped the tape out from around the pickup head; the music from the big speakers overhead ended with an ungainly squelch, and the big reels on the deck started to speed up as its tension control sensed a lack of resistance. Somebody might hear, somebody might wonder; perhaps even the managing director, who was notorious for calling people to account for fluffs and glitches that had happened at the most ungodly hours. Given time, somebody might even come to see what had gone wrong.

And then they'd probably find her, making up a foursome with Don and the others; because time was something that she was almost out of.

There was a soft thump from just outside; it was the sound of the studio's outer door as it closed behind someone. Someone who was about to open the inner door and step through into this one-exit, soundproofed killing pit. Mercedes was looking, but she couldn't even see any scissors or used blades for tape editing.

The door opened with a hiss; he came in sideways with his eyes glowing like coals under darkened brows, a single strand of damp hair hanging forward over his face. He was hiding something from her, and it was as he turned to bring it into view that Mercedes found the will to move. She snatched up one of the metal reels from the stack beside her and, with grace and an accuracy that wouldn't have been possible with forethought, threw it edge-on and Frisbee-style toward Derek. It zipped through the air, spewing out tape as it spun, lifting in flight and making straight for his face. He ducked, but not fast enough. The edge of the reel clipped him neatly on the forehead and he staggered back.

He fell against the door, but the door gave only reluctantly as its damper resisted. He was pitched down onto his side as the reel clunked onto the floor and rolled away, still leaving a trail of tape behind it. Derek was struggling feebly. Mercedes came around the desk, sick at what she'd done and unable to resist her own feelings of guilt; she'd never killed anything, never even burt anything before, and now here she was, plunging into the major league with a human target. She hesitated when she saw that Derek was moving to get to his feet again; she'd slowed him, but it seemed that she hadn't stopped him.

He pushed himself up against the doorframe. His movements were stiff, his eyes empty and dazed-looking; when he glanced down, it was with a thick, liquid slowness.

"Shit," he said bleakly. "You spoiled my surprise."

He was looking down at his right hand; this was gripping a wooden plate that Mercedes recognized, after a moment, as the newsroom bill spike. There was a lag in recognition because of the fact that only a couple of inches of the spike itself were visible. His hand was held out in front of his chest, just where the breastbone ended and the soft tissues began; the point was marked neatly by a dark stain that was beginning to spread through the material of his sweatshirt.

The fight to get upright was obviously proving too much for him. With a sigh of regret, he gave up and began the return slide to the floor. He hit with a grunt, and his hand fell from the spike's wooden base; this stayed in place like some king-sized hatpin pushed into some life-sized voodoo doll, and now Mercedes saw that his eyes were fixed on nothing in particular.

It took her several minutes to raise the courage to step over him; time in which Derek didn't move, didn't blink, and didn't even bleed much any more. A tiny bubble of blood appeared at one nostril, stayed for a while, and then popped as the last breath slowly left him. The overhead speakers hissed with the no-transmission phenomenon that was called—with grim appropriateness—dead air.

Between this and the four lifeless bodies in the room—none of them, thankfully, her own—Mercedes found herself being driven from the studio by an urge that was almost physical. She stepped carefully over Derek, forcing herself to watch him in case this should turn out to be some elaborate and impossible trick to get her within reach, and then she fell thankfully through the outer door and into the low air-conditioned hum of the corridor. The first sight that met her eyes was that of a long trail of yellow papers, scattered around the corridor floor and stretching back and around the corner toward the newsroom; these were all of the bulletin scripts from the past few hours, ripped from the spike and discarded en route to the studio. He must have been pulling them off one at a time, she realized, like the petals from a flower or the legs from a fly.

Her own legs were feeling none too steady, but they held her up well enough as she headed toward the offices. There had to be a phone somewhere, at least one outside line that Derek (or, as she was thinking, the potent force that had expressed itself as Derek) hadn't remembered or managed to block. She wanted to call somebody—it almost didn't matter who any more...the police, the boss, her mother in Bristol, any human voice or contact.

Surely the director's office would have its own outside line; probably more than one. She expected to find the door locked, but it wasn't. She felt around for the light switch before she entered, not wanting to step out into darkness; the lights came on to reveal the quiet expanse of executive furnishing. The carpet was thick and soft, the wood panelling warm and mellow. The phone on the desk was ivory-white.

And it rang.

Mercedes lifted the receiver slowly, and listened. The voice that came down the line was a signal now stripped of any pretence at humanity.

"*Men may come, and men may go,*" it quoted softly, "*but I go on forever.*
"*Happy New Year, Mercedes.*"

The Beautiful Feast
OF THE VALLEY

SOMETIMES I SEE her. Magdalena, late at night, in the stacks on the seventh floor where she used to work and study. I know she isn't there, and I don't believe in ghosts. This is something else.

I'm taking out my keys as I approach her carrel. At this hour there's only the night cleaning crew and me, and they're somewhere on another floor. We close the library at nine, but I have staff privileges. It's a modern building, low ceilings, open plan. The lights are turned low but the air conditioning is a constant; old books need a steady climate, and the bound volumes on the seventh are among the university's rarest. It's always quiet. On warm summer days our undergrads will seek out the cool air and fill the study areas but at other times, not so much.

The carrel was Magdalena's private space, and now I suppose it's mine. It's at the end of the building with a corner view over the campus. An odd shape, thin-walled, hardly big enough to call a room—just a desk and chair, a lamp, and her boxes. The sense of her presence is strong.

But I think I've told you already, I don't believe in ghosts.

I'm working my way through Magdalena's boxes. Two were here when she died, and I retrieved the others after her mother and sisters had been through her flat. The boxes contain her work diaries, her notebooks, all the background research for her doctorate, even lecture notes and timetables from her student days. I gave the hard drives to Henrik in Computer Sciences, and he gets back to me for anything he needs explained. Henrik claims that he's mastered classical Greek, but he's joking. With his programmer's mind he quickly grasped the alphabet, and he enjoys my show of faux-horror when he mangles the words.

I switch on the lamp and draw out the chair. The folder on the desk is open, the papers arranged as I left them.

I admit that I struggle. I used to manage with a big magnifying glass, but now I've an app on my phone that does the job almost as well. Eyesight problems apart, I found her handwriting almost impossible at first. Some of it's in a personal shorthand that no optical scanner could ever decipher. Now I know it as well as my own.

Halfway down an old shopping list, which has no relevance to the project but which fascinates me nonetheless, the phone vibrates in my hands. I still jump when that happens. I answer and it's Henrik.

He says, "Do you have a copy of the index?"

"Not to hand. Why?"

"I've some content with no attribution. Thought you might know it."

"You want to send it over?"

"I could read you the first few lines."

"Just send it."

While I'm waiting for the attachment to show up, I look out of the window. I can see; I just can't see well. The campus is deserted, though the main walk-through stays lit for student safety. I can see across to the white tower of the Computer Sciences building where I imagine Henrik alone in the basement, surrounded by his technology, while I'm here in the sky amongst my centuries-old texts. Two lonely souls in our different spheres, working on into the night.

One of us haunted by a dead spirit, the other working to recreate one.

My phone vibrates again as the attachments come in. The Greek text is accompanied by a crude machine translation, which I ignore.

From the Greek I read, *"This story was told to me by a priest. It concerns a slave who had been one of the many prisoners of war taken by Sesostris, men of the vanquished countries who were brought home and set to work on great monuments to their conqueror's name."*

I don't recognise it but I'm thinking that it reads more like Herodotus than Plutarch. Magdalena was familiar with both. It's no more than two or three hundred words, but I save it for later when I can view it on a bigger screen.

It's after eleven when I leave. With its long rows of shelves and the whisper of hidden engines, the seventh floor has the feel of an empty aircraft on a long night's flight. Hard to believe that such shiny modern architecture can house spooks and shadows, but there it is.

No, she isn't here now. I can look for her in the stacks, but that isn't how it works. I travel down in a glass lift, I walk out across the concrete way. I suspect that architects love concrete far more than people love architects.

The roads around the university are older, tree-lined, the houses tall and Edwardian. I live only three streets from here, in two rooms and a kitchen on the second floor of a mid-terrace villa. Walking home through fallen leaves and autumn chill, I see haloes around every street lamp. Magdalena's been dead almost a year, and I should be feeling her absence by now. But she hasn't left me.

Going blind has few compensations, but I found one.

This story was told to me by a priest. It concerns a slave who had been one of the many prisoners of war taken by Sesostris, men of the vanquished countries who were brought home and set to work on great monuments to their conqueror's name. You may choose to believe or disregard these Egyptian tales, however you wish; for my part, I set them down just as they were given to me.

The name of the slave is not known, but I will call him Fahim. After capture he had been set to work on the building of a causeway. Along this causeway, mighty blocks of stone were to be hauled from the Nile to the Libyan hills. The blocks had been cut in the Arabian quarries of Fahim's homeland and ferried over to Egypt; it was an enterprise involving a hundred thousand slaves, and many would not live to see the work completed. Fahim was one such. He had risen in the hierarchy of slaves to a position of some responsibility when, despite a strong constitution and better nourishment than most, he succumbed to a fever.

Sesostris had closed all the temples and forbidden the religions of the vanquished, so Fahim was buried in the manner of the Egyptian poor; which is to say, with little preparation or ceremony in the dry desert soil where natural processes would imitate—or so it was hoped—the more elaborate preservation rituals of the high-born.

One year after his death, on the morning that followed the ceremony of The Beautiful Feast of the Valley, Fahim dug his way out of the sand.

I write up my translation of the fragment, along with alternate word choices to reflect shades of meaning. Late in the morning I receive a text from Henrik, and I call by to see him in the afternoon.

He says, "I've run a search against all the digitised material. I can't link it to anything in the dialogue corpus. Nothing even close."

"Then where did it come from?" I say.

"That's the thing. Nowhere."

"You don't mean the machine wrote it." I wait. Then, less certain, "Do you?"

"That's not how it works," he says. "Everything has to be sourced from in-domain data. Did you find any clues in the handwritten stuff?"

"That's going to take a while," I tell him.

I should explain the situation. For several months before she died, Magdalena had been providing library support for Henrik's interactive AI project. She wasn't our most senior classicist but she was a Plutarch specialist, and Henrik is building a database of literary material with the aim of creating a virtual personality based on an ancient writer's works. He chose Plutarch of Chaeronea because of the sheer volume of the philosopher's output and legacy, passing over a more obvious choice like Shakespeare—the low-hanging fruit of linguistic analysis, and too well-used a figure to bring much glory to a new researcher. And Shakespeare hid behind fictions; Plutarch was chatty, personal, immensely prolific, and available.

Also, he'd approached the English department and they didn't want to know.

Henrik's aim is to recreate Plutarch the man, within the machine. To be able to ask a question, and have Plutarch answer, by triangulating a personality from the texts and incorporating multiple translations, along with commentaries and monographs, to eliminate linguistic bias and reach the author's bare thoughts.

Behind the gimmick lies some serious AI research but I'll be honest, from the moment we heard the pitch we all thought the idea was Gold-Standard bonkers. Our Head Librarian thought so too, but Magdalena spied an opportunity to digitise the collection on another department's budget, and he was talked around.

Henrik says, "Can't we speed things up a little? I'm not having a go at you. Maybe we could put a student on it."

"There's no money for that," I say.

"For the experience?" he suggests, hopefully.

"Not at this uni," I say. "They just don't have the Greek, Henrik."

It's true. A Classics education isn't what it was.

And the fact is, I don't want anyone else let into this... I almost called it a relationship. When Magdalena died I volunteered to step in. I'm no Plutarchian, and I've no interest in computing. I'm doing it for her.

And in case I've been giving you the wrong impression...no, there was nothing between us. To Magdalena I was just a colleague, no doubt an unremarkable one. I'm sure she had no feelings for me at all. Mine for her stole up on me over time, and I knew better than to declare them.

Oh Magdalena, Magdalena; name from a Hungarian father, looks from her Italian mother, an accent from the Western Isles of Scotland where she grew up. She ran, she swam, she sang, and it's fair to say that I loved her from afar. Loved her and lost her; she was killed on the way back from a climbing weekend with her similarly sporty and outgoing group of friends. Their minibus ran off the road at two in the morning and she was thrown clear. They say she died instantly.

Now I have what I often wished for, though by the most terrible means. I have her to myself. I sift through her papers, through her notes, through her stray thoughts jotted in margins; I transcribe, I upload, and every now and again Henrik bothers me for some further detail.

They say we live on in the memories of others. I find that more sentimental than useful. Remember me all you like but if I'm to live on, I need to know about it. Henrik talks of a future when we'll be able to upload our thoughts and live for ever. I don't see it. Copy what you may into a machine, I'll still be here. And when this life ends, I'm still gone. My own perception is that every one of us is a conscious mind in a private box, self-contained, looking out. Henrik's vision is a future of empty boxes, pointlessly interacting, endlessly pinging each other in a space without voices.

Naturally, he doesn't see it that way.

Fahim stood upon the hot sand and looked down at his hands, at his funeral clothes. He remembered nothing of his burial. He did, however, recall his suffering and being aware of his impending death, and he recalled the grief of those who wept at the prospect of his departure. Although a slave, Fahim had a home and a family, and friends to mourn him. On the ground around him lay evidence of their devotion in the remnants of bread and leeks and rotting fruit, all scattered by his emergence along with a spilled half-cup of wine.

He lifted his gaze to the necropolis across the plain. There, some distance away, stood the tombs and the chapels of the wealthy. Spread far and wide across the ground between were the graves of the poor, in shallow pits marked by nothing more than a reed mat or a stone. Some, like his own, bore the signs of a feast day celebration—The Beautiful Festival of the Valley, on which day a procession bore the sacred image of Amun from city to necropolis. There its followers made music and performed rituals to honour their ancestors, while outside the necropolis those of lower birth performed their own humbler, though no less heartfelt, ceremonies. They dined, they drank, and through drinking they often fell asleep on the graves to dream of their dead.

Fahid was not alone. Others had risen, and stood looking lost. Others before them had risen and departed, leaving the ground disturbed and the grave-offerings strewn about. Fahim's one urge was to

follow their example. Cramped and stiff from a year crouched in the pit,
he began to make his way home.

She sits in the corner and watches me. I've never known her so close. If I
turn my head, she'll be gone. So I don't turn.

I'm working on the new material from Henrik. I don't know where it's
coming from but it isn't Plutarch, nor is it Herodotus as I'd thought, although
it mangles Egyptian history as cheerfully as that ancient did. I do find it hard
to concentrate, feeling her so near.

As my grandfather grew deaf, he began to hear music. Not to imagine
it, but to hear it. He feared that it was the beginning of dementia. Doctors
explained that he'd no mental impairment but as his hearing declined, his
brain was replacing the missing signal by releasing stored memories into the
auditory channel. Once my grandfather knew what was happening, he wel-
comed it. With me it's in the eyes. Magdalena is my music.

This old Egyptian tale, it puzzles me. Nothing in any version of Plutarch's
Moralia corresponds to it. If Henrik's program is restricted to in-domain
data, where's it coming from? A machine can't create. Henrik is getting
excited, of course, persuading himself that it might.

I go down to see him.

It's mid-afternoon, and he looks as if he hasn't slept since yesterday. Turns
out that he hasn't. Around him are stacked the different components of his
project, no one machine but a lash-up of many, always running, processing,
crunching, rendering. At the heart of it all sits an enhanced keyboard and
an ordinary monitor. Henrik's screensaver is a spinning representation of the
bearded Plutarch in marble, minus most of a nose. Henrik hits a key and the
bust disappears, revealing the torrent of type that's going on behind.

"I'll say it now," Henrik tells me, "I don't know what we have here. It
looks like it's the same unfolding narrative but it's flipping back and forth,
Greek and English."

I observe for a while. "Is it broken?"

"A glitch wouldn't explain it."

"There's nothing in the index to match the fragment."

"You're way behind. It's not just a fragment now."

"There's more?"

"It's fascinating to watch. It juggles the words and phrases until they settle and make sense. What's coming out... I don't know, it's not like the usual parroted stuff."

What he doesn't dare say is, it has the feel of new thought.

I say, "This is what you wanted, isn't it?"

"Early days," Henrik says. "Early days."

On the road to Karnak he saw Ahmose, son of Hekaib, whom the gods had taken at the age of nineteen; Fahim approached him with a cry of delight, but became more solemn as Ahmose told his story. Ahmose had risen some hours before and with the same desire to see his family once again. What a welcome would await him, he imagined. But it was not to be.

At first there was joy. But they brought him food and he could not eat. They brought him water and he could not drink. When the knife slipped as he sliced the fruit they offered him, he did not bleed.

His sisters fled in terror, and his uncle barred the door. When his mother could be persuaded to come out and speak to him, she wept and begged him not to stay. We mourned you, she told him, we honour you at the Beautiful Feast. We do not know how to greet you in this form, your place is no longer here with us.

As Ahmose spoke they were joined on the road by another of the risen, and a third. All had attempted to return to their homes, to be met with the same response.

Uncertain now of where to go, they returned together to the field. On every side the dead were rising in increasing numbers, spitting and clearing the dirt from their eyes. Among them Fahim recognised Khalidin, his father's cousin and a much older man, taken into slavery in the same great raid by Sesostris but fated not to survive his first year in the Black Land.

They sat on the ground together. Fahim told of events that the elder had missed in his absence from this earthly life. Fahim refused to bow to misery; if a return to the old life was not possible, he would seize the new.

At this, there came a distant roar from the direction of the necropolis, and Khalidin turned to look at the far-off site, its walls and taller structures shimmering on the horizon. Others of the risen were beginning to move in its direction, as if summoned.

And Khalidin said, as the poor rise from the ground, so do the rich emerge from their tombs. Death offers no release. The order will be preserved. Slaves we were and slaves we will remain, required always to serve.

I can see why Henrik's excited. To him it suggests a breakthrough; that his virtual philosopher is evolving a philosophy of its own. There's no internet link, nothing in the enclosed system beside the code that he's written and the immense volume of raw material supplied by Magdalena. Has he done it? Has he created the beginnings of a conscious mind, self-contained in an actual box? Will Plutarch eventually speak to him? Or is he merely creating for himself the experience of hearing Plutarch speak?

If we raise the dead this way, can the dead ever know?

Later on, I go back to the library. No cleaning crew tonight. I swipe my pass and ride the glass elevator up to the seventh. I think she's there, but she doesn't appear. When I reach the carrel I leave the door open, and when I look back she's a small figure at the end of the row, watching me from afar. When I turn away I can feel her gaze upon my back, like a faint electric touch.

I take my seat and open the next folder.

All her important material has been scanned or transcribed and uploaded now. I'll be surprised if there's anything here that will be of use to Henrik. It's from her undergraduate stuff, mostly timetables and reading lists. I'd taken a quick look through everything when I'd first taken over, and I'd put this folder to the bottom of the pile. After this it's mainly old bills and receipts, and then I'll have reached the end of it all. The boxes will go back to her family, and I'm not sure what I'll do with my evenings from there on. It'll be a wrench.

There's something handwritten on the back of her Year Two Classics book list. I flip it over and hold the phone where it can magnify her scrawl.

It's no more than a few lines. It begins, *Idea for Story* and offers just the bare bones of a thought.

> *Idea for story—Egyptian slave revives after death—the myths are true—struggles out of the ground where he/she was buried intact for inexpensive mummification in dry hot sand.*

And then underneath it, written in different ink and in what I recognise as Magdalena's more mature hand, the note-to-self comment, *NB: Think of an ending!*

NOW I'M IN the Computer Sciences block and Henrik's not here. They wouldn't let him bed down in the building so I expect he's given in to exhaustion and gone home to sleep. As far as I'm aware, the rendering is a hands-off process and doesn't happen any faster if you watch. I can understand his urge to be in the room as it all comes together, but adrenaline and caffeine can only do so much.

I have the paper with me. It's no more than a scribble, an idea jotted down in a spare moment, returned to once and then almost certainly forgotten. All her later creativity was channelled into academic rigour. I've seen her teenaged poetry and in the course of the project I've turned up some of her short amateur fictions, mainly written for school magazines, but this didn't become one of them.

The screensaver is up on the monitor, that noble head rotating in imaginary space. A touch anywhere on the keyboard will make it vanish and reveal what's going on behind. I don't *think* it will interfere with the running of the program, but I don't know enough to be sure.

Henrik will kill me if I'm wrong. But I have to know.

I touch the space bar.

It's revealed. The torrent of type has given way to a static page of text.

When Fahim and Khalidin reached the necropolis, they found themselves at the back of a vast and growing crowd of their own kind; and far from being downcast at the prospect of a return to servitude after death, those before them seemed to be in a mood of celebration. They jeered and roared as if at some sport or entertainment that Fahid could not yet see.

He pushed through the crowd and found that, at its heart, they'd created a circle of bare ground resembling an arena. In this space several of the risen were stumbling blindly, back and forth, to the great amusement of all.

Each stumbling figure wore gorgeous attire. Some were still bandaged. Most prominent among them was a figure in the robes of a high priest who, as Fahim watched, staggered with outstretched arms into the ring of spectators and was repulsed back into the circle.

The priest was trying to scream. But his screams were silent, for he was without lungs, without organs, without eyes. All had been removed in the elaborate funeral rites of the high-born. Unwisely, it now emerged. Dried onions plugged his eye sockets, peppercorns his nose. The stitches that sealed up his flank had broken, and from this wound in his side the embalmers' linen packing trailed and was causing him to trip.

In this manner the well-heeled dead lurched back and forth, colliding, causing laughter, capable of nothing other than suffering, unable to find any escape from their pain.

From a group of nearby buildings came a cheer, as a tomb was broken open and another rich official dragged out. A chant was raised to fetch the old king himself, and a party was assembled for the task. These were slaves who had built the royal tomb, and knew all its secrets. They moved off with assurance and impunity; for what punishment can be exacted on the unwanted dead?

Then a gap of a couple of lines.

And then the words, *NB: Need a closing line!*

It stops there. The cursor blinks, ready to accept—what? An instruction? A question? I look down at the paper in my hand.

I hesitate.

Then with one finger I type in, *Magdalena, is that you?*

I'm not sure how this works so I just hit *Enter*.

And now I wait.

One
DOVE

O N THE WALK to Bethlem he had time to compose the report he'd be making to Sir James. It had been a depressing trip to Hastings, and the sight of a little sunshine out over the sea had done nothing to improve it. Sebastian's train was late back into Waterloo, and there was a further delay as the Metropolitan Police briefly closed off one of the platforms to make an arrest. Outside the station, the forecourt was jammed with motor cabs attempting to turn in a space meant for the passage of horses.

Such a racket, accomplishing so little.

His employer had grown suspicious about the mental health of a prominent solicitor, a man of means with a City practice and a house in fashionable Mortimer Common. Rumours of his distressing behaviour had reached the Lunacy Commission through colleagues. But whenever Sir James had tried to arrange an interview, his efforts were met with some plausible evasion or a breaking of the appointment.

It was for such cases that Sir James kept Sebastian Becker on his private payroll. Sir James Crichton Browne was the Lord Chancellor's Visitor in Lunacy, Sebastian his Special Investigator. Sebastian soon established that the solicitor's diary was a sham, his reported movements those of a wraith, his signature on any correspondence forged. Sebastian had followed a weekly money order to Hastings, where he'd found the man in a two-roomed house in St Leonards. He was confined there under the care of husband-and-wife servants who took most of the money intended for his keep. His dementia, worsened by these conditions, was now profound.

His fortune was not at stake—power of attorney would surely have been granted to his brother with no need to involve the Masters of Lunacy in his financial affairs—but Sebastian had uncovered a darker reason. A daughter's society wedding plans were threatened by any question of madness in the family. So the madness must be hidden.

Sebastian had called in doctors who arranged the man's transfer to the East Sussex County Asylum. He was half-starved, his lower limbs covered in sores. The couple were in the hands of the police.

Of the wedding plans, Sebastian knew little and cared less.

It was a half-mile walk from the terminus to his place of work. His office was a basement room in Bethlem Hospital, Lambeth's once-notorious asylum for the insane, but he spent as little time there as possible. He shared it with the suitcases and trunks of those who'd died in the place they called Bedlam, forgotten by the world, their effects unclaimed.

The door to his basement room stood open. Inside he found Thomas Fogg, one of the Men's Ward assistants, struggling to reach down one of the topmost bags.

"You're standing on my chair," Sebastian said.

"Beg pardon, Mister Becker," Fogg said, "but I did bring a rag to wipe it with."

The back half of the room was like the end of a baggage car, floor-to-ceiling with the luggage of the departed. Sebastian gave Fogg a hand to climb down with the case, which went onto the table that served for a desk.

Sebastian said, "Is it to be claimed?"

"No, sir," Fogg said. "I've to return this letter to its rightful place and then back up it goes."

"Twice in one day," Sebastian said. "Beware of altitude sickness."

"We're below ground here, sir."

"I was aware of that."

Sebastian glanced at the envelope in Fogg's hand. It was addressed to one Joseph Sachs, care of the hospital.

"When did Sachs die?" he said.

"The day he got the letter," Fogg said. "It was found on his body in the laundry. The coroner took it in evidence and returned it just now."

"Sachs was the suicide?"

"The same."

"Let me see that."

Fogg gave up the letter without protest. Becker had no official status in the hospital, but everyone knew he was the Visitor's man. Joseph Sachs had been resident in the hospital for a year, overcome by a disabling melancholy after the death of his young wife. His house had been sold to pay for his keep. Male patients were not generally to be seen in the laundry rooms, but after receiving his letter he'd gained access and there drank a fatal dose of lye.

In the envelope was a single sheet of folded paper. The stationery was of the best quality. Nothing was written there, but within the fold were two items: a lock of dark hair, and a pressed flower.

"If you speak to the gardeners," Fogg said, "they'll tell you a white tulip's the flower of remembrance."

"And that's what this is?"

"That's what they say."

"So what was the coroner's conclusion? That the letter reawakened his grief?"

"I wouldn't know, sir. I was just told to put it back."

"Leave it," Sebastian said. "I'll sort it out."

Fogg paused for long enough to polish the footprint from Sebastian's chair with the rag he'd brought for the purpose, and left.

Sebastian sat, and examined the stationery again. The dead man's sense of loss was something that he could well understand. He looked more closely at the franking. The ink was blurred but the date was readable.

Then he turned to the suitcase. It was mid-sized, of splitting black cardboard with reinforced corners and two straps to hold it together. Inside it were a gentleman's grooming kit with its silver all tarnished, some Christian tracts, personal cutlery, shoe cream, old pyjamas. Of most interest to Sebastian was an ivory portrait miniature in an oval frame. Small enough to hold between his thumb and forefinger, it showed a young woman with an elaborate coiffure. A flower in her hair, a thick braid over one shoulder.

Was this the departed wife? If so it was an oddly old-fashioned image, and one in which she was barely smiling. He turned it over. The reverse was glazed to reveal a single lock of dark hair, laid on brown silk.

"For a while the police thought he'd killed her," Fogg said from the doorway.

"I thought you'd gone."

"I'm going now."

"THE HAIR IN the envelope was of the same colour as the lock of hair in the miniature," he told Frances that evening after supper. They were seated by the coal fire in Sebastian's rooms above a Southwark wardrobe-maker's shop, enjoying the last of its heat before retiring to their separate rooms. Frances was the unmarried sister of Sebastian's late wife. She'd lived with them for years, and stayed on as his housekeeper now that he was alone.

"Just because it's the same colour," she said, "that doesn't have to mean it came from the same person."

"But the intent was there, I think. For the association to be made."

"Perhaps so."

He said, "Whoever sent the memento could hardly expect such an extreme response. But why send it at all? Was it an accusation? An attempt to stir guilt? Is there some message here I'm not seeing?"

"What did the gardeners tell you about the flower?"

"I didn't ask them. I just took Fogg's word on that."

"May I see?"

"I put the letter back."

"Did you really?"

He hesitated. But she was giving him that look, the one where she dared him to deny something. It was half-amused, but mostly knowing. He gave in and took the envelope from his inside pocket.

"I'll return it to the suitcase in due course. No one's in a hurry to collect it."

"And the miniature?"

"God help me if I ever try to keep a secret from you, Frances." Sebastian hitched over sideways in his chair to dig the miniature out of a side-pocket, where he'd been keeping it wrapped in a handkerchief.

He watched her as she held one item after another close to her face. Her eyes were blue, her skin pale, porcelain by firelight. She'd been their silent helper as their son had grown, as loyal over the years as she was dependent. Through circumstance alone, the marriage season had passed her by. In all their years together, he'd only really begun to know her after Elizabeth died.

As Frances turned the miniature around he wondered whether a decade of needlework in poor light served to strengthen the eyes, or to ruin them.

She said, "In the language of flowers, a bloom can have more than one meaning."

"Is that so?"

"It is. Do you plan to look into this any further?"

"No one's asked me to," he said.

THE NEXT MORNING he stopped for his usual breakfast at the pie stand under Southwark Bridge. Bread and butter, and a mug of cabman's tea. He'd not slept well. Thoughts of Hastings troubled him. Not thoughts of the squalid conditions in which he'd found his man, but of seeing street after street of those divided St Leonards houses. They were the one and two-roomed apartments of so-called "remittance women", the spinster relations of families that had no place for them. They lived out their years, dependent and alone. He thought of Frances and her situation, and it made him feel uneasy.

Or perhaps it was the grief and mystery of Joseph Sachs that played on his mind. On reaching Bethlem he went to the Physician-Superintendent's office and asked to see the dead man's records.

They were already to hand, for archiving. Along with Sachs' admission papers and medical notes, there was a police report.

As Fogg had suggested, Sachs had been a suspect in the disappearance of his wife. His story—of a handwritten note that had sent him to find her shoes and coat, neatly folded by the river—had not rung true. He said he could not locate the note, though he swore it had been lying on the kitchen table when he left the house. Its contents were burned into his memory, he said. He insisted that her stated intention was take her own life. He'd raced out in the hope of preventing this. He could quote her words, but he could not produce them. Or her.

No wonder the man had been driven to the madhouse.

But then there was more. Rumours, but only rumours, that she'd been sighted alive in Birmingham. Further police investigation revealed that she'd given false information on their marriage certificate. No trace could be found of her 'brother', to whom Sachs had been persuaded to lend several large sums.

The real story there was plain to see.

To everyone, except for Joseph Sachs.

NORTH OF OXFORD Street in the heart of the West End, the Langham was one of London's premier hotels. Perhaps even the premier hotel of its time, its clientele a regular mix of rich Americans and European aristocracy. Sebastian had rarely felt more shabby and out of place in his heavy coat and one good suit than here in its busy entrance hall. Even the bellboys were better turned out than he.

The General Manager could hardly refuse to cooperate with Sir James' man, but he made his reluctance all too clear.

"I can't discuss the private affairs of guests," he said. "If Sir James were here himself, I'd say the same thing. They have a right to my discretion."

"I understand that, Mr Robarts," Sebastian said. "But you will at least confirm that this letter was posted from your hotel?"

"It's our mark," Robarts conceded. "But that's all I can say."

The Langham was the only hotel in London with its own post office and the right to frank its guests' mail. Sebastian had this information from an avid philatelist on the incurables' ward.

"And your stationery?"

"It looks very much like it."

"I'd say that's a woman's handwriting on the envelope. Would you agree?"

"Mister Becker, I'm no detective and you're keeping me from my duties. You have as much from me as I can give you. You will please excuse me. I have a fire drill to supervise."

"Of course," Sebastian said. "But before I go. This woman. Is she in any way familiar to you?"

He was holding up the miniature and watching Robarts' expression; but the manager's face gave him nothing.

"Really, Mister Becker," Robarts said.

"My apologies, sir," Sebastian said, pocketing the image. "If you think of anything further, I can be reached at the Bethlem Hospital."

"Bethlem?" Robarts echoed. "Are you talking about Bedlam? That place for the insane?"

"I can also receive messages at the pie stand on Southwark Bridge Road," Sebastian said.

"A pie stand."

"Any cabbie will oblige you."

"Good day to you, Mister Becker," Robarts said.

SEBASTIAN SAT IN the public entrance hall, the miniature close to hand for easy reference, watching guests come and go until an assistant manager came over. He leaned close to Sebastian's ear and murmured, "Please forgive me, but I've been sent to ask you to leave."

"Am I causing a disturbance?"

"Mister Robarts fears you'll try approaching the guests. I'm very sorry, sir, but Mr Robarts can be very protective. He's been known to turf out the blind for lowering the tone."

"Then I must lower it no further." Sebastian rose to his feet, turning his hand to ensure that the assistant manager caught a glimpse of the mystery woman's face. The man looked for a moment. Then gave a nod so brief that it would pass unseen from across the lobby.

"Guest or staff?"

"Guest," the man said, as perfectly as any stage ventriloquist.

"I thank you for your courtesy," Sebastian said.

"My father was in Bethlem, sir," the assistant manager now spoke quietly but in a normal voice. "He was returned to us cured."

ACROSS OXFORD STREET, in a coffee shop down by the Palladium, Sebastian took a corner table and perplexed the waitress by asking for a fork with his brew. With the tip of one of the fork's tines he popped open the miniature frame. It fell into two halves, revealing a trade label on the portrait's backing paper.

The London Stereoscopic Company. Their new studios were in Hanover Square, not five minutes' walk away.

The move from Cheapside to Mayfair had brought the company a corner showroom in a tall Regency-style building close to Regent Street. On sale and display were all kinds of hand and stand cameras, telescopes, enlargers, and cases of field and opera glasses.

The clerk was a man of less than thirty, but with the birdlike frame and thinning hair of a classics professor in a Punch cartoon. He'd grown his remaining hair long, and arranged its darks strands across his dome in an effect that was more of a reminder than a disguise.

He took the disassembled miniature, inspected it under a glass, and said, "This isn't an ivory. It's an overpainted photograph. They were a fashion for a while and cheaper than the real thing. This style would most likely have been a wedding gift from wife to husband."

"But it *is* one of yours."

"We still offer the service, but most people can appreciate the art in photography now. It's just that to some…"

"They mistake tradition for taste?"

"I would never say that to a customer."

"Can you tell me anything more about *this* customer?"

The clerk consulted his glass again. "We'll have the plate on file. Along with any record of prints and payments made."

All of the newly-moved company's records were in cabinets and boxes, stacked up in the storeroom to await unpacking. But their filing system was efficient and the glass negative was quickly located. It had been stored upright in a numbered tray, along with a paper proof and a sales slip.

"Well, that's strange," Sebastian said. Though the miniature was no more than two inches high and showed a woman in an evening gown, the proof was taken from a half plate negative and showed a full-length figure in a different costume.

The clerk said. "With a portrait on file, there'd be no need for Miss Hannigan to bear the expense of another sitting. We could just print the head and shoulders from this one. The dress is easily painted over."

The future Mrs Sachs stood before a canvas backdrop of a classical garden, with an urn of flowers for a foreground prop. Her dress was ruched at the shoulders, corseted in the bodice, and flared out from the waist over white tights. Though hardly dressed for ballet, she wore laced pumps and stood in a dancer's third position. Her right hand gripped a riding crop, its other end laid in her left palm.

"She was a theatrical," Sebastian said.

"Our cabinet cards are very popular with the profession," the clerk said. "We give discounts on large orders."

"May I take this?"

"The proof? I don't see why not."

HE SHOWED THE bromide paper proof to Frances that evening over supper.

"She was an equestrienne," Frances said.

Sebastian looked at it again. "You think so?"

"The ballet shoes and riding crop. They're not the usual photographers' properties. We saw costumes like it on riders in the Ringling Brothers shows. And no woman would be seen wearing a dress like that outside the circus."

"The name on the invoice was Joan Hannigan," he said, "Though that could be another alias."

"Will you take this to the police?"

"Only if I can find a crime to take along with it. If they ask me how a lock of hair might drive a man to suicide, I've nothing to offer."

"You always tell me there are only two likely keys to any mystery," Frances said. "It's always love, or money."

"Well, he'd already lost his money. He'd dug into his capital to lend it to her so-called brother. The sale of his house barely covered his keep at the asylum."

"You believe she's alive."

"I'm sure of it. And no doubt she's working her next scheme in a hotel full of dukes, princes, bankers, and railroad tycoons that I can't even get near."

Frances said, "I went by Borough Market this morning. I took the chance to speak to the man on the flower stall. I asked him about white tulips and the language of flowers. I was sure they have another meaning, and I was right."

"So what can they mean, besides remembrance?"

"Apology," she said. "A plea for forgiveness."

IT WAS TWO days before Sebastian could return to the Langham, during which time he secured the liberty of a widow in Chatham, unjustly committed by two local physicians at the behest of concerned relatives. The relatives were concerned at the prospect of their inheritance being spent on ocean travel. Later in the day he'd an appointment to swear an affidavit in Temple Bar. He could spare an early hour or two, lurking and watching from across the street, and if she didn't appear in that time then he'd have to move on.

But the wait took only minutes, not hours, as he saw the former Mrs Sachs being ushered by the doorman to a waiting taximeter cab. She was dressed in a short jacket and a riding skirt. The cab headed north toward nearby Regents Park. Sebastian followed it as far as he could and then crossed the park to the Gloucester Gate entrance, where he was just in time to see his quarry riding out on a rented hack from one of the many nearby stables.

She was beyond hailing distance. The animal broke into an easy trot, and horse and rider disappeared from view in the direction of the Outer Circle. The park had become more popular for early-morning canters when, earlier in the year, Queen Mary had issued a royal ban on women riding astride in Rotten Row. Rather than go side-saddle, most had chosen to exercise elsewhere. These were modern times, where the word of a queen no longer carried the force it once had.

Sebastian waited under a group of trees close to the Broad Walk, and within half an hour saw her returning, still alone. As she drew level with some bushes a small terrier—brown and white, angry-looking and spiky, a classic ratter—dashed across her path, pursued by a small boy.

The horse reared. The rider fought for a few moments and then, when it was clear that she couldn't keep her seat, did an athletic dismount, landing on her two feet without releasing the reins. The horse tried to pull away, but by the time Sebastian reached her she had it under control.

Rather than remount, she had begun to lead the animal the short distance back to the gate. "Thank you, sir," she said breathlessly as he approached, "but I need no help."

"May I at least walk with you?" he said.

"That's hardly proper," she said. "I have told you, there is no need."

"I feel I should," Sebastian said. "Since I'm acquainted with your husband."

Her manner changed. She brightened. She immediately entered her latest role and said, "You have business with Sir Robert? Then be assured that I welcome your concern."

"Not Sir Robert," he said. "The man you married. Joseph Sachs."

She grew pale. Then set her face and walked on.

"You've mistaken me," she said.

"I don't think so," Sebastian said, keeping up with her and holding out the miniature for her to see. She glanced, and knew it straight away. Her accent slipped from Mayfair toward Manchester.

"Did he engage you to find me? I took steps against that."

"By ruining him and then driving him into the madhouse?"

"That was never my intention."

"He thought you were dead. But then you sent him anonymous proof that you were not. Your mistake was to send it from the only London hotel that franks its own letters."

"If it was grief that sent him to Bedlam, then knowing that I am alive and unworthy of his love may lift him out of it. Tell him I am sorry and not to seek to contact me again. No good can ever come of it. He'll think me cruel but he is a good man who deserves better. He should despise and forget me, and put an end to his mourning."

"It's too late for that."

"It's all the apology I can offer."

"After receiving your letter he took his own life. Believing you dead robbed him of his peace of mind; but knowing how you deceived him took away his will to live."

She was shocked. She appeared to weaken. It was real. He offered his arm, but she did not take it.

"So," Sebastian said. "You're playing the Lady now. And is Sir Robert the same man who posed as your brother while the two of you hollowed out your husband's fortune? I imagine he's another con merchant from the Music Halls. I've met many such. Masters of the patter and of separating people from their money."

She took several deep breaths. In her portrait she was plain. In person it was possible to see how men might be so willing to be taken in by her.

She said, "Joseph knew what I was. I was no soiled dove in his eyes. He took me from the life and I let him believe that he'd saved me. The plan was always to take his money and disappear. But he was so decent. The first truly decent man I'd ever known.

"Conscience is a luxury I cannot afford. I made enquiries, hoping to hear that his spirits were on the mend. But instead I learned of Bedlam and a life ruined. I knew I couldn't put things right, but I hoped to ease the pain I'd caused. What will you do?"

"What can I prove?" Sebastian said. "But the power to change is yours. You can start with whatever bogus scheme the two of you are running from your fancy hotel address."

They were almost at the exit to the park. She walked with her head down for a few paces. As they reached the street and its traffic, the horse slowed without being told.

"If you don't change your ways and restrain your man," Sebastian said, "be assured that I will."

"You can have no idea what you're asking," she said.

Sebastian said, "There's a suitcase waiting to be claimed. Joseph's personal effects were few. You're still his wife—if you don't claim them, can you name someone who might?"

She gave no reply. But she gave him a look; brief, sideways, and haunted. The kind given to the well-meaning by the truly damned.

He waited by the gates as she led the horse, now calmed, across the road toward the mews where he was stabled.

Sebastian watched her for a few moments, then turned and walked back into the park.

The boy was waiting for him by the great stone drinking fountain at the Broad Walk's north end. The terrier was by his side, a yard of string serving for a leash.

Handing over the money he'd promised, Sebastian said, "You were only to distract the horse, not throw the rider."

"I told that to the dog, sir," the urchin said, "but the dog dint listen."

THE WAS A message waiting for Sebastian at the pie stand the next morning. A request to contact Mr H B Robarts at the Langham Hotel on a matter of urgency. Rather than telephone, he went.

When he arrived he was ushered into Robarts' office. Robarts closed the door. He was tight-lipped and furious.

He said, "You're a detective of sorts, are you, Becker? I want to engage you. The people you were looking for have been calling themselves Sir Robert and Lady Cransfield."

"And they've skipped?" Sebastian hazarded.

"With their champagne suppers and entertaining, the bill is close to seven hundred pounds. Last night some of the staff heard voices raised in their suite. Then this morning, Sir Robert settled his account and departed before breakfast. By the time the bank refused the cheque, they were long gone. They even stole the sheets!"

Sebastian had a moment to ponder that last point, as it was here that the telephone rang. Robarts picked it up and, without waiting to listen, said, "Not now!" and ended the call.

He said, "There's no Sir Robert Cransfield listed in the Peerage."

"You didn't check before?"

"There was no reason to be suspicious. Sir Robert lodged a number of bonds in the care of the Cashier's Office. I considered them adequate surety."

"And the bonds now prove to be worthless."

"Newspaper. I saw them go into the envelope and watched him seal it. But newspaper is all we found."

Sebastian said, "A little sleight of hand would be nothing to them. They are a pair of known fraudsters with music-hall skills."

"You couldn't warn me of this?"

"I was seeking your help in establishing it, but you turned me away. Call in the police."

"I would rather this were not brought to public attention. *WHAT?*"

This last was directed at a nervous-looking hotel employee who had dared to put his head around the door.

He said, "Beg pardon, Mr Robarts, but there's a problem with the water supply. We may need to warn the guests."

Robarts said, "We'll do no such thing. Open the connection to the Hampstead reservoir and have the master plumber inspect the well." The

Langham was famed for the purest and softest water in all of London, rising from deep underground through its own artesian bore.

"It's not the well, sir. The pumps are working fine. It's the cistern that's blocked, and what little's coming through has a funny old smell."

Sebastian said, "When Sir Robert left the hotel. Did you see the woman?"

The manager was slightly thrown by the sudden switch back. "No. He'd sent her on ahead. Why?"

"An argument between fraudsters, the man leaves alone, you're missing a sheet and now there's something blocking your water tank," Sebastian said. "If you don't summon the police and have them look in the cistern, I will."

"HE'D STRANGLED HER," Sebastian told Frances. "That was his answer to her change of heart. A woman who could feel pity for their victims—what use was she to him now? And if she gave in to the urge to confess, she'd most likely take him down with her. She wouldn't fit in a trunk so he wrapped her in a weighted sheet and sunk her to the bottom of the tank where she wouldn't be found for a while. He may have imagined that he'd bought himself a day or two, but detectives tracked him to King's Cross and the police took him off his train in York the same afternoon."

"They should thank you."

"I don't deserve thanks. If I hadn't intervened, she'd still be alive."

"She's the author of her own fate. All you did was expose her actions. If you're responsible for anything, it's for showing her how she might redeem herself."

"Which cost her dear. But I can always rely on you to lift me up, Frances."

They were passing down Southwark Street by Borough Market, a maze of halls under railway arches where the yelling of stallholders and costermongers was in regular competition with the thunder of steam trains right above their heads. The alleys here were a regular jam of wagons and handcarts, the public houses with their doors flung open, keeping market porters' hours. Frances had linked Sebastian's arm for safety.

She said, "What will happen now?"

"She'll get a parish burial, and he'll be hanged." The counterfeit knight had been identified as Octavius Hannigan, failed Shakespearian, second comedian, and sideshow three-card swindler. Joseph Sachs' suitcase would rejoin all the others. Like a trapped and forgotten soul, parked for all time, soon lost to notice.

Frances said, "She was the fool. Joseph died for love. She left it too late and died for nothing."

"Dead is dead," Sebastian said.

"If you say so," Frances said, in an airy tone that said she would indulge his inclination to argue without for a moment accepting his argument.

Sebastian glanced back toward the market. He'd decided that he would return, later on, and seek out the flower seller.

Frances ought to know that she was appreciated. Not like all those forgotten women in St Leonards, parked in their remittance homes like unwanted baggage, paid off to keep their genteel distance. He valued her, but he could not find the words. Perhaps something in the language of flowers would express what he wanted to say.

A flower seller should know.

And if no advice was forthcoming, there were always white tulips.

The Visitors'
BOOK

"SOMEONE'S TORN A page out of this," she said, turning the book toward me. "Look, you can see."

She was almost right. The page hadn't been torn, it had been cut; taken out with a blade that had been run down the middle of the book as close to the centre as it was possible to get. It was the kind of cut you make when you don't want your handiwork to be noticed. The only thing that gave it away was that when the book was closed, a slight gap appeared as if a bookmark had been lost in there somewhere. It made me faintly curious, but no more than that. I really didn't think that it was any big deal.

"So it has," I said, and tried to look more interested than I was.

Some time later, I remember getting it out of the drawer to look at it again. It was a big book, album-sized, and it was two-thirds filled with handwritten entries by many of the families who'd stayed in the summerhouse before us. Only one or two of them were in a language I could understand, and they gave a few hints about the place—how to puzzle out how the circuit breakers worked, where to get English newspapers two days out of date—as well as the standard, had-a-lovely-time kinds of sentiments. There were some people from Newcastle, others who'd come up from Dorset. Many of the others were Germans, a few French. Sally hadn't come across the book until we'd been in the place for three days already, and then she'd found it while rummaging around in the sitting-room furniture for maps and brochures.

When I eventually went back and brought it out again, I turned to the place where the missing page had been and looked at the entries before and after. I couldn't read anything of what had been written, but by then I was only interested in the dates. The gap seemed to correspond to a two-week period exactly one year before.

No, I remember thinking. It can't have any significance. All that it probably meant was that someone had messed up their entry and had taken the leaf out to try it again. The paper-cutter they'd used was still there at the back of the drawer, a little plastic block with just the corner of a razor blade showing.

When I turned the paper to the light, I could see that some of the missing writing had pressed through onto the next page. Not to the extent that I could make out any words, but enough to get an idea of the overall style. It was neat, it was rounded. A feminine hand.

And it didn't match with any of the entries that came before or after.

But that was later. Back on that third day, there was no reason for the Visitors' Book to bother me at all. I left Sally looking through the remaining pages, and went out onto the covered terrace on the front of the summerhouse.

"Watcha doing, Minx?" I said.

The Minx looked up at me from the table. On her birth certificate and by her grandparents she was called Victoria, but to us she'd been the Minx for so long that we had to make an effort to remember that she had any other name. She was four years old that autumn, and was due to start at school the following spring. She'd have her own books, name tabs, a uniform, everything. We'd always told ourselves that we could look forward to this—like all children she'd hit our lives like a hurricane, leaving us dazed and off-kilter and somehow feeling that we'd never quite be able to make up the ground again to become the people we'd once been—but I found that I wasn't quite anticipating the event in the way that I'd imagined. I suppose I was just beginning to realise how closely the growing and the going away were entwined, and would ever be so.

"I'm colouring," she said.

She was, too. She'd coloured the page in her book and a good piece of the old vinyl tablecloth around it. She'd coloured a cow blue, and the sky behind it black.

I said, "That looks really good. Are you going to do another?"

"I'll do another next Tuesday," she said, Next Tuesday being her way of indicating some undetermined time in the future. "Let's go and look for froggies."

"Clear your lunch away first," I said, "or you'll bring in all kinds of creepy-crawlies."

She climbed down from the bench to the wooden planking of the terrace, and surprised me by doing what I'd asked of her. Then we set off down the steps and into the grounds to find some froggies.

It was a pretty good house. I'd felt a twinge of disappointment when we'd first rolled up the grassy drive after a long haul by road and ferry, but within a few hours of unpacking and beginning to unwind it had started to grow on me. It was bigger than we needed, but I liked the sense of space. So what if it was a little shabby around the edges and the shower arrangements were kind of spartan and the beds were dropped in the middle in a way that would have suited a hunchback perfectly and nobody else at all; after a while this only seemed to add to the atmosphere.

It was late, a quiet time of the year. Almost all of the other summerhouses, including the newer one that shared this grassy clearing in a thicket just a little way back from the beach, appeared to be unoccupied. When the road gate at the end of the driveway was closed, it was almost as if we were shutting ourselves into a private world. When the Minx had spotted the horde of tiny frogs that seemed to migrate across the drive at around four o'clock every afternoon, that more or less confirmed it. It seemed that we were going to be okay.

"Have you found any?" she said brightly, but I had to tell her that I hadn't. She liked to hold them on her hand. By now they probably just sat there toughing it out and thinking, *Oh, shit, not again* and *Why me, God, why me?*

"No," I said. "It's the wrong time of day. Look, I saw a bike in the garage yesterday. Why don't you ride it around the garden?"

"A big bike?" she said warily.

"No, just a little bike."

So we spent the afternoon playing with the house's rusty old tricycle and a football that we'd picked up from Willi's Market about a half-mile down the shore road, and after we'd eaten picnic-style out on the terrace we all took a walk along the beach until it was too cold for everybody but the Minx, who had to be picked up out of the sand hole that she'd dug and carried home squalling.

And as we were tracing our way back through the upturned boats and then across the strip of coarse grassland that divided the shoreline from the shore road, I found myself thinking: Maybe the people who wrote the page weren't the ones who took it out. Maybe it was something that the owners didn't want the rest of us to see.

The owners.

Those shadowy people who weren't actually present but whose mark was everywhere, so that they seemed to stand just out of sight like a bunch of watchful ghosts. Their pictures, their ornaments, their old castoff furniture—their house. Maybe they came in after each new tenant and read the book, and there was something here that they'd censored.

Maybe.

Exactly what I had in mind, I couldn't have said. Something uncomplimentary, some insult even; written by someone who perhaps didn't have a good time and blamed the place and not themselves for it. Or worse. It could have been something worse. I was surprised to find that the possibility had been playing on my mind. I said nothing to Sally, but I decided there and then that I'd think about it no further. I mean, you worry at something to which you know you can never find the answer, and where does it get you?

Nowhere. So I thought I'd better stop.

That night, after the Minx had been installed in her room and had exhausted every avenue for stories and drinks and had eventually exhausted herself as well, we got a couple of the local beers out of the fridge and turned on the sitting-room lights. Sally flicked through some of the magazines that she'd picked up on the boat coming over, and I hunted around for the paperback I'd been reading. I'm not much of a reader, and thinking of the two weeks that lay ahead I'd bought the book for its size and weight as much as for any other reason. Every other page was dotted with CIA and MI5 and KGB, and the plot went on and on and had about as much grip as a wet handshake; after a while I gave up looking for it, and went over to the shelves instead.

There had to be something here I could read. There was a cabinet full of books and overseas editions of *The Reader's Digest*, most of them probably abandoned and accumulated from visitors over the years, but there wasn't much that was in the English language. There was a fat book by Leon Uris that I put back because it looked such heavy going and, besides, I'd already seen the movie, and an old and brittle Agatha Christie which, on a quick check, appeared to have lost its last ten pages. The only decent bet seemed to be a two-fisted private-eye story titled *Dames Die First*.

When I pulled it out, a photograph dropped to the floor. It had been between the books. I picked it up and looked at it, and saw that there was the sign of a crease across the middle. At a guess, it had been slipped in between the volumes for the pressure to flatten it out, and then it had been forgotten. It was of a blonde girl of about six or seven, and if it had been taken anywhere around here I didn't recognise the spot. I carried the picture over to the chest of drawers and then started to go through them, much as Sally had earlier in the day. After a while, I became aware of her watching me.

"What's the matter?" she said.

"Just checking on something."

She didn't seem to think much of my answer, but it was the best one I had. As she was laying down her magazine to come over, I found what I was looking for; another, different photograph that lay in one of the drawers underneath some boxed games and out-of-date timetables.

It was a family group. Nothing formal, just a snapshot. The house was recognisable in the background, although they'd added to it since. These, I'd been guessing, were the people who actually owned the place and who let it out through an agency for the times when they didn't need it themselves.

I laid the two photographs side by side on top of the dresser. The girl who appeared in one didn't appear in the other.

Sally picked up the portrait shot and said, "She doesn't look local," before dropping it again and going on through the kitchen toward the bathroom.

Yeah, fine.

That's probably what I'd been thinking, too.

SATURDAY CAME AROUND.

I didn't actually realise that it was Saturday until I saw a strange car coming up the driveway that morning. At first I thought that it was somebody on their way to speak to us, but the car turned off and pulled in by the other of the two houses that shared the driveway and the private clearing at its end. Suddenly, it didn't seem so private any more.

The family got out and we nodded to each other. They didn't seem to have brought much in the way of luggage and they went straight into the house as if they already knew their way around. My guess was that they were another set of owners, just up for the weekend. I went back into our own place and warned Sally and the Minx, just in case either of them happened to be wandering around after a shower in less than their underwear. There was just a stretch of open ground between the two buildings, nothing screening them at all. The other house was newer, neater. I know it was theirs, but I couldn't help thinking of them as intruders.

I looked at the two children. Neither of them was anything like the girl in the photograph.

So then I wondered if they might be able to tell me what had happened here, in this same week exactly one year before.

But I never asked.

On Sunday we took the Minx on a long drive to the zoo, where she acted up so much that we had to threaten to leave her there and halfway meant it. When we got back late in the afternoon, our short-term neighbours were apparently loading up to go. We nodded as we passed just as before, and then they went.

I gave it a few minutes after their departure and then I took a walk down the driveway to check that the gate was secure; the driveway curved and was lined with dense bushes, so the gate couldn't be seen directly from the house.

The Minx came after me, on the prospect of froggies. She squatted down looking hopefully at the ground while I rattled the wide gate, but the bolt was secure.

"Why are you doing that?" she said.

"So that we can let you wander around without worrying about you getting onto the road where the cars are," I told her. "Haven't you noticed how one of us checks on it every morning?"

"I check on it too," she said.

"Really."

"Yes," she said. "Someone keeps coming in and leaving it open."

Either the frogs had already been and gone, or else they were getting wiser and waiting. We walked back up to the house. The day was dying and the shadows were long and deep, and the houselights glowed yellow-on-blue like a twilit jack o'lantern. The Minx took hold of my hand as we climbed the wooden steps. Only a couple of hours before, she'd been winding me up to bursting point outside the monkey house and she'd known it. Now this. I couldn't help thinking, and not for the first time, that the worst thing in the world for me would be to lose her.

And, of course, eventually to lose her was one of the few things in my life that could fairly be called inevitable.

WITH ONLY A few days left of our stay, we found ourselves less inclined toward loading up the car and going looking for late-season amusements and so instead we just stayed around the place. I'm not exactly sure what we did, but the time carried on leaking away from us anyway. Anything we needed, we could usually get it from Willi's Market. The only problem was that we couldn't mention the name of the place when the Minx was in earshot without her latching onto it and getting us helpless with laughter.

Sometimes the Minx walked down with me. Thursday was one of the days when she didn't.

It was a rambling, one-storey building set back from the road with space for about half a dozen cars in front of it, and although it wasn't big it sold just about everything from fresh bread to padlocks. It was clean and it was bright and it was modern, and the only note that jarred when I compared it to similar places back home was the sales rack of shrinkwrapped pornography stuck in there by the checkout between the Disney comics and the chewing gum. One man seemed to run the place on his own, at least at this quiet time of year when there were only the few locals and late visitors like ourselves to keep it ticking over. He wore a sports shirt and glasses and combed his thinning hair straight back, and whenever I went in we communicated entirely by nods and signs and smiles.

As he was punching up my stuff on the till, I brought out the little girl's picture and showed it to him.

He paused in his work, and looked at the picture. He wasn't certain of why I was doing this, and so he looked closely without any reaction other than mild puzzlement for a few moments. Then he glanced up at me.

He shook his head. There was sadness and sympathy in his eyes.

And he said something, and right there and then I'd have given almost anything to know what it was; but I just took the picture from him and stowed it away again, and I nodded my head as if I understood. The words meant nothing to me, but I thought I knew the tone of them.

It was the tone, I believed then, that one would use when speaking of someone else's tragedy.

As I was walking back along the side of the shore road, I felt as if the formless apprehensions of the past few days had suddenly come together and made a creature with a name. Its name was dread, and it sat in me like an angry prisoner with no sight of daylight. A few cars zipped by me, one with a windsurfing board on its rack. I knew I'd closed and bolted the gate behind me, I knew it, and yet...

In my mind's eye I could see the Minx running hell-for-leather down the drive, giggling in mischief the way she often did, with Sally screaming a warning and falling behind and the Minx too giddy to realise what she was being told... *Someone keeps coming in and leaving it open,* she'd said, and I'd paid her no attention...

But who? Apart from our weekend neighbours, we were the only ones to be using the gateway at all. Was there someone who'd been prowling around the place, and I'd overlooked the evidence because it was the Minx who was telling me and I was so used to the workings of her imagination that I was dismissing the truth along with the usual dose of unreality?

Come to think of it, the garage door had been standing open when we'd gone to get the bike a few days before.

And I still hadn't found that damned paperback, even though I was pretty sure of where I'd left it.

And there was the Visitors' Book, which had planted the seed of my unease.

And the reaction of the checkout man in Willi's Market, that had brought it into flower…

Pretty thin fabric, I know.

But by the time I reached the house, I was running.

SALLY SAW ME coming up the drive. I must have been a sight. Breathless, my shirt half-out, the bag of groceries crushed up against my side. She was out on a sun lounger in front of the house, and she raised her head and squinted at me. I slowed. Everything seemed normal, and I was a dope. But I wasn't sorry.

"Where's the Minx?" I said.

"She's set herself up with a picnic on the porch," she said. "What's the matter with you?"

"Nothing," I said, almost sharply, and I walked past her and up the steps to the covered terrace. As my eyes adjusted to the shade, I could see the Minx: in a world of her own as she so often was, with plates and crockery from the kitchen set out on the outdoor dining table and her all-time favourite doll, clothes long gone and the rest of her distinctly frayed around the edges, propped up opposite. She'd hijacked the big tub of margarine and a packet of biscuits, and Sally must have opened a bottle of Cola for her to round off the feast. She was just raising it to her lips and tilting it as I came into sight.

Nothing amiss here.

And then, in an instant, I saw that I was wrong.

I don't know exactly what happens when you're in a situation like that. You can see the most minor detail with the utmost clarity, and it burns itself deep into your awareness; but it's almost as if the sheer volume of information suddenly slows the speed of processing, so that you don't seem to act or react in any positive way at all. You see your own failure, even before it's had the chance to happen. Disaster's heading straight for you like a rocket, and your responses are moving like letters in the mail.

If I had any talent with a paintbrush, I could probably reproduce the scene exactly. The well-worn sheen on the checkered vinyl cloth. The sunlight, backlighting the Minx's hair as she raised the bottle. The mismatched china and the scattering of crumbs. The open margarine tub, its contents churned like an angry sea. The last inch of flat cola.

· And the live wasp in the bottle, floating toward the neck as the bottle was tilted.

SHE SCREAMED AND dropped the bottle, and clapped both her hands to her face. The wasp was on the deck boards now, buzzing furiously but too wet or too damaged to rise; she'd squeezed it between her mouth and the rim of the bottle as it had tried to escape, and it had reacted the only way it knew how. Which got no sympathy out of me at all. I stepped on it quickly, and it popped like a grape.

The Minx was still screaming as I hauled her up and onto my knee. Sally was already on her way up the steps. I tried to pull the Minx's hands away, but she was hysterical. Sally was saying "What is it, what's happened?" and I remember thinking, completely unfairly but in the lash-out, bite-anything manner of a run-over dog, that she should have been right there and this should never have been allowed to happen. Which makes no sense, of course, but that's the way I was thinking. I don't think it showed on the outside, but I was in a panic. I didn't know what to do. We were in the middle of nowhere in a place where we didn't speak the language, and there was a crisis here and I didn't know what to do.

The stinger was still in the Minx's lip, like a tiny yellow thumbtack. I managed to pick it out carefully with my thumbnail. And what then? I tried to have a go at sucking out the poison, but the Minx beat me away. Sally ran to the kitchen and brought back half an onion to rub the wound, but the Minx batted that away too. She was screaming for a plaster, the little-kids' answer to every hurt. I handed her over and went for the first aid kit in the car.

There were Band Aids, there were bandages, there was a folded sling for a broken arm. I'd bought the kit as a ready-made box and I don't think I'd even looked into it since I'd taken a curious glance over the contents and then stowed it away in the car at least three years before. I fumbled it, and the contents went everywhere. I saw some antiseptic wipes and grabbed one up and went back to the covered terrace.

The Minx, still tearful, was quieter. Sally was rocking her and whispering *Sshh, sshh,* and the Minx was sobbing. I tore open the sachet and crouched down before them both and managed to get a few dabs in with the wipe. Her lip was already beginning to swell.

I was scared.

When the swelling grew steadily worse over the next half-hour, we loaded her into the car and went out looking for a hospital. I had no idea. We were already on the road and moving when I thought that I should have checked through the old brochures and guides for an area map which might have some indication on it. I had a terrific sense of desperation, as if there was a bomb ticking in the back of the car. I hardly knew what I was doing. In the end it was the cashier at a big Shell service area who marked the nearest hospital on a tourist map and then waved me away when I tried to pay for it.

Carrying the Minx into the Emergency Room, I felt like a wrecked sailor reaching the shore. I mean, for all I knew she could have died—she could have been dying right then, and I'd have been no more useful. As it was they checked her over, gave her a couple of shots, painted the sting site with something, and then sent us away. The Minx stayed quiet in the back with Sally as I drove us all home. It was dusk when we got there, and it was to find that we'd gone off leaving every door and window of the place wide open. Even the gate at the end of the drive was swinging to and fro, and I knew that I'd stopped and jumped out of the car to close it behind us.

I knew that I'd never feel quite the same again, about anything. I'd crossed a line. I'd peeped into the abyss.

Nothing much more happened those last couple of days. I put the child's photograph back on the shelf where I'd found it, and I made no further enquiries. The Minx looked like a defeated boxer, five rounds and then out for the count, but by the next morning we were even able to make jokes about it. They were morale-boosters, not the real thing, and I suppose they must have sounded pretty hollow to both of us. The camera stayed in its case for the rest of the trip. Nothing was said or agreed, but I think that this was something that none of us would ever want to be reminded of.

So, no more photographs.

We'd probably have gone home early if we could, but the boat ticket couldn't be transferred. And, besides, there was so little time remaining. The weather held good, but we stuck around the house killing time as if on the rainiest of rainy days.

On the last day we packed almost in silence, and the Minx went for one last froggie-hunt while I loaded up the car. Sally stayed in the house. When I went inside to bring out the last few items—the boots, the overcoats, the radio…all the stuff that didn't belong in any particular box or bag—I found her at the big table in the sitting room. The Visitors' Book was open on the table before her. She looked up, and she seemed almost defensive.

"We've got to write something," she said. "It's not the house's fault. Not to put anything at all would be rude."

I shrugged, and didn't say anything. We hadn't been saying much of anything to each other since the accident, at least not directly. I picked up the stuff that I'd come for and went out to the car.

Half an hour later, with everything loaded away and the house locked up for the last time behind us, we rolled down the driveway and out through the open gate.

"Say Goodbye, house," Sally told the Minx, and the Minx turned and waved through the back window and said, "Bye!"

I stopped the car.

"I just realised, I left my sunglasses," I said.

"I checked everywhere before we locked up," Sally said. "Are you sure?"

"I only meant to put them down for a second," I said. "I know where they are. Let me have the keys."

The keys were to be dropped off at the agents' office in the nearest town as we drove on by to the ferry. Sally got them out of the big envelope and passed them forward to me, and I got out of the car and walked back up the drive. I left the engine running. This wasn't going to take very long.

Already the house seemed different. No longer ours, it was a place of strangers again. I felt out-of-place, almost observed, as I walked up the steps with the door key in my hand. I could hear the car's engine running at the end of the driveway, over on the far side of the bushes.

I entered the newly-regained silence of the place. There was no sign of my sunglasses but then, I'd known there wouldn't be; they were in their case, safe inside my jacket.

I didn't have much time. I crossed the room to the chest of drawers and crouched, pulling open the one which I knew held the Visitors' Book. It was uppermost on all the brochures, and I took it out and laid it on top of the chest before feeling around at the back of the drawer. Then I straightened, and opened the book to the latest entry.

I didn't want to read it. In fact I'd turned the book around so that all of the entries were upside-down to me, on purpose. I didn't know whether Sally had mentioned anything about how the visit had ended, and I didn't want to. I spread the pages flat and I took a grip on the little cutter and I ran it, firmly and neatly, down the final page as close to the spine as I could get.

A firm tug, and it came out cleanly. I screwed it up and stuffed it into my pocket, for quiet disposal at a stopover point somewhere on the journey ahead.

And then I closed the book, returned it to the drawer, locked up the house, and walked away.

Forever.

In
GETHSEMANE

THERE WAS A thick haze in the sky, and rain on the stones out in Station Square. Borthwick the press agent was waiting for them, stepping out through the crowd with his arm raised. The crowd parted and pushed on around him, heading out into the drizzle.

"I've a taxi for the boarding house, and a boy with a handcart for Mister Goulston's boxes," he told the travelling-party of five.

"A boy, Mister Borthwick?" Goulston spoke up suspiciously from the back.

"A reliable boy, sir," the press agent assured him. "I've used him before. He'll get your trunks to the hall and he'll see them secure. His father's the doorkeeper there. Now if you'll follow me, gentlemen, I've some journalists waiting."

Two petrol-engined taxicabs awaited the party by the railway station's awning, between the row of charabancs and the stop for the new electric trams. Borthwick rode in the first with Goulston and Frederick Kelly. The others followed behind. Goulston looked back through the cab's tiny rear window, but in all of the activity out in the crowded Boulevard there was no boy or handcart to be seen. He settled uncomfortably in his seat, and tried to turn his thoughts to other matters.

He hadn't been to Blackburn in ten years. No bookings here, no reason to. He looked out and saw yet another cotton town in the rain, glory and squalor all pushed up together. It was a market day, caps and clogs and baskets much in evidence. He was half listening as Borthwick discussed arrangements with Frederick Kelly, but he played no part in their conversation.

Their lodgings were on one of the streets that inclined steeply toward the moors on the northern side of town. The cab laboured to make the climb, and their driver repeatedly crashed his gears. Goulston winced at the sound. When they'd finally stopped before the genteel but sturdy redbrick villa that was to be their base for the next three days, Borthwick got out first and led them into the house. Walter Ward, Kelly's secretary and keeper of the purse, stayed behind and settled the tariffs. Some bicycles leaned on the fence alongside the path to the front door; the press party had already arrived and were inside. Goulston and Kelly were greeted by the landlady, handed over their wet coats to be hung in the scullery, and then were shown through into the stifling warmth of the drawing-room where their first audience waited.

Six chairs had been set out for the journalists, and two facing them for the key performers of the troupe. They were arranged before the hearth, where a mature fire glowed with the intensity of lava. Not all of the newspapermen's seats had been filled.

"What kind of a show can we expect tonight?" was the opening question and it was fielded, as always, by Frederick Kelly. Kelly was an unlikely-looking captain, with his pale skin and broad forehead and fine moustache; he looked like a young man of delicate health who only ever ventured out of doors after a stern warning from his mother. But his apparent frailty was misleading, Goulston knew. Tireless was not the word to describe him, for Goulston had seen him in a state of complete exhaustion on more than one occasion; but however low his energies might fall, Frederick Kelly always found the strength to rise again and go on.

He said, "Mister Goulston will begin with a demonstration of spirit effects and fake mediumship. I can tell you now that he's very impressive."

"And yourself, sir?"

"I then do what little I can in the face of the scepticism he engenders."

"Mister Kelly is being extremely modest," Borthwick the advance man put in from where he stood at the side of the room. "His appearances have caused a sensation in every town on the tour so far."

"We end the evening with comments from the audience and a debate on the spiritualist issue," Kelly added. "Mister Goulston gives me no quarter in this, I can tell you."

Two of the four journalists present made notes, and the man from the Northern Telegraph said, "Can I ask Mister Goldston why he consents to appear on a bill with a practising medium, when he's declared all clairvoyants to be frauds and charlatans?"

"That's very simple," Goulston said, with a glance at Borthwick to be sure that the error over his name would not go uncorrected. "I'm here to catch Mister Kelly out."

"Have you done that, yet?"

"Perhaps tonight."

The man from the Blackburn Times said, "What are we going to see? Do we see physical manifestations?"

"Goulston does all of those," Kelly told him. "You want to see a table tip and fly, Goulston does it better than anyone I've ever seen. I practice a form of clairvoyance that is far less spectacular. I handle objects and I say whatever comes into my mind. Rarely do I see more than that."

"Do you raise the dead?" the Telegraph man said, and there was a tone in his voice and a look in his eye that seemed to urge Kelly to say yes, just so that the Telegraph man could go on into print and make him regret it.

"I do not raise the dead," Kelly said and then he added, with care and certain emphasis, "Sometimes I believe the dead can speak through me."

The Telegraph man switched his gaze. He looked like a bank clerk, but his manner showed the wiry energy of a whippet. "Mister Goulston?"

"Let me be diplomatic," Goulston said. "I believe that Mister Kelly is an exceptional performer of his type."

"Do you think he's a fraud?"

"I have no doubt."

"But no proof."

"Proof will come."

Three pencils scratched away in three notebooks, the exception being the cheerful-looking young man at the back of the room whom Goulston had already concluded was congenitally damaged in some way. He had a notebook like the others, but he'd so far written nothing. Coals settled in the grate, the only other sound to break the patient silence.

The man from the Blackburn Times said, "Mister Kelly, you make much of the fact that Goulston is an independent observer. He freely asserts that he's looking to expose the means he thinks you use. So if we can assume there's no collusion between you, what exactly is the advantage to you in his presence?"

"Publicity," murmured the cheerful-looking young man from the back but Frederick Kelly, seeming not to hear him, said, "I can give you two answers to that. The first I'll state freely. Goulston is a showman. I am not. His performance and our public conflict fills more seats than I could hope to fill alone. I'm raising funds to build a spiritualist temple. Empty halls will raise not a single stone of it and the law will have me if I use my talents to raise money in any other way. If Goulston doesn't feel that he's made a deal with the devil for his ends, then neither need I."

"But you travel and lodge together," the man from the Times persisted. "Do you argue in private?"

It was Borthwick who broke in with a reply. "Constantly," he said, and with such a long-suffering air that all were prompted to smile.

The Telegraph man said, "What's the second answer?"

Kelly considered his words before he spoke. His long fingers intertwined before him, almost as if in prayer.

"I am human," he said, "and the pressures are many. But Goulston's eyes are always on me." The medium looked at the stage-conjurer then, and the conjurer returned his gaze steadily.

"Goulston is my conscience," Kelly said. "And my guarantor."

Kelly went upstairs to rest, the newspapermen fell upon the tea and cakes that Borthwick had thought ahead to arrange for them, and Goulston made his way through to the back of the house to find his overcoat and to ensure that he had, as he'd thought, left his keys in one of its pockets. His bags had been taken up to his room, but he would unpack them later. Goulston always made a point of unpacking, even for a single night's stay. The party would be here for three days, and then they would move on. They had one night's engagement in which Goulston would be performing, the remaining time being set aside for Frederick Kelly's private consultations. It was always the same. Goulston would take the stage first and thoroughly discredit every trick and technique that Kelly might use. And yet still they would line up after the public show, begging for the medium's private attentions.

His coat was damp, but he had no other. He said to the landlady, "I need to find King George's Hall. Is it far from here?"

"Five minutes to walk it, sir, no more," the landlady told him. "Shall I send you someone to show you the way?"

"Just point me in the right direction. I can ask as I go."

King George's Hall stood with its back half-turned against the middle of town, huge and solid and bursting with civic dignity. Goulston's heart sank a little when he saw it. Already he could imagine it inside, a great gilded barn of a place. The main doors were locked but he found a stage door in a yard around to the side, and he banged on this. A handcart stood in the yard, its wheels braced with iron and its well-worn handles tilted toward the sky. Goulston looked up. The drizzle had cleared, but the sky had not. It was a yellowish-grey, the colours of soot and ochre.

"I'm Goulston," he told the doorkeeper when the door was finally opened. "Did my boxes arrive?"

"Ay, they did, sir," the doorkeeper said, moving back to let him enter.

"I want to check my properties and look at the stage. You have all-electric light here, I assume?"

"We do."

The doorkeeper moved ahead of him. His frame was that of a powerful man but it was bent as if by injury or long misuse, and he shuffled. He'd a walrus moustache, and blond stubble on the back of his neck. Goulston had noted that his blue eyes were as pale as water. His hands touched almost everything that he passed; door handles, newel posts, the angles of walls.

Goulston's boxes had been placed in a bare room under the stage. The room was undecorated and had illumination from a single, unshaded bulb. In the middle of the floor stood a wickerwork livestock basket and two big metal-bound trunks, rugged enough for a long safari. He'd bought them at a railway company sale and they now held all of his effects and properties. Firstly he counted his doves, checking their water and grain. All were alive, all seemed alert. Then, taking out his keys, he unlocked the first of the trunks and opened it up to check its contents.

It had not always been so. Goulston's properties and major illusions had once filled a railway car and required a full-time baggage master on the payroll to get them around the major cities of Europe without loss or damage. He'd employed a staff of eleven and his own small orchestra and with them presented a full-evening show.

How the wheel could turn. Now he opened for another headline performer, and had to rely on doorkeepers' boys and push-along wagons for transport.

All was in order. He closed the boxes and relocked them.

He said, "I'll be here to set the stage at six. Can you put someone to watch my properties between then and the time of performance? It's essential that once I've laid them out they shouldn't be touched."

"I'll see they're safe," the doorman said.

They went from the room and along a narrow, black-painted passageway to reach the stage. Some carpenters could be heard working up on the balcony, and the house lights were already on. He walked out onto the stage, and looked into the auditorium.

It was more or less as Goulston had expected. An assembly hall, rather than a playhouse. Limited space in the wings, no rake to the seats in the stalls, and a distant, shallow balcony that was like the spectators' gallery in a public swimming baths. Space and civic pride, but no intimacy. Good for a big temperance meeting with a brass band and all the lights on, but not for much else.

"I'll have a list of cues for the house electrician," Goulston said dispiritedly. "I'll need to go through them with him before the performance."

He walked forward and clapped his hands once, to gauge the acoustic. Almost immediately one of the carpenters upstairs began to hammer.

The doorkeeper waited with patience, breathing steadily and noisily through his nose.

Goulston turned to him and said, "Has anybody been asking to see a seating plan?"

"I couldn't tell thee that," the doorkeeper said. "I wouldn't know."

"Could you ask around for me? Not just about the seating. I'd like to know of anything unusual. Anything. Strangers asking questions. New wiring or mirrors fitted in odd places. Someone buying more than one ticket for tonight, but for seats in different parts of the house. I'll pay you a guinea for any information I can use."

The doorkeeper's face creased, knowingly. "I know what tha'rt after," he said. "But watch who tha asks. There's some round here, they'd take tha guinea and they'd tell thee owt."

GOULSTON LOOKED OUT across a packed and half-illuminated house and said, "Tales of ghosts and spirits have been with us since early man cowered in his cave and sought some form of expression for his fears of the darkness outside. When daylight entered the cave and the fears departed, the ghosts departed with them. Today, when mediums claim to conjure spirits, what is the first step in what they do?"

He raised his hand and, after a second's delay, the house lights began to lower.

"Are there any spirits with us tonight?"

There came a loud bang, apparently from the very air above the stalls, that electrified the house.

"Have you a message for anyone here?"

Two rapid bangs now, close together, and someone up on the balcony shrieked and giggled and was hushed.

Goulston pressed on, "Can you spell out a name for us?"

"'*Ang on*," came a sepulchral voice from midair, speaking with a local accent that was as thick as newly-dug peat, "*I've dropped me 'ammer.*"

There was a braying laugh of released tension from the audience, and Goulston lowered his hand and smiled. It was a simple effect using stereophonic speaking tubes and concealed horns, but it always set the mood. He'd refined and adapted his act considerably in the weeks of the tour, ever since that first night when he'd peeped out from behind the tabs and seen, to his dismay, that a good one-third of the night's audience had been in mourning. He'd played some tough houses in his career, but never before had he been obliged to walk out and begin his act before row upon row of stone-faced widows.

He'd made it through, all the same. Empathy was the key. They were wound up like springs, and in order to let it go they needed permission. Goulston let them believe that he understood their pain. They ached for the unknown, and the unknown was his business.

When their reaction began to die down, he went on, "To those who are here to be amused I say, you shall not be disappointed. To those who come in grief and hope—and I know that the Great War has made so many of you—I say this. See what I am about to show you, and be on your guard thereafter. Grief makes us vulnerable, and death is life's greatest mystery. All that you are about to see is achieved by natural means. You will not think it so. But that, ladies and gentlemen, is the very soul of the conjurer's art. I do not show you magic. I show you wonder."

He performed the white dove production then, sending it out from his fingertips to fly up to the rafters. During the distraction that it caused, he let his hand move back to load his next effect from the profonde in the tail of his coat.

"I stand before you as an honest deceiver," he said. "I stand here and I say, beware of those who are not."

The act ran a little over forty-five minutes. After a few simple sleights to get them warmed up he brought forward the spirit cabinet and, after having himself bound to a chair by audience volunteers, he ran through much of the old repertoire of the Davenport brothers; then he turned the cabinet around and did it all again with the back open and the interior exposed, with his volunteer observers at the back of the stage being duped in plain view. The house roared. He let them see what he was doing; but as to the exact details of the escapes and rope releases that let him do it, he left them wondering.

Then some billet reading and mentalism, a display of muscle-reading down on the floor of the hall and then, for the finale, a table levitation in which the table flew about the stage under the hands of a dozen volunteers. He revealed no more tricks after the first, and there he revealed little that wasn't either obvious or hackneyed in terms of technique. He had them, he knew. The grievers and the good-timers, all of them were his.

And then he handed them over to Frederick Kelly.

"Thank you," Kelly said. "May I ask you all for a moment of silence as I concentrate."

Despite the way that the medium had presented it to the pressmen, Kelly was the one they'd really come to see. Goulston might be the showman, but Kelly was the real draw. The advantages that he held over Goulston were of promise and challenge; for whereas Goulston assured them of the fakery they already suspected, Kelly purported to offer them genuine entry into the unknown. Bogus or not, the invitation was one that could not be resisted.

Goulston did not leave the hall, but took a position where he could observe both the audience and the stage. His purpose in this was to use his professional experience to watch for evidence of fraud. Occasionally he'd intervene and request some change or modification, like an opposing counsel.

Kelly's approach was a straightforward one, and Goulston had yet to fathom it. He used no apparatus, none of the usual routines. Walter Ward or one of the other young men of the party would bring from the audience an object, any kind of an object. Sometimes a laundered handkerchief, sometimes a pipe or a snuff-box, often it was a medal. The medals were of least use, most of them never having been handled by the recipient. Personal items were supposedly the best. Kelly would hold one for a while, and then speak about the life and sometimes the afterlife of its owner. Then the person who had brought the object would be invited to stand, and Kelly's story would be checked against the reality.

There would be gasps, sometimes. Often tears. Kelly's part of the performance rarely ran for less than three hours, and then Goulston would return to the stage where he and Kelly would stand, alone and on opposing sides of the platform, to rehearse some well-worn arguments for and against a belief in the spirit world.

Tonight it went as it almost always did. Even the audience questions had grown familiar.

"Mister Goulston," said a man of about thirty-five years old, standing halfway down the hall and wearing a long overcoat. "You've asserted that the spirits only ever bring us knowledge that is already available to us by common means. Does anything you've seen tonight alter that view?"

"No sir," Goulston said, "it does not."

"Mister Kelly was extremely detailed and convincing in a large number of his perceptions."

Goulston shaded his eyes and peered at the man, and seemed to give a start. "Sir," he said, wonderingly. "What if I were to say that I see the shade of a woman standing beside you? Her hand is on your shoulder and she looks on you with love. I believe she very much resembles your mother."

"My mother is very much alive, sir," the man said, with a glance down to his side.

"I did not say she was your mother," Goulston snapped before the audience could react. "I said she *resembled* your mother."

A mature woman, seated beside the man and partly obscured by the person before her, was heard to exclaim, "Lillian!"

"Lillian is speaking," Goulston said, "but you don't hear her. She says a name. Edward?"

"My name is Albert," said the man, extremely dark-faced.

"Then, who is Edward?"

"I do not know," the man said, seeming deliberately to ignore the woman's tugging at his sleeve.

Goulston turned to the rest of the house and said, in a passable imitation of Frederick Kelly's rising agitation, "I see Edward now. He's a young man, I see him in uniform. He looks weary. He has passed on and he is lost. Anyone. He's appealing to you. Will anyone acknowledge Edward?"

In various parts of the house, hands began to rise. Goulston nodded, and his manner abruptly changed.

"Who could deny the appeals of the dead?" he said. "Sit down, sir. And lower your hands, my friends. At least I have the grace to apologise for raising your hopes. The dead sleep on. They tell us nothing."

A man in uncomfortable-looking Sunday-best clothes stood waving his hand and, when acknowledged, said, "Are you familiar with the suggestion that spirits are actually the telepathic constructs of the living?"

"I am, sir," Goulston said. "I give it no more credence than spirit photographs or flying tambourines."

"So you're saying, then, that Mister Kelly's character is that of a cheat and a liar?"

Goulston hesitated. He did not look at Kelly who stood some yards away, content, as always, to let Goulston run the debate. Apart from having been exhausted by what he claimed was the personal toll taken by the use of his powers, he had few arguments to advance. He claimed no great understanding of his gift. It was there, he said, and it functioned, and he could explain it no better than the next man. See what you see, he would say, and judge for yourself.

Goulston could feel the tension of the house. There had to be close to a thousand faces out there, millworkers and shop workers and professional people, and their will to believe in Kelly was almost palpable. He did, after all, offer them a hope that they could carry away. What could Goulston offer them? A much colder certainty. But it was like prizes at the fair. Even though they might be worthless, who could want to go home without?

He said, "I have, in these past weeks, spent much time in Mister Kelly's company. As to his character, I believe him to be a sincere man." He looked across at Kelly then. The medium stood with his gaze directed down, swaying slightly. His shirt was damp with perspiration from the evening's efforts, and his fine hair stuck to his forehead.

Goulston was telling no less than the truth. He had entered into this arrangement without a trace of doubt that here was a fellow-practitioner who abused their common craft. Nothing in that belief had changed. But his personal impression of the man had been utterly at odds with that certainty, and he had yet to find a way to reconcile the two. Only one possible explanation had suggested itself.

"Which is to say," Goulston went on, "that I must number him among the ranks of the deceived."

THEIR LANDLADY BEING used to the hours kept by theatricals, as she called them, there was a hot supper waiting even though the hour was close to midnight. The lady's husband had been deputed to wait up and he let them in, locked the front door, showed them where to find the kitchen and then disappeared off to bed.

As ever after a show, nobody was quite ready for sleep. After they'd eaten, the two assistants went off to their shared attic room to play cards (they'd flatly refused to play with Goulston after he'd demonstrated a few simple lifts and steals and flourishes by way of a warmup on a train out of Harrogate) and Walter Ward took a table in the front parlour to check receipts and to read and sort the various messages that had been delivered to the stage door in the course of the evening. Goulston and Kelly each took a glass of port before the embers of the drawing-room fire. As always, Kelly had the wan but bright-eyed look of a man who'd just shaken off a fever and found a reason to live. After a while, Walter Ward brought in the accounts for Kelly to check, along with the letters and messages and a dampened towel on a tray.

The letters went to Goulston first. One of the conditions that he'd set was that all advance correspondence had to be held, unopened, by the theatre's management until after the performance it anticipated. He would check the seals and postmarks before passing them over. Had any been tampered with, he would know. A halfway competent medium would be able to construct an evening's revelations out of the contents of such letters alone.

The night's stage-door messages went straight to Kelly. Two or three would always contain banknotes as a sign of gratitude or support. The rest would mostly be direct appeals or invitations from which something more might follow. Goulston glanced across and said, "More donations in prospect for you, Kelly?"

"Perhaps," Kelly said as he first took the books and looked over Walter Ward's figures. "I won't deny it. Do I prostitute my gift in your eyes, Goulston?"

"You have no gift in my eyes, as well you know. You have a skill. If you'd only be content to have it recognised and admired for what it is, you and I would have no argument."

Kelly seemed not to hear or, if he did, to take no offence. "Look at these," he said, turning from the books to the first of a number of engraved visiting-cards with messages or requests written on their backs. "Tonight we had the public show for the souls of the infantry. Now even in death, the officer classes expect some privileged consideration."

Kelly did little more than glance through the notes and cards, leaving Walter Ward to make any necessary appointments and replies. He lay back and placed the dampened towel over his forehead as Goulston opened and read through a few of the notes at random.

He looked for cues, for clues, for recurrences of handwriting or paper. Many were barely literate, some were in educated hands. Private séances and the donations that followed them were almost as profitable as ticket sales, the difference being that Goulston took no share in these. He still attended when invited, as many of the requests were from prominent families and those notables in some of the larger houses. Like any professional player or performer, he never passed up an opportunity to move in exalted circles—even though the circles in some towns were rather less exalted than elsewhere. He'd go along and say his piece, and then withdraw.

He gave the letters back to Walter Ward, who inclined his head and returned with them to the drawing room.

"Ever-vigilant, eh, Will?" Kelly said as he took the linen compress from his brow and refolded it.

"You're good, Frederick, I'll give you that."

"Does the possibility of authenticity appear nowhere in your considerations?"

"You know it does not," Goulston said, taking out his pocket watch and checking the time. It was getting late.

"A scientist should exclude nothing."

"I'm no scientist."

"But you know what you know."

"I know what is real," Goulston said, preparing to rise, "and what is not."

"Oh!" said Kelly. "Then your faith is as blind as any other man's. May I?"

Kelly was holding out his hand for Goulston's watch. Goulston hesitated, then handed it to him and settled once more in his chair. But not so comfortably now, in the knowledge that he'd be moving again in a minute or so.

As Kelly turned the watch case over in his hands, Goulston said, "From where do you draw your confederates? I don't believe I've seen the same face twice."

"I have none," Kelly said with a smile, and without looking up from the timepiece. "Keep trying."

"Who scouts ahead for you?"

"You watch me all the time. I know you've had me followed. I've found the secret marks you've made on my bedroom windows. When would I ever have chance to confer?"

"I'll expose you, Frederick," Goulston said calmly. "Believe that I will."

Kelly opened the watch's cover, looked at the face, and then held it to his ear as if it was a small animal for whose heartbeat he listened. He smiled when it came.

"I can tell you one thing," he said. "If you can ever work out how I do what I do, I'll be the happiest man alive. Because it's God's own truth, Will, I do not know it." He closed the cover on Goulston's watch, and held it out to him.

"Your father's work?" he said. "I know he was a watchmaker. What better training for the design and construction of a magician's stage effects?"

Goulston took it. The metal felt warm. "That won't wash, Frederick," he said, with a warning in his voice. "Don't attempt to tell me you learned all of that from the handling of a timepiece."

Kelly laid his head back on the chair again.

"No," he said. "I learned all of that from the London *Times* when you were headlining at Maskelyne's."

Leaving Kelly to finish his port and watch the embers fall, Goulston climbed the stairs to his room. There was a streetlamp outside, and it threw a watery shadow of lace curtain across the wallpaper. Headlining at Maskelyne's. That had been two years before. Eight weeks as a featured performer at the end of a European tour that had barely broken even, but no matter; the set-up costs of the show had been immense but now the sets and properties had almost been paid for and would go on to earn him his fortune. Everything had been run-in to perfection and the show was ready, bar a few running repairs and adjustments, for an extensive North American tour. He'd moved everything to his Manchester workshop and gone ahead by liner to New York, only to learn of the fire on his arrival.

Everything had gone. Everything. The timber and canvas and size had burned with utter ferocity and made the place unapproachable. Nothing had been saved. Two people had died, along with all his animals. With every borrowed penny sunk into his show, Goulston was underinsured; he hadn't been able to envisage losing everything, all at once, and had thought instead that it would be better economy to make up any losses or damage himself as he went along.

He'd gone out to New York on a first class passage. He'd returned steerage after only two days, and had been forced to leave his hotel bill unpaid to afford even that. Now in essence he worked for Kelly, to clear his debts and to keep his name before the public until his show might be rebuilt.

Whenever that might be.

Goulston drew the curtains in his room, splashed his face at the washstand, and tried the bed. It was cold and lumpy and smelled of new laundry, with a weight of covers that would hold him down like six feet of dirt over a tomb.

Perfect. He slept better than he had in a week.

THE NEXT MORNING, Goulston bought all of the northern newspaper editions that he could find and set himself up at a corner table in Booth's

Café where he could read through them undisturbed. Frederick Kelly was still up at the boarding house. He would seldom rise before noon, claiming the need to recover from his evening's exertions. Sheer sloth, was Goulston's interpretation. Once awake, Kelly would rarely go out but would spend the afternoon writing letters or reading. He found it difficult to walk abroad without gathering a crowd, some merely curious but most wanting a part of his attention for some pressing and personal need. He couldn't begin to satisfy them all. He'd once spent an hour simply trying to cross the lobby of a large hotel. So instead he stayed in, and only ventured out to keep appointments or to make unannounced evening visits to local spiritualist circles.

A strange kind of professional, in Goulston's view. The very inverse of a showman. No mauve limousine, no monkeys, not even a visiting card. Something new in the art of misdirection, perhaps.

Kelly never even troubled to read his notices.

There was a piece in the early edition of the Northern Telegraph, something in the Standard, one in the Times. Only the Telegraph man gave a good account of Goulston's involvement. Out of interest, he then turned to the advertising and announcements to see who might be playing at the local halls. There were some names that he knew, but no one that he cared to look up. Selbit was touring, he noted, but it was advance publicity with no firm dates. Selbit was the magician who had taken up a five-hundred-pound spirit challenge from the Sunday Express and fooled a committee that had included Conan Doyle. When the truth had been revealed, the committee had clung to its belief in the clairvoyant demonstration and expressed doubt over the explanation. Selbit's tour was built around his new sawing-through-a-lady illusion.

And good luck to him, Goulston thought, and made a face which caused the waitress to look twice.

Not for the first time, his thoughts turned to his difficulties over Kelly.

Frederick Kelly was artless, and from Goulston's point of view that was the problem. He simply did what he did, with no apparent technique. One of Goulston's theories was that Kelly might be a kind of *idiot savant* of the craft, functioning in a way that even he himself didn't fully recognise. This

was an explanation that had gained ground in his mind of late. It allowed
for Kelly's sincerity without opening a door into realms of patent unreality.
Exactly how the man worked was something that Goulston had still to determine. The method had almost certainly been staring him in the face from
the beginning, and was no doubt elegant and utterly simple. Simplicity was
always the hardest to spot.

And when he spotted it, what then? He'd have to sink the raft on which
he stood. End of tour, end of contract, end of income. And he'd do it, as well.
His pride would allow nothing less. He'd come to realise that until then he'd
be like some emasculated courtier, not a true and principled opponent at all.
His function here, he'd realised, was to fail; and in his continuing failure, to
prove Kelly's authenticity so that the show could go on and the temple could
eventually rise.

That evening, he put on a clean shirt and his formal wear and accompanied Kelly and Walter Ward to one of the large houses that overlooked the
east side of the town's Corporation Park. It was the house of the Graingers,
a family whose money came from three generations of rope-making in the
town. The pattern was familiar to Goulston. A son had been lost in the war.
Bereavement so sudden, so out of time, and at such a distance...it evaded
the normal processes of grief and left people suspended, uncertain, unable to
respond. They'd fall gratefully upon someone like Frederick Kelly, as those
lost in a strange land might fall upon an English-speaking guide.

A housemaid showed them through a stained-glass vestibule into a pleasant, panelled hallway, where Mrs Grainger emerged to greet them. She was
well-spoken and well-mannered, graceful but without pretensions. She introduced them to her sister Dora Isabel and her daughter Enid, and directed
their attention to the wall where hung a picture of her son James in his uniform. The picture's oval frame had been draped with black crepe ribbon.
James had been a smooth and good-looking boy, in the manner of all who
had sat for such photographs. Smooth and good-looking boys just like him
had gone to their deaths in their thousands.

They moved into the drawing-room, which had been prepared for the
séance. Goulston introduced himself, and gave the short lecture-demonstration

that he always gave on such occasions. He sought to inform rather than to entertain, and to encourage a healthy scepticism in Kelly's audience-to-be. He showed them how a glass could move, how a table could be turned and tilted. He demonstrated rappings. Kelly stood there nodding, he realised. Kelly seemed entirely on his side.

"Spirit effects are fashionable tricks," he concluded. "They did not exist before they were devised. The skills used are exactly those I have shown you. If all expect the table to turn, it will turn without help."

Through all of this, Enid Grainger had been watching with great intensity and Goulston had found himself responding to her attention, to the extent that he'd had to remind himself to favour the others equally. Now she said, "Will you be staying for the séance, Mister Goulston?"

"No, Miss Grainger," he told her. "I've said all that I can say."

He walked the half-mile or so back to the boarding house. He felt like a drink, but he was overdressed for any of the public houses or hotels that he passed.

So grave. So serious.

He found himself envying Frederick Kelly for the comfort which he would be bringing to Enid Grainger and which he, Will Goulston, could not. All that Goulston could offer her was the certainty that her pain had no remedy.

And who, anywhere in this world, could find a shred of comfort in that?

OVER BREAKFAST THE next morning, he managed to quiz Walter Ward on the progress of the séance. It had, from Ward's account, been one of Kelly's finer performances. Mrs Grainger had fainted and the evening had ended in great consternation all around, with neighbours hearing the cries and summoning the police.

At ten, soberly dressed, Will Goulston presented himself at the house and was again shown inside. Mrs Grainger consented to see him, and he waited in a first-floor library that contained a number of rare-looking coins and documents and illustrated manuscripts under glass. The collection of Mr Grainger, he supposed. According to Walter Ward, Grainger had busied himself in this room after refusing to attend any séance, and had appeared amidst the uproar to insist that it ended and to forbid any repetition.

"Mrs Grainger," Goulston said respectfully as the lady appeared. She was pale and her eyes were reddened, but she held herself with dignity.

"If you are here to debate with me, Mister Goulston," she said, "I will have to decline."

"I am here to enquire after your health. I understand the evening was a harrowing one for you."

She hesitated and then inclined her head, as if in apology for her mis-apprehension. She said, "My son died a terrible death in a terrible place. We relived it in his presence last night. Mister Kelly tells us that we helped to bring his soul to peace by doing so."

"My warnings meant nothing to you, then."

"I wish you had stayed. You might now understand more. My health is good. My mind is calm. I have a strength I did not have before. Nothing in your parlour tricks could bring me to this."

Goulston descended the stairs to find, not only the housemaid waiting to hand him his hat and stick, but Enid Grainger as well.

She said, "May I ask you a question, Mister Goulston?"

"Of course."

"Have you never considered that your participation in these events may validate Mister Kelly's work far more than it can debunk it?"

"I struggle with that thought, Madam," Goulston said. "Believe that I do."

She seemed in no hurry to see him go. She said, "Mister Kelly seemed drained last night. Is that common?"

"It would appear to be. He's an enthusiastic performer."

"He did none of the things you talked about. He wouldn't even have us turn out the lights."

"I'm aware of that," Goulston said.

"I feel the need of air. Would you walk with me through the park?"

Goulston declared himself at her service. She disappeared and returned a few minutes later, dressed for outdoors and carrying a spray of cut flowers from the garden which she laid along her arm.

Once outside, they crossed the street and entered the park by its East Gate. The slope of the land here had been tamed a little by terracing and landscaping, but still the park fell away to a wide and open view across the slate-and-soot vista of the roofs and chimneys of the town. Here a broad promenade passed above formal gardens, while below could be seen a band-stand and a succession of ornamental ponds.

Enid Grainger said, "My mother is utterly convinced."

"And you?"

"I have an open mind. I believe it's important to have an open mind on everything. You don't."

The assertion took Goulston aback slightly. "How so?" he said.

"You're certain he's a fraud and you've set out to prove it. That doesn't sound like an open mind to me. That's like a scientist who fixes his result and then rejects the experiment that doesn't give it."

"I'm not a scientist, ma'am," Goulston said, doing his best to hide his irritation. "I'm a common man with a common man's sense. The only thing that sets me apart from a common man is the knowledge of how these effects are achieved."

"That sounds rather like a person trying to make a virtue out of ignorance."

"Let me try to explain it." They descended a flight of stone steps that would lead them down from the garden terraces and into the landscaped field at the heart of the park. Miss Grainger seemed to know where she was going, and Goulston was happy to go where she led.

He said, "When I was a boy, I saw the great Kellar on tour. I sat through the show three times and I was convinced that his powers were genuine. I left my seat and tried to get backstage to see if it was true, but they were used to boys like me. It was two years before I was able to watch a magician work. That was at the Salford Hippodrome, in nineteen hundred and one. He was old and he drank, but he was a craftsman. And I watched the secrets unfold, one by one, and I saw...that they were nothing. Most of them were so simple, just a matter of timing and misdirection…and preparation. Preparation was everything. I felt then that I had a vocation. To make such wonder out of dust seemed to me like one of the most subtle achievements of man. But the wonder lies in that moment of uncertainty. It's a trick. But how can it be? And what Frederick Kelly and all the other false mediums do is to betray that moment. They betray my vocation. They tell you yes, it is so, when they *know* it is not. They show you false heavens where the dead wander and spout rubbish. And my sense at that betrayal is one of outrage."

Enid Grainger said drily, "I take it you give no credence to any part of the spirit world."

"No."

"No kernel of truth, obscured by the deceits of the ill-intentioned?"

Again: "No."

Now they had crossed the open spaces, a matter of a hundred yards or so, and had picked up the carriage drive that would lead them on down to the lowest point of the park. The drive was scattered with yellow seeds and shaded by overhanging trees that threw patterns of gently-moving light across the ground.

Here Enid said, "Did you go to war, Mister Goulston?"

"I was in uniform," Goulston said.

"But did you go to the front?"

Uncomfortable now, Goulston found some cause to look at the ground and said, "The army looked at a showman and saw a recruitment officer. I toured the halls with a call to arms. I did not go to the front. But many of the boys who died there were sent to it by the likes of me."

But Enid was not seeking to embarrass him, nor to question his courage. She'd another purpose in mind.

She said earnestly, "James wrote in his letters of a wondrous happening at the Battle of Mons. He had it direct from a man who'd been there."

Goulston nodded his head, slowly. "The Angels of Mons."

"You know of this?"

"The bowmen of Agincourt appeared in the sky and rescued British troops whose retreat had been blocked. It's a tale."

"I am telling you it is true. The bodies of Prussian soldiers were found with the wounds of arrows."

"It was a published fiction, Miss Grainger. It's there in the files of the Evening News for anyone to check."

"So how, then, were these arrow wounds caused?"

Goulston was helpless. "What would you force me to say?"

"That my brother was a liar?" she said, almost daring him to agree.

"Your brother was misled," Goulston said. "The tale was a persuasive one. There is something in us all that aches to believe. A well-chosen tale can sway millions."

They were almost at the park's ornate lower gateway now. But here, revealed to view as they followed the curve of the driveway, stood a few square yards that had been set aside to create a garden of remembrance.

In the garden was a War Memorial. Behind an oval pool fed by twin fountains stood a larger-than-life bronze on a plinth, showing a young woman draped in folds of cloth who appeared to be raising one of the dead or wounded to his feet. Already the bronze was beginning to darken and turn green, as if the entire construction was being absorbed by the nature that surrounded it. From somewhere behind came the tumbling sound of a stream running down the hillside and through the trees. The trees were waxen-leaved evergreens.

They stood in silence, looking up at it for a while.

Then Enid said, "And how do you stand on the Resurrection, Mister Goulston? Was that another trick, or another myth distorted in the retelling?"

Such was dangerous ground, and Goulston declined to walk upon it.

"I'm no theologian, Miss Grainger," he said.

"Suddenly, no," she observed. "But don't worry. I shan't embarrass you further."

She laid the cut flowers with others that had been placed on the stones before the pool. The flowers for the boys that had no tombs, who slept in anonymous communion with their brothers. James had been brought home, as far as Goulston understood, and buried in the family grave in the town cemetery.

As they were walking back, Enid said to him, "You don't seem like a happy man to me, Mister Goulston. I wonder whether it might have been different for you if the boy had stayed in his seat."

THAT EVENING—HIS LAST in the town—Goulston sat quietly behind his whisky and soda in the bar of the White Bull Hotel until someone recognised him, after which he was drawn into performing some table magic for the other patrons. He was hardly in the mood, but he rose to the occasion. But then they started pressing him to repeat some of the effects, which he would not do, and then someone tried to catch him out by snatching away the handkerchief during a coin exchange, after which he contained his anger and made a cool and courteous withdrawal.

Walking back through the night-lit streets, past the silent marketplace and across the tramlines before the old Cotton Exchange Hall, he felt as if some force were compressing his temples and weighing heavy on his heart. He felt as if the direction of his life had become a punishment for something that he was not even aware of having done. It was unfair. Kelly fed them guff, and they were happy. Goulston shone the light of truth into their darkness, and they turned from him.

He didn't choose the truth. The truth was there. And it stayed there, whether they chose to acknowledge it or not.

For once, he found, he was starting to envy them. Almost wishing not to know what he knew, almost aching to share the uncomplicated bliss of their ignorance.

To be the little boy, back in his seat, and never to have sneaked backstage at all.

Walter Ward was writing letters in the drawing-room. "Where's Kelly tonight?" Goulston asked him.

"He went with a Mr Tyrell to give a reading at a local temple. He left you the address, for if you cared to have him followed."

Goulston went upstairs and sat on his bed for a while and then, unable to settle or rest, he put on his coat and went out again.

The spiritualist meeting was in an unassuming back-street hall with a sign over the door. The sign had been lettered with more love than skill, and was misspelled. The door was open to all.

Goulston went through a tiny cloakroom with a stove in it, and emerged into a place that was like a raftered, high-ceilinged schoolroom. Union flags and bunting hung across from wall to wall, leftovers of some past celebration. There were dark wooden benches on a plain board floor. The seating was about two-thirds filled. Goulston moved into the shadows beyond the pillars at the side of the room.

Kelly was up at the front, speaking. A working woman of about fifty years old stood beside him and he held her by the hand, his other on her shoulder. Goulston glanced at the rest of the crowd. They were ordinary people. Just ordinary people.

"I see green," Kelly was saying. "The colour green."

"His favourite coat was green," the woman said.

"Don't help me! This is a field. It's on the side of a hill but it's so smooth. It doesn't look real. The sky's a deep blue. Deep, like…like iron, when you cut it."

The place was freezing. Why was it so cold? All this stone, and only the heat of the gaslights. But no one seemed to mind. Kelly would be working this crowd for no reward. He did this everywhere. The idly curious could pay into the cause, but to the genuinely dedicated he gave and asked nothing.

The door opened again, and Goulston glanced toward it. Everyone else kept their attention on Frederick Kelly. Two young women entered and quickly made for the nearest available seats; there was a moment's lapse in time and then Goulston recognised them. Enid Grainger, and the maidservant from the big house.

He felt shocked. He couldn't have explained why, but he did. Enid hadn't seen him. Her eyes were on Kelly and she was pulling off her gloves, settling in.

Goulston knew that look. It was the look of the lost. The look of those who, instead of seeing the world as it really was, preferred to gaze out into the vaguest of mists where they could imagine a sunlit landscape of ghosts and unicorns.

Staying out in that part of the hall beyond the pillars, he moved to the door in order to leave. As he reached it he heard Frederick Kelly calling his name.

No. This was the last thing that he wanted.

But he turned.

"You don't have to leave us, Will," Kelly said. "There may be something here for you."

"I don't believe so, Frederick," Goulston said, uncomfortably aware that every face in the hall was now turning toward him. He wouldn't look down and meet Enid Grainger's eyes, but he knew that she'd turned and was gazing on him too.

"You walked the streets to get here," Kelly called to him, "but you don't walk alone. You think you do, but you don't."

"Please," Goulston said with a pained expression, and threw open the door to the cloakroom.

Kelly's raised voice pursued him.

"I can't give you what you need," Kelly called after him. "No one can. You create wonders for others, but you've lost the faculty of wonder in yourself. It doesn't matter what shape your faith takes, Will. What matters is that you have some capacity for it in any form."

These last words followed him almost out onto the pavement. And then Kelly was in the doorway, in his waistcoat and shirtsleeves, and he was holding onto the sides and calling out after him.

"He cries tears for you, Will," Kelly shouted down the street. "They're not of pain or of joy. I don't understand them. But his tears run black. Does that mean anything to you, Will? His tears run black!"

Goulston made a sound that he meant to be defiant, but which came out like a growl of pain.

Goulston ran. He turned a corner, saw the lights of a public house, and slowed. He smoothed down his clothes, got a grip on himself, tried to control his breathing. He drank in moderation, but never had he felt the need for a drink as he felt it now.

He pushed open the doors and went inside. The warmth of the place stung his eyes. He pushed through to the bar and ordered himself a glass of whisky.

Of course the tears ran black. It was the black of soot and mucous.

For the coroner had told him that when his father had died it was the smoke from the burning paints and canvases, not the heat or the flames, that had first choked and then killed him.

He swallowed the whisky, let it burn its way through him. And then he looked around.

He remembered this place. Ten years before. The Theatre Royal stood next door, and this was where the artistes came to drink. He searched for any face he might know.

Then he spied one.

And as recognition dawned, something else—akin to elation, not far from disbelief—began to rise in him and swell.

THE NERVOUS-LOOKING MAN in the shabby clothes stood before a hastily-convened gathering in the offices of the Northern Telegraph and, turning his hat in his hands, said his piece.

"I have been a confederate of Mister Kelly's," he told his audience. "I would go in advance to the towns where he planned to appear. I would intercept letters that people would send to him. I would read them and then place them in new envelopes and send them through the post a second time so that they would appear not to have been tampered with. I'd get other names from newspaper files and from recent headstones and sometimes I would pass out free tickets in public houses to be sure that the right people came."

The man from the Telegraph said, "Why are you making this confession?"

The ill-fitted man glanced toward the figure by the door.

"Mister Goulston recognised me last night," he said. "I have done similar work in the past for mind reading acts and mentalists. I specialised in being a plant or a confederate for a number of magicians. I had the look and I could carry it off. Ours is a small world. Goulston knew me of old. He bought me a drink and we talked. I was on my guard, but he tricked me into confessing."

"Does Kelly have any psychic powers at all, to your knowledge?"

"Ask Goulston," the man said.

Well, that was it. It was over. The man went on to respond to some detailed questions with dates and case histories, but as far as Goulston was concerned the job was at an end. He left the offices and spent an hour at King George's Hall securing his properties and exercising his doves before arranging the dispatch of everything to the station, and then he gave two interviews over lunch in the Adelphi Hotel alongside the Telegraph's offices on Station Square. By the time that he returned to the boarding house to pick up his luggage, the late editions were out and the word was all around. There was a crowd in front of the boarding house, and an ugly crowd at that. He pushed his way through and learned that Frederick Kelly had left some time before, making a hasty exit through the back yards behind the buildings to avoid attention.

When Goulston brought his bags downstairs to the hallway, he found Enid Grainger there hearing much the same story from the landlady.

She looked at Goulston as if dazed.

"I am dismayed," she said.

"I'm sorry."

Enid made an effort to gather herself. She held up an envelope, unsealed. She said, "I had this draft to give to Mister Kelly. How will I get it to him now?"

"Mister Kelly is exposed," Goulston said gently. "The charade is over."

"Then he will need his friends more than ever," Enid said, offering the envelope and leaving him with no choice but to receive it. "Please see this safely into his hands."

Goulston began to attempt to protest, but already she was turning away. "Miss Grainger," he began, but she was walking out of the door without a backward glance.

He took a look inside the envelope. She could hardly have intended it to be a secret, or she'd have sealed the flap before handing it to him.

It was a Banker's Order, left open, for the sum of eight hundred pounds.

Goulston's mind reeled. What moved these people to the extent that, despite discredit and disgrace, they persisted in their sympathy and support? No truth, no logic could touch them. Now Enid had made him responsible for a sum that could have bought out the very house in which he was standing. His impulse was to chase her down the street and hand it back.

But he could not bring himself to do it.

He'd heard that Frederick Kelly had travelled to Preston in the hope of avoiding notice at the railway station there, but when Goulston arrived by taxi it was to find that another mob had tracked him down and, by one means or another, had managed to get onto the platforms and were gathered outside the waiting-room where Kelly and his party now hid. The police had been brought in to keep order, and their uniformed presence was considerable. They presented an intimidating wall of blue to the crowd, and refused Goulston entry until one of them recognised him from his photograph in the newspaper. The wall parted, the crowd yelled, and Goulston squeezed through with his collar split and his hat gone missing. He stumbled as he fell in through the door, and a hand caught and helped him.

The hand was Frederick Kelly's.

"They're like dogs," he told Goulston as he raised him to his feet. "Right now they'll tear at anything that moves."

The windows of the waiting-room were of obscured glass, like those of a saloon bar. They admitted light and a sense of the turmoil outside, but none of the details. Goulston did his best to straighten himself as Kelly stepped back and looked on. He didn't know what to say.

He said, "Do you have adequate protection?"

Kelly gave a slight shrug. "I'll change trains," he said.

Goulston made a helpless gesture, and said, "I'm sorry, Frederick. This is not as I'd expected."

"I had far to fall. Why did you come?"

Goulston glanced across the waiting-room. Walter Ward sat there, head down, lost in his own concerns. Of the two paid assistants there was no sign.

Goulston pulled out the envelope and said, "I was placed under an obligation. Miss Grainger asked me to give you this."

Kelly took it and briefly checked the contents, but beyond that he seemed to give it little attention. "I thought you might have more to say."

"It's over. Nothing to be said."

But Kelly obviously thought differently.

He said, "Why?"

He was looking at Goulston with complete intensity, and Goulston had to look away.

Kelly said, "If you were so sure of your case, why didn't you put some trust in it? Why resort to this?"

Goulston gave him no answer. Kelly moved closer to him, and put his face only inches from Goulston's own.

"Who was he, Will? One of your old employees? One of your own confederates, or just someone you could trust to perform the lines that you gave him?"

"I had to end this farce," Goulston said, his voice almost a whisper. "Conscience demanded it. I'd have exposed you in the end. All I did was make it sooner, and cut down on the mountain of lies."

"But don't you see? You've robbed only yourself. Now you can never know for certain."

Somebody blew a whistle outside. A dark-uniformed arm came up against the glass as if out of a fog, and rapped against it hard. Kelly's train was about to depart, and it was time to get him onto it. Walter Ward was getting to his feet. He seemed slow, broken.

"Tell me, then," Goulston said with urgency. "Now that you have nothing to lose. Tell me how it was done."

Kelly drew himself up straight. In the midst of everything, he seemed almost composed. He said, "You're sincere in your way, Will. How can I blame you for doing wrong when you don't know how wrong you are?" He looked at the banker's draft, still in his hand. "There'll be no temple now," he said, and then he leaned forward and stuffed it into Goulston's handkerchief pocket.

"Tour's cancelled," Kelly said. "I can't meet your contract any more. But you can rebuild your act with this. I know it's important to you."

"Are you mocking me?" Goulston said. He'd meant it to sound indignant, but somehow he failed.

"No," Frederick Kelly said. "I'm forgiving you."

The waiting-room door slammed inward then, and a corridor of uniformed bodies showed the way across the platform to the waiting train. Beyond the corridor was a sea of snarling faces and waving fists. Kelly went out without hesitating, and the uniforms immediately closed around him and carried him forward; the mob went after and Kelly was almost lost to Goulston's sight, buffeted and borne along until he reached the carriage door. Kelly was hauled up and pushed inside, the door was slammed, and the policemen formed a line to hold the crowd back from the carriage as the train made ready to depart. Other doors could be heard slamming all the way down the platform, and then the guard's whistle sounded. Goulston could see Kelly through the window now.

The train began to move, and the angry crowd broke through and tried to keep pace with Kelly's compartment. Their rage seemed to be formless, reasonless, something abstract that opportunity had made personal. They beat on the windows. Kelly was looking down, and he didn't react.

Goulston watched him go. He didn't see Kelly raise his eyes, or look back.

Five minutes later, the platform was clear. Walter Ward had scuttled out and boarded the train somewhere further along. Only Goulston remained. Steam and coal smoke were dispersing from the empty track.

He waited around for a while, but there was nothing left to do or see. He found his trampled hat. It was almost as if he was reluctant to tear himself from the spot.

But finally he moved, walking to the end of the platform and climbing the steps toward the station exit. He did not feel as he'd expected to feel. He could not have explained how he was feeling at all.

On the far side of the ticket hall, the conjurer hesitated. It was a fair day and there was a fine breeze. There was nothing to regret. He had done no wrong. With this thought running insistently through his mind, Will Goulston walked onward and out into a world without angels.

Men and women moved by, heads down, lost in their own concerns. Goulston moved through them, unseen. It didn't take a Frederick Kelly to attune to their thoughts. They ached for some comfort, as he'd said to Enid

Grainger. And how hard they found it to accept that the ache did not prove the existence of some remedy.

People could not quite bring themselves to believe in the death that surrounded them, that was the root of the problem.

But oh…how they longed to believe in the dead.

Life
LINE

I STOOD BY THE phone booth while Ryan made his call, watching the Camden Town traffic and only occasionally glancing his way to see how he was getting along. He was standing with the phone to one ear and a finger stuck in the other, and he was almost having to shout to make himself heard. Ryan being intense always looked like a schoolboy getting excited over a packet of stamps. Hardly surprising I should think that way, because this was almost how long I'd known him; we'd met at Art College and hung around a lot together over the years since.

Too many years, I was beginning to feel. And probably too much hanging around, as well.

Even the best traffic can lose its fascination pretty quickly, so then I turned to look through one of the broken side-windows of the booth. There were dayglo stickers all over the back wall behind the phone, each the size of an envelope label and all offering personal services that were either improper, immoral, illegal, or physically improbable. Some were printed, but all the phone numbers were handwritten. Ryan must have landed either a really bad line or a really thick tele-ad girl, because he was having to repeat his entire message with painful slowness.

"Suitable for spares," he was saying, "No MOT," and then he faltered and came over with such a look of utter blankness that I could only assume that she'd asked him how to spell it.

I love those stickers. Big busty blonde and madame de paris and shy schoolgirl needing correction. All the professional ladies that I've ever seen have reminded me of somebody's grandmother, except for the Awaydays who come in by train from the provinces and do the hotels and then go back to their unsuspecting husbands, and they've always reminded me of prim little typists on an outing. Not that I've ever made a study of the subject, you understand.

I read on; horny black bitch. randy mandy. venus in chains. You dial the number, you make your assignation, you dream Jane Fonda, you meet somebody who looks like a tortoise in a fright wig and they bring their own handcuffs.

Nutcracker. See Niagara falls. tv/rubber/pvc/leather, fantasy cp, uniforms/dom.

And there, almost hidden from sight under the directory shelf; life line. I may have wondered what it meant, briefly. I know that it barely stayed in my memory at the time.

Ryan came out, looking slightly punchy, and he gave me back some change. As we turned toward the Parkway I said, "Just explain something to me."

"Name it," he said.

"You just placed an ad with your phone number in it, which kind of suggests that you've still got a phone. So why drag me out here and sting me for the price of a call?"

"Simple," Ryan said, and he took a deep breath of road air as if he'd just been set loose in the country somewhere. Parkway lorries rumbled on by like a dinosaur herd. "If I miss a meal here and a meal there, I can just about afford the rental."

"So have the phone taken out, and eat more often."

He gave me a look which seemed to suggest that all the patience in the world wouldn't be enough to lead me to the obvious. " I couldn't do that," he said. "Belinda might call."

I wanted to say something. Honestly I did.

But I couldn't.

We ended up about half an hour later in a poky little café somewhere around the back of St Pancras Station, one of those hole-in-the-wall places where everybody crams in shoulder to shoulder and the old pair in the tiny space behind the counter shuffle around on bad feet after years of standing. The tea was lousy and the place had all the charm of a *pissoir*, but it was cheap.

I said, "I'll stand you a sandwich," which under the circumstances should have been about as welcome as a death threat, but Ryan brightened. I guessed that he probably hadn't eaten at all that day; blown all his giro on riotous living, no doubt.

"You're a saint," he said.

"Don't believe it. I'll be around to collect when the car gets sold."

"You're still a saint, but don't hold your breath."

We got the corner table and settled ourselves in. I didn't really expect ever to be paid back. Ryan's car, his last and only asset, stood on four flats in a borrowed garage and had a family of cats living in its engine compartment. Ryan himself wasn't in very much better shape. At least I made the effort to pick up some undeclared income whenever I could, but ever since Belinda had gone away Ryan's life had been steadily falling apart like a wreck trying to roll home unaided from the demolition derby. Don't get me wrong, Belinda was no picture—at least, not to anybody's eyes other than Ryan's—but he missed her with a grief that was almost more than his underfed and under-sized body could hold. She'd been plain and a little too heavy for a woman so young; in fact they'd been an odd-looking pair altogether, but somehow they'd found each other and been as devoted as a couple of dogs'-home strays after a Monday-morning rescue. Their breakup had been sudden and dramatic. I didn't know what was behind it, but Ryan had told me that it was over nothing and I could well believe it. They'd been in so deep that they were as touchy and insecure as fifteen-year-olds; now Belinda was gone, and Ryan was going hungry to keep on paying his phone rental on the off chance she'd call.

The food came, and he went at it like a stoker. I said, "You won't be seeing me around much for the next few weeks. I've picked up a job."

"Doing what?"

"Exhibition work."

"Design?"

"Nah, just putting up and taking down. Calls for a pair of hands, a back, and no brain. Nothing you'd want to put in the CV, but it's cash in hand and no questions asked."

He gave a faint, faraway smile and said, "Couldn't put in a word for me if the chance comes up, could you?"

"I will if I can," I said. "But you know how it is."

Yeah. I think we both knew how it was.

Later, when we'd worn out our welcome and taken ourselves out onto the street before we could be ejected there, we walked along for a while and talked about the old days again and finally reached the midpoint where there was nothing to do other than split up and go our separate ways.

Ryan said, "Well, I'd better get back. See if there's anything new on the answering machine."

"You've got an answering machine?"

"Office surplus. Dirt cheap, but it works."

"What do you want it for? You never go anywhere."

"Not often. But now when I do, I'll be covered if Belinda calls."

I couldn't let this go by. Not twice, in one day.

I said, "Belinda's dead, Ryan."

But again, he smiled a little, as if mine was a common ignorance that he'd just about learned to put up with, and he gave me a brief wave as he backed off and then turned in the direction of home.

I DIDN'T GET to see him for a while after that. Every morning I was down in Soho before eight, waiting for the van that would pick me up and take me out to Olympia, and every night I'd be dropped off in the same area sometime after six and often later. I was mostly working with strangers, raising frames and rigging lights and laying cable ready for some kind of a home computer show. It wasn't exactly skilled work, but it wasn't tough and it was all indoors.

I think it was on a Thursday evening that I hopped down out of the van just as someone familiar was coming out of a Wardour Street newsagents' with a sports bag slung over his shoulder and a copy of The Stage in his hand; I said, "Hey, Lyle, what's new?" and stepped through the usual pile of trash and cardboard boxes to reach the usable part of the pavement. We walked on more or less together, although the pavement was narrow and there was a lot of dodging around involved.

Lyle scowled and said, "I'm wearing roller skates to serve hamburgers and I'm telling people with salad in their teeth to have a nice day. Life's fucking wonderful. What's new with you?"

So I told him about the job and then said, "Seen Ryan around the house?"

"Seen him? I'm halfway to strangling him."

"For what?"

"He's right above me. His boards creak, he never sleeps. When he isn't walking the floor, he's on the phone."

"But he told me never uses the phone."

"Well, then, he's talking to himself. I'd say he was on something, if I didn't know how broke he was."

We headed up toward the lights of Oxford Street, a little faster than the taxis that were jammed nose-to-tail in the roadway alongside us. Lyle was a dancer, and probably regarded waiting on tables with the same kind of feeling that I had for my own efforts with a staple gun. I said, "Perhaps he isn't broke. I know he was selling his car..."

"Yeah, was," Lyle said. "The day the ad came out, someone called him and fixed up to see it. When he got to the garage, they'd already been and gone and the car with them. Now he's got no car and a bill for a busted door and he's more broke than ever."

Walking home across town, I started to wonder. I wondered how Ryan might have taken this, on top of everything else. I wondered if I ought to overcome my growing reluctance and make the effort to seek him out and try to raise his spirits yet again.

But mostly, I wondered how they'd managed to get the damned car started.

∽

AT THE WEEKEND, I got a call.

The nurse from across the landing came and knocked on my door, and I hurried down to the pay phone in the hallway.

"It's me," Ryan said.

"Astonishing," I said.

"I've been trying to call you since yesterday."

"I've been working."

"Still? Anyway, I need your help."

I leaned against the wall, suddenly feeling somewhat weary. "Go on," I said, "I'm listening."

"Can you come over?"

"It's my day off. I'm really whacked."

"Please," he wheedled, and Ryan wheedling is a terrible sound to have echoing in your guilty dreams, so in the end I said, "Give me half an hour."

It was actually an hour before I got there, because I was damned if I was going to come running. I'd helped Ryan through just about every one of his life's crises in the last ten years, from his lousy diploma marks to the day that Belinda's unrecognisable body had come home in a welded coffin. I don't know exactly what it was between us. I didn't even always like him, that much. But he could be so hopeless in so many ways—some people can square themselves and walk away from someone like that, but I've never been one of them. Lousy luck, I know, but there it is.

His flat had never been much to look at. Now there was even less of it. I didn't ask straight out, but I was pretty sure that he must have been selling off pieces of the landlord's furniture to raise a few scrapings of cash. As he ushered me in I saw a big empty room with just a sofa bed, a table and a couple of kitchen chairs; a Belling cooker and a sink were half-hidden behind a curtain in the corner alcove. His hi-fi and his portable TV had gone along the same route as his cameras, many months before. Now the phone and the linked-in answering machine stood alone on the table—alone, that is, apart from a buff-coloured window envelope that couldn't be anything other than a bill.

"It's this," he said, and he picked the bill up and held it out. He looked thinner than he'd been, and red-eyed as if he hadn't been sleeping much.

"What am I supposed to do with it?"

"Open it for me. Please."

This was it? Ryan had broken into my weekend, not merely out of friendship or because he missed seeing me around, but because neither he nor any other soul in North London had the requisite skill for the opening of an envelope with a Telecom overprinting? Well, naturally I was flattered.

"Fuck off, Ryan," I said, and threw it back at him.

He fumbled and then caught it and said, "Please. I know it sounds stupid, but I can't bring myself to open it."

"Couldn't you ask Lyle? At least he's only downstairs."

"He'd think I was an idiot."

"I think you're an idiot."

"I know, but you're different."

In the end I had to do it, or we'd have carried on like this for the rest of the afternoon. I ripped the envelope open, threw out the junk that they always put in along with the bill, and folded out the main paper and read it aloud.

I said, "You've got basic rental. You've got two engineers' test calls. You've got VAT." I scanned it over again, just to be sure. "And that appears to be it."

Ryan looked blank. He looked like a man who'd just surprised himself and shit a billiard ball. He reached for the bill, took it from me, and studied it hard.

I said, "What were you expecting?"

"Pull up a chair," he said, "and I'll tell you."

ANYBODY TAKING A look in through the window from the top deck of a passing bus would have seen first a smeary layer of grime, and then beyond that the two of us sitting head-to-head across the table like a couple of chess players in a championship. As he talked, Ryan kept pushing a hand through his thinning hair. Belinda used to cut it for him, once; I don't think scissors had been near it since.

"You remember how it was, the last time we met? That was the day I placed the ad." I remembered. "Well, I hit a low patch after that, not just because of what happened with the car but because of that and everything else. I didn't want to call you because I didn't want to be a pain in the arse. You're the best friend I've got, and I think I was starting to wear out my welcome. I mooched around for a few days, but I couldn't get it together. I'd heard about Life Line, but I didn't want to risk using the phone. And then I thought what the hell, if it's either that or a rope over the rafters let's give them a try."

"Who?"

"Life Line. You never heard of it?"

"I've heard the name, I just don't know what it is."

"It's kind of… I don't know how you'd describe it. You call the number, and there's an operator who puts you into a conversation with about half a dozen other people."

"Yeah," I said, "you're talking about a chat line. They got banned, didn't they?"

"Not banned. I mean they can't be banned, or it wouldn't be there. They go for a lower profile now, that's all. And Life Line isn't like the others; it isn't listed and they don't advertise. They say it's only for the right kind of people and you wouldn't believe it, but somehow they find their way in."

I really didn't know what to say. What, exactly, were the 'right kind of people'? If Ryan was anything to go by, I wouldn't have cared to meet a bunch of them all together in the back room of a pub. Don't get me wrong, Ryan was a friend; but one of him was enough for anybody.

And now I had to hand it to him because when he decided to fall, he certainly went the distance. The big problem with the chat lines had always been that it was too easy to be seduced into forgetting that there was a meter running and it ran at premium rates, calculated by the minute. Kids were calling when their parents were out, office phones would start ringing up the charges when the afternoons got slack. And cost wasn't the only problem;

there was supposed to be monitoring, but people still managed to talk dirty and make dates. Paedophiles would hook into the teenaged lines and sit listening and jerking off to the sound of girl talk.

Ryan said, "It's not what you'd expect."

"So, what gets talked about?"

"Life. Dreams. The things you want to be, instead of what you are. I can't explain it to you."

"It's a ripoff, Ryan."

"I know it is. But I can't help it."

"How deep are you in?"

"This deep," he said, and he got up from the table and went over to the sofa bed. He came back with a box that I recognised as the one in which he'd always kept his music collection. And still did, I supposed from the rattle of cassette cases as he dumped it on the table between us; but then I took a closer look and realised that most of the titles on the liner inserts had been crossed out, and a recent date and time pencilled into the space around the edges.

I looked up at him. I could hardly believe it. There was hours of stuff here. "You taped over all of these?"

"Most of them," he said.

Exactly how long had he been hooked into the line with his answering machine turning, feeding it with fresh cassettes as the disembodied party rolled on through the ether? And what could possibly have been so gripping that he'd want a record of it anyway?

I said, "Have you considered a cocaine habit? It would work out cheaper."

"I know. Why do you think I was too scared to look at the bill?"

"It'll catch up with you. If not now, then with the next one."

"I know."

"You'll have to jack it in."

He sat down again. "I can't."

"Now listen," I said. "Think about it for a minute. You didn't drag me all the way over here just to open an envelope. You called because you knew you needed to hear some sense, and this is it. You're a lonely person, Ryan, but you're also broke. You run a phone you can't afford because you think a dead woman's going to call, and now you're into serious debt because of conversations with a bunch of nobodies telling lies about themselves and you don't even know their real names."

He nodded, as if none of this was news. "Right on every count, except for one."

"So you'll stop?"

"I can't."

"Why not, for Christ's sake?"

"Because I heard Belinda on the line!"

I sat back in the chair. I closed my eyes.

"Oh, fuck," I said.

When I opened my eyes again, Ryan was still there. He was leaning forward and his own eyes were two bright little beads, like a rabbit's.

"I know what you're thinking," he said, "and you're wrong. You think I wiped my entire Led Zeppelin collection for a bunch of dickheads droning on about how inadequate they are? She's the reason I had to keep phoning. You don't get into the same group every time. It's random, and you can't rig it. I heard her once, I had to keep going back."

"You heard somebody like her."

"There *is* nobody like her. Don't anybody ever try to tell me that I don't know her voice. And she knew mine, I'm sure of it. She's out there and she's lonely too, and I know she's trying to get back in touch."

"So why doesn't she call you direct?"

"I don't know. Maybe she can't. Maybe she's even scareder than I am, it's impossible to tell."

I was stuck for an answer. "I don't know what I can say to you."

Ryan broke into a kind of sheepish, lopsided grin. "How about, 'could you use a loan?'"

"Sounds like I might as well dig a deep hole and throw money into that."

"If it's any help to know it, I seem to be on some kind of suspension. Last night I said the wrong thing, and the operator came in faster than a lighted fart. I tried again, but they wouldn't take the call." He started to pick out certain of the cassettes, and I felt my heart sink as he said, "Do something for me, listen to some of these. Then come back and tell me if I'm fooling myself."

"And if I do? You still won't believe me."

"It won't happen," he said with utter conviction.

And what could I do? I took the tapes.

There were only about half a dozen of them, each marked with an asterisk to distinguish it from the others in the box. At least I was getting the action highlights, and not the entire festival programme. All the same I wasn't much looking forward to it, any more than I'd look forward to being in a locked room with a doorstep evangelist. I tried the first as soon as I got home, and it was very much along the lines of

Hey, y'all right?

Yeah, I'm all right.

What's new?

Nothing much, What's new with you?

and so on, until the participants either got bored or they bored each other or else they ran foul of the ban on names or personal details and were pulled without ceremony, voices dwindling rapidly as if they were being yanked off into the night.

But this in itself seemed to work as a process of selection. It was slow going, but gradually a tone and a sense of theme began to emerge.

Most of the time, I wasn't paying too much attention to what was being said. I got on with other things while keeping an ear cocked for a voice that might sound enough like Belinda's to have fooled Ryan, given that he was so raw on the subject that he'd be wide open to any suggestion.

Ryan wasn't stupid. Show him Belinda's dead body, and even his belief would have to falter; the problem lay in the manner of her disappearance and the way that her family had handled it afterwards, leaving Ryan on the outside and with a desperate confidence in her survival that was fuelled by his own dismay. Nobody had heard from her for several weeks after the breakup, and the police had only been able to come up with one doubtful sighting on a train out to the coast; nearly two months had gone by when a badly-decomposed body washed up onto a beach in Holland. The effects of the long immersion had been compounded by the attentions of various marine life and at least one encounter with a boat propeller. Belinda's older brother went out to identify the little that was identifiable, there was a Dutch post-mortem, and the sealed box that he brought home with him went straight into the ground. Ryan was told to stay away. She was pregnant when she died. That was the rumour, anyway.

I think I was spraying roach poison around under the carpet for the third time that week, when I heard a voice that made the hairs on the back of my neck start to prickle.

I stopped what I was doing. It couldn't be Belinda, of course.

But it did sound so much like her.

I set down the spray can and went across the room and stopped the machine, and then I rewound the tape about a minute's worth before sitting and listening to it again. I turned the volume up loud. Ryan wasn't speaking, but I could almost feel the tension of him gripping the phone and listening. I forget exactly what she said. It was nothing much in itself, and she didn't speak again until some time later when one of the others mentioned the fact that the sun was rising, and there was a general agreement for everyone to ring off. There was a silence, and then I nearly got all of the wax blown out of my ears by a burst of unerased Bowie before I could hit the off switch.

I put in the next tape. Ryan didn't seem to be talking on this one, just listening. She came up again, but again only briefly. She had the sound of someone who was trying out the water. A gruesomely apposite image, I suppose, but there it was.

I put in another.

Someone was saying, *"I remember the worst thing I ever saw. I was fourteen. I was at school, and we were having a biology lesson. The teacher brought out this frog. It must have been dead, but I'm not really sure. He did something to it, I didn't quite see what; but then he just pulled, and the whole thing turned inside out like a glove. He did it like it was his party piece. Everybody shrieked, and some people laughed. I still get nightmares about it."*

I settled back to listen for as long as it would take.

Someone said, *"I had a dream, once. I was walking toward this car. I knew there was a bomb inside it but I still couldn't help walking. When I was about ten feet away, the bomb went off. The whole world went white and I could feel this hot wind washing over me, and I knew that it was taking my skin away and that I was going to die."*

The Belinda-voice spoke.

"That must have been terrible," she said.

"It was the most beautiful thing I ever saw in my life," the storyteller said simply.

There was silence for a while. Nobody seemed ready to jump into the breach. I don't know how many were in the circle at this stage but it was another of those conversations with a late-night, before-dawn feel to it. I glanced at the dates on the stack of cassette cases and realised that this was the last one in the sequence.

After a few moments' hesitation, the Belinda-voice came again.

She said, *"My dream happens on a cliff. I'm standing on the edge and I'm looking out to sea, and it's night and all I can see are these distant lights somewhere out across the water. I keep thinking they're the lights of home, and all I have to do is take one step out and I'll be there. One step. All it takes is the nerve to do it."*

And then I heard Ryan say, *"And do you?"*

Did she falter, there? Did she recognise him as he believed he'd recognised her?

She said, *"What?"*

"In the dream. Do you take the step?"

"I can never remember."

I looked at the turning reels. There was about twenty minutes left to go. I let it run.

Neither Ryan nor the woman spoke again, and then when somebody mentioned the hour and people started to say their anonymous goodbyes I reached for the switch. But I didn't press it. Of the two voices that I was most interested in, neither had joined in.

About a minute passed before I heard Ryan say, *"Is anyone else still there?"*

There was a pause. Then...

"I'm still here," she said.

"I've got a confession to make. I was waiting for the others to go."

"So was I."

"The sun's coming up."

"Is it? I can't see it from here."

Another pause. And then -

"Belinda, why don't you call me?"

She started to answer. She started to answer but by God, they were quick on the button. She'd barely drawn breath and then the line was suddenly dead.

But she'd started to answer.

And I'd have sworn she was saying his name.

THEY OFFERED ME Manchester.

What it meant was the use of the van, expenses in cash, find my own lodgings, and three days re-setting the same exhibition under the high glass arch of the GMex Centre in the middle of town. They asked me if I could find another pair of hands and I half-heartedly phoned Ryan to let him know, but his line was engaged and by that afternoon they'd already found someone else.

I called around to return his tapes when I was on my way home to pack.

He looked worse. He'd never looked good, but he looked worse. The room was stuffy, as if all the air in it had been used and then used again, and Ryan himself had that raw-eyed, burned-up look that you see in anorexics and junkies in withdrawal. The place itself was as spartan as before.

"You heard her, didn't you?" he said, even before I was through the doorway. "You know I'm not wrong."

"It sounded a lot like her," I conceded, and Ryan smiled and shook his head as he closed the door behind me. The implication was that I was the one clinging to the irrational belief, not him; and to be completely honest, that was the way that it was beginning to feel.

He told me that he'd been unable to get reconnected. He'd been trying almost constantly, but couldn't get through. Not even on a different phone. But even this failure couldn't diminish the fierce elation that was bearing him along.

"It's simple enough," he said. "They found some body and they stuck her name on it and they couldn't really know. It was like they'd rather have her dead, than to carry on not knowing. And if you want something like that badly enough, you'll convince yourself of anything."

He offered to make me coffee. I cast an eye toward the roach motel of crockery that he'd piled up alongside the overfull sink, and made some excuse. He barely noticed.

He said, "I've got something that most people want and not everybody gets. A second chance. I'm not going to blow it, this time."

Either he was mad, or I was, or else there was actually something in it. I said, "How do you plan to make it work? You don't know where she is, they won't take your calls. And if they do, they'll cut you off the moment you try to make contact."

"I've been thinking about that," he said.

SO THAT SAME evening, when I was already supposed to be about halfway up the motorway with a vanload of display boards and bunting, I was actually cruising the West End with Ryan in the passenger seat, checking out every phone booth and stand-up kiosk that we could find. The load shifted in the back whenever we took a corner, and I was doing mental calculations of how fine I could cut it and still be at my destination for the start of the next working day. I'd already intended to stop off somewhere along the way and grab a few hours' sleep in a layby, and this was the margin that I would be having to shave.

There can't have been many that we missed. We did the back alleys between the main Soho streets, the ornate kiosks in Chinatown, a slow roll-past of the bright lights and the big crowds in front of the Palace Theatre, and then when we'd covered them all we went around again.

I was sweating, a little. What if somebody recognised the van? But then I thought, And what can they do? Fire me? Since in the eyes of the law they'd never officially taken me on, I supposed they'd find that kind of difficult.

It got later. The theatres filled, the discos began to open. As we nosed through the stop-start of the fun crowd traffic, Ryan told me of how he'd first begun to search.

"I started with the Yellow Pages," he said, "but there was nothing listed. Then I checked the regular phone book, but that was the same. The enquiries operator had never heard of them and the commercial desk in the library couldn't find them in any register. So I called the engineers to see if they could trace it through the number, but they tried to tell me that the exchange was an old one."

"You mean, out of use?"

"Not used for ten years or more."

"So how do the calls get through?"

"That's what they couldn't tell me. They seemed to think I was winding them up. I even rang the accounts department and queried the bill, but they'd still got nothing showing anywhere. If this doesn't work tonight, I don't know what will."

By eleven I was starting to check my watch, and wondering how I could let him down gently. We were just coming around the end of Denmark Street, which was pretty well dead at this hour, when he said "There's one!" so loudly that I stepped on the brake without even thinking and nearly got the front end of a taxi through my rear doors as a result. The taxi driver sounded his horn as Ryan threw back the door and leaped out, and then as soon as I could I cut out of the traffic and got the van half-up onto the pavement in front of a music shop with electric guitars behind thick wire mesh. By the time I caught up with Ryan a couple of minutes later, he was well into conversation with somebody.

The somebody was a youngish man in a stained old suede jacket, with big eyes and a fuzz of beard and a skin so pale that he looked as if he rarely saw daylight. The two of them were by the phones in the shadow of the big old church at the end of the road, lit by the warm yellow light from inside the old-style booths. The youngish man carried a shoulder bag like a delivery boy's. As I got near, I could see that the bag was crammed with sheets of dayglo stickers.

Well, there went another illusion. I'd naively supposed that all of this was simply some kind of X-rated version of the classified ads, small-time enterprise in a wide open market, and I felt strangely let down to see that it was organised enough to have pieceworkers walking the streets and keeping one step ahead of the cleanup squads. The man glanced at me as I approached, and Ryan turned. There was a certain look of triumph in his eyes.

"He says he can take me to them."

"Who?"

"The people who run Life Line."

I looked at the youth. He looked at me. There didn't seem to be much to him, as if a life on the margins had faded him to a shadow of a person.

I wondered what he saw.

Maybe the same, only older.

He sat in the van with us and didn't say much, just enough to direct me back up toward that home territory where the West End gave way to one big railway terminus after another, acres of brick and rail and the grime of the steam age. I was expecting Ryan to be pestering him with questions, but no. I finally turned into a long street of empty houses, windows boarded and roofs mostly open to the night sky, and we came to a halt under what appeared to be the last working street lamp.

We all got out. There was broken glass underfoot. Nobody else was around. I could hear a train passing on the far side of the row and could imagine how, in times past, people's lives would have moved to the rhythm of that basement-level thunder; now there was just this oasis of light and beyond it, the darkness.

"I don't like this," I told Ryan in a low voice.

"Don't worry," he said.

"What if it's a setup?"

"To achieve what? I'm wearing a Timex watch and I'm carrying the price of a newspaper. I've got absolutely nothing to lose."

He wouldn't let me go with him, and I suppose I didn't push as hard as I might. He showed no sign of nerves and seemed completely at ease; if it had been anyone other than Ryan, I'd have called it serenity. He was going to Belinda, and nothing else in the world mattered. The two of them crossed the street, Ryan following the wraith of a boy, and I watched as they went into one of the houses. I waited and watched for a while longer, but nothing more seemed to happen.

And then when I checked and saw that it was after midnight, I got back into the van and drove away.

I WAS IN Manchester by dawn and dead on my feet by lunchtime, but somehow I managed to make it through. I'd had a word with Lyle and he'd put me onto some theatrical digs out in Didsbury, and after checking in I went looking for a takeaway and then returned to my room with a newspaper that I'd scrounged from the residents' lounge. I stretched out on the bed and scanned the headlines, fairly sure that I was going to fall asleep in my clothes and too exhausted to get up again and do anything about it.

The item on page four was a sure-fire cure for drowsiness.

I sat up and read it twice. Three times. With repetition, it slowly began to sink in. I picked up the receiver on the bedside table but it was only a house phone, and nobody picked up at the other end. So then I went down to the pay phone on the ground floor and tried Ryan's number. I got his answering machine, tried to think of something to say, and then gave up.

So then I went back and read the item again.

London man's bizarre rail death, I read. Just after midnight, the driver of a local train out of King's Cross had looked ahead out of his windshield to see a man planted squarely in the middle of the track, facing the train lights and leaning forward as if braced for impact; I could picture it in my mind, a shabby Superman and a speeding locomotive, only here was a scenario that was set to change from heroics to horror in the space of a panel. The driver had hit the brakes, but he didn't have the distance. According to the report, the last thing that he'd seen was the man kind of grinning with his eyes tightly shut, his hair whipped up by the onrushing wind, and then had come the inevitable impact. I could imagine it. Didn't much want to, but could hardly help it. That flat, shit-thrown-at-a-wall sound. A spray of muck up the windscreen that the wipers wouldn't clear, smearing it around and maybe jamming on it as the train finally came to a halt on well-greased wheels about half a mile down the line. The paper only said that the driver was in deep shock and under sedation. Passengers had glimpsed a youth running from the scene, but he hadn't been traced.

No name was given, but I didn't doubt that it was Ryan any more than I doubted that it had happened on the stretch of track behind those empty houses. I had another cruel thought that I couldn't help, I wondered if they'd pick up the pieces and find his Timex still ticking. I wondered if I should phone in and identify him, but I didn't.

They'd have some way of finding out.

BUT WHATEVER WHEELS there were turned slowly, because when I got back into town and went over to Ryan's place I found it empty and unvisited, the air stale and only one message on the answering machine, my own. I wiped it. Then I looked at the pad alongside and saw a number and a name.

The name was mine, the number wasn't. So I picked up the phone, and dialled it.

In under a minute, I found myself on Life Line.

I didn't say anything, just listened.

"Doesn't anybody remember it? Someone must remember it. God, it was the best thing on television. It was everything to me!"

"One day I'll go back. I've promised myself I will. The only problem is that the longer I leave it, the more scared I am of what I'll find."

"I've learned one thing. Everything you love, you lose. Everything."

And then—

"I had a dream, once. I was standing on a railway line, and a train was coming toward me. I just had to stand there as its lights got bigger and bigger. I could hear brakes, but they made no difference. It came up so fast that it filled the world from one side to the other."

There was a voice in the room.

It was unexpected, but it was mine.

It said, "That must have been terrible."

There was the faintest of echoes, as if I'd been calling down a well, and then I heard, *"It was the most beautiful thing I ever saw in my life."*

I said quickly, "Ryan, where are you?"

But I was cut off before I got an answer. I quickly pressed the cradle and then dialled again.

But nothing happened. The line was dead.

Not Here,
NOT NOW

HE CAME AROUND the corner too fast, there was no denying that. But it wasn't his fault, it was the way they'd laid out the road. The Mondeo's offside wheels veered out over the double white lines and hogged a piece of the opposite lane, but he had a clear run at the bend and so that was no problem. He took it wide to avoid dropping his speed. He hated to brake. Only bad drivers braked on bends.

Bad drivers, faint hearts, and life's born losers.

Oh, shit, was the thought that then flitted through his mind in the two-fifths of a second before disaster struck.

Because what lay beyond the bend was all wrong. There was a school on the far side of the road and a line of parked cars half on the pavement where they shouldn't have been. A big yellow refuse cart was coming the other way and it had swung out to pass them. There was room to squeeze by it to the left, just…but the way wasn't clear.

Just beyond the dustcart, someone was crossing.

A mother and child, the girl holding the woman's hand and pulling ahead. What happened then happened in an instant, and it both amazed and dismayed him.

He was going to hit something, that was inevitable. He was going too fast to stop and there was nowhere to swerve. The refuse cart was like a lumbering wall of glass and metal and shiny hydraulics. The girl was about seven years old. And…

It was already too late. There was no point in trying to make any kind of a thought-out decision because some part of him had already reacted.

He'd chosen the child.

There was a thump and a flurry as they went by, just like an empty cardboard box that he'd once struck on a windy day on the motorway. He was braking hard and he was thrown forward against his seat belt, the car sliding to a halt a good fifty or sixty yards on.

Then he dropped back into his seat as the car finally stopped.

The accident was way behind him now. He gripped the wheel, blinking. He was so out of phase that he wouldn't have been surprised to look in the mirror and see nothing unusual, no sign of anything having happened at all. As if it had all been one of those little flash effects one saw in movies, a few frames of nightmare and then back to normal. Like God saying, *Boo*! and then you look and nothing's changed.

But when he did raise his eyes to the mirror, he could see that the child was lying in the road like a dropped sack and the woman was crouching over it, shouting. He could hear her, now. He turned in the seat for a better look back. People were running to them. The men from the dustcart, in those shiny yellow jackets. More women, from the direction of the school.

All converging. All so far behind him. For a long moment he sat there, knowing that he had to get out of the car and that he would have to go back and confront what he'd done.

Everyone was concerned for the child. Any moment now, some of them would raise their heads and transfer their attention to him.

He floored the accelerator, and took off.

He didn't breathe until he was around the next corner and out of their sight. Some of their faces were like little painted dabs of outrage in his rear view mirror. It took only seconds, but those seconds seemed like an hour. He knew that he should have gone back, but what could he have done? The child was already getting help. He couldn't change anything now. He'd get abuse, he'd get blame, no one would want to hear him explain…

And it hadn't even been his fault.

He drove like a robot, hardly aware of the moves that his body was making. His mind was racing hard on a track of its own. The traffic was thinning out at the tail end of the rush hour; it was almost nine and most people had made it to where they were going by now. Just the flexitime crowd and the late-spurters. Late for the shop or the office.

Late for school.

At least the ambulance wouldn't have to fight its way through.

Damn that kid. *Damn* her! And her mother too! What the *fuck* did they think they were *doing*?

His rage was sudden and real. Half of those cars had been parked on double yellow lines and a couple of them had been left on the zigzags where even the Pope couldn't stop if he'd wanted to. It was as if women dropping off their kids thought that rules didn't apply to them. They parked like shit, they pulled out without looking, they'd even stop in the middle of the road and walk their darlings to the pavement if there were no spaces left. They put the hazard lights on and seemed to think that was some kind of a charm. *It's only for a minute*, they'd almost certainly say. But how long did it take? They'd as good as condemned that kid.

It was their fault. They deserved the real blame.

Not him.

He'd gone past the building where he worked before he'd realised it. He drove on anyway. He couldn't face the idea of going in now. He'd call in later with some excuse, but for now he had to think.

Had anyone taken his number? Or a description of him or the car? He hadn't been aware of it, but there was no way to be sure. Apprehension sat in him like a sickness. As he joined the traffic on the ring road he began to wonder if the car might be carrying any telltale marks. He tried to raise himself in his seat to peer at the wing, but the angle was impossible. There were no shop windows on the ring road, which mostly went through industrial land. So no chance of catching a reflection there.

He could always stop and check, of course. But that would mean getting out of the car.

He needed some time to think, and he felt more at home behind the wheel than anywhere. He was a good driver, one of the best. There were five accidents on his insurance record but not one of them had been down to him; idiots pulling out ahead of him, most of them, or taking too long to manoeuvre or moving too slow.

Like that dustcart. Chugging along like an ocean liner down the middle of the road, guaranteed death if he were to hit it head-on at the speed he'd been going. It wasn't as if he'd consciously decided to hit the child. Some reflex had been responsible for that, some uncluttered animal circuit in the brain that saw certain mortality and acted for survival. No questions, no considerations. You couldn't plough into a truck like that and live; whereas with a seven-year-old, you could.

It was basic human programming. Automatic, and beyond conscious reason. Surely anyone would have done the same.

He watched for police cars. If they had his number, they'd certainly be watching for him. But the chances were that they didn't. People didn't think that fast in a crisis. He had to stay cool and he hadn't to panic. It was sad—no, it was worse than sad, it was lousy—but it wasn't as if he'd knowingly opted to do harm. Harm had simply chosen him as its messenger that day. It could have been almost anyone. That didn't make him a bad person.

Just unlucky.

He knew the woman's type. Middle-class parents. He saw ones like her every morning, hanging around and chatting on the pavement outside the school gates. Dressed up, made up, nowhere useful to go until pick-up time but, God, couldn't they complain about how busy they were. When it came to whining, they were experts.

So even with all that screaming, it was entirely possible that the child hadn't actually been hurt.

The bump had been nothing and he'd all but brushed by. The more he thought about it, the more certain he became. The image of the small body sprawled on the tarmac would be a hard one to get out of his mind, but things like that always looked worse than they actually were. If he'd hit the kid, really hit her, then she'd surely have been thrown somewhere further along the road.

A tiny pocket of chilled sweat had collected under his waistband at the small of his back. He arched slightly in his seat, and shivered as he felt it run.

The ring road was curving through the edge-of-town industrial estates and bringing him back in a full circle toward the area of his home. He was about ten minutes away from it and he could think of nowhere else to go. Once there, he could phone work and say that he was unwell. He could pretend he hadn't even left the house yet.

No one would ever know.

But when he was making the turn into the road where he lived, he saw that there was a police car across the end of his driveway. Its lights were on and its engine was running. He quickly cancelled the indicator and went on past the junction. He wasn't sure whether he'd seen anyone in the car. If they'd gone around the side of the house, they wouldn't have been able to see him at all.

What was he going to do?

What *was* he going to do?

For a few desperate seconds he actually tried to make some other kind of sense of the situation, but that wouldn't work. They had his number, and he was sunk. He'd left the scene of the accident. They had a name for that: hit and run. It wouldn't matter that he could explain, that there was a perfectly rational sequence to what had happened; hit and run would stick, and the truth would go unheard.

He'd been driving like an old woman since it had happened. He'd just gone along with the flow and hadn't overtaken a single car in the past twenty minutes. He checked his mirror and saw that the police car was emerging from his road, blue lights flashing but with no siren. So they'd seen him, then. He changed down the gears and tried to get ahead of the car in front, and that was when the siren started up.

This was all wrong. This wasn't the day that he'd set out to have. The car in front was a white Fiat and it shifted out of the way when he blasted on his horn. He was desperately trying to think of some way that he could turn it all around and make it come right, but everything was moving too fast. He shot through the space that the Fiat had made, and crossed traffic lights on amber. The police car came through on red a few seconds later, slowing for safety as the cross-traffic braked and gave way, but already he'd doubled his lead. He floored it, he sped. Within the minute he was back on the ring road and the police car was a distant howl. Still behind him and still chasing, but losing ground in the traffic rather than gaining it. Some tangle must have held it back for a few seconds for him to get so far in front. He didn't know what, and he wasn't inclined to hang around and look.

He had to get away from all this. He had to buy some time to think.

He cracked open the window an inch or so, just enough to be able to listen out for his pursuers and judge how far they were behind him. At first all that he could hear was the roar of the wind, but then the sounds began to separate out. It was as if the siren had an echo, but then he realised; there were at least two of them now, two wolves on his trail, both howling as they picked up the scent.

And then a third, a different kind of two-tone altogether. One of the blue vans, perhaps, or something bigger. The van they were going to throw him in. Word was going out on the radio, and they were converging in pursuit. The howling of the sirens would then give way to the howling of a mob and once that began he could never, ever hope to be heard above it.

The road was dropping into an underpass, traffic noise turning to thunder. The articulated lorry ahead of him began to pull out, and he got close up behind and pulled out after.

Much of the traffic here was made up of trucks and vans, big freight and delivery wagons. They lumbered along and it took one hell of a surge in acceleration to pass them sometimes; you were out there and exposed for what seemed like forever, a real test of the best. Getting in behind a lorry and using it for cover felt almost like a wimp's way out, but right now he was desperate. He checked his mirror, and saw the blue van. It was some way back, still, but must have joined the chase from somewhere close. Its twin blue lights were like captured stars, and they were reflected over the cars in a sea of metal.

The underpass was open to one side, daylight coming in through an endless temple of concrete columns. Slowly, achingly, the lorry ahead of him drew past the long flatbed vehicle in the inside lane. He was right up against its tail and hanging on close. The flatbed carried roadbuilding machinery and could probably go no faster; the roar of engines in the enclosed space made his chest vibrate. As the back end of the overtaking lorry moved ahead of the flatbed's cab, the flatbed driver flashed his lights and the lorry signalled to swing back in.

The way ahead would be left clear, and he could floor it and go through.

He'd better. Because the two big lorries were nose-to-tail in the inside lane now, and there would be no space for him to get back in.

Elementary mistake.

The articulated's driver had judged it perfectly. He'd seen the oncoming Volvo truck some way ahead, he'd worked out that he had exactly enough time to make his manoeuvre and get back in, and he'd carried it out with neatness and precision. The trucker's calculations hadn't included a Mondeo tagging along behind. Why should they? Controlling one of those big lumbering dinosaurs was enough of a job on its own.

He'd been left out in the wrong lane, heading the wrong way, racing head-to-head with a vehicle ten times his size. The Volvo truck was blasting its horn, flashing its lights. Warning him to get out of the way.

But how could he do that? He gripped the wheel harder, willing something to happen.

He couldn't drop back, there wasn't time. He couldn't return to his lane, there wasn't a space. If he tried to swing wide, he'd hit the pillars.

And the truck driver's options were exactly the same as his own.

In the two-fifths of a second before disaster struck, he knew exactly what had to be going through the truck driver's mind. Knew it probably better than the driver did himself.

When it came down to it, the man's options were limited. Swerve into the other trucks, and die. Swerve into the concrete pillars, and die. The choice he had to make was really no choice at all.

Whether he knew it or not, he'd reacted already.

He'd chosen the car.

The
PLOT

I T WAS A grey February morning in the Northern hills and Matthew Price, vicar of a rural parish, was crossing the graveyard that stood between his parsonage and the church. The church stood above the town, and the churchyard was exposed. The wind had driven a rim of last night's hail around the headstones, piling it up against them in a shallow tide of gruel.

There was only a short dash to make, but the wind was bitter. Matthew kept his face turned from it, and failed to see the young woman until she stepped out into his path.

She was red-haired and pale. Her thin shawl was plastered to her and her dress whipped around her legs. She was nineteen.

"Mary," said Matthew, taking a moment to overcome his surprise. "You should not be out."

"I am well enough," the young woman said. "And someone sits with my daughter."

"Your daughter? Where is she now?"

"In the cot the parish gave me."

He was shocked at this news.

"Still?" he said. "A week has passed."

"She keeps well enough in this cold."

"Mary," Matthew said. "You must bury her."

She looked away. A tendril of hair fell across her face, and she pushed it aside.

"Not in your unhallowed ground, Reverend. Will you not relent and baptise her?"

"Baptism is for the living."

"She looks just as she did in life," Mary offered.

Matthew felt something close to despair as he looked upon her. She meant her words to be taken seriously. It was as if she hoped that, with a little haste and a show of conviction, even God himself might be misled.

The young girl was returning his gaze with a mixture of wariness and defiance. She had a face that was doll-like and pure when she washed it, save for a faint childhood scar that divided her right eyebrow. She was without family and without much education; and now she was without her child.

"Walk with me to the church," he said.

The path took a haphazard course through the yard, cutting this way and that: here around an iron-railed sepulchre, there to avoid an angel. These were the tombs of country families who built their graves like they built their houses: solid, massive, ugly, and for all time.

Matthew said, "I don't say no to punish you, Mary. God makes provision for the unbaptised."

"Amongst the suicides and heathens."

"In limbo."

"A place of nothing."

"Limbo is not a place of nothing, Mary. It is a state in which the innocent can look forward to the day when they receive God's grace."

"And be denied it until then."

There was no persuading her. What she lacked in sophistication, she more than made up for with directness and tenacity. As they reached the church's oak door he said, "Why did you not bring the child to me before she died?"

"The midwife said she was too poorly to be moved."

"Then you had only to send word of your need," he said as he unlatched the door and pushed it inward, "and I would have come to you."

"I came to ask," she said. "But I was turned away."

He turned back and looked at her in dismay.

"When?" he said.

But she had stopped at the threshold. She looked in and all around, like a person whose way had been barred by an invisible hand. She took in every corner of the cold church, as if to remember it.

"I will not enter this house," she said.

"Mary!" he said, but she had nothing more for him. She turned and walked away.

He tried to follow, but he could not catch up with her. He stopped at the church gates and watched her departing figure as she descended the hill. It was a cobbled street that ran down through the middle of town to the river and the mill. It did not run straight, and in less than a minute she was lost to his view.

Matthew went back inside, and closed the door. The chill of the wind gave way to the bone-cold stillness of stone. There was an iron stove against the church's third pillar. Jacob had cleaned out the ashes and laid a new fire the night before, and it waited now to be lit. Jacob had begun his working life as the gravedigger's boy. Now in his sixty-eighth year, he served the parish as verger, sexton and churchwarden.

By the time of the morning service the stove was glowing, the pipes were clanking, and the difference they made was imperceptible. It was a midweek matins and poorly attended, the usual roster of widows and cripples and indigents. They hurried for the best pews near the stove, and gave up their places to no one.

The coughing was louder than the singing, and a mite more musical. Not for the first time, Matthew looked over his midweek flock and reflected that the people who clung most fiercely to their God always seemed to be the ones who'd received the worst of his favour.

But perhaps even a God could go too far. Matthew spoke the words and led the hymns, but his thoughts were elsewhere. They were of Mary Tolliver and in particular of her child—one scant week of life, and an eternity dead.

∽

BACK AT THE parsonage, the service over and his body chilled to the core, Matthew did his best to warm himself at the big fire in the kitchen. He could hear Mrs Temple moving around upstairs. He waited for her to appear and then, when she did not, moved to the stairway and called to her.

Like Jacob, Constance Temple had been a fixture when he'd come to the parish. And like Jacob, she'd embraced Matthew's new ideas for managing the household while somehow managing never to act on any of them. He felt guilt as he listened to her descending. Her back was as straight as an artillery-man's, but she moved with the slow dignity of joint pain.

When she was with him, Matthew said, "Mary Tolliver was waiting for me in the churchyard this morning."

"Was she," Mrs Temple said, in a tone that somehow took the query out of the words and gave them a critical edge.

"Did you ever turn her away from the door?"

"I turn away anyone who will not disclose their business."

"You must have known her business. Everyone in the village is aware of her state."

"And a fine state it is. There's a word for her and there's another for her child."

"Please don't speak it."

"I would not soil the air."

So that was it. Matthew knew that if he argued further, Mrs Temple would remain calm and he would grow more agitated and in the end, she would acknowledge no fault and nothing would change. Her opinions had stood for a long time, and their foundations went deep. For two years he'd been trying to persuade her to bring in a housemaid to help with the more onerous tasks. She would listen and promise to consider, but nothing would be done. He might as well argue with the land itself.

He said, "She lodges in Mill Row, does she not?"

"Along with the rest of them."

The rest of them being unmarried mill girls and servants who lived out. Some had privacy in rented rooms, most had to share. The Row had a certain reputation.

"Thank you," Matthew said.

He had a funeral to conduct that afternoon, and an important letter to write in the evening. Perhaps a few hours would give Mary time to regret her words and reconsider. First thing tomorrow, he would seek her out and see to what extent the church's forgiveness might move her.

BUT IT WAS not to be. At four in the morning, he was awakened by the barking of Jacob's dog. The dog was as touchy as its owner and often barked at any sound in the night, but would normally fall silent after a while. This time it did not. Matthew climbed out of bed and moved to the window, where he looked down and saw the light of a lantern moving in the church-yard. He dressed over his nightshirt and went out.

He found Jacob standing over the grave that he had filled in only a few hours before. The wreaths and flowers had been scattered from the fresh-ly-turned earth, and some of the exposed mound had been excavated.

"Grave robbers, Reverend," Jacob said. "In this day and age."

Matthew had him raise the lantern higher, and studied the work. A piece of broken fencepost lay close by. Someone had been scraping into the dirt with it, to little effect.

"They don't seem to have achieved much with their efforts."

"And the hard work already done for them, as well," Jacob said contemp-tuously. "That ground was like iron when I broke it."

But Matthew's gaze had been led to the dog, quiet now and sniffing around at some short distance.

"I think our dead are safe from an earthly resurrection," he said. "I sus-pect a different motive."

They moved over to where the dog had stopped, and Jacob shooed it away. It hovered at the furthest reach of the lantern's throw as Matthew bent to inspect the bundle it had found.

"Not here to raise a body," Matthew said quietly, "but to leave one."

It was the body of a week-old child, pale as the marble angels and wrapped in stiff linen.

"In another's grave?" said Jacob.

"Where better to lie undiscovered?" said Matthew. "Please. Steady me."

Rising with the child, he felt the usual rush of blood from his head and waited, the sexton's hand supporting his arm, until the dizziness abated.

Once he was confident of his balance again, he had Jacob light the way to the church. The dog followed behind.

"I should fetch the constable," Jacob said.

"Wait until the morning," Matthew said. "If call him we must."

He laid the dead child before the altar in the side-chapel, and took a seat in the front pew. He said a prayer, but once again found his thoughts taking him to a place where he felt less than comforted. He wished that Mary had not fled before he had arrived. He wished that he could have sat here with her in the presence of her daughter, and persuaded her back to God. She was distraught, and it was natural. She retained her sense of what was right, or she would not have attempted to place the child in consecrated ground. Were she truly lost, consecrated ground would mean nothing to her.

If only he could make her see that even to deny God was to acknowledge his presence. Matthew's fear now was that this failure to secure a burial in the churchyard might drive her further from the light. Wasn't that it? Wasn't that the source of his discomfort?

But faced with the dead child, its eyes closed, its mouth open, its cold fingers crooked, an ivory doll from a nativity scene, Matthew was not so sure. He could feel no sense of justice at the exclusion of its soul from heaven. Not for a promise of eventual bliss, not for even for the briefest moment.

He'd baptised many children. He'd performed the service so many times that sometimes his mind wandered as he said the words. The water came from a tap in the churchyard. Godparents stumbled through vows they could neither repeat nor remember. The child knew nothing of its state before, nor of any difference after.

He put his head in his hands. He wore the robes and stood for the Church's authority in all things spiritual. But could it be that, if there was a conflict here, his sympathies were not entirely where they ought to reside?

After a few moments, he had regained himself. Mary Tolliver's bitterness might be justified, but it was not right. If he allowed his sympathy to undo him, he could be of no help to her. Ministers must not question their duties.

Allow them that option, and even the Kingdom of Heaven might fall.

THERE WERE STARS still visible in the morning sky as Matthew and the constable made their way to Mill Row. Matthew had not slept. The constable had been roused early, and had little to say. Matthew was directed to a communal loft that ran the length of four stone cottages in the roof space, where more than thirty young women and girls made a home. Some slept on mattresses on the floor, others had strung up blankets for privacy. The girls were awake and dressed but many had yet to leave for the mill.

Matthew recognised some of them. There were other churches and chapels in town, but Mill Row fell within his parish. The girls were reluctant to speak, until Matthew caught the constable yawning and sent him to find a chair.

He learned that Mary Tolliver had made a brief return to collect some possessions but had fled before first light, telling a few close friends that it was her intention to make her way to the city. The nearest city was at least two days' walk away for a person in the best of health, and Mary was still weak from childbirth.

"Has she lost her wits?" Matthew said. "She could die on the road."

"She spoke of a married sister," one of the girls said.

"In town?"

"In her old life."

As Matthew was leaving, he noted that the cot from the parish stood out on the landing. Mary's space had already been claimed by another.

A plan of sorts had begun to form in Matthew's mind. There seemed little that he could do for Mary now, and the course that had suggested itself to him was hardly a correct one. But it had a sense of necessary decency about it.

As they walked from the Row and over the river he conversed with the constable, and easily persuaded him to take no further interest in the matter. He argued that any offence here was spiritual, and need not trouble the law. The constable offered no argument in return.

Then Matthew made an early call at the offices of Henry Munby, the solicitor who handled all of the parish's legal affairs. An hour with Munby got his designs off to a start, and he climbed the hill back to the parsonage with renewed purpose.

He found Jacob, and walked with him to the place where the churchyard ended and the moor began. The division was marked by a stone wall with a gate in it. Beyond the gate was an unmade path that led off into rolling hill country and a sea of ferns. It was lush in summer, blighted now. By the gate stood a massive elm.

Matthew said, "I want a child's grave dug under that tree."

Jacob gave him a suspicious look. "I can't dig if it's not church land."

"It will be. I've taken steps to acquire the plot outside the gate. It won't be consecrated, but I can bless the ground and the child that lies in it. And Jacob…please. Tell no one for now."

He did not mean to, but he glanced toward the parsonage as he said this. And Jacob brightened; any scheme that merited Mrs Temple's disapproval was guaranteed to secure his.

The job would take Jacob the rest of the day. He went off for his barrow and tools, and Matthew went to the church. He'd closed it up with the dead child inside, locking the doors and keeping the keys on him. His intention had been to send a local undertaker with them to collect the body, but that intention had now changed.

If the church had made no provision for the unbaptised, he would make his own. It was not unknown for a churchyard to have sections both consecrated and unconsecrated. As communities grew, people took less of an interest in the fates of the strangers around them. An unknown suicide might rest in an anonymous corner nowadays, where once they would have been banished to a crossroads burial. There was even a time set aside for such interments, the grim hours between nine and midnight.

So might it be here. This bastard child could be denied the full service of burial, but need not be denied Matthew's prayers or his compassion. And if no one else knew of it, then none need debate it.

They laid the child to rest that evening, wrapped in the simple linen in which they'd discovered her. Jacob and his dog were the only witnesses. There was no marker but Matthew made a careful drawing of the spot, measuring and noting the distances from gateway and tree. It was important to have a record, in case the plot should ever be needed again. Mary Tolliver was not the first of her kind, nor did he expect her to be the last.

IT WAS MORE than a week later when Matthew read of a theft at a coaching inn that stood out on the city road some fifteen miles from town. Baggage had been left unattended for a few minutes when a horse had thrown a fit, and a young woman had seized this opportunity to rifle the passengers' goods. She'd left valuables and fled with only money, but a substantial sum of it. A reward was being offered by the carriers. She was described as pale and red-haired, and bedraggled from the road. Those who'd seen her before the theft described her as 'glocky', or half-witted, talking to herself and shunning company. She'd been begging money for herself and her child, although no child was seen with her.

It was little enough to go on, but Matthew was convinced. Red-haired, bedraggled, an imagined child—it seemed likely to him that Mary Tolliver was the thief. If so, she was pursuing a downward course. And pursuing it in a way that he had done nothing to prevent.

But perhaps he might act to halt or even reverse it. More than anything, he wanted to show her the plot under the elm and to tell her of the blessing. Her child might not lie in the Bishop's ground as she'd wished, but she surely lay in God's own earth.

Letters were sent that same day, and replies received the next. A curate from the adjacent parish would take over his duties during a few days' absence. A carriage and driver were borrowed from the Wetherbys, a local family who were rich and had several and could be persuaded that the loan of a spare would gain them some extra credit with the Almighty. Matthew weathered Mrs Temple's disapproval as she packed for him.

"Be sure you let Jacob carry your bag," she said.

"That hardly seems right," said Matthew. "He's close to seventy years old."

"And he spends all his days in a hole with a shovel," Mrs Temple said bluntly. "He's used to the strain. You've had your doctor's warning."

He reached the coaching inn at around three in the afternoon. He gave the driver a shilling, and half an hour to spend it in. Matthew himself had no appetite, and was relieved to stand on firm ground for a while and not be shaken. He took a walk around the yard. He watched the horses being watered, and spied a white-bearded, bald-headed man in a tattered army coat, striding about with a hefty staff and slamming the end of it down on the cobbles whenever he stopped. His frame was aged, but his gaze was fierce.

Matthew caught his eye. Aware of his attention, the old man drew himself up a little taller.

"A formidable weapon," Matthew observed.

"And I'll use it," the old man said, "before I see property interfered with again."

"I take it you speak of the woman who rifled the luggage."

"She took advantage of her sex and struck at me like the harpy she was." He tapped his waistcoat with his finger, just below the breastbone. "Struck me right here and drove the breath from this old body. A pitiable object she made of me."

"Would you know her again?" said Matthew.

"In an instant," said the old man. "And so might you, by the mark on her brow."

And he touched a finger to his own white eyebrow, in exactly the place where Mary Tolliver's had been divided by some long-forgotten hurt.

✍

ONCE IN THE city, Matthew took a room in a small commercial hotel and sent the carriage driver home. He ate little and retired early. His stomach was unsettled and his head ached. Matthew did not travel often, and when he did he rarely travelled well. The ache was still there when he woke, dull and specific like a blunt nail in the brain. But he ignored it, and with breakfast it faded.

After the small mill town that he was accustomed to, stepping out into the streets of the city both excited and threaten to overwhelm this country parson. So many people. So many streets. The noise, and all the smells. But it was only novelty, and it soon began to pass.

He began his search with the aid of a sixpenny gazetteer and a street map. His plan was to visit every hostel and charitable institution, but after three or four of these he began to realise that he was wasting his time. All had some form of religious patronage or other association, the very thing that Mary had set herself against. Even the hospitals bore the names of saints.

But a sister had been mentioned. A married sister, so she would not be a Tolliver. But she had been a Tolliver once. Matthew abandoned his tour of charity houses and set himself instead to visit the various parishes of the city, asking to see their marriage registers. He was dismayed by the scale of everything—the distance between parishes, the sheer number of them, the size of the record books in each. His own modest register recorded perhaps a dozen weddings in a year. These churches were putting them through like factories.

On the second day of his search he found a likely candidate, married seven years past. The wedding of one Albert Wardle to one Dorothy Tolliver, spinster of this parish. He took a note of the husband's address, and found the house in a dark terrace by a canal. Here lived Albert's mother, widow of the one-time lock-keeper. From there he was sent to the tenement where Albert now lived with his fast-growing family.

Dorothy Wardle received him with eagerness and some embarrassment at the state in which he found her. Her husband was at his job in the docks, and her children were everywhere around them. Matthew counted six, or it might have been eight. They moved about too much, and too quickly. Not all were her own; she minded the children of neighbours for payment.

Mary had been to visit her, but she had not stayed. She'd looked weary, but she had new boots and nearly-new clothes. Dorothy was shocked when Matthew told her of the theft that had paid for them.

"She said it was money she'd saved," Dorothy said. "She told me that her mind was set on something to buy with it. That was her reason for coming to town."

"Did she say what she intended to buy?"

"No."

"It is important that I find her," Matthew said. "I believe that I bear some responsibility for the course that she follows."

"Surely not, Reverend."

"Although I did not judge her, I fear I left her feeling judged. Might she return here, do you think?"

"I could not swear to it. But her parting words had the sound of a goodbye."

She had to break off their conversation for a moment, to scold one of the smaller children who was picking mouldy wallpaper from the wall and eating it.

Matthew said, choosing his words with delicacy, "Did she seem…entirely herself to you?"

He could see that Dorothy understood his meaning well enough. But she shied from it. "How else would she seem?" she said, uneasily, and her very unease was the answer he sought.

He said, "Do you know where she went to from here?"

"She'd a list of some addresses that she wanted to visit. I gave her Albert to lead her. Albert!"

A boy of six or seven came forward. His head was the shape of a battered turnip, his eyes the eyes of a frightened doe.

Dorothy said, "Show the Reverend the penny that Aunt Mary gave you."

Albert produced a grubby handkerchief and carefully unfolded it. From its heart, he took out one new penny.

"Very shiny," said Matthew. "If I can match it with another, can you tell me where your Aunt Mary went?"

"Albert does not speak," Dorothy said. "Will you not sit for a while, Reverend? You seem drained by your journey."

"I shall rest once she is found," Matthew said.

Albert might not speak, but Albert could lead, and so Matthew followed him through streets and down alleys and into a district of warehouses and sweatshops. Albert hopped and ran, dodging through handcarts and porters laden with bales and bolts of cloth, and every now and again would stop and look back to see that Matthew was still with him. More than once, Matthew feared that he'd lost sight of the boy. At the next glimpse, off he went again.

Beyond the warehouses was a broad street, and beyond the street was a sooty park with factory chimneys in the distance. The houses around the park were tall and fine and many had porches and railings. The pavements here were broad, and flagged with stone. At the end of the avenue leading up to the park gates stood a white tower. Here, Albert stopped.

An engraved brass plate was fixed below the bell-pull.

"She had you bring her *here*?" Matthew said. "Are you sure it's the right house?"

Albert stared up at him and waited for his penny.

By the time Matthew had done ringing the bell, the boy had disappeared. Looking around for him, he missed seeing the door open and turned quickly at the sound of it.

He was surprised to find himself faced by a man whom he guessed to be the householder or tenant. He'd expected a servant. But no servant would appear at his master's door in a faded Turkish robe and carpet slippers. The man before him was pale and fair, his face strangely undefined and smooth. He had a fringe of beard around his chin.

He took in Matthew's clerical garb and said, "Arthur Halifax, sir. How may I help you?"

"I seek a young woman with a scar on her brow," Matthew said. "She was led here."

"Won't you come in?"

On entering, Matthew perceived the white tower to be a house of books and cats. He saw the books everywhere—on shelves down the hall, on shelves in those rooms that he could see into, stacked in deep piles on the treads of the stairs leaving barely enough room for a person to ascend. The cats he didn't need to see at all.

There was nowhere to settle, but Arthur Halifax led the way down the hall and into a kitchen and scullery at the back of the house. It had a view over a yard filled with broken furniture and rolled linoleum.

After Matthew had explained himself further, Arthur Halifax said, "She was here. She was lucid. She was bright and composed. But she had a strange idea of the kind of service that I might do for her."

"Your plate declares you a bookseller, yet I see no shop."

"I have no use for a shop. I seek out rare volumes for particular clients. I suppose some might imagine that because I handle knowledge, I must therefore be in possession of it."

"What service did she ask for?"

"Help in obtaining the unobtainable. She had made a list of many items—I cannot remember them all. But they were odd. The life of a dying child, a face of innocence, the power of a serpent's poison. As if these were things that one might touch and trade. And yet she asked with such sweet earnestness that at first I thought the flaw was in my understanding, and that her requests were no less than reasonable."

By now Matthew had noted that Arthur Halifax had eyes that did not entirely fix upon the person that he was addressing, but rather on some point in space to one side or the other. Yet he seemed sufficiently aware of who or what he was looking at.

Matthew said, "She has suffered much, of late. Her grasp may not be complete."

"Is she kin to you? My sympathies if she is."

"A parishioner. I have made it my task to bring her home."

Halifax nodded, slowly, and then picked off some cat hairs from the front of his robe.

He said, "However strange her purpose, it seemed to be sustaining her. But a fire that burns so brightly can never burn for long. Search where you will. But may I suggest that you also call on the madhouses."

LEAVING HIS COMPANY, Matthew found himself wondering whether the volumes that left the house bore the same feline history that his clothes now seemed to carry. He took a brisk walk around the park, flapping his coat to dispel the odour, while he considered what his next step ought to be.

It was surely as he'd begun to fear. Grief and frustration had unbalanced her mind. It was mainly in the theatre that mad people gibbered and rent their clothes; in life they often presented themselves with no perceptible change, save that their aims and reasons followed a logic entirely their own, until self-neglect or some worrying encounter drew attention to their state.

He could return to the sister's house and see if Albert would be good for a second address. Or he might try to determine from which directory or magazine's advertisement columns she had compiled her list. But his time was limited. As was his money, and as were his energies. There seemed little point in continuing his pursuit at a distance that he could never diminish.

He sat on a bench by a stone urn that had been blackened by factory air, and took out his sixpenny gazetteer. No asylums were listed; but he did find an entry for the city's Lunacy Commission, at an address close to the courthouses. If her state grew worse, eventually the Commissioner would come to know of it.

AND SO, EARLY that evening, the Reverend Matthew Price found himself before the gates of a public asylum on the outskirts of town, its high brick walls surrounded by open fields and its barred upper windows opened to the clean country air. In his hand was a letter from the Lunacy Commissioner. In his heart, sadness and dread. The gatekeeper let him in and led him up the driveway toward the home of the Superintendent.

The asylum was not one building but many, occupying an estate of its own. Were it not for the workhouse-style construction of its wards it might have been taken for a veritable village of the unfortunate, with a duck pond and a chapel and a farm manned by inmates to supply its needs. It had a one-platform railway station with a line that ran out from the city, with special trains for visitors at weekends.

There had been twelve new admissions in the month. Three of these had taken place in the past week and one of them had been of a young woman of roughly Mary Tolliver's age and description. This woman had been found screaming and breaking mirrors in a public house, and had to be prevented from tearing at herself with the shards. When they took the broken glass from her, she attempted further damage to herself using her nails. Her clothes had been good but were ruined, and when committed she was penniless.

There was a trade in pauper lunacy, Matthew knew. With a grant of seven shillings a week for their keep, they could find themselves sped from the streets and into a system from which they might find it hard to escape. If she was here, the fault was his. And if she truly was mad, then here she would probably remain. Here or somewhere else like it, perhaps for the rest of her days.

His letter was read, and an attendant summoned to take him to view the patient. As he followed the attendant down the corridor, he felt his pulse racing and his heart pounding. A part of him hoped that he would find himself facing some stranger. But to have such a hope was to wish a misfortune onto someone that he did not even know. All the same, if the misfortune was a given, would it be wrong to feel relief?

They passed day rooms where inmates warmed themselves, and then left one building and passed through yards and airing courts into another. Matthew felt as if he were moving deeper and deeper into a place from which all sense of the world outside was being lost. They came to a locked cell; he waited alone as the attendant went for a key.

She lay on a cot with a single blanket. There was little chance of her clawing herself now. Her arms had been bound from her fingers to her elbows, and some blood had seeped through the bandages.

His heart sank as he crouched beside her and, sensing his presence, she turned her face toward his.

"Do you know me?" he said.

Her eyes showed no recognition.

"Can you remember your name?"

Her bandaged hand went to her face, but stopped short of touching it.

From behind him, the attendant said, "Tell the reverend your name."

Matthew winced at the sharpness of his tone and would have remonstrated with him, but the young woman said, "My name is Bridget Fagan."

"No," Matthew said.

"My father was a bricklayer."

"Your name is Mary Tolliver. You had a child that died. Do you understand me? Think on it, Mary. Grief has driven you from your senses."

Her gaze wandered from him, past him, taking in the room as if she'd never seen it before and could not comprehend its planes and angles now.

"I broke a mirror in Molly's shop," she said.

"Do you understand me, Mary?"

"My name is Bridget Fagan."

Matthew was growing dizzy. He knew that he ought to stand.

"May God forgive me," he said. "Have I found you too late?"

And in that moment it was as if a veil had dropped, and her eyes fixed on his and grew fiery, as she said in a low whisper that the attendant could not hear, "Too late for you, Matthew."

Startled, Matthew drew back. He tried to rise, but halfway up his balance failed and he stumbled and had to grab for the rail at the end of the cot. He missed it, and would have fallen had the attendant not reached him in time.

Normally these episodes would pass in a moment. This one did not.

There was no chair in the room. The attendant lowered him to sit with his back against one of the walls, and then ran for a doctor. Matthew felt as if he was in a sea, a blood-warm sea, and he was rising and falling with its motion. Each rise and fall, he knew, was a beat of his heart. Each surge of the tide was a flush of his life's-blood through his head, the barriers broken, its flooding unchecked.

He saw the young woman sit up, and swing her legs off the cot. Her bandaged arms were like paws, blunt and bloodied. She sat there, staring at him. Her face was slack. Where for a moment there had been fire, now there was an absence behind it. He could see that there were red marks on her cheeks where scratches had been made and had begun to heal.

She rose to her feet, and began to move across the room toward him. Crouching down, she stared blankly into his face. He tried to speak, but it was as if a great weight had been hooked into the corner of his mouth.

Her gaze roved over his features. Something flickered there.

Then she rose and returned to her cot.

The attendant arrived with the doctor no more than a minute or two later. The doctor spoke to Matthew in scrambled words that he could not understand. Beaten and drained, he did not even try to listen. He knew only one thing.

The young woman on the cot had the face of Mary Tolliver.

But the face bore no scar.

MATTHEW'S GREATEST FEAR, as the days passed, was that they would keep him here and he would eventually be forgotten. How easily that could happen. He was unable to speak, or even move. He lay in a whitewashed room with a wooden cross upon the wall. Weeks seemed to pass without news, and no one ever thought to tell him anything. Or did they tell him, and he failed to remember?

Some days a female inmate was sent to sit with him and read aloud from the bible. She read random pages, without order. But even then the scriptures retained their power; he began to feel a limited strength returning to his left arm. After a while he could lift it a few inches from the bed and push against the mattress with his knuckles. With persistence, he might soon be able to grip.

Then, one day, instead of a lunatic with a bible at the end of his bed, there was Jacob. Nervous and uncertain, with the brim of his old hat clenched in his hands and a suggestion of tears in his eyes. Jacob had come to take him home. He'd brought a wagon borrowed from the next parish and a fourteen-year-old girl to nurse him on the journey.

His doctor gave him a final examination, and a few parting words.

"I am encouraged by your recovery," he said, "as you should be." And he held Matthew's face in his hands and turned it, first this way and then that. "I am optimistic that the power of speech may return, and I see no reason why your power of movement should not continue to increase. I have known patients with your condition make a full and complete recovery. But their attacks were less severe. And they were younger and stronger than you. I think you should continue in hope. And be grateful for whatever you receive."

Two of the asylum's attendants dressed him for the journey in the clothes in which he'd arrived. They bundled him in blankets, sat him in a chair, and then carried man and chair down to the yard where the wagon waited. They sat him in a corner of it, and wedged him there with pillows and cushions.

Jacob drove the horses. The child sat with Matthew and watched. Where the road was rough and he started to slide, she moved over and righted him. She was small, but surprisingly strong. When they stopped at the coaching inn where he'd talked to the old soldier, she fetched water and held the cup to his lips. As Matthew drank, he raised his eyes to her face. It was unfamiliar to him, but he saw the scar that divided her brow. Their eyes met, and he knew.

She settled opposite and watched him for the rest of the journey.

He ached to tell her of the plans he'd had to make amends. Of the plot of ground and the quiet grave under the elm, of the prayers he'd said, of the prayers he'd hoped they might say together. But it was all hollow. It had been for his comfort, not for hers. Salve for his conscience, where there could be no balm for her pain.

The child disappeared after they'd reached the parsonage. Jacob was joined by the blacksmith from the Wetherby estate. They didn't use a chair but faced each other and gripped each other's elbows to make a seat on which they carried Matthew to the house, one to either side. The toes of his dangling shoes skimmed the longer grasses, as if he hovered above the ground without touching it.

"See, Reverend?" gasped Jacob as they shuffled him up the path. "See what it is to fly with the angels."

Mrs Temple was waiting to see them in, and directed them toward the sitting room. Matthew saw that his bed had been brought downstairs. He had not been forgotten, as he'd feared. He had never been forgotten.

Mrs Temple took off his shoes, and they laid him on the bed in his clothes. She sent the men away and then stood before him. He tried to smile. He knew that his effort would probably look bizarre.

"Oh, Reverend," she said. "Matthew. Promise me you will not give in to despair, and I shall do the same. We may question God's will but we cannot hope to know his mind."

Her use of his name did not escape him. He had never heard her be so familiar before.

She went on, "This is Bridget."

Matthew was able to turn his head sufficiently to see that the young girl had entered the room, and was standing behind Mrs Temple. "She'll be helping me to care for you," Mrs Temple said. "She came to us with a reference from your asylum doctor. You see how God provides?"

But Matthew could remember that when she'd arrived with Jacob to collect him, the asylum doctor had shown no sign of knowing her.

That night, Mrs Temple fed and bathed him, and then she retired and the girl named Bridget came in to sit with him.

The hour grew late, and the house grew quiet. Jacob's dog barked once, and far away. Bridget sat with the oil lamp dimmed, and an open book unread on her knees. Her eyes were on him, and she never seemed to blink. Matthew thought back over that mysterious list…the life of a child, a face of innocence, the power of a serpent's poison. What did it mean? And what else might it have contained?

He saw her lay aside the book. He watched as she drew a plain silk handkerchief from her sleeve. She reached for his water glass on the bedside table and spread the handkerchief over it, pulling the silk tight so that it stretched across the opening like the skin of a drum.

Then she raised it to her lips and tilted back her head, unnaturally far. He saw teeth that were hooked like cats' claws, but only for an instant; they burst through the tight silk with an audible pop, and then he saw a milky fluid dribbling down the inside of the glass as she chewed at the fabric.

When she was done, she unhooked herself from the silk and used it to wipe her lips before returning it to her sleeve. There was now about an inch of cloudy water in the glass.

Moving with a rustle as her dress brushed along the length of the sheets, she brought the glass to him. She reached across the bed, and he felt her breath against the exposed base of his throat where the collar of his nightshirt began.

She picked up his left hand and, bringing it across his chest, wrapped the fingers of it around the glass. He hadn't the strength to resist her. With her hand over his own, she raised the glass to his lips.

As he felt its touch, he heard her whisper close to his ear.

"By your own hand," she said. The first and the last words he would hear from that mouth.

And then she tipped the poison into his.

CONSTANCE TEMPLE, A light sleeper who refused any opiate to ease her pain, was alerted by a scream from the girl followed by the sound of a glass breaking. By the time she reached the sitting room, it was too late. Matthew had half slid out of his bed and onto the floor, and was stone dead.

The girl named Bridget had backed off as far from him as it was possible to get, and was distraught.

"I saw him with the glass and dashed it from his lips," she said, "but it was too late."

Mrs Temple carefully picked up the intact base of the glass. There was a drop of white fluid in the angle. She sniffed it briefly, and recoiled.

"But I thought he could do nothing for himself," Bridget said.

"Perhaps he exaggerated his infirmity," Mrs Temple said, carefully setting the broken glass down, "so no one would interfere." Then she looked at Bridget.

"Hush, child," she said. "Do not be afraid. Nobody will blame you."

And no one ever did, although no one could account for the poison. Bridget vanished soon after, and the one person who might have explained it was no longer of this world.

There was hope of some leeway, but the Archbishop was adamant. The child's account of the parson's last moments left no room for doubt. The Word of the Lord was clear: *Know ye not that ye are the temple of God, and that the Spirit of God dwelleth in you? If any man defile the temple of God, him shall God destroy; for the temple of God is holy, which temple ye are.*

So Matthew Price, servant of God and defiler of his temple, was buried outside the churchyard in the very plot of land that he'd been securing for others' use. He was laid to rest one week after his suicide, sometime between the hours of nine and midnight. Only Jacob knew the hour for sure, and Jacob made no note.

It may be assumed that he'd have needed help with the body. It's possible that Constance Temple may have been at the graveside. A woman was seen there, it was said.

But all that can be said with certainty is that Matthew ended his earthly existence with no prayers, no marker, and no eternal company in the ground save that of one unshriven babe.

O, VIRGINIA

I GREW UP ON those stories where the circus comes to town. You know the ones. It's always a circus or a travelling fair, and the people who come with it are always somehow *other* and scary. A small and placid community gets all shaken up, the town's suddenly full of magic, and everybody's life is changed and made mysterious.

I don't know why those stories meant so much to me. I read them in books I got from the library, but they might as well have been taking place on Mars. Our town had a visit from a circus twice a year, and it was nothing like that.

Ours was a circus and travelling fair combined. It was family-owned, with the same name appearing on the show posters, the booths, and the sides of the clapped-out wagons that brought it all in. They pitched on a rubble-strewn croft and they stayed for four days at a time. When they went, the croft reverted to a parking place for lorries and haulage vehicles. During those four days and nights, crime rose, drunkenness increased, and the streets all around were measurably less safe. There was a concentration of lights like an electrical storm. There was the noise of old pop records, played at a deafening level that was way beyond the limits of the equipment.

Naturally, for an eleven-year-old it was a magnet.

It was magic of a kind, I suppose. Not the magic of the stories, but a sweaty, oily, ugly kind of magic. Mine wasn't one of those stable, self-contained little communities, it was an industrial suburb in the north-west of England. And the show people weren't in any sense ethereal. My memory is that the rides were all supervised by medically classifiable morons, and the sideshows by change-counting fishwives with hands like tree bark.

A couple of times I went on my own, but mostly I'd go with Otto. Otto was a half-German boy, an oddity in the school, and I expect that this was part of the reason why we were friends. While the fair was in town, we'd go just about every night; we scrounged what money we could and pooled it and made it last, but even when our money was gone we still went along anyway. We'd hang about. Walk around. Watch. Occasionally some of the people who ran the stalls would tell us to get out of the way of the paying customers, but mostly we were invisible.

We'd stand outside the Wall of Death, and we'd watch the walls shake as the motor bikes went around inside. That was when we couldn't afford to go in. The Wall of Death was one of the few attractions where they didn't turn us away because we were too young. They wouldn't let us into the knife-thrower's show, because they made this big thing about how the woman who stood there would have to take most of her clothes off to make her the least possible target so she could avoid the blades. Crowds of young drunks would suddenly develop an animated interest in the knife-thrower's art.

Otto and I were still in short trousers. We weren't even tall for our ages. Over the past three years' worth of visits we'd been frequently rebuffed. When we tried to get into the freak show, it was the same kind of story.

The woman in the pay booth looked down on us and said, "How old are you two?"

"Eleven," Otto said.

"Twelve," I said, lying.

"Can you see that?" the woman said, and she pointed at something that was pinned up in the booth beside her. Obediently, we looked. It was one of those joke car number plates and it read, RU21.

She said, "What does it say?"

"It doesn't say anything," Otto said.

So now she pointed to the letters and numbers, one at a time. "It says are…you…twenty-one. Are you?"

I was ready to slink off, but Otto was genuinely puzzled. "How does it say that?" he said.

"This is a show for grownups. And you're little kids. So bugger off, boys, and don't mither. Come back when you're older."

Crestfallen and embarrassed, we retreated to a distance.

"Rotten cow," Otto said.

"Yeah," I agreed, unable to think of anything of equal daring.

We went to look at other things, but we kept coming back to the same spot. I can't speak for Otto, but even the outside of the freak show had a terrifying fascination for me. It was basically a lorry, but the shape of it had disappeared because fold-out sides and add-on pieces had turned the whole thing into a shanty building. Lurid sign-writing on the sides, more vivid than it was accurate, read: *Abominations of Nature, Freaks and Monsters*.

And, most mystifyingly, *Parts of the Stars*.

For a while, we watched people going in. Then we watched them as they came out, and we tried to read their expressions to get some idea of what they might have seen inside. Most were talking or looking ahead to whatever it was they were planning to do next. It was as if the show had already passed from their mind and left no impression. But not everyone was like that. There were quite a few nervous gigglers, mostly girls with their boyfriends piling it on. Odd ones—and these were the ones who caught my imagination—emerged and slipped off into the night, faces pale and dismayed.

What had *they* seen?

And what exactly was the meaning of that expression they wore? It wasn't just the susceptible ones. Some of them looked like quite hard types. It was as if they'd been hit with something they'd never even imagined they could feel. I can't describe it. They looked suddenly fragile.

Disarmed.

Otto wanted to see if we could peek into the circus, so I went along. There was an open flap at the back where the acts came and went, and sometimes you could get an angle and see a six-inch-wide slice of the action for nothing.

The circus wasn't much. An aunt took me, once. There appeared to be three performing families and they swapped around and helped in each others' acts. I counted four horses, three camels, and one sad-looking elephant. The trapeze family had a certain glamour, but that was helped by distance. The man who did the catching got drunk and picked fights in local pubs while the two women, awesome in flight, looked flat-footed and stocky when you saw them shopping in Tesco's. The circus had no band, just an amplified Hammond organ, and there were rumours about the organist that small boys like us were never supposed to hear.

Neither of us could see anything, and Otto finally had to concede that we were wasting our time, and then it started to rain so we moved to another part of the ground.

Now we were close to the knife thrower's tent, where there was a man who kept up a constant come-along drone over the loudspeaker system. The knife thrower was up there on the forestage in his fringed jacket, and there alongside him was his moll who promised to take her clothes off. This was no dream girl. Only in retrospect do I realise what she actually looked like: a hardened, tired, working-class woman with bottle-blonde hair that didn't match the colour of its roots. The two of them were just disappearing inside.

It must have been the middle of a slack evening. I suppose that the pitch-man must have been aware of us hanging around all night because suddenly, over the loudspeaker system, we heard, "All right then, lads. Do you want to see the show?"

We blushed, we panicked. Yes, he was looking our way; and just about everyone in the fairground, we imagined, would be able to hear him calling to us.

"We're just waiting to meet someone," I called out, and we backed off further.

"We could have gone in, then!" Otto said to me a couple of minutes later, furiously and under his breath. I pointed out that he hadn't shown any noticeable courage when the offer was being made.

I realised that, somehow, we'd gone full circle and we were back at the freak show.

The rain had started to come down heavily now, and we were cold. We'd no gloves, but we dragged our pullovers down over our knuckles. Avoiding the mud, we found a bit of canvas to stand under.

From here, we could see all the misspelled publicity and the amateurish paintings on the sides of the boards. All right, so we couldn't get in. But speculation was free.

Otto said, "If a calf's got two heads, how does it know which way it wants to go? I mean, do they both have control of everything?"

"It could be that one of them's just like a passenger," I suggested. "Otherwise they'd have to work something out and I don't think cows are all that bright."

I was keeping one eye on the people coming out. Not so many of them, now. Apprehensive though I was of what might be inside, I started to envy them. They'd *seen*. Their score in life was higher than mine. I felt a kind of rage against my limitations. There was somehow no dignity in being so protected.

One came out with his head bowed, and I could have sworn that he was in tears.

After some further discussion about the coordination of six-legged sheep, I suddenly said, "What I'm wondering is, what does it mean by *Parts of the Stars?*"

Otto got smug. "I know that," he said.

"How?"

"I just do. It's pieces of famous people's dead bodies. If you're famous and you die, they don't just bury you like they do anyone else. They make you have this special operation."

"What's the point of an operation when you're dead?"

"It's not like an ordinary operation. They cut you right open so everything comes out," Otto said, with an all-encompassing gesture that made the entire process only too vivid. "Then they cut the top of your head off with a saw, and get your brain."

"What for?"

"It's the law. My grandmother got all upset because they wanted to do it to my granddad."

"Your granddad wasn't famous," I said, thinking that I'd spotted the flaw and that this was all turning into an enormous con on Otto's part.

He wasn't fazed. "You don't have to be," he said. "But if you *are* famous and you die, you get it done to you for certain."

That was it, I'd bought it now. My imagination was hooked, and I started to get into the swing of it.

I said, "Imagine not being dead, and waking up while they're doing it."

"If you weren't dead when they started, you'd be dead afterwards."

"What's the point of it?"

"It's so they can look at everything and work out what you died of," Otto said with assurance. "They have doctors who don't mind that kind of thing. Everything they take out doesn't get buried, it gets put in jam jars in stuff like vinegar. They only bury the part that's left over."

I said, "What kind of things are you talking about?"

"Brains," Otto said. "Eyes." I imagined people lining up to get into heaven, reamed out and flip-skulled. Daylight shining through the holes where their eyes had been. If they had such a thing as daylight in heaven.

But Otto wasn't finished yet. He lowered his voice. "Rude parts," he said.

My heart did a somersault.

"Titties?" I said in a breathless, anguished whisper.

"Of the Stars," said Otto. Then he said, "And, you know what I heard they've got?"

I waited.

He told me.

After that I looked across at the freak show with renewed angst and interest. Rain had more or less settled in for the night. Drops of it were sizzling on the hot light bulbs. The fairground was emptying, and some of the stalls were already closing up. Someone with a pole came along and lifted some of the overhead canvas, and a couple of gallons of rainwater hit the ground only yards away.

They closed up the freak show, then, and Otto and I finally gave up and went home. We had to walk home in the rain, because we were pennies short of our bus fare. I got shouted at for getting my hair wet and my clothes soaked through. That night I slept deeply, and dreamed of the Parts of the Stars.

The next day was a school day.

During the lunch hour, Otto and I went to the pie shop and then took our pies down to the canal. We sat on a bench and ate the pies, and then we screwed up the white paper bags and shied them at the ducks on the murky, reed-clogged water. The ducks squawked and made a fuss because they thought the bags were bread, but then they quickly lost interest.

"You can see the circus and the fair from the bridge," said Otto.

The intention was that we'd just go to the bridge and look. I don't recall the exact sequence, but I know it was inevitable we'd end up at the fairground. By then we had about fifteen minutes of the lunch hour left, and I was optimistically thinking we'd have plenty of time to get back, even though it had taken us the best part of half an hour to get down there.

It all looked quite different in daylight. It was just as tacky, but with none of the redeeming excitement. Dead bulbs hung on their lines. The sideshow stalls had been emptied of their cheap soft toys and plaster ornaments.

Otto said, "The Wall of Death's gone."

I'd felt that something was missing, and I saw that he was right. There was a bare churned-up space where the Wall of Death had been, the shape of a raw O still imprinted on the ground. They'd struck it and moved on already. It wasn't even the weekend, yet.

Looking around now, I could see that some of the other attractions had been partly dismantled. The cars had been taken off the Spider, and its legs hinged up in the middle. There was no roof on the Waltzer. They were no longer fairground rides, but more visibly machines on trailers.

Free-standing metal barriers had been put across to close off the area, but there was no one around. It was lunchtime, after all. The fairground workers were probably over in their caravans, which from here looked like a gathering of wedding cakes.

"The freak show isn't locked," Otto said.

He was right about that, as well. There was a big padlock on the entrance door of the shanty building, but the hasp was turned back and the padlock was hanging open.

"Fancy a look?" Otto said.

"We'd get done," I said.

"Not if we're quick."

Otto didn't even wait. He slipped around the barrier and walked straight across the open ground toward the freak show. I didn't move. He stopped by the door and turned to look back at me. We had one of those silent arguments over a distance, all mouthings and exaggerated gestures. I was trying to point out to him that we were in school uniform; even if we were spotted and ran, we'd be traceable. He didn't get it. He carried on not getting it for a while, and then he opened the door and went in.

My heart was hammering like a drum filled with stones. I was convinced that Otto was about to be caught. It was perfectly possible, even probable, that someone was working inside; but I heard no bellowing, no shouting, nothing.

Inside me, something seemed to burst. Before I even knew what I was doing, I ran over and went in after him.

The shanty had a canvas roof, and the light inside was like the light in a tent. The floor creaked as I stepped in and closed the door behind me. I was working out my excuses. I was taking my cat to the vet's and I saw it run in here. I'd heard someone shouting for help. Something. Anything.

I looked around.

My first feeling was of an enormous sense of cheat. There was a two-headed calf, all right. It was a photograph, pasted onto a board. Almost everything was a photograph, apart from the tallest and smallest people in the world, who were life-sized but incredibly lousy painted figures on hinged sheets of hardboard. In a display case there was a pair of tiny boots and something that appeared to have been stuck together out of a dried fish and a monkey. In a frame behind that was a birth certificate for the oldest man in Britain. It was on shiny photocopier paper that had faded to the point where only parts of it were at all legible.

Something snorted behind me, and I almost hit the roof. I turned around. In a waist-high pen was a sheep with matted wool. It was a live one, but it seemed to be kneeling. When I looked more closely, its front legs were oddly bifurcated so that a pair of spare and useless hooves stuck out behind.

This, presumably, was the six-legged sheep. It wasn't six-legged at all; it was just desperately, sadly crippled. It made a scrabbling sound as it hitched itself around in the confined space. Coordination would never be a problem for it. The poor beast couldn't even stand.

And then I heard Otto call out in a whisper, "They're down here."

He'd come around a corner, and was beckoning me down into the back part of the shanty. He disappeared out of sight and before following him, I looked at the sheep again. Its eyes were dull, and it had no interest in me. It didn't appear to have any interest in anything.

It was darker at the back of the building. Set apart from the rest of the non-show, this section led to the exit. I saw shelves. I saw jars.

"Parts of the Stars," Otto said proudly, as if they were here to prove him right.

I wasn't looking at the parts of the stars right then. I was looking at the Medical Mistakes that began the section. Mostly these were plaster casts of deformities, but there was one big jar with a tiny, drowned-looking body squashed up into it. It looked like a baby mouse before its fur grows and its eyes open, so pale that you could see the entire map of veins through its skin. It was floating in murky fluid and it was heartbreakingly human.

Then there were more jars. They weren't jam jars at all, they were far too big. Otto seemed to have come straight to these and to have noticed nothing else.

"Look," he said.

I looked. He was pointing to a half-gallon container with its lid sealed all around with sellotape and a handwritten label that read, in big block capitals, THE PENUS AND TESTICCLES OF ERROL FLYNN. Down in the bottom of the jar was something that looked at first like a bowel movement, and at second glance like an oversized gherkin.

I looked at the next one. BOGEY'S LUNG. I remembered my dad saying that Bogey had died of lung cancer. My mother had almost run from the room. Cancer was a word you only whispered, back then, and never in the presence of children; it was like the name of one of the major demons.

The object that was supposed to be Bogey's lung resembled a stiff, cooked liver. The next jar had the same murky fluid but nothing obviously in it. No label, and just a residue of sludge at the bottom.

I said, "What's that supposed to be?"

"Bogey's bogies," Otto suggested, and we had a cackling fit made even more intense by my terror of being heard.

I moved along, and looked at some of the others. Some of the subjects dated way back, and a lot of the so-called stars I'd never heard of. All the time, I was tensed for the slightest noise from outside. As far as sound was concerned, the walls were so flimsy that there might as well have been no barrier between us and the rest of the world.

Otto was skipping everything, looking only at the labels until he found what he was looking for.

"It's here," he said excitedly.

I moved to join him. On the top shelf, just out of reach, was THE VIR-GINIA OF MARILYN MONROE.

I said, "What's a Virginia?"

Otto said, "I think it's another name for…you know."

I peered.

"I can't see anything," I said.

"Reach it down."

I was startled at the very suggestion. As if we weren't criminals enough!

"No," I said.

"You're soft, you," Otto said scornfully. "I'll do it."

"You'll get us both killed!"

"That's about the only thing that would shut you up from whining."

He stretched up his arms to reach it down. Otto had begun to outgrow his school blazer and it was a size too small, so the sleeves rode up to somewhere around his elbows. They stayed there as he lowered the jar.

The object inside the jar bobbed as the fluid tipped. Clouds rose inside as years-old sediment was disturbed. I looked around, terrified, but I couldn't bring myself to leave. I had to see.

"It's like piss soup," Otto said, holding it up before his face and inspecting it closely.

He gave it a shake.

I think they were old confectionery jars, the kind with the plug-in glass stopper for a lid. The stopper just sits there, held in by its own weight. The lid had been sealed into place with sellotape, but the sellotape had dried out completely until it was brown and crackly, like insects' wings. As soon as the surging fluid hit it, the lid flew off.

The stink was incredible. The stuff showered onto the floor and with it slithered something about the size and colour of a rotten banana peel.

"That's it!" Otto said excitedly.

I was horrified. Otto had put the jar aside on the floor, and was crouching over the mess on the boards. How he could even breathe the air without keeling over, I don't know.

I was trying not to cough, because of the fumes. It wasn't vinegar, it was something else.

"I don't want to see," I said, with my own breath catching in my throat.

"You've got to!" insisted Otto, as if his own experience wouldn't be validated without someone else along.

I could see more than I needed to from where I was standing. The jar exhibit resembled a piece of brown leather, like one of those ancient sandals they dredge up out of a peat bog. Part of it had bristles, like pork rind. I didn't want to look any closer. If it genuinely was what it purported to be, I suddenly wanted to see it even less.

It wasn't the reaction I might have expected to have. I mean. The Virginia of Marilyn Monroe. A boy could only dream.

But these weren't the kind of dreams that I wanted.

The stink was indescribable, and it was getting even worse.

"It's melting," Otto said, incredulously.

He was right. Exposed to air, the object was deliquescing before our eyes. In less than a minute, it was slime.

He stood up. Our eyes met.

"Come on," I said.

We burst out of the exit door running. I don't know if anyone saw us, and we didn't stop to see. We didn't even slow until we reached the canal and then, even though we were a good ten minutes late for afternoon school, we had to slow to a walk.

Otto seemed exhilarated. I remembered the reactions we'd observed on people emerging, the only evidence on which we could try to gauge the emotional temperature of what lay inside. It was only years later that I was to realise that whatever was in the shanty was emotionally neutral. It was the interior architecture of the people that governed their reactions.

Otto was high. My timing was bad, and he looked at me as I was wiping my eyes on one of my sleeves.

"You fucking baby," he said. But not just with the contempt I would have expected; there was a certain wonder in his tone as well.

"Shut up," I said.

Nothing more was said after that. We could each incriminate the other, so probably nothing would be. We braced ourselves for terrible consequences, but none came. One of the girls complained about the strange smell in the French classroom that afternoon, and asked for a window to be opened. Even that might have been for some other reason, although I don't honestly think so.

The next time I was in the library, I looked up Virginia in the dictionary. It puzzled me, because it was a place in the United States and not a part of the body at all. Otto talked about our exploit a few times, but I never encouraged him and after a while we let the subject drop.

The next year, we went again. The knife thrower didn't return in that next season but the Wall of Death and the freak show were there, both unchanged and as dilapidated as before. We hovered outside the freak show for a while, and then we decided to try it on. Our voices had dropped in the course of the year, which I suppose meant that a couple of other things had dropped as well. There was someone different in the booth, a teenager who looked as if he only shaved once every couple of weeks, and then only to take the tops from off his spots. He took our money and let us in without a murmur.

Everything was the same, even the sheep. It shuffled and it stared into nowhere. A few other people were in there with us, trying to make the most out of a lousy-value deal. Otto and I went straight through to the Parts of the Stars.

There they were. Errol's tacky tackle. Bogey's bogies.

And there, at the end, in the same jar, in fluid that wasn't noticeably fresher than the rest; magically restored or somehow otherwise replaced, The Virginia of Marilyn Monroe.

I suppose we should have drawn the obvious conclusion, but we didn't. I think we still assumed it was real. Trust and gullibility are things that we're born with, and they can take time to unlearn. Perhaps we can only absorb one of life's big lessons at any given moment, and I'd already had one of mine when my heart had moved in a way that I could never have imagined before, and that I would never afterwards forget.

That's my excuse, anyway. I can't think of any other way to explain without shame how, for the rest of that year and for some time thereafter, I went around holding the awed conviction that our experience had been an authentic one and that when it came to Virginias, every woman had a minimum of two.

MISADVENTURE

FOUR OF US waited in the van, parked under a streetlamp on the bridge. Below us ran the motorway, a river of light in a valley of steel, a steady flow of people with somewhere to be. Beside the motorway stood the gym and the parking lot that served it. Well-lit, but almost deserted now.

Outside the van, our foreman paced up and down. He had his phone in his hand. Every now and again he'd glance at it, checking the signal.

"They call him the Sheriff," Peter the Painter said.

No one else responded, so I did.

"Why?"

Peter had his little finger stuck in his ear. He waggled it with a crackling sound and then inspected the result.

"You'll find out," he said, and wiped off on his overalls.

To look at us, you'd think we were a gang getting ready to rob the place. We were a rough-enough set of characters and nobody was in a mood for conversation. There was Peter the Painter, who I knew, and a couple of others who I didn't. Miserable-looking types, both. Disappointed men who'd reckoned themselves cut out for something better. We all sat as far away from each other as it was possible to get. One of them lay across the back seat with his hand over his eyes, shading them from the lights.

"What's going on down there?" Peter said, so I took a look.

"I think the boss is coming out," I said.

The gym's parking lot was floodlit but close to empty. The last of the customers had left about fifteen minutes before, and staff had been drifting out steadily ever since.

Two figures were now emerging through the glass doors. Outside the van, our foreman stopped his pacing and shaded his eyes for a better view. Way down below, the two appeared to be bidding each other goodnight. They were so far off that you'd need a sniper's eyesight to be sure.

The last man waited until the other had driven away, and then he started to make a call. Almost immediately, our foreman's phone played a tune.

It was a conversation that was over in just a few seconds.

"We're on," our foreman said as he got behind the wheel.

It took us no more than a couple of minutes to get down there. A gym doesn't really describe it. You'd think you were looking at a factory unit, an immense low-rise building with no visible windows and all its air ducting on the outside. Inside it were tennis courts, squash courts, swimming pool, sauna, and a weights room the size of a zeppelin hangar. On the outside, a second swimming pool and a barbecue terrace.

By the time we arrived, two more vans were onsite. Unlike ours, these were clean and had all their original doors and didn't look as if gypsies had been keeping dogs in them. They had ladders on their roofs and the name of a building maintenance company on their sides. When we went into the club's foyer to be briefed, the two men who'd arrived with them stayed apart from the rest of us.

Outside the doors, our foreman exchanged a few words with the gym's manager and then the manager got into his car and drove away.

Then the foreman came inside.

"Right," he said. "Here's how it's going to be. We've until the end of the week to get everything done. We can only work when the place is closed, which means from ten at night until seven in the morning."

He winced, hitched up and scratched his nuts through his pants, and carried on. "Tonight we mask off all the switches and skirting boards. There's some filling and sanding to be done. We need to drain the pool and clean it out—it's a two-day job just to empty it, so there are waders on the van.

Once it's empty we need to recaulk the expansion joints and fill it up again. There are tiles to replace in the steam room, and locker doors to rehang in the changing areas. I'll do a walk-around and show you where the work needs doing. Any questions?"

I said, "What about cameras?"

"The manager's switched them off."

And one of the men I didn't know said to no one in particular, "I suppose that means he's in on the deal."

"Enough of that," the foreman said. "You don't care."

It was about ten-thirty.

I wondered why they called him The Sheriff.

DON'T EVER LET anyone tell you that a modern building with all its lights on can't feel spooky. Only the tennis courts were dark, separated from the main walk-though by hanging nets. Also, the grille was down on the sports shop and they'd locked up the crèche. Otherwise everything was wide open and ablaze, and as we walked around it was like one of those movies where you wake up and you're the last person on earth and you can go any-where. The world's your playground but it still feels as if you're being daring. Someone had been through ahead of our arrival, spray-marking each of the job sites with a white arrow or otherwise pointing them up with coloured tape or a note.

It was just snagging work, really. The building had been up for five years and the faults were no more than routine wear and tear. They were superficial but they made the place look bad. If the place looked bad then the members would complain. The membership would be families, mostly—so this wasn't like a boxing gym or a backstreet hangout for bodybuilders, where a bit of exposed brick or a leaking roof only added to the ambience. This was pastels on the walls and ciabatta in the restaurant, and you'd better believe it.

The Sheriff assigned me to help Peter. The two newcomers, who he called Geordie and Jacko, were to work around the pool. They had to chisel out broken tiles in the steam room until the pool's water level had dropped low enough for them to put on the waders and start scrubbing. All four of us stood there and watched as the Sheriff flipped back a cover and opened the sluice, and while he was doing it I heard the one called Geordie say, "Hey. What was that?"

He was looking out at the pool. After an hour without use it had settled to almost complete tranquillity, and its surface was like a vast blue gel. We were at the deep end, where it seemed to go on down for ever and ever.

"What was what?" I said.

He seemed about to answer, but then he changed his mind.

Peter the Painter lowered his voice to me as we were all walking along the side of the pool toward the exit.

"This is going to be fun," he said. "Not even got started yet, and already he's seeing ghosts."

I saw Geordie looking back again as we filed out of the door to go back to the foyer. I was last out, and I lingered.

Maybe I saw what he saw, I don't know. But I saw something. A dark shape in the deep end, like a big fish making a fast turn. But only the turn, and then there was nothing.

Which only made sense when you considered that the main drain was down in the deepest part of the pool and that as the sluice opened and the pump started, it would create eddies right down at the bottom. All right, so for a moment it had looked like something black and muscular, limbless and featureless and turning on itself like an eel, vanishing as quickly as it had been called into creation. But an eddy in any great weight of still water would bend the light in exactly such a way.

And if anybody ought to know a ghost when they saw one, it was me.

WHEN I WAS thirteen, I had a bad fall. I hit my head and they tell me that my brain swelled up and it almost killed me, and I suppose that's the reason I started to see things. It ended when I finally got better. But while it lasted, it was quite something.

It happened when I was playing with some friends in the ruins of Feniscowles Hall. It was a building that had been around as a ruin for almost as long as it had stood as a house. Pollution from the river had driven the family out of it, and for the same reason no one had done anything with the land since. Back in the 'thirties they'd ripped all the timbers out and left the walls to fall in on themselves. Everything had become overgrown, the formal gardens had turned to jungle, and the surrounding woodland had grown dense and blocked off any access. The estate was surrounded by a barbed wire fence, but no one seemed to maintain it. It was a great and secret place to play. But the worst possible place to have an accident.

When I came to I was lying on my back and in pain, and my friends had all disappeared. I imagined that they'd gone to get help, but I later found that they'd all run home and quickly tried to establish alibis.

But I wasn't alone, that was the thing. When I managed to sit up I could see people moving through rooms and doorways that weren't even there. And I knew they had to be ghosts because there were too many of them in the same place at the same time—they were overlapping and passing through each other, as if I was seeing events that had been separated by years but were now replaying themselves all at once. The entire building was like a transparent shell before me, the broken walls of the ruin merging seamlessly up into the frozen smoke of the original lines.

I watched for a while, convinced that if I tried to rise then the spell would be broken. And then I tried to rise, and it wasn't. Everything lurched and changed a bit but the basic picture stayed the same. Maybe there were fewer layers now, but that was all.

I didn't know what to do. I knew that I'd been hurt but your thirteen-year-old self doesn't think in terms of damage—you just want it to stop, and then you'll be back as you were. I just stood there with this great silent dolls' house of activity going on before me, in a kind of stupor. After a while I saw someone coming out toward me.

She was a couple of years older than me. I don't remember what she was wearing. She was quite pretty but her teeth were bad. She looked straight at me and then she started to walk away. Not back to the house, but toward the woodland beyond it. I watched her go, and when she'd covered a few yards she came back and stood looking at me again. The way a dog does. It was then that I realised that, like Lassie, she meant for me to follow her.

She took me to a cobbled track ascending through the woods. It led up from some kind of a yard at the back of the house and I imagine it was the way they would have brought goods and supplies in. It was so overgrown that in places you'd hardly know it was there, and there were whole stretches where it had disintegrated into a rockery.

Despite the pain, it didn't seem to be taking me much effort to climb. I'd a sense that there were other figures amongst the trees, watching as I passed, but all my attention was on my guide. I don't think she looked back at me once.

I know it sounds strange as I'm telling you this. You're probably thinking that I was delirious or having a dream. All I can say is that it's what I saw. If I close my eyes I can see it almost as clearly now.

At the top end of the old driveway was a farm gate with a Keep Out notice that I was on the wrong side of. The gateway led into a posh close of big houses; nothing as grand as the ruined hall down in the wooded valley, but big enough for driveways and tennis courts and all that Agatha Christie stuff. The gate was chained and padlocked and I don't know how I got over it, but I did.

The next thing I recall was walking up one of the driveways with my ghost guide no longer in sight. A teenaged girl in riding gear came out of the house looking as if she was about to order me off the property, and I saw hostility turn to horror when she got a good look at me. She fled back into the house and I sank down to the gravel. It bit into my knees and then into my hands and finally into my cheek as I laid my face on the ground.

The earth seemed to hum, as if I was hearing its entire secret machinery for the first time.

I slept, then.

WHEN WE GOT back to the foyer, it was to find that the two regular building-company employees had stacked the ladders, sheets, paint and all the other equipment in the middle of the space and then gone. It was unlikely that we'd be seeing them again. They'd get a cut of the money but it would be us, the casuals, who did all of the grafting.

That was the arrangement. On paper it was a full-price company job, but in practice they were fielding a second team of cut-rate unskilled labour at a fraction of the cost. We took cash, we paid no tax, we got no benefits. No insurance, no security, no rights of any kind. I'd done two years of a college course that I didn't finish and three in the army, and now this was all I could get. In principle I was doing it until something better came along but in truth, I'd stopped looking.

I won't say I was happy with the station I'd reached in life, but I didn't openly resent it the way that Geordie and Jacko obviously did. Jacko more than Geordie, if I read them right. As we laid the dust sheets and put up ladders in the squash court corridor, Peter told me about them.

"A right pair of wheeler-dealers," he called them, "in their dreams."

They'd gone into business together but it wasn't a real business, more of a franchise deal where they interposed themselves as middlemen between some company with an overpriced product and a group of buyers spending someone else's money.

Peter said, "You know there's got to be something wrong with the world when a box of office widgets that cost pennies to make comes all the way from America and gets hand-delivered out of the boot of a BMW with a gimmick number plate. Blokes like them dream big but it's always on the never-never. It never lasts and they never see the end coming."

The end came when the supplying company stopped taking calls and the latest widget shipment failed to materialise. Geordie and Jacko had mortgaged their houses to buy the franchise, and now lost their shirts. They tried to get into the air-conditioning business and attended a couple of recruitment seminars for the pyramid-selling of kitchen products, but the end was already written. First the cars with the personalised plates had gone, and then the suits. Geordie had grown surly and sarcastic. Jacko had grown a beard.

It was at this point that the Sheriff came by to check on our progress. He saw us talking as he came down the corridor.

"Come on, lads," he said, "What's the hold-up?"

And Peter looked at me with one eyebrow raised.

"Nothing, boss," he said.

Then the Sheriff said to Peter, "I'll give a hand with this. You nip down and straighten that Jacko out. He won't go in the steam room. Find out what he's moaning about and get him sorted."

"I'm not the foreman," Peter said. "Why aren't you doing it?"

"'Cause I'm so sick of his fucking whining," he said. "I'm seriously worried that if he starts it up again, I'll deck him."

"Hey," I said. "I'll do it."

Well, it was nothing to me, so down I went.

I followed signs marked *Hydrous*, through the empty restaurant and down to the pool area. There wasn't just the pool and a steam room, there was the sauna and the cancer beds and both sets of changing rooms. I cut through the women's, just because I could.

Jacko and Geordie were arguing at the poolside when I got there. There was a whirlpool over the drain in the deep end and the water level had already begun to drop.

"What's the problem?" I said, and Jacko fell silent.

"He says he saw someone in there," Geordie said, and Jacko flared up again.

"I didn't say anything about that," he said. "I didn't say anything about *anything*."

"Well," I said, "let's have a look."

The steam room's door was a single sheet of toughened frosted glass, and the steam room itself was about eight feet by twelve with a tiled bench around three of its walls. The steam had been off for ages now but the starlight effect in the ceiling was on, tiny points of light that changed pattern every few seconds.

I came out and looked at Jacko.

"There's no one in there and nowhere to hide," I said. "So what exactly was it you didn't see?"

Nobody spoke and then Geordie said, "Tell him, you daft get."

"Nothing," Jacko said.

"Someone through the glass, just standing inside?"

The way his eyes widened was answer enough.

"This is what's probably doing it," I said, and I stuck my hand in through the open doorway and showed the effect when the lights played on it. It looked nothing like a person standing there, and he didn't seem impressed.

I said, "There's not enough light in there to work by, anyway. Nip up to the foyer and get a lamp with an extension lead. Nobody's going to get paid for arguing about it."

Jacko went off. As well as the beard he'd let his hair grow, and it made him look like a bony hermit type. When he was gone, Geordie said, "That's not what he told me."

"What did he tell you?"

"He said he could see a little lad in there."

"A little lad?" I said. "Can't you see when someone's trying to wind you up?"

WHEN I CAME to in the hospital, I was in a room on my own just off the medical assessment ward. My head was bandaged and I was on a drip to reduce the swelling, and loads of painkillers as well. I'm not saying I felt good, but I suppose I was mostly insulated from my injuries.

My parents came, and my aunts came, and in amongst the relief and concern there was dark talk of the police turning up as well. But I don't think anybody had the heart to give me a hard time. Back in those days they wouldn't let parents stay in hospital with a child, so I spent that night in the side ward on my own.

I don't know what hour it would have been, but I woke in the night with the certainty that there was someone in the room with me. What little light there was seemed grey and grainy and my eyes were almost gummed shut with sleep crystals, so it was hard to get a focus. But he was there. I could see him against the Venetian blind. Sitting. Half-turned away. Grey like a stone, or like some kind of a golem. A jaw like a shovel and, when he turned toward me, eyes that were just fissures.

I closed my eyes to make him go away and, when I felt as if I'd waited long enough, cautiously opened them again. It was then that I found that he'd crossed the room and was inspecting me closely. I quickly screwed my eyes shut and I didn't open them again, or relax or find sleep, until dawn came a couple of hours later. They had to change my sheets that morning.

In the course of the day my best friend Malcolm was brought in for a visit and my memory is of him holding onto his mother's hand at the end of my bed looking green and unsteady, a state which she put down to empathy but which I knew was terror at the prospect of being challenged or exposed. Malcolm was the one that I'd have least expected to run off and leave me there, but he had. We'd continue as friends, but I'd never forgive him. I hadn't thought it all the way through at that stage, but it seems to me that it was only the dead who'd shown any concern for me. The living had thought only of themselves, and left me to struggle.

Everyone seemed pleased with my progress that day and I was told that in the morning I'd be moved onto an open ward with all the other children, as if that was something I ought to look forward to.

I was feeling stronger, and I spent most of the day sitting up. So when the shovel-jawed figure came again that night I found the strength to get out of bed and flee.

I hadn't seen outside the room before, so I'd no idea where I was or which way to go. I ran blindly, convinced that he'd be right behind me. I just wasn't ready for the hospital. It was like the haunted dolls' house all over again, but this time it went on and on.

Hundreds of them. More than a thousand, maybe.

Everywhere I looked, there were more of them. Many were very old, and most were just standing. The entire building, which had been on this spot for more than a hundred years, was like a refugee station filled with the lingering images of those who'd died there. I saw people with terrible injuries, and those wasted by their suffering. I saw children, bald and bloated with drugs. Babies the size of my fist floated like bubbles through the air before me, trailing their bloody cords like the tails of kites.

When a hand fell on my shoulder from behind, I screamed out loud.

But it was only someone from the nursing staff, catching up with me to take me back to my room

JACKO NEVER CAME back. Geordie said he'd go to look for him and he didn't come back, either. It seemed to me that for men without options, they scared off far too easily.

But they were also men in a low state, and I had a theory that it took a troubled mind to see what they might have seen. I went and stood at the poolside and looked into the vortex that swirled over the drain pump. All I saw was water, twisting around and looking like something alive. I turned and looked toward the steam room, but nothing moved behind the frosted glass. Once I might have seen more, but these days I was healed. I saw no more than most other people.

When I told the Sheriff that we appeared to have a couple of deserters, he put his hands to his head and cursed them loud and long, and then got out his phone and disappeared for a while in search of a signal. Peter and I carried on with the preparation work until he returned.

"We're on our own for tonight," he said. "We need to get as much done as we can."

Over the next few hours the three of us pitched in and got as many of the jobs started as we could manage. Tomorrow there'd be some new faces brought in, but on our tight schedule we needed to grab all the ground we were able. Peter carried on with his preparation, the Sheriff started breaking tiles out with a cold chisel, and I got a bucket of filler and a ladder and started patching the cracks where plaster had shrunk away from joints.

A couple of odd things happened. Like when I threw the wrong switch in the cardio suite and all the empty running machines started up together, and Peter nearly crapped himself on the spot. I found a couple of excuses to visit the pool area again, but the Sheriff started looking at me suspiciously and so I just went back to my work.

I might not be able to see my ghosts any more, but that didn't mean they weren't there. So I took an interest when others did.

৶

THEY KEPT ME on the open ward for a couple of days and then they let me go home, with strict instructions that I was to stay in bed and take no exercise. Little did they know that they were setting a lifestyle choice that was to see me all the way through my teenaged years.

My bedroom was at the top of the stairs and my grandmother's was across the landing. She'd lived with us for two years and she'd died there the previous summer while I was away on a school trip. She'd been a widow for almost as long as I could remember, but toward the end she'd grown vague and forgetful and developed some odd ideas that meant she couldn't be trusted to look after herself. She couldn't be trusted not to empty the occasional pot of her pee into our kitchen sink, either.

For three days and nights after the ambulance brought me home, I saw nothing unusual. I had books from the library and the radio in my room, but the hours were endless and if there had been anything there to see, there's no way I would have missed it. I wondered if my so-called gift had been a short-lived one, and then after a while I began to wonder whether I'd really experienced it at all. What's memory, after all? Just certainty in retrospect. And mere certainty's no actual proof of anything.

On the fourth day, when my mother went out for an hour, I went and took a look in Grandma's old room.

The bed was still in there but the mattress was gone and the carpet had been taken up, and now it was mainly used to store empty suitcases and broken furniture that my father had ideas of someday repairing. My dad could never pass up a useful-looking piece of wood. He might never be quite sure what he wanted it for, but he always knew it had to be handy for something. He held onto one piece of driftwood for at least twenty years, moving house three times and taking it with him. After he died and I had to clear everything out, I put it in with other stuff from the garage and took it all to the local recycling point. Three or four old guys watched me dropping it into the skip, and before I left I saw one of them carrying it back to his car.

Grandma was by the bed. I'd half expected her. What I hadn't been prepared for was the massive blow to the heart it gave me to see her again. All the other ghosts had been strangers and, naively, I'd expected this one to feel the same. I don't know if she saw me or if she knew me. I don't think she did. She moved about the room, her hand outstretched, touching for things that were no longer there. For some time afterwards I tried to think what her action reminded me of, until it struck me. She was like a lone fish in a bowl, circling, the days all the same and the scenery never changing.

I'd noticed back in the hospital how all these people seemed to be hanging around near the spot where they'd died. As if they were anchored to it somehow, and unable to leave. Repeating actions that they'd once performed in the places where they'd once performed them, never straying too far.

Did this mean that they were just mindless after-images? Photographs of past actions, fading slowly with time?

No, seemed to be the answer to that one. Otherwise that girl would never have come over and led me to safety. The dead were aware. Of the living, if not of themselves.

Grandma saw me and smiled. Then seemed to forget me again, and moved on.

I STOOD AT the edge of the pool and looked into the deep end. The level had fallen but with a pumping-out rate of more than eighty gallons a minute, it should have fallen more.

The waders were a size too large for me, but no matter. I'd manage. I took the long boathook from the wall and climbed down the steps with it. The pole was about fifteen feet long and the double-hook on the end was a small one, meant for snagging the cord on a life preserver to pull it over to safety. I moved gingerly down the sloping tile, and when I reached the water's edge I went in up to my waist and then extended the hook down toward the drain cover.

It shouldn't have lifted as easily as it did. It should have been bolted down, but it wasn't. I lost my purchase on it and the water pressure sucked it back into place again, but when I got the hook in for the second time I was able to pull it completely clear. The grille spun around in the water and settled with a muffled clank. I advanced a little further and probed with the hook, down into the darkness of the uncovered drain.

I've a theory, of sorts. I don't think that ghosts are the people they were. They're more like the husks of people, the stuff left behind that the dead don't need. Shedding the earthly form like a reptile with its skin. It just doesn't make sense to me that we move on into any kind of afterlife with every scrap of material baggage that this life has thrown our way. We all have that experience of looking at the body of someone we love and knowing in an instant that they're no longer there. That they've dumped the body and flown.

And yet with ghosts, an image of the physical body is exactly what we see. Even down to clothing. Where's the sense in that? Where do you draw the line? Jewellery? Dandruff?

My dad's collection of useful-seeming timber?

Down there in the drain, my hook met resistance. I pushed a bit harder and felt it yield. It was like pushing into soft wax. I turned the pole in my hands and tried to work the hook around, looking to see if I could get any purchase.

So my theory is this. There's a condition where you can see things that aren't there to be seen, but which you've picked up with other senses. It's called synaesthesia. You taste words, you feel colours as texture. It's real to one sense, but manifests as another.

I reckon there has to be an equivalent condition where we pick up on the presence of those shed husks with whatever primitive antenna we've forgotten we have, and something makes us render it as a visual experience. The presence is real. And we really see it. But we're summoning the picture out of more subtle information.

I heard the steam room door. Out came the Sheriff, spitting dust and cursing. "Bloody thing."

I didn't look up. "What?"

"Got a piece of shit in my eye."

"Should have worn the goggles."

I'm guessing it must be a brain thing. I had it in spades for a while, and as my injuries got better I lost it. Some people reckon they're born with it. But usually you get it when your head's in a state. You don't have to fall off a wall like I did. Fear, loss, grief—anything that makes you susceptible will do it.

The invisible, made visible. For as long as it lasts.

I could feel something against the hook, so I renewed my grip on the pole and pulled. Nothing happened at first, but I kept up the pressure and then, slowly, I felt something beginning to slide. It was like drawing a cork. Steady pressure, steady pressure, and then out it came.

It erupted out of the drain in a cloud of matter, which immediately swirled around and was sucked back into the hole like a genie into its bottle. I walked backwards out of the water, pulling the cargo on my hook like a sack of mussels up the beach.

The Sheriff gawped, and forgot the splinter in his eye.

"What the fuck is *that*?" he said.

"I think it *used* to be a little lad," I told him.

And I was glad that I was out of the water by then, because he puked in it.

THEY LINGER CLOSE to where they died.

That was something I understood from very early on. I don't know how long for and I don't know why, but it's what I'd observed.

His name was Johnny Jaggs and he'd been missing for almost a year. They'd looked all over for him, but they hadn't looked here. Why would they? Only members used the pool.

But Jaggs and a couple of others had climbed over the fence on the barbecue terrace on a crowded summer's day and once they were in, they hadn't been challenged. Jaggs was the youngest, and the smallest. The others had brought him along because they thought he'd be small enough to get into the swimming pool drain and pick up the loose change they'd convinced themselves would be down there.

They were wrong about the change, right about his size. Small enough to get in, but not strong enough to fight the current and get out again. Instead of raising the alarm when he didn't resurface, they'd reacted in a way I recognised only too well.

They'd run home and established alibis, and kept their silence as the search began.

In the end it took a couple of child psychologists to get the full story out of them. As concerns had risen, the price of confession had quickly become too high until, after a while, they'd begun to believe in the tale as they told it.

I'd pulled only a part of him out of the drain. The chlorinated water had done things to the flesh and they took the rest of him out in pieces, like a late abortion. He'd only partially blocked the pipe. The efficiency of the pumps had been reduced, but not enough to make anyone act. There's a high turnover of staff in these places and it's hard to get anyone to care.

Our bosses took a hammering over our black-economy working setup, but not as much as they deserved. There was talk of nailing me and Peter for benefit fraud. I don't know about Peter but I'm still waiting to hear.

I didn't tell anyone what had led me to the blockage. I let them think it was the slow rate at which the pool had been draining, and left it at that.

Whatever haunts the pool and the steam room, I don't believe that it's little Johnny Jaggs himself. It's something he left behind at the moment of his passing, the pattern of the form in which he walked in this world, a coat that he shucked off and let fall. It's same with all of them. Incomplete, discarded, abandoned. Left to hover, to wander, and eventually to fade. To be sensed and, when conditions are right, to be seen.

But whatever they might be, whether or not they remember what they were, I do know that they see us too. They know when something's not right, and they'll try to get our attention. It seems to worry them. If there's anything I can do to ease that worry, I won't hesitate. I don't care if it costs me a job, or gets me into trouble.

When others ran or looked away, one of them was there for me.

So what if they're only the dead? I still owe them my life.

Little Dead Girl
SINGING

HERE'S ONE YOU won't have heard before.

If you're a parent with a musical child then you'll know the festival circuit. I don't mean anything that's big business or in any way high-profile. I'm talking about those little local festivals run on dedication and postage stamps, where the venue's a school theatre or a draughty church hall and the top prize is nothing more than pennies in an envelope. I'm talking about cold Saturday mornings, small audiences made up of singing teachers and edgy parents, judges whose quality varies depending on how their judgements accord with your own, and shaky little juvenile voices cracking with nerves.

As you might have guessed, I have been there.

Never as an entrant, of course. Even the dog leaves the house when I sing. But every young singer needs an adult support team rather like a racing driver needs a pit crew, to provide transport and encouragement and to steer them through the day's schedule. That's where the parents come in. Some children turn out with their entire extended families in tow, decamping with them from class to class like a mobile claque.

But not us. By the time Victoria was twelve we'd reached the point where she wanted as little fuss or pressure as possible. The thought of one of those three-generation cheer squads would have filled her with horror.

"One of you can come," she'd say. "And you're not to sit right at the front. I don't want to be able to see you."

This was last year. She liked to sing and she sang well, but she didn't like to make a big deal of it. So on the Saturday of the festival just she and I made the hour's drive to this tiny little town you've never heard of, way out in the middle of the flat country between home and the coast, with her entry slips and her piano copies and a bottle of mineral water.

They'd been running an annual festival here since nineteen forty-eight, and we'd done it twice before. This year Vicky's singing teacher had entered her for four different competition classes, spread throughout the day. The room where the earliest would take place was the one we liked least, the village hall with its high ceiling and tiny stage and no acoustic to speak of. Well, you could speak of it, but you'd have to shout to be heard at the back. And it was always so cold in there that at this time of year you could see your breath.

We sat outside in the car for a few minutes.

"All right?" I said. "Anything else you need?"

She shook her head. She didn't seem keen. I knew she'd had a bad throat for a few days and wasn't feeling entirely at her best, but in we went.

They'd already started and so we waited for an interval between competitors to find a seat. When the opportunity came, we dodged around empty chairs and a photographer's tripod and made our way down the hall.

The judge had her table out in the middle, while the spot for the singers was by an upright piano before the stage. The stage had a home-made backcloth for *The Wizard of Oz*. The judge was a woman in her late 'fifties, straight-backed, powdered, a little severe. None of which meant anything. I'd found you could never really get the measure of them until you heard what they had to say.

Vicky's name came halfway down the programme, so we settled in. The class was *Songs from the Shows* and the age group was the youngest. There was low winter sun coming in through the windows at the back of the hall and it was making the singers squint.

Early morning voices, little kids singing. Some in tune, most not, every one of them the apple of someone's eye.

Andrew Lloyd Webber was getting a real hammering. In the space of half an hour we had three *Whistle Down the Wind*s relieved only by a couple of *I'm Just a Girl Who Can't Say No*s. I recognised a few of the entrants from previous years. Only two young boys got up to sing and, bless 'em, you could tell that this was not their chosen element.

Vicky got up and did her piece. As she sat down beside me again she said, "That was rubbish."

It wasn't, but I knew that it wasn't a patch on what she could do at her best. But I also had that sneaking feeling that I'm sure I shared with every parent in the room, that out of this bunch I had the only real singer and the rest of them might just as well give up and go home.

We had a song from *Annie* and a song from *Les Miserables* and then another *Whistle Down the Wind*, and then the judge did some scribbling and called the next name.

She mispronounced it the first time and I looked at my programme to check…Cantle? But the name was Chantal, exotic enough amongst the Emmas and the Jennies. There was movement over on the other side of the room and I craned to see what a Lancashire Chantal might look like.

Up stood this little girl in a cardigan, with a bow in her top-knot and a dress that looked like funeral parlour curtains. She was tiny, and I reckoned she couldn't have been more than eight or nine years old.

She stood by the piano and waited for the judge's nod and then the accompanist started up, and then little Chantal sang a perfect piping rendition of *Don't Cry for Me, Argentina*.

Let me qualify that. It was perfect, but it was also horrible in a way that I still can't quite put my finger on. Her diction was clear and her intonation was bright. She hit all the notes dead-on, and she even acted the whole thing out.

But to see this eight-year-old doing such a precise imitation of mature emotion was like watching a wind-up doll simulating sex. She'd been drilled to a frightening degree. On one line her hand moved to her heart, on the next she gestured to the crowd. When the lines were repeated later in the song, she did exactly the same movements again in exactly the same way. There was a slightly American intonation there, as if she'd learned the words by listening to the movie soundtrack so many times that it rang in her head like tinnitus.

I looked for her mother. Sure enough, there she was. She had a little boy of about five or six beside her. The little boy was ordinary, fidgeting, eyes wandering, all his little-boy energies struggling against the imposed stillness like cats in a heavy sack.

The mother, though...she was as much of a study, in her way, as the little girl.

She wasn't old, or even middle-aged. But her youth was only there in traces, as if it had been harried out of her too soon. Her hair was a dirty-blonde froth of curls, cut short and pushed up high on her head above her ears. She was staring at her daughter as she sang, her lips twitching along. She wasn't mouthing the words as some of the mothers do, vicariously living the performance or, even worse, trying to conduct it from the sidelines. To me it seemed that she was just rapt, quite literally lost in the song, as the tenderest of souls might be overwhelmed by the greatest of artists.

I reckon you could have wheeled out Madonna herself and the London Symphony Orchestra, but you couldn't have given her a performance that could affect her half so much. And my cynical heart softened then, because whatever form it comes in, however it's expressed, it's hard to be critical of such uncompromising love.

The song ended. There was the standard scattering of applause, and the little girl's smile switched on like a bulb. Two seconds later it switched off again and she walked back to her seat as the next singer went up to take her place. Her mother bent over to whisper something but I was distracted then by a metallic bang from the back of the room, and I looked around to see a nondescript man noisily folding up his camera tripod.

The father, I assumed. My heart promptly hardened up again. I don't like it when people make it so obvious that they've no interest in the efforts of any other child than their own. It may be a universal truth, but I think we've all got a responsibility at least to pretend otherwise. Yet still you see them at school shows and concerts, not looking at the stage, flicking through the programme book, sometimes not even bothering to join in the applause. They're here to see the Third Wise Man triumph, and to them all the rest is just noise.

We've got a camera of our own, but I'd stopped taking it along. I'd started to find that if you make a big thing out of recording the moment, what you lose is the moment itself.

They stuck it out for one more song, which was about as long as it took for him to pack the video gear away, and then in the gap between entrants the four of them got up and left. The girl went out in front and her brother got dragged along behind, bobbing around in his family's wake like a ragdoll caught up on a motorboat.

We slipped out ourselves about ten minutes after that. Done quietly, it was no breach of etiquette. The class was running late and we had another one to get to, so for this one we'd check the results and pick up the judgement slip later in the day. That was how it worked; young singers and their minders in constant motion from one hired room to another, getting nervous, doing their best, hoping for praise, fearing the worst.

We planned to get some lunch after the English Folk Song. They always set up a tearoom in the church but, being no lover of grated cheese and pickle sandwiches, I had other ideas. On our way to the car, we stopped to pick up the slip from that earlier class and to check on the list of prize winners.

Strange little Chantal had taken the first prize. Second and third places went to performances that I couldn't remember.

Well, what can you do? You note it and move on.

We got into the car and drove out toward the coast, which was only another three or four miles. I thought a change of scene would be a good idea. I could sense that Vicky was unhappy; not peevishly so, just unhappy with her own performance, unhappy with the way she felt, unhappy with the day ahead and the sense of a course to be run that had no great promise of satisfaction in it.

After being quiet for a few minutes she said, "I don't think I want to go back."

"No?"

"I just want to go home. There's no point."

I said, "If that's what you want, then fine. I'm not going to force you to stay. But be sure in your own mind that you're not throwing it in for the wrong reasons. All right?"

"Mmm." She was looking out of the window.

We found a cafeteria over an Edwardian parade and, wouldn't you know it, they'd run out of ham for the sandwiches but had no shortage of grated cheese and pickle to offer.

Over lunch, we talked about the morning. Specifically, about Chantal's win.

"I can't say she didn't deserve it," I said. "Technically she's very impressive and in two or three years' time there's a chance she'll be really good. Right now I'd say she's been drilled too much. She's very mechanical and over-controlled. But I'd also have to say she's got an obvious natural gift. From here it'll depend upon how naturally it's allowed to develop, as opposed to being forced."

Vicky sat there sucking her Coke through a straw, not overhappy but not disagreeing, either. She needed a straw to keep the ice from bobbing against the metal of her brace.

I said, "And of course, we know for a fact that the room's got a curse on it and the judges are always peculiar."

I said it as a joke, but felt there was a grain of truth in it. This was the third time we'd had the same experience. It was a catch-all class that started the day, with the age range heavily weighted toward the very young. The prizes had always gone to shrill little girls who maybe didn't get the notes but did a lot of eye-rolling and arm-waving. The judges marked high on smiling and gestures, and some of the teachers played to that. A real singer probably flew right above the radar.

Well, it got her laughing when I said it was no insult to miss out on a prize in a freak show. And as we were walking to the car she said, "I think I *will* go back."

So instead of going home, we went back.

I was glad, because later in the day was when the big girls came in and the musicianship got more serious. Vicky was caught somewhere in between the moppets and the teenagers but when she sang amongst the best, she sounded as if she belonged there. Even if she didn't get a prize, it would be good for her to see it through. Prizes are nice, but what really matters is who your peers are. The quality of the people amongst whom you clearly belong.

We were laughing about something else in the car when it came to me. The little girl had stuck in my mind and had been troubling me for some reason, and I suddenly realised why.

I found myself recalling an image from a TV documentary that I'd once seen. It was about the second world war, the London Blitz. I don't know how old I'd been when I saw it, but it was an early and shocking memory. Outside a bombed-out house, this family had been laid on the pavement. One was a baby, clearly dead, but not in repose. Its mouth was open, as if caught in mid-chortle.

The image was in my mind now because it shared something with the face of the girl I'd seen that morning. I'd hate to say what. But if I close my eyes I can still see her now, eyes hooded with dark rings under them, her downturned mouth hanging slightly open, her tiny teeth like points.

I saw her again, about half an hour later.

We'd moved over into the church, which was a big improvement. Inside the church there were several large informal rooms as well as the wood-panelled nave, and they were decently heated. In the nave was the best acoustic of them all, and the best piano to go with it.

I slipped out while we were waiting for Vicky's turn in the British Composer set piece. She was complaining that her throat was dry and the water bottle was empty. She stayed behind in the hall.

The tearoom was in the middle of the building and had no windows. Metal-legged tables and plastic chairs had been set up amongst the pillars, and service was through a hatchway from a kitchen staffed by volunteers. There were some uncleared plates and crumbs on the tables but otherwise the seating area was empty apart from me and Chantal.

I recognised her easily, even from the back. That topknot, that cardigan. Just like a dressed-up doll. She was drawing something aimless in spilled sugar on one of the tables, and she was making a singsong whispering sound as she did.

"Hello, there," I said.

She jumped. Not literally, but you could see her start. She turned around.

I said, "I heard you this morning. Congratulations. You sang really well."

I was sorry I'd started this. She seemed panicked. I'd spoken to her and she didn't know what to do or how to respond. Her eyes were looking at me but her eyes were empty.

I didn't know what I could say now.

"Chantal," I heard from behind me.

It was her mother. I glanced back and saw her. She didn't meet my eyes but her gaze kind of slid around me to her daughter, as if she knew I was there and she ought to acknowledge me…and she *was* acknowledging me in her own way, but her own way was not direct.

She muttered something about being late and the two of them went off together, with me stepping aside to let them by. I don't know if she'd been speaking to me or to her daughter. I felt like an idiot, to be honest, and I wished I'd kept my mouth shut.

More than feeling stupid, I felt a little bit spooked. That was one creepy family. Chantal's eyes had been empty until her mother spoke. But I can't say for sure what I'd seen in them then.

The rest of the afternoon passed by. Other classes came and went and the voices got better and better. We heard some thrilling sopranos and one beanpole of a teenaged boy who ran in late and sang Handel like a spotty angel.

Our final session was in the nave of the church. Vicky was more or less resigned to the fact that this wasn't her best day, and she was taking something of a gonzo attitude to it all now. By which I mean that she wasn't worrying about placing or prizes, but was just getting in there and doing it. Which I've always liked better. Do a thing for its own sake, and let anything else that comes along be a surprising bonus. That's how to be an original. That way you can't lose.

So there we were. The first thing that I noticed on entering the church, up on the empty balcony above our heads, was the nondescript man with his tripod and camera. Once we were in our seats, I looked around for the other three.

And there *they* were. The boy was in the middle. Slumped, glowering. He was the one I felt sorry for. He looked like the normal one in the family and I could imagine his patience being tested to near-destruction by a day like this. It must have been Boy Hell, having to get scrubbed-up and endure hours of boredom and sitting still in the company of grownups, and all for your sister in the spotlight.

Vicky was up third. She sang her piece, and sang it well. The throat problem hadn't gone and she was up against her limit by the ends of some of the lines, but in contrast to the morning she was warmed-up and relaxed, and it was a great room to sing in. The atmosphere was completely different. The piping-little-kid factor was almost completely absent, but then I had to remind myself that all these mature and impressive young singers had probably been piping little kids once.

While Vicky was singing, there was a sharp noise from one of the rows. It didn't throw her—in fact she told me afterwards that she hadn't even noticed it—but it made me look back.

Chantal's brother had dropped something, I guessed. Probably a hymn book from the rail in front of him. His mother was giving him a kind of gritted-teeth, staring-eyes silent scolding. I looked past him to Chantal. She was completely slack, as if she'd been switched off.

That was when I started thinking of her as a little dead girl, in her funeral-home curtain dress. In fact I fantasised about the whole family of them living above the funeral parlour, and climbing into the boxes to sleep at night.

But not for long. My kid was still singing.

Even the applause sounded better in here. She sat down flushed, and I could see that she was pleased with herself.

Chantal was the youngest entrant in this class. She went up about twenty minutes later.

If anything, her performance was more extreme than the one I'd seen that morning. Her diction was so sharp that it was unpleasant to the ear. Every *r* was rolled, every *t* was a gunshot. Whatever had served her well before, she was doing more of it now. The lightbulb smile was a bizarre facepull.

I nudged Vicky and she followed my glance over at the mother. The mother was doing it again, her mouth unconsciously making the shapes of the words, living the song with her daughter. I couldn't see the balcony from my seat but I knew for sure that Cecil B would be up there, capturing it all on tape for endless home replay.

It was only the youngest member of the family who seemed to have used up all his reserves of team spirit. He wasn't paying his sister any attention at all. To be fair to him, he'd probably sat through this a hundred times at home. He squirmed in his seat and stuck an arm up in the air, stretching. His mother quickly pulled it down so he stuck it up again, instantly computing that he'd found a way to annoy her. She pulled it down almost violently now and he tried it a third time, but by then the damage was done. The movement must have caught the little girl's eye and distracted her for a second. She'd stumbled on her words. I'd only been half listening but when she went wrong, I knew it at once.

So did her mother. God, now *there* was a look. Medusa would have asked for lessons.

When it came time for the judge to give his results, Chantal got a kind mention along with everybody else but Vicky got a very respectable second prize. It was all the more welcome for being unexpected, and she was only one point behind the sixteen-year-old who took the first. I'd have been happy at the fact that she'd held her own so well amongst such a high class of singers. But what the hell, it was nice to get an envelope as well.

"I bet you're not sorry you stayed," I said to her as everybody was gathering up their papers and their coats, and she made a face that could have meant anything.

Outside the church, the sky was mostly dark and streaked with red but there was just enough light to see by. Some of the sessions would go on into the evening, but quite a few of us were dispersing to our cars.

This was never my favourite kind of countryside. Far too flat and featureless. I imagine it had all been under the sea at one time, and the best thing you could say about it was that the views were uninterrupted. Looking out now, across the road and the fields beyond, I realised that I could see all the way to the far horizon. On the horizon sat the disappearing rim of the sun, on a strip of ocean that was like a ribbon of fire.

In a minute or less, the sun would have dropped and the effect would be gone. I wasn't the only one to have my attention caught by it.

I could see Chantal about halfway across the parking area. She was out where there were few cars and she was alone. She was little more than a shadow-silhouette in the fading light but, as before, she was immediately recognisable.

I saw this little ghost take a faltering step, and then another. And then I saw her break into a run.

I don't know why. But it was as if she'd seen a doorway open up between the sun and the sea, and she'd set her mind to reach it before it closed.

Whatever was in her mind, she was running straight for the road.

I wasn't near enough to reach her. I looked around for her parents and saw them, loading their stuff into a brown Allegro. I'll swear to what happened then, because I saw it. I don't think anyone else did.

Her mother looked back over her shoulder. That's all she did. She didn't call out and she didn't even change her expression. Just looked at the running child, and the running child stopped about a dozen yards short of the road.

A couple of cars zipped by. Then the child turned and started back.

She climbed into the brown car without a word and they all drove off together.

As I said, that was last year.

This year, we went again.

Vicky had picked up a first prize in one of the classes in the city festival a few months later, and it had raised her enthusiasm enough for her to want another crack at this one. When the time came around, we sent in the forms. We skipped that perverse morning session, finally giving in to the lesson of experience, and went straight for the afternoon.

I remembered little Chantal, and when we got there I looked for her name in the programme. I felt a slight disappointment when I didn't see it. I was curious to see how she might have developed—at that age, a year can make a lot of difference in one way or another—but it seemed that I wasn't to find out.

Well, it was only curiosity.

But here's the odd thing. Chantal wasn't there, but her family was.

I knew it as soon as I saw Cecil B up in the gallery with his camera. Of course I immediately looked around the pews, and saw the mother with the boy. But no little dead girl.

The boy was in short pants and a clean shirt with a little bow tie. He was behaving himself. Or was he? By the look of him, you'd think he'd been drugged. He certainly wasn't the squirming livewire I remembered from the year before. In fact he had the same kind of slack, dead-eyed expression that I'd seen on his sister.

So if they were here, where was she? Could she have changed so much that I'd passed her outside and hadn't recognised her? I looked toward the doorway, expecting her to walk in and join them, but the stewards were closing up the room ready to begin.

The competition started, and the boy just sat there.

Until a name was called, and with a nudge from his mother he got to his feet.

Surprised, I watched him move to the piano. He took short steps. If body language could show a stammer, I reckon that walk is what you'd see. When he reached the piano, he turned to face the audience. And when the accompanist hit the first note, he switched on his smile.

The woman leaned forward in the crowd, her gaze intent, her lips already beginning to shape the first of the words. Upstairs, the man rolled the tape.

I looked at Vicky, and Vicky looked at me.

And down by the piano, when the moment came, the boy placed his hand over his heart, opened his mouth, and sang like a clockwork nightingale.

Doctor
HOOD

AT THE TOP of the narrow garden, Miranda climbed the steps to the front door of her childhood home and rang the bell. Then she waited.

No lights were showing in any of the windows. The lane on which the big house stood was a pocket of old-fashioned stillness in the city, tucked away behind the Cathedral and especially quiet at this hour of the night. You turned in through a gated opening half-hidden from the main road and seemed to enter an older, gentler, and more tranquil world. The lane was narrow and tree-lined. It wasn't maintained by the city but by the residents, who mostly left it alone.

She gave it a minute before producing her key and letting herself in.

"Dad?"

Now she stood in the hallway, and waited for an answer that didn't come. She set her overnight bag down on the floor. There was light somewhere upstairs but none down here at all, apart from the watery street lighting that shone in through the windows.

Miranda started to ascend, calling to her father as she went.

There was apprehension in her, but she wouldn't acknowledge it. She'd come here to establish that nothing was wrong. Not to flirt with dread. Dread's day would come regardless, she'd learned. Why spoil other days by anticipating it?

The next floor was also dark. The light came from the one above, where her old room had been. She stood on the landing and looked up the stairs.

"Dad?"

Something moved in the darkness behind her.

She spun around. In the space of an instant she felt her heart rate spike and a cold shockwave pass through her. It seemed to take the breath from her body while lifting every fine hair on her skin.

"God Almighty," Alan Hood said, no less taken aback.

He was a pale and insubstantial shape in the darkness, but as he moved forward into the light she could see him better. He had some sort of technical device in his hand that he glanced at and then shoved into his pocket.

"Where did *you* appear from?" he said. "You frightened the life out of me."

"I let myself in," Miranda said. "What was I supposed to do? You didn't answer when I rang the bell, and that was after I'd been trying all night to phone."

"Well, why not just call me tomorrow?"

"Well, why do you *think?*"

It came out a little more stridently than she'd intended, but it gave him an accurate snapshot of her mood. What could he expect? That she shouldn't worry? Her father lived alone in this enormous empty house, and she lived a hundred miles away.

He ran a hand through his uncombed hair and glanced all around him, in an attitude that was somewhere between distraction and embarrassment.

"I suppose I can see what you mean," he said, and then, "Why don't we go downstairs?"

She couldn't help looking at him critically as he moved past her. His clothes were clean, but didn't match and looked as if they'd been slept in. He was turned out the way a man might dress for gardening.

As she followed him down, the thought in her head was both an uninvited and an unwelcome one: *He's doing his best, but he's looking old.*

He apologised for the state of the kitchen, as well he might.

"I'm due a tidy-up," he explained.

Miranda looked through towers of pans and dishes at the phone extension on the wall. This was the message phone. No wonder there'd been no
answer when she'd called.

"Why's it unplugged?" she said.

Her father had to move some of the dirty stuff in the sink just to get the
kettle underneath the tap.

"I was working on something," he told her as it filled. "I needed to
concentrate."

If he'd disconnected the bedroom phones as well, her attempts to raise
him must have rung out unheard in the basement.

There were no clean mugs, but he rinsed a couple and set them on the
kitchen table. As he was pulling out a chair, she said to him, "Your head of
department called me. He got my number from your doctor. He wanted to
talk about something."

He looked at her in puzzlement as he sat. "What, exactly?"

"He didn't say. Just left me a message."

"And you couldn't leave it until the morning?"

"No."

"You didn't have to race over. Everything's fine."

"It doesn't look it," she said, and waited.

He looked around and past her, anywhere but at her. He clearly didn't
have a ready or an easy answer to her concern.

"I don't know how to say this," he said. "Which is why I haven't tried.
But since you've come all this way and you're obviously worried, I'd better
tell you. I've been aware of your mother."

"That's no surprise," she said. "There can't be a thing in this house that
doesn't remind you of her."

"More than that."

His gaze was on her and steady now, and she didn't like the way it was
making her feel.

"What are you saying?"

"It's a perception thing," he said. "You want the science of it? There's no
obvious cause but there can be a definite physical effect. The temperature

falls. The electromagnetic potential at a given point changes. I can measure it. I'm not about to start believing in ghosts," he added quickly. "But maybe this is what makes people fall for the idea."

"Ghosts? Jesus, Dad..."

"That's exactly my point."

"So being you, of course you've got to study it."

"I can't dismiss any of it, can I?" he said. "It's first-hand experience. The alternative is to pretend it didn't happen. How professional would *that* be?"

What she really wanted was for him to stop right there, to change the subject, or even better to tell her that he wasn't really being serious.

Anything that meant she wouldn't have to deal with this.

She said, "What form does the awareness take?"

"Mental certainty," he said. "For no apparent reason. Nothing seen, nothing heard, I just know she's there. While I fully accept that she isn't."

"All the time?"

"No."

"Okay. Right."

There was an awkward silence.

"So how's everything at your end?" he said.

PAUSING ON THE way to collect some bedding from the half-landing cupboard, Miranda trudged up the stairs that had once been so familiar to her. Most of her childhood and all of her teenaged years had been spent in this house. She'd never imagined there could be a day when it wouldn't feel like home. But the day had come, nonetheless.

The suite of attic rooms had been her exclusive territory. The Independent Republic of Miranda. They'd redecorated the one room she'd painted black, but otherwise they'd left everything pretty much as it was. Now she saw cables on the upper landing and boxes in some of the rooms. They were like the boxes that computers came in.

So what was the purpose of all this? When she elbowed open the door to her old bedroom, a sudden flash half blinded her and she almost dropped the linen right there.

On a tripod in the middle of the room, a Polaroid camera spat out a print.

"Oh, for fuck's *sake!*" she said, and when she'd tossed the linen onto the bed she lifted the entire apparatus, tripod and all, and shoved it out onto the landing. There were microphones in the corners of the room, and they followed the camera along with their cables.

Lying in her old bed, in her underpants because she'd forgotten to bring nightwear, too exhausted to stay awake, too upset to go to sleep, her mind wandered a little and then settled into its well-worn small-hours track. The one she never chose, but couldn't avoid.

Just like tonight, for her it had started with a phone call. She'd made the same long drive, although she remembered nothing of it. At the hospital she'd found her father waiting, rudderless and dazed; Miranda had more or less had to take over, talking to the medical staff and then repeating their words for her father, who wasn't listening. She was, she realised, playing a part in a sad and sorry spectacle. The great Doctor Hood, major figure of international science, one-time Nobel co-nominee, the Northern Hemisphere's leading authority on Dark Matter, rendered almost childlike by personal disaster.

He'd discovered his wife at the bottom of the stairs, where she'd been lying for some time. But it wasn't a simple matter of a fall. For a week or more she'd been suffering from persistent headaches and had been sleeping for as many as twenty hours out of the twenty-four. The best guess was that she'd woken alone in the house and been unsteady or disoriented. Further investigation showed an unsuspected brain tumour that had already grown to inoperable size.

Over the next few weeks, they moved her from ward to ward and tried different combinations of drugs to reduce the cerebral swelling and raise her from the coma she'd fallen into. It had worked for a few days and for a while they'd had her back, lucid and aware even though her thinking had been a little strange. But then she'd relapsed and died. It had been a rapid decline, but at the time it had seemed to take forever.

Now this. With her mother gone, her father was falling apart. It didn't seem fair. So much that she'd always taken for granted was no longer there. Much of the pain she felt was that of a lifetime's support system being kicked away. When she tried to explain it to Dan, his idea of sympathy was to match her troubles with competing ones of his own.

She'd been pressed into membership of a melancholy club where the options were limited. One either died young, or eventually one joined it.

Like it or not, she was the grownup now.

SHE WAS FIRST downstairs the next morning. The day was a bright one. After loading the dishwasher and setting it going, she went into the basement and did the same with the laundry.

He hadn't quite been letting himself go. Most of his clothes were clean, and had been hung to dry on fold-out racks. Miranda suspected that they'd probably stay there until he came to wear them, skipping the need for an iron to press them with or a closet to put them in.

The mail arrived, and she went back up to get it. Her father appeared then, bleary and tousled, in a paisley bathrobe knotted over mismatched pyjamas. He followed her into the kitchen.

"This place is a tip," she told him.

"I know."

"Then why don't you do something about it? Where's Mrs Llewellyn?"

He settled back into the place where he'd been sitting the night before.

"I let her go," he said.

"Why?" Miranda said. "You've had her for years."

"She kept offering to stay late and cook me a meal. And I don't think that feeding was all she had in mind. You know what I mean? I'm not up for that."

"If I mark up the Yellow Pages for you, will you promise to sort out a replacement?"

"Yes, miss."

"I'm serious, Dad. It's such a big place. You don't want it turning into a sty. Once it gets past a certain point you'll be like one of these old guys the council sends a hit squad to fumigate."

"Thanks very much."

"You know what I mean."

"When I'm done with the observations I'm making, then I'll get a house-keeper in. I don't want someone fussing around and messing up the data."

Miranda set coffee in front of him while he looked through the days's letters. He glanced at each and then laid them aside without opening any.

She waited until he'd gone for a shower before letting herself out of the house and heading over to the University.

THE PHYSICS BLOCK was way out at the back end of the campus, the last major building before the playing fields and the sports centre. It had won architectural prizes in the 'seventies and was hideous beyond belief.

Duncan Dalby was neither as senior nor as well-qualified as Miranda's father, but even Doctor Hood would have to agree that Dalby was a better choice for department head. He might have been a mediocre scientist, but he was a born administrator.

Informed of her presence, Dalby came out of a budget meeting to see her.

"Do you have any influence with your father?" he said.

"Why?" she said.

"Because, to be frank with you, he's giving me problems I can't handle."

"So you're asking me, can I tell him what to do? You're talking about the infamous Doctor Hood."

"Thanks to whom we've got a physics department that's on a par with the best in Europe. But for how long? Someone needs to make him aware of what will happen if his behaviour doesn't change. I can't get through to him. I was hoping that you might. The only times he ever makes an appearance, it's to help himself to equipment which he doesn't account for. He's done no teach-ing. He's got five postgraduate students who've been getting no supervision.

Our participation in the Dark Matter Project's fallen through and I can't pin him down to discuss it."

The Dark Matter Project was an EU-funded venture to build a specialised particle detector at the Bern underground laboratory in Switzerland. Alan Hood had been one of its most active lobbyists, and had been an obvious choice to chair the project's governing committee.

"Look," Dalby said, "I know he's had a tough time. But it's been nearly a year."

"He isn't losing his mind," Miranda said. "He's coping."

"Not professionally, he isn't."

"I'll talk to him," she said. "I'll see what I can do."

Five people were waiting for her in the building's smart but draughty foyer. Three young men, two young women. They were all older than the average undergraduate, but not by much. Their spokesman looked as if he was at least part Chinese.

"Are you Miranda Hood?" he said.

She was wary. "Yes?"

"Can we speak to you?" he said. "We're your father's research students."

THEY ALL WENT over to the Union bar. The lunchtime rush hadn't started yet and they had their pick of the circular tables. One of the researchers brought teas and coffees from a machine on the counter where you fed it a plastic sachet and it peed you a drink.

The part-Chinese boy's name was Peter Lee. He told her, "We're all just marking time with our own research. Duncan Dalby wants us to inventory everything in the labs for a full picture of what's gone missing."

"We daren't tell him exactly what's involved," added a young woman named Kelly. "There's a thermal imager alone gone missing that's worth fifty thousand. Have you any idea what he's doing with it all?"

"If I were a scientist," Miranda said, "I might be able to tell you. As it is…"

She was hesitating because her natural instinct was to defend her father, but she couldn't come up with any account of his activities that didn't put him into a bad light. Poor old Doctor Hood. Poor old man. Those whom the gods would destroy, they first soften up with a whiff of the occult.

She was still hesitating when the time alarm on her phone went off.

"Oh, shit," she said as something dawned on her.

Peter Lee made a polite face. "Something wrong?"

"Can you excuse me for a second?"

She left them talking amongst themselves and moved to an empty table, where she took out her organiser and ran through her schedule for the rest of that day. Miranda made her living as a private singing teacher, mostly coaching teenaged sopranos through the ABRSM grades. She wasn't going to make it back in time to take any of her lessons, it was as simple as that. She'd have to be on the road within the hour, and that clearly wasn't going to happen.

By the time she'd finished making calls and leaving messages, the bar was filling up. Of the physics department party on the next table, only Peter Lee was left waiting.

"Sorry," Miranda said as she rejoined him, and he shrugged and smiled as if to say, not that it didn't matter, more that it did and he'd be lying if he pretended otherwise.

Miranda said, "What's the chance of getting a list of the missing gear?"

"Tricky," he said. "Nobody knows exactly what's gone. We've spent many an hour trying to work out what he might be using it for. Why?"

She was thinking of the cardboard cartons up in the attic. She'd peeked into some of them, and they hadn't even been unpacked. "Maybe we can get some of it back to where it came from."

"The gear's not really the main issue for us. It's more about the academic ground we're losing."

"But it's a place to start."

SHE WALKED IN the open for a while, wondering what best to do. She was hardly up to this. She felt like a person charged with stopping a rock slide, armed only with a couple of sticks and a handkerchief.

When she finally got back to the house, the day was all but over and there was a note waiting for her on the door.

Experiment in progress, it read. *Enter via back door.*

In no mood to be messed around, she used her key and walked straight in.

The first thing that she noticed was a deep bass *wub-wub-wub* sound permeating the entire building and pitched so deep that she mainly felt it through the soles of her feet and in the pit of her stomach. The neighbours were probably watching their furniture walking around on its own and asking themselves what the hell was happening. As Miranda moved toward the foot of the stairs there was another flash, just like the one she'd experienced the night before but this time from a different camera. This one had a motor drive. It was aimed at the spot where her mother had fallen.

The throbbing noise stopped abruptly. She could hear him heading down. She didn't wait, but went up the stairs to meet him.

"Didn't you see the note?" he called out.

"Yes," she shot back, "I saw the note. You want to carry on like Professor Branestawm, fine. Just don't expect me to pretend this is normal and play along with you."

They met up on the middle landing, where there now stood a loudspeaker that wouldn't have been out of place at a Grateful Dead concert.

"What do you mean?" he said.

She looked at the speaker, and wondered how he'd managed to get it up the stairs without help. Her mental picture of his struggle didn't help his case.

"I'm not going to humour you in this," she said. "You are seriously making an idiot of yourself while your students' careers are going down the toilet."

"What have *they* got to do with anything?"

"Given the consideration you've shown them, nothing! That's my point!"

"Who've you been talking to?"

She took a deep breath and steadied herself and then she said, "I can imagine what it's like for you. It almost made sense when you explained it to me last night. But to everyone else you're coming over as a...a..."

"A nutcase?" he suggested.

It was as good a word as any, and more polite than most of the ones she'd been thinking of.

"They're making plans, dad," she said. "Everything you spent your life putting together, you're losing it all."

To her irritation, right at that moment her phone timer went off again. Or did it? As she pulled her phone out, her father searched around and produced an identical one of his own.

"It's mine," he said, killing the beeper. "I have to be somewhere." He slid past her without touching her and started to make his way down the stairs.

"That's right," she called after him in exasperation. "Walk away."

From down at the rack in the hallway, shrugging into his big overcoat, he looked back up at her and said, "Walk with me, then."

WHAT HAD ONCE been a densely settled part of town was now a wasteland. Some of the old pubs had been left standing, only to turn rough and then die in their isolation. Now they stood amidst blown litter and weeds, bereft, boarded and vandalised.

Hood said, "Your grandfather used to look at the houses and say he could remember when all this was fields. I wonder what he'd say now."

Miranda walked on with her head down, and didn't respond.

Without changing his tone, her father said, "I do know what you're thinking. The simple fact of it is that I can't deal with anything if I don't deal with this."

"Can't you deal with it outside office hours?"

"If it's any consolation, I find it all as ridiculous as you do. I'd love just to nail it and get back to normal."

Not quite everything had been razed. A pillarbox here, an old church up ahead. Miranda was taking her father's words on board when she realised that not only was the old church not deserted, but it was their destination.

Some cars stood on the street. Bodies were getting out of them and one or two elderly-looking people were already going into the building. One of them waved, briefly.

Her father raised a hand in acknowledgement.

Miranda's heart sank.

On the pavement outside the door, as her father was making his way in, she stood and looked up at the hand-lettered board above the entranceway.

It had been nailed over the original church sign. It was in Gothic script, painted by a non-professional with only an approximate idea of what Gothic script ought to look like and an even more hazy notion of spelling.

It read *Lane Ends Spiritulist Church* and underneath, in smaller letters, *Healing, Open Evenings and Sunday Services.*

Someone behind her said, "Don't be shy!" and a batty-looking woman just inside the doorway called out, "You must be Miranda! Come in! Come in!"

And before she knew it, she'd been swept inside.

The building was in bad shape but it was still recognisably a church, albeit a peeling and crumbling one. The congregation numbered about thirty, and Miranda was the youngest amongst them. Everyone was in a group at the end of the nave, chatting enthusiastically. The woman who'd greeted her by name made something of a fuss of her and offered to take her coat, urging her to have a seat by one of the pillars with a radiator.

"They're the most popular spots," she explained. "They always go first." The woman was wearing a blue cardigan and had a lazy eye. Miranda had to make an effort not to glance back over her shoulder to see who she was talking to.

Her father was a few yards away, in the middle of the group. It was obvious that he was some kind of a regular here. As soon as she could, Miranda disengaged herself and moved to his side.

"I'm not staying," she said in a low voice when she had his attention. "I'll see you back at the house."

"Don't leave now," he said. "You might learn something."

"*Dad…*" she said, but was unable to continue as an excited murmur rose up at the appearance of a late arrival. He was standing in the doorway, and a couple of senior members of the congregation broke away to greet him. He was one of the worst-dressed men that Miranda had ever seen.

"That'll be Doctor Arthur Anderson," her father murmured to her. "He's come over from Leeds."

Anderson was a shrunken-looking homunculus in a brown checked suit that looked as if it had once been put through the wash with him inside it. The points of his waistcoat were curling up even more than the tips of his shirt collar. With this costume and his wispy moustache and a chin that almost vanished into his neck, he'd have passed for Ratty in a low-rent theatrical production of *The Wind in the Willows*. He was declining a cup of tea, rubbing his hands together, expressing a wish to be getting on with it.

"Doctor of what?" Miranda said.

Her father mimed clicking a mouse. It was an old family joke. Click 'print' to download your diploma.

Miranda realised with an even-further sinking heart that she'd left it too late to escape, because the street doors had been closed and everyone was moving to the pews to be seated. As predicted, the seats around the radiators filled up first.

Her father ushered her to a side-bench. From here they could observe while sitting some way apart from the others.

"It's a clairvoyance evening," he said as the babble was quietening down. "They have them every now and again to raise funds."

She was still eyeing the exit as the service began, but one of the elderly men had set a chair beside it. Someone started to sing an unaccompanied hymn and, after a bar or so, thirty reedy voices all joined in. It wasn't any tune that she knew.

Then Doctor Arthur Anderson, the man in the flood-salvage suit, took the floor and began to speak. He didn't use the pulpit, and he didn't use notes. This was clearly a speech that he'd made many times on similar occasions.

He said, "The spirits are all around us, they say. Well, it's true. And I know that because when the moment's right and the will is there, I can see them as plainly as I can see you. And people say to me, Arthur, they say, you've described them to me just as they were in life, but how does that work? How come uncle Bert's still got his glass eye on the other side? How come mum's still in her favourite cardigan, did that pass over too? Because I thought we gave it to Oxfam. And what I say to them is this. I don't know. Because I don't. I just see what I see."

He paused for a moment and looked aside at the floor, as if to gather his thoughts, and then he went on, "Do I see the spirits? I believe I do, but I don't *know* that I do. It's a much-abused word, is spirit. We can't hear it without thinking of ghosts and spooks. The whole point of a spirit is, it isn't a thing. It's the essence of something without the form it comes in. But that's a bit deep for most of us, which is why we can't think of God the Father without making him into an old man. And in the same way, we can't think of the dead without making them into the people we knew. So what I think happens is, the spirits decide, I think I'll go and talk to old Arthur. And what Arthur's going to see will be something that looks like the form that spirit left behind, because poor Arthur's only human and his mind needs something to fasten onto."

Miranda cast another look in the direction of the exit, where the elderly man on the chair was nodding in agreement.

"Daisy," the visiting speaker said with a sudden change of tone. "Who's Daisy? Whoever you are it's not your real name, it's your nickname, I know. I know you're here somewhere, put your hand up, love."

Nothing happened for a few moments but then, almost masked to Miranda by one of the church pillars, a tentative hand was raised.

"Someone used to call you Daisy, didn't he?" Anderson said. "And it's a name you've not heard for a long time. We're talking about someone who's passed over."

Miranda couldn't quite hear the response but it sounded like, "My brother." She tried to lean out a little way to see more, but it didn't help.

She knew how these things worked. He'd start fishing now, building on the woman's responses, shaking plausible-sounding information out of the tiny cues she'd be giving him.

"Just a minute, love…" Anderson said, and then he turned and spoke to the empty air beside him. Spoke to it as if there was a person standing there.

And Miranda thought, *Oh, come on.*

She thought, *They may be old and they may be credulous, but don't treat them as if they're stupid.*

"What are you telling me?" Anderson was asking the air. "It wasn't just Daisy, it was Daisy May?" He turned his attention back to the woman in the audience. "Is that right?"

"I had an Auntie May," the woman said, her voice barely audible even though she'd raised it.

"*That's* what he's trying to tell you," Anderson said with the triumph of a hard-won discovery. "That's who he's bringing the message from."

The message was something about the fears surrounding a medical procedure. The drift of it was that all would be well in the end. He went on like this, working his way through the audience, picking people out and talking to the spirits that he insisted were at their shoulders, sometimes bantering or making a friendly argument out of his dialogue with the invisibles.

It was fascinating, in its way. Even though she found it ludicrous, Miranda didn't move or try to escape. She didn't want to do anything that might draw the speaker's attention. She sat tight, like someone scared of making an erroneous bid at an auction.

When she caught a movement from the corner of her eye, she looked and saw that her father was studying the handheld device that he'd been using the previous night. It was about the size of a TV remote and showed its information on a liquid crystal screen. He was holding it low, so it would be concealed from the—what could she call them? Congregation? Audience?— by the empty bench in front.

It didn't end until more than two hours later. Anderson had talked himself hoarse, but looked as if he was game to go on indefinitely. The man who'd introduced him moved a vote of thanks, and everyone applauded. Miranda joined in, enthused by the prospect of unpeeling her rear end from the woodwork. After the time she'd spent seated, it was as if she had nothing beneath her but thin flesh pinned to the bench by the pointed ends of her pelvic bones.

There was a bucket collection for the roof fund, and then there was an announcement of a small spread in the vestry consisting of tea and packet cakes and buttered malt bread.

"I'm not staying," Miranda warned her father.

"Neither am I," he said. "Just give me one minute."

She was assuming that her father wanted to talk to the speaker, but Hood ignored him and exchanged words with some of the others. They crowded around him, all but neglecting their guest. One woman had brought along a magazine that she produced and now pressed on him.

"I saved this for you, Doctor Hood," Miranda heard her say.

"*Did* you, Mrs Lord?" Hood said. "Thank you."

"They've got a psychic's page where people write in. One of the letters is just like the experience you told us about."

"I shall read it. Thank you."

And even though Miranda was trying her best to find it all too ridiculous for words, she couldn't help feeling a twinge of envy at the genuine warmth that surrounded her father in this unlikely place.

He'd promised her a minute. They were out in just under twenty.

They walked some of the way home in silence. But then Miranda couldn't help herself.

"Please don't tell me you were taken in by any of that," she said.

"Not the slightest danger," he told her. "Don't worry."

"He was a total fraud."

"Ah," Hood said. "You can be wrong without being a fraud. Just as you can be sincere without being right."

"What were you measuring?"

He showed her the instrument. "It's called a tri-field natural EM meter. They were developed to measure the activity in electromagnetic storms. Ghost hunters use them."

"And what did you pick up tonight?"

"Nothing at all."

The main road was ahead. There were no cars to be seen, but the traffic lights changed and then changed back.

As they crossed, Miranda said, "They treated you like one of the family."

"I'm their pet sceptic," her father said. "They appreciate me. I give them open-minded attention without prejudice."

As they made the turn through the gateway that led into the private lane, she said, "I don't know where I stand with you. One minute I'm convinced you're off your trolley. Then I can see a kind of sense in what you're doing. Then suddenly I'm in the middle of a freak show and I don't know *what* to think."

"Don't think, then," he told her. "Just observe. I'm not going insane, however it looks. You could say that I'm just finding ways of preserving my sanity in the face of pressure. You should leave me to it."

"Don't think I wouldn't, if I could."

"Miranda, my problems are not your problems. I'm bright enough and old enough and ugly enough to sort them out for myself."

"Well," she said, "two out of three isn't bad."

When they got near to the house, she paused in the lane to check on her car. She couldn't remember locking it earlier, but it turned out that she had. Looking up from the vehicle, she saw that her father had gone ahead and was at the top of the house steps with his key already in the door. He seemed to hesitate, and then he pushed the door open and went inside.

It had only been a moment, but in that hesitation she believed that she could read him exactly. It wasn't as if he'd paused in apprehension of what he might find.

It was more as if he was bracing himself for the disappointment of finding nothing.

THE NEXT MORNING Miranda slept late, but was still up and about before her father. She'd spoken to Dan for half an hour the night before and given him a list of people to call. She could get away with a week's absence, she reckoned. In one week, she'd lose only money. More than a week, and she might begin to lose students. Two cancelled lessons in a row might not bother her less committed pupils, but with the more competitive ones it would start to count against her.

She filled a dish with boiling water to steam her vocal cords, and made a pot of tea with the rest. Then she poured herself a mug without milk and took it into the dining room, ready to run her voice exercises.

She'd always found this room a little bit intimidating. It had a clubby, Edwardian billiards-hall look, dark and high-ceilinged, done out in maroons and greens with dado rails and panelling. A low chandelier hung over the dining table. A hundred or more family pictures hung on the walls.

And there was the piano, of course.

Her mother's upright Bechstein. Her father had offered to let her take it, but where would it go? The most that her own tiny lounge could run to was a Yamaha keyboard stowed off its legs in the space behind the sofa. And besides…moving in with Dan had been one of those try-it-and-see decisions, not the whole starry-eyed hog. She suspected that moving in and bringing a piano would have been rather more than their tentative relationship could take.

She raised the lid to play herself a starting note, and was appalled at the thickness of the dust that had been allowed to gather on it. There was more on the lid than on anywhere else, and her fingers left marks where she touched it. The sooner he found a replacement for Mrs Llewellyn, the better.

Then she frowned. She rubbed her fingers together and felt the texture of the powder that clung to them. Silky. Then she sniffed. Lavender.

Lavender?

It wasn't dust at all. It was talcum powder.

He'd dusted the piano lid with her mother's talc.

For what? Ghost prints?

She felt helpless.

Fortunately he hadn't dusted the keys as well, possibly out of a scientist's respect for their underlying machinery. She struck a C and began her scales.

Few people had any idea of the sheer physical technique involved in producing vocal sound. After all, they probably reckoned, who taught the birds to sing? She heard plenty who believed that you just stood there and did it, and who stood there and did it down their noses, in whiny fake accents, off-key, off-note, off the beat and with their voices full of breath and strain.

Miranda's mother had taught her in this very room. She'd coaxed her through the grades and driven her to the festivals. Miranda could remember running up to her father's study to show him her prizes; second, third in the class, the occasional first…and always the same reaction. He'd look over his reading glasses and say something along the lines of, *That's very good, Miranda. You'll have to sing something for me later.*

Always later. And somehow he was always occupied elsewhere when she sang.

Miranda sensed that she was not alone.

She became aware of him standing there in the doorway. She didn't have to turn. She saw his reflection move in the glass of the photo frames, broken up and repeated like an image in an insect's eye.

"This is where it happened to me," he said.

She looked at him. He'd drawn a mug of tea from the pot and was there with it in his hand.

"How?" she said.

"The piano lid was open. I tried to pick out a scale. You know how much musical ability I've got. For once, it just came. And I had an overwhelming certainty that I wasn't alone."

"But you didn't actually see her."

"I saw nothing. I'm talking about awareness. Something I realised I had no definition for. Utter conviction without sensory evidence. I took my own pulse, and it was racing for no reason."

Mug in hand, he moved around the room. This side of the house got the worst of the morning light, and was often gloomy. As now.

He said, "I looked for some kind of explanation. Because something here required one. It's said that sometimes you can get a sense of presence or foreboding caused by a low-frequency standing wave from a fan or a vibrating object. But I tested the entire room and found nothing. Or stimulation of a certain part of the brain can induce a sense of formless apprehension, like there's someone standing uncomfortably close to you." He stopped by the enormous fireplace. There was a fire screen in the empty grate and a basket of dried, dead flowers before it.

He said, "I had an encephalogram check over at the psych department and there's nothing to that, either. All I know…is that for a moment I knew she was here. It happened again a week later, in one of the rooms upstairs. I don't know what triggered it that time. Something did, I'm sure. Something must."

He was behind her now. He leaned past her to reach the dusty piano, and started to pick out a scale with one finger.

Five notes into it, he went wrong.

The bad note jarred, and a mood was broken.

"Don't hang around here," he said. "Time's not for wasting. Get on with your life."

She hoped he wouldn't look at her. But of course, he did.

He seemed bewildered. "What did I say?"

But all she could do by way of an answer was to turn away from him and run from the room.

LATER THAT MORNING, she met up with Peter Lee in the University library. He'd told her that with his own work on hold, he was making a little extra money researching old science journals for one of the other professors.

The library was an 'eighties addition, and such a monolith of a building that it looked as if it ought to have Stalin's picture hanging down the side of it. From there they walked across the campus to the visitor parking where Miranda had left her car. She'd asked Peter Lee to go to the house with her to see how much of the borrowed equipment could be spirited back to its rightful place. She was hoping that her father would be out when they got there. But he wasn't.

They could hear voices coming from the kitchen. When Miranda went through she found her father sitting at the kitchen table with a woman that she didn't immediately recognise. Both looked up at her. Peter Lee hung back in the hallway, but Hood spotted him and called him in and then made the introductions.

The woman's name was Yvonne. Yvonne Lord. She was the woman who'd saved a magazine to give to Miranda's father the previous evening.

"Yvonne's been describing her experience for me," Hood explained. "It makes quite a story."

"I'm sure it does," Miranda said.

"Tell it again," he suggested, and at that point he cast a look in Miranda's direction. "We're all open minded, here," he said. "Aren't we?"

"Well, I don't know what you'll make of it," Yvonne Lord said. "I'm afraid it might sound stupid." She was a broad-shouldered, blonde-rinsed, quite handsome-looking woman of around fifty or fifty-five.

Peter Lee was pulling out a chair and sitting down, so Miranda reluctantly did likewise as the visitor began.

"It's happened to me five times in the past three weeks," she said. "Always when I'm just drifting off to sleep."

Yvonne Lord was a widow. Her husband, much older than her, had been dead for almost three years. Even though she was a believer, she'd had no paranormal experience during most of that time. It was only when she'd had the bedroom redecorated that the apparitions had started.

"I see him in the room with me, over by the wall," she said. It didn't matter whether the light was on or not, she could see him whatever. He seemed to be calling to her but making no sound, reaching for her but making no progress. It was as if he was pulling against something, like a man harnessed to a big sled with weights that he could barely move.

The first couple of times it had happened, she'd been unable to react or speak. The third time, she said his name and believed that he responded by renewing his efforts. It was then that she became aware of other presences. These were much vaguer, and without faces, and they came right out of the wall. These, she realised, were the forces that were holding him back. As she watched, their strength overcame his and they pulled him away. Though he fought them every inch he eventually vanished, silently screaming, into the new Sanderson vinyl that she'd picked out to match the carpet.

She was doing fine until the screaming part. Then her voice betrayed an unsteadiness that gave Miranda a moment's feeling of guilt.

After that, she fell silent. Doctor Hood, who'd been taking notes, laid down his pen and said, "Is that everything?"

Yvonne Lord nodded.

"Right," Hood said, "Thank you. I think we can dismiss the idea of a poltergeist outbreak because it has none of the features. And it's not a crisis apparition because they only happen once, at a time closely related to the moment of death. Which leaves us with a residual or an intelligent haunting."

Peter Lee said, "What's the difference?"

"A residual haunting is just imprinted, usually on a location. Something triggers it and it plays back without variations. There's no life or actual presence involved. An intelligent haunting is more interesting because it implies the existence of life after death. The apparition can vary its behaviour and interact with the observer. On what I've heard so far, this could make a claim to fall into either category. Everything depends on whether the apparition was merely following a pattern, or whether it really did alter its actions when you called your husband's name."

Peter Lee looked at the woman. "What do you think, Mrs Lord?" he said. "Can you say for sure that there was a response involved?"

Yvonne Lord spoke carefully. "I think there's some part of my husband that's still with us," she said. "I think he's aware and in distress. The very thought of that is very hard for me to bear. I'll do whatever it takes to get him out of it."

"Dad…" Miranda said then. "There's something I need to ask you. Can we…?"

She left the question hanging, and Hood got to his feet. Leaving the graduate student and Yvonne Lord together, they moved through into the dining room.

Hood got in first, saying, "Where did you meet Peter Lee?"

"He's helping me to sort out the mess you've got into. I bring him home, and what do I find? Tales from the Frigging Crypt in our own frigging kitchen! How embarrassing is that?"

She couldn't help her voice escalating in intensity, but she did manage to keep its volume down. The effect was that she could barely prevent it from turning into an indignant squeak.

"Separate this out," Hood said, dropping his voice and almost matching her tone. "There's what she saw, and what she thought she saw. The distinction between the two is exactly the area I'm interested in."

"Yeah, well give some thought to what *she* might be interested in."

"Oh, for God's *sake*, Miranda!"

"You were quick enough to spot the glad eye from Mrs Llewellyn when there was no hocus-pocus involved!"

"Do you really not know someone's genuine pain when you see it?"

She wanted to say that the reality of the pain didn't prove the authenticity of its supposed cause, that maybe the mind just cut and shaped its own expression where the distress had no ready form... until she realised that she was getting perilously close to quoting the dubious wisdom of Doctor Arthur Anderson, at which point she broke off the argument and went to haul Peter Lee out of the kitchen. He and Yvonne Lord were making polite conversation, but he got to his feet and came at her command.

"We're going out," she called back over her shoulder.

She took Peter Lee to a corner pub a couple of streets away.

"Sorry about that," she said as they walked toward it. "Had to get away. I've heard more intelligent noises coming out of a colostomy bag."

The pub was city-centre cod-Victorian in an authentic Victorian shell, open at both ends and filled with a lunchtime business crowd. She managed to catch someone's eye and got herself a pint of Jennings and the grapefruit juice that Peter Lee had asked for.

"Is that all you drink?" she said as she put the glasses down on the half-a-table that he'd managed to bag while she was at the bar.

"In the middle of the day, it is," he said. "Anything stronger puts me to sleep."

"Me too," she said, and knocked back a third of the beer in one go. "God," she said when she'd set the glass down again, "I just don't know what to do with him. All those years, he was like a giant to me. Now it's like..."

Whoa. She was beginning to hear how she must be sounding.

"I'm sorry," she said. "You've got your career on the line. You don't want to be hearing my problems."

Peter Lee shrugged.

"'Sokay," he said.

"What do you make of all that, though? How can an educated person even start to entertain such a notion?"

"Sometimes it takes an educated person to know enough to say, 'I don't know.'"

She looked at him, eyebrows raised. "That's deep," she said, suddenly realising that thanks to the beer she was getting the first warning signals from a low-down and dangerous-feeling belch.

Peter Lee started picking the ice out of his grapefruit juice and dropping it into the ashtray.

"I had a strange experience of my own, once," he said.

Which he then went on to tell her about.

MIRANDA WOKE UP on the sofa in the ballroom-sized lounge a few hours later, living proof that she and daytime drinking were necessary strangers. Her head felt bad, in the way that fruit goes bad. Soft, rotten, ready to split.

She went up to the bathroom to look for some aspirin. It was a room that she rarely saw when she visited, having a bathroom of her own on the attic level. When she opened the door of the wall cabinet, it was to find all of her mother's toiletries lined up on the shelves. The bottles, the lotions, the perfumed bath cubes that people bought each other as presents but no one ever used. The home colour kit, the highlighting shampoo, the lavender talcum powder.

She knew that most of her mother's clothes were in the wardrobes, still. He'd told her as much. He was waiting until the time felt right to let them go, he said.

She found some soluble aspirin, but no glass to dissolve them in. On her way down to the kitchen she was vaguely aware that something was different, without immediately being certain of what...and then she realised that not only was the enormous speaker gone from the landing, but also the wiring that had hung down the stairwell. All removed. Various cameras and other ghostbusting items appeared to have been stripped out as well.

That brightened her, a little.

In the kitchen, sipping from a clean glass out of the dishwasher, she picked up Yvonne Lord's magazine and leafed through it until she found the page of readers' letters to Rita the Psychic. The first was from a woman whose husband had died and who was now being visited regularly by a pigeon that stood on her bedroom windowsill and tapped at the glass with its beak. Could this be my husband, Rita, the reader wanted to know, returning with a message for me? Yes, replied Psychic Rita, I believe it almost certainly is, which caused Miranda to blow soluble aspirin down her nose.

The phone started ringing then, and she was still choking when she picked up the receiver. It was a real effort just to manage, "Hello?"

"You're awake, then," she heard Peter Lee's voice say.

"What makes you think I was asleep?"

"The sounds you were making when I left you at the house."

"Did you move some of the gear back to the lab?"

"We're not at the lab," he said. "Are you fit to drive? There's something going on here that you maybe need to see."

IT WAS A suburban close of modern houses, none of them more than ten years old. They'd been crammed onto the available land like penguins on a rock. Each had a one-car garage and a driveway and an immaculate Brazilian strip of garden, and the convenience of being able to step straight out of your front door and into your neighbour's face.

The horseshoe end of the close had turning space for one car, and there were seven non-resident vehicles in it with their wheels up on the pavement. The biggest of these was a white University service van. There was no mistaking the house Miranda needed; the kids from the department were all over it.

She parked the car as near as she could. Two of them were up ladders, fixing plastic blackout sheeting over the upper storey windows. Down below them she recognised one of the graduate students hooking up a heavy-duty generator cable between the house and the van. Others were stepping over it with boxes, taking care not to trip. Some of the boxes looked familiar.

Miranda followed the students in. No one challenged her. The front door was pinned back, the house opened up to the world as if for surgery. A boy in the hallway was fixing up an array of six Pentax cameras in a framework. She heard her father's voice somewhere upstairs saying, *Check the walls for buried wires. Anything that conducts. Start at the manifestation point and work outwards.*

Hard to tell for sure from down here, but it sounded as if he was enjoying his evening.

The stairs were impassible for the moment and so she made her way through the house, looking for someone that she could recognise. She found Peter Lee in the glazed conservatory on the back of the building. The invading party had taken over the space, and Peter Lee was setting up a command centre here. At this moment he was down on the floor trying to link up four portable TVs with the outputs of four separate video recorders, which in turn had to be matched with switchable input from somewhere near a dozen cameras.

She stood over him for a while, watching without being noticed, and then to get his attention said, "When did all this get under way?"

He looked up, squinting with one eye because of the bright tungsten working light behind her shoulder.

"While you were sleeping," he said. "We brought all the gear from the house and a vanload more from the lab." Then he grinned. "Duncan Dalby's going to hit the roof."

"Nobody seems worried."

"It's a ghost hunt!" he said.

She gave up on Peter Lee and moved back into the main part of the house, where her father was now in the hallway. As soon as he spotted her, he broke off his conversation and said, "Miranda! Don't just stand there, make yourself useful."

Someone bumped past her with a laser printer.

"Doing what?" she said.

"Help Mrs Lord with the coffee."

As she took a breath to tell him what she thought of that idea, there was an approving chorus of voices from all the rooms around her. So instead of responding, she clamped her lips shut and went through into the kitchen.

By late evening, everything was in place. Video cameras were tested and running. The house had a complete new nervous system and a brain room to drive it. Devices in the upstairs rooms ranged from a state-of-the-art ion cloud detector to an array of cheap motion sensors from the home security section of a DIY store. Spot-temperature observation, infra-red profiling, electromagnetic field detection…in the midst of directing the installation, Doctor Hood had taken the time to liaise with anxious or indignant neighbours out in the Close. She'd heard him soothe them, reassure them, convince them that the work here was crucial and without any attendant dangers to the surrounding property…

And all without ever once mentioning the 'g' word.

Everyone gathered in the sitting room to hear Mrs Lord tell her story once again and to discuss a strategy for the evening's observations. It had been impossible for Miranda to get a head-count before this, because everyone had been constantly on the move and there had been some people who'd turned up with gear, worked for a while and then hadn't been seen again.

Now she counted nine, including Peter Lee and three of the graduate students she'd met back at the Physics department. All listened intently as Yvonne Lord went through the story that Miranda had heard earlier on in the day. Miranda had the worst spot, right at the back of the crowd, almost pushed out into the hallway, trying to see over everybody's heads.

When Yvonne Lord's story was done, Hood sent her upstairs to take a Valium and get herself ready for bed before the cameras went live. Once she was out of earshot, he opened the matter up for discussion.

Someone said, "What if we're looking at something purely psychological?"

"You mean, is it only in her imagination?" Doctor Hood said. "That's entirely possible, but we're not going to start with a conclusion and then cherrypick our evidence to fit. I know that's a bit radical for this profession, but let's give it a try for once. As long as ghosts wear clothes I'm inclined to be convinced that the psychological is a major element. But let's not be closed to the possibility of the actual existence of some underlying physical trigger, here. So-called spirit photographs often show a ball of fog where a live observer sees a human form. That factor alone is of serious interest to me."

Everyone was assigned to a post. Nobody said as much out loud, but Miranda's role was to keep out of the way. Yasmin the medical technician went up to attach a pulse monitor to Mrs Lord, and on returning gave Doctor Hood the go-ahead to send all the cameras and monitoring equipment live.

Miranda felt herself prickle all over as the ghost house went on-line.

EVERYONE FELL SILENT, and tried to settle. There was no way of knowing how long they'd have to wait for something to happen. Maybe nothing would. Maybe their presence would be enough to upset the conditions that had caused the phenomenon. Or maybe ghosts just didn't like a crowd. As far as was possible, they'd confined their wiring and mess to the downstairs rooms and kept the upstairs looking normal. That meant a lot of gear hidden behind furniture, in the loft, and even in the wall cavity.

Under these bizarre conditions, artificially relaxed by the Valium, Yvonne Lord had undertaken to lie in her own bed with a pulse meter taped to one hand and a signalling device adapted from a PlayStation joystick in the other, and in that unnatural state to wait for her dead husband to make his nightly appearance.

In a creaky cane chair at the back of the conservatory, Miranda let out a long breath and felt much of her energy following it. Her main view was of the backs of her father and Peter Lee, watching over all the monitors and readouts, observing, tweaking, calibrating, swapping theories in the lowest of low voices.

Looked at from any angle, it was a joke, wasn't it? Spook hunting was for the oddball, the damaged, the credulous. Bobble-hat people. Not bright kids like these.

And yet…

Under more normal academic circumstances, under the tutelage of the world-famous Doctor Hood, these same bright kids would be exercising their intellects in the search for and study of Dark Matter. And what was Dark Matter? Miranda was no scientist but she was a scientist's daughter, and knew that her father's regular field of study involved a material of unknown composition that had never been seen, measured, nor even proven to exist, and yet was reckoned to comprise more than ninety per cent of the known universe. The strongest argument for its existence was that without it, the heavens would fall. Spiral galaxies would fly apart and the light from distant stars would bend without reason.

Despite nobody knowing what it was or what it was made of, Dark Matter had to exist in *some* form, because otherwise certain phenomena lacked any rationale.

Which of course had no parallel in anything that was going on here.

She could hear Yvonne Lord's breathing over an intercom-sized speaker on the main desk. Every now and again there'd be a rustle of sheets as the woman shifted her position.

Everyone waited, and nothing much happened.

Miranda was looking at Peter Lee.

I had a strange experience of my own, once.

He'd been walking home late one night, he'd told her. This had been some years before, when he'd been a second-year student. He'd had a lot on his mind and had only been vaguely aware of a figure walking ahead of him. When he thought about it later he realised that the figure had been dressed in very old-fashioned garb, gaslight-era clothing, but the fact hadn't struck him as anything remarkable at that moment. All that he'd registered was the presence of a man in front of him, heading in the same direction as himself.

When the man reached the house where Peter Lee was living at the time, he stopped as if to enter. Peter Lee registered this, and took an interest. The gap between them was closing as Peter Lee approached. The man met his eyes, smiled…and then walked right through the closed and locked door.

That was it, and that was how he'd told it. His only such experience, ever. The significant element to Peter Lee's mind was not that he'd seen a ghost, but that the ghost had so obviously seen him.

Miranda's father was looking pensive.

"Nothing much happening here," he said. "Let's run some juice through the wall. See if we can start something rolling."

Peter Lee got up and moved out of the conservatory and into the main part of the house. Yasmin the medic, half-hidden by monitor screens, said,

"How do you record an observation when your observer's asleep on the job?"

"Already?" Doctor Hood said. "Are you sure?"

"I'm on sound. Her pulse has slowed and she's making z's."

Miranda turned her attention toward the intercom speaker and, yes, she could hear a faint snoring coming out of it as well.

"I don't want her *that* relaxed," Doctor Hood said.

"Does she do Valium every night?" Miranda ventured. "Maybe the whole thing's no more than a recurring dream."

"Ion surge," someone said then, with an edge of excitement that everyone immediately picked up on. Other voices chipped in with further observations, some called through from the adjacent room.

"I'm picking up an EM field by the wall."

"Temperature down two degrees."

Doctor Hood looked at all the TV monitors and switched cameras on a couple of them. Miranda looked over his shoulder and saw the same thing that he did. Nothing. Empty stairs, empty landing, empty bedroom apart from the half-visible figure of Yvonne Lord in one corner of a screen, nothing happening in the box room on the other side of the bedroom wall. All in grainy digicam night shot vision, images magically pulled out of the darkness.

"How closely did that coincide with the voltage?" Hood said.

Peter Lee stuck his head around the door.

"I hadn't started the voltage yet," he said.

"High, high activity," said the boy who'd reported the ion surge. "I've got levels jumping all over the place."

"Sound?"

"Woman in a room breathing," the girl said. "Slow breathing, slow pulse, same as before."

"Is she reacting to anything?"

"Nope."

"Is she even aware?"

"Doesn't look like it. We've got an independent phenomenon. It isn't coming from her."

Then there was a sound that made everybody gasp and jump at the same time, as six Pentax cameras fired off all at once and only inches from the room microphone. The switchblade sound of the shutters was followed by a chorus of motor drives as the film rolls advanced.

On the monitors, there was nothing to see. Yvonne Lord stirred a little.

Responding to movement within the range of their infrared trigger, the reset cameras fired off again.

And still, in the room, there was nothing.

Doctor Hood was on his feet. "For God's sake, woman! What do you think we're here for? Wake up and look!"

"Live body on the stairs," somebody said then. "Moving."

There was a whimper from one of the students nearby. A few heads turned in the direction of the hallway. Miranda realised that her fists were bunched up so tight that her nails were hurting her hands. Those all around her were focused on the work they had to do, but she could sense without looking that in this little chintzy house, on its quick-build middle-income suburban dormitory estate, there was a sudden and shared terror in the air. The theoretical had suddenly become all too real.

She glanced at those students she could see from where she was seated. One was flushed, another bloodless, one was actually shaking.

"Moving up or down?" Hood said.

"Up."

Miranda said, "It's Peter Lee."

She'd just spotted him on one of the screens, crossing the upper landing. As he entered the bedroom, he passed from one screen and onto another in a different part of the array. Greyed-out, featureless, and leaving a streaky trail of fading pixels as he moved, on the screens he looked as convincing a ghost as any spirit footage.

"He's compromising the experiment," someone said.

"Quiet, there," Doctor Hood said. "Stick with your observations."

She saw Peter Lee cross the room and crouch by the bed, just his shoulder in shot and nothing visible at the wall where the apparitions were supposed to take place.

"He's talking," the girl on sound reported.

"Put it on the speaker?"

"He's on it," she said. "The mike's barely picking him up. I don't know why. He ought to be coming through loud and clear."

Doctor Hood bent to listen more closely. But most of what Miranda could hear was just loud static hiss with the odd, formless surge of sound pushing up through it without actually breaking into clarity, like bad short-wave after midnight. And on that same soundtrack the cameras kept firing, winding, firing again...

"Whoever's there, he can see them," Hood said.

...and still the video monitors showed an all-but-empty view of a suburban bedroom where Peter Lee, seen from above and behind, stood and faced a cleared space before a blank and newly-decorated wall.

And yes, he seemed to be talking to someone that the cameras couldn't see.

"The needles are dancing off the scale," someone said and then, "Oh my God, I think they're answering him."

And someone else said, "She's waking up."

And then there was a real, honest-to-God, first-hand sound as a muffled cry was heard through the fabric of the house; the awakened Yvonne Lord had sat up in bed and was shouting out her husband's name at the top of her voice.

Scientific discipline finally cracked. Everyone rose to their feet. Someone screamed and it sounded as if someone else in the next room was throwing up. In the turmoil, Doctor Hood pushed his way through the clutter of people and equipment and disappeared into the hallway. Miranda could see him on the monitor then, making his way up the stairs two at a time.

"Temperature up two degrees," called a lone, conscientious voice, but no one else was paying any attention. At least one person was in tears. Everyone was talking at once and somebody was saying, over and over, *I want to go, I want to go...*

MIRANDA FOLLOWED HER father.

When she reached the upper landing she could still hear the racket going on downstairs, like a noisy party where the music suddenly stops. No one had tried to come after her.

The room lights were on. They were so bright, they hurt. Yvonne Lord was sitting up and crying uncontrollably, and Miranda's father was at the side of the bed with his arm around her shoulders. Peter Lee stood a few feet away, his features drained and shocked-looking, his stance a little unsteady. The cameras were silent now, their rolls of film all used up.

Miranda said, "What did you see?"

Peter Lee said. "It's not what she thinks."

"Did you interact with the manifestation?" Hood said. "Did he answer you?"

"He wasn't aware of me. All he can see is her. He doesn't even know he's died, yet. The others answered for him."

"What others?"

"I don't know who they are. They're trying to help him over." He looked at Yvonne Lord. "But it's her. She won't let him go. Every night she keeps on calling him back. Every night he tries to reach her, and every night they have to pull him away. He fights them. Sometimes she sees what's happening. Whether she sees it or not, it still goes on."

Miranda looked at her father. He was still holding Yvonne Lord, rocking her for comfort, but absently. He didn't appear to be listening.

"You'll see nothing on the film," Peter Lee said, and wiped his dry lips with the back of a shaking hand. "It's not like he's haunting her. It's more like, *she* won't stop haunting *him*."

SHE DROVE HER father home. He sat beside her in the car and said almost nothing.

Yvonne Lord had gone to relatives and a couple of the more iron-nerved of the graduate students had made the equipment secure in the house for the night. They'd done it on the condition that all the others waited right outside, and they worked with all the lights on. Angry neighbours tried to make a scene, but nobody would talk to them. The Close was silent now. The vehicles were gone and the house stood empty.

It was well after midnight when they turned into the quiet lane of big houses behind the cathedral. Someone was walking a dog, pausing under a streetlamp down at the far end while the animal stopped to sniff and pee, but that was the only life around.

She followed her father into the house. There was a vague sense of *deja vu* about the moment, and she knew why.

This was exactly the way that it had felt, coming back to the house from the hospital on the night that her mother had finally died.

She'd always had the guilty feeling that her mother's death had never hit her as hard as it should. She'd rationalised this in various ways, telling herself that she'd channelled her own grief into concern for her father. But she wondered if instead she'd merely used him as a buffer, hiding behind him while he took the full brunt of the hurt.

Just as they'd done that night, he switched on lights and she went to make tea. Little rituals. Little comforts.

As she was swilling out the pot, she heard him in the dining room. She heard the sound of the piano lid being raised and then she heard him playing a halting scale on the keys.

Just a simple one. Do, re, me, fa…

And then a wrong note.

He didn't try again. She heard him close the lid and then she heard him going upstairs. Slowly, as if in defeat.

She felt her heart lurch, momentarily overcome with a weight of love mixed with self-pity. He'd always been able to lessen her sorrows just by being there, but she felt that she could offer nothing that would lessen his. And she could no longer pretend or imagine that he'd be there forever. When he was gone for good, who would she hide behind then?

The night beyond the kitchen window was blacker than black. There was a blind, but they never drew it down. Her reflection looked back at her, a creature drawn with a neon wand in liquid crude. The water on the hob made a sound like a jetliner streaming ice vapour from its wings. It was as if all of her senses had edges. This was how she could remember feeling sometimes as a little girl, when she'd stayed up too long and too late but wouldn't admit that she was tired.

A thought crossed her mind, and made her skin prickle.

She went through into the dining room and, gently so as not to announce it with a sound, lifted the lid on the piano. As she settled onto the stool, she inhaled the deep scent of lavender and it was as if she felt her heart flood.

Delicately, walking her hand up the keyboard, she played a chromatic scale. Then triads in various keys. Then a melodic and a harmonic minor. Though she played them softly, they broke the silence like pistol shots. These were the patterns of notes underlying the vocal exercises that her mother had taught her to warm up with. How many times must they have been heard in this room?

Not often, of late. But once, long ago…

But nothing.

It wasn't working.

The notes were just notes. They brought no sense of presence. Not beyond anything she might be imagining, anyway. For a moment she'd thought that it might have been within reach, but already she could feel the magic leaking away.

Until she heard her father's voice upstairs.

They were alone in the house. But that wasn't how it sounded.

She couldn't hear words, just the low rumble of his speech. She held her breath, the better to hear. Held it for so long that she was getting lightheaded. Although she couldn't be sure of exactly what was being said, it sounded like some kind of a question or perhaps an entreaty. Was he on the phone? Could it be something as stupid and obvious as that?

But in the moment that Miranda finally let go of her breath and exhaled, she could almost have sworn that she heard a woman's voice replying.

Her head snapped up and she looked at the ceiling, as if by sheer intensity of will she might be able to look right through it and on into the rooms above. She could have cursed herself for her timing. She listened even harder, but now she heard nothing.

If there had been a response, it had been a brief one. One word, two words, no more. Maybe just an echo in her head. Maybe just the blood pounding in her brain.

She wanted to run upstairs. But her finger was still holding down the last key on the piano. Even though the note had long faded, the action was not yet closed.

Close it, and the moment would be over.

Which it was anyway, as she heard the heavy tread of her father descending the house stairs.

SHE FOUND HIM in the kitchen, finishing what she'd started. Steam from the kettle had fogged the kitchen window. His back was to her and as he sensed her, he turned his head to look over his shoulder.

Something was different.

Miranda said, "Was it her?"

He winked at her and smiled, as fathers do at their little girls when life's in order and much as it should be, and returned to his task.

He didn't acknowledge her again.

Back in the dining room, she lowered the lid on the piano. What had originally been an even dusting of talc had become well messed-up. Any apparition that now cared to leave its mark would have to take its chances at passing unseen.

Miranda paused, staring at something she hadn't noticed before. Had her father done this? She was certain it hadn't been her.

Scrawled in the powder, lightly drawn with an idle fingertip, all but faded and blurred, there were two words.

Release me.

Nothing else.

Miranda leaned forward, her face only inches from the lid. She could see every trace, contour and swirl of the letters, every grain of the powder.

The grains on the lacquer like stars in empty space. She took a deep breath, pursed her lips, and blew. Not hard like someone trying to blow out a flame, but gently, steadily, like someone cooling an angry patch of skin.

As she blew, the words faded. After only a few seconds they were all but gone. And when they really were gone, gone for good, she sat back and felt a peace like nothing she'd ever experienced before.

From the kitchen, she heard her father call her name.

Nothing here was anything that she could explain.

"Coming, Dad," she said.

Knowing that, for this moment at least, all was well.

My
REPEATER

WHAT CAN I say? It was a job, and I was glad to get it. The money wasn't great, but I had no skills and nothing to offer beyond a vague feeling that I was meant for something better. My mother knew someone who knew the owner, and I got a message to go along and show myself. I started two days later. Training was minimal. Customers were few in number.

I'd been there six weeks when I saw my first returnee.

He must have got off the bus at the far end of town, and it had started to rain on him as he'd been walking through the centre. I saw him coming up the road. The road was called Technology Drive, and it had been built to run north out of town and into the hills. Ours was the only building on it. You walked about two hundred yards to get to us, with open scrub on either side. If you wanted to follow the road further you could, but there was nothing much to look at unless you wanted to see how the weeds had broken up the concrete.

He walked with his head down, and with his hands in the pockets of his brown overcoat. The rain was light but he walked as if he was taking a beating.

He looked vaguely familiar. But at that point I hadn't considered the possibility that any of the people I'd been dealing with might ever come back.

He came in and went straight to the ledge under the window where we kept the boxes of forms. He didn't have to ask for any help. When he brought the paperwork over to the counter, the boxes had been filled in and the waivers were all in order and I'd little more to do than run through the questionnaire and then take it all through to my boss for his approval.

Morley was in his little back office, where he spent most of the days reading old magazines. He had a desk, a chair, and an anglepoise lamp that couldn't hold a pose without slowly collapsing. I think he had a framed picture on the wall but I can't for the life of me remember what it was of.

"Customer, boss," I told him, and showed him the papers.

He looked them over, and then tilted his chair back a couple of extra degrees so that he could see through the doorway to the main part of the shop. He stared at the waiting man for a moment, then gave me a nod and returned his attention to his reading. Most of his magazines were old technical publications, filled with page after page of fine print. They carried long lists of obsolete gear and they looked about as much fun as telephone directories.

I went back to the counter, and worked out the charges on the spreadsheet. The further back in time you wanted to go, the more it cost. Then there were other complicating factors, like bodyweight and geography.

When we'd sorted out the payment, I gave him a key card to put in the machine.

"Booth five," I told him.

He went inside and closed the door. I made all the settings and locked off the switches, and then there was nothing else to do but press the big red button.

"Are you ready, sir?" I called out to him.

"Get on with it," I heard him say.

So I got on with it. It was no thrill, just a routine—any buzz had gone out of it very quickly. But something jolted me in that moment as I realised why he'd seemed just a little bit familiar. It was the target settings that I recognised. I'd set them before. He'd been in about twelve days previously and he'd specified exactly the same destination.

But he'd been at least ten years older then.

∾

IT WAS A nothing job in a run-down travel bureau in a town in the middle of nowhere. I could have been stacking shelves in a supermarket or earning merit stars in a fast-food franchise, but instead I was sending a small group of losers back in time to relive their mistakes. I know that's what they did, because the same bunch of people brought us so much in the way of repeat business.

There must have been hundreds of bureaux like ours, small-town operations all scraping by as the last of their investors' capital dwindled. They'd been set up as a franchise network when the technology had first become available. They were like those long-distance phone places where you buy time at a counter and they assign you a booth while they set up the call; only here, you paid your money to be sent back to a date and a place of your choice.

Anyone could walk in and do it.

But only a strange few ever did.

The predicted boom had been a bust. I suppose it was like space travel. Full of romance and possibilities until it became achievable, and a matter of doubtful value ever after.

Here's what I learned when I talked it over with Morley:

He laid his magazine face-down on the desk and said, "I bet there's something in your life that you'd change, if you could."

"That's got to be true of everybody," I said. "Hasn't it?"

"So why don't you consider going back?"

I suppose the correct answer was that it would be a huge and scary one-way trip, and to make it would involve abandoning the life I now had. And for what? No certain outcome.

But what I said was, "You don't pay me enough."

"I'm not talking about the cost of it," Morley said. "Say I offered you a free one. Would you consider it then?"

"That would depend if you were serious."

"I'm serious. You're hesitating. Why?"

"I haven't thought about it that much."

"Think about it now. It sounds like a great idea. But why doesn't it *feel* like a great idea?"

"I don't know," I said. "It just doesn't."

But the more I thought about it, the more I thought I understood. It was obvious that I would never successfully go back and fix everything with Caroline Pocock, the proof being that she despised me so thoroughly in the here and now. Whatever I might try to amend, there was a known outcome.

I said, "Does that explain why the only people I see coming through that door seem to be life's born losers?"

"That's exactly what they are," Morley said. "They're the ones who can't accept what became common knowledge after the first few years. Which is that you gamble everything, and nothing changes. Nothing significant, anyway. The status quo is like one big self-regulating ecology. All that happens is that the balance shifts and whatever you do to try to upset it, it just sets itself right."

"How does that work?"

"Nobody knows. The rules are beyond grasping. If you go back to meet yourself, you won't be there. The past that you return to may not even be the past you left behind. Whatever you try to alter, somehow it all still comes out the same. Or else it's different in a way that suits you no better. There's a whole new branch of fractal mathematics that tries to explain it and what it all comes down to is, there's an infinite number of ways for something to go wrong and only one way for it to go right."

I said, "So the overall effect is like, when you pee in the swimming pool and nobody notices."

Clearly this was an analogy that had never occurred to him, because he stopped and gave me a very strange look before carrying on. He wasn't a healthy-looking man. He had pale eyes and grey-looking skin. His hair had lost most of its colour, as well. He dressed as if he didn't care about his appearance, in clothes that most people would have bagged up and sent to a charity shop.

He said, "The people who set these places up thought they'd make a fortune. Most of them went bust within ten years. The rest of us squeeze a living from the same bunch of hopeless romantics who think they're the ones who'll beat the system." He gestured toward the public area beyond his office door. "You've seen enough of them by now," he said. "They keep coming back. They're older, they're younger, they're just in a loop thinking, *I almost did it then, I'll do it for sure next time.* Next time, next time. They scrape up the money and they come limping back. They can't even see how they've thrown away the lives that they set out to fix."

THAT FIRST RETURNEE of mine was back within the week.

This time, he was much older. I mean, seriously. He was recognisable but he looked as if he'd spent the last couple of decades scavenging for his life in a war zone. Maybe I exaggerate. But not by much. He didn't seem to have washed or shaved in ages. I could smell him from across the room. He just stood there holding onto the wall by the door, as if that last long walk up the road had taken everything out of him.

I said, "Hi."

He fixed on me. I wondered if he was drunk, but when he spoke I was fairly sure that he wasn't. The messages were just taking their time to get through.

He said, "I'm sorry. I've come a long way."

"Can I get you anything?"

He shook his head, and then moved over to where the forms were and pulled out a chair. I made a mental note to tell Morley that the whole area would need a scrub-down with disinfectant and then I realised, with gloom, that the job would fall to me.

I watched the man. The one I now thought of as My Repeater. I'd seen other returnees by now, but he'd been my first. It wasn't so much that he was now old, more that he'd become old before his time. He looked as if he'd been sleeping rough, and I wondered how he'd managed to get his latest stake together. By years of begging and spending nothing, by the look of him.

He brought the paperwork over. I held my breath.

"Just a few last details to get," I said.

"I know," he said.

I went through the usual questionnaire as quickly as I could and when he emptied the money from his pockets onto the counter, I had to force myself to pick it up. The grubby notes were in bundles, and there was a lot of small change. I felt as if I wanted to scrub the coins before touching them.

It always had to be cash. Travellers weren't creditworthy. They walked away from their futures when the Big Red Button was pressed, leaving no one to pay off the debts.

I said, "Do you want to take a seat while I count this?"

"I'll just wait here," he said.

And he did, too. He leaned on the counter and watched, with me breathing as shallowly as I could and trying not to rush it so much that I'd make a mistake and have to do it again.

Only days before, I'd seen him in good health. Now he was a shocking wreck. I couldn't imagine what he'd been through and I didn't want to ask. The part that I couldn't get my head around was that although the change seemed like a magical stroke that had happened in a matter of days, it wasn't. While his younger self had been standing before me, this older version had been somewhere out there, probably heading my way. They were *all* out there, at more or less the same time—every one of his repeated selves, going over and over the same piece of ground. Never meeting, never overlapping, co-existing in some elaborate choreography managed by forces unknown. Causing no ripples, accomplishing nothing, scraping up their cash and heading right back here. The person he was, and all of the people he would ever be. Fixed. Determined. Tripping over the same moment, again and again and again.

I felt a sudden and unaccountable sympathy. It bordered on tenderness, and it was an awkward and unfamiliar feeling; doubly hard to deal with, considering the scent and the state of him.

Lowering my voice so that Morley wouldn't overhear, I said, "Second chances don't come cheap, do they?"

"You give it whatever it takes," he said.

He looked so bleak and downcast that it made me sorry I'd spoken at all.

I HAD AN idea, and I pitched it to Morley.

I said, "If we kept one file on each repeater, it would save us having to cover the same ground every time."

"You lazy little bugger," he said.

"I'm not being lazy," I protested. "I thought I was being efficient."

"So somebody comes in here and we face him with a file that shows half a dozen returns that he doesn't even know he's going to make yet. What's that going to do to him?"

"Stop him from wasting his life?"

Morley said, "Watch my lips. It's already happened. Nothing's going to change it. All you can do is add to his misery."

And that was the last of my employee suggestions.

I GOT AN hour for lunch, and some days my old school friend Dominic would turn up and we'd walk out along Technology Drive until we reached its lonely end way up in the hills. There we'd sit on a rock and throw stones at bottles until it was time for me to go back.

I must have seemed down that day, because Dominic said, "What's the matter with you?"

"Morley," I said.

"What about him?"

"He's depressing me."

Dominic knew Morley. Partly because it was a small town and everybody knew everybody, if only indirectly, but also because in my first week Morley had made one of his few front-of-house appearances to tell Dominic to stop hanging around the shop and making conversation with me.

He said, "Morley depresses everybody. Even his daughter took her own life rather than listen to his conversation."

This was a surprise. "Seriously?" I said.

"Far as I know."

"When?"

"Years back. When Dinosaurs Ruled the Earth."

I didn't know what to say to this, so I pitched a few more stones at the bottle we'd set up. One of them caught it a glancing blow, and knocked it over. It didn't break, but it fell amongst the remains of countless others that had.

"Who says so?" I wondered aloud as I went over to set it up again.

"My mum," Dominic said. "She used to know him, in the days when he was a human being."

On the walk down, he told me what he knew of the story, which was very little...just that Morley's daughter had written a note and then opened her wrists while stretched out fully-clothed in the bath. She'd cut them lengthways rather than across which, according to Dominic, was proof that she'd meant it. She'd been nineteen. No one knew for certain what her reasons were. Morley had burned the note.

Technology Drive was like an abandoned airstrip. Just being there made you feel guilty and excited with the thrill of trespass, and for no reason at all. It was as wrecked and overgrown as any Inca road, and in its time had served far less purpose. We picked our way down it, stepping from one tilted block to another. The drains had fallen in and all of the roadside wiring had been dug up and stolen. There was also about seven miles of buried fibre optic cable that no thief had yet been able to think of a use for.

They talked of it as the Boulevard of failed business plans. The cargo-cultists' landing strip for a prosperous future that never came. Crap like that.

Nineteen years old.

I wondered what she'd looked like.

THE AFTERNOON WAS uneventful. That evening, I borrowed the car and went out with Dominic. We spent most of it in the Net café attached to the local Indian restaurant, and then after I'd dropped him off at home I contrived to drive past Caroline Pocock's house a few times, which is no mean trick for a place down a cul-de-sac. Then I parked and watched for a while. I didn't know which of the windows was hers, but long ago I'd picked one at random and by now I'd convinced myself that it was her bedroom. I stayed there until her father came out in his pyjamas and stared at the car and then I took off.

It was after one in the morning when I passed the end of Technology Drive and saw lights in the Bureau's windows. I stopped the car and walked back to the junction. Someone was moving around inside.

Burglars? Looking for what? There was nothing in the place worth stealing. I didn't get too close because I didn't want to be seen. I stayed back in the darkness and waited for another movement. After about a minute, I saw who was in there. It was Morley. He wasn't doing anything much. He was just mooching around.

I saw him polish the glass panel in one of the booth doors with his sleeve, I saw him straighten one of the disclaimer signs on the wall. He mostly looked as if he couldn't quite bring himself to go home.

I couldn't imagine why. He lived on his own. There'd be no one waiting there that he might want to avoid.

I didn't get to bed until after two o'clock. I had a restless night. My thinking kept going around in the same circles. If life is lousy and you go back to change it, all that happens is that you fulfil the pattern that delivered your lousy life. Your choices are no choices at all. It seemed all wrong but think about it long enough, and you'd be scared even to breathe.

After all of that, I overslept and had to scramble.

I was late getting in. Morley was there already. I don't *think* he'd been there all night. He muttered something sarcastic and went off into the back office. The fact of it was that he could have run the place single-handed and saved himself the cost of my miserable wages, if he'd chosen to. What he had me doing was mostly dogsbody work. When I wasn't behind the counter I pushed a mop or answered the phone. The technology, though it was getting pretty old, was maintenance-free and the operation of it was idiot-proof.

I think it was just that he didn't like to go out there and face the clientele any more.

Around ten-thirty that morning, a taxi drew up outside and this young male of around my own age got out. He was well-dressed and had a sharp-looking haircut. You could tell just by looking at him that here was someone from a good family with money, and that he'd been favoured by the education system. Almost everyone from my school slouched, and their mouths hung open in repose. He stood looking the building over as the taxi pulled away, and then he came inside.

He spent twenty minutes or more reading through the forms before he brought them over to the counter.

He said, apologetically, "You'll have to help me with these. I can't work out what I'm supposed to do."

"Sure," I said, and I started to go through everything with him. He'd filled in some of the stuff, and he'd left blank the parts he wasn't clear about.

This time, I knew it way before I saw the name.

"You've never done this before?" I said.

"Nope," he said. I tried not to stare at him. Here, in the midst of his pattern of recycling visits, was the visit that began it all. He was bright, springy, full of confidence. The only giveaway was a dangerous-looking light in his eyes, but it was like the nerve of a bungee-jumper getting ready to go. In his own mind he knew exactly what had to be done, and he was about to step out and do it.

I went to get Morley's approval on the paperwork. My thoughts were racing.

Back at the counter, the young man was waiting. He was tapping out a drumbeat on the counter's edge with the fingernails of both hands.

"Everything all right?" he said.

"Everything's fine," I said with forced brightness.

"When do I go? Do I go right now?"

I lowered my voice and said, "Can I say something to you first?"

My repeater stopped his nervous drumming and looked at me; polite, puzzled, curious.

I said, "Walk away from this. Get on with your life. Whatever you think you're going to change, I can tell you for certain it won't work."

"Thanks for the advice," he said. "But I know exactly what I've got to do."

So then I did what I'd been warned against. "Just one moment," I said.

Then I went and got the records of his last few visits. The ones that I'd witnessed, but that he'd yet to live through.

I laid them on the counter for him to see.

He looked at them. Then he looked at me. The light in his eyes was still there, but it had changed. He wasn't so certain any more, and I could see that he was scared.

"What's all this?" he said.

"That's you," I said. "Your entire life if you don't walk away."

He stared down at the papers again. They all carried his signature.

I've got him, I was thinking. *It was a risk, but it's working.*

"Fuck is this?" he said. "Do what I've paid for, or get me your supervisor."

But Morley was already coming out of the back office. "All right," I started to say, "forget I even spoke." I could hear the desperation in my voice as I started to backtrack, but it was too late.

Morley said, "What's the problem?"

"I thought you people gave a service," my repeater said, and he pointed toward me. "Since when was it his job to interfere in my private business?"

Morley looked down, and saw the files on the counter.

"There's been a misunderstanding, sir," he said then, raking them toward him and dropping them under the counter without giving them a second glance. Then he looked at me and said, with a considerable chill factor, "Go and wait in my office."

I went into the back, but I could still hear them talking.

"*Booth four, sir*," I heard Morley say. "*I hope it works out for you.*"

"*I reckon it will*," I heard the young man say.

A couple of minutes later, the young man was on his journey and I was on the carpet.

"What do you think you're playing at?" Morley said.

"I was just trying to save him a load of grief."

"He's *got* a load of grief. Sometimes it's just a person's lot to live it out."

"You didn't see his face when he looked at his file."

"I told you, *no* files. Didn't you hear me?" He rammed the point home with his forefinger in my chest, stabbing me with every word. "You don't… show…the clients…their…fucking…files."

"If you'd only stayed out of it," I pressed on, "I'll bet you I could have convinced him. I was almost there. I could have rescued a wasted life."

"You know nothing," Morley said, but I was warming to my theme now; now that there was no chance of being proved wrong, I was starting to believe that I'd had control of the situation prior to Morley's interference.

"I bet he was just about to turn," I said, "and then you had to come wading in."

"He's on rails," Morley said dismissively. "We're all on rails. Knowing it won't make any difference."

"But what if things *do* change?" I argued, and suddenly the doubts that I'd been unable to articulate all fell into place like jointed plates.

"What are you talking about?"

I said, "Maybe things change all the time and we just don't know it. Maybe your daughter wouldn't be dead now if you weren't too pig-headed to go back and fix what went wrong."

Bad move.

I knew then that I'd gone too far. I also knew that it was too late to take it back.

Morley just stood there and closed his eyes. I could see the whites flickering where the lids didn't quite meet. He took a shuddering breath and swayed a little. I thought for a moment that he was starting a fit, but it was just that I'd never seen anyone in the grip of such bone-shaking, overwhelming anger before.

He said, "Get out of my place."

He was barely audible. My hands were shaking as I gathered my stuff together and as I was going out of the door that he held open for me, I couldn't bring myself to look back at him.

I heard him say, "I've forgiven you an awful lot since you came to work here. I can see now I let you get away with too much."

"Sorry," I said.

"Not sorry enough," were his last words to me.

I COULDN'T EAT that night, and I felt so sick about it all that I couldn't tell anyone why. It wasn't just that I'd never been fired from a job before. And it wasn't because I'd failed with my repeater, because I'd been onto a loser there from the beginning—the very evidence that I'd tried to show him had been proof in my hands that he'd continue. I just wished I could have taken back what I'd said to Morley about his daughter.

But there it was. You can't change what's passed.

Unless.

Unless I was right. For some odd reason I kept thinking about the spreadsheet we used to work out the charges. When you changed one little thing deep down, everything shifted around as a result. It made a whole new picture.

Maybe we're just talking about the spreadsheet of everything. There's no past as such, there's just the big '*is*'. No final, bottom line, just an endless middle. Updating all the time, undergoing constant changes in the always-has-been. Our certainties rewriting themselves from one instant to the next. For every miserable repeater, maybe there are a thousand happy and successful travellers whose journey simply vanished from the record once their misery was removed and the journey became unnecessary.

Not a bad leap. For someone so young, naïve and stupid.

I know that there are brain-damaged people who live entirely in the moment, whose memories fade in the instant they're formed. They need a notebook so they can keep checking on who they are, where they live and where they're from, who all these strangers around them might be.

Maybe this whole time thing's just a magic notebook.

And we're just the readers who believe all we see.

THE NEXT MORNING, I confessed to my mother about losing the job. It was that, or go through the pretence of getting dressed and going out early with no reason. She wasn't as surprised as I thought she'd be, but she asked about my unpaid wages. I hadn't even thought about them, and I really didn't feel like facing Morley again. But then when she started to talk about going with me to make sure that I got what I was due, I made hasty arrangements to go back alone.

The building on Technology Drive was all closed up. I looked in through all the windows but nobody was there.

So I went away, and returned late in the afternoon. By then someone had called the police out. Two uniformed officers had turned up in a van, along with a man that I recognised as the owner of a big womenswear shop in the middle of town. I mean it was a big shop, not that it sold stuff to big women. It was called "Enrico et Nora" and he was Enrico. I didn't know it at the time but he was Morley's sleeping partner in the business. The policemen were getting ready to break the door in.

I said, "Can I ask what's going on?"

"It's bolted on the inside," Enrico said. "Who are you?" The police wanted to know who I was as well, so I told them.

Then they brought this heavy thing on handles out of the van, and used it to batter the door in.

Nobody said I couldn't follow them inside, so I did.

I'd walked through the same door every working day for the past couple of months, but now it didn't feel right. All the lights were on, even though it was daytime. I was tensed for something awful. I know it may sound melodramatic, but it felt like the kind of scenario that precedes the discovery of a lonely death.

One of the officers had his head inside one of the booths. He pulled it out and said, "How do those things work?"

"It takes two people," I explained. "One to travel and one to operate from the outside. There's a system so one person can't do both."

They started looking in each of the booths, I'd guess in case Morley was lying in one of them.

But I was looking over at the counter.

The anglepoise lamp from Morley's office was standing on it. When I glanced over into booth five, I could see that there was one of our key cards in the activating slot. Back on the counter, the lamp was positioned in such a way that the edge of its metal shade rested squarely on the Big Red Button.

He'd have had maybe a minute to get himself into the booth as the lamp slowly descended.

The settings on the machine meant nothing to me, but I could imagine where they'd led. I don't know if he'd aimed to get there hours before, to prevent the child from killing herself, or months before, to divert her from wanting to.

I told them all about it.

And even as I was telling them, I looked out through the window.

I knew that he couldn't have succeeded, of course. I knew it because I lived in a world where Morley's daughter lay long-dead in her grave and I'd seen the damaged plaything that loss had made of her father. If he'd gone back and saved her, then none of that could ever have happened. But it had.

I could see a figure heading up Technology Drive, walking from where the bus had dropped him off. I couldn't see his features yet, but I could read the determination in his stride.

Next time, his attitude seemed to say. *I almost did it then, I'll do it for sure next time.*

The police went into the back to look through the papers in Morley's desk. Enrico went looking for a phone to call his lawyer. I moved around to my usual place behind the counter.

And there I waited, to see which of my repeaters it would be.

The Governess
An Introduction

I'M NOT AN obsessive collector but I'll admit to owning more than one copy of Arthur Conan Doyle's dinosaur epic *The Lost World*. It all started with the version I bought in paperback after discovering an omnibus volume of Professor Challenger stories in the children's library, since they ungenerously expected me to return theirs. If I thought the paperback would scratch the itch, I was wrong. I was missing the other material so as soon as I could scrape together enough pocket money I bought my own *Complete Stories*. Jump forward a few years and I'd acquired the shabby-but-nice first edition that I got cheap because it was short of a couple of plates, the fit-for-the-bin early reprint that I rescued for small change from a Spitalfields stallholder (only to find that it contained intact the very plates my other copy was missing), the Pilot & Rodin annotated edition, bound copies of *The Strand Magazine* with the story's original appearance in serialised parts, the *Eagle* strip with Martin Aitchison art and the Ladybird Book with different Martin Aitchison art, the 'Graphic Classic'...

All right, then...*you* define 'obsessive'. I just call it legitimate interest.

It's fair to say that in any list of books that I've loved and been influenced by, 1912's *The Lost World* is right up there. It's a bold, light-touch, groundbreaking popular entertainment of lasting cultural heft. For BBC Films in 2001 I built my *Murder Rooms* screenplay around a fictional scenario planting *Lost World* seeds in the young Conan Doyle's imagination. If you've read my novel *The Bedlam Detective* you'll recognise something of Professor Challenger in the guilt-driven delusions of Sir Owain Lancaster, back from his own Amazonian expedition where his entire party was wiped out. *Spartans vs Dinosaurs* is the grindhouse peplum spectacular that I'll never get to make.

And now here comes *The Governess*.

Stories usually happen for me when two disparate ideas link up. Each begins to connect with the other in a process that feels more like one of discovery than an act of imagination. Somewhere in my notes were a few lines of speculation in which Edward Malone, the *Lost World*'s journalist narrator, revisits an ageing Challenger. Elsewhere I'd jotted down a supernatural notion that needed a context for it to go anywhere.

Doyle had used Challenger as a spokesman for his own spiritualist beliefs in *The Land of Mist*. It's a late novel that reads more like a tract, but it put Challenger firmly in touch with The Beyond. That's the element I was able to run with; that, and the mention of Malone's marriage to Challenger's daughter at the end. Such is the nature of art that, despite embarking on a pastiche, I found my way to areas and themes that I can recognise as my own.

It's not my only love-and-influence title. Another is *The Odyssey* in E V Rieu's novelistic prose translation—just the three shelved copies of that one, at last count, and if you've been reading in order then you've already seen one story owing something to it. We echo those who went before, whether we plan to or not.

But for now, *The Governess*.

—SG

The
GOVERNESS

HADN'T SEEN OR spoken to Professor Challenger in four years, since the day he cut me dead at John Roxton's funeral. Enid was on his arm then, and would not acknowledge me either. Still my wife in the eyes of the law, but her affections lost to me for good. I dare not complain about that, even now—I had no one to blame but myself. Though I'm not sure which I regretted more: the deed of mine that had caused the rift, or my ill-advised confession of it.

It was in the Albert Hall, one Sunday evening in the July of 1930, that I laid eyes on Challenger again.

The occasion was a memorial service for an author friend of the Professor's; a popular figure, and they say that ten thousand people packed the Hall that night[1]. I can easily believe it. I'd been sure that I'd find Challenger there, but now my hopes of reaching him for a word were not high. He sat unaccompanied in a second-tier box while I was above in the standing gallery, shoulder to shoulder with the mass of my social peers.

My fortunes had declined since my separation from his daughter. Not as a consequence of our parting, but in the way that tribulations seem to gather where they sense an opening. Beaumont's line for the Gazette was that all matters Spiritualist were bunkum, and with McCardle's retirement I had no

---

[1] 10,000 was the figure estimated by the event's organisers; the true number was closer to 6,000

news-editor to champion my efforts for even the occasional piece. These days I wrote what I could, and I sold it wherever I might. I'd perhaps get five hundred words out of tonight. But this was not my reason for attending.

I could see that Challenger had aged. He didn't once look my way, and I could study him at length. The black of his mourning attire showed up the silver in his beard which, unlike the days of old, he now wore trimmed. I could only imagine that Enid had persuaded him to a concession that her mother had never managed. Perhaps time and grief had done their work, but the Wild Man of Science seemed relatively dapper and almost subdued.

An hour of hymns and speeches was followed by a much livelier hour of clairvoyance, reaching its height with the manifestation of the deceased author in the empty chair beside his widow. That is, if the medium were to be believed, which few saw any reason to doubt. When the meeting ended and the excited crowd moved as one into the streets, I fought the tide to reach the carriage entrance before Challenger's motor car. I got there just as it arrived to collect him. When his driver returned to the wheel, I jumped in from the other side.

"Sir," I began, "I know I'm unwelcome here. But please—" And that was as far as it went, because the Professor had me by the collar and was flinging open the door to throw me headfirst into the street.

I said quickly, "Hear me out and I'll agree to the divorce."

His grip didn't lessen, but he stayed his hand.

He said, "You dare to offer terms?"

"No terms," I said. "I'll take whatever conditions you name."

I was released. As I eased my collar and dropped back onto the seat the Professor commanded, "Once around the park, Austin." And then, to me: "I don't want Enid getting sight of you."

"I appreciate this, sir."

"Save your appreciation. Say your piece and then get out."

"Do you recall the children at Chorley Grange?"

Those fierce eyes narrowed, and I had his attention.

"I do," he said. "What of them?"

Chorley Grange was a burned-out manor house where the four of us—Challenger, his daughter Enid, the medium Algernon Mailey, and myself—had once responded to reports of a juvenile haunting. It had begun as a whispering in the ruins, followed by sightings of movement through the window of the former nursery. Someone appeared to be inside, yet the room always proved to be empty. We spirit-hunters set up camp, with Challenger and Mailey at the house while Enid and I looked into its history. Enid reported 'powerful vibrations' from three unmarked graves in the nearby churchyard, while Mailey contacted the spirits of those who'd died in the fire. Ghosts and graves proved to be connected. They were children who had strayed from the *limbus infantium* through which they were meant to pass, and did not know how to return.

A common occurrence with children who predecease their parents, according to Mailey. With no one to shepherd them, they wander; and having lost their way, can only cling to the familiar.

I said to Challenger, "I've been visited by the boy."

I didn't need to say which.

"You mean the *b*—," he said.

"I mean my son."

"And you dare speak of this to me."

"You've agreed to listen."

"My tolerance has its limits," he said, and then, to his driver, to call our meeting to an end, "Austin!"

"The boy is dead," I said.

There was a long silence. The driver awaited instruction which did not come.

Challenger said, "Go on."

"I saw him first at the end of my street, then three nights later at my window."

"This was when?"

"Last week. When I went out, he was gone. I took it as a sign of trouble and sought out the mother. She confessed that the boy died last winter. She'd kept silent in order to continue receiving the money."

"You can't expect honesty from a blackmailer."

"There was no blackmail. I paid willingly. But through my solicitor—there had been no contact between us since the child's birth. I refused to see him, but I had enquiries made. At the time it seemed for the best."

"Then how could you know him now?"

"I knew him," I said.

The child had been the outcome of a pre-matrimonial experience. This was the substance of the confession I'd made to Enid when, swept up in our newlywed bliss, we had sworn to a shared life with no secrets between us. Our union was broken there and then, in the sitting-room of Folkestone's Imperial Hotel, never to be restored.

At that time the child was three years old. The mother was a woman I had barely known. In the past week I'd learned that she had taken the role of a widow and raised the boy alone. Their life had been difficult. He had died a charity case, I was told, in the Evelina Hospital for Sick Children.

"He's lost, George," I said. "A lost soul. We helped the Chorley Grange children to peace. He deserves no less. Blame me as the sole author of Enid's pain, George, but the boy is an innocent."

For all his ire, bluster, and ego, I knew that Challenger was a decent man. I saw that I had reached him when he let my slip into familiarity pass. He had the reputation of one who did not suffer fools gladly, which was an understatement. He suffered nobody gladly. He looked out of the window for a while, thinking. The park outside lay silent under the light of the quarter moon.

He said, "Mailey has passed beyond."

"I know," I said. Our late colleague had used his powers to engineer the delivery of the Chorley Grange children to some higher care.

"With Mailey gone we need some other way," the Professor said.

He leaned forward and gave his driver an address in Bloomsbury, whereupon the motor vehicle turned from the park and we headed east along the Bayswater Road.

∽

WE VISITED THREE different houses, finding no reply at the first and only a maid to answer at each of the others. At the last of them, in Bedford Square, Challenger sought the use of a telephone and returned to the vehicle after ten minutes. His expression was dark. On this night, perhaps the most significant of the Spiritualists' year, it seemed there wasn't a single reputable psychic of his acquaintance who'd stayed at home.

I dared not suggest that we might call upon Enid for help.

I asked what joy, and he ignored me. "To Ralston Street," Challenger told his driver. "Number One."

When we arrived at the Chelsea address, he told me to wait in the car. I recognised the house, a tall narrow building with railings around the basement and seven steps up to the door. It was here that Miss Gwendoline Otter held her regular salons, attended mostly by young actresses and literary figures. I wondered at the point of our visit until Challenger emerged a few minutes later, followed by a jowly, balding man of fifty-something years in a shapeless brown suit and floppy bow tie. Though I recognised the man I wasn't sure of his name, because he had several; I knew only that he preferred to be known as La Paix.

I moved over as he made for the seat beside me. He landed heavily, looked me over and then said to Challenger, "Is this him?" There was nothing of the French about his accent, unless I'd missed the news of France annexing Warwickshire.

"Tell him your tale, Malone," Challenger said. I couldn't say if the distaste in his manner was for my story, or for our new companion.

As we headed for our guest's Paddington apartments, I went over it again. When I was done, La Paix turned to Challenger and said, "Took something for you to come to me, George. What do I get out of this?"

"You get the satisfaction of hearing me ask," Challenger said.

La Paix settled back into the limousine's upholstery.

"Worth it," he said happily.

We ascended to La Paix's flat, to be met by a startled and nervous male companion who seemed to be part dependent, part housekeeper, part something I couldn't define. The two men left us alone and for a few seconds I could hear furious whispering in the next room. The chamber we were in was run-down, dark, and unsettling, with a round wooden dining table and half a dozen chairs. Soot had blackened the ceiling above the table, and damp had stained the walls.

The companion reappeared and, with ill grace and a foul expression, spread a circular cloth on the table. The cloth was decorated with various occult symbols. In the centre of it he banged down a bowl containing dried weeds which, after several attempts, he managed to set to smouldering.

La Paix then rejoined us. He'd changed his clothes and was now barelegged in a dressing gown that I think was meant to be some kind of ceremonial robe. The companion made a noisy departure to the kitchen and the three of us sat around the table, forming three points of a triangle.

"Breathe deep of the incense," La Paix said. "It's essential to the ceremony."

Stove heat had already made the air in the room close and oppressive, and at the very first whiff of incense my head began to ache. This was no séance. Or at least, it resembled none that I'd ever attended. Unable to locate a psychic, Challenger had been forced to resort to a mystic. La Paix produced a tattered scroll from his sleeve and read from it, and then he made an incantation. All of this in a language that might, for all I know, have been of his own invention.

Then he asked me, "The boy's name?"

And I had to admit, "I don't know."

"I need to locate his vibrations in the ether. For that I will require certain information. Tell me about the mother. Was she pretty?"

"In honesty? No."

"The truth."

I had no escape. I was painfully aware that I was speaking in the presence of my estranged father-in-law.

I confessed, "She appealed. In the moment."

"The moment is where we begin," La Paix then said.

What followed was an interrogation on matters of such intimate detail that I'm convinced the questions were more for the man's private gratification than for the gathering of any useful facts. I grew more embarrassed. Challenger grew increasingly angry, and rose to leave.

"It's essential that you stay, Professor," La Paix said mildly. And then he leaned forward and fanned the incense smoke toward himself with both hands, inhaling deeply.

Then he sat back with his eyes closed.

"The boy follows you," he said. "He's close to you. But as you've denied him, he can never come near."

I said, "Tell me what to do."

"Find the Governess, and place him in her care."

There was a puzzled silence from both of us, and then Challenger said, "The Governess?"

"The entity charged with the care of young souls in limbo," La Paix explained. "Not a job you would envy. Those souls are legion. Their noise is deafening. And they never stay put."

"Good Lord," Challenger said.

And I said, "How do we find her?"

La Paix bent forward again and took another deep draught of the fumes, so deep that he couldn't catch his breath and went into a coughing fit. We waited until he'd done spluttering. Then he wiped his eyes and composed himself.

"I see another boy. Atop a rock or a broken tree. Spirits and creatures swirl around it. He blows a pipe."

I recognised the description immediately. "The Pan statue," I said. "Peter Pan. The bronze in Kensington Gardens."

"I was getting to that," La Paix said, irritated. "It draws those young souls entranced by it in life. The Governess knows the place well. It's one of her regular collection points."

Challenger said, "Will we find her there?"

"If you hurry," La Paix said. He dug in the pockets of his robe, and brought out something that he slid across the table. "Show her this. It will tell her you came from me."

I expected some kind of personal token, but it was a coin. A foreign coin, one of those odd ones with a hole in the middle. I picked it up and saw that it was an ordinary ten-centime piece.

Challenger said, "Why should she care who sent us?

"She's the Governess," La Paix said. "She has a duty to the lost. This creates a debt that I can someday call upon."

The Professor's patience had now worn thin. He pushed his chair back and said, "Are we done? I'll have Austin bring the car."

"No," La Paix said. "Walk."

SO WE WALKED, from Praed Street to Kensington Gardens, through empty streets and into the park, with Challenger's man in the Daimler following at a distance. It was a mile or less. When street lighting fell behind us, the vehicle's lamps helped to show the way.

Every now and again, I would look back. If I turned quickly enough, I'd catch the silhouette of a small figure in the corner of my eye. I was in no doubt that it was a genuine presence. Yet whenever I tried to bring him fully into focus, he'd be gone.

Challenger said, "Is he with us?"

"He is," I said.

Among the things I'd learned in my confrontation with the boy's mother; she'd told him that his father had been a soldier, an officer, a hero who had died in some foreign war that was never specified. She supported the fiction with two medals bought from a pawnbroker's. These had become the boy's proudest possessions, kept in a tin box under his bed.

We were well into the park now. Down the path by the Long Water we could see our way to the clearing around the statue. Pale stone around the base, a gleam of polished bronze above. There seemed to be movement around it, but when we reached the spot there was no one.

We stood there, looking around. I was about to express my disappointment when Challenger said, "I hear them. Don't you?"

"Who?"

"Children. I hear children's voices." And before I could respond, he'd raced off into the dark. I tried to follow, but I'd already lost him.

Then I heard him—or someone—crashing around in another part of the undergrowth. Then a silence; and then, somewhere in the near distance, a soft whistle.

"You heard that, I hope," the Professor said close to my ear.

I turned and found him behind me. He quickly raised a finger to his lips for silence and beckoned me to follow.

"See," he whispered.

The fresh air had done little to clear my head after the poisonous fug of the mystic's lounge, and now I began to doubt my senses. I knew Kensington Gardens as a park of broad walks and wide open spaces, but it was as if we'd struck out from the statue in a direction with no counterpart on any map.

As we pressed onward the shrubbery grew ever denser, the pathways more confined. Our way was crossed by a broad grove, of the kind you'd expect to lead to a garden temple or other such feature.

At the far end of the grove, I saw children. Spectral children, a dozen or more of them, small and shining with a faint light all of their own. And at the centre of the group, towering above them, a dark figure that gave no light at all; but rather absorbed it, drawing it in, creating a centre of night around which those little planets revolved. This swirling group was there for a moment, and then it moved from the end and out of our sight.

"Quickly," Challenger said, and as he moved I followed.

We reached the turn. The temperature seemed to fall where the paths met. The last traces of a moving glow drew us on to the next juncture. And then again and again, turn after turn, with Challenger setting a pace.

"Wait," I said, but he wouldn't wait. My head spun. I looked up and saw no clouds, no quarter moon, no stars. Yet there was light enough to see by, as if we now moved in a luminous mist.

And then, as I lowered my gaze to look back, there he was. Not the Professor, but the boy, fully disclosed to my sight and closer than ever.

I turned to tell Challenger, and saw snow. Falling snowflakes, in July. And the foliage around us crusted with ice. I looked for the boy again.

"It's working," Challenger said. "He's being drawn in with the others."

"Professor, I'm confused," I said. "I don't know where we are."

"You're right to be," he said. "I believe we stand on the threshold of the *limbus infantium.*"

And then I heard a woman's voice behind us, saying, "Go back, gentlemen. There's nothing for you here."

The dark veil mostly shadowed her face. I think she was young. It's impossible to say. The snowflakes fell around her head and shoulders. Instead of settling they seemed to pass on through.

"Now, Malone," Challenger said in a low voice. "Remember what you came for."

My legs were unsteady but I felt Challenger's strong grip on my shoulder, and I was able to find words.

I said, "Might you be the Governess?"

She made no move to reply but then I was distracted for a moment, as another stream of young figures flickered right by me. I had my answer. They were like children called home for supper. Except that they were only briefly substantial, barely on the edge of existence, and I thought I saw the boy among them.

"Now go," she said. "Return. Before you forget the way."

But there was business to transact before we could leave. I reached into my pocket for the ten-centime piece and held it out.

"Here," I said. She looked at the coin. She made no move to take it.

"We brought you a soul," I said. "This is a token so you'll remember the debt."

She sighed, then. Not the reaction I'd expected.

"Don't tell me," she said. "La Paix."

"You're acquainted?"

"Far too well."

She moved on without taking the coin. I wasn't sure what to do next. But Challenger was there by her side, moving with her, the scientist in him compelled to seize this unique opportunity.

"You seem weary," he said. "Why?"

"For the children this is a place of passage," she said. "For me it's hell. The innocent will eventually move on. I never will."

"Why not?"

"For a sin I can no longer remember. Bound by my duty, and now at the beck of the likes of La Paix." She almost spat his name with bitterness, and I began to imagine being a trapped soul condemned to be at a disadvantage to any low wretch who could mangle a spell.

We reached a clearing then. But what a clearing. Here the children were waiting. Imagine a field of a billion young souls, their faces turned toward us, a vast army, on and on until their outer numbers were lost to view. My very breath stopped in my body at the overwhelming sight.

The Governess paused and looked at me, as if an idea had occurred to her.

"Let me discharge the debt, and owe La Paix nothing," she said. "Take back your boy."

I failed to understand. "Take him where?" I said.

"To life," she said.

But Challenger said, "Take him back into life? Can that be done?"

"I don't see why not," she said. "I can hardly be damned for it."

She held out her hand. I placed the coin in her cold palm.

"It's done," she said. Then she smiled. "But only if you can find him. And dawn approaches. The door between the worlds is closing as we speak."

A trick. I'd fallen for a trick. I looked back toward that endless gathering, a single night's work for the Governess. How could I ever hope to find one half-glimpsed face among so many?

But the Professor strode forward, and with all the power and force of the old Challenger that I remembered so well, bellowed, "Which of you is this man's child? Cry out and take your place back in the world!"

I was hit as if by a blast as a billion yearning voices answered him. I clapped my hands over my ears, but Challenger stood firm before the inrushing tide of sound. I was overwhelmed, I had no chance...but the Professor knew what he was doing.

"There," he said. "Tell me I'm wrong."

And with the noise still raging, I followed his pointing finger to the one child who stood, mute and silent amongst all the others, with his accusing eyes upon me.

The roar subsided. The Governess shrugged.

"Fair enough," she said. "Now I suggest you go back while you still can."

"And the bargain?" Challenger said.

"Will be honoured," she said.

WE EMERGED IN West Norwood. Do not ask me how. With no way of getting a message to Challenger's driver, we walked to Gipsy Hill Station for a train on the Crystal Palace line.

Challenger said, "I'll have the divorce papers delivered for your signature."

I'd completely forgotten my promise. But a deal is a deal.

I said, "Please tell Enid I wish her well."

That, it seemed, was expecting too much. But I could not complain. I'd been given the help that I'd sought, and we'd found a resolution of a kind. Though what form that resolution would take, I had yet to discover.

It was grey dawn when I reached my lodgings on Gower Street. I threw my coat on a chair and prised off my boots and dropped onto the bed, exhausted. Though my body was spent, my mind spun like a dynamo. I had acted, but I had no idea what would happen now.

As the events of the last few hours moved from the immediacy of experience into the memory of it, I began to examine the evening's narrative as a third party might, and to interrogate it with a journalist's eye. Just how much of the story could I 'stand up' from the moment we'd settled around that filthy table in that incense-choked room? La Paix was a known self-promoter and charlatan. He couldn't be compared to a reputable psychic like Algernon Mailey. In his daily life, Mailey had been a barrister and family man. La Paix flirted with the occult, and his powers were rooted in narcotics and depravity.

The longer I spent fending off sleep and reviewing my thoughts, the more that last night took on the character of an opium dream.

And yet.

And yet, if it could only be.

I thought of the boy with his medals in a tin box, worshipping a father who lived only in his imagination. A man next to whom I cut a much diminished, far less admirable figure.

No wonder we are seduced so easily by fantasies of second chances, by the dream of turning back time. Once I'd had a career, and once Enid had loved me. But now I was finding that the greater torment drew its power from a charity bed in the Evelina Hospital for Sick Children.

By now the city's birds had begun their chorus and I was no closer to sleep. I'd run out of new thoughts and my mind was just rehearsing the same themes, over and over. It was at this point that a tentative knock came at my door.

I froze. I listened.

The rest of the house was silent. And then, just as I was becoming convinced that I'd imagined it, the sound came again.

Someone knocking, for sure.

A light rap, as if by a small fist, tapping with a coin against the wood.

MAGPIE

MR MCCLURE LOOKED us over from the head of the classroom, and said, "Who's running in the school cross-country on Wednesday? Let's have some hands in the air, here."

Let me tell you the worst thing about being a fat kid.

It has nothing to do with how you feel or how you look in the mirror; you feel okay and you see exactly what you want to see, so no problems there. The worst of it lies in those little incidents and throwaway remarks that stick in your memory and become an unwelcome part of your life for good.

Because the picture that I carried around in my head wasn't the same as the one that the rest of the world seemed to see, I'd fall for trouble every time. So there we were one day, about thirty-five of us in Latin class, and Mr McClure the Latin teacher was asking us which of the boys were going to be running in the school's annual cross-country race. This was a once-a-year three-mile slog across the local golf course and along muddy woodland tracks, and I had about as much chance of making it around the circuit as I had of levitating.

The girls nudged each other and all sixteen of the boys stared back with a kind of bovine stupidity, and so he changed his tack and asked who wouldn't be running.

And me, like a fool, I stuck my hand up.

He asked me why not and I told him that I had a dentist's appointment, and everybody roared. I sat there bewildered, because it happened to be true.

The loudest of the barnyard sounds were coming from Colin Kelly and his cronies at the back of the room where they regularly shoved their four desks together and whiled away the hours defacing things. I suppose you'd have called Kelly the form's athlete; he had a collection of those little gilt cups and medals that the school bought cheaply out of a catalogue and handed out once a year on sports day. He was long-limbed and bony and he could dodge like a mongoose...and as far as the contents of his head were concerned, analysis would probably have yielded a teaspoonful of brains and a cupful of snot and a smattering of earwax, end of story.

McClure walked down the room toward them, and as they hushed and looked sheepish I could feel the heat moving away from me. McClure said, "What's the matter with you, Kelly?" and Kelly, surreptitiously trying to cover his exercise book with his elbow, said, "Nothing, sir."

"Are you running tomorrow?"

"Yes, sir."

"Don't mumble, Kelly."

"Yes, sir."

"Think you might win?"

"Yes, sir."

To be honest, this wasn't necessarily vanity on Kelly's part. He was probably fast enough to run on water without getting wet. McClure moved around to stand behind him and Kelly, beginning to sweat a little, fiddled with his pen as if trying to make out that he hadn't been using it for anything at all.

McClure said, "I know you've been training. What about the school record?"

"I'll get it easy," Kelly said.

"The word is *easily*, Kelly," McClure said, and he reached down and yanked the ineptly-hidden exercise book by its protruding corner from under Kelly's forearm. Kelly's elbow hit the woodwork with a loud *clunk* and McClure said to the class in general, "Does anybody here doubt Kelly's chances?"

Not a hand went up. McClure was holding the book in front of him to study the result of Kelly's efforts; knowing Kelly, it was probably something obscene. "So we all know that Kelly can run," he said. "And we all know that

Thomas can draw and tell stories, and that Kelly couldn't wield a pen to save his life." And then there was more laughter as McClure tore the page from the book before walloping Kelly over the head with it and dropping it back onto the desk before him.

He screwed up the page and put it into the pocket of his tweed jacket as he moved back up the room at that slow, patrolling pace known only to schoolteachers and drill sergeants.

"We've all got something we're good at," he said. "It's putting the same kind of effort into everything else that's the real test of character. Wouldn't you say so, Kelly?"

"Yes, sir," Kelly mumbled, in a tone that was both dull and dark. I looked back and he was staring down at the desk with a face that looked like a sky just before a really bad rain.

As he drew level with me, McClure stopped and lowered his voice.

"Who's your dentist, Thomas?" he said. "Is it Norman Hope?"

I said that it was. Norman Hope was an old boy of the school with a surgery in one of the big old houses at the head of the golf course. He picked up most of his custom amongst the kids and couldn't even see a tooth without drilling and filling it. He was cheerful and friendly and milking the system for all it was worth.

"I'll phone him for you this afternoon," McClure said.

"Thank you, sir," I said hollowly.

The lesson went on. But I was too miserable to take much of anything in.

I suppose that McClure must have been one of the old-school generation who believed in all that stuff about sport being some kind of metaphor for life. He'd been decorated in the war and he'd taught for more than twenty years, so you'd think he'd have known better. It was tough enough being a kid at the best of times, without having to fall victim to someone else's philosophy; but he was decent enough in his way, and in that country of memory where I so often go stalking with machine gun and machete he tends to die less lingeringly than most.

The prospect of having to put on the kit and run was making my heart sink like a stone into deep, dark water. But even then an alternative strategy was starting to shape up in the back of my mind, and it wasn't the biggest of my worries; that was reserved for Colin Kelly, a more immediate and less predictable concern. McClure had done me no favours by using my name to bring him down a peg or so; Kelly wasn't likely to take it with good grace. He could move like a cat, but he had the mental acuity of a paperweight. You don't ask the Colin Kellys of this world to take a broad view of anything. You just throw in their bananas and slam the cage door, fast.

The lesson dragged on, the incident apparently forgotten.

The four of them were waiting for me when school let out for the afternoon.

"Well, fuck me," Kelly said. "It's Thomas the Tank Engine."

I stopped in my tracks, mostly because three of them had spread to block my way and I could hear the fourth moving around behind me.

"Yeah," I said pleasantly, and with a confidence that I didn't feel. "Just steaming back to the old engine shed."

I'd emerged from the asphalt yard into the street only seconds before. Why couldn't I have taken another exit, just for today? Behind me was the main building of one of the last of the old-style grammar schools, a redbrick structure of moth-eaten charm with a gaggle of overspill prefab classrooms gathered around her skirts like bastard children. There had to be about twenty different ways in and out of the site; about five of these were official, the rest would have been impossible to cover.

But it was the end of the day. There was a hint of thunder in the air. I was toting along the great overstuffed briefcase that I always carried, everything that I could possibly need in one place because I could never rely on my memory to turn up with the right books for the right classes. And I was no great planner of battles, just an averagely-bright kid who read a lot and didn't move around much and whose physique nature had adjusted accordingly. All I'd had in mind was getting home.

Kelly made a kind of frowning squint at my remark and said, "You being funny?"

"You started it," I said.

"He thinks I was joking," he said to the others, and they made a noise like a chorus of cows. Damned if I can remember much about any of them today; their names and something about the way that one or two of them may have looked, but that's about all. They were just the crud that stuck around Kelly.

As they lowed and snickered Kelly said to me, "You want to try watching yourself sometime."

"For what?"

"Fucking entertainment, that's for what. You know what you are, don't you? You're a queer. You know what a queer is?"

"No," I said.

Apparently neither did Kelly for sure, because all he could say was, "It's what you are. Get his bag, Richard."

The one from behind me had a hold on my briefcase before I could get it up to hug it protectively to my chest, and he dug his nails into the flesh of my fingers to make me let go of the handle. We were right out in the middle of a dead-ended street, but I knew better than to hope for any help from behind the windows of the houses.

Just kids playing. Ignore them, they'll go away.

They tossed my bag from one to another and I made a few half-hearted lunges to get it back but I knew that I was wasting my time and in the end I just watched them, resigned, until they began to get bored. I knew how it would go, I'd been here before.

"It weighs a ton," Richard complained, so then they stopped and Kelly opened it up to take a look inside.

"No wonder," he said. "Look at all the crap in here."

What they were doing now was terrifically personal to me, and they knew it. When Kelly turned my bag upside down and emptied everything out onto the ground, that sudden shower of trinkets and books that flapped like birds was like the slamming of a door on some inner happiness. Nothing from the bag would ever be quite the same for me again.

He looked down at where my felt-tip pens had scattered. It was a bundle of about two dozen of them, a range of colours brighter than any rainbow, and the bundle had split so that they lay in a heap like a half-finished sky-scraper at the end of a Godzilla movie.

"Thinks he can draw," Kelly said, and he hawked up snot with a sound like Norman Hope's suction tube; and then he spat right into the middle of the tangle of pens, and it landed in a slug with a sound like a chunk of meat propelled from a catapult.

"Draw with that," he said.

The others followed suit. One of them, a plug-ugly kid called Doug, managed to spit down his chin and onto his own trousers.

When they'd gone I picked up all of the books, but I left the pens where they were. It didn't much matter, they were cheap and I had others.

But these were the ones that I'd always remember.

THAT NIGHT, AROUND seven, Keith came over to my house.

We'd fixed this the day before. Keith was another of the regular gang of freaks who could be found shivering in their games kit around the goal-mouth while the real play was all taking place downfield during the football season. His aversion to the track was as powerful as my own, and he'd asked me for some specialised help. He was short and skinny and pigeon chested, and when stripped for the showers he looked like a long-legged duck. He was so nervous when he said hello to my mother that I had to bundle him upstairs before he could give the game away.

Keith said he was impressed by my bedroom, so he passed the test. This was my true home, the one place where the person that I was and the person that I wanted to be were merged into one. I had my drawings on the walls, my model aircraft suspended from the ceiling on cotton lines so that you could half-close your eyes and imagine them in flight, my stacks of Sexton Blake and Tarzan paperbacks from the local market bookstall (where, in truly philistine manner, they clipped off the corners of the covers to mark a new price in the space; I'd spend hours with card and watercolours restoring the copies that I'd rescued), an old Dansette record player under the bed with a stack of well-worn ex-jukebox singles and only one middle between all of them, some much-prized copies of *Famous Monsters of Filmland* which made me hunger for a film called *Metropolis* that I'd never seen, more models, more books...

And, in what to the untrained eye would look like a disorganised mess on the chipped blue desk, my stories.

Keith said, "I brought some paper."

"What about the handwriting?"

"This is all I could get."

It was a note to the milkman, hastily written on a sheet torn from a cheap lined pad. Keith's mother's writing had the look of the hand of someone faintly retarded. Keith said "Will it be enough?" and I said, "It'll have to do."

So then I settled down with a pad of Basildon Bond and *The Family Book of Health* for reference, and started to compose. Keith peered over my shoulder for a while, but then his interest started to wane. I hadn't minded him watching just as long as he didn't start making suggestions, but now he wandered off and looked out of the window.

"It's starting to rain," he said.

I didn't say anything. I wasn't the one who was going to have to walk home in it later.

"If it rains tomorrow," Keith said, "they'll have to call off the run."

"Don't bet on it," I said.

The signature was the easiest part. You wouldn't think so, but it was. I'd worked out a technique which involved placing the two sheets against the shade of my bedside lamp and making a rough trace of the original lines in pencil. With this as a guide it was simple to do a quick, straightforward signature in ink, and then remove the pencil lines with a soft eraser when the ink was completely dry. The final forgery wasn't going to be exact, because I'd felt it necessary to tidy up the original a little—what schoolteacher was going to believe in the authenticity of a note from a woman who couldn't even spell the days of the week? But the overall effect was just about right.

Keith had discovered the stories by now.

"Don't mess them up," I warned him. This was a time when I'd already laid down my belief that there was a special circle in Hell reserved for the abusers of books, somewhere midway between the cat poisoners and the child molesters. Keith said that he wouldn't and then sat there hamfistedly turning the pages, and I winced every time like I'd just taken a slap on a bad sunburn. The second note, which would be my own, took me almost twice as long as the first because of this.

As I was finishing, he held up the pages stapled to imitate a magazine and said, "What's this one about?"

"You just read it, didn't you?"

"I was only looking at the pictures."

I went over and took it from him, and began to turn the pages with rather more care. "It's about a man who loses his dog and goes to the dogs' home looking for it. When he gets there he finds they've sold it to this professor who's used it in experiments, so he goes to the professor's house and kidnaps one of his children and does all the same things to it, so when the professor finds out the next morning he goes mad."

Great, subtle stuff. I paused at my favourite page in the entire story, the one showing the professor tearing his hair out at the Corporation Tip as he confronted a great mountain of waste bags from the medical school that were just in the process of going under the bulldozer. Most of the bags had split and there were dead dogs and monkeys hanging out, and from somewhere in the middle of the charnel heap a plaintive voice was crying *Dad-ee! Dad-ee!* in a shivery-edged balloon.

"What's happening in this bit, here?" Keith said as I turned to the next page, and I said, "That's afterwards. The dog comes back."

"Isn't it dead?"

"No, it was all a mistake. It was another dog that looked just the same."

Keith made a sick-face, and shuddered. He'd actually gone a shade paler.

"Got any more like that one?" he said.

So I took him through some of the others, me curious to see if I could scare him enough to make him ask me to stop, and him grappling with his awe as if he'd found some streak of the spirit that he'd never even sensed before. I showed him the one about the solitary morgue attendant getting drunk on New Year's Eve as all the lonely suicides were brought in, and his reaction at midnight when they all rose up and started to party. I showed him the one about the slaughter-house worker who built up such a terrific charge of bad karma during working hours that disasters happened to everyone around him as he unwittingly dis-charged it like static, but this one wasn't too effective—Keith didn't understand the concept of karma and, to be honest, I was a little shaky on its details myself. So then I showed him the one about a man who set a trap for a rat and instead caught some miniature, blind armadillo-like creature that bit him as he released it, and who started to pee tiny worms the next morning.

Yuk, Keith said, and crossed his legs and squirmed.

And then I showed him the one called *Magpie*.

This was my magnum opus. It concerned a man who trapped eight mag-pies and kept them in a cage in his darkened attic so they'd make his wishes come true in accordance with the old children's chanted rhyme that began *One for sorrow, Two for joy* and went on up to *Eight for a wish*. The story turned on the fact that he was cruel and neglected them, so that his wishes came true but all went bad in the end. Finally he repented of his wicked ways and returned to the attic for one last wish that would get him out of the big trouble that he'd brought upon himself, only to find that seven of the birds had starved to death and that only one—one, for sorrow—remained alive. And then there was this heavy knock on the attic door.

Keith didn't get this one, either. He said he'd never heard the rhyme, which I could hardly believe, and then he started arguing that it wasn't eight for a wish anyway, which was a pretty difficult line to pursue in view of what he'd just told me, and in the end it came down to me demanding Who's tell-ing this story? And then finally it was time for Keith to go home, and I was so peeved at him I almost didn't hand over the note that I'd done for him.

Afterwards, when it was a couple of hours later and I was on my way to bed, I took another look at the note that I'd drafted for myself. It read *Please excuse William Thomas from the cross-country run as he has a touch of sciatica*, and it was signed—although she'd never know it—by my mother. It was a less certain strategy than the dental appointment ploy and slightly compro-mised in that I'd already promised something similar for Keith when my other plan had fallen through, but still it looked pretty good to me.

I opened my wardrobe door and cleared back the shirts on the rail. *Magpie.*

I put the note in the chalk circle on the floor of the wardrobe. Pinned to the back boards, in a line, were eight identical bird pictures. I touched each in turn, and then I touched the note, and then I closed the door.

Eight, for a wish. Did I dare to wish for something bad to happen to Colin Kelly? Did I have that much of a nerve?

I already knew the answer to that one.

But the note came first. I'd leave it in there until morning, and then I'd present it without the slightest doubt that it would be accepted and believed. Keith would just have to take his chances. I'd done something different for him, of course…different paper, a different wording, and a different disease from *The Family Book of Health*.

I didn't know what leukemia was, exactly, but something so tough to spell ought surely to have been enough to keep a kid out of games for a week.

WILSON, THE GYM teacher, read the notes and made no comment. I took this as a tribute to my skill instead of seeing the truth of the situation; that to Wilson we were flyspecks almost beneath notice, and that whereas under normal circumstances he'd simply have bawled us out and sent us to get our kit and given us some added humiliation as a penance for our effrontery, today he had more important things on his mind. He was a hatchet-faced Scot, always in a tracksuit and a hurry, and the gym-teacher God had seen fit to eliminate every trace of humour and sense of justice from his nature. He spent nearly all of his time and energy on those sporty kids who needed him least, and maybe they saw a different aspect of him. All I know is that he made kids like me feel like human ballast.

He told us that we were going to be race marshals, which I thought sounded great. The reality of it would be that we'd have to stand at some cold, wet spot in the woods where the track turned, waving the runners through and noting their names and times. But what the hell, it would be better than having to be one of them.

He kept us hanging around the tackle room for half an hour before giving us flags and a clipboard to carry and leading us out to the distant spot on the circuit where we'd have to stand. There was no conversation as Keith and I trooped in his wake toward the golf course. He didn't even look back at us, apart from when we were crossing the road. Without him along it would have been perfect because the school world seemed to fade out behind us as we pressed on into this different territory of birdsong and tree shadows and wide acres of grass just the other side of the pathway rail.

The day was clear and cold. Rain had continued through the night, becoming so hard and fierce around one in the morning that it had sounded as if the roof above my bedroom had been stretched like a drum skin, but by dawn it had stopped to leave the sky washed-out and clean.

Walking was no problem for me. I could walk for ever. But on that circuit or anywhere else, I could run maybe two hundred yards before slowing to a plod like a gyroscope with a busted wheel.

"You'll wait here," Wilson said. We'd followed a muddy track, rutted and stony, that had led us to a spot in the woods where a stile marked the point where the pathway and the dirt track separated. Digging in the pocket of his tracksuit pants he said, "If anyone's not certain of the way, you wave them on over the stile. You don't leave until I come back and say you can go. Do you hear?"

We said we heard.

"You note the name and the time of every boy who goes through. You note them in these columns on this page, and I want to be able to read every one of them. Do you understand?"

We said we understood.

He'd taken out a small felt bag, from which he took what I'll always think of as an old man's watch. "This comes back to me in perfect condition. Anything happens to it and I guarantee, your feet will not touch the ground."

By which I took to mean that he'd probably knock us around so badly that we'd have to be carted home in a wheelbarrow. I looked at the watch and saw that it was a cheap Timex, probably cheaper than the one I'd been given for Christmas. But I didn't say so.

Wilson's retreating presence was like a thumbscrew being released. We were out of the race and we were no longer under supervision. We began to breathe the clean air of a couple of freelancers.

Keith said, "Got any more stories?"

"I might," I said.

And then, to pass the time until the first of the runners should appear, I broke a rule and told him a story that I'd dreamed up but hadn't yet put onto paper. Keith's wide-eyed awe made him a great audience in many ways, although his regular failure to grasp the most central detail in a narrative tended to throw me a little. But it didn't seem to bother him, so I didn't let it bother me.

The story was about a struggling writer who couldn't get his book published and who finally in desperation went to the Devil to try to work out some kind of deal for the book to become a bestseller. In my story, the Devil had a shopfront office with the windows painted black and the word *Loans* in flowing gold script on the outside of the glass. There was such a place, right on the busiest road in the old town about ten minutes' walk from where my grandmother lived, and it had spooked me ever since infancy. I think it was that black glass and the overheard phrase *loan shark* that did it. Sometimes an image can get into your mind early and rearrange the furniture to make itself at home, so that even when the light has been let in and the demons turn out to be just shadows you find that you're stuck with the new floorplan for life. The writer haggled with the Devil for most of an afternoon, but they couldn't come up with a deal that suited them both; until finally the Devil suggested taking one year from the very end of the writer's life in exchange for huge sales and a Hollywood deal, and the writer said okay. Who'd miss just one year, he thought, when by the time that it comes you'll be too old to enjoy it anyway? So he left his manuscript with the Devil and walked out into the street, and was promptly dropped by a massive heart attack as soon as he hit the pavement.

"What was his book about?" Keith said.

"That doesn't matter."

"Well, how come he dies?"

"Because he only has another year to live anyway," I explained patiently. "Only, he doesn't know it."

Keith contemplated the abyss of unexpected mortality for a while. Somewhere further along the dirt road on which we stood, there were the faint sounds of an approaching van or tractor.

Keith said, "You want to try selling some of those."

"The world's not ready for me yet," I said modestly.

The tractor, when it came into view about a minute later, proved to be that of the course greensman. It jarred and splashed through the ruts in the track, the greensman peering forward over the raised front shovel that had been loaded with fencing posts and about half a dozen rolls of new barbed wire. I don't know which was the more ancient, the man or the vehicle, and he had a skinny grey dog of similar antiquity that rode along on the platform behind the saddle. Keith and I backed off nervously to let them pass, even though there was plenty of room on the track. I'd never seen or heard him speak directly to anyone before, apart from a shout of *Git off of there!* heard from about a quarter mile's distance, and that fairly frequently.

But he pulled up level, and throttled back, and raised his voice over the sound of the hammering old engine. "What's all this about?" he called down to us.

"It's the school cross-country run," I said. "It happens every year."

"Not this year, it won't," he said. "Not through here. Who's organised it?"

"Mister Wilson," I said.

"And has he bothered to check on his route this morning?"

"I wouldn't know."

The greensman glanced heavenward, and my heart leaped happily at the thought of Wilson the Terrible being cast as a buffoon in some other adult's drama. "Well," he said, "you can tell your Mister Wilson that the rain's washed out the path and if he'd bothered to consult with me, I'd have told him so. You'd better not let anybody down there."

"It's too late," Keith chipped in. "They'll have started by now."

"Well, you turn them when they get here. That path drops away so sudden, you wouldn't see it coming. Send 'em around the outside of the wood and tell them to keep off the greens or I'll have 'em strung up like Nellie's bloomers." And then he slammed the tractor into gear against its noisy protests, and said, "Bloody Wilson again. I wouldn't pay the man in bottle tops." And then the tractor lurched forward and the skinny dog, which had hopped down to mooch around and piss on something, hastily wound up business and galloped after.

When he'd gone, Keith looked at me.

"I'd better go and see what it's like," I said.

I climbed over the stile and followed the path for some way into the woodland before I reached the spot, and then I came upon it so suddenly that I almost lost my footing even though I wasn't even taking it at a run. The path was cut into a steep gradient with a streambed below, and it was just beyond where this stony yard-wide shelf went out and around a big old tree that the washout had occurred. The land above had come down in a great wave of earth and simply erased the path, and an old retaining fence from somewhere up above had been dragged down out of line and across. Because of the way that the big tree screened it, the whole arrangement was as neat and unexpected as any prepared deadfall.

From where I stood I could look down and see the broken wire of the fence tangled into a rusty skein and half hidden by raw earth and roots and leaves. The birds sang unconcerned and the stream bubbled in the middle distance and I was struck by a sudden and awesome thought, a realisation that seeped in as slow and as warm as a pee in the pants...

Colin Kelly would undoubtedly be the front runner in the field.

It was like a door opening out into a dark and inviting land, and I slammed it as quickly as I could.

I was back at the stile a couple of minutes later.

"What are we going to do?" Keith said.

"We'll just have to send everyone around."

"That means messing up all the timings. Wilson'll kill us."

"He'll be just the same whatever we do," I said, taking the marker flags and trying to stick them in some kind of crossed arrangement in front of the stile. "And somebody could really get killed back there."

"Is it as bad as that?"

"You want to see it."

I was still messing with the flags, trying to get them to stay in some arrangement that had a look of warning about it, when Colin Kelly came pounding into view venting steam like a train.

As predicted, there wasn't another runner within sight of him. Loose-limbed and sullen, bottom lip hanging to show his teeth as he sucked air, he looked as if he'd been put together out of coat hangers. He knew the route, and all he could see as he came up the dirt track was a familiar fat kid blocking it.

"*Fucking get out of the way,*" he screeched as he bore down on me.

I stood my ground. "You can't use the path, Kelly."

"Says who?"

"It's all washed away. There's no way through the woods, you'll have to go around."

"Fuck off," Kelly said. He'd had to break his stride because I hadn't moved, and now he swung his arm to knock me aside; I ducked, and felt it pass through the air close to my head like a bony club. He ran into me and I pushed back at him, hard, and he stumbled and then recovered himself with an expression of rage and disbelief.

"I'm telling you to go around, Kelly," I tried to say in the brief half-second that was available to me, but he was beyond listening; from that day to this I've never seen a sight uglier than his twisted face thrust up against my own or heard a sound more vicious than his scream of "*Shift!*", delivered at maximum decibels as he grabbed hold of me and threw me down into the dirt with a yank that jerked my shirt entirely out of my pants.

By the time that I'd struggled to my knees, grazed and winded but barely aware of either fact, he'd hurdled the stile and was gone.

Keith was standing pale and scared, his mouth hanging open in a dark little O.

"You'd better go back and tell Wilson what he did," I said, only my voice came out as barely a whisper. I sat heavily on the step-up part of the stile.

"Me?" Keith squeaked.

"Yes, you. Tell him everything that Kelly said to me and that I said to Kelly."

"Can't you do it?"

"No," I said. "It has to be you, you're my witness. I'll stay here and stop the others. I think the race is over."

So he went, and I stayed, and about four minutes later the rest of the field started to arrive.

THREE WEEKS AFTER that, during school time, I went around to Colin Kelly's house. It was mid-morning, and I was lucky; I caught his parents just as they were getting ready to go out.

Mr Kelly answered my ring at the door. It was a pleasant house on a road that had some trees along it, a few rungs upmarket from the place where I lived; there was a paved drive out front to park a car, instead of just the street. And the car looked nearly new.

"Yes?" Mr Kelly said, squinting down at me as if his mind was running just a few steps behind his senses, and I said, "I'm from Colin's class. I've brought something for him. Is that all right?"

"Oh," he said, making an effort, and he smiled a forced and hollow smile. "Come in, won't you?"

I went into the hallway. Mr Kelly was in a suit and tie and the atmosphere of the house seemed to be like that of the preparations on the morning of a funeral. The door to the kitchen was open and I could see all the way through to the back of the house, but I didn't see any Mrs Kelly.

I said, "We had a sponsored swim last week and I volunteered to get the present and the card. We all signed it." And I held up the carrier bag for Mr Kelly to take. As he took it, there was a sound from upstairs; I couldn't even have identified it, let alone understood it, but Mr Kelly raised his voice to carry and said, "It's one of Colin's friends from school." And then he looked at me. "I'm sorry, er…?"

"William. William Thomas."

"I'm sorry, William. We were just getting ready to go back to the hospital. I suppose you'll have to hear about this sometime. Colin lost the infected leg last night."

"I'm really sorry," I said.

"You can imagine, we're very upset."

"I wish I'd come another time."

"No. It's a very nice thought and a very nice gesture. I'm sure Colin will appreciate it. Let's have a look, here."

He seemed to have trouble telling one end of the carrier bag from the other, but finally he found his way in and partway drew out the item that I'd spent half the morning searching for.

"Trains," he said, looking at the picture on the front and trying to come up with something to say about it. "Colin likes trains."

"It's a Thomas the Tank Engine drawing pad," I explained. "It's a bit young, but it's the biggest one they did. Do you think he'll like it?"

"I'm sure he will."

"There are some felt tip pens in there as well, all different colours. And I drew the card myself."

"Yes," he said. "A bird. How nice. We'll have to be going soon, ah…"

"William. William Thomas."

"Can we give you a lift anywhere, William?"

I politely declined, even though they'd be passing the school. I was out on licence, and I had no plans to hurry back. And I didn't much take to the idea of sharing a car with the so-far-unseen Mrs Kelly.

I glimpsed her, briefly, as the car passed me further down the road; she was just an anonymous woman, yet another kid's mother in a world that was full of them, and her head was bent as if in prayer. Or perhaps she was reading the card, signed by all of the form and with the bird that I'd drawn on the front.

A dark bird.

Just the one.

One, for sorrow.

∽

I BURNED THE magpies shortly after that.

It wasn't that I'd ceased to believe in them. My faith was undiminished; it was like a child's touching faith in the baby Jesus, only darker and more ritualised and somehow more personal. It was as if I saw the outlines of forces unseen by others, the shapes of those great sombre machines that worked under the surface of reality to keep the show seamless and complete and which, if you knew just the right place to push, might occasionally yield to persuasion. I think the truth of it was that I felt scorched by their primitive heat. They saw through me too clearly for comfort, and I was unnerved by their ability to spit out the twisted progeny of my unformed wishes and appalled by my own willingness to offer a secret embrace to such malevolent offspring.

And then time passed by, and even that conviction faded.

When I reached sixteen, the excess weight abruptly burned away as if a hoop of fire had been passed over me. When you start thinking about sex for roughly eighteen hours a day, I suppose the energy has to come from somewhere.

Colin Kelly didn't return to the school. His parents moved him to a bungalow somewhere out on the coast, and by all accounts started to smother and to treat him like he was five years old again. He got one of those legs that looks like something made out of Airfix and Meccano. I've no idea what happened to Keith. Wilson quietly left the school at the end of the year but I don't know what happened to him, either.

Make of it what you like. Maybe it was chance, it all just happened. Maybe there's a callous God with a sick streak of humour who's fond of setting up these little ironies every now and again. Maybe there was some power locked up in those bird pictures that only someone who'd been cut deep enough could release.

Or maybe it was the dogshit that I found and smeared all over the barbed wire in the deadfall before I returned to the stile. Who can ever say?

The Boy Who Talked
TO THE ANIMALS

DID YOU EVER see the kid they called Pugsley, in the old Addams Family TV show? Well, that's what my sister's boy looked like, the first time I saw him in seven years. At first he didn't even come out when she knocked on his bedroom door, but finally he emerged and shook hands very solemnly, and that's when the thought struck me. He was ten years old, short for his age, and he was carrying more weight than looked healthy on a child or on anybody else. When I glanced over his shoulder through the open doorway behind him, I saw drawn curtains and more hardware than you'll find in Radio Shack.

"I get worried about Petey," Janis said to me in a low voice about ten minutes later, when the kid had quietly faded from the scene again and disappeared into his bedroom. Janis glanced in his direction, extra nervous of being overheard. "He never brings friends home, never goes to another boy's house. He spends all his time in his room, in the dark. I sometimes wish we'd never bought him any of that stuff."

"It'll pay off in computer classes," I said, stretching back on Janis's chic beige sofa and hoping that I was going to be able to stay awake for the duration of the reunion. I'd had a hard interview followed by a long drive, and there wasn't much energy left in the batteries for counselling about somebody else's problems. With no job and a big loan that I couldn't pay off, I felt I had enough of my own.

"But he isn't," Janis said. "That's the part we can't understand. You'd think he'd be way ahead, but he comes in near the bottom of the class. Craig went to school, talked to Petey's teacher. She said that Petey had picked up so many bad habits by working on his own that she was having to work twice as hard with him to get him up to standard. She said he wasted his time just going around and around in circles on the simple things."

"And what did Craig say?"

"He said the teacher was full of shit. Not to her face, but he said it when he got home. Anybody could see that there was more value in trying original solutions instead of just learning the accepted ways, a lot of stuff like that. But none of it helps Petey with his grades, and Craig's never home, so neither does he. And what can I do?"

I don't know what she expected me to say. "Pull the plugs and kick him out of the house to play," I suggested, but she just gave a little smile as if I'd made a bad joke, and then she turned to the window as if to check the drive. Craig wasn't due home for at least another hour, but Janis was looking out toward that far-off horizon where the dreams and the disappointments meet. In the soft light thrown by the net curtain, she was my little sister again; only a few minutes before, I'd been thinking how seven years had played some tricks on her, and of how they hadn't all been kind ones.

I got up off the sofa and walked over to her. I stood behind her and put my arms around her shoulders, wrapping her up as completely as I used to when boyfriends threw her over or when life got so tough that she was grateful to be out of it, if only for a moment; and she relaxed a little and let herself sink back, just as she always had.

"He talks to it," she said miserably. "Not only the computer, he talks to all his stuff. It's like he had a little zoo in there. I've got a boy who holds deep and meaningful conversations with an Atari."

We stood there for a while longer, and then she sighed and slid out of my hug like a fish. "I'm sorry," she said. "It's good to see you again, really it is. You didn't come here to listen to our troubles."

I managed not to agree; in the state that I'd reached, it would have been awfully easy for something like that to slip out. Instead, I heard some dumbfool part of me saying, "Why don't you give me some time with him? See what I can do?"

"In three days?"

"I can at least get him out of the house for you. I don't suppose he sees much sunshine with the drapes closed all the time. Which of the big places hasn't he seen?"

"Sea World, Disney World, you name it. Craig took him along to see the Space Center a couple of times when he was working there, but the rest of it's just been good intentions."

"O.K., then. You sell him on the idea tonight, and tomorrow we'll make the trip."

"You're on," she said, and for the second time she smiled; only now there was something noticeably warmer in it. Nothing as warm as hope, but it was getting part of the way there.

It was a plain white Florida house in a development of fifty or so near identical houses. They had shared lawns fed by buried sprinkler systems, and snaky service roads named after exotic flowers. There was a residents' committee, and a hired man who kept the public grass short and the woodchip borders neat. Craig may not have been so happy any more, but at least he wasn't poor.

He never had been, although the letters I'd got from Janis after the six-week stretch that he'd spent between jobs had almost made him out to be like a character from one of the seamier Steinbeck novels—basically decent, but cast down about as low as a human being can get. The truth of it was that they'd already been in their present house when the components company lost its NASA contract and folded, and I knew for a fact that they had some good investments. Six weeks' living expenses wouldn't have made much of a dent in them, and Craig's new job with the management of a TV-repair firm paid almost as well as his old position…but Craig was determined that there was going to be some tragedy in his past, and there was no taking it away from him.

Petey didn't come out to dinner that night, so it was just the three of us. Janis said that he'd had a sandwich while I was in the shower; she said it almost apologetically, as if she was embarrassed at the presence of the empty chair.

Craig wouldn't have been recognizable from his wedding photograph; he'd gained about twenty pounds, and lost a lot of his hair. He had his first drink in his hand within ten minutes of arriving home, and within an hour he'd built up a lead that I couldn't hope to catch. He laughed a lot, and he made jokes. I don't think he said one word about his son.

By ten o'clock, I'd had as much as I felt I could take. I was feeling like a shirt looks when it comes out of the spin-dryer. I made my excuses and dropped out; Craig was back at his little cocktail-cupboard, and he said good night from there. I kissed Janis on the cheek, and left them to it.

By Petey's bedroom, I stopped for a moment and listened. Janis had said nothing about my earlier proposal, neither to Craig nor to me; now I was left wondering whether she'd even managed to cover the subject with Petey. A part of me wouldn't have been too unhappy if she hadn't—I'd never had children of my own, and talking to them was like a whole new language to me.

Well, he was still awake; and he was talking.

I listened for a while, but I couldn't make out what was being said. Either the words made no sense or the door just made it sound that way...I really don't know. There was some urgent whispering followed by a long-drawnout-groan of disappointment. There were no other sounds from the room.

I left his door and went to bed. I fell asleep faster than a falling rock.

THERE'S ONLY ONE place you can take a kid who's looking so down, and that's the Most Wonderful Place in the World.

At least, that's the advertising line that the Byron's Wonderworld people used to promote their theme park, one of many that had chased Disney money and arrived in the area close to Orlando. When I trailed a few ideas past Petey over the breakfast table, this was the one that got his attention; Sea World and Gator World went by him without a blink, but something here struck up a spark that kept on burning. While he went to get into his newest jeans and his baseball shoes, I borrowed some cash float money from Janis and told her that it was going to be a good day. She said that she hoped so, but she didn't really look as if she believed it.

We set out in my rented Chevrolet to cover the ninety miles or so of the journey. It was a bottom-of-the-range car, a Monza, and riding in it was pretty much like sitting in a launderette at gunpoint. Petey said hardly anything, and then only in response to some comment of mine; for most of the time he simply sat with his hands folded in his lap, watching the landscape unroll. His eyes were wistful, his hands small and delicate, and I began to revise my opinion of him a little. He wasn't so much a Pugsley, more a pocket-sized Oliver Hardy.

The road was long, straight, and not very exciting. There were wide grass verges on either side with occasional tracks cutting through where someone had swerved after bursting a hose or having a blowout. The vegetation beyond the verges was low-rise, dense and impenetrable, and it seemed to go on forever. If I'd been of the kind who's easily spooked, I might have been disturbed by the idea of that solid-looking, endlessly deep wall of greenery to either side, mile after mile; crowding in close as it did, it made the road seem almost temporary. It was with a sense of near-relief that I finally pointed out to Petey the spot ahead where the jungle turned to dust and the first of the smart new hotels appeared.

"Dad said you worked in a hotel," Petey said as we left it behind. It had been a two-story chain motel, blazing white stucco, fairly upmarket and with room prices to match. Large asphalt parking lot sectioned by tasteful planted borders, probably a couple of tennis courts around the back, certainly a pool with night lighting. Deep-pile carpets in the rooms, and air-conditioning units so powerful that they'd constantly drip water onto the outside walkways. Little nailhead rust spots would just about be starting to appear on the stucco, betraying the speed with which the whole structure had been thrown up to get in on the vacation boom of the past decade. My mind had run through the checklist and filed it away in the few moments that it had taken to drive by. Force of habit, I suppose.

"That's right, Petey," I said, "except that I didn't work in any one hotel. I worked for the management people. We had lots of hotels."

"Does that mean you got free rooms whenever you went somewhere?"

"That's right."

"Sounds neat. Why did you quit?"

"A good question," I said, and left it there.

I suppose the park management would have called it a slow day, but as far as I was concerned, it was just about right; we didn't have to push through the crowds to get from one section of the park to another, and the waiting in line didn't take long enough to wear the edge off anticipation. In the high season it might have been a different story, but this was the odd part of the Florida year where the sun hardly shines and the sky is never blue but a bright, hazy gray.

Petey had his own list of priorities, and for me it was a simple matter of letting him loose and then following. First it was the Hall of America close to the cable-car station, where we saw a lifelike animated George Washington make a crackly recorded speech, and then it was into the main part of Wonderworld to look for the Pirates of the Spanish Main. By one o'clock we'd seen the Pirates, the Hoe-Down Hillbilly Bears, the Haunted House, and the City of Tomorrow. Petey was hovering over whether to give Washington another look when I called a halt for lunch.

By now I'd more or less worked out what was governing his choices. Hardly any of the rides interested him (although we'd already planned the Interstellar Switchback for the end of the day, when the lines would be getting shorter), and a place like Cannibal Island didn't even rate a second look. Petey's fascination was with the virtuoso displays of high-tech to be found in the life-sized talking figures that he'd read so much about.

Whether he'd ever expressed this enthusiasm to Craig and Janis, I really couldn't say. He'd probably kept it well under wraps, knowing how they'd take it; I was a little uneasy myself, wondering if I wasn't just helping to reinforce his obsessions when I was supposed to be giving him a day out away from them.

"The whole park's really a deck," he said, "a concrete deck about thirty feet up with all tunnels and everything underneath. All the workpeople are down there, and the big computers that control the robots. It's where they got the idea for Westworld."

"Is that right?" I said vaguely, watching as a park employee in a heavily tailored chipmunk suit went skipping by the hamburger concession, waving at all the terrace tables. I waved back. I was in shirtsleeves, and I was warmer than I needed to be; whatever they were paying him, it wasn't enough.

"Yeah," Petey said, and he started to elaborate. Well, I thought, hardly listening any more, isn't this fine? It was probably the most talking that he'd done in months, at least to someone or something that didn't have a slow-beating lizard's heart of silicon. I could report some success back to Janis. Petey, meanwhile, was talking about wisecracking parrots and small dancing prototypes.

Our table was in the open air against the terrace rail, overlooking a part of the river where the Mississippi steamboat ran. From where I was sitting, I could see some incongruous waist-high boarding alongside the Indian Center where a piece of the decking was being ripped up and relaid. It looked all wrong, seeing that caterpillar-tracked digger in the middle of all that careful set design. Although this particular park was new to me. I'd visited plenty as part of my old job; that included the original Byron's Wonderworld in southern California, and I'd never noticed so many running repairs going on at one time. Okay, so they'd had to update and renew, but they'd always managed to carry it off without being obvious; here I'd already noticed three or four examples of off-limits areas, closed down rides, high makeshift fences with apology boards.

Perhaps the designers had finally overreached themselves, I thought, like building a tower too high or a bridge too wide; they've created something larger than they can control, and now they've got to run around at full stretch just sealing up the cracks. And the idea gave me the usual buzz that you get when you see someone else, usually with an inflated idea of his own capabilities, take a graceless fall and land on his backside.

Petey pulled me down with a bump, too, with his next question.

"Uncle Ray," he said, "why did you quit your job when you can't get another?"

I looked at him across the tray debris of our lunch. It was a straight question, even if it was one that I hadn't been expecting. I said, "Didn't your mother tell you?"

"They talked about it once last year, but not to me. They stopped when I came into the room."

"Well," I said, "that would be about the time when I left. But I didn't quit; I was fired. They fired me because I was going to jail."

Petey was saucer-eyed with amazement. "Were you framed?"

"No, I wasn't framed; I was guilty. I stole four hundred dollars from one of our own hotels, and I got a year for it. I came out a month ago with no job and no money, so I had to start looking. I came to Florida for an interview, and I'm staying with you because I've got another in Miami the day after tomorrow. I'm not making any secret of what I did, because I reckon that's my best guarantee that I won't do it again." The only problem was that nobody so far was taking the bait.

"Wow," Petey said, genuinely impressed. "Was it tough in jail?"

"Not for most of the time. Not after I moved to what they call an open prison. Not many walls and not too many guards, because they trust you not to run away."

"Didn't you plan jailbreaks? Weren't there any fights?"

"No jailbreaks. And only one fight, and that didn't come to anything. I talked my way out of it." At this, Petey looked disappointed. "I had to," I explained. "The guy was twice my size. He'd have killed me."

"I suppose," Petey said, but I'd obviously tarnished a little of the gold leaf on his new discovery.

Anyway, this was an area of the conversation where I wasn't feeling too comfortable. "Look, Petey," I said, "wouldn't you say I've been pretty straight with you? Jail's not something to be proud of, but I didn't lie or fob you off."

"I guess," he said, somewhat suspiciously.

"So, do the same for me. Why do you talk to your toys?"

"I don't."

"Straight talk, now. It goes no further than this. If something's getting you down, I might be able to help you with the way out."

"I don't think so," he said, and he looked out over the rail toward the water. The Mississippi steamer was cruising by for the second time, its rear paddle wheel slapping at the river and boiling up white fire.

"O.K., Petey," I began, and found immediately that he was facing me again.

"Please," he said, "don't call me Petey. Just Pete will do. Pete's just fine."

I shrugged. "Whatever you say. Is that what your friends call you?"

"No," he said, and he started to put the burger wrappings and the wax cups back onto the tray to be cleared away. "They call me Pugsley."

I SUPPOSE IT was inevitable that we should wind up visiting the Hoe-Down Hillbilly Bears for a second time. The wait for the Interstellar Switchback was even longer than before—presumably nothing sets you up for a roller coaster ride better than a good, greasy fast-food lunch—and we'd more or less run through Petey's (sorry, Pete's) short list of urgent must-sees. The Bears had put on probably the most technically complex show of all those that we'd seen so far; the Pirates, like old-time vaudeville artists, had simply repeated the same basic routines for each passing boatload of audience. The same was true of the waltzing ghosts in the Haunted House, whilst the talking man-nequins in the City of Tomorrow had been too bland and sanitized to set anybody's imagination running.

And it wasn't going to kill me to sit through a twenty-minute show for the second time in one day, so I said Okay. As we headed for the wide front-age of the three-story log cabin that was the entranceway facade, I saw myself doing something similar at Pete's age: sitting twice through the same movie and being yelled at when I got home, or running the same four-minute clip of an eight millimeter Chaplin film over and over on a junkshop projector. It seemed a long way from Atari and Speak-and-Spell...but was it, really?

Inside the theater, it was a different story. Nothing of the backwoods here, but a small Victorian auditorium in deep red velvet and gilt. There was a center stage with two half-round side stages, and an orchestra pit with a low brass rail along its forward edge. We got ourselves seats about halfway back and on the end of a row; besides us, there couldn't have been more than three dozen people present when the automatic doors closed and the lights began to dim.

"Showtime," Pete whispered, and I had to smile.

It was still impressive, even though I'd seen the performance through only a couple of hours before. The curtains opened, and an ursine jug band came forward on a sliding rostrum, mechanized bears of all sizes, keeping time and changing their expressions along with the music track. There was a bass player almost seven feet high, one with a banjo, a cub-sized player with a washboard; I glanced down at Pete and saw that he was totally absorbed. He wasn't just happy-fascinated like most of the kids in the rows before us; he was watching like one guitar player watches another, eyes fixed on the hands to study the technique as much as the music.

Now, I don't make myself out to be any kind of a child psychologist, but the details were starting to pile up. Probably without even realizing that they were doing it, Craig and Janis were shutting him out of the important areas of their home life; the way they'd obviously clammed up about my difficulties when he was around was just one example. And they went on calling him Petey as if he were still a baby; add this to Pugsley from the kids at school, acting with all the usual kindness and concern that a group of ten-year-olds will show a fat boy in their midst, and you'd have an equation that would factor down to one simple conclusion.

He talked to his toys only because no one else would talk to him, not in a way that recognized him as an equal. Everybody gets that feeling at some stage, but it's the nonstandard kids, the no-good-at-games kids, who get it in a form so sharp that it can sometimes draw blood.

The rostrum with the jug band started to withdraw into the carbon pine forest that was the stage set, and the audience began to applaud. I was joining in before I realized how ridiculous this was; the bears couldn't hear us, the original performers were no more than taped voices, and the people who took the real credit—the technicians and the animators who'd designed and programmed the whole show—would be in some design studio or workshop way over on the far side of the park complex, dreaming up something new to make our jaws drop when singing bears had become passé.

Then I looked down at Pete. He was clapping harder than anybody else. Whatever I thought, he knew different. The bears could hear.

The main curtains closed, while those on one of the side stages opened to reveal the master of ceremonies. He was a reddish brown bear in a starched collar and a top hat, and he wore a wide-eyed expression of polite surprise.

THE BOY WHO TALKED TO THE ANIMALS   465

"Glad to see y'all here," he said, scanning not only the audience but also a lot of empty seats on the outer fringes, and he emphasized the welcome with a small gesture of his paw. Those paws with their pointy black claws were the most truly bearlike thing about him; the rest was just comic-book stylization, a baggy fur suit topped by a talking rubber mask.

But still, it was fascinating to watch. Even knowing that he was just a mass of gears and relays, that everything that really made him tick was down below stage level and feeding signals up through the armatures that anchored his legs to the floor, that his voice was the voice of an actor, and that his performance had no more spontaneity than a tune on a piano roll...even then, the effect had something of the unnerving echo of real life in it.

He introduced the first solo act, a light-colored bear with a stupid look, a single tooth, and a ukulele. The kids all started to laugh at the first sight of him, and they laughed all the way through his number.

Then the spotlight swung back to the MC, and that's when we all saw something go wrong.

He started into a link; as far as I could remember, the next move would be for the ornate petals that formed the theater's roof decoration to open like a flower so that a chubby white she-bear could descend on a trapeze. The MC got going well enough, and when I looked up, the petals were already starting to open; but then, when he gestured upward, something in him seemed to lock.

The sound track ran on, but suddenly nothing was happening.

Presumably, bells would be ringing down in the basement somewhere, but the belowground staff took a while to respond. Meanwhile, the MC stood with his arm raised and his head thrown back and a goofy expression frozen onto his face, and the kids and the adults in the audience shifted uneasily and glanced around. I know what they were feeling, because I was sharing it; talking bears were weird enough if you stopped and thought about it, but this sudden halt was downright spooky. It was like the shock of the incongruous that you'd get if a ballerina paused in her dance to spit on the stage.

I looked down at Pete. His disappointment was obvious.

"Do you think they'll be able to get it going again?" he said, but all I could do was shrug.

"You're the expert," I said. "You tell me."

Another number started, a rousing fiddle tune that wasn't going to get anybody clapping in this performance, but we didn't get more than a couple of bars in before the speakers abruptly went dead. A few seconds of silence, and then up came a taped message in the down-home accent of one of the bears.

"Sorry about the break in the show, folks," it ran, "but it seems we got some problems in the back room... Us bears is going to get ourselves some root beer and lemonade, so why don't you do the same? And we'll see you back here when all the little details have been taken care of..."

There was more, but nobody was going to stay to listen to the public relations. Most of the crowd was already on its feet, and those down at the front were moving as the automatic side doors opened and let the daylight in. The curtain of the half-round of the MC's side stage was closing in slow jerks, cutting him off from sight like a sheet being drawn over an unusually distressing corpse.

The rest of my row couldn't get out as long I was there. I stood up, trying not to let my seat fly up too fast, and said, "Well, Pete, if you're still game, we can give them an hour to get it fixed, and then..."

But there wasn't much point of going on, because Pete wasn't there.

I let the tide of people carry me out into the foyer, looking around as I went. I expected to see him waiting and watching for me, but all I saw was a park employee setting out apology signs on metal stands to keep a new crowd from forming. The foyer filled and then emptied fast; nobody was smiling much, and at least one child was crying because he couldn't understand why he was leaving before the end.

But no Pete, not anywhere: not in the foyer, not outside on the forecourt, not looking in through the glass of the doors to see where I might be.

He couldn't have run off. For one thing, there hadn't been time; no more than a few seconds had elapsed between the automatic doors opening and me glancing down at his empty seat. And why do something like that, anyway?

Why, indeed. I could think of only one reason, only one place that he could have gone. So while the employee was still turned away, I detached myself from the tail end of the moving crowd and stepped back into the auditorium.

The small theater was now empty, and it was just me and the red velvet seats, red velvet carpets, and red velvet drapes with the brass rail of the fore-stage showing like a streak of gold in the dim house lights. Half expecting a shout or a challenge, I made my way down to the front. It wasn't far, and when I got there, I found what I was looking for. The corner of one of the stage curtains was hanging wrong, just the way you'd expect it to if a small and not particularly agile boy had lifted it and crawled underneath.

I took another look behind me. This was the point at which I should have gone along and raised the management, explain what had happened so that they could send someone backstage to find him.

But there was nobody on hand…and besides, to them, Pete would have been just another brat who wouldn't stay on his own side of the line. So instead, I hopped over the rail and crawled after.

It wasn't as easy as you'd expect, because there were lead weights in the hem of the curtain to give it the right kind of hang. My collar was up, my knees were grimy, and my hair was a mess when I got to my feet on the other side; there was a smell of dust and ozone like you get around the back of a new TV set, and I was almost touching noses with a seated bear with a fiddle on his knee.

He was a sly-looking red beast in a derby hat with a feather. Seen this close, he looked larger than life-sized, although I have to admit that I've never tried facing a real grizzly to make the comparison. His eyes had a dull glitter in the green of the backstage safety lights, and they seemed to be look-ing straight at me.

"Pardon me," I said, and eased around past him.

The first surprise was to find that I was actually on a three-part carousel, with a different figure in each section. They all faced outward, so that the carousel could turn when the curtains were closed, and it would simply seem that one act had replaced another on the same piece of stage.

The second was that there was no backstage area, not in the usual sense: no wings, no flies, no waiting areas for performers. Behind the carousel was just a narrow catwalk of perforated metal, and then banks of side lights for the main stage area.

Still no Pete. I wanted to call out for him, but I didn't dare. I stood on the metal catwalk and tried to see across to the far side of the stage. It wasn't easy, because the safety lights were few and none of them seemed much brighter than a candle; the jug band on the sliding rostrum was just a series of hulking shapes sketched in the darkness, and they were framed against pine-tree cutouts that had become sinister by green moonlight.

Since I couldn't call out, I tried listening.

Air conditioning. From somewhere far below, a harsh clicking like the line selectors in some distant telephone exchange. The low hiss of live speakers on an open circuit with nothing coming through.

And also—was it there, or was I simply reading it into the random sound picture that was around me? The sibilants and pauses of a small boy, whispering.

I strained hard to make it out, but no joy. Pete, you little beast, I was thinking, you've just about used up all the sympathy you had coming to you. And then I tried calling his name once, not so loud that anybody working down in the basement level would be able to hear.

Well, there was an immediate response...but not the one that I'd expected.

The fiddle-playing bear on the carousel suddenly sprang to life. One moment he was completely still, the next he was rocking back and forth and sawing away at the mute strings with his bow; the shock of it all happening no more than three feet away nearly sent me running up the wall like Spiderman. He rocked and fiddled, and the only sounds were the pops and groans of the little air pumps and servomotors that made him live. And then, just as abruptly as he'd started, he stopped and held the pose; I found that I was staring at him as if there were some chance of catching him out, of seeing him blink or take a breath like an out-of-work actor pretending to be a showroom dummy.

But I had to tell myself that the movement, not the stillness, was the illusion. They must have been checking the programming down in the control center, so that what I'd just witnessed would have been just a small segment of the fiddler's subroutine. It made sense, since they'd obviously be probing around to find out exactly what had gone wrong...but it would also make sense for me to stay well back from any of the other figures. I thought of the MC, of those broad sweeping gestures and those dangerous-looking claws; skin and bone wouldn't be much defence against their slashing power, hydraulically driven.

And then I thought of Pete, wandering around in the darkness alone, and most of the annoyance that I'd been feeling turned to real fear.

I was guessing that he had to be over on the far side, unless he'd found a trap or a service door that would let him into some other area. I also had a moment's passing doubt, which tried to tell me that I was all wrong, that even now Pete was wandering around outside wondering where I'd disappeared to; but now that I'd come this far, I couldn't allow myself to believe it. I was in charge of my sister's kid. In loco parentis, you might say. The responsibility was too heavy for me simply to walk away.

"Pete!" I said loudly, no longer caring that I might draw attention to myself. "Pete, are you there?"

I might have been mistaken, but I thought I could make out a response; not a sound, as such, but more a few moments' alteration in the texture of those faint background noises that I'd first noted as I'd emerged from under the curtain. It was as if the whisperer had stopped, listened out for a while, and then carried on.

It was all I needed. Pete was over there somewhere, talking to the bears. How could I ever explain that to Janis?

So I started out across the stage, and after three strides, I stumbled and fell over one of the recessed rails that would carry the jug band's rostrum forward. The noise that I made would have alerted any park employee or technician within earshot, and the word that I used was definitely no part of the show. But by now I'd concluded that there was nobody around up here but me and the bears and the boy, and the sooner we reduced that to just the bears on their own, the happier I'd be.

I managed to miss the second rail, and reached the flats screening the main stage from the other carousel. Now I was more certain about the whispering; I could even recognize Pete's voice. It was just like I'd heard it the night before, when I'd stood outside his bedroom for a while and listened.

Even so close, I still couldn't make out the words. It sounded more than ever like some made-up language of his own. I ducked under an angled spotlight to get to the carousel, and there I stopped.

The circular stage section was no longer angled as it had been when the show had reached a premature end; it had made a one-step revolve, which meant that the section carrying the Master of Ceremonies was now turned toward me. The figure had moved, too—his arm lowered, his whole body tilted forward…the new pose looked almost like one of attentiveness, because the lowered head, still with its surprised expression, was almost on a level with Pete's own.

WHATEVER HE WAS trying to say, it seemed urgent. But now I knew for sure that Pete was talking gibberish, a long stream of unconnected syllables punctuated with strange, hiccuping guttural sounds and the occasional click; and all of this with a look so earnest that he obviously meant every meaningless word.

I was going to have to dump all of my amateur analysis. The boy needed help, headshrinker style—and the sooner I could tell Janis, the sooner he'd get it.

"Pete?" I said, gently.

Two heads turned to look at me.

I swear that this is exactly how it happened; it was as if I'd broken into a conversation between two strangers in a coffee shop. The bear's eyes were fixed on mine. They had a dull gleam, like old money. Slowly, he straightened up. He was at least seven feet tall.

Testing again. That was the explanation for it. If those broad paws suddenly started to swing around, Pete was close enough to be hit and perhaps badly hurt.

"Pete," I said, "come over here with me. It's time to go home."

But it was the bear who answered.

Or rather, his mouth worked and his face moved, but there was no sound track for him to be synchronized to; and since he didn't have lungs or a larynx, he couldn't produce any vocal sounds of his own. The only noises were those of the servos and little compression pumps that animated him. They sounded like an approximation of the noises that Pete had been making only moments before.

"He says you shouldn't be here," Pete told me. "He says you're in trouble."

"Never mind what he says. Just step over here toward me."

The bear looked down at Pete. The boy looked uncertain, as if loyalties were in conflict.

"Look at him, Pete," I said. "Look at what he is. What you're doing isn't safe."

That shaggy, bottom-heavy shape, so much like a cartoon figure played for laughs in the show, had become in the half-light something far less reassuring. From Pete's angle, he must have seemed immense. Pete stared up at him, as if he was realizing for the first time that there was a choice to be made, that this was a zoo where there were no visitors, only new inmates; and he glanced once at me, as if to remind himself of what his own kind looked like.

And then, reluctantly, he made his decision.

He started to step off the carousel toward me.

The bear moved with frightening speed. One massive paw slapped down on Pete's shoulder and jerked him back as the carousel began to turn; it moved rapidly and in silence, and that tableau of intimidation was gone before I'd even taken half a step toward it. The MC's place was taken by the pouting bear in the blue jeans and the red bandanna, and he was already rising from his stool as he swung into view; only one of his feet was anchored to the floor for the passage of his control cable, because the designers had left the other free for stamping out a rhythm in time with the banjo. This gave him about another three feet of reach, which put me well within clawing distance. I couldn't go forward, so I quickly tried to back out through the flats and onto the stage.

But when I looked over my shoulder, I could see that they were there ahead of me. The forward edge of the jug band's rostrum was sliding across, just closing off the gap—a couple of seconds earlier and I'd have made it with no trouble, although the thought wasn't much consolation now. The rostrum itself was no more than a yard high; the real barrier was the jug band itself, every member standing up and facing toward me, arms spread and ready to grab.

I was well caught, the narrow gap between flats plugged at both ends. But surely, the flats themselves could be only canvas or thin ply? I could kick my way through.

But I never got to find out, because that's when the banjo smacked me on the back of the head.

I went down like a sack of pebbles. I could feel myself going, but there was nothing I could do about it. Something hooked me by the leg and started to pull me in; I felt the bump as I was dragged over the edge of the carousel, and got a momentary burst of basement sounds and metallic air as my face came close to the perforated catwalk around the outside. Then I was on solid ground again, and being rolled over, and the shooting stars and singing birds were subsiding and giving me a chance to concentrate.

The pouting bear was standing over me. The banjo, which seemed to be permanently anchored by the fingerboard to his left paw, hung in two pieces held together only by the strings. His mouth was working, but I couldn't guess what he was telling me.

And then there was a tearing sound, and the brown dividing curtain on my right began to come down in long, ragged strips. The banjo player leaned over and held me in place, his free paw bearing down on my chest like a hydraulic press. I didn't doubt that he had the power to push on through and out the back; but I didn't have to think about it much, because I was too scared to struggle, anyway. I could smell machine grease and nylon and a weird tangy smell like battery acid. The whites were showing all around his dim glass eyes.

What made it worse was that I'd been here before. Big Mick Dunleavy had squatted over me in just the same way, one hand pinning me like a bug to a board while the other raised up ready in a fist of impossible size. We'd been in one of the prison workshops, hand-painting little plastic superhero figures on an outside contract for fifteen cents an hour. It was the only work left that they'd allowed Dunleavy to do; he'd tried to take a saw blade out of the machine shop and a chisel out of the carpentry shed, and he'd added six months to his sentence when he'd worked in the laundry by grabbing the hand of a forger named Gilbert Mercado and holding it down in near-boiling water until it was halfway cooked. The word was that Mercado had made a pass; according to others, he'd rejected one. Either way, I still couldn't say what it was in my manner or what I'd said that had caused Dunleavy's flare-up and turned me into his target of the morning.

And I hadn't told Pete the truth; I hadn't managed to get out from under, even though that's the way I'd have liked to be able to remember it. It was the worst feeling I'd ever known. I was completely powerless, and Dunleavy put in four or five solid blows like he was trying to pound a melon into the floor before one of the guards finally ambled over and laid him out with a sap behind the ear. They had to reset one of my cheekbones, and my eye swelled up so badly that I saw nothing out of it for a week, and everything in Cinemascope for two weeks after that.

So pardon me when I explain that as I lay on that carousel with all the weight and the power of the banjo playing bear devoted to keeping me there while his pal tore a way through to us, I was only one spasm away from crapping my pants.

The curtain between the two sections of the carousel finally came down. It was almost in shreds; everything that I'd first suspected about those claws had been true. The Master of Ceremonies stood there with the green light behind him. Pete held one-handed against his side like an awkward parcel. He was struggling, but it was getting him nowhere.

The banjo player looked at the MC, as if for a signal. The movement was too smooth, a point-to-point glide, as inhuman as anything could ever be. It was something colder and even more remote than the madness in Dunleavy's eyes.

The MC inclined his head, once, and I knew that I'd had it. I'd crawled under the velvet barrier into something else's world, a place where there was no welcome. It was the sign that my captor had been looking for, a definite thumbs-down.

The free arm went up, banjo dangling in two pieces like a flail. I could hear all the motors that were working together to raise it, muffled by the fur-fabric of his outer skin. I took the only way out that I could. I closed my eyes, as tight as they'd go.

Now, I know that somebody's sense of time can be quite badly affected in circumstances like these, but after a while of lying there with my face screwed up and the rest of me as tight as an overstrung piano, it started to become pretty clear that things were no longer happening in the anticipated order. The weight was still there on my chest, but my head was still there on my shoulders. I hardly dared to open my eyes again, but toward the end of the longest minute I've ever known, I found that I had to.

Nothing much had changed, but the banjo player was looking over toward the MC. The MC was looking down at Pete, and Pete was doing all the talking.

It was that same weird parody of a language again, sounding like distant echoes down an air shaft. Whatever he was saying, they were listening and listening closely. Claws were digging into my shirt and making exquisite little needlepoints of discomfort, but I didn't try to move.

Suddenly, like a trap springing open, the pressure was gone. Pete was released in that same moment, and he scrambled toward me across the car-ousel and the ruins of the dividing curtain. The banjo player straightened slowly, almost with reluctance, like a sadistic interrogator being ordered off a prisoner.

Pete was at my shoulder. "Come on," he said urgently. "They're thinking it over. I don't know how long we've got."

I made sure that I pulled myself out of reach before I tried to stand. The banjo player watched, his rubber face dull and slack. The Master of Ceremonies was a dark silhouette. As I took this in, Pete was tugging at my sleeve, pulling me toward the flats and the main stage.

We ducked under the lights and through the cutout trees, and climbed up onto the rostrum that was blocking our way. None of the jug band made any move toward us, but they were all watching; their heads tracked us in perfect synchronization as we went to the front of the stage and I hauled up the weighted curtain. Pete slid through the gap in a second, and I dropped to my knees and wormed my way after. It wasn't easy, turning my back on the band and knowing that at least a couple of them could lean forward and catch my ankle or my pants leg even as I got my nose out into freedom, but moments later I was rolling out over the brass rail and falling to the safety of the auditorium floor.

SWEET AIR. IT was probably no different than the air on the other side of the curtain, but you couldn't have told me that. My knee was throbbing where I'd knocked it on the rail, and there was a kind of crescent of sore points on my chest; they meant nothing at all.

"We'd better leave before they catch us," Pete said. Amen, I thought, and I didn't stop to ask whether he meant the bears or the park security people. The auditorium was still empty; so was the foyer when we got to that, and the apology signs were still posted outside the doors. They'd been locked, but each had a crash bar for fire safety. An alarm may have sounded somewhere as we left, but we'd be in amongst the crowd before anyone knew.

I was starting to shake. Pete was a marvel of ten-year-old calmness, and there was I, going to pieces and wondering if there was anywhere inside the park itself that I could get a decent stiff drink. Of course there wasn't; there's no room for booze in the Happiest Place on Earth. But he took me by the hand and led me to one of the concession stands and sat me down, and then he took the five dollars I gave him and returned with two root beers and a fistful of change.

I had to turn away as an actor in a fox costume, frock-coated and top-hatted, went by looking for somebody to be photographed with. It was stupid, really, but I was feeling kind of sensitive. An actor in a suit was just an actor in a suit. But how could I ever handle another plug-in appliance without wondering if it had some small, dim share of the alien intelligence that I'd met on the other side of the curtain? Would I ever be able to watch TV without the uneasy feeling that it might be watching me back?

Pete set the root beers down, and climbed up onto the seat alongside me. Even though he was only a kid, he had that bright, confident look of somebody who's had a sudden insight into the layout of his world and—more important— has been able to decide on his own place in it.

He was watching the fox. If anybody was going to make the first pitch here, it was going to have to be me.

I said, "They're hiding it, aren't they? What they can do."

He looked at me. "They're waiting," he said. "They haven't known for more than ten years or so. The microchip was a big boost for them…kind of like an evolutionary step. Before that, they were only dreaming."

"How far's it spread?"

"I know only what I've heard. The more complicated we make them, the brighter they get. They talk to each other, they make plans. They're waiting for the day when we get too smart for our own good."

"And then? "

He shrugged. "Who knows?"

Who knows, indeed. I took a drink. I hate root beer.

I said, "You don't think that's something to be worried about?"

"Not if some people know how to control them."

"And you know how?"

"I know a way."

Now he was teasing me, leading me on and enjoying every minute of it. He drew on his multicoloured straw, swung his legs, and squinted out across the bright plaza by the concession stand.

The fox crouched, arms spread wide in welcome as two small children ran toward him. Their mother followed, floral print blouse and stretch slacks that were being stretched to their limit and a little bit beyond. As she walked, she was unhitching a Polaroid camera from her shoulder.

Pete had me by the nose…but I needed to ask. "What did you say to them?"

The fox hugged the children close, the woman raised the camera. I thought of a living insect trapped in amber, waiting its time. A small intelligence smouldering like a flyspeck of plutonium.

Pete said, "I told them that you were my uncle who worked for Con Ed. I said that's why they had to let you go."

And then he sat back, as if that explained everything. But I didn't understand, and it showed.

"Con Ed supplies the power," he said patiently. "Who do you think they pray to?"

The
BACKTRACK

I PICKED UP A rental car at the airport and some flowers from a teenager at a roadside stand. We could barely hear each other over the roar of traffic. I chose two bunches from the buckets next to her canvas chair and she wrapped the stalks in a page from a magazine. The blooms lay in the passenger footwell as I drove on.

An hour later I left the highway to cover the last few miles on the Old Mine Road. It sounds grim, but the mines are long gone and the valley's mostly been reclaimed by nature. Now the road carries mainly local traffic through a forest of mixed oak and Virginia pine. It's well kept but you can go a mile or more without sight of a truck or another car.

Just short of town I stopped and backed up a way. I'd almost missed Shawn's sign. When I reached it I pulled onto the verge and got out.

It was the standard state-issued memorial, a generic plaque that read *Drive Safely in Memory of* and then, on a separate plate below that, *Shawn Richard Kinney*. There were a few personal tributes around the base. A couple of unopened soda cans so old that the branding had faded right off, some ribbon that had once tied something, handwritten notes with the ink washed away. I had to be the first person to have stopped by in a long time. I went back to the car and took out a couple of stems to lay across the remains of the old tributes. The flowers were for my mother's birthday but I was sure she wouldn't mind.

Then the final mile, passing the derelict chicken restaurant. No one could ever make a go of that place. Even the local ghost, the Gray Lady, was said to have moved down the road a way to avoid it.

My mother came out to meet me when she saw the car pulling in.

"Hello, stranger," she said.

To be fair, it was my first trip home since my dad's funeral. We were never a hugging family, but with the first awkward minute out of the way we were fine. We went inside. While she was fetching a jug to put the flowers in, I spotted my book on top of her display cabinet. It was propped upright among the family photographs.

"That's just the advance proof," I said when she came back. "I'll swap it for a good one."

"Whatever you like," she said. "I keep it there so I can look at it."

"Did you read it?"

"Of course I read it. Your Aunt Rose wants to read it too, but I told her where to buy her own."

"I could mail her a copy," I said. "I only brought one other and it's spoken for."

"Let her pay for one," she said. "She was looking to borrow mine but she's not getting it. I still remember when she folded your baby pictures."

The author copies were in my overnight bag, safe as bullion between layers of clothing. I took the bag into the smaller bedroom. It had been my room once, and later my dad's. Same carpet, different paint. I anticipated some rush of nostalgia but I felt nothing.

I checked one of the books for dings or scratches and then went back with it into the kitchen. My first novel, and from a big New York publisher. In the months ahead I'd try to be self-deprecating but I was desperately proud of it. Five years later I wouldn't be able to look at my own prose without wincing in embarrassment. Now whenever I look at my early words, it's like a more capable stranger wrote them.

"Happy birthday," I said.

The proof was just a proof, a functional softcover with no art. They'd done a great job on the real thing, a three-piece case with a nice headband, coloured endpapers, the works. The dust jacket had commissioned art and my paid-for headshot on the back. She gave it due admiration and said, "Now I can read it again."

"I brought one for Mr Kinney," I said.

I sensed a change. She didn't look up and she didn't do much to show it, but she seemed to grow a little wary.

"You did?" she said.

"In a way, he started it all. I thought he might get a kick out of seeing it."

"I'm sure he will."

"Is he all right?" I said, feeling that something was a little 'off'.

"He's retired," she said, which wasn't really an answer. "You don't see him around much."

I was in Ward Kinney's English class at high school. At the end of one of my assignments he wrote, *I like your style!* Until then, I wasn't even aware that I had a style. He had a son who was my age. I'd known Shawn, but not too well; the Kinneys had sent him to a different school. He was part of our group but not part of the gang, if that makes any sense.

I said, "I passed Shawn's memorial on the way in."

"The roadsign?"

"It looked kind of neglected."

"It's not the only thing. So you plan on visiting his father?"

"I thought I would."

I retrieved the proof and she set the new copy in its place, and we went on to discuss evening plans. The options ranged from college student dives to fine dining aimed at their visiting parents. Anywhere you like, I said. It's your birthday. Go mad. She chose the senior special at the Country Kitchen buffet, where the tables were wipe-down and the waitress uniform was house-maid from the 1890s.

She didn't ask about Caroline and I didn't push it. They'd never really liked each other. I told her how my work was going and she caught me up on local gossip. All of it was news to me. Facebook was around then, but it wasn't such a thing; any homecoming always meant a picking-up of lost connections.

∽

ONE SUCH CONNECTION was Clem Henry. We had a lunch date lined up. I dropped my mother off at the hairdresser and we met in a Pizza & Brew place just behind the Art Deco movie house.

Clem had very much been one of the gang and—to my knowledge, at least—was the only one of us who'd stayed around. He'd finished his education locally and now he taught at our old school. Our parents' generation had seen their dying community reborn as a college town, with a modern campus and sports arena just a couple of blocks from our historic Main Street.

"I don't see many changes here," I said, looking around after the waiter had taken our order and the menus. The décor was the same as I remembered it, bare brick and grey linen, and featured an open kitchen with a wood-fired oven.

"Why mess with perfection?" Clem said.

"You hear much from the gang?"

"Only what I hear from Justin. Taryn got married. Gabby's not well."

"She okay?"

"I don't know the details. It sounds bad. How's Caroline?"

"She's fine," I said. "She sends her love. She would have come along with me but…"

"I expect a couple of days without you around was more appealing."

"That may have been an element," I conceded. And then: "You remember old Mr Kinney? Do you ever see him around?"

"Kinney? Hmm." There it was again, the same expression as my mother, falling somewhere between pity and regret.

"Meaning?"

"He used to show up for school events but he hasn't done that in a while. Now he's on his own, he's kind of let himself go."

"Really? That's sad."

"Yeah, well. After Shawn…"

"Is he still in the Rosebery house?"

"No, he moved somewhere up the Backtrack, I couldn't tell you where. He's on his own now. You sometimes see him when he comes into town for his mail."

The food arrived, and we talked of other things. He asked for more on Caroline and I told him about her new job at the museum. She'd also been part of the gang, but the two of us hadn't been a couple then. She'd dated some of the others, Shawn included, and when we both left town and launched out into the wider world it had been with other partners. Only later on did we meet up and get involved. Hand of Fate, I called it. It was as if the home town and the years we'd spent there had created some kind of gravity. You'd feel it all your life and sometimes it would draw you back together.

AFTERNOON RAN INTO evening but I stuck to one beer and kept a clear head. The Country Kitchen was in the retail plaza, close to where many of the motels and suite hotels stood. There was no game this week, so not many visitors around.

"So," my mother said. "How was Clem?"

"Still Clem," I said.

"I was talking to Maybelle. She saw the strange car and guessed you might be home."

"She did? How is she?" Maybelle had been my babysitter, back in the day.

"She's well. She was asking how you were."

"Nice of her."

"She says her son-in-law downloads books for nothing off the internet. Do you get money from that?"

"Not if he's getting them for nothing, no."

"I'll tell her to tell him."

"I imagine he knows."

The Senior Special was popular. Some of her friends stopped by to say hi. We were home by nine.

∽

I'D PROMISED CAROLINE that I'd bring home some of the local pepper jelly and apple butter, so in the morning I walked into town. Little had changed, though the comic book store was now a bakery for pet treats. As I waited for the crossing lights, I saw this scarecrow figure walking out of the bank to a yellow Toyota with a long, loping stride. Some local eccentric that I didn't immediately recognise. His sparse hair was over-the-collar long and gray and he had the look of a stoop-shouldered tramp. He didn't look up or around.

The lights changed but I stayed frozen to the spot as Ward Kinney started up the Toyota and drove away.

I still hadn't moved. I quickly thought of a number of reasons why I hadn't approached him. Too much traffic. He was too far away for me to call out. My book was back at the house.

Excuses, really. None of them valid.

He turned at the next lights and was gone. The truth was that I was shocked and a little bit scared. After the way my mother and Clem had been talking I'd been picturing someone a little careworn, frayed at the edges maybe. Not someone so transformed. Mr Kinney had never been dapper or over-correct, but in the classroom he'd been neatly turned out with an air of relaxed authority. Now he looked like something broken at the back of a thrift store.

The Samaritan in me wanted to chase him and reach out. The real me briefly wondered if I could just mail him the book instead, though that would be the coward's way.

I was tempted, all the same.

As I walked the last block to the deli, I was thinking it over. I could abandon the whole idea. Or I could catch up with him and make amends— that is, if I could find out where he lived. Clem had mentioned something about the Backtrack and he'd promised to check at the school for an up-to-date address. After I'd picked up the preserves I texted to ask if he'd found anything. Then I went into Spinks' to get a coffee and wait for his reply.

When the reply came it was no, the school didn't have anything current, just the old one on Rosebery. I already knew where that was. We all knew it as Shawn Kinney's house, when Shawn Kinney was alive.

Back when we were all seventeen, falling in and out of love and filled with angst and joy, Shawn died after turning over the car he was so proud of. No seat belt, neck broken as he was thrown from the vehicle. Troopers looked at the scene and concluded that he'd been practising stunt turns in the relative quiet of the Old Mine Road. He ran off the roadway and struck a culvert.

His was the first death of our generation, of someone we actually knew, and it hit us hard. Death was only supposed to happen to other people, old people, strangers. Not us.

When the news got out someone tried to start a Gray Lady rumor but no one was in the mood for campfire stories. This was too real. We all knew how Shawn liked to drive too fast. We were upset and his parents were devastated. He was their only child.

I picked up my car and drove over to the Rosebery house. It was a single-story place with a big front yard, set well back from the street. I didn't know the new people so I made a cautious approach. The garage door was raised and I called out before I got near. A man of around forty came out. He looked guarded until I explained why I was there.

"Kinney?" he said. "Haven't seen him since we bought the place."

"Did he leave a forwarding address?"

"No, but I can tell you how to get there. I helped him move his stuff."

It seemed that Kinney and his wife had been separated for some time before the sale, but several boxes of his books and other effects had been stored in the garage. Kinney had promised to move them but there was no definite arrangement in place. Rather than risk being stuck with the clutter, the new owners had lent a hand.

"We were annoyed," the man said. "But when we saw how he was living, you just had to feel sorry for him."

I FOLLOWED DIRECTIONS. The Backtrack was a turnoff on the Old Mine Road, easily missed. It ran up into the hills, ran out when it got there, and was all but abandoned. They say that slaves had been buried alongside it, but no one knew for sure where the graves were. I found it passable, but broken-up enough to make me glad I was driving a rental.

I wasn't sure what to expect when I got there. With care it took me a the best part of half an hour to reach Kinney's house, which stood by a clearing about a mile in.

The house had the look of a frame building that had served out its useful life somewhere else only to be hauled up here and dumped onto its base from a height. You'll rarely see a structure like it that hasn't been boarded up for demolition. I knew he was here because the yellow Toyota stood before it. I pulled in alongside.

There was a porch. A brace of cottontails hanging from its rafters gave it all a certain *Texas Chainsaw Massacre* chic.

I climbed the steps with book in hand, and knocked on the door. The door wasn't secured. I called out, tentatively, and there was no reply.

I was wondering what to do next when I thought I heard a sound, so I descended and went around to the back. Something skittered off into the trees as I got there, too fast for me to see what it was. A deer, maybe. By then my attention was fixed.

Despite the state it was in, I recognised Shawn's car. Up on blocks, smashed and rolled, the roof half-in and a canvas lashed down over the windshield. But instantly recognisable.

I didn't know what to make of it. In Kinney's place I imagine I'd have wanted it crushed and gone. Perhaps this was why the roadside shrine had been neglected? Here was a better one, bigger, more significant, more private. But somehow wrong, too much the macabre memorial.

Then I heard a gunshot somewhere close in the woods. I looked at the wreck and I remembered the barely recognisable creature that Kinney had been twisted into, and decided that I didn't want to be here at all.

I didn't run but I wasn't slow, either, getting myself back around the house. I still had the book in my hand. I couldn't bring myself to drop it in the blood and dirt on the porch so I pushed at the door and it swung inward; I saw a hall table almost within reach so I dropped the book onto that and turned to go.

My timing couldn't have been worse. As I came down the steps I heard an angry yell from up in the trees and a dog started to bark. If I hadn't just heard gunfire I might have stopped to straighten everything out, but I panicked and ran for my car.

The dog kept on barking. I didn't see Kinney. But then I didn't stay around for long enough. I'd done my duty.

I drove back thinking how it wasn't the best idea I'd ever had.

MY MOTHER ASKED, "Did you see him?"

I said, with some understatement, "There could have been a misunderstanding," and went on to explain. She was unsurprised by most of it.

She said, "That old car's been up there for years. He used to keep it in the yard. Maybelle says it's the reason his wife threw him out."

"It's a wreck."

"She said in the divorce that he'd go out and sit in it. All night, sometimes. Talking to himself. You can't explain grief."

Apparently he'd promised to send the wreck to a breakers' but he'd stalled and stalled until his wife's patience snapped. After the separation he'd had it towed up the Backtrack to its new home. In a half-assed romantic way, I thought I understood. Its presence kept his pain alive, and in that pain some part of Shawn lived on.

"Weren't you going to call home?" my mother said.

I checked the time. Caroline would be on her break around now. Even though there was a good cell signal in the house, I went outside to make the call. It was on the point of going to voicemail when Caroline answered.

I told her I'd had a good journey, the birthday dinner had gone well and I'd seen Clem for lunch, and she said, *Just Clem? No one else?*

"Just Clem," I said. "Everyone else is gone, but Clem's never going to leave." Then: "I did manage to track down Kinney."

I heard her sharpen up. *"And?"*

"He lives out of town now. He all but chased me off the property. With a dog and a squirrel gun."

"*Why? What did you say?*"

"Never got to say a thing. He's living up there like Grizzly Adams. He still has the car."

"*No.*"

"It's on blocks behind the house."

I was trying to keep it bright, but I could hear the short breath she let out and the despondency that drove it.

"*He won't let it go,*" she said.

"You don't need to worry."

"*You say that.*"

I didn't know what to tell her, but I was saved by my mother waving for my attention from the doorway. She had the house phone in her hand and she held it up for me to see.

"I've got another call," I said. "Speak later?"

"*Sure,*" she said without enthusiasm.

Who'd be calling me here? Was there someone I hadn't accounted for?

But I got a different kind of surprise. It was Ward Kinney.

"*I'm sorry about the welcome,*" he said. "*I didn't recognise you.*"

"No, you were completely in the right," I said. "I shouldn't have walked into your house like that."

"*I understood when I found the book. I'm very impressed. Will you come back and sign it for me?*"

"If that's what you'd like."

"*I would. Very much.*"

WHEN I STEPPED out of the car he was waiting on the porch. He called to me and said, "Come on in."

In the few hours since that morning he'd shaved and changed his clothes. From the evidence, his razor needed a new blade and he didn't own an iron. Something tugged at my heart to see the effort that he'd made.

We went inside.

"I know how all this must seem," he said, waving to indicate the room. I saw a TV, a chair, and a footstool, with only a dining table where two people could sit at the same time. "Old Mister Kinney, eh? Look at him now. But that's a long and dull story. Tell me about you."

My book lay in the middle of the table. He was moving around as I started to tell him of my life after high school, and out came a bottle and a couple of whisky glasses.

We sat and he poured, and with some embarrassment on my part we toasted my so-called success. I became aware of an elderly beagle watching me from a basket. In a minute or less the dog had dozed off again.

He asked after my mother. Then we got onto the book. Kinney read the title aloud, *A Full Side of Blank Chrome*. I told him he was the first person not to ask me what it meant, which wasn't quite true but did have some truth in it. If you haven't read the novel, the springboard is a message from a dead lover on an audio cassette. It's a ghost story where you never see the ghost. You'll have to buy it if you want to know how that works. Or what an audio cassette is.

He said, "I liked it. A lot. I knew you had promise."

"You read it?"

"It was a skim. I'll give it another read. A real one."

"This feels weird," I admitted.

"For me too. I never turned out a writer before."

"Don't feel you have to grade me on this one. I'll actually be grateful if you don't."

"No, I got swept up in it. You brought the whole town to life, with so much I could recognise. Those two friends in the story," he said, "the steady one and the wild one. Did I see a bit of Shawn in one of them?"

My mother had picked up on that too. I said, "I stole from everybody. Observation filtered through imagination. You told us how writers do that."

"I did, I did. You'll have to forgive me. I may be seeing things that were never there."

"I'm not saying you're wrong," I said. "I'm sure I got some inspiration from Shawn. But he was never wild."

"Tell that to the County."

Now I wasn't sure what to say. The coroner had accepted the investigating troopers' conclusion, that Shawn had lost control while using the empty road to push the car beyond its limits. Drifting around the bends, pulling handbrake turns. Mechanical examination of the wreck appeared to confirm it.

The silence went on and he stared into his glass. Without being in Kinney's position, it's hard to say what he wanted. Nothing was going to bring his son back. But I think he would have taken any explanation—a bolting deer, a crack in a rod, a bird strike—over something so avoidable, so self-inflicted.

Kinney said, "You write the spooky stuff. I don't mind that. Not what I call literature but it has its place. Does it make you money?"

I ignored the bait and just answered the question. "Not the kind you can live on," I said.

"But you *are* a pro. That's great."

"I like the feeling of making something. Same as anyone who creates a pot or a painting. Everything beyond that is a bonus."

"So," he said, getting down to it. "Can we talk about the supernatural?"

Again, I felt I was on the back foot. "If you like."

"Have I said something wrong?"

"No," I said. "Go on."

"Is it something you believe in?"

"I don't think you have to," I said. "Any more than you need to worship Greek gods to get *The Iliad*. You taught us how the real story's always in what's underneath."

"But you must have looked into it. For research or whatever. Give me your opinion."

It was like I was back in the classroom. But I could see where he was going, and there was something more to it than intellectual enquiry.

So I said, "People don't need to believe in ghosts to appreciate a ghost story. They affect us on a primitive level for a very good reason. We're hard-wired to interpret every shape in the dark as a possible threat, that's our evolution. Lock me in an attic at midnight and I'll be as creeped-out as anyone. It's a shared experience that everyone can relate to. But it's no more than that."

"Not every ghost is a threat."

"Depends on your story, I suppose."

"What if I told you I'd seen one?"

"A ghost? Have you?"

"Not seen, exactly," he admitted. "But what if I told you he spoke to me?"

"You mean Shawn."

"Suppose I heard him."

"Okay." I didn't know how else to respond.

"I mean, I used to sit in the car and talk to him, but it's not like he ever answered back. But then one day I was out in the woods and I heard someone call. Plain as anything. I came back to the house and there was no one here. But then I was drawn to the car and I could feel him. It wasn't like the other times. I can't explain it, I just knew he was close. And nothing will ever convince me otherwise."

"I don't know what to say."

"It happened again, twice. Some nights I go out and sleep on the backseat. I can sense his presence growing stronger. It's like he's getting closer. Maybe one day I can ask him."

"What do you think he could tell you?"

"What really happened. I can feel that he wants me to know." He could see that I was lost for words, so he went on to explain. "Some questions never got answered," he said. "They never followed up on that girl."

"What girl?"

"Seen walking by the road that same night. I told them, it could have been a witness. They said it wasn't a reliable sighting. Just one of those Gray Lady stories that kids like to tell. I don't suppose you believe in the Gray Lady either?"

"No."

"I don't know what to think any more. You must remember me back in the day, I was always a rational man. Now I don't know what I am. This world has let me down. I can't make sense of it." He glanced toward my so-called spooky book, in which he was desperate enough to look for answers, and I felt a weight of responsibility that I'd never signed up for.

He said, "I don't expect you to believe everything I say. But I thought you might understand."

"Yes, Mister Kinney," I said. "I do understand." He wanted his world to make sense again, to be able to say what agency had intervened and taken his innocent son. He wanted someone or something to blame. The world could turned and the sun could rise but his soul remained trapped in the attic at midnight, listening for cries and making shapes out of the darkness.

"Thank you," he said. "That's all I can ask."

He saw me out, and the old beagle got to his feet and followed us as far as the porch. I shook hands with Kinney and I nodded to the dog.

WHEN I GOT back my mother was in her favorite chair, reading her new copy.

She looked up and said, "It's not the same. The boy doesn't die the same way in this one."

"I changed it," I said.

"They let you do that?"

"They don't like you making too many changes. But the proofing stage is your last chance to get everything just right."

"I thought it worked very well before."

"It had to come out," I said.

She held her look for long enough to make me a little uncomfortable. But I said nothing more, and she returned to her reading.

After a while she had to break off and go out to fill a prescription. No more than half an hour, she said. As soon as I was alone in the house, I called Caroline.

"*Did you get it back?*" she said.

"It's safe in my bag. I swapped it for a finished copy. And Kinney got in touch."

"*What did he want?*"

"Just to talk."

"*About Shawn?*"

"You were right. He hasn't moved on."

"*So he doesn't know?*"

"No," I said.

There was a long silence; I wanted to break it but I didn't know how.

In that first version of the story, my "wild" character—I called him Josh—had died in an argument with a girl he was seeing. When he wouldn't stop the car she reached over and angrily pulled on the handbrake, not realising the likely consequences. I thought it a neat plot turn that made sense of the incident.

Let's just say that the woman I lived with told me something that obliged me to take it out.

One person dies, one walks all the way home without a scratch and never speaks of it. I'd heard those Gray Lady stories. Did a part of me know? Was I testing when I asked her to look at the proof for typos? I can never be sure. And I suppose when you lance an old wound, intentionally or not, bad stuff's going to come out. I can see now what my mother saw, that Caroline was more attractive than she was likeable. Men often struggle to know the difference. As always I did what she wanted, but it was the beginning of the end for us.

I keep thinking I should go back. I've thought it often, though I know it's been far too long and it's too late to bring the closure that Ward Kinney was aching for. Maybe he found it anyway, responding to that siren call from the wreck behind his house, feeling the shade of his dead son drawing ever nearer.

That, I can never know.

So I guess I've no option. I'll just have to stay haunted.

Live from
THE MORGUE

THE BUZZER SOUNDED some time shortly after eleven. I put down my coffee and my magazine and went to look at the little screen. It showed five people waiting outside the door, two men and three women. Well, I say men and women. Boys and girls, really. Grown but not mature. Lots of swaggering from the boys and giggling from the girls. I can remember being that age. It was not so long ago, but it feels like a world away. The giggles stop and the swagger wears thin. Then the real work of living starts.

I said, "Yes?"

The boy nearest to the camera said, "Is Sheila there?"

My name's Sheila. I work nights at the mortuary. I used to work days but the nights suit me better.

I said, "What do you want?"

The boy said, "George sent us. He said…" and then by way of explaining what George had told him, he held up a roll of money. Close to the lens, where it looked enormous.

"Wait there," I said.

I didn't move right away, but watched them for a while in case they'd drop their guard if they thought no one was looking. I can't be too careful. But from their body language, tense and edgy and full of anticipation, they were just what they seemed to be. Partygoers looking for a party, or maybe ducking out of one for a different thrill. Now they stood on one of the dark service roads around the back of the teaching hospital, waiting to be let into the morgue.

The night shift is just caretaking, really, and those you're in charge of don't make many demands. Sometimes the phone will ring for an out-of-hours admission, but you always get a warning. Some cleaning-up, some filing…otherwise the time is yours to pretty much do as you please.

I opened up the door and there they stood, five of them in the stark glare of the security lamp, their breath feathering in the cold air. Somewhere in the distance, an early firework popped in the sky. I forgot to mention, it was New Year's Eve.

I said, "Did George tell you how much?"

"Twenty each?" Now that I could see him, this first boy was really tall.

"Twenty-five," I said.

One of the girls chipped in, "George said twenty."

"When did you hear that? It's been twenty-five for a year."

You charge what the market will bear. I reckon I can get more for these events but only from perverts, and that's a very narrow field. Plus they always want you to go out of the room for a while, which I don't do.

They exchanged glances and shrugs and then he paid up for everyone. I ushered them in and resecured the big door.

I counted the money first. "Follow me," I said then. "Don't make any noise. Don't touch anything, and no souvenirs."

"You've got it, Sheila," the tall one said.

"I'm serious. There's a risk." And as they followed me up the empty passageway I said, "What else did George tell you?"

"Just that you give a tour and it's worth it."

"Did he say why?"

"He said we'd find out."

"Okay, just to be clear. We're not bending the rules here, we're breaking the law. That's not only me, that's all of us. So if you do anything that gets us caught, that's not just me losing my job. That's you going to court."

One of the girls seemed unhappy. From the back she said, "Shall we not do this?"

"You can back out at any point," I said, "but I don't do refunds."

"That's not fair."

"Take it up with George."

I always start them off in the chapel. Its main entrance is in one of the hospital's basement corridors but we have our own access from the back. It's not where the bad news is given, that's the Quiet Room upstairs. The chapel's an all-purpose worship space with nothing on show that's specific to any religion, though there's a cupboard full of holy books and hardware that can be used to dress it for one faith or another. As I'm explaining this I use the opportunity to weigh up who I'm dealing with.

There's the tall one and there's the blonde, pretty and she knows it, obviously his girlfriend. Call them the Alpha couple. The ruddy-cheeked boy is the tall one's best mate, the one the girls look past. I sense an intention to set him up with the blonde's friend, the dark one, and she isn't interested. So she's pulled in the third girl, the outlier, the one who'd spoken up from the back, to keep it from becoming a two-couples thing.

I decided I'd keep an eye on the third girl. She was possibly the sharpest of the five. I knew her type too well, independent but not confident.

Our first stop out of the chapel was the receiving area. As we went through I said, "You'll have noticed there was no signage on the outside of the building. We keep things as discreet as possible." I placed myself so they wouldn't see the numbers I put into the keypad lock. I mean, 007. You see that, you remember it.

"When bodies arrive and leave we use unmarked vans. Anyone who dies on one of the wards is brought down here on a special trolley. The trolley's enclosed and it can take two patients at a time, one above and one below. A lot of people see it and think it's a lunch delivery."

By now we were standing in Receiving and they were looking all around as I spoke. I felt the tension rise a notch. The whiteboard, the wall of brushed steel doors. The classic image of a mortuary. Where the chapel was decorated with the dull taste of a motorway hotel this area was stark and functional, almost crudely so. We keep it clean, but it's not like the clinical areas. The tiles are swabbed with Jeyes Fluid and we wash the instruments in a sink.

I said, "The hospital had an old Victorian wing across the road, we don't use it now, but it was connected by a tunnel that used to flood when there was heavy rain. The porters on the night shift used to run the trolley down the slope to pick up speed and then jump on board to ride through the puddle. One night there was a hard rain, the flooding was a couple of feet deep and you can probably guess what happened. They had to go back, clean everything up, and try again."

I moved to stand in front of the whiteboard. "The first thing we do is label the body and record it on this board. Before you ask, no, we don't put a tag on the toe. It's a plastic band that's fixed around the wrist or the ankle."

"Like a baby," the blonde girl said.

"You leave this world pretty much as you came into it."

Girl #3 said, "What's that name down in the corner?"

No one else had spotted it. I said, "That's John. He's our oldest resident. I'll be telling you about him when we get next door. First let me show you this." I dug in my overall pocket for one of my props. "We undress the body and bag up all the clothes and any personal effects, and they go into secure storage. If there's to be a viewing we may need to close the eyes. In those cases we use a pair of these." It was a small pink hemisphere of flexible rubber. I held it out to Tall Boy and he looked alarmed, then forced himself to take it.

"It's an eye cup," I said "You can pass it around, don't worry, it hasn't been used, it's fresh out of the box. The way it works is, the cup slides over the eyeball and those little hooks you can see on the outside hold the eyelid down. Otherwise the eyes sink back into the head and that changes the facial appearance. Before these they used to glue the eyelids shut. I know at least one technician who got himself glued to a body that way."

The eye cup went around the houses and then the ruddy-cheeked boy handed it back. They were an obedient bunch so far, easier than some.

I went on to say, "In some cultures the family want to wash the body themselves, and we can accommodate that. What happens after depends on a number of things. Whether there's to be a post mortem, or if it's just a pickup by an undertaker. Sometimes we can be involved if the dead person is an organ donor. One time I was shaving the arm on someone who was freshly deceased. I'm running the razor over and I lift it and turn it and suddenly the hand grabs me and won't let go." I illustrated the moment by snatching at the air and got a satisfying gasp in response.

"It's a reaction," I said. "The same thing can happen if you're trying to get to the axillary artery to put in a drain. You press on certain tendons and trigger a grab reflex. Doesn't matter how often it happens, it's always a shock."

Tall Guy said, "Has anyone ever…you know…"

"Been declared dead and come back to life here? Most of those stories have a medical explanation."

Girl #3 picked up quickly. "*Most of?*"

"Let's go through," I said.

I didn't take them through the double swinging doors to the post mortem suite but instead we went up the three steps to the viewing gallery, from where I'd be able to switch on all the lights for a dramatic reveal. The gallery doubled as a meeting room, with a conference table and a large TV that could take a feed from the overhead cameras at each table. The day shift sometimes ate lunch in here. The old TV gag of the doctor snacking off a corpse needs to be retired. If anyone knows about pathogens, it's a pathologist.

I stayed by the switches and as they filed past me I said, "The question was about signs of life after death. The dead don't only give you goosebumps. They get them, too. The *arrector pili* is a tiny muscle attached to each hair follicle in your skin. Like any other muscle it's subject to rigor mortis. When that happens…goosebumps after death. It's called horripilation. It's where we get the word 'horror'." And with that I switched on the lights to the theatre below.

We have five dissection tables in a long row, though it's rare for all of them to be in use at any one time. They're in stainless steel, each with a drain and a hose. All were empty; another TV misconception, we don't keep bodies lying out. Some mortuaries have one big cold storage room rather than individual refrigerator pods, but that's as close as it gets.

೧

I SAID, "YOU see the wall of refrigerator doors at the end of the room. Those are the same units you saw in the receiving area. So bodies go in on that side and come out on this. Now follow me."

I could almost hear the thumping of their hearts now. We were dancing around the dead and the longer we danced, the closer we came.

I said, "On the question of a dead person coming back to life. Those rare cases you read about, and it's usually somewhere on the other side of the world, they've invariably been called wrongly and that's not the same thing. But has anyone heard the expression, 'agonal breathing'?"

I gave it a moment, just enough to establish that no one had.

"But we've all heard of 'the last gasp'."

Nods all around.

"When the brain dies, it's game over. But not right away. The heart stops beating, the blood stops pumping, the brain ceases function and the organs shut down. But the brainstem—the reptile brain, the primitive part of our nervous system—that's the part that fights on past the end. Every other process has closed down for good. Permanently. But the signals keep coming out of that last flickering corner, firing out like the last soldier in the final trench, refusing to give up the fight. And that's the agonal breath, the dead corpse sucking in air, a sound you can never forget. They tell us, don't worry, it's just a reflex. But it's never easy to watch. And it's always hard to deal with."

And Girl #2, who hadn't spoken at all since the start of the tour, piped up impatiently, "When are we going to see a dead body?"

"Do you want to?" I said, looking at all of them.

Girl #2 didn't give anyone a chance to say no. "What do you think we're here for?" she said.

"Fine," I said. "As long as everyone's on the same page."

I wheeled the transfer gurney over to the refrigerated lockers and positioned it under a particular door. As I turned the handle to release the seal I said, "Remember John? He's actually what we call a male unknown. He collapsed in the street and died in the ambulance. There was no ID and they couldn't match DNA or fingerprints."

Out he rolled and onto the gurney, a long form under a plastic shroud. No one moved.

I forget which of the boys said it but one said, "What about dental records?"

"There's no database of dental records. If you think you know the name of a dead person you can track down their dentist and get a confirmation. But that's no help to our John."

I drew the sheet down to the middle of his chest, revealing the top of the post mortem incision, closed up with the duty assistant's big stitches.

Sometimes people faint. Sometimes nervous laughter. Very few of the young have seen a dead body for real. The vibe that I usually get on the reveal is an odd one. I'd describe it as a sense of queasy disappointment.

"I know," I said. "You're thinking, is that all there is to being dead? You build it up in your mind. You're afraid of what you'll see. Your heart beats faster, your mouth gets dry. But yes. This is it. This is all there is. When you leave here, I can guarantee you. You'll leave with one less fear."

John lay there, quietly composed. He was not much older than they, but refrigeration had slowly been drawing moisture from his flesh. It gave him a noble skull and sunken cheeks. People compare the colour to wax or marble, but neither quite conveys the texture. But then there's the hair; you see it on Egyptian mummies, and on those bog people. Sometimes I wonder if hair lasts for ever.

"John's been with us for some time," I said, "You could say he's fallen through the cracks in the system. I don't suppose anyone here knows him?"

No one here knew him.

No one among the visitors, anyway.

Girl #3 said, "How long will a body keep for?"

"Without embalming? Normally two weeks, tops. But if it's in one of these negative temperature cold chambers, then months." I drew the sheet back over the mundane reality of John's remains and said, "Are there any other questions?"

There weren't, but there was a sudden shriek from Girl #2 followed by a showering of metal onto metal. She'd jumped back and banged into the instrument table behind her.

"Please," I said with clear annoyance. "I told you the rules."

"The sheet moved!"

"The sheet did not move."

"I saw it!"

"You imagined it. You're not the first."

Then the sheet really did move, as if all the noise had awakened something under it. There was a big reaction with everybody shouting at once and Tall Guy said, "Oh, come on. You're doing that."

"I'm doing nothing," I said. "If you're going to get stupid on me the door's right there." I pointed angrily to the emergency fire exit. It opens with a crash bar into an alley behind Oncology. I needed at least one of them to be aware of it.

"It's a trick," Girl #3 said. "You've got a mate under there."

"You think so?"

The blonde joined in with, "You promised us a real body."

In one quick movement I drew away the plastic shroud. John lay there, naked except for a pair of cotton boxers. For a while he'd been covered by one of the modesty towels but the boxers had been lying around spare. The more you saw of him, the harder it was to argue. John had been dead for a very long time.

They all fell quiet.

Then the blonde said, doubtfully, "It's makeup."

I looked down. "Is it makeup, John?"

John's bony hands gripped the side of the gurney. Then with the sound of air being driven out of a leather bellows, John slowly sat up.

"*Sheila*," he slurred. "*'Lo, Sheila*." He swung his legs off the table, as if to stand.

The clamour that followed was less like pure terror than a ghost train or rollercoaster scream, halfway to hysteria and a few steps short of heart failure, the product of a big burst of adrenalin that leaves you exhausted and drunk. I raised my voice and said, "People here think you're faking, John."

John was fumbling out his eye cups. The second boy cracked and tried to run but immediately skidded on the fallen silverware and fell.

"Show them, John. You know what to do."

Legs dangling, John had stopped and was now picking at his post mortem sutures. Usually they're knotted off, but his ended in a bow. When he tugged on it, the stitches loosened.

Then, like Superman ripping open his shirt, he pulled the two sides of the incision apart.

"*S'all gone,*" he said. "*See.*"

By the time his bare feet hit the floor, the second boy had picked himself up and they'd all stormed across the room. I didn't see who got there first but someone hit the crash bar and the doors flew open into the alley. They tumbled out like a ball of fighting cats, and in the next instant they were gone. I quickly went over and closed the doors after them, resetting the bars. There's an alarm, but I always disconnect it.

With the building resecured, I turned back to John. He'd dropped back against the gurney. He can't balance on his feet for long.

"They're gone," I said.

"*I do good?*"

"Yes, John. Good work. We made some good money tonight."

"*Don't know what I'd do without you, Sheila.*"

"Thank you for saying so. It's nice to be needed."

I draped the shroud around his shoulders and gave him the big needle with some fresh thread. I'd taught him how to restitch himself using the same holes. He was a careful worker, which was just as well. Some of them were starting to pull and I didn't know how much longer they'd last.

I counted the money again. I'd keep some of it back but most of it I'd add to the hidden stash behind the secret panel in my locker.

As he worked, John said, "*Anyone know me?*"

"No, John," I said. "Sorry."

"*Maybe next time.*"

"Yeah," I said. "Next time."

A funny coincidence, his name really is John. What people don't know is that he was my boyfriend. We were going to get engaged. I wasn't there when they brought him in, but I saw him the next day when he was brought out to prep. I heard somewhere that a person's spirit can't rest without a name. Actually it wasn't just somewhere, it was in *High Plains Drifter*. Anyway, I stole the admission record and switched the samples for ones I knew they couldn't match. No one's ever found me out and that's how I kept him.

John doesn't remember who he is. Or me. He thinks I'm his new friend. That's all right. I know what we have. It's special. There'll never be anything like it. I switched to the night shift so we can be together. After a while we went into business. A lot of couples do.

Still bent to his work, John said, "*I don't know what I'd do without you, Sheila.*"

"You just stick with me, John."

He coughed, and a loop of intestine fell out. He tucked it back in.

"*I wish I could remember who I am,*" he said.

"Don't worry about it," I said. "Listen."

He stopped, and we both listened. The post mortem suite has windows, but they're just wide slits very high up in the wall.

"Do you hear the bells?" I said.

He listened a while, and then nodded slowly.

"*And fireworks,*" he said.

"Happy New Year, John."

"*And to you, Sheila.*"

At that moment, the buzzer sounded. So close to the stroke of midnight, it came as a surprise. But business is business.

"Customers," I said.

"*Cuthtommns,*" John mumbled, his head down into his chest as he tugged the sutures closed.

I gave him his eye caps and helped him to swing his legs back onto the gurney, and then I covered him with the shroud. When he gave me the signal I rolled him back into the storage chamber and closed the door. Then I resited the empty gurney against the wall. The fallen instruments would have to wait, there wasn't time. I dashed through the viewing gallery, turning off lights as I went, and by the time I reached the office we were set to go again.

The magazine lay where I'd left it, and my coffee was cold. I'd make fresh afterwards. I checked the little screen to see who was next.

I know it's wrong. But it's just so hard to let go.

Especially when they pay so well, and you're saving for a ring.

Shepherds' BUSINESS

PICTURE ME ON an island supply boat, one of the old Clyde Puffers seeking to deliver me to my new post. This was 1947, just a couple of years after the war, and I was a young doctor relatively new to General Practice. Picture also a choppy sea, a deck that rose and fell with every wave, and a cross-current fighting hard to turn us away from the isle. Back on the mainland I'd been advised that a hearty breakfast would be the best preventative for seasickness and now, having loaded up with one, I was doing my best to hang onto it.

I almost succeeded. Perversely, it was the sudden calm of the harbour that did for me. I ran to the side and I fear that I cast rather more than my bread upon the waters. Those on the quay were treated to a rare sight; their new doctor, clinging to the ship's rail, with seagulls swooping in the wake of the steamer for an unexpected water-borne treat.

The island's resident constable was waiting for me at the end of the gang-plank. A man of around my father's age, in uniform, chiselled in flint and unsullied by good cheer. He said, "Munro Spence? Doctor Munro Spence?"

"That's me," I said.

"Will you take a look at Doctor Laughton before we move him? He didn't have too good a journey down."

There was a man to take care of my baggage, so I followed the constable to the harbourmaster's house at the end of the quay. It was a stone building, square and solid. Doctor Laughton was in the harbourmaster's sitting room behind the office. He was in a chair by the fire with his feet on a stool and a rug over his knees and was attended by one of his own nurses, a stocky red-haircd girl of twenty or younger.

I began, "Doctor Laughton. I'm…"

"My replacement, I know," he said. "Let's get this over with."

I checked his pulse, felt his glands, listened to his chest, noted the signs of cyanosis. It was hardly necessary; Doctor Laughton had already diagnosed himself, and had requested this transfer. He was an old-school Edinburgh-trained medical man, and I could be sure that his condition must be sufficiently serious that 'soldiering on' was no longer an option. He might choose to ignore his own aches and troubles up to a point, but as the island's only doctor he couldn't leave the community at risk.

When I enquired about chest pain he didn't answer directly, but his expression told me all.

"I wish you'd agreed to the aeroplane," I said.

"For my sake or yours?" he said. "You think I'm bad. You should see your colour." And then, relenting a little; "The airstrip's for emergencies. What good's that to me?"

I asked the nurse, "Will you be travelling with him?"

"I will," she said. "I've an aunt I can stay with. I'll return on the morning boat."

Two of the men from the Puffer were waiting to carry the doctor to the quay. We moved back so that they could lift him between them, chair and all. As they were getting into position Laughton said to me, "Try not to kill anyone in your first week, or they'll have me back here the day after."

I was his locum, his temporary replacement. That was the story. But we both knew that he wouldn't be returning. His sight of the island from the sea would almost certainly be his last.

Once they'd manoeuvred him through the doorway, the two sailors bore him with ease toward the boat. Some local people had turned out to wish him well on his journey.

As I followed with the nurse beside me, I said, "Pardon me, but what do I call you?"

"I'm Nurse Kirkwood," she said. "Rosie."

"I'm Munro," I said. "Is that an island accent, Rosie?"

"You have a sharp ear, Doctor Spence," she said.

She supervised the installation of Doctor Laughton in the deck cabin, and didn't hesitate to give the men orders where another of her age and sex might only make suggestions or requests. A born matron, if ever I saw one. The old salts followed her instruction without a murmur.

When they'd done the job to her satisfaction, Laughton said to me, "The latest patient files are on my desk. Your desk, now."

Nurse Kirkwood said to him, "You'll be back before they've missed you, doctor," but he ignored that.

He said, "These are good people. Look after them."

The crew were already casting off, and they all but pulled the board from under my feet as I stepped ashore. I took a moment to gather myself, and gave a pleasant nod in response to the curious looks of those well-wishers who'd stayed to see the boat leave. The day's cargo had been unloaded and stacked on the quay and my bags were nowhere to be seen. I went in search of them and found Moodie, driver and handyman to the island hospital, waiting beside a field ambulance that had been decommissioned from the military. He was chatting to another man, who bade good day and moved off as I arrived.

"Will it be much of a drive?" I said as we climbed aboard.

"Ay," Moodie said.

"Ten minutes? An hour? Half an hour?"

"Ay," he agreed, making this one of the longest conversations we were ever to have.

THE DRIVE TOOK little more than twenty minutes. This was due to the size of the island and a good concrete road, yet another legacy of the army's wartime presence. We saw no other vehicle, slowed for nothing other than the occasional indifferent sheep. Wool and weaving, along with some lobster fishing, sustained the peacetime economy here. In wartime it had been different, with the local populace outnumbered by spotters, gunners, and the Royal Engineers. Later came a camp for Italian prisoners of war, whose disused medical block the Highlands and Islands Medical Service took over when the island's cottage hospital burned down. Before we reached it we passed the airstrip, still usable, but with its gatehouse and control tower abandoned.

The former prisoners' hospital was a concrete building with a wooden barracks attached. The Italians had laid paths and a garden, but these were now growing wild. Again I left Moodie to deal with my bags, and went looking to introduce myself to the senior sister.

Senior Sister Garson looked me over once and didn't seem too impressed. But she called me by my title and gave me a briefing on everyone's duties while leading me around on a tour. It was then that I learned my driver's name. I met all the staff apart from Mrs Moodie, who served as cook, housekeeper, and island midwife.

"There's just the one six-bed ward," Sister Garson told me. "We use that for the men and the officers' quarters for the women. Two to a room."

"How many patients at the moment?"

"As of this morning, just one. Old John Petrie. He's come in to die."

Harsh though it seemed, she delivered the information in a matter-of-fact manner.

"I'll see him now," I said.

Old John Petrie was eighty-five or eighty-seven. The records were unclear. Occupation, shepherd. Next of kin, none—a rarity on the island. He'd led a tough outdoor life, but toughness won't keep a body going for ever. He was now grown so thin and frail that he was in danger of being swallowed up by his bedding. According to Doctor Laughton's notes he'd presented with no specific ailment. One of my teachers might have diagnosed a case of TMB, Too Many Birthdays. He'd been found in his croft house, alone, half-starved, unable to rise. There was life in John Petrie's eyes as I introduced myself, but little sign of it anywhere else.

We moved on. Mrs Moodie would bring me my evening meals, I was told. Unless she was attending at a birth, in which case I'd be looked after by Rosie Kirkwood's mother who'd cycle up from town.

My experience in obstetrics had mainly involved being a student and staying out of the midwife's way. Senior Sister Garson said, "They're mostly home births with the midwife attending, unless there are complications and then she'll call you in. But that's quite rare. You might want to speak to Mrs Tulloch before she goes home. Her baby was stillborn on Sunday."

"Where do I find her?" I said.

The answer was, in the suite of rooms at the other end of the building. Her door in the women's wing was closed, with her husband waiting in the corridor.

"She's dressing," he explained.

Sister Garson said, "Thomas, this is Doctor Spence. He's taking over for Doctor Laughton."

She left us together. Thomas Tulloch was a young man, somewhere around my own age but much hardier. He wore a shabby suit of all-weather tweed that looked as if it had outlasted several owners. His beard was dark, his eyes blue. Women like that kind of thing, I know, but my first thought was of a wall-eyed collie. What can I say? I like dogs.

I asked him, "How's your wife bearing up?"

"It's hard for me to tell," he said. "She hasn't spoken much." And then, as soon as Sister Garson was out of earshot, he lowered his voice and said, "What was it?"

"I beg your pardon?"

"The child. Was it a boy or a girl?"

"I've no idea."

"No one will say. Daisy didn't get to see it. It was just, your baby's dead, get over it, you'll have another."

"Her first?"

He nodded.

I wondered who might have offered such cold comfort. Everyone, I expect. It was the approach at the time. Infant mortality was no longer the commonplace event it once had been, but old attitudes lingered.

I said, "And how do you feel?"

Tulloch shrugged. "It's nature," he conceded. "But you'll get a ewe that won't leave a dead lamb. Is John Petrie dying now?"

"I can't say. Why?"

"I'm looking after his flock and his dog. His dog won't stay put."

At that point the door opened and Mrs Tulloch—Daisy—stood before us. True to her name, a crushed flower. She was pale, fair, and small of stature, barely up to her husband's shoulder. She'd have heard our voices though not, I would hope, our conversation.

I said, "Mrs Tulloch, I'm Doctor Spence. Are you sure you're well enough to leave us?"

She said, "Yes, thank you, Doctor." She spoke in little above a whisper. Though a grown and married woman, from a distance you might have taken her for a girl of sixteen.

I looked to Tulloch and said, "How will you get her home?"

"We were told, the ambulance?" he said. And then, "Or we could walk down for the mail bus."

"Let me get Mister Moodie," I said.

MOODIE SEEMED TO be unaware of any arrangement, and reluctant to comply with it.

Though it went against the grain to be firm with a man twice my age, I could see trouble in our future if I wasn't. I said, "I'm not discharging a woman in her condition to a hike on the heath. To your ambulance, Mister Moodie."

Garaged alongside the field ambulance I saw a clapped-out Riley Roadster at least a dozen years old. Laughton's own vehicle, available for my use.

As the Tullochs climbed aboard the ambulance I said to Daisy, "I'll call by and check on you in a day or two." And then, to her husband, "And I'll see if I can get an answer to your question."

My predecessor's files awaited me in the office. Those covering his patients from the last six months had been left out on the desk, and were but the tip of the iceberg; in time I'd need to become familiar with the histories of everyone on the island, some fifteen hundred souls. It was a big responsibility for one medic, but civilian doctors were in short supply. Though the fighting was over and the Forces demobbed, medical officers were among the last to be released.

I dived in. The last winter had been particularly severe, with a number of pneumonia deaths and broken limbs from ice falls. I read of frostbitten fishermen and a three-year-old boy deaf after measles. Two cases had been sent to the mainland for surgery and one emergency appendectomy had been performed, successfully and right here in the hospital's theatre, by Laughton himself.

Clearly I had a lot to live up to.

Since October there had been close to a dozen births on the island. A fertile community, and dependent upon it. Most of the children were thriving, one family had moved away. A Mrs Flett had popped out her seventh, with no complications. But then there was Daisy Tulloch.

I looked at her case notes. They were only days old, and incomplete. Laughton had written them up in a shaky hand and I found myself wondering whether, in some way, his condition might have been a factor in the outcome. Not by any direct failing of his own, but Daisy had been thirty-six hours in labour before he was called in. Had the midwife delayed calling him for longer than she should? By the time of his intervention it was a matter of no detectable heartbeat and a forceps delivery.

I'd lost track of the time, so when Mrs Moodie appeared with a tray I was taken by surprise.

"Don't get up, Doctor," she said. "I brought your tea."

I turned the notes face-down to the desk and pushed my chair back. Enough, I reckoned, for one day.

I said, "The stillbirth, the Tullochs. Was it a boy or a girl?"

"Doctor Laughton dealt with it," Mrs Moodie said. "I wasn't there to see. It hardly matters now, does it?"

"Stillbirths have to be registered," I said.

"If you say so, Doctor."

"It's the law, Mrs Moodie. What happened to the remains?"

"They're in the shelter for the undertaker. It's the coldest place we have. He'll collect them when there's next a funeral."

I finished my meal and, leaving the tray for Mrs Moodie to clear, went out to the shelter. It wasn't just a matter of the Tullochs' curiosity. With no note of gender, I couldn't complete the necessary registration. Back then the bodies of the stillborn were often buried with any unrelated female adult. I had to act before the undertaker came to call.

The shelter was an air-raid bunker located between the hospital and the airfield, now used for storage. And when I say storage, I mean everything from our soap and toilet roll supply to the recently deceased. It was a series of chambers mostly buried under a low, grassy mound. The only visible features above ground were a roof vent and a brick-lined ramp leading down to a door at one end. The door had a mighty lock, for which there was no key.

Inside I had to navigate my way through rooms filled with crates and boxes to find the designated mortuary with the slab. Except that it wasn't a slab; it was a billiard table, cast in the ubiquitous concrete (by those Italians, no doubt) and repurposed by my predecessor. The cotton-wrapped package that lay on it was unlabelled, and absurdly small. I unpicked the wrapping with difficulty and made the necessary check. A girl. The cord was still attached and there were all the signs of a rough forceps delivery. Forceps in a live birth are only meant to guide and protect the child's head. The marks of force supported my suspicion that Laughton had been called at a point too late for the infant, and where he could only focus on preserving the mother's life.

Night had all but fallen when I emerged. As I washed my hands before going to make a last check on our dying shepherd, I reflected on the custom of slipping a stillbirth into a coffin to share a stranger's funeral. On the one hand, it could seem like a heartless practice; on the other, there was something touching about the idea of a nameless child being placed in the anonymous care of another soul. Whenever I try to imagine eternity, it's always long and lonely. Such company might be a comfort for both.

John Petrie lay with his face toward the darkened window. In the time since my first visit he'd been washed and fed, and the bed remade around him.

I said, "Mister Petrie, do you remember me? Doctor Spence."

There was a slight change in the rhythm of his breathing that I took for a yes.

I said, "Are you comfortable?"

Nothing moved but his eyes. Looking at me, then back to the window.

"What about pain? Have you any pain? I can help with it if you have."

Nothing. So then I said, "Let me close these blinds for you," but as I moved, he made a sound.

"Don't close them?" I said. "Are you sure?"

I followed his gaze.

I could see the shelter mound from here. Only the vague shape of the hill was visible at this hour, one layer of deepening darkness over another. Against the sky, in the last of the fading light, I could make out the outline of an animal. It was a dog, and it seemed to be watching the building.

I did as John Petrie wished, left the blinds open, and him to the night.

My accommodation was in the wooden barracks where the prisoners had lived and slept. I had an oil lamp for light and a ratty curtain at the window. My bags had been lined up at the end of a creaky bunk. The one concession to luxury was a rag rug on the floor.

I could unpack in the morning. I undressed, dropped onto the bed, and had the best sleep of my life.

WITH THE MORNING came my first taste of practice routine. An early ward round, such as it was, and then a drive down into town for weekday surgery. This took place in a room attached to the library and ran on a system of first come, first served, for as long as it took to deal with the queue. All went without much of a hitch. No doubt some people stayed away out of wariness over a new doctor. Others had discovered minor ailments with which to justify their curiosity. Before surgery was over, Rosie Kirkwood joined me fresh from the boat. Doctor Laughton had not enjoyed the voyage, she told me, and we left it at that.

After the last patient (chilblains) had left, Nurse Kirkwood said, "I see you have use of Doctor Laughton's car. Can I beg a lift back to the hospital?"

"You can," I said. "And along the way, can you show me where the Tullochs live? I'd like to drop by."

"I can show you the way," she said. "But it's not the kind of place you can just 'drop by'."

I will not claim that I'd mastered the Riley. When I described it as clapped-out, I did not exaggerate. The engine sounded like a keg of bolts rolling down a hill and the springs gave us a ride like a condemned fairground. Rosie seemed used to it.

Passing through town with the harbour behind us, I said, "Which one's the undertaker?"

"We just passed it."

"The furniture place?"

"Donald Budge. My father's cousin. Also the coroner and cabinet maker to the island."

Two minutes later, we were out of town. It was bleak, rolling lowland moor in every direction, stretching out to a big, big sky.

Raising my voice to be heard over the whistling crack in the windshield, I said, "You've lived here all your life?"

"I have," she said. "I saw everything change with the war. We thought it would go back to being the same again after. But that doesn't happen, does it?"

"Never in the way you expect," I said.

"Doctor Laughton won't be coming back, will he?"

"There's always hope."

"That's what we say to patients."

I took my eyes off the road for a moment to look at her.

She said, "I don't do my nursing for a hobby. And I don't always plan to be doing it here." And then, with barely a change in tone, "There's a junction with a telephone box coming up."

I quickly returned my attention to the way ahead. "Do I turn?"

"Not there. The next track just after."

It was a rough track, and the word boneshaking wouldn't begin to describe it. Now I understood why the Riley was falling apart, if this was the pattern for every home visit. The track ran for most of a mile and finally became completely impassable, with still a couple of hundred yards to go to reach the Tullochs' home.

Their house was a one-storey crofter's cottage with a sod roof and a barn attached. The cottage walls were limewashed, those of the barn were of bare stone. I took my medical bag from the car and we walked the rest of the way.

When we reached the door Nurse Kirkwood knocked and called out, "Daisy? It's the doctor to see you."

There was movement within. As we waited, I looked around. Painters romanticise these places. All I saw was evidence of a hard living. I also saw a dog tethered some yards from the house, looking soulful. It resembled the one I'd seen the night before although, to be honest, the same could be said of every dog on the island.

After making us wait as long as she dared for a quick tidy of the room and herself, Daisy Tulloch opened the door and invited us in. She was wearing a floral print dress, and her hair had been hastily pinned.

She offered tea; Nurse Kirkwood insisted on making it as we talked. Although Daisy rose to the occasion with the necessary courtesy, I could see it was a struggle. The experience of the last week had clearly hit her hard.

"I don't want to cause any fuss, Doctor," was all she would say. "I'm tired, that's all."

People respect a doctor, but they'll talk to a nurse. When I heard sheep and more than one dog barking outside, I went out and left the two women conferring. Tulloch was herding a couple of dozen ewes into a muddy pen by the cottage; a mixed herd, if the markings were anything to go by. Today he wore a cloth cap and blue work pants with braces. I realised that the tweeds I'd taken for his working clothes were actually his Sunday best.

I waited until the sheep were all penned, and then went over.

I told him, "It would have been a girl. But..." And I left it there, because what more could I add? But then a though occurred and I said, "You may want to keep the information to yourself. Why make things worse?"

"That's what Doctor Laughton said. Chin up, move on, have yourself another. But she won't see it like that."

I watched him go to the barn and return with a bucket of ochre in one hand and a stick in the other. The stick had a crusty rag wrapped around its end, for dipping and marking the fleeces.

I said, "Are those John Petrie's sheep?"

"They are," he said. "But someone's got to dip 'em and clip 'em. Will he ever come back?"

"There's always hope," I said. "What about his dog?"

He glanced at the tethered animal, watching us from over hear the house. "Biddy?" he said. "That dog's no use to me. Next time she runs off, she's gone. I'm not fetching her home again."

"A DOG?" NURSE Kirkwood said. She braced herself against the dash as we bumped our way back onto the road. "Senior Sister Garson will love you."

"I'll keep her in the barracks," I said. "Senior Sister Garson doesn't even need to know."

She turned around to look at Biddy, seated in the open luggage hatch. The collie had her face tilted up into the wind and her eyes closed in an attitude of uncomplicated bliss.

"Good luck with that," she said.

That night, when the coast was clear, I sneaked Biddy into the ward.

"John," I said, "you've got a visitor."

I BEGAN TO find my way around. I started to make home visits and I took the time to meet the island's luminaries, from the priest to the postman to the secretary of the Grazing Committee. Most of the time Biddy rode around with me in the back of the Riley. One night I went down into town and took the dog into the pub with me, as an icebreaker. People were beginning to recognise me now. It would be a while before I'd feel accepted, but I felt I'd made a start.

Senior Sister Garwood told me that Donald Budge, the undertaker, had now removed the infant body for an appropriate burial. She also said that he'd complained to her about the state in which he'd found it. I told her to send him to me, and I'd explain the medical realities of the situation to a man who ought to know better. Budge didn't follow it up.

The next day in town Thomas Tulloch came to morning surgery, alone. "Mister Tulloch," I said. "How can I help you?"

"It's not for me," he said. "It's Daisy, but she won't come. Can you give her a tonic? Anything that'll perk her up. Nothing I do seems to help."

"Give her time. It's only been a few days."

"It's getting worse. Now she won't leave the cottage. I tried to persuade her to visit her sister but she just turns to the wall."

So I wrote him a scrip for some Parrish's, a harmless red concoction of sweetened iron phosphate that would, at best, sharpen the appetite, and at worst do nothing at all. It was all I could offer. Depression, in those days, was a condition to be overcome by 'pulling oneself together'. Not to do so was to be perverse and most likely attention-seeking, especially if you were a woman. I couldn't help thinking that, though barely educated even by the island's standards, Tulloch was an unusually considerate spouse for his time.

Visits from the dog seemed to do the trick for John Petrie. I may have thought I was deceiving the Senior Sister, but I realise now that she was most likely turning a blind eye. Afterwards his breathing was always easier, his sleep more peaceful. And I even got my first words out of him when he beckoned me close and said into my ear:

"*Ye'll do.*"

After this mark of approval I looked up to find the constable waiting for me, hat in his hands as if he were unsure of the protocol. Was a dying man's bedside supposed to be like a church? He was taking no chances.

He said, "I'm sorry to come and find you at your work, Doctor. But I hope you can settle a concern."

"I can try."

"There's a rumour going round about the dead Tulloch baby. Some kind of abuse?"

"I don't understand."

"Some people are even saying it had been skinned."

"Skinned?" I echoed.

"I've seen what goes on in post-mortems and such," the constable persisted. "But I never heard of such a thing being called for."

"Nor have I," I said. "It's just Chinese whispers, David. I saw the body before Donald Budge took it away. It was in poor condition after a long and difficult labour. But the only abuse it suffered was natural."

"I'm only going by what people are saying."

"Well for God's sake don't let them say such a thing around the mother."

"I do hear she's taken it hard," the constable conceded. "Same thing happened to my sister, but she just got on. I've never even heard her speak of it."

He looked to me for permission, and then went around the bed to address John Petrie. He bent down with his hands on his knees, and spoke as if to a child or an imbecile.

"A'right, John?" he said. "Back on your feet soon, eh?"

SKINNED? WHO EVER heard of such a thing? The chain of gossip must have started with Donald Budge and grown ever more grotesque in the telling. According to the records Budge had four children of his own. The entire family was active in amateur dramatics and the church choir. You'd expect a man in his position to know better.

I was writing up patient notes at the end of the next day's town Surgery when there was some commotion outside. Nurse Kirkwood went to find out the cause and came back moments later with a breathless nine-year-old boy at her side.

"This is Robert Flett," she said. "He ran all the way here to say his mother's been in an accident."

"What kind of an accident?"

The boy looked startled and dumbstruck at my direct question, but Rosie Kirkwood spoke for him. "He says she fell."

I looked at her. "You know the way?

"Of course."

We all piled into the Riley to drive out to the west of the island. Nurse Kirkwood sat beside me and I lifted Robert into the bag hatch with the dog, where both seemed happy enough.

At the highest point on the moor Nurse Kirkwood reckoned she spotted a walking figure on a distant path, far from the road.

She said, "Is that Thomas Tulloch? What could he be doing out here?" but I couldn't spare the attention to look.

ADAM FLETT WAS one of three brothers who, together, were the island's most prosperous crofter family. In addition to their livestock and rented lands they made some regular money from government contract work. With a tenancy protected by law, Adam had built a two-storey home with a slate roof and laid a decent road to it. I was able to drive almost to the door. Sheep scattered as I braked, and the boy jumped out to join with other children in gathering them back with sticks.

It was only a few weeks since Jean Flett had borne the youngest of her seven children. The birth had been trouble-free but the news of a fall concerned me. Her eldest, a girl of around twelve years old, let us into the house. I looked back and saw Adam Flett on the far side of the yard, watching us.

Jean Flett was lying on a well-worn old sofa and struggled to rise as we came through the door. I could see that she hadn't been expecting us. Despite the size of their family, she was only in her thirties.

I said, "Mrs Flett?" and Nurse Kirkwood stepped past me to steady our patient and ease her back onto the couch.

"This is Doctor Spence," Nurse Kirkwood explained.

"I told Marion," Jean Flett protested. "I told her not to send for you."

"Well, now that I'm here," I said, "let's make sure my journey isn't wasted. Can you tell me what happened?"

She wouldn't look at me, and gave a dismissive wave. "I fell, that's all."

"Where's the pain?"

"I'm just winded."

I took her pulse and then got her to point out where it hurt. She winced when I checked her abdomen, and again when I felt around her neck.

I said, "Did you have these marks before the fall?"

"It was a shock. I don't remember."

Tenderness around the abdomen, a raised heart rate, left side pain, and what appeared to be days-old bruises. I exchanged a glance with Nurse Kirkwood. A fair guess would be that the new mother had been held against the wall and punched.

I said, "We need to move you to the hospital for a couple of days."

"No!" she said. "I'm just sore. I'll be fine."

"You've bruised your spleen, Mrs Flett. I don't think it's ruptured but I need to be sure. Otherwise you could need emergency surgery."

"Oh, no."

"I want you where we can keep an eye on you. Nurse Kirkwood? Can you help her to pack a bag?"

I went outside. Adam Flett had moved closer to the house but was still hovering. I said to him, "She's quite badly hurt. That must have been some fall."

"She says it's nothing." He wanted to believe it, but he'd seen her pain and I think it scared him.

I said, "With an internal injury she could die. I'm serious, Mister Flett. I'll get the ambulance down to collect her." I'd thought that Nurse Kirkwood was still inside the house, so when she spoke from just behind me I was taken by surprise.

She said, "Where's the baby, Mister Flett?"

"Sleeping," he said.

"Where?" she said. "I want to see."

"It's no business of yours or anyone else's."

Her anger was growing, and so was Flett's defiance. "What have you done to it?" she persisted. "The whole island knows it isn't yours. Did you get rid of it? Is that what the argument was about? Is that why you struck your wife?" I was aware of three or four of his children now standing at a distance, watching us.

"The Flett brothers have a reputation, Doctor," she said, lowering her voice so the children wouldn't hear. "It wouldn't be the first time another man's child had been taken out to the barn and drowned in a bucket."

He tried to lunge at her then, and I had to step in.

"Stop that!" I said, and he shook me off and backed away. He started pacing like an aggrieved wrestler whose opponent stands behind the referee. Meanwhile his challenger was showing no fear.

"Well?" Rosie Kirkwood said.

"You've got it wrong," he said "You don't know anything."

"I won't leave until you prove the child's safe."

And I said, "Wait," because I'd had a sudden moment of insight and reckoned I knew what must have happened.

I said to Rosie, "He's sold the baby. To Thomas Tulloch, in exchange for John Petrie's sheep. I recognise those marks. I watched Tulloch make them." I looked at Flett. "Am I right?"

Flett said nothing right away. And then he said, "They're Petrie's?"

"I suppose Thomas drove them over," I said. "Nurse Kirkwood spotted him heading back on the moor. Is the baby with him?"

Flett only shrugged.

"I don't care whether the rumours are true," I said. "You can't take a child from its mother. I'll have to report this."

"Do what you like," Flett said. "It was her idea." And he walked away.

I couldn't put Jean Flett in the Riley, but nor did I want to leave her unattended as I brought in the ambulance. "I'll stay," Nurse Kirkwood said. "I'll come to no harm here."

On the army highway I stopped at the moorland crossroads, calling ahead from the telephone box to get the ambulance on its way. It passed me heading in the opposite direction before I reached the hospital.

There I made arrangements to receive Mrs Flett. My concern was with her injury, not her private life. Lord knows how a crofter's wife with six children found the time, the opportunity, or the energy for a passion, however brief. I'll leave it to your HE Bateses and DH Lawrences to explore that one, with their greater gifts than mine. Her general health seemed, like so many of her island breed, to be robust. But a bruised spleen needs rest in order to heal, and any greater damage could take a day or two to show.

Biddy followed at my heels as I picked up a chair and went to sit with John Petrie. He'd rallied a little with the dog's visits, though the prognosis was unchanged. I opened the window eighteen inches or so. Biddy could be out of there like a shot if we should hear the senior sister coming.

"I know I can be straight with you, John," I said. "How do you feel about your legacy giving a future to an unwanted child?"

They were his sheep that had been traded, after all. And Jean Flett had confirmed her wish to see her child raised where it wouldn't be resented. As for Daisy's feelings, I tried to explain them with Tulloch's own analogy of a ewe unwilling to leave its dead lamb, which I was sure he'd understand. John Petrie listened and then beckoned me closer.

What he whispered then had me running to the car.

I'd no way of saying whether Thomas Tulloch might have reached his cottage yet. My sense of local geography wasn't that good. I didn't even know for sure that he was carrying the Flett baby.

I pushed the Riley as fast as it would go, and when I left the road for the bumpy lane I hardly slowed. How I didn't break the car in two or lose a wheel, I do not know. I was tossed and bucketed around but I stayed on the track until the car could progress no farther, and then I abandoned it and set myself to fly as best I could the rest of the way.

I saw Tulloch from the crest of a rise, at the same time as the cottage came into view. I might yet reach him before he made it home. He was carrying a bundle close to his chest. I shouted, but either he didn't hear me or he ignored my call.

I had to stop him before he got to Daisy.

It was shepherds' business. In the few words he could manage John Petrie had told me how, when a newborn lamb is rejected by its mother, it can be given to a ewe whose own lamb has died at birth. But first the shepherd must skin the dead lamb and pull its pelt over the living one. Then the new mother might accept it as her own. If the sheep understood, the horror would be overwhelming. But animals aren't people.

I didn't believe what I was thinking. But what if?

I saw the crofter open his door and go inside with his bundle. I was only a few strides behind him. But those scant moments were enough.

When last I'd seen Daisy Tulloch, she'd the air of a woman in whom nothing could hope to rouse the spirit, perhaps ever again.

But the screaming started from within the house, just as I was reaching the threshold.

The Butterfly
GARDEN

WAY BEYOND TOWN and out along the river, there was a place known to all as Shitty Hollow. It was a real name. It had disappeared from every official map and record more than two hundred years before, but there was no erasing it from the hearts and minds of the people thereabouts. Some things in life are just too dear to let go.

Early one summer, at about ten o'clock on a weekday morning, Louise Tanner was being driven by her father along the hollow's narrow lanes. They were in his old Humber, a car with the grace of a tank and the colours of a battleship. Behind her in the back-seat footwell was the overnight bag that she'd packed in a hurry. She was squinting; the flicker of hard sunlight through the overhanging trees was giving her a headache.

He hadn't told her where they were going, or why.

She hadn't asked, but waited to hear.

He wasn't in a talkative mood. His was more a do-it-and-get-it-over-with frame of mind. He'd done a lot of pacing and fretting last night, and sometime between then and now he'd come to a decision.

"Get your things together, Louise," he'd said. "Enough for a day or two." And although she was no more than eleven years old, she'd sprung to it like a soldier. That was how it had to be, at home in their motherless household.

Now she tried closing her eyes, and found that it helped with the ache. There was nothing to see here, anyway. Nothing to the area other than endless woodland and dead-looking farms and long, twisty lanes with no names on them. No pubs, no shops, no schools or churches. The land was poor and the scenery was dull. People didn't come out to the hollow because nobody had much reason to.

"Ach," her father said, and braked so suddenly that she had to open her eyes and put out a hand or be pitched forward. She could hear locked-up wheels sliding on the road as the car stopped. Then he stirred the gearshift around like a stick in a bucket of stones. Once he'd found reverse, he backed up the twenty yards or so to the turnoff they'd missed.

A couple of minutes later, they were there.

The lane curved through the middle of the farm and disappeared behind it. The farmhouse stood on one side of the lane, its outbuildings over on the other. The outbuildings were low and mismatched while the house was a great, neglected wedding-cake of a place. It had probably been built for a farmer who was the richest in the area, and wanted everyone to know it. Now it looked desperate and haunted, like a big toy broken beyond repair.

When they'd pulled into a dirt yard off the lane, her father turned off the engine.

"Where are we?" she said.

"An old friend of mine lives here," he said. "I'm going to leave you with him for a while."

"Why?"

"Unfinished business with Mister Taylor. Something I've been avoiding. Nothing I want you around for."

So that was it? Because he had some business she was to be dropped off among strangers, like a dog at the kennels?

"I don't want to stay," she said.

"You haven't even met him."

"I don't want to."

"You'll be all right," her father insisted. "It won't be for more than a couple of days and then I'll come back and get you. You won't be short of company. His children are about the same age as you."

"Big deal," Louise said. "That makes no difference."

"I think you'll like them," her father said. "If they're anything like Colin, they'll probably teach you to swear and play poker."

He started to get out of the car.

"Please, Dad," she said, but he wasn't listening any more. He'd left her alone in the Humber and was crossing the yard to the main door of the farmhouse.

So she stayed there, sullen and alone.

Life stank.

"I already know how to play fucking poker," she said when she thought he was out of earshot.

"What?" he called back.

"Nothing," she said.

COLIN KELLY SNAPPED awake in his farmhouse bedroom and had instant cause to regret it. It seemed that he'd failed to make it into bed last night, because he was still sprawled across the covers. All his bones hurt. The coverlet under his face was damp, where he must have drooled.

Rebecca was shaking him. "Someone's outside," she said. "Don't think I'm dealing with them."

Colin Kelly made a halfhearted attempt to focus.

"Who is it?" he said.

"Go downstairs and you'll find out."

He didn't hear her leave, but he heard the door to her room slamming a few moments later. A visitor? Visitors never found their way here. Only the education people who came to talk about his children, and that was Rebecca's department.

This didn't sound promising, and his head was in no shape to deal with anything too complex.

But Rebecca had shut herself away again, all bad mood and banging around, so it seemed as if he didn't have any choice. He went to the window, retying his dressing gown cord. He didn't own pyjamas, never had, couldn't quite bring himself to change now. So he always slept in the big old dressing gown, with his underpants on.

When he looked down from the window he saw a banged-up grey Humber that he didn't recognise. A child was sitting in it. Someone was hammering on the door down there, and he heard a voice call his name.

Colin left the room and headed down toward the stairs. The stone house was almost mansion-sized, big enough for the four of them to lose each other in; which was about the wisest thing that they all could do, given that none of their lives seemed to intersect much these days for anything other than all-out arguments.

Many parts of the house were unusable. When a window broke or the damp came in, Rebecca would close the room off and they'd all leave it alone. It was hard to imagine doing much else. Colin didn't do practical stuff. One day soon he'd settle on what he was meant for, and then the world would take notice. Invent something amazing. Finish the book he was going to write.

Or start it, even.

He opened the door, and looked blankly at the man who'd been calling his name.

"Hello, Colin," he said.

He was no better off.

"It's Frank," the man said patiently. "Frank Tanner."

"Oh shit," said Colin.

"Don't have kittens, Colin," the man said. "I just want to ask for a favour."

"Is it optional?"

"Hear me out."

Colin led the way inside, and down the hallway to the kitchen. His children were at the kitchen table, which was covered in American comic books and breakfast debris. Ralph and Catriona looked up blankly as the two adults came in.

"Go and play," Colin Kelly told them, and they got up and left without a word.

He closed the door behind them. Then, turning back to face the room, he tugged the sides of his dressing gown together, and wished he'd taken an extra minute to pull on some trousers.

Tanner said, "Yours?"

"So I've been told," Colin said, and saw the look on Tanner's face as he glanced around. People had said that there could be an odd smell to the house sometimes, although he'd never noticed anything himself.

He said, "What's the matter?"

"Nothing," Tanner said.

"Place needs a lick of paint," Colin explained. "Never my strong suit."

"Who's running the farm?"

"Nobody," Colin said, pulling out a chair and sitting down. Frank stayed on his feet. "What happened to the child of nature who was going to live off the land?"

"When it came down to it, the land couldn't quite match the convenience of the weekly Giro. Let's cut right to it, Frank. We haven't seen each other in years, and we didn't like each other then. What do you want from me?"

"I need somewhere to leave my kid for a couple of days while I straighten a few things out with my employer," Tanner said. "It's way overdue and it's not something I want to involve her in."

Colin said, "Why here?"

"I don't know anyone else who inherited a hundred-acre farm in the middle of nowhere. If you don't want to help me, Colin, just say so."

For a mind still befuddled by bad sleep, Colin's was doing a pretty good job of racing. He had his memories of Frank Tanner, and they weren't fond ones.

"Sounds like trouble," Colin said.

"That's none of your concern."

"I'm a parent with responsibilities. I nearly paid the council tax, once." He saw Tanner's face and said, "What are you laughing at?"

"Come on, Colin. I doubt anything's changed. I'm perfectly aware that every spare penny you ever had went straight into that big vein in your dick. If it's money, I'll pay you."

Colin was about to come winging back with a sharp reply of some kind. He was sure that he would have thought of one, but the sudden involvement of money brought him up short.

"How much?" he said.

LOUISE DIDN'T LIKE the look of the farm, or the farmhouse, or the man whom she'd seen briefly at the door, or anything about the entire setup. When she saw her father coming out again she quickly hunched down in the seat and pressed her knuckles into her temples.

"It's turned into a migraine," she said accusingly when he reached the car.

"That's good timing," her father said, strangely unmoved by her suffering. "You can go straight upstairs and have a lie down."

Reluctantly, she gave up the attempt and climbed out of the car. As she walked across the yard she thought that she might have seen a couple of figures disappearing behind one of the shanty outbuildings, but she couldn't be sure.

She didn't want to be left here alone. She didn't want to face the effort of making new friends. And that business with the knuckles in the temples had been a mistake—she still had the headache for real, and now she'd made herself feel queasy on top of it.

A minute or so later she was standing with her father in the kitchen, which smelled vaguely of drains and stale vegetable juice. Colin Kelly looked no better close-to than he had from a distance. His hair was all up on end and his face resembled the unmade bed that he'd almost certainly crawled out of. He was still wearing the immense moth-eaten dressing gown, under which his two pale stick-insect legs showed.

"Louise reckons she has a migraine," her father said.

"Really?" Colin Kelly said, and looked at her with a fellow-sufferer's sympathy so palpable that her heart, which had been as cold toward him as the stone of the kitchen floor, could only soften a little. But it was only a little, and it mostly dissipated when he stuck his hand inside the bathrobe for a scratch.

"You'll be fine here," her father told her as he moved toward the door, and then he shot Colin Kelly a look and a movement of the head that was a pretty clear summons for one last private word in the hallway.

She waited until they'd both left the room and then shot across to listen at the door.

"Make sure you keep a close eye on her," she heard her father say. "Don't let her leave the farm and don't let her use the phone."

It was only after he'd gone that she realised he'd driven off with her overnight bag in the back of his car.

COLIN KELLY SAID, "This way," and led her up the stairs. She looked around her as she went. The paper was peeling off the walls, and the walls were in no great shape beneath. Half museum, half haunted house.

When they'd reached what seemed like the top of the house, he opened a door to reveal a windowless stairway climbing to a further attic level above. There was no carpet on these stairs, just the brown felt that usually showed through when carpets wore out.

She followed him to the top, holding the rail because the climb was so steep. This attic level was even more run-down than the rest of the house. They came to a landing under a skylight with four doors leading off it, all identical. He opened one of them, and indicated for her to go in.

One half of the room was cleared, the other was filled with junk. Neither half could remotely be called tidy but in the clearer part, a striped mattress lay on the floor.

"There's bedding and pillows in a box over there," Kelly said. "Sort yourself out and take whatever you need. I'll…"

And then he seemed to lose the thread of whatever it was he'd intended to say.

"Just take what you need," Kelly said again, and then he left her there and went downstairs, switching off the stair light when he reached the bottom. She heard the lower door close a moment later.

Louise looked around. She didn't want to be here. If she could have seen a way out, she'd have taken it.

But at eleven years old, you tend to have to stay where you're put.

It was an odd-shaped room. It was right up under the eaves of the house, so that half of the ceiling angled down to make a wedge shape and the window stuck up out of the sloping roof.

She went over to the junk pile and poked around at some of the stuff in there. Against the wall there were some old prints in frames, the prints all but destroyed by damp. A bag of lampshades, dusty enough to make her sneeze. She found the bedding box but there were no sheets, no covers, just the pillows and some old-style quilts.

She didn't undress but she took off her shoes, which she lined up on the floor alongside the mattress. She noticed that where the brown felt of the floor covering had worn through to the boards, most of the holes had been patched with strips of parcel tape.

Louise spread out the best of the quilts and then lay down fully clothed on the mattress and drew it over herself. It felt cold and scratchy. She'd closed the curtains, but they hadn't made much difference. They were ratty and yellow and the light coming in through them gave the perverse impression of a glorious day outside.

Her head *did* ache. At least she could try to get rid of that.

She said her usual little prayer, and closed her eyes.

AFTER SLEEPING LIKE a dead thing for the rest of the morning, Louise awoke. She had that thick, druggy feeling of having been disturbed before she was ready. She tried to close her eyes and slide off again. She was alone, it was quiet, there was nothing to stop her. But somehow it wasn't working.

At first, she wasn't sure why. Then she became aware of it; somewhere in the house, someone was arguing. It was muted by floors and walls and all the other fabric of the building so that nothing of any detail came through, but like the echo of a battle from the next valley its general nature was unmistakable.

A man, a woman, and at least one temper. Colin Kelly didn't seem to have the energy, so at a guess the temper was all coming from the woman.

There were probably lots of possible reasons for the argument, but her mind leapt directly to the only one she could imagine. They must arguing about her. Which meant that as far as *someone* was concerned, she was unwelcome.

She got up and, yawning, opened the yellow curtains.

Outside, the sun really was shining. From this side of the house the miles-wide valley stretched out and away, a repeating mosaic of fields, walls and woodlands in an enormous random design. As she was looking out, she heard a door slam somewhere down below.

From the window she saw the man called Colin going out in a well-rusted white van. It went off down the lane, reappearing in little flashes wherever there was a gap in the wall.

She tried her window. It rattled in its frame, but the catch had been painted shut. Outside there was a decorative stone parapet marking the edge of the roof. Beyond that, there was some scaffolding up against the side of the building. It looked as if it had been put up and then forgotten, months or years before.

She sat on the mattress for a while. She folded up the bedding and put on her shoes. Her stomach rumbled.

Finally, she heard someone coming up the narrow attic stairs.

The footsteps came in a rush. The woman entered the room abruptly and without knocking, as if she'd been blown in through the door by a whirl-wind or a storm. But then she slowed down to normal speed as soon as she'd entered, almost as if she'd been working herself up to confront something enormous and was now deflated by the lesser reality before her. The reality being Louise, and her neatly-made bed on the floor.

"So," she said.

She was a handsome woman, but looked as if she either didn't know it or didn't care. Her hair was tied back and the way she was dressed had a neglected, thrown-together look, like gardening clothes. "I'm Rebecca," she said. She wasn't openly hostile but she wasn't exactly friendly, either. Louise didn't know what to make of her. "Who are you?"

"Louise Tanner," Louise said. She didn't meet the woman's eyes, but kept her gaze lowered. The woman's hands, she noticed, looked strong like a man's.

"You've no other clothes?"

"No," Louise said. "My dad forgot to leave me any."

The woman made an exasperated noise, but then seemed to gather herself as if there was no choice but to take it in her stride. "I'll have to see what I can get together," she said. "Come and have some lunch."

Louise followed her downstairs. She was hungry, but she also carried a small stone of dread inside her at the thought of having to meet even more strangers. Young strangers, now. She hoped she'd get through it. She hoped they'd be nice. Rebecca didn't seem too bad, but it was almost as if she was forcing herself to it.

The house looked just as weird and unprepossessing on her descent as it had when she'd arrived.

Two faces looked up as she entered the kitchen. A boy and a girl, the boy her own age or slightly younger while the girl was older and, though seated, looked a lot taller than herself. Both were in T-shirts over shorts and trainers. Not identical dress, but near enough the same to look like a uniform.

"This is Ralph and Catriona," Rebecca said. "And you're…?"

"Louise Tanner," she said.

They stared. Not with any conscious rudeness; they just stared. They appeared to be having breakfast cereal for lunch. Nobody seemed to think it strange. Louise supposed that she'd be getting the same.

They watched her as she sat down at the table across from them. Rebecca gave her a bowl, found her a spoon and rinsed it, pushed the Shreddies and the milk cartons within her reach, and then left the room.

Then they started.

Louise didn't know if they'd been told about her, or how much they knew, or anything. But they wasted no time in awkwardness or formalities.

Ralph said, "Is that your watch?"

Louise hesitated over her Shreddies, spoon in midair.

"Yes," she said.

"Can I have a look at it?"

She was reluctant, but she couldn't see any other way. It wasn't a demand, or anything. But how could she refuse without seeming impolite? She unbuckled the strap and handed it over. It left a pressure mark on her skin, which she rubbed at before she picked up her spoon again.

"Ingersoll?" Ralph said, peering at the tiny face of the watch. "Who are they? I've never heard of them."

"It's very old," Louise said.

"Is it valuable?"

"I don't think so."

It had been her mother's.

She was aware that Catriona was watching her at the same time. Louise had been hungry before she'd come downstairs, but now it was as if she'd lost all sense of taste and appetite. These two made her ill at ease.

Catriona said, "Where do you go to school?"

"All different places."

Ralph said, "We don't go to school. Do we, Cat?"

"Not in the conventional sense," Catriona said, the big word seeming to come quite naturally to her. "We're being home educated."

Louise couldn't think of any reply to that, so she simply said, "Oh."

Louise was aware that Ralph was watching her now, and it was as if he'd seen a chance here to catch her out. That seemed to be the pattern. One spoke, the other studied. He said, "Do you know what home educated means?"

"No," Louise admitted.

"It means we can do what we like, all day. We're following our own lines of enquiry. It's Rebecca's idea. Dad got her here to be our teacher."

Which settled something in Louise's mind; Rebecca wasn't their mother. No one had said as much, but it was something she'd quietly picked up. There hadn't been much to go on, but from the way she'd looked Louise had the feeling that Rebecca didn't even like the two of them.

She said, "Does that work?"

"It wouldn't for just anyone," Catriona said. "But we've got a genetic advantage. Our father's a genius. He's the most intelligent person in his family, ever. He's got an IQ so high, no one can measure it."

Now, this was news. From what she'd seen of Colin Kelly she could only conclude that his genius was well-disguised. He didn't give the impression of a man who could be trusted to make a pot of tea without a set of instructions and a handy first-aid kit.

But still, you never could tell.

Ralph said, "Cat can't read. Can you, Cat?"

"No," Catriona said with what appeared to be great and genuine pride.

Then Ralph scraped his chair back and stood up. "We're going out, now," he said. "You have to come with us because we've got to watch you. I know it's a pain, but you're not to go anywhere on your own."

Louise hastily shovelled in as much of her Shreddie-mush as she could manage. She couldn't be sure if Ralph was apologising because it was a pain for her, or complaining because it was a pain for them. She had her eye on her wristwatch, hoping that this might be a good opportunity to rescue it. But Ralph was putting it on. When he'd got the strap fastened, he held it out at arm's length and considered it.

"It's a girlie watch," he said.

But he didn't take it off.

They all went out. Now that they were all on their feet, Louise could see that Catriona was a full head taller than herself. She had bumps in her T-shirt as well, which Louise could only look upon with envy.

The air was still and warm, and there were tiny fireweed seeds drifting in the air across the yard. Apart from birdsong and crickets, there was dead quiet. Ralph and Catriona walked out onto the lane without looking, like wild creatures in the bush whose first experience of traffic would be the car that hit them. Across the road was a gateway leading to pens and cattlesheds and other outbuildings.

Louise said, "Is your dad a farmer?"

"No," Catriona said. "He sold off the land. He sold it to idiots."

"Dad doesn't work," Ralph explained. "He's too brilliant for that kind of thing. It makes him all angry and depressed."

They walked on, and Louise heard a sound. A moment later, she found out why. Out of the nearest building erupted the dog she'd heard earlier; only then he'd been locked away, and now he quite obviously wasn't.

He was big, angry, and yellow. He came at them like a rocket until his chain stopped him with a violent jerk that almost took him off his feet. Then he danced around on the spot making savage noises and focusing all of his apparently limitless supply of hatred on Louise.

He couldn't reach her, but she couldn't move. Ralph looked at her and said, "Lantern's harmless. Dad got him to chase the idiots away when they came to complain. He can't do anything while he's on his chain. Don't be such a crybaby."

"I'm not," Louise said. "I don't like dogs. They scare me."

"Dogs can smell fear," Ralph told her.

"And farts," Catriona said.

"Dogs can smell everything that's happening for miles and miles."

"I don't like dogs," Louise repeated.

The two Kelly children took affectionate swipes at the dog's head as they passed him. He ducked away from their hands, and carried on yowling and spraying spit at Louise. She made a wide circle around him, and he danced after her in an arc at the end of his chain.

OVER THE NEXT couple of hours, she had to follow them everywhere as they made a tour of each complete building and falling-down shell on the property. There were a lot of them; big sheds and barns, open-fronted tractor ports, a cattle parlour and a dusty dairy and a few poky storerooms. There was a garage with no roof and a years-old petrol handpump inside, rusted through to a skeleton. Behind the garage was a big decayed fuel tank, corroded right through like the carcase of a rotted whale.

Some of the buildings weren't so old, but all of it had an air of dereliction. Weeds forced their way up through the concrete setts underfoot. Some of the windows had thick plastic sheet instead of glass, and the sheet had been torn out and in places hung in ribbons.

It would have been a great place to explore and play, if only Ralph and Catriona hadn't been here. They weren't rude to her, and they weren't exactly cruel to her. They were just…strange.

The business of the afternoon seemed to be to check a succession of boxes in a very strict order. The boxes were all in out-of-the way places around the farm, and seemed to be wooden traps of some kind. They looked like the long, narrow boxes that sherry bottles came in at Christmas, and they had sprung flap ends that were a home-made addition.

Louise was tagging along, but they didn't particularly exclude her. She learned a few things along the way. Like, Rebecca was a properly qualified teacher, but they never had lessons. They got by because Rebecca lied a lot to the inspectors and showed them project work and homework that she'd either forged or was recycling from some earlier time in her career. And that worked? No, it didn't. Their father was in big trouble because of it. The children themselves seemed unconcerned by this. They seemed unconcerned by anything.

Louise said, "But if she doesn't actually teach you, what does she do?"

"She shops and cooks, mostly," Catriona said. "And locks herself in her room and does things. She writes letters all the time. I don't think she posts them. No one ever sends her any."

Ralph brought out one of his boxes from the darkness of a coal shed, the shed roof so overgrown with moss that it had the appearance of having been turfed. The flap on the box was closed, and weight shifted inside it with a scratching sound. Ralph seemed pleased.

Catriona was looking back at Louise.

"What's the matter with you?" she said.

"Nothing," Louise said, and wondered what might have been showing on her face.

They went into a long shed that was mostly empty space apart from something stacked up under tarpaulins at the far end. The floor was concrete, with a slight dip toward the middle and a long drain running down its length. There was dried-up straw on the concrete, and cow dung so old it had set there like cement.

Where the bottoms of the boxes showed under the tarpaulin, they were gnawed and sodden-looking. Some had been moved around to create a little sheltered area, and within this area was a makeshift pen of wooden posts and very stout wire. There was something inside the pen, something that started to move and boil around as they approached.

Louise craned to look, warily. Were they ferrets? She'd seen some ferrets on TV once. People kept them on farms, and in cages not unlike this one.

Holding his box, Ralph looked down through the wire top of the pen and said, "Good morning, Colonel, and how are you today?"

Now she could see. They weren't ferrets. They were the things that ferrets were bred to catch.

Ralph looked over his shoulder, and saw her standing well back. "What's the matter with you now?" he said.

"They're rats," Louise said.

"Scared of dogs, scared of rats…there's something wrong with you."

"Rats aren't pets."

"They can be."

"Not those kind."

Catriona said, "We don't keep them as pets. They're an experiment."

"Rats are amazing," Ralph added. "They can live on almost anything. We've proved it." He pointed into the pen, moving his finger to track one of the animals. All that Louise could see was a mass of heaving brown, their tails flicking up here and there like whips. "This big one's called Colonel Wish," Ralph said, "and the rest are his ladies. The more food you put out, the more rats they make. Now we've stopped feeding them to see if they'll eat each other."

"It's better than school," Catriona said, almost daring Louise to challenge her by saying otherwise.

Ralph carefully unhooked one corner of the wire, and he lifted the box to the gap. There was a crude loop on the hinged end, and he hooked his finger into the loop to open the flap.

"Because this one's a stranger," he said, "they might turn on him."

He tipped the box. There was a frantic scratching as whatever was inside scrambled to keep a purchase on the tilting floor, but then the battle was lost and a dark blur dropped into the pen like an aid delivery being airdropped out of a plane.

As the newcomer hit the scrum and the scrum boiled up with renewed energy, Ralph and Catriona leaned forward to see. Their faces were right above the wire, and their expressions were of transfixion. They looked like two saints in a stained-glass window, gazing on the awesome beauty of heaven. They were innocent. They were damned.

And in realising this, Louise could see that they were more than strangers to her. They weren't even like her; they were some different species, quite unlike her kind.

She wanted her father to come back, right now.

And she passionately, *passionately* wanted the return of her wristwatch.

"SAY IT AGAIN," Ralph demanded.

Louise could see no way around it, so she tried it again.

"In brightest day, in darkest night…"

"It's not *darkest*," Ralph exploded, "it's *blackest!*"

"What does it matter?"

"If you don't say it right, what's the point of saying it at all?"

"Exactly, Ralph," Catriona put in drily from the wall she was lying stretched-out on, chewing a fresh grass stalk that dipped and waved around as she worked it. "What *is* the point?"

"It's Green Lantern's oath!" Ralph said helplessly, and it was clear that in his mind the others were stupid not to see it.

They'd finished checking all the traps and she'd hung back while Ralph counted his rats after their feeding frenzy, and then they'd set out away from the farm and across the fields.

For a while, they followed the river. Drought had taken it low, almost down to a dry bed, slate-coloured water shining as it descended over shallow rocks as if finding a path down a well-worn stairway. On the riverbank pathway, tree roots stood out like veins in mummified flesh.

Now they were in a glade, between overhanging cliffs of striated rock so lush with clinging ferns and grasses that Louise half expected the face of some Mayan temple god to be peeping out of the overgrowth.

Ralph got bored very quickly, she noticed. Catriona didn't seem to care where she was. Ralph squelched ahead of them as they moved on toward the next place. He'd waded into the water after an interesting-looking stick without bothering to take his canvas shoes off.

As they walked, Louise said to Catriona, "What's a Green Lantern anyway?"

Catriona shrugged. "I don't know," she said. "Someone in one of his comics."

The next question came out almost against her intentions; Louise wanted to know the answer, but she had no idea how it would be taken.

She said, "Can you really not read?"

Midges danced in the sunlight, like motes over the path; Catriona waved some of them away from her face, "It's a waste of time," she said. "Nobody's going to read in the future."

So that was that.

They'd been climbing for a while. Ahead of them, the track narrowed to a stony single-file path through some dense foliage. On the slopes above, there stood a neglected woodland of tall, straight, once-cultivated trees. Some had fallen like soldiers, caught and supported by their comrades, rotting where they leaned.

Ralph stopped and turned where the path narrowed and said, "Come on," before heading onward. The greenery pushed in so close that he almost had to part it, but there was a clear way through.

"Follow him," Catriona said. "I'll be right behind you."

There was something odd in their attitude, but Louise couldn't work out what it was. She concentrated more on keeping her footing; the path here was of closely-packed stones through foliage that pressed in from either side. One or two of the stones were loose, but it wasn't that much of a problem.

"Stop a minute," she heard Catriona call from some distance behind her. Louise looked back.

Catriona hadn't followed her at all, but was watching down the narrow alleyway of green. Ralph had skipped ahead and stopped, and now Louise was at a point midway between them.

What were they doing?

Ralph said, "I think I dropped something in the bushes right around where you are. Can you have a look for it?"

"What did you drop?" Louise said suspiciously.

"I think it was your watch. Just have a look. Right where you are."

Ralph's hands were behind his back, so she couldn't tell if he was still wearing her watch or not. He seemed to be hiding them deliberately.

She still didn't get it. But wary now, she looked all around her and then, hesitantly, she parted the foliage to one side. It was dense, with broad waxy leaves.

As an armload of the leaves pushed away, she expected to see bare ground starved of sunlight. But there was none. She turned to the other side and it was the same; no ground, more greenery, and gaps and shadows that hinted at serious depth below.

She wasn't on a stony path at all. She'd been walking along the narrow top of a high wall. She was halfway across it with still some distance to go. The bushes weren't bushes, but the tops of trees to either side.

Ralph and Catriona were still standing there, one either end, just watching. Not cracking their sides in laughter, or even treating it as a joke; it was more as if they were interested to see what she'd do.

Everything had changed now. Where before she'd slipped and scrambled on the loose stones without any concern, now she could hardly bring herself to take a step. She didn't know how much of a drop there was on one side or the other. It could have been twenty feet, it could have been thirty.

Wobbling slightly, she raised her arms and stretched them out for balance like a tightrope walker. She wanted to freeze up and not move at all, but she knew that this wasn't an option. And besides, they were still watching. She wished that she could have looked more unconcerned, but she couldn't do it.

She tested the first step, and made sure that her footing was firm before she dared to transfer her weight. Her legs were rubbery. Heart-in-mouth time.

At her next step a stone moved as she began to shift her weight onto it, and adrenaline shot through her in a dizzying rush so that for a moment, fizzing with its surge, she could hardly see or hear.

Slowly, she dropped to her hands and knees. With one hand, she felt ahead. The loose stone rocked, and she prised it out and let it fall from sight.

She heard it crash back and forth as it dropped through the greenery, and it seemed to take forever before it stopped.

Still crouched low, she began to crawl forward. It wasn't dignified, but it was all that she could do. The Kelly children were still watching her.

Twenty yards, ten yards, five.

When she reached the solid ground where Ralph was standing, she stood up shakily.

Catriona came hopping across after her, showing no fear at all.

"See?" she said to Ralph, as if resolving some long-running debate. "Knowing shouldn't make any difference, but it does."

They went on.

Louise said nothing. As her heartbeat began to return to normal, she noticed that some kind of a tick had fastened itself to the back of her hand and had begun to feed greedily, as if she were the tick's birthday buffet. She knocked it away, and felt the tug as it pulled out. The warm weather seemed to have brought entire new species out of nowhere.

"Why are you in long sleeves when it's so hot?" Catriona said. "Are you covering up a Popeye tattoo?"

"My dad drove off with all my other clothes," Louise said. "I've got nothing else with me to wear."

As they were walking along, Catriona said, "This used to be one big estate. There was a big house, and these woods were all like part of the gardens. You can see where there used to be walks and waterfalls. Our house was the estate farm. It's the only part that's left standing."

"Apart from the butterfly garden," Ralph added, and he looked at Louise. "Do you want to see it?"

"Not particularly," Louise said, disinclined to trust either of them in any way now.

"You're going to see it anyway," Ralph said.

A small footbridge led over a stream to a door in a wall. The wall was of stone and about eight feet high, the door was solid with a black iron ring for a handle. The wall disappeared into the woodland in either direction.

Ralph turned the ring and leaned on the door, and it opened inward with a squeal.

They entered into an enclosed acre of ground. As far as Louise could see, the wall encircled it completely and there was no other way in or out. There was a small pond to the left, dried-out down to a stagnant puddle surrounded by a bed of mud. To her right lay what looked like the overgrown lines and pathways of a vegetable garden, with anything useful having been long strangled and overrun by weeds. Nettles stood like trees and the fireweed had burst out into exotic pinkish-purple flowers, so excessively developed that they were like foliage from Mars.

Overgrown, still, lush, abandoned. Even in the bare light of day, Louise found it spooky. But she was stuck with the timetable of her hosts, and was subtly at their mercy.

Catriona wandered off. Ralph found a spot and stretched out with his hands behind his head. Louise took the opportunity to move to a distance on her own.

Looking down, she saw something that hit her with a slight shock. It was a patch of black and white tile in a diamond pattern. A building of some kind had stood here, and this was all that remained of it. The space where she stood had once been a room. Now it wasn't. She couldn't say why that felt odd.

She heard Ralph say, "Do you know what kind of butterfly that is?"

She looked over at him. He was shading his eyes and pointing at the tall weeds that surrounded the pond. Their blossom was like spiders' webs, and it stripped from them in a fine cloud whenever the wind blew.

Louise said, "I don't know the names of any butterflies except for Red Admirals and Cabbage Whites."

"It's a Painted Bride," Ralph said. "I bet you don't know why it's called that."

Louise was in no doubt whatever that he was going to tell her, and so felt no urge to say anything.

Ralph said, "Once it's mated, the female kills the male and eats it. Then when the eggs hatch out, it kills the grubs and eats them too. The blood gets all over it and stains it red. That's what makes it into a Painted Bride."

That made her look. She could see something fluttering, but it was too far away to make out any details. It looked like a bog-ordinary Red Admiral from here.

"Really?" she said.

"The dark patches are the oldest blood. The bright spots are from the blood of the babies."

From almost on the other side of the garden. Catriona called out, "That doesn't make any sense."

"But it's true," Ralph insisted.

"If all the grubs get eaten, where does the next lot of grownups come from? They can't get wiped out and then still carry on."

"It's a mystery of nature," Ralph said.

Louise was genuinely uncertain now. Her imagination was gripped by the tale, but the rational part of her mind recognised the sense of Catriona's argument. Kill all the babies, no more bugs. A one-generation aberration.

She said, "Are you making it up?"

"I certainly am not," Ralph said.

Catriona said, "Maybe some of the grubs escape."

"That's right," Ralph said.

"I thought you didn't know."

"It's coming back to me now. What happens is, some of the grubs deliberately smear blood on themselves while the others are being killed. Then they lie very still under the pile of bodies and pretend to be dead."

Louise was still doubtful, but still felt herself being drawn along. She said, "Doesn't that mean they just get eaten alive?"

"The unlucky ones do," Ralph said, really warming to his theme now. "But a few always escape because the butterflies get full very quickly. They can't eat everything."

"I know, I know!" Catriona said eagerly, moving back over to join in. "And having the blood on them's like a curse, so when the grubs turn into butterflies they're doomed to do the same thing all over again."

It went on. Catriona seemed able to switch sides on a whim, while Ralph seemed to be making it up as he went along and incorporating every new notion into a scheme of increasing elaborateness.

Anyone could do that, she thought.

Anyone.

They weren't only making it up. The moment they'd made it up, they seemed to believe it. Then they made up something else which they roped in as proof. Meanwhile reality was out there on the horizon, and retreating fast. Louise didn't know what to believe or what to dismiss.

Spend enough time in such company, she thought, and you'd face a stark choice of options. Be their constant victim, or become like them.

When Louise wasn't expecting it, Ralph got to his feet.

"I'm hungry now," he said.

And suddenly they were all up and moving and starting back toward the farm.

LOUISE HAD MANAGED a retreat to her room at the top of the building. She'd told Rebecca that she needed to lie down again, and so she'd been allowed upstairs alone. Which meant that to her great relief, she was without the company of the two Kelly children for the first time in hours.

She didn't know what time it was. She had no way of checking because Ralph still had her watch. She'd managed to raise the nerve to ask for it back, one straight and polite question, and he'd ignored her. She'd started to repeat the request but he'd walked away, already talking about something else. Louise didn't know what more she could do.

She'd have to tell her father, if and when he ever came back.

Ralph would probably be unfazed by adult disapproval. He'd told her that he and Catriona regularly stayed up until after midnight with nobody telling them otherwise, and Louise could believe it. It might have been bravado, but still she believed it. Their day so far had been completely unstructured, completely without adult direction. When they were hungry, they went into the kitchen and helped themselves; a fistful of cereal, a slice of bread, some biscuits...they grazed on junk instead of dining, and Louise had to do the same or go without.

Hugging her knees tightly, she sat on her mattress and rocked.

They hadn't allowed her a minute to herself. The lowest point had been when she'd wanted to go to the toilet. They'd prevented her from closing the door, and pushed it all the way open. They'd said they'd been ordered to watch, and then they'd stood there waiting for her to perform.

Louise had seriously wanted to go, but faced with this she'd abandoned the idea, pretending that the urge had passed. It hadn't. It had receded for a while, but then it had crept back and steadily grown worse. Her belly was tight, her bladder hurt when she moved now; she couldn't even straighten herself up without it hurting. She'd tried the window, thinking that if only she could get it open she could go out and squat inside the safety of that narrow parapet and relieve herself into the guttering. Even thinking about it was enough to add to the torture. But the catch had been painted over and was solid.

So the only answer was to wait until she couldn't possibly hang on any longer, and then quietly make her way downstairs in the hope that they wouldn't be waiting.

That would be the nightmare scenario; to last out for so long, and for nothing. They'd probably think it a great joke. Even the thought of it was enough to make her redden with humiliation.

It was no use. She had to go. The last possible moment was now.

Carefully, achily, she got to her feet. The house had been quiet for a while. No doors, no voices. Her bladder hurt so much that she could hardly stand. But she only had to get down as far as the next floor and then she could do what she had to in privacy. She opened her door, and started to make her way down the attic stairs.

One tread creaked as her weight went onto it, but she couldn't stop herself now. She went all the way down the stairs with no further sound, and emerged through the narrow doorway onto the landing.

Cold air blew across her feet as she passed a couple of the doors. The rooms with the broken windows, imperfectly stoppered. She'd left her shoes upstairs, to make less noise.

She made it to the toilet. Closed the door. Slid the bolt. Dropped her pants and got seated in a panic, terrified of losing it in the last few seconds. She had no clean clothes to change into if she were to soil these.

Then...

Well, for what seemed like ages, nothing. After all her suffering, it was as if there was a lock on her bladder. When it finally came, it wasn't with the satisfaction she'd been expecting. It came in a long, thin, burning stream that went on and on with no particular relief. It left her wrung-out and exhausted, almost in tears.

She tore some of the paper off the roll, and blew her nose on it. Then she dropped the makeshift tissue into the pan behind her and sat with her elbows on her knees and her head hanging down, miserable. It was as if she'd been cheated of even that one, tiny, hard-earned bliss.

That was usually it. You got through the hurt because you were sure that when you reached the end of it, things would be better.

But not in this house.

She sighed, and sniffed, and decided that she'd finished.

Pulling the chain was going to make a lot of noise. But it would be too embarrassing to leave the bowl full of her stale, hot, stored-up pee and, besides, she'd finished what she needed and there was nothing for them to watch.

The chain looked as if it had been broken a few times over the years, and remade a few inches shorter every time. She had to reach way up for the wooden pull-handle, and in reaching for it she noticed something odd.

Just visible over the edge of the cistern was a stub of pencil. It had been pushed through a knot in a plastic bag, and hooked there so that the bag itself hung out of sight inside the tank. The pencil kept it from dropping all the way down into the water.

Louise glanced back over her shoulder. The bolt was on the door and she couldn't be discovered. So, knowing herself to be safe for the moment, she climbed onto the seat and reached up to get a look at whatever the bag might contain.

It was something pretty interesting.

When she eventually pulled on the chain, the rush of water sounded like a flash-flood in a bowling alley. After waiting a few seconds for the worst of it to be over, she eased open the door.

Nothing stirred. She hurried down the landing, and almost bumped into Colin Kelly as he emerged from the stairs to her attic room. He'd been hurrying down, and he looked anxious.

She didn't know what to say.

It took him a moment to recover and then Colin Kelly said, "I thought we'd lost you."

"I needed the toilet," Louise said lamely, as if it wasn't already obvious.

He said, "Have Ralph and Cat been looking after you?"

Here was her chance. An invitation to come forth with a flood of all the day's petty injustices, the curtailment of her liberty, the complete lack of respect for her privacy.

But she only said, "Yes, thank you."

She wondered if he could have any inkling of how strange and twisted his children were. Maybe he just didn't see it. They weren't exactly savages, and it wasn't exactly cruelty that she'd felt from them; they were more like aliens, their agenda an impenetrable and uncomfortable one. As if she was the first ordinary child to have strayed onto their patch, and now they wanted to take her apart and see how she worked.

Kelly said, "Is there anything you need?"

"I don't think so," she said.

"Say if there is. We don't get many visitors here. We're not really set up for it."

There was an uncomfortable silence as she waited for him to signal an end to the conversation and move out of the way so that she could go back upstairs. She wondered what the signs of extreme genius might be. She wondered how he managed to keep them so well-hidden.

He said, "I can see a bit of Frank in you, now. I couldn't before."

"Everyone says we're alike," she said.

He was about to say something else.

Then he seemed to think better of it, and stepped aside to let her go.

"WELL," REBECCA SAID brightly the next morning. "I'm not used to having help in the kitchen."

Louise said, "What do you want me to do?"

Rebecca didn't seem to have thought that far ahead; she wiped her hands on her apron with a nervous, smoothing motion and looked around and said, "You can try peeling some of those vegetables. Have you ever done that before?"

"No," Louise said. "I've been a table monitor, though."

"Then perhaps you can set the table for us later."

Something wasn't right, here. Rebecca was going through all the motions of being friendly, but something about her manner didn't ring true. The woman was all smiles and sympathy, but there was a brittleness under it all as if someone was holding a gun to the back of her head. She found some excuse to get out of the room, and left Louise on her own.

Louise thought it over. Rebecca was tall, and unusually attractive in a non-delicate way. Which meant that she probably had mental problems, since no such woman without them would stay with a man like Kelly out of choice.

So that was Rebecca sorted out.

Some carrots, a few potatoes, and an undersized turnip lay in a nest of crumpled newspaper on the kitchen table. A suspiciously large amount of farm dirt clung to everything, as if Kelly had perhaps cut out all the middlemen and grubbed them up himself from the edges of a growing crop.

Whatever she and her father ate at home came frozen or in tins or as ready-meals. Louise wasn't used to food in its raw state, although she'd an idea of what to do. She searched through all of the drawers until she found a bone-handled paring knife, and with this she began to cut careful slices off the outside of a potato. The pile of slices grew, and the potato got smaller. After a few minutes, she was left with a small pale cube. She put this to one side of the draining board by the sink, and started on the next. She'd never realised how much waste there was in a potato before.

She'd slept well, considering. She'd said her usual prayers, and prayer had eased her mind. Her father didn't know that she prayed. She suspected that he might not approve. Sometimes she wondered if there was anyone out there actually listening. The safest way not to find out was to avoid asking for anything specific. Far better to spend your life wondering if your God was real, than to receive certain and early proof that he wasn't.

Helping Rebecca had been her strategy to avoid spending more time with Ralph and Catriona. She'd almost despaired at the prospect of having to be at their mercy again. When she was with them, it was as if time stopped while the misery went on and on.

Louise had made a small pile of the potato cubes and was wondering how she might tackle a carrot when Rebecca came back.

She looked at Louise's handiwork for a while and then said, "That's probably tired you out. I'll do the rest. Would you like to sit and read a book or something?"

"I don't have one," Louise said.

"No? Come with me."

Rebecca led Louise up the stairs and along to her own room, the one into which she disappeared and did whatever it was she did in there. Wrote letters, or whatever. Louise felt her heart beat a little faster as Rebecca unlocked and opened the door.

This was how she always felt whenever she explored some place where children weren't supposed to go. In a convent school called St Xavier's where she'd attended for more than a year, she and another girl had crept up to the staff quarters and, through a half-open door, glimpsed one of the senior nuns lowering herself stark naked into a hot bath. Louise was thankful that they hadn't been seen and was starting to make a silent withdrawal when the other girl, overwhelmed by that same tension and possessed of some perverse and irresistible urge, had suddenly roared at the top of her voice, "What a *BIG ARSE!*" and they'd had to scramble for their lives.

They'd never been identified or caught, but for ages Louise had carried around the uneasy feeling that it was still only a matter of time before she was summoned for a reckoning. But it never happened. When the nuns had finally thrown her out of the school, it had been for the same reason as all the others.

She followed Rebecca into the badly-lit room.

In any other house it might have been remarkable, but in this junkshop of a place it was mainly a matter of more of the same. More junk, more dust overlying the junk. It was almost as if Rebecca had dragged her entire past along when she came here, like a fisherman hauling a net full of rocks up a beach.

Louise saw dolls and soft toys, baskets full of them. All the dolls looked a little bit strange. Some of the china ones had no tops to their heads, as if they'd been trepanned. One had a face with a rictus grin, as if it had died in a fit. Clothes hung on hangers on the front of the wardrobes, whose doors wouldn't close on the bulging stuff inside. The ornate mantelpiece above the fireplace was solidly cluttered with a zoo of plaster animals and ornaments and photographs in frames. There were books everywhere; on the table, on the floor, in cardboard boxes under the chairs. Almost all were children's books—Nancy Drew, Malcolm Saville, the Chalet School.

Rebecca said, "You can borrow something of mine, if you'll promise to be careful with it. Do you know how to look after books?"

"I got a Bookworm badge in the Brownies," Louise said, without adding that her time as a Brownie had been restricted to the single term she'd spent at St Bartholomew's, and the Bookworm was the only badge she'd gained.

She'd thought that it would be interesting in here but instead it was a little frightening, like being inside another person's head and hearing worms slither in the darker corners. It would have been tempting to grab the nearest book and go, but Louise took several minutes over her selection. She could sense Rebecca's patience, not great to start with, getting less and less as she stood behind her and waited. This one? That one? Old books looked like such hard going.

Finally she made a choice, a fat and friendly-looking volume bound in green cloth. It would have been hard to say which of them, she or Rebecca, was the more relieved to get out of the room as they returned to the landing.

Rebecca relocked the door. Louise felt her flesh creep a little as the image of the room's interior persisted in her mind, fading far more slowly than she would have liked.

"Off you go, then," Rebecca said.

With the book under her arm, Louise climbed the stairs to her attic room. She went inside, and closed the door behind her. There was no furniture in here other than the mattress, so Louise sat crosslegged on that.

She set the book on her knees and inspected it. THE BRITISH NATURE BOOK, by S N Sedgewick. Profusely illustrated. It had decorated boards like a storybook. Louise opened it, and read the handwriting on the flyleaf; *To Rebecca, with love from Auntie Hilda and Uncle Bill.* The flyleaf page was brown around the edges, the colour of weak tea.

She turned some pages and began to look through the contents list. It was a big book, and almost everything seemed to be in there; animals, birds, insects, even plants. The pages gave off a musty, heady smell.

Lepidoptera. Butterflies and moths. Page two hundred and eighteen.

After about ten or fifteen minutes of intense study, Louise was more or less satisfied. She'd examined every caption on the four colour plates, looked at all sixty-seven entries for species of British butterflies and then, just to be certain, skimmed the forty-odd pages of un-numbered moth species.

There was not, nor had there ever been, any such species of butterfly as a Painted Bride.

It was all lies.

All that stuff about the blood, and the bodies, and the curse—all a fantasy. She hadn't doubted it for more than a moment, of course. But she felt a fierce sense of elation in having her doubts confirmed.

She sat back, almost in triumph. It was as if Ralph and Catriona had attacked her very hold on reality, and now she had it back again.

She wondered what they were doing now.

Outside her room, a board creaked.

Louise stiffened. Her head turned quickly as her gaze went to the door. She didn't otherwise move.

Whoever it was, they must have tiptoed up the stairs. Otherwise she's have heard them. Even someone with a naturally light tread would have been betrayed by that creaky board halfway down. Unless they knew it was there, and avoided it on purpose.

Who could it be? Louise had her suspicions. She cocked her head like an animal, trying to pick up any sound that she could. There had to be breathing. But why just stand there?

A click. Very gentle, almost like watch parts working. It came from the handle as it started to turn.

Louise rose to her feet. She moved to the door and stood only inches from it, still listening. This was absurd. She could all but see the two of them on the other side of the door, like something in an airport X-ray. When she grabbed the door and flung it open, she had the satisfaction of jerking the handle out of Ralph's hand and seeing him standing there completely wrong-footed. Catriona was right behind him and she had that same right-off-guard, paparazzi-blinded look.

It was a small triumph, but a satisfying one.

Catriona recovered first.

"Someone's poisoned Lantern," she said.

"You have to come and look," said Ralph.

SOMEONE HAD POISONED Lantern, all right. The dog had died an unpleasant death, and in the process had voided every available bodily fluid around its narrow pen. Blood, bile, urine, liquid feces. In the middle of it all, the animal lay in an attitude of comparative peace.

Ralph and Catriona were watching her for a reaction. She was determined to give them none.

She looked at Ralph.

"Did you do it?" she said.

Ralph seemed genuinely shocked. "No!" he said.

Catriona said, "It was probably one of the idiots, coming back for revenge."

Louise looked at the dog again. Not scary any more, just pathetic.

She said, "What am *I* supposed to do about it?"

"You have to touch him," said Ralph.

"No way."

"You have to."

"Let's see you do it first."

"We already have," Catriona said. All three of them knew she was lying but in this little democracy, it was always going to be two against one.

"There's no way I'm touching the dog," said Louise.

Ralph said, "Then you'll have to do a forfeit."

"I'll do a forfeit," Louise said, and then before Ralph could open his mouth again she added, "but I get to choose it. Not you."

"Where's the point in that?" said Catriona. "You'll just choose something easy."

"Here's the deal," said Louise. "I know the kind of thing you want to see. But whatever I decide on, you have to do it too. The same thing after me. If I pick on something and you think it's easy, then you'll have no trouble matching it. But if you wimp out, I've won. Then you have to tell me you're sorry and look as if you mean it. And then you have to fuck off out of my sight until it's time for me to go home."

They blinked at her daring, as if they'd been threatened with a savaging by Bambi.

"Well?" she said.

Ralph looked at Catriona. Louise saw uncertainty between the two of them for the very first time.

Catriona said, "What happens when we win?"

Louise said nothing. Just waited.

And after a while Catriona said, "Okay." She tried to be cocky about it, to throw it away as if it didn't matter to her one way or the other.

But it didn't come off. Not quite.

COLIN KELLY HAD been spending Tanner's money in his head. He didn't have any of it yet, but that was no obstacle to his imagination. Not that his imagination had much of a journey to make.

He hadn't mentioned any prospect of payment to Rebecca, certain that she'd instantly produce a long list of domestic necessities if he did. He'd hired her to teach, not to nag. Kelly was the master of this house and had needs of his own.

Tanner hadn't been wrong about his little habit, but Kelly was under the impression that he had it well under control. He based this on the fact that he'd set himself rules, and he stuck to them. He was no addict. He only indulged when he really, really needed to. When he was down, for example, because obviously he needed the lift. Or when he was up, to celebrate feeling good and because it was self-evident that he'd earned the treat. And if his emotional temperature indicated neither one state nor the other, then a little chemical bracer was a justified answer to his uncertainty.

He'd been inching toward a crisis, of late. He'd had no ready cash for weeks, and a line of credit wasn't the kind of line that his supplier ever dealt in. His stash was low and he'd been making it last, as best he could. But if it's forward planning and thoughtful, careful management that you're looking for, it's best not to look to a junkie.

No particular troublemaker himself, Kelly had always seemed to get sucked in when trouble was passing by. He'd been the brightest in his family, where it has to be said that the competition had never been stiff. His aunts and uncles had always talked with pride about "the scholar", a pride that was real but which had been based on a meagre handful of very modest exam results that he'd never managed to repeat. A quiet boy, a dreamer, unable to handle pressure, he'd been into drugs at fifteen and had tried suicide two years later.

Right now, his mood was down. The dog's death had rattled him and he'd had two panic attacks already that morning. It would only get worse. Before he could do anything about it he needed to check on Rebecca, to ensure that she was occupied somewhere and wouldn't be likely to walk in on him. She probably wouldn't interfere, but he could do without her disapproval. That look of hers could wither a person's spirits like nothing else he knew.

It wasn't that he'd had any affection for the dog. He'd bought it from the shelter cheap as an ill-tempered adult, and it had liked him no better than it liked anyone else. It had been intended to provide a quick conversation-stopper back when the idiots had still been on the land and kept trying to bring him their complaints. Like they imagined he'd act, or even care.

The way that he'd dealt with his inheritance had been typical Kelly. For him, it had been something of a grand scheme. He'd subdivided the land into plots, and onto them put a job lot of old sheds and mobile homes. These he'd sold off to individual buyers as inexpensive dwellings. But it was grade three agricultural land, fit only for grazing, with no services, no planning permission for buildings, and no chance of any.

Kelly's logic was that as it took at least two years for the local council to process an eviction order on each individual plot, and the plots had been sold cheaply in the first place, then what he was actually selling was a couple of years' worth of low-cost accommodation. It was a great deal. How could anyone complain? He swore that he'd made all this clear at the time of sale. His buyers thought differently. For a while, hardly a week had gone by without an eviction order being served on the farm and some ramshackle hut or old signal box being dragged down by a bulldozer as its owners watched, destitute and in tears.

So what did they think they could expect, trying to make a home in a place with a name like Shitty Hollow?

Now peace had returned and they were all gone. So was the money he'd taken from them. So was most of his stash. So was the dog, under worrying circumstances, because anyone who could get at the dog could probably get at the house.

Which, to Kelly's mind, made it time for a little something.

Rebecca had retreated to her room with the door locked. She didn't respond to his knocking or calling, which usually meant that they wouldn't be seeing her for a full twenty-four hours or even longer. Whatever she nursed in there, she never shared. Which suited him fine.

Flexing his fingers and with sweat on his lip, he made his way to the upstairs toilet. He bolted himself into the narrow room with trembling hands and then reached up to the cistern, where the knotted bag hung inside the edge…

And that was all he got. The bag had no weight at all because it was empty, just a tube of plastic all ripped open at the bottom. The syringe, the spare needles, the razor for cutting and the candle for cooking, and most importantly the airtight packet of Shanghai Sherbert that he'd now started to ache for. All gone.

"Oh hell," he said, and put the wooden seat down so that he could clamber up onto it and reach into the tank. Without stopping to roll up his sleeve and without being able to see, he plunged his hand into the water and started to feel around. The packet was the one that mattered. It had to be in there. Floating, hopefully.

But clearly it wasn't, and so with increasing desperation he raised himself up onto tiptoe and felt right down into the sludge at the bottom of the cistern.

He didn't find the packet, but he found something.

His roar of pain, audible to anyone who cared to listen and sounding all the way from the bats in the rafters down to the rat-infested cellar, was evidence that he'd at least found his spare needles.

They stuck in his hand like porcupine quills, bristling in all directions when he pulled it out of the water.

"HERE WILL DO," said Louise.

They'd come to the shed with the drain down the middle of its concrete floor. She'd rejected the first couple of places that they'd shown her, just on principle. This was a big space, light and airy, but with a hint of something grim about it. She knelt on some old straw and emptied her pockets onto the floor in front of her.

"Those are Dad's!" Ralph said, and would have said more but Catriona elbowed him. They got down cross-legged on the ground to watch.

"I'm only going to use this and this," Louise said, picking out first the piece of rubber tube and then the razor. The tube was about the same length as the gas line on a school bunsen burner. The razor blade had a piece of sticking plaster along one edge, making it safer to hold. Especially if the regular user was a person with an unsteady hand.

"Where's all the rest of it?" Catriona said.

Louise looked up from under her brows. "You mean the drugs?" she said. "I fed them all to your dog last night. Why do you think he's dead?"

"Lantern?" said Ralph, in a voice that sounded slightly strangled and faraway.

"You couldn't," Catriona said. "We'd have heard him bark."

Louise sat back on her heels, rolling up the sleeve on her left arm.

"He only barked once," she said. "Then God made him quiet for me. My God. Not yours. Assuming you've got one."

Catriona didn't respond. She was staring at the uncovered inner part of Louise's forearm as she got the sleeve up and above her elbow.

"How did you get those?" she said.

"It's how I keep track and make sure that I never miss a prayer," Louise explained. "By the time I've moved the safety pin back to the beginning, the first holes have healed and I can start working my way down again. I won't need it for this," she added. Unhooking the big pin, she took it out and laid it aside. The holes that it left hardly bled at all.

"Pay attention to this part," she said. "It's the bit you'll probably find the most tricky."

Quickly and expertly, she threw a loop of the rubber tube around her upper arm and pulled the other end tight with her teeth. When she made a tight fist, all the scars stood out.

"Now, the forfeit here is an act of worship. I'm going to carve my name on my arm with this, so God will know it's me that's praying. God understands pain, whether it's on a cross or with a razor. It's the only way you can ever get really close to him. Don't think of it as self-harm because that's not the same thing at all."

Not an argument that had cut much ice with the nuns, of course. Not them, nor any of the schools that had tried to cope with her as an individual but had drawn the line at her recruitment of others. Nails and a cross were fine. Show them stigmata and they'd make you a saint.

But let an otherwise timid girl start her own Church of the Holy Razor, and she could expect no sanction.

She said, "I could cheat and use my old nickname, Lulu, but I won't. Ralph, it's not too bad for you because your name's quite short. But Catriona, you're shit out of luck. I suggest you take your turn before Ralph while the blade's still nice and sharp, or you'll never make it through to the end. Everybody ready?"

Eyes wide, mouths open. Human polaroids.

"I'll just tighten this a bit more," she said. "It stops most of the blood and if you have it tight enough, you don't even feel anything until after it comes off."

She got the rubber end into her teeth again, pulled it taut, and then started in with the blade. She held her breath while she carved the first letter, and then she let both breath and tubing go.

The rubber held. After her breathing had steadied she said, "An L's pretty easy. But I'll have to be more careful with the O. You have to leave it connected in a couple of places or there's a chance that the circle of skin in the middle could fall right out like a plug and you'll have a hole that won't ever heal. Don't forget, Ralph, that applies to R's and A's as well. The holes may be smaller but you'll bleed like a pig."

She started on the O.

Ralph threw up then.

IT WAS TWO days later when her father came back. The first she knew of it was the horn sounding outside in the yard. After a quick glance from the window she ran to get her own clothes from the drying rack.

The clothes were still damp, so she folded them for taking with her. She'd stayed in them for as long as she could, but in a house like this it wasn't too long before a person started feeling grubby. Right now she was wearing one of Catriona's newer T-shirts and a pair of shorts that she'd probably outgrown.

Catriona hadn't objected. She hadn't even been present to express an opinion. In fact, Louise hadn't seen either Catriona or Ralph since that session in the long shed. They were around and she was aware of them, but they were keeping themselves out of her way like a couple of small and panicky mammals in a carnivore's cave. She'd quickly learned that as long as she gave some audible signal of her approach, they'd be gone from any room before she entered it.

Which suited her fine.

Between their scuttling around and Colin Kelly's absence—he'd roared off to town in his van and had yet to return—it had been a tolerable end to her stay. Rebecca's natural reclusiveness had completed the illusion that Louise had the run of an empty house. She'd placed the British Nature Book on the floor leaning against Rebecca's bedroom door, and it had disappeared at some time when Louise wasn't looking.

The first thing her father said was, "You forgot to take your bag."

"You drove off with it," Louise said.

"I only found it this morning. Sorry."

"'S'all right."

She looked him over and said, "Did you sort everything out with Mister Taylor?"

"Everything's settled now," he said. "It had to be faced. The longer you put it off, the harder it is. But when it's done, it's done."

When he reached to open the door for her he moved slowly, wincing as if his back hurt. Much as a man might do who'd taken a severe kicking around the kidneys. As far as visible marks went, two of the fingers on his left hand were splinted together. One eye was closed in a magnificent shiner and, most conspicuous of all, a long stitched cut ran from his right ear to his chin like a zipper. It must have taken twenty-five sutures or more to pull it together.

Her father had always said that Mister Taylor was a hard employer for those who displeased him. But if you stood up and took your discipline, he could be a forgiving one.

Frank closed the door on her and limped around to the driver's side. She'd said nothing about his splints or his stitches, just as he'd said nothing when he noted her self-bandaged arm. He lowered himself gingerly into the driving seat and, once he'd made it all the way, sighed with satisfaction like a man settling into a hot bath.

Then something crossed his mind and he said, "I promised Colin I'd pay him something."

"I wouldn't bother," she said. "He isn't even there."

"What about that T-shirt you're wearing?" he said.

"They told me to keep it."

"What about saying goodbye?"

"We did all that."

All of which seemed to suit him fine. He started the engine. Louise took one last look at the house, and in her heart she bade it good riddance.

As they headed off down the lane and back toward civilisation, her father said, "So, tell me what you got up to."

"All kinds of things," she said.

"Anything in particular?"

"We went for long walks. I played with their dog."

He nodded, as if this was all fine and good, and said, "Anything else?"

Once again, Louise found herself screwing her eyes up against the play of light and shadow through the overhanging trees.

She flipped down the sunshade, and that helped.

"Yes," she said. "We went to church."

Copyright Information